To Jane
With Love
John (Ken told me to say
that !)

The Carrington's
In search of a legacy

www.echo-books.co.uk

ECHO BOOKS

York Hub, Popeshead Court Offices, Peter Lane, York, YO1 8SU

A Queue Press Company

www.queuepress.co.uk

First published in Great Britain
in 2014 by Echo Books
an imprint of Queue Press

A CIP catalogue record for this book
Is available from the British Library

ISBN 978-0-9930069-0-6

Printed and bound in Great Britain by
Queue Press Limited, York

1 3 5 7 9 2 4 6 8 10

Acknowledgments

This novel was inspired by and is dedicated to my uncle and godfather A.J Downes. My hero and a real life James Carrington.

When I murmured to David Nobbs, undoubtedly the best humourist writer of our time; that I was nurturing the idea of writing a novel. His reply was – If I might plagiarise CJ speaking to Reggie Perrin- 'I didn't get where I am today by talking about it –so get on and write your book!'

My thanks also to my darling wife Lindy who encouraged me to continue writing a book that had slumbered in my computer for years .

I am also indebted to Sarah Standeven for proofreading and organising the original chaos and turning it into a hopefully readable manuscript.

With regard to the front cover : I would also like to acknowledge the skilful architectural assistance of Colin Britton ARIBA who has, with the help of some old family photographs, coaxed Milford Hall back to life

Finally a thank you to the good friends who accompanied me on this journey :-
TWLC ; APJ ; DBJ ; JWP

The Carrington's - In search of a legacy
Principal Characters

Robert Carrington	James Carrington's father
Elizabeth Carrington	James Carrington's mother
Edward Lawson	Close friend & initial business partner
Connie Lawson	nee Cummings – Edward Lawson's wife
Jack Priory	Close friend & eventually business partner
Kate Palmer	James Carrington's wife
Jeremy Palmer	Kate Palmer's father
Angela Palmer	Kate Palmer's mother
Anthony Jayes	Solicitor in Jeremy Palmers law firm
Tim Cooper	Architect & close friend of JC
Charles Latimer	Regional Manager Martin's Bank
Sir Julian Abbercrombie	Chairman APP Merchant Bank
Henry 'Porky' White	Racehorse Trainer
Miles Stanhope Court	Senior Banker APP & friend of JC
Nick Carter Brown	Racehorse owner & friend of JC
David Barrington Jones	President RIBA & friend
Sally Parkinson	Daughter of Sir Robert & Lady Camilla Parkinson
Johnnie Mortimer	Friend of Kate Carrington

The Carrington's
In search of a legacy

PROLOGUE
CAMBRIDGE : OCTOBER 1980

James Carrington was a successful man, a man of infinite ambition. There was a demon that drove him relentlessly on: It was the vow he had made when, as a fourteen year old, his parents' financial collapse meant the loss of the family estate and his transfer from Public School to the local Grammar. A fate he had sworn his children would never know. Since then work had dominated his life, he could not take his hand off the tiller and yet today, in the warm autumn sunshine, an event was transcending all those financial dreams.

Today, his son had come up to Cambridge to take his place at St John's College, the very same college that a quarter of a century ago his father had also dreamed of attending. As father and son walked briskly along The Backs each with their own thoughts, the father's happiness was dramatically derailed by a beady malevolent eye that observed them from the fence. A single magpie; that ancient portender of doom. James's heart sank. Surely fate would not again deny him and then, just as suddenly it soared, as the bird's mate squawked angrily into view. One for sorrow, two for joy, he mentally chanted the old folklore.

As they approached the Bridge of Sighs, so called because of its similarity to the original in Venice, the son instinctively stepped to one side to allow his father to lead him across and into the third and second courts, which are known as quads at Oxford. Finally into the first court of St John's where opposite from where they were standing, a heavy oak door was open to reveal the staircase that had for three centuries guided hesitant young men from youth into manhood, imbuing them in the process with a sense of privilege and learning, of responsibility and leadership.

Mission accomplished, he grasped his son's hand, no words were necessary, the warmth and affection were evident.

As his son disappeared into the doorway opposite, James Carrington cast his mind back a quarter of a century when he too had hoped to enhance his education in this same college. With complete clarity he remembered spending the night prior to his interview in a cold and rather barren room and an even colder bathroom which had occasioned thoughts of his hero, Scott of the Antarctic.

The following morning breakfast had been a rather subdued affair, after which he reported to the Porter's Lodge and was sent to room H13 where he was told Dr Pickersgill would be expecting him. He made his way up the stone staircase to see another boy disappear through the doorway opposite the green leather couch on which he now perched himself.

He remembered him from the dining hall, he had a shock of ginger curly hair and his arrogant manner and self- confidence had both antagonised and intimidated the others on his table. Apparently his father and grandfather had been at St John's; it was a family tradition he assured them. James had wished he could get hold of him on a rugby field and show him how much tradition counted there.

At his Grammar School, his Headmaster Dr Stanley was a John's man and had, without alerting James, had a word in the ear of the Master, extolling the boy's academic ability and of equal interest to the college, James's exceptional promise on the games field. Dr Stanley had forecast that he would play for Cambridge and gain his Blue in the Varsity Match and the expectation was that he would be capped by England at senior level in the not too distant future.

But the youthful Carrington was unaware of this, so sat nervously awaiting his opportunity. Finally the door opened and the tousled haired youth of yesterday was ejected, his shoulders slumped and his face no longer exuding haughty arrogance. James was invited in by a friendly looking man in a black gown, in his mid- thirties. He introduced himself as David Creswell and led James through to the Master's study where the occupant waved him into the chair adjacent to his desk.

Apart from the chimney breast which housed several sepia coloured photographs, the room appeared to be entirely filled with books and manuscripts in haphazard bookshelves which appeared to be on the point of collapse. The enormous desk too was similarly decorated, this time with a mass of files through which its leather surface was occasionally revealed as green. One of these files, was headed Carrington JRS.

The Master, Dr Pickersgill, flicked his way through the file; eventually he looked up. 'I see you play rugger, are you any good?'

'I'm very keen sir.' The modest reply.

'Come on Carrington, you have captained both the England Schoolboy and Youth teams. This is a place where being good is very important, it is what marks you out.' James allowed himself a hint of a smile.

'I am very keen to pursue my rugby here, although I realise that must not be at the expense of my studies; perhaps I should take Professor Cresswell as my role model?' They both smiled, they both knew why the younger Don had been scheduled to attend the interview of this candidate. Professor Cresswell had captained the Light Blues against the Dark Blues in the Oxford v Cambridge match on two occasions, he had also played for the Harlequins and England, so was well qualified to assess the eighteen year old interviewee.

James had opted to read English, so the next half an hour followed the traditional pattern. He was asked to discuss the Romantic poets and draw comparisons with the Pre-Raphaelites. James particularly admired Ruskin whose heroes in turn were Turner and Wordsworth. Like them, he enjoyed the swirling colours of the former compared to the minute attention to detail of the Pre-Raphaelites. Also Craftsmen like William Morris, who was both a Poet and an Artist and also a very fine Designer. He was, James had ventured, also a very influential social reformer.

Dr. Cresswell interrupted. 'What posthumous legacy if any, do you think Keats left behind?' 'I believe he had a huge influence on Tennyson and indeed on Wilfred Owen.'

The interview continued with a vigorous but fair exchange of ideas, the would-be undergraduate not afraid to admit if he was not sure and equally eager to hear the opinions of his mentors.

Finally Dr Pickersgill called the interview to a close. 'I am sure that I speak for Dr Cresswell when I say that this has been an interesting discussion and

I am delighted to observe that you appear receptive to new ideas. In a place like Cambridge we are of course very conscious of the past, but we also recognise the present and indeed the future, which lies in the hands of young men like you. However, I am afraid that we will not be able to find a place for you at St John's; I suggest you try Trinity College.'

It was like a dagger to the heart; he had let so many people down.

The master saw the acute disappointment in the handsome, youthful face andlaughed. 'The Gods too are fond of a joke.'

'Aristotle.' The immediate response.

'Excellent Carrington; a knowledge of ancient Greek as well as an understanding of the golden age of English literature.' He stood up indicating the interview was concluded but his handshake emitted warmth, that same sentiment echoed by the younger Don who confided, 'It would be good to see you in the pale blue and white hoops putting those damned Oxford people to the sword! – You will be hearing from us.' He promised.'

He remembered these details with complete clarity, but then put them quickly to one side and walked swiftly through the Gateway with those four tall brick towers which have been described, with some authority, as the noblest entrance in Cambridge.

Turning right along the High, he marched past the majesty of King's College Chapel, one of the great religious statements of this nation, and into Trumpington Street. He was savouring every moment of this day and not even the sight of a warden decorating his car with a parking ticket could disturb this satisfaction as he looked forward to arriving home and relating to his wife the events of the day, realising for the umpteenth time just how much he loved her. From the moment they had met she had never failed to excite and inspire him. He remembered too, how she had insisted that he and Charles come up to Cambridge together, just the two of them, knowing instinctively how much this occasion meant to her husband.

But enough of daydreaming, he had a business empire to run, the thought of which quickened his step even more and, having removed the parking ticket, he slid into the sculptured leather seats and contemplated the two bookends which sought to contain his Aston Martin.

One a gaudy yellow and black Volkswagen masquerading as a tiger and the other, a very old Rover, black and with dark blue leather seats he guessed? His mind pondered that memory, re-awakening again the demon that sat on his shoulder and reminding him vividly of the last time he had sat in just such a motor car.

CHAPTER ONE
In search of a legacy

March 7th 1948.

The heavy man in the brown chalk stripe suit slammed together the doors of the furniture van, checked the back and advised that it was time to go. Robert Carrington nodded his agreement and passed the man a white five-pound note, which he promptly palmed with that adroitness known only to tradesmen and professional illusionists.

From the rear of the car James saw his father look back, just once, at the splendid proportions of the magnificent stone house remodelled by his grandfather more than a century ago. Now with its great stone tower there stood, instead of the previously weary looking 17th century manor house, a proud and imposing piece of architecture.

The Staincliffe family had farmed this part of the Nottinghamshire, Leicestershire borders for centuries and, until Matthew Staincliffe, remained content with their lot as yeoman farmers. Matthew however, awakening with his fellow Victorians to the dawn of industrialisation had seen the coming of a new age, full of promise for those prepared to accept new challenges and new opportunities.

Through a friend, he had met Richard Kirtley, an up and coming railway engineer. He was immediately impressed by the man's commitment and confidence in the changes that would soon be brought about by the disciples of George Stephenson. His enthusiasm for the new mechanical alternative to the horse had led Richard Kirtley to suggest he went to see the railway line already installed by Stephenson, which ran from Leicester to Swannington. Here they were able to deliver coal, the very lifeblood of the industrial revolution, for less than ten shillings a ton.

The Nottingham coal owners with only horse drawn carts and barges could not compete. With that perception and pragmatic thinking peculiar to all innovators and men of vision, Matthew Staincliffe had enquired; 'Why do we not join on to that line?'

'We are thinking of just that,' the engineer replied before adding. 'If you have funds you could join us in the proposed Midland Counties Railway Company.'

So it was that on August 16th 1832 he went with others to the Sun Inn at Eastwood, a small town on the outskirts of Nottingham, later to become synonymous as the birthplace of D.H. Lawrence.

Here he vouchsafed the considerable sum of £2,000 towards the building of a railway line from the village of Pinxton to Leicester. The coal owners to whom this meant so much were wary and then intrigued by the enthusiasm of this farmer who stood with them. He had a persuasive manner however and the prospect of running part of the track across his land, which stretched into both counties, plus his financial commitment, were enough to convince them of his genuine belief in the project. Thus was established the cornerstone of the considerable fortunes of the Staincliffe family.

Their influence grew steadily until, at the turn of the century, Matthew's grandson Albert, the so called Furniture King was made a Baronet by King Edward the Seventh. It must have seemed then that they would be forever the masters of this house, the fate of which was now to be decided by an auctioneer's gavel.

His father turned the handle and opened the car door; he sat behind the wheel at the side of his wife. 'I am so very sorry Elizabeth,' he whispered. 'Don't worry; everything is going to be fine.' Her gentle reassurance belied by the steely look in her eyes.

James in the rear seat, heard the affirmation of his mother's love, sensed too that had she been the man, they would not be leaving the family home. From where he sat he could not see his father's face but, in the driving mirror, caught a momentary glimpse of his eyes, moist with emotion and he defiantly blurted out;
    'One day we shall move back into our house.'
As he said it, he instantly wished that he had not, as he realised that it must cause further anguish for his father. They drove down the drive and out, for the last time, past the high iron gates with the imposing rising sun motif. The rest of the journey was without comment; even the sight of the large Pickford's van with their possessions on board failed to evoke any comment.

James awoke early next morning, unaware at first of his surroundings then slowly realising that the heavy low beams were neither part of Milford Hall nor his dormitory at Uppingham School. Instead they now lived in the Vale of Belvoir in a farm house with about thirty acres bequeathed to his father some six months ago. This inheritance had mitigated the loss of his mother's long time family home and, since it was free of debt, it gave Robert Carrington a small degree of dignity and the possibility of earning a living, albeit initially considerably less than he had been used to.

For a fourteen year old, James was an assured and confident boy and yet he admitted to himself a degree of apprehension at the prospect of meeting his new schoolmates at the local Grammar School. He wished now that they had lived nearer the town so that he might have forged more friendships with local boys. His concern was interrupted by his mother's voice insisting he hurry down to breakfast.

He leapt from his bed, drew back the curtains and saw his father in the field beyond the gaunt dead beech. He was bending over, opening one of the feed hoppers, the pullets milling around him expectantly and Henry, their old pointer, still going through the motions of his antecedents and setting up the stray birds. Even at a distance the son could sense his father's contentment, he was a country man and, but for marrying his mother, would still be running the large family farm, now under the stewardship of his brother. How his father must have hated those years sat behind a desk at Staincliffes.

The firm, started by Matthew Staincliffes son Benjamin, had grown rapidly until as the new century dawned, it had become the largest manufacturer of furniture in the country.

In the hands of his son Albert, later to become Sir Albert Staincliffe and Elizabeth's own father Charles, the firm continued to flourish. All these Staincliffes possessed tremendous driving energy and expanded the company in an aggressive transatlantic style rather than the more English approach typified by their contemporaries. They had gathered around them a team of similarly eager salesmen and designers to whom Robert Carrington, when he took his place on the Board of Directors and later when he took control, must have seemed, popular though he undoubtedly was, the very voice of doom for this great battleship company still privately owned.

'James.'

His mother's voice once again broke his reverie.

'One minute,' he called, dashing to the bathroom.

He rode slowly to school, not wishing to stand around any longer than need be. Bad enough, he thought, that his striped blazer looked so new, his cap and badge so bright that they seemed to yell out 'new boy.' How he wished for the crumpled black blazer now resting in the second hand shop at Uppingham.

The school gates loomed up, he swung through them, glad of the others around him, realising he needed their unspoken guidance to find the cycle shed. Past the impeccably mown square lawn in front of Founder's Hall; for prefects only, he rightly guessed and around to the back of the school where stood the bike-shed, as always striving to exist amidst the great piles of coke that threatened to engulf it.

He poked the wheels of the Raleigh into an empty slot, pulled his trousers out of his socks, and turned to see a large fair haired boy observing him.

'You're new here,' he accused.

'Yes,' admitted James.

'My name is Edward Lawson,' the giant advised, a pleasant smile lighting his strong open face.

'I'm Carrington. James Carrington,' he quickly corrected, realising that the more formal tones of his previous school would probably not apply here. 'We heard you were coming, I'll show you to the form room,' the other invited.

James followed, thankful that once again his good luck had held; it would seem that this blonde giant's friendship would smooth his way. They made their way to form IVA, deposited their satchels and joined the lemming like mob en route to morning prayers. The boys filed in and sat in rows according to age, James's year being about half way back. The Headmaster, Dr Stanley, whom James had liked when they met at interview, intoned the morning greeting in Latin and announced the first hymn.

'I vow to thee my Country, all earthly things above';

The six hundred voices ploughed through it mechanically, as they did through various hymns every morning. The hymnbooks closed in unison; it was followed by the lesson read by a prefect.

Dr Stanley summarised the week ahead, appealed for volunteers for the school play, chastised the miscreants and led them through prayers and into the second hymn. The school filed out, mostly without noise, preparing to resume their tussle with Pythagoras and Shakespeare. Some, with more optimism than others.

Form IVA stood at the end of a corridor next to its partner IV Alpha. James followed Edward into the classroom.

'Mr Carrington I presume,' said a deep voice with an air of amusement.
James turned and a saw a smallish powerful man in his early forties.

'Yes Sir,' he said in awe, for this was the legendary R.S.G. Dickson who was, according to his father and by common consent, the greatest rugby scrumhalf that this country had ever produced.

The master handed him a set of textbooks, Thomas Carlyle, Paradise Lost, The Nun's Tale and Hamlet.

'Do you know any of these?' he enquired.

'I have read Carlyle, sir, and we saw Hamlet in town last year.'

'Well if you need any extra prep or any other help don't be afraid to ask, boy.'
English Lit passed comfortably as did French and James was amused at his introduction to maths. Mr JC Barnsley, Bonzo to all the boys when out of earshot, carefully laid his cane across the two hooks above the blackboard and announced, as he did prior to every lesson, that Dr Cane cured all mathematical ills. Rarely was James to meet a man who could so easily inspire both fear and humour, and yet be accorded respect by the recipient. Bonzo too had been a fine sportsman, uniquely playing for Wolverhampton Wanderers whilst still a student at Oxford, although his thick stature denied all trace of that now.

James cycled home, relieved that the day had passed so uneventfully, not even the prospect of homework dulled his pleasure. There was after all something special about writing in new exercise books, as if all the mistakes of the past had been erased and a new start made.

The atmosphere at home was pleasant, perhaps it was just a relief for his parents to be free of the tensions of the last few months; they had tried to shield him and his sister Louise from these pressures but, despite their efforts to shield the children, he was acutely aware how difficult it must have been for both parents.

It was a feeling of failure for his father, but one of deprivation and isolation for his mother as, since that fateful day when they knew they had to sell up, his mother, devoted to golf and bridge had ceased to play either. Her friends no doubt embarrassed at their changed circumstance had, whilst making the right noises, not pressed their invitations.

James entered the house by the back door and carelessly hung his blazer and cap in the hall. After the extremes of 1947, the winter had been mercifully mild and the spring gave optimism for a hot summer. His parents being out, he set about his homework and the essay he had to write for Mr Dickson, the master who had so impressed him today.

Even now the man had such an aura, an understated affirmation of everything that James had heard from his father, a good rugby player himself and a member of the Leicester side just after Dickie Dickson as he was always known. It was fourth year games tomorrow and the boy wondered if the great man helped out with the coaching.

He had just started his essay when he heard the noise of an engine and, not recognising the sound, was surprised to see Henry bounding in, his tail wagging ferociously. Inquisitively he went to the kitchen door and there in the yard was an Austin Pick-up truck from which his parents were alighting.

'Far more useful than the Rover.' His father anticipated his question. The boy nodded, anxious to convey his own information.

'Guess whose form I am in?'

'Do we know him?'

'Yep, it is Dickie Dickson.' He yelled before picking a cabbage from the back of the truck and slinging it at his father's head. 'Too high,' counselled Robert, plucking it from the air and returning it like a bullet, waist high. The boy, to his father's delight, gathered it effortlessly.

That evening father and son went on what had become an evening ritual, a tour of the property.

'Quite a bit of hedging that the Parsons never got around to and one or two of those chicken houses have seen better days,' observed Robert.

'Why not cannibalise the oldest ones?' the boy suggested.

'Good idea, I will start on those nearest the house tomorrow,' affirmed his father.

'What about restocking?' James enquired.

'I thought we would take a ride up to Yorkshire during half-term and choose some point of lay pullets. Meanwhile I have ordered two thousand day old chicks from Golding's and I intend to sort this lot out before then and get rid of those who are not paying their way.' 'How do you know which ones are laying?'

James was interested, aware for the first time that in business matters his father now needed no prompting.

'Come on, I will show you.'

His father strode into the nearest hen house where, in the gloom of evening, the birds were settled on their perches, approachable now, unlike the squawking, cackling rabble that resisted capture during daylight. He lifted the nearest bird and put it back apparently satisfied, the next one he handed to James.

'Put its head under your left arm and see how many fingers you can place between its pelvis bones.'

'One,' replied the boy.

'Then that is one for the pot, three fingers mean a really good layer, two is still earning its keep, but that one is way past its best and there are no eggs coming out of there,' declared Robert.

'If you will help me to keep on top of this culling it will provide a good cash flow in terms of oven ready birds and keep the feed bills down no end.' In the darkness James felt such warmth towards his father. To see such happiness greatly diluted the giving up of Milford Hall.

Darkness had fallen when they heard his mother calling them to the supper table. His sister Louise had gone back to Cheltenham Ladies College today; the school governors generously deciding that in view of the numbers of Staincliffe girls educated there, his mother Elizabeth included, that a bursary should be found to enable the girl to stay at the school. James was pleased for her, although he would miss her infectious laughter around the house.

Without bidding, he rose early next day and cycled hard to school in time to join in one of the many games of football being waged across the schoolyard. Morning lessons dragged, as they always did, prior to games afternoon but finally they were over and the boys took their places in the dining hall. Stew, followed by apple pie, or more accurately apple pie crust noted James. Apparently the undercutting of the pie filling by the older boys was not exclusive to his previous school!

Lunch over; he wandered with Edward Lawson to the games field. On the sheet in the entrance he saw that his year was split into three groups. The first two groups, A and B were to go to Beeches Field for rugby, whilst the other, group C was down for cross-country running.

'You are with us,' Edward Lawson observed.

'Come on, Tommo will sort us out.'

James looked at the mass of black and gold hoops, rather like being in a wasps' nest he thought.

He was uncertain which jersey to wear, finally opting for the old and familiar crumpled white shirt he had worn at Uppingham, less presumptuous he thought. The boys came racing down the steps in sixes and sevens, the balls being kicked high in the air, howls of derision greeting the clumsy catchers. Tommo, viz Mr Thomas brought them to the centre of the field with a loud blast on his whistle. The sixty boys were split into groups of ten for thirty minutes devoted to ball skills and tactics. James followed Edward, his heart like his step, light, anticipating as he always did the thrill of running and physical contact.

Mr Thomas's whistle finally interrupted the session. He counted each group, seeing James apparently for the first time.

'Where do you play Carrington?' the soft Welsh voice enquired.

'Fly half sir,' came back the reply.

'Are you any good?' The master was genuinely interested, he had seen the boy run, his action fluid and he caught the ball with that light economy of movement found only in a natural games player.

If this lad could play as well as he looked then this team, already promising to be the best in his fifteen years at the school, might well realise its full potential.

'Not too bad sir,' the modest reply interrupted Mr Thomas's dreams.

'Right, Robinson you move from stand-off to centre and Carrington you take his place with the Whites.'

He swapped around the front rows trying to even up the scrums but deliberately left his first choice back row playing for the colours - they would soon let him know if the boy could play rugby.

The first scrum came and white's hooker struck quickly, the ball coming almost immediately through to the number eight, who stepped neatly over it allowing his scrum half to deliver a perfect pass to James. His first inclination to run was tempered by a momentary thought not to show off and, in that same instant, a great blonde shape buried him, leaving him with an aching leg and an even more aching heart as he saw Dickie Dickson standing on the touchline. Mr Thomas too was disappointed; he had played many times against James's father and had hoped for better.

The game continued, the hoops scoring a push over try in the corner and failing to convert a long wide kick. From the kick-off an infringement meant another scrum for the whites and again their hooker won the strike but the scrum was under pressure and the pass from the scrum half was wild and short. James still smarting and with now no other thoughts than the game swooped on the ball, picking it off his ankles, instinctively side stepping the menacing fair haired giant on his right and moved in a great electrifying arc across the field, over the goal line and then straightening to place the ball neatly behind the posts.

'Take the kick yourself Carrington.' Mr Thomas tried to keep his voice calm, in all his years of playing and coaching, he had never seen such potential.

Mr Dickson, watching from the touchline also sensed that a new star had arrived. The boys too were pleased, it made Saturdays match with St Thomas's, whom they rarely beat, something to anticipate rather than fear.

Saturday came and went; James Carrington had come to stay. Two tries, both converted and a dropped goal made him the hero of the hour, particularly as both the A and B teams suffered their conventional heavy defeats.

He rode home, pleased not to be at boarding school, anticipating sharing the day with his father. After the tensions of the last two years, life was suddenly worthwhile.

CHAPTER TWO

They went to Yorkshire at half term.

'   Always buy your stock from up north, preferably raised on the moors, they come hardy and do well,' Robert Carrington had knowingly advised his son.

James nodded, conscious once more of the change in his father. He looked so fit, had an air of authority, even his mother was surprised, reminding her just how handsome and engaging he had been when they first met.

They lunched at York, at The Chase overlooking the Knavesmire, that majestic racecourse set on the outskirts of the city. In the dining room enjoying a good lunch, they forgot their changed circumstances.

Inwardly however, James was still conscious that here, in these genteel surroundings was where he belonged, where he was comfortable and the resolve burned within him to re-establish his family once more to this lifestyle.

They returned to the pick-up, a further reminder of their changed circumstances and travelled in silence, each with their own thoughts. But James was glowing with pleasure remembering the half pint of beer pressed into his hand by his father.

'I think you are big enough to fool them,' his eyes twinkled.

'But, don't let your mother know or she will skin us both alive.'

They continued on the A19, seeing from a distance the great White Horse which had been carved out of the hillside in 1857 by the schoolchildren of neighbouring Kilburn. This is home to the famous oak furniture maker 'Mousey Thompson', so called because all their products from cheese board to sideboard are adorned with a carved mouse. The company was part of the revival in craftsmanship inspired by the Arts and Crafts movement led by William Morris, John Ruskin and Thomas Carlyle and in the north by Robert Thompson in Yorkshire and Stanley Webb Davies inWindermere.

Heading north the road swept them past Easingwold and its delightful Georgian market place and, skirting Thirsk, turned off on the Scarborough road making their way through Sutton under Whitestonecliffe - the longest place name in England - his father advised him, and then up one of the steepest and most testing roads for cyclists, Sutton Bank itself.

The air was magnificent, the trees starting to assume the green mantles of summer, the houses mostly in stone or burnt yellow bricks that resembled the locally quarried stone.

As they passed the various finger posts it was interesting to note how many of the local areas bore the same names as those in the Nottingham and Leicestershire borders from whence they had come.

Carlton, Mowbray, Husthwaite, Sutton, Tollerton etc., proof indeed of the voracious appetite to conquer of our Viking forebears.

Turning off before Helmsley they arrived at Beck Farm and were welcomed by a large bluff man with a pronounced Yorkshire accent. Robert introduced them and they were taken into the fields to see the pullets.

The birds, mostly Rhode Island Reds and Light Sussex, were healthy specimens, clucking happily, pecking with that quick darting action, seeing specks of food in the grass quite invisible to the human eye.

James moved away, leaving his father to negotiate the price and delivery. He saw the men nodding and laughing and then, with a shake of the hand they came over to where he stood.

'Now then young sir, what do you think of them?' enquired Mr Willoughby.

'Very good sir' the boy replied, 'I was wondering how much the turkey poults were.'

'Five shillings each,' came the reply.

'Do you think I could have twenty?' James asked, feeling the money drawn from the Post Office in his pocket.

'Fancy your chances as a stockman?' Duncan Willoughby smiled, liking the boy's keen open face with its steely, determined gaze.

'I'll tell you what young fella, you pick yourself a couple of dozen with my compliments.' He brushed aside the boy's embarrassed protest.

'Look upon it as an investment on my part, - when you are buying them in thousands, don't forget to get a quote from Beck Farm first.'

James selected his poults, loaded them into a crate and stowed them in the back of the pick-up. His eyes sparkled with anticipation, he saw no problems, he was too young for that, he could not wait to be back on their own farm to install his birds in the chicken house he had been preparing, unbeknown he imagined, to his father.

The journey home was pleasant, each of them anticipating the pleasure of seeing the birds mature.

'So that is why you have been so busy on that old shed in the orchard.' Robert smiled, the rhetorical question needing no reply. His son, however, was more than ready to talk about it.

'I reckon that if they run out and I supplement their diet with meal I should have a good return on my capital by Christmas.'

'What do you plan to do with your profit?' his father enquired.

'If you will allow me to use the small three acre field near the house I intend to invest most of the money on more poults for next Christmas. I have spoken to our butcher, Mr Bradley, and he will take fifty off me for his shop and I thought if we made a sign and hung it near the gate we could easily sell the another fifty to passing traffic, it will also help with the egg sales.'

The boy spoke confidently, with the sound commercial instincts of his maternal forebears.

The weeks leading up to the summer holidays were busy ones for both father and son. As each batch of new chicks arrived they were lifted individually from the crates, and their beaks dipped twice into dishes of milk to provide them with nourishment before they were placed carefully into the incubators. No chick ever passed through Robert Carrington's hands without this ritual and, as they grew and were introduced to the rearing pens in the fields, the same trouble was taken to ensure they were roosting and not huddling in the corners where they could so easily suffocate. All this James observed and absorbed. He noted too that they rarely lost a bird, unlike the majority of poultry farms who accepted 6-7% losses as normal.

Finally the summer holidays arrived, exams were over and James organised his workforce.

He had co-opted Edward Lawson and two other boys, the agreed fee being an oven ready turkey for each family. During the past weeks James had approached Mr Jackson, Chairman of the Parish Council and suggested he would arrange to remove the old cricket pavilion, flattened during the storms of 1947, in return for the materials.

This was sanctioned by a somewhat surprised Parish Council, and the boys with the aid of two handcarts moved the lot, bricks, beams and all to the field next to the orchard. James drew a further £12 from his rapidly dwindling Post Office account and paid for the brick base to be built on the concrete foundations laid by himself and Edward and other friends. They levered the boards off the framework and de-nailed them prior to delivery so the next part was easier, although they learned very quickly that what appeared so easy when done by a tradesman, was rather more difficult, particularly cutting the larger timbers so that the ends were square.

The design of the building was very dear to James's heart as he had determined to be an architect eventually and saw these designs in a very practical light. From the time spent helping his father repair the chicken houses he realised how much easier it would have been if they had been sectional, and to a modular scale. This, his prototype turkey house was 56 feet long and 24 feet wide.

It stood 8 feet to the eaves on a two foot brick wall which served not only to keep the timbers off the ground but also to contain the foot or so of shavings on which the birds walked.

His father watched with interest, watching what the boy was doing, offering advice but not pressing it; the odd mistake would not go amiss.

'Why the shutters?' he asked, intrigued.

'So that I can control the daylight,' his son confided. ' I have read the results of some experiments which confirm that fixed periods of daylight and darkness ensure the birds rest and gain weight.'

'That makes sense,' agreed Robert, 'but what about the winter months?'

'In the case of the turkeys it doesn't matter,' said James, 'but with hens it is helpful to extend the daylight hours and make them think it is summer - come and see what I have rigged up.'

He led Robert into the garage and pointed out the alarm clock from his bedroom. He set the alarm and fixed a string to the winder on the back. The alarm rang, the winder revolved, tugged the string attached to it and the garage light came on. His father laughed, with a mixture of pride and admiration.

'Well I never, and it is so simple.'

'It's a bit crude.' The boy modestly pointed out, 'And fixing the string to the switch is not easy.'

'Why not use one of those old fashioned brass switches with a little knob on the lever?' Robert suggested.

'Great idea Dad'; the son enthused. Sharing the moment and happy to make it sound as if his father had invented the whole idea.

The holidays seemed to go so quickly and it was back to school once more. This time without the apprehension of a new environment, but with the knowledge that school certificate awaited them and that decent 'O' levels were essential to providing the springboard to 'A' levels and university.

Christmas finally came, and with it James's first business coup. Of the original twenty four free turkeys and the extra fifty he had bought only two failed to survive and even after presenting his willing helpers with their share of the spoils, James could scarcely believe it when he added the £150 from Mr Bradley to the £61 from his own sales at the gate. After paying Mrs Pettifer and Mrs Hughes who had heroically done most of the plucking and dressing, Mr Carrington Junior had a £142 surplus. On the strength of this he opened an account with Martins Bank, the Post Office seeming suddenly not quite suitable for a man going places.

Apart from James's first financial success, Christmas was a great time for all the family. Elizabeth and Robert, more relaxed than for many years and with Louise home for the hols, all of them had thrown off the blues of the last few years.

On Boxing Day, the whole family went as usual to Welford Road to see the Leicester Tigers take on their traditional foe at this time of the year, The Barbarians, or the Ba-Ba's as they were affectionately known; a team drawn from a cosmopolitan mix of established internationals and exciting newcomers. The game, as always, was a fast and open end to end encounter in which the Tigers surrendered the spoils in the dying seconds. James stood with the others to applaud the teams off the field, he saw his mother look at his father, remembering the day when Robert Carrington had been the toast of the county, the only man ever to score four tries against the *Ba-Ba's*.

CHAPTER THREE

March 13 1949.

James drifted with the other boys into morning prayers. As usual they went through the normal procedure of hymns and announcements, whilst his mind crept back to the farm and his plans for enlarging his turkey house by utilising the same modular concepts he had initially instigated. The sound of his name broke through his subconscious.

'Will Carrington and Lawson step forward?'

Bewildered, they made their way through the throng and on to the dais, to stand next to Dr Stanley who was leaning on the lectern. He turned to the school.

'Because of the actions of these two boys the match with Oakham is cancelled.'

He turned towards them, placed his spectacles on and read from a card in front of him.

'You are required to be at Twickenham on Saturday March 25th to represent England in the Schoolboy International against Wales.'

The Headmaster smiled and extended his hand.

'Congratulations both of you, you bring great credit to the school.'

They stood there both of them, hearts pounding, trying not to let the excitement be too apparent;

A great cheer went up from the school, the staff too joining in the clapping.

Dr Stanley signalled them to stay on stage and announced the next hymn.

'Number 357, Fight the good fight with all thy might.'

The following twelve days were the longest that James had ever known. He spent them dreaming of scoring winning tries and then, just as often, dropping final passes.

Finally, it was the Friday prior to the match and they travelled up to London and to the 'Stoop', that famous London ground which is the home of the Harlequins Rugby Club. This is adjacent to Twickenham and they were to have their final training here. First though they were issued with their kit and the dark blue satin caps proudly embroidered 'England v Wales 1948.' The training session was vigorous and thorough, James quickly re-discovering the rapport with his scrum half John Murray that had proved so decisive in the trial matches.

The following morning after a late breakfast they idled away the time as they nervously waited for the coach to arrive. The atmosphere as they travelled to the ground was an electric mix of fear and determination, finally after what had seemed an eternity the coach drew into the car park. They collected their kit from the boot before walking towards the great green stands, sensing as they did, the envy of the crowd around them as they passed through the doorway proudly bearing the legend 'Players Only.'

The cool corridor redolent with the smell of embrocation finally brought home the realisation of what they had achieved and what they might accomplish this afternoon.

In the stands, Dickie Dickson and even Mr Thomas, forgetting for the day his Welsh antecedents, saw England achieve a hard fought win, the culmination of which was a try three minutes from the end. Murray performing Herculean feats for such a small chap somehow wrestled the ball from the Welsh number eight and sent out a long spinning pass to James who, without hesitation, set off for the try line.

With those long legs pumping he drew the inevitable cover from the defending red jerseys and, at the last instant, released the ball to Edward Lawson. As he hit the ground he saw the big flanker crashing over the try line with two red limpets attached to his back.

The stadium was hushed as James with trembling fingers carefully wiped the ball before placing it on the divot he had heeled out. He was suddenly calm and, as if in slow motion, saw his boot strike the ball, which soared in a great arc over the Welsh crossbar.

It was all over, the greatest day of his life; he looked into the stands but, even with a much smaller crowd than for a full international, he could not pick out his parents. However, he knew they would see him and share in his triumph.

The following morning his parents collected him and Edward, and on the way home treated them to a family lunch at the George Hotel in Stamford. Here they were joined by Dr and Mrs Lawson in what turned out to be a very convivial occasion, the parents striking up an immediate rapport, so much so that a bridge evening was arranged as was golf for the men at Melton Mowbray Golf Club. In the midst of all this bonhomie James suddenly remembered they were to collect his sister Louise from Leicester railway station as she too was coming home from boarding school for the Easter holidays. Fortunately he had remembered in time and a very happy family eagerly anticipated relaxing together; after all the hardships of the past few years, at long last they could relax and enjoy family life.

January 13 1951.

An ominous date, mused James; he hoped not for today the Oxbridge results would be through.

He sat in the library waiting for the news, gazing abstractly and idly around, seeing properly for the first time, the fine hammer-beam trusses which sprang from richly gilded octagonal posts and supported the huge timber roof.

He turned to admire more closely the workmanship that craftsmen had laboured to create with such effect four hundred years ago, and through the irregular leaded lights of the arched windows he saw with the concentrated thoughts of a condemned man the distant playing fields and a group of juniors practising with Mr Thomas those same skills, he too had been taught those few short years ago.

This fine building with its gothic strength was the original school, endowed to the town by Lady Jane Seagrave. The rows of tables and benches inscribed with the initials of lesser craftsmen, giving testimony to previous generations. How many before him had sat here waiting to hear news close to their hearts. He rose, casually looking at the oak bookcases, their carved ends replicating the plaster bosses high in the ceiling. He allowed himself a wry smile seeing the cheeky arrangement of books, the titles artfully arranged to compose saucy sentences.

'Carrington,' his daydreaming was interrupted by the school secretary.
'The Headmaster would like to see you.'
He followed her, his heart pounding so loudly he thought it must be heard. He tried to arrange his thoughts, to compose himself for the dreaded news... he would stay on and try again next year...
'Come in Carrington,' Dr Stanley's calm voice invited.
He held a slip of paper in his left hand, placed his spectacles on and extended his now unencumbered right hand.
'Well done James, very well done, a place at St John's College Cambridge.'
His face and voice reflected the pleasure of delivering such good news.
'You have brought much credit on yourself during your stay here and this is a fitting reward, an opportunity well earned and one I know you will grasp.' James heard him speaking, catching the odd word, pulling himself together to hear the Head say 'I expect you would like to let your people know, so cut along and we will see you in the morning.'
He left the room, his feet felt as if they were hovering above the elm planks, crossed the gallery to the main stairs and, coming through the doorway broke into an exuberant run to the bike sheds. Stopping briefly to put his trousers into his socks he pulled his cycle from the rack and set out for home.
For once he rode slowly, savouring again his great news, knowing the pride his parents would take and appreciating too the sacrifices they would make, without hesitation, to send him to Cambridge.
Cycling to the back of the house he left the machine in the stable that served as a feed store and, followed by Henry, ran across the yard and into the kitchen. He heard music coming from the drawing room, Mendelssohn's violin concerto, his father's favourite. He heard too a whispered voice.
'Don't despair Elizabeth.' It was his mother's sister, Margaret.
'It is no use,' his mother replied,
'The doctors say it is too advanced - why oh why?' she entreated,
'Why after all those years in that office should he be given so few years to enjoy working on the land again and enjoy a sense of achievement; it is so unfair.'
His aunt took her sister's hand. 'Have you told James and Louise?'
He heard his mother's whispered voice. 'Robert asked me not to tell them, he wants the time he has left to enjoy them, to discuss the future with them positively. Their grieving can come later rather than now, particularly with James's exam results being so important.'
James crept from the house, took his cycle and rode furiously, his lungs bursting, but he could not stop, he wanted to delay as long as possible the moment when he must face the reality of what he had overheard.

Eventually he felt his legs slowing, conscious that he was riding up the steep hill that led to Milford Hall. At the crest he threw the bike down and sank on to the bank. Through the fingers clasped to his face he saw the stone front of this great house rebuilt by his forebears. Overhead he was aware of the rooks, their vicious squawking an obscene intrusion to his grief. They wheeled and jostled in the tops of the elms seeking the nest to perpetuate life, to secure the future, the very future that was to be denied his father.

The boy wept great sobbing tears that made his head pound and, through the tears, he saw again the great stone facade he had last seen as a fourteen year old when his parents had been forced to sell his mother's inheritance.

Seeing once again his parents in the front of the Rover, he swore, this time without regret, that one day he would, as he had promised his father, be master of this house.

He rode home slowly dreading the conversation with his parents.

Robert Carrington met him on the drive and smiled. 'Hello son, are you feeling okay? Your eyes look red.'

'I'm fine, I am afraid I didn't get in at Cambridge.'

He lied, knowing that it was impossible for his mother to carry on here without him.

'Never mind,' his father's kind voice comforted, 'There is more to life than Cambridge.'

He hugged his father burying his head in his shoulder, the bereft voice whispering.

'I know Dad, I heard mother talking to Aunt Margaret.'

Neither could think of the right words. Finally Robert managed to choke out.

'When you go back to Milford Hall, promise me you will take your mother with you. I will be up above making sure you do!'

In the next eight weeks his condition deteriorated rapidly and on March 15th, the Ides of March, Robert Carrington's life, like that of Julius Caesar's, ended. The turnout at his funeral, like the one in Rome, was attended by the great and the good of the Midlands; the Rugby and the Hunting fraternities alone would have filled Leicester Cathedral; in the event, because of the numbers, most had to stand outside to listen to the service through the loudspeakers. In his address, the Bishop of Leicester recalled how as a young man he was a regular visitor to Welford Road and to his generation and the next, Robert Carrington epitomised the expression of sportsman and gentleman. In this respect he had few peers.

CHAPTER FOUR

March 1953

James Carrington at 19 stood a couple of inches above six feet in height and had the hard muscular physique of his father. His wavy hair and deeply set blue eyes   gave testimony to his Staincliffe origins.

He switched off the engine of the MG, parking it outside the bakery just behind the proprietors van. Gathering his briefcase, he zipped the cars protective tonneau cover and walked casually across the road to the local branch of Martins Bank.

One minute to ten he noted, looking at his watch and at the same time stealing an admiring glance at the little red sports car that occupied pride of place in his life.

The welcoming smile of the cashier advised him that he was expected and he was directed towards the door emblazoned with the manager's name.

'Good morning Mr Carrington.'

'Mr Osborne?'

'Yes, do come in,' the manager invited.

He ushered James to a chair and sat himself behind the large leather topped desk.

'Not another car is it?' Mr Osborne enquired, referring to the notes in which his predecessor had sanctioned the £150 needed to purchase the MG.

'Rather more interesting,' replied James.

'This is a business proposition; I need £3,000 to build a row of houses.'

The manager winced. He liked the young man sitting opposite, admired him for the way in which he had shouldered the family responsibilities but, with the cautious instincts of his breed, felt that James was getting out of his depth, was trying to do things too quickly.

'Mr Carrington, that is a great deal of money and your experience of the building industry is, to put it mildly, virtually nil.'

'It is something in which I have always taken a great deal of interest,' the would-be speculator countered.

'Nevertheless, it is far more than I could sanction to an unknown company, unless of course you have considerable equity as security.'

'Unknown company.' James Carrington stood up.

'My family have banked here for more than a hundred years.'
The neck stiffened, the blue eyes bored across the desk, the iron will normally disguised beneath the affable exterior could be felt in the room.

'I really must explain,' the manager started.

'Explain,' James's cold voice rapped out.

'I came here to explain; to explain how it could be profitable to both of us.'
He thrust the papers back into the brief case and flung open the office door.

The bank staff concentrated on their tasks, trying to appear unaware of the open door and their superior's red face. James strode across the street, his thoughts once more under control. He slipped into the red car and drove through the town, it was still only ten fifteen and he could drive the eighty miles to Birmingham before lunch.

As the miles sped past his mind wandered back to his family, to the wealth they once had, to their changed circumstances, how he resented their present comparative poverty.

He thought of his father, through whose fingers their fortune had slipped away and, just as suddenly, the hatred disappeared. No disappointment ever seemed quite so important when he remembered his father's kind voice. No rebuff or business refusal would ever seem as harsh as those dread words between his mother and her sister, words that had altered his life and signalled the end of life itself for his father.

The countryside changed, the trees and hedges giving way to suburbia, the endless ribbon developments leading to the heart of this great city, unmatched by any other in its diversity and dynamic growth. The impressive buildings, many now sadly engulfed in industrial grime. Though now tawdry, their shabby exteriors still failed to disguise the energy of those who had commissioned them. They stirred in James a craving for success, a feeling so intense that only those who have experienced it can comprehend.

He would not have been able to describe this yearning; it would, however, have been understood by the giants that had made Birmingham the second city in the land and, in terms of industrial wealth, unequalled in size and influence.

The disappointment of the early morning had disappeared; instead, as he parked his car near the Bull Ring shopping centre, he savoured the prospect of the contest ahead. He walked as far as New Street Station and, from a telephone directory, elicited the address of the Regional Head Office of Martins Bank.

Steeling himself, he walked through the revolving doors and walked, apparently confidently, to the enquiry desk. A very attractive girl with auburn hair smiled at him, wishing as she did so, that all her customers were as handsome as the healthy figure standing in front of her.

'Do you have an appointment?' the faultless voice enquired.

'No I am afraid not, but it really is most important.'
James's face wore that small boy look that was both defenceless and defied rejection.
The girl walked away, promising to do what she could.

James idly watched the small feminine cheeks of her bottom as she disappeared and let his thoughts stray somewhat from the purpose of his visit.

She returned shortly to convey the news that the Manager had a lunchtime appointment and would be engaged with clients all afternoon.

'I will wait,' he blurted out defiantly.

'If he has a few minutes between interviews then perhaps he will see me.'

'But sir.'

The girl's voice trailed off, realising that only closing time and the Bank's Messengers would prise this determined young man from the capacious confines of the bank.

The hours dragged by, he read and re-read the bank leaflets, the investment journals and the dates in his diary; he mulled over his scheme and watched the large overhead clock tick its way through the afternoon. At three twenty, the girl appeared again at the desk.

'The manager will see you now,' she smilingly confided. 'Thank you.'   He turned towards the manager's office.

Suddenly, his heart pounding, he heard himself saying,

'May I see you again?'

The girl blushed, the red of her face almost indistinguishable from the colour of her hair.

'What time do you finish?' he persisted.

'Why five o'clock,' she replied.

'Then I will wait outside the main doors.'

Before she could answer he turned again.

'I must dash, I have an appointment.'

His laugh rang out, leaving the girl totally bewildered and more than a little excited.

The Manager's clerk directed James towards the enormous mahogany door and ushered him into the large meticulous office. The Manager rose, extending his hand and indicating his young visitor towards one of the leather chairs facing his desk.

'Thank you for seeing me.'

'I really didn't think I had any alternative,' the manager replied with an amused air.

James seized the initiative. 'I expect you are wondering what this is all about.'

He had determined during his long wait to initiate the questions and thus conduct the interview from his side of the desk. It was a formula that he would employ many times in the future.

Without waiting for a reply he opened the case and produced an architect's drawing.

The manager saw opposite him an animated face, the expression determined and intent. 'What do you think?'

The manager considered the row of cottages shown on the plan.

'Do you intend to convert them?'

'I intend to build them,' stated James.

'Build them; they already appear to be quite old.'

'Let me explain,' James outlined his career to date.

After his chosen decision to leave school to help his mother, he had employed a man to do the more mundane jobs around the farm, spending his time instead in building portable chicken houses, farrowing pens and other similar buildings for smallholdings.

He explained that other manufacturers were now seeing the market potential, much larger concerns with considerable capital to invest in automated production.

He had defended his share of the market by personally conducting a vigorous sales campaign, by calling on the farmers and, rather than drop his prices to below a viable level had increased them, offering instead to fill the chicken houses with day old chicks from off the Yorkshire moors. - Finally, able to repay Mr Willoughby for the vote of confidence given to him as a young lad those years ago.

'Where did you get the capital to buy the machinery?' Mr Lattimer was genuinely interested; the young man's enthusiasm was infectious.

Small wonder that he had sold so many buildings.

'Do you remember Staincliffes, until a few years ago the largest furniture manufacturer in Europe.

The Bank manager nodded. 'I believe they banked with Martins for decades.'

'For ninety eight years to be exact. They were my mother's family.'

The intent young face confided before continuing...

'After the Staincliffe collapse, the receiver sold off all the modern equipment. However, there was still some of the older machinery left in the now disused factory and, with my mother's influence, we bought some of this and negotiated a short term lease on a small industrial unit near to Grantham.

'If then you have been so successful, why do you not fund your new venture from your own capital?' The manager assuming again his professional hat.

'When father died,' explained James, 'We still owed £1,800 on additional land he had acquired, a debt which I have now paid off. In consequence I do not have any capital, but the equity in the property is in the region of £5,000, so your loan will be assured.'

'Proposed loan,' corrected Mr Lattimer.

'Now, these cottages look attractive on paper, but where do you get the materials and expertise to build them? Your experience is after all limited to small sectional buildings.'

'Remember that I live in the country; I have seen barns and other farm buildings fall into disrepair over the past few years. I now have a large stock of old bricks, beams, pan tiles etc. all gleaned from these ruins in return for either clearing them away or, in some instances, trading a pig arc or similar.

James leaned forward taking another file from his case.

'These are the costings and cash flows; you will see that the full £3,000 will not be required until near the end of the development, the main requirement is for stage payments to progress the construction.'

'What about buying the land?' interrupted Mr Lattimer.

'I already own it and have planning permission. Remember too,' he added, 'that, as the scheme develops we have a growing equity to further guarantee the loan.'

Mr Lattimer pursed his lips, the intense face opposite had done his homework, the bank would be safe.

'Very well Mr Carrington, subject to the usual formalities, I will authorise your local branch to make the facility available to you.'

'No,' James voice rang out.

There would be no profit or kudos in this deal for the doubting Mr Osborne.

And then, more diplomatically, 'I think I would prefer my company to have a major bank as its address - I do not intend to stay a small country builder for very long.'

The manager stood up.

'To the start of a successful partnership,' he held out his hand.

'Try not to be so hard on us the next time you come to Birmingham.'

James looked puzzled.

'I am a lifelong member of the Moseley Rugby Club,' he explained.

James grinned. 'I will try and miss a couple of penalties on Saturday.'

'So long as you don't miss them the following week against Scotland,' Charles Lattimer's smiling rejoinder.

He watched the tall athletic figure disappear through the doorway and congratulated himself on acquiring for the bank a potentially important customer. He wondered too who the dunderhead was at the local branch that had not even put this idea up for consideration.

James, suppressing the joy on his face, walked slowly through the banking hall. A glance at the overhead clock showed him it was just turned five o'clock, he wondered if she would be there.

She was, dressed in a camel coloured swagger coat that emphasised the colour of her hair.

'Hello,' they both spoke in unison.

'Where does a poor country boy take a girl for coffee in this great city?' he teased.

'I will show you Mr Bumpkin.' She entered into the spirit of the moment.

They walked towards Snow Hill railway station and the Burlington Arcade, pausing when they reached a terra cotta façade which announced itself as the popular Kardomah coffee house. Inside the atmosphere was redolent with the inviting aroma of freshly made coffee and, still in a trance, they followed the smiling dark haired waitress to a corner table where they sank into the bright red leather bench seat, keeping ever so slightly apart.

'We had better introduce ourselves, I am James Carrington.'

'I know, and you are quite famous,' cut in the girl.

'Two of the clerks recognised you.'

This time it was his turn to go red.

'I am Kate Palmer, and am not at all famous,' she announced through the cascade of long hair that had fallen across one side of her face.

James was enchanted by her, the atmosphere was light and they found that both enjoyed the same zany sense of humour, Hancock and the Goons. They sipped coffee unconscious of time until Kate suddenly glanced at her watch and announced.

'I am sorry James, but I have to go, I have arranged to go to a concert at the University with a couple of girls from the bank; It is to hear Chris Barber and Ottilie Patterson, Peggy queued for absolutely ages to get the tickets.'

James suddenly remembered the other great love of his life, 'At least let me give you a lift.'

He drove slowly, dragging out the journey to Edgbaston as long as was seemly and refusing to let her go without the promise of seeing her the following Saturday.

'Come over to Moseley Rugby Club, it's not far, the ground is called The Reddings.' She noted the name in her diary.

'I will look forward to it.' The tone of her voice leaving no doubt as to her sincerity.

He did not remember much of his trip back home. His thoughts were racing ahead, to conveying the joyful tidings to Edward Lawson and with him, organising the start-up date for their first development. He turned into the drive and as he swung around the back of the house saw, from the corner of his eye, the signboard already painted.

The red and grey letters on the white ground announced FORDMILL DEVELOPMENTS.

The name, an inversion of Milford, he had chosen to serve as a reminder of the past and as an inspiration for the future.

CHAPTER FIVE

The early friendship with Edward had blossomed so that, when they left school, it seemed natural to extend the embryonic partnership into the real thing. Many times, particularly when they were digging footings for the poultry houses etc., he had been grateful for the big man's great strength and resilience. His easy manner with other workmen and natural aptitude made him a natural leader and his powerful physique deterred any serious argument.

They started building the following day and on the third morning received their first enquiry.

The Simpsons, a couple in their mid- fifties with a Victorian home too large now that the family had married and flown the nest, fell in love with the olde worlde charm they saw growing from the stacks of bricks and tiles.

What had begun as a day out in the country now saw them excitedly pouring over plans in the site office, already mentally disposing of the surplus furniture. James winked at Edward, certain they had just hooked their first customer.

The project was a complete success. War weary Britain had a surfeit of town life, the lure of the countryside and the prospect of a postcard cottage, with all mod cons, proved James's judgement to be exactly in tune with the moment.

Fordmill Properties after its early success grew rapidly, the timing for the building industry was absolutely correct; the war had changed so many concepts. Mr and Mrs Average saw it as their right to have indoor lavatories and their own patch of garden and, perhaps more significantly, an inalienable right to own their own house.

Fordmill grew from strength to strength, the company headquarters progressed from a room at home to a small office in town and, within five years to a three storey development with spacious offices and an entrance hall exhibiting some better examples of modern art and furniture, copies of chairs by Mies van der Rohe, teak tables from Sweden and other contemporary pieces, all underlining the aphorism of the Bauhaus school of architecture that 'God is in detail.'

This was the creed in which they all passionately believed, a credo they wanted to impart to their work, to awaken and stimulate a public awareness for good design.

The same care was taken in the offices. The staff, suffused in this modern environment, found it easy to extend a client's thoughts from not merely a building but a complete package. So often a company would build new premises and then, packing it with dreadful pre-war artefacts, destroy the illusion they had created. The dream that a designer had pondered for weeks on their behalf was destroyed in the time it took for the removal men to deliver the chattels and files from their previous place of work.

The home may be cosy, but the office must exude efficiency if it is to generate quality of output; this they all firmly believed in.

James Carrington, rugby now a spectator sport, locked the door of the Jaguar XK150 and strode into reception,

'Is Mr Lawson in yet, Connie?' he enquired

'He is with Mr Cooper the architect; I believe they are in the conference room.'
He nodded.

'Good, save the day and organise some coffee - make it strong, it's been a long night.'
He joined and greeted the others. 'Edward, Tim.'
Without further preamble, James outlined his latest thoughts.

'I have an idea I want to run past you. There are three types of people buying homes:-
One - Young first timers.
Two - Couples with two kids moving out of their smaller houses, either because they now earn more money or because they need the space.
Three – Finally there are older couples either retiring or preparing the ground for retirement.
Do you agree?'

Edward nodded. 'Very succinct, but in its simplest form, quite true.'
The other two in agreement, waited for the big story to be delivered.

'We are catering for the first two categories' observed Tim Cooper, his mind wondering what new schemes his imaginative client would come up with next.
'Blocks of luxury apartments,' James announced.

'Full of all the latest gadgetry, most of which these people will never have seen. You make them inviting from the outside, Tim, and we will leave them convinced that they must have one.'

'We could maybe have some girls dressed as French maids to show them round.'
Edward was warming to the idea!

'I might have known you would come up with something like that,' James laughingly accused his partner.

'On the other hand, just this once, your trousers may just have come up with a good idea.'
'They usually come down with one.' Edward's reply had them in hoots of laughter.

For several minutes the conversation degenerated in to a mixture of ribaldry and good humour that close friends can, for the moment, find so amusing and yet, when related later, loses so much in the telling.

'Order, order. Now, as you seem to think it such a good idea, where do you propose we should build these apartments?
He smiled encouragingly at them.

'Don't call them condominiums or we shall be back where we started a moment ago.'
They looked at him enquiringly.

'By the sea,' he enthused.

'I have given it a lot of thought, we need to be within the reach of the family and we need a carrot to entice the relatives to visit. If you have kids, the prospect of visiting Granny at the seaside has to be a winner. The Grandparents hog the kids and the parents are then free to go out and enjoy themselves.'

'The apartments need to be big enough to house a family on a temporary basis,' Tim interjected.

'Good point,' affirmed James.

'Find a way of making the 'extra' accommodation useful, maybe a studio or something.'

'The location is the key.' Edward pondered the options.

'Devon and Cornwall; wonderful holiday spots, but not easy to get to, particularly in the winter. The Welsh are so damned parochial, East Anglia is superb but, until they build some decent roads, rather impractical, so I favour the south coast.'

'Excellent,' appraised James, 'Your logic is impeccable, but precisely where?'
He threw the question back at them, sensing they were by now enthusiastic to be going down his latest tangent.

'Bournemouth!' He delivered the goods.

'Well within reach of most parts of the Midlands and even London and I just happen to know a girl down there whose parents have friends, potentially in the right places.'

'Of course, the red head from the bank.' Edward smiled.

'Now I know why we have such extortionate petrol bills, you sly old dog.'

'Actually she has left the Bank; she is in PR with the International Seating Corporation. Mother knows the chairman from the Staincliffe days so was able to put in a word for her.'
The blue eyes twinkled.

'I bet she paid for it.' Tim shook his head.

'Do you never stop wheeling and dealing?'

'Nope, life is too short, I will not, cannot stop, until I have regained my inheritance.'

A telephone call to Kate Palmer fixed the visit to Bournemouth and elicited the anticipated invitation to stay for the weekend.

He collected her from High Wycombe and enjoyed again the easy friendship they had shared from the start. They arrived about six thirty and were announced by a pair of black flat-coated retrievers who fell over themselves to welcome Kate home to 'The Cedars.'

Jeremy Palmer, a solicitor, was a tall erect man with a strong intelligent face. He emerged with his wife and, from the vantage view on the porch gave James the sort of appraising look that parents cannot resist. Angela Palmer's face indicated she had already given the seal of approval. They shook hands and led their guest through the oak panelled hall and into the drawing room.

'You have a beautiful home, sir.' The comment sincere and genuine.

'Far too big for us now my boy,' the host confided, quite unaware that, at a stroke, he had validated his guest's raison d'être.

'Do you miss the rugby James?' The older man was interested and anxious for every scrap of gossip from his famous visitor.

'Well I tell you what Mr Palmer, I don't miss the training.'

'In that case we can have a drink right away. Kate dear, be an angel, there is some bubbly in the refrigerator.'

The drinks were served and the conversation was as easy and relaxed as it had been with Kate that first time at the Kardomah. So much so, that freshening up and changing for dinner was all a bit of a rush.

The Palmers had invited two other couples to join them. Dickie Jackson and his wife were locals, the others; Wendy and Peter Charlton were mutual friends from Northumberland.

The conversation was relaxed and convivial and well informed on many subjects, not least food and wine. James who subconsciously admired perfection, so had always found older women more interesting was particularly aware of Rachel Jackson. She was Dickie's second wife and, at thirty four, had the advantage of stunning good looks and a husband who could afford to indulge her expensive tastes.

The starter was a terrine of crab and Dublin prawns exquisitely served on a sauce of yoghurt and dill, accompanied by Chablis.

The meal continued in fine style with Saddle of Lamb stuffed with asparagus and served with mint flavoured Hollandaise sauce. Carefully putting down his glass of Margaux, James looked from his hosts to his fellow guests.

'Is there a long waiting list for this club?' he asked approvingly.

'Not if you are well in with the right people,' Rachel's mischievous observation, causing Kate's face to change colour to match the Titian hue of her hair.

Jeremy Palmer interrupted, to spare his daughter's blushes.

'Any member of the committee will do.'

The conversation continued with James content to sit in the shade, knowing instinctively that, sooner or later, the topic would inevitably turn to rugby and he would be centre stage.

He was after all the only new face and most of the current conversation, vis-à-vis this chateau and that had been mulled over endlessly on previous occasions. He knew enough to join in occasionally and they respected his polite indulgence.

The food though was awfully good; he wondered if Kate was as talented as her mother, he rather hoped so. Eventually, the men wanted to know about the recent British Lions rugby tour of South Africa. He fed them a few inside details re the training and match tactics and, much to the obvious enjoyment of Rachel, a few anecdotes about the antics off the field.

'I notice you were never involved in any of these excesses,' she chided.

'Certainly not,' the blue eyes unconvincingly protested.

He attempted to adopt a naive expression. 'I was always resting for the big occasion.'

The inference was not lost on Rachel who, at thirty-four, was only ten years older than him and was coyly letting him know that she belonged to his set rather than the others.

'What about golf?' Dickie Jackson enquired.

'A rather bad eleven.'

'Do you play often?'

'About once a week, but I do intend to apply myself rather more in the future. Now that the rugby is out of the way, I will have more time. What I really need is someone to prompt me.'

'That's it then, Peter. We had better take the lad to Ferndown on Sunday morning and concentrate his mind. Eight thirty suit you? '

'I should enjoy that sir.'

James noted the amusement in Rachel's eyes as, by deferring to her husband he had once again assumed her wavelength in terms of age, he was building a bridge, one that was probably a slippery pole rather than a Brunel-like structure. He would not however know what lay on the other side without crossing it. 'Lay' being the operative word. He smiled, inwardly relishing the thought of the chase.

James and Kate spent Saturday together. They set out for Buckler's Hard, the humour flowing effortlessly .The Jaguar burbled through the New Forest, the hood down, the sunlight piercing the leafy canopy overhead and dancing on her face so that she looked like a wonderful porcelain doll. Through the large sunglasses she stared ahead, aware of his gaze and thrilling in his company, wishing this weekend would never end.

'Ye Master Builder's House on the port bow.' He nautically pronounced their arrival, disturbing her daydream.

A simple ploughman's lunch, after the banquet of the previous evening was all they could manage. In the afternoon they strolled around the moorings, lazily holding hands, deliriously content with life.

In Lyndhurst on the way back they stopped opposite a jeweller's shop.

'There is something I want to get for you.'

Before she could answer he was out of the car and running across the road towards the jewellers. At the last second he swerved to the left and disappeared into the ice-cream shop next door. He returned bearing two large cones, a large smile lighting his face.

'I bet that had you worried.'

'You are a fool, you had me terrified.'

On the Saturday evening they went to a hop at the village hall which developed on the way back into a fairly steamy affair.

'She is overheating' he said, switching off the ignition and putting his arm around Kate at the same time.

'James's...' her voiced tailed off

She trembled slightly but protested no more as he lowered the front seat and gently kissed her. He needed no caution to be gentle; she was very special to him, the only girl that he had not tried to get into bed. He had sensed from the start that any premature moves on his part would only build barriers. But now, not at all where he had planned it, the moment was right and she allowed his hands to become ever bolder. As they finally reached that divinely silky area above her stocking tops he felt his lungs must burst, he felt a great flood of longing burst from her and now it was her turn to prompt and lead.

She stroked him and he thought of England, of garden walls, of anything that would not cause a premature moment.

'Please,' he pleaded, 'it is more than flesh and blood can stand.'

Without speaking she guided the cause of all this trouble to the place it so anxiously sought.

The excitement, the pent up emotion, all exploded with fervent calls to the almighty and then, with a shuddering and ecstatic sigh he was thanking her and apologising to her, all in one jumbled sentence.

'God, I love you Kate Palmer.'

'So you ought Mr Carrington, I have given to you something I can give to no other man, but then I guess I knew it would be you since that first day at the bank.'

'Thank you, thank you.'
He held her tight and then, to release the tension, as they disentangled themselves.
'If you think this is difficult thank goodness we never tried it in the MG.'

James awoke through habit at six thirty the next morning and slowly allowed himself to surface, he felt relaxed, the joyous delight of the previous evening and the prospect of seeing Kate again made life seem so very worthwhile. He showered, and dressed in his bathrobe skipped lightly downstairs. Apart from the housekeeper the house was quiet and he wandered out onto the lawn, glad of the opportunity to compose his thoughts. He had no set plans to further his ideas on the apartments, but knew instinctively that the three men at the dinner table last night could be crucial to his ambitions.

Kate came down at eight fifteen and the knowing looks they exchanged confided more pleasures to come. Their reveries were interrupted as Jeremy Palmer entered the morning room looking very spry and ready for action in his plus two's and Slazenger sweater.

'Ready to take a pound or two off them James?'
His manner light, yet competitive.

'It will help pay for the petrol.' The enthusiastic reply.
They enjoyed a light breakfast of bacon and scrambled eggs, glancing through the newspapers as they did so. Jeremy, very much aware of the warm feeling his daughter was radiating to the good-looking young man opposite her.

He dusted his mouth with his napkin and stood up.
'Goodbye Kate darling, see you about two o'clock I guess.'
They strode out of the house to the waiting Jaguar.

'Good job I keep my clubs in the locker.'
The father's observation, looking at the tiny luggage space, blissfully unaware of the contortions his daughter had performed only hours earlier on the same red leather. They drove the short distance to Ferndown Golf Club and here in this most attractive setting amidst the pine and heather, James was introduced to the various members gathered around the first tee. One of these was a young man of his own age, who was equally as famous in his own sport as was James in his.

'Peter Allis, James Carrington.'
Dickie Jackson introduced them. The two young men liked each other instantly, an appreciation born of respect for the dedication as well as the skill that both had applied to achieve the honour of representing their country.

'Your father is the professional here, I hope he will not be scrutinising my swing too closely.'

'He is more likely to try and persuade you to put me on some rigorous fitness plan,' the effortlessly charming Allis retorted with a wide grin.
The conversation was interrupted by the late arrival of Peter Charlton.

'You are too old to do it every Sunday.'
The ribald comments flew as they placed the balls in the rack adjacent to the first tee. The customary stakes of half a crown first nine, second nine, and ten shillings on the game were agreed along with the usual sixpenny birdies.

As always, the challenge ahead had activated the adrenalin and for James, who even as a small boy at prep school had always been instinctively competitive, the desire for success even on these friendly occasions was never far below the surface, although his good humour usually disguised it.

37

Dickie Jackson off six was first to play and hit a very respectable drive into the middle of the fairway. This being the first hole, the pairings alternated and James played next. He teed up, breathed in and was now, as he had been at Twickenham, perfectly under control.

The clean thwack and the willowy follow through, the ball flying into the distance, evinced a contemplative observation from their opponents,
'Good shot, looks like we have been set up,' and a similarly appreciative and generous remark from Peter Allis as he emerged from the Pro's shop.

The day was perfect; everyone played well, the match decided at the 17th when Jeremy holed his bunker shot. They took their opponents' silver with that relish peculiar to golfers and then, being the victors, promptly spent it and more buying the whisky to go with the coffee back in the clubhouse. On such occasions the conversation between men is free and easy and ranges effortlessly over all manner of topics, usually interspersed with the latest humorous tales. James was introduced to several members and, perhaps more importantly, Dickie invited James and Kate to a day on his yacht at Poole.

They departed, with James promising his good offices to arrange tickets for the French match the following year in Paris. They drove back, the conversation still flowing easily as they swept into the drive to be greeted by the ladies drinking sherry on the porch. After a cold lunch in the conservatory, they spent the afternoon sunning themselves on the lawn and idly doing the various Sunday crosswords. James keeping a sly eye on the clock, waiting for the hour to be decently near to six o'clock and the excuse to go to his room to change. His loins activated by the same instinct as last night, also anticipated the opportunity to be next to Kate.

Hope springs eternal but, with watchful parents never too far away, a gentle embrace and murmured love and affection was what they had to make do with prior to supper, at which Angela Palmer had mysteriously and seemingly effortlessly produced a splendid joint of beef with which to seduce their appetites. The conversation continued to be both stimulating and easy, James innocently enquiring as to the effects, if any, that the war had wrought upon Bournemouth. Jeremy excused himself and disappeared into his study whence he returned with a newspaper yellowed with age.

'Take a look, you will see that the damage was quite extensive, the building minus its roof and windows is only about fifty yards away from my office.'
James took the parchment-like edition of the Evening Echo and nodded appreciatively
'Have the buildings been rebuilt?'
'Some have but, go out of the town a short way and there are still quite a few spots that remain grassed over and covered in that damned weed.'
'Rosebay willow herb.'
Kate and Angela chorused in unison, it was an old family joke, Jeremy could never remember the name of this or Christopher Columbus' three ships and, consequently, these two questions were always fired at him in any family quiz.

He acknowledged their laughter with an assumed frown.
'Unusual for a young chap like you to be interested in the war, I thought you were only interested in the future.'
'True, but to be quite honest, since I have been down here an idea hascrossed my mind on which I would very much welcome your advice.'
His host crossed to the drinks cupboard and signalled James to continue.
'Without being rude, sir.'

Jeremy interrupted him. 'Now if you have designs on our daughter and you seem a decent sort - well compared with some of the others! - we would prefer you to call us Angela and Jeremy and no, I do not like to be called Jerry, it reminds me of things that used to go under the bed or people that keep wanting to cause the sort of collateral damage you observed in that photograph.'

James dipped into his trouser pocket and took out a white handkerchief which he waved before crying out 'Pax.'

This was well received and prompted him to light the potential touch-paper.

'There are quite a few older people living down here in properties that are far too large and difficult to run. Many of your generation, yourselves included and I include my own parents, will have employed maids and gardeners and the like and, without being cynical, the war will have changed much of that. Working people have their own expectations, they will not see themselves in service any longer and with more people enjoying the mobility of the motor car there will not be the emphasis on maintaining the family home that the professional classes previously found themselves incumbent to do. I can see commuting growing, perhaps with a small flat in town and a more acceptable house for the weekend.'

James inwardly flinched at the slight bending of the truth, deciding that it was worth it, rather than insult either his hosts or their daughter who had shown him such warm hospitality.

Jeremy smiled, remembering his own such admission when he welcomed his guest to his home and then, assuming his professional stance, turned to the handsome face with its steely blue eyes.

'How can I help?'

'Do you know a good firm of solicitors; not too expensive mind, us northern lads are pretty canny with us brass.'

'Tomorrow morning then, but you don't fool me Mr Carrington.' They both smiled.

'Enough talk of business, we are due at the tennis club.'

Angela rose from the sofa to curtail the business talk and Kate laughingly warned James that they were going for cocktails and not, she insisted, to look at the girls' legs.

CHAPTER SIX

After golf the previous day, Dickie had passed on Rachel's request that James and Kate come over for drinks the following evening. They duly arrived at six thirty and once more Rachel drooled over the Jaguar. Her husband attempted to fend off her pleadings by stating quite correctly, that there was a long waiting list for the car.

James confirmed this, at the same time mischievously suggesting that as he had had his fun in the car he was considering selling it. The raised eyebrows that accompanied this disclosure were not wasted on Kate who, unseen by the others, gave him a coy yet piercing flash with those large green eyes that so fascinated him.

'Oh Dickie darling, please, please, please.'

Rachel went into overdrive and the poor man besotted by this exquisite woman had no chance, even though James, feeling rather guilty, attempted to come to his aid. The pouting face however was not to be denied and with a sigh of resignation Dickie, without realising he was aping James's trick of yesterday, put one hand into the pocket of his slacks and raised a white handkerchief above his head and with the other hand he pulled a cheque book from his jacket and turned to James.

'You are a very expensive chap to know.' He proffered the cheque book to James, who was beginning to wish he had not become quite so carried away and yet at the same time he knew that this was a small pawn he was losing in his game plan.

He wrote £2,1250 on the back of the cheque book, this being the cost of the car plus the £200 he had paid the dealer to jump the queue. He put a line through this and the figure £1,500 in the box on the cheque.

'That is very fair.' Dickie symbolically spat on his hand and offered it to James.

'I forgot to mention the bottle of Bollinger.'

'You are not smashing that on MY car,' the exultant Rachel cried as she smothered her husband in kisses.

'And the taxi fare home,' Kate laughingly joined in, pre-empting with feminine intuition Rachel's next move, the suggestion that James take the new owner for a spin in her new car.

'Only five minutes mind,' Kate warned.

'To the cliffs and back,' yelled Rachel.

They slid into the car and James took the wheel, noticing as he did so the long creamy thigh that rested against the gear stick. The Jaguar growled and within seconds they were hurtling down the road, the g-forces pushing them back into the sculptured hide seats. He noticed Rachel's face, sideways on it was lit with an ear splitting grin, the mixture of ecstatic pride and exhilaration at the speed, it was difficult to differentiate. He glided to a halt and opened the door so that she could take the wheel.

'James's, she reached forward to switch off the throbbing engine.
Her voice was husky and excited. 'Now is not the time, but I will reward you for this like you have never been rewarded before.'
'I will hold you to it.' The double entendre slipped out before he knew it.
It was however sufficient to lower the temperature, not to mention the problem in his groin. This time she let him change places in the car.

'Steady with the clutch, it is a little fierce.'
The Jaguar leapt forward but she was a natural and accomplished driver, soon in tune with the car she quickly mastered the art of easing into the bends and then powering out of them. The others heard the deep resonance of the approaching engine and pretended to throw themselves to the ground as Rachel swung the car into the drive. She leapt out, totally ignoring James and ran across to her husband.

'Thank you darling.' It was said with such warmth and affection, as if the invitation made to James five minutes earlier had never existed.

James took the champagne from an unsuspecting Kate and squeezed her other hand with a genuine desire to communicate the love that was growing apace for her.

The evening continued with yet more champagne, with the conversation flowing as easily as the Bollinger and with no look or hint of the interlude in the car. James introduced the idea that he had mooted to Jeremy Palmer and was encouraged by the response it elicited. Rachel not surprisingly was all for, as she put it, 'Lowering the local geriatric age.'

Dickie with more commercial instincts saw the additional benefits to the local economy.

'I would appreciate picking your brain on this Dickie.'
James's voice invited and elicited the appropriate invitation.

'As opposed to pickling it as we are doing at the moment.'
Kate joined in, her humour as on that first meeting, very much in tune with James.
They finally left in a black cab, but not before Peter had insisted, as part of the deal, to pay the cabbie. The poor driver, used as he was to all sorts, could not for the life of him, imagine what all the laughter was all about.

As they pulled out of the drive, James looked through the back window and was rewarded with hint of a wink that spoke volumes from his hostess.

Their homecoming in a taxi catapulted the Palmers from the seats on the porch, both faces alive with anxiety and overflowing with relief when they discovered the reason.

The concern gave way to a mixture of relief and amazement that this young man could, at the drop of a hat, sell something as precious and cherished as his car, and a very special car at that.

This was clearly something the Palmers were going to have to get used to. They were after all, people who had always lived in the same house, the very house that had belonged to Jeremy's parents before them; they were thoughtful people, who had never made an instantaneous decision in the whole of their lives.

Angela stood up and signalled Kate to follow.

'Shall we make do with sandwiches?' she appealed to the others for affirmation.

'You had better ask James if you want a quick answer.' The amused reply.

'We had had a few nibbles at the Jackson's so something very light, how about cucumber sandwiches, Hovis bread, no crusts and Earl Grey of course.'

His reply instantly entering into the spirit of things, and at the same time indicating just how far the relationship had developed over the course of a weekend. As the ladies left the room Jeremy walked across to his pipe rack and selecting an old favourite, indicated as he filled it for James to follow him out on to the porch.

'I have been thinking, and I hope you will not consider me interfering if I suggest that in the event of you taking forward your idea on the apartments, that you will need an office down here.'

He continued, 'since old Wooler the accountant died, the adjacent office to my own firm is now vacant and might be worth considering.'

'Jeremy, that would be marvellous, such august neighbours, it will also give us an air of respectability and I will be able to nip round next door and pick your brains, or are you going off the idea?'

'We will look into it in the morning, but I warn you it is not like those swish Scandinavian places you design for your clients up north.'

James had warmed immediately to Jeremy Palmer; having an older man in whom to confide was new to him, particularly one whose values he respected.

'Did you always you want to go into the law?'

He remembered his own father and the expectations that had given him little option but to join the family firm.

'No explicit pressure was ever applied and yet as my time came to go up to Oxford I was aware of Grandfather suggesting he had a word with the Master of Balliol with whom he had been an undergrad. To be fair, I had no set plans, although I guess I would have read Classics and probably gone into teaching. However, the law has been pretty good to me and has certainly given me more of an insight into the real world than I might have seen as a school master. What about you James, you obviously have a good brain, did you never want to go up yourself?'

'It was the thing most precious to me.'

James related to his host the events of that day when his highest hopes had been realised and then crushed when overhearing the conversation between his mother and his aunt. The blue eyes were moist as he confided for the first and only time of his cycle ride to the great stone house that had once been the family seat and the oath he had made to deliver those proud acres back to the family from whom they had been snatched by the bank.

'Sorry Jeremy, it is something I keep under wraps, not even my partners know the full story. I know I can rely upon your discretion and, to be honest, it was good to get it off my chest. Perhaps, if I sometimes seem a bit passionate or determined, you will know now the demon that drives me.'

'Ambition,' he confided, 'is like heartache, it is like a lump of stone in one's chest, only achievement can make it go away. One day, my sons will take my place at Cambridge.'

His voice tailed, off embarrassed that he had, for one so self-contained, said so much 'Thank you James, I am honoured that you should feel able to make me privy to these very special thoughts and ideals that you so commendably have.'

'Maybe sir, it is that you hold the key to my ambitions, at least in terms of Cambridge.'

They looked at each other and smiled.

'Maybe I do, maybe I do,' Jeremy smilingly acknowledged.

The new high ground the two men had established was invaded by the sound of the trolley laden with sandwiches, cakes and a silver tea service from the spout of which Angela had hung a sign bearing the legend, Earl Grey.

The following day the two men went into town, both in pinstripe suits, only the lack of a bowler hat denying James his partner's obvious calling in life. Although the large overnight bag carried by the younger man as opposed to Jeremy's brief case was another.

Jeremy Palmer's office was proclaimed on a brass plate bearing the legend Palmer, Braithwaite, Palmer & Jayes.'

'That is me.' He confided, touching the second of the Palmer names etched upon the sign.

'The first was my grandfather and, since my father was killed in the Great War there was a bit of a gap until I came along. Old Braithwaite is dead, but his son is still with us and we made Anthony Jayes a partner last year. Actually, as he is only about thirty, he is probably the best chap for you to deal with.

They entered through a heavy panelled door and walked to the staircase pausing to enquire at a small sliding hatch if there had been any urgent messages. James followed his host to a first floor room at the front of the building. The whole atmosphere reeked of respectability, the oak bookcases groaning with legal expertise, unchanged it appeared since the time that Kate's Great Grandfather had occupied the same desk.

'Dreadful news about the Titanic,' observed James, casually returning the yellowing copy of Country Life to its position amidst the other fading glossies.

'Touché,' laughed the lawyer, 'but then I did warn you not to expect anything too swish, or up to date.'

'Actually it is perfect, it will, as you said, give us that solid look of respectability that most of our clients are going to consider important'

'In that case I will take you along to meet young Jayes.'

James followed his host along the corridor and up a further set of stairs to a door announcing its occupant as A. P. Jayes.

Anthony Jayes stood up, hand outstretched and, after the introductions, assigned James to a comfortable leather sofa in the bay window. He telephoned down for coffee and in a totally business- like manner took out a foolscap sized journal and headed the next empty page, James Carrington. He paused and James took up the running.

'I suggest Anthony that I outline the idea and you knock some holes in it.'

'We know that since the war, people, all sorts of people, have re-defined their ideas and expectations and that a very big part of that new thinking is the home. The right to own your own house and the need for mobility will be an essential aspect of the new careers being created by the new technologies. Older people are realising that their offspring will not only not be following them into the family firm, neither will they be moving into the family home. Kate for instance does not expect to be tied down to living in Bournemouth, nice place that it is. Ergo, Jeremy will eventually find The Cedars too large for Angela and himself;- he has in fact already alluded to this.'

Anthony interrupted his new client, 'How do you propose to cater for this brave new world? It seem to me that inducing people to abandon their family homes for a new apartment may in essence be a good idea, but it will founder on the very strength of that logic, i.e. unless you can unlock the equity they have in the bricks and mortar they will not have the capital to buy the new dream home.'

'Precisely,' James affirmed the problem.

Now he needed to know if Anthony Jayes was a man of initiative or just a good solicitor.

He sought to tease a reaction from the earnest face with the open journal.

'How do you think we should approach it?'

'It would help if we could find someone to buy the client's house,' he mused.

'Come on, if you are going to benefit from all these conveyancing fees you will have to do better than that.'

James leaned over and took the virgin page from Anthony's hand. He wrote a series of headings.

Initial funding
- Acquisition of land
- Build Apartments
- Lease Properties
- Re-invest capital
- Long-term goals

'I am not a rich man, but I do have a reasonably substantial sum that I can inject into the project. Your first task, Anthony old bean, is to draw up a shortlist of people that might have the wealth and the inclination to join us in this little venture. On second thoughts, you draw up the list and I will do the persuading.

- As to acquiring the land, I will comb the town for prospective sites and it will then be up to you to establish title to these properties.
- The actual building procedures will be taken care of by my own Fordmill people.
- When the buildings are ready for occupation you will once again be centre stage to arrange the leases. These will be fair but totally under our control.
- The re-investment of capital will be done through a merchant Bank, possibly the one that Dickie Jackson represents, although he does not know this yet.
- The long-term goal is to make us all extremely wealthy.
- As to releasing the equity in the unwanted family bricks and mortar; I am formulating an idea about that.

'Any more questions? No, then do I assume you are with me?'

A bemused Anthony Jayes found himself nodding his head, outwardly calm, inwardly his thoughts were in turmoil. Solicitors did not make far reaching decisions of this kind without long and tedious thought processes.

'Great'. James reached across and shook his hand, 'I will leave you to fill in the journal whilst I square it with Jeremy.'

He left Anthony's room and returned to find the senior partner working his way through a mound of legal documents. His host pointed towards the coffee pot and carefully stacked the papers whilst the younger man filled two cups. That done he looked enquiringly at James who gave him the thumbs up...

'The arrangements you suggest, they are perfect. However, I have to go back to Nottingham for three, maybe four days, could you possibly ask one of your juniors to get things moving for me?' The solicitor nodded.

'It will be good to have the office taken again, especially if it is in the family.' He gave a knowing wink.

'Ah yes, that is something else I have to speak to you about, but perhaps on a more appropriate occasion.'

'Plenty of time, be careful driving back.'

He said it without thinking and then, realising James no longer had a car, immediately offered his guest the Daimler sitting in the road outside.

'No thanks Jeremy, I am quite looking forward to travelling back by train.'

He rose to his feet, appreciative of his newly acquired friendship, but anxious also to be starting out on this exciting and important new phase of his life.

James glided down the stairs, swinging on the newel post much to the amusement of the three middle-aged secretaries, collected his bag from reception before striding purposefully through the Square, past the Post Office, and up Richmond Hill to Horseshoe Common and then turning right was soon within sight of the Railway Station.

He didn't have long to wait, he knew he wouldn't, not when you are on a roll like this. The train arrived and he was soon ensconced in first class, scribbling away at the figures that were roaming around in his head. The master plan was evolving. He had telephoned Connie and asked her to arrange to bring Edward and Tim Cooper and to join him for dinner at the Black Boy Hotel in Nottingham.

God, life was good!

CHAPTER SEVEN

After a fairly liquid but thoroughly good working dinner they decided on impulse that it would be sensible to stay the night.

He was awake at around five thirty, the combination of alcohol and the excitement engendered by the meeting having kept him awake most of the night. He decided to go on ahead of the others and not having a car, he summoned a taxi. They inched out of the car park at the back of the hotel into a deserted Parliament Street and made their way towards Trent Bridge passing on either side of the river the two rival football grounds and then the majestic Trent Bridge cricket ground, home of Nottinghamshire County Cricket Club and host to so many famous Test matches including the very first against Australia in 1899.

They headed south towards Ruddington and entered the grounds of what had once been a fine Victorian house. They had acquired the building last year and added a modern wing in tone and sympathy with the gothic splendour bestowed on the original by that giant of late Victorian architecture, Watson Fothergill.

Nottingham is so fortunate he mused, to be so richly endowed with these fantastic Dracula like homes of incredible complexity, in which turrets and gables vie with enormous chimneys to catch the discerning eye.

Intent as he was upon getting to his desk, James could not but glance and be uplifted by the splendour of what he saw. He felt pride too in the sympathetic addition they had made to the building; this enterprise that had won them an award from the Royal Institute of British Architects.

He paid off the cabbie and opened the great panelled door leading into the reception area. To dado height the walls were panelled in oak which complemented the doors that led to the various rooms. The cool painted walls above the panelling were hung with a mixture of their own projects and the works of Le Corbusier and other major architectural figures of the twentieth century, the centrepiece of which was the original plans and water coloured elevations of the building, signed by the master himself, Watson Fothergill.

He switched on the electric kettle before sitting at his desk and placing all the paperwork into the in-tray. He leaned back in his chair and cast his mind back… he had been lucky in his choice of partners, they rarely disagreed and if they did, each would usually defer to the one whose arguments were logical and appropriate. James had a genial nature, at least on the surface, and the others recognised him as the natural leader, they all understood who would make all the core decisions.

Importantly, they were able to do this without having to sacrifice their own self-esteem. Today he recognised, he must assert that leadership as never before.

How to play it, - most of the best ideas had come from batting an idea freely around the table, enjoying the ensuing humour as when they first conceived the Bournemouth concept, or the ribald amusement when two or more of them had stayed overnight after a site visit.

He decided to stick with the proven format, they had after all produced a skeleton of an idea at dinner last night, today they would attempt to flesh it out.

First however, he decided to catch up on the post and was more than a little surprised to open a letter from the Bank advising that they had been unable to clear the cheque from Dickie Jackson. While he was still pondering the problem, Connie who had also come in ahead of the others, buzzed him to say that Dickie was on the line for him.

A very apologetic and shamefaced voice on the other end was clearly distressed at the embarrassment and James tried to defuse the situation by acknowledging that 'these things do happen.'

'I will of course see that you get the car back.'

'That will not be necessary, things are pretty good for me right now and I can quite comfortably stand the fifteen hundred quid. I am sure you will not want to tell Rachel and neither do I, let this be a private matter between us and I will cash the cheque when it suits you.'

'James you are a brick, what can I say?'

'Let's forget it Dickie, as a matter of fact I was intending to telephone you anyway.'

'In that case I have a brilliant idea, can you and Kate manage a day at Goodwood races later this week? The Bank is inviting a few high flyers down so it could be quite interesting - bring the Palmers of course.'

'As a matter of fact I am planning to return to Bournemouth so that would be marvellous; I shall really look forward to it.'

'That's settled then and James, I really won't forget this.'

You certainly will not, James mused as he put the receiver back on the hook.

It was all coming together and the car, which he had seen as the centrepiece of his manoeuvring was doing just that, without any steering on his part.

He leaned back in his chair and with eyes closed contemplated the latest throw of the dice, it was his throw next and he must go for a pair of sixes.

His concentration was broken by Edward and Tim Cooper, the procession completed by Connie and the coffee tray.

'I will not ask how you feel; I can only hope it is better than you look. However, when I have imparted my latest tidings you will surely be uplifted.'

James outlined the telephone call from Dickie Jackson and Edward, with his many years' experience of James's ability to turn defence into attack, knowingly observed;

'The poor bugger's going to pay for that car many times over and he won't even realise it.'

'What I have in mind will give him a good return on his investment with 'Carrington Cars' - actually that has a ring to it don't you think?'

'Oh no, no more new ideas please, let's get this off the ground first.' A plea from the still pallid, overhung face of Tim Cooper.

'OK, so let's draw up the battle plans; open forum as usual, just bounce a few ideas around.' The others nodded.

ITEM ONE

'First we need to establish a line of cash and we are talking serious money.'

Edward's brow was furrowed with concentration, he stroked his chin, a sure sign that he was thinking of matters financial. Because of his great size and affable nature not many people were aware of just how astute he was and James, who had sometimes considered taking on a Financial Director, had sensibly decided that it would be a quite unnecessary salary in view of the skills, as yet not fully exploited; realising too that it would hurt his friend to even contemplate such a move.

Edward gave him a considered look. 'We need a Bank, James'.

'But we have a Bank and Charlie Lattimer has been as good as gold to us ever since that day when that idiot Osborne wouldn't play ball.'

Tim sided with the big man.

'Edward is right, James. What you are contemplating will take us into the big time and we need to be able to talk money, big money, on a regular basis, we cannot be telephoning old Lattimer every time we want to move the goal posts a little.'

'So what do you suggest?'

James was enjoying this debate; the two directors sitting across the table were delivering the goods, effortlessly. It gave one confidence for the future.

'Your pal Dickie Jackson, he works for APP doesn't he?'

'Why yes, Abercrombie Pope & Plummer. Now we are talking big time.'

'Losing your nerve old son,' Edward pretended to duck.

'   Cheeky bugger, all I was going to point out is that I believe he is responsible for European investments - but at least he could maybe give us an entrée to the right person.'

Edward's gaze circled the boardroom table as he continued, with ever increasing enthusiasm.

'We really are on to something here but we must set out our terms so that...' James interrupted, like Edward now fully warmed to the task.

'We will insist on it being at Head Office. I believe their H,Q is in the Strand, thank you Edward, you have really got the ball rolling.'

ITEM TWO

'Tim can you give us a ball park figure for overall costs?'

'Give or take, I reckon on around seventy thousand for a complex of twenty flats and six integrated shops. If we go for under floor car parks which is very bold and maybe too forward looking , then you can add a further ten thousand.'

'Let's skip that for the moment although I personally think that will make us a lot of money in the future but, if we have to trim our costs it will be a simple option to delete.'

ITEM THREE

'What will the market stand in terms of selling price?' No reply from the others.

'We are now moving into an area where we have no local knowledge and that will be vitally important, particularly when we make our presentation to APP.'

The others nodded and he continued.

'You will remember I mentioned Anthony Jayes to you last night over dinner at the Black Boy. It will be interesting to see how he has got on, to see if he has the nous to realise the opportunity we are presenting to him.'

'I agree and move that we delay that decision until James gets back from his next trip to Bournemouth - agreed?' Tim looked at the others for approval.

The heads around the table nodded their acquiescence and he continued...

ITEM FOUR

'You mentioned Jeremy Palmer's idea of us taking the rooms adjacent to him.

I think it makes a lot of sense; it might make even more sense if we could secure two or three other adjacent rooms and perhaps convert them into a mews type of cottage. This would be handy - not just for James as he now has his leg under, or should I say over the table at the Palmers, but for entertaining business customers or potential buyers from further afield.'

'Tim, that is a brilliant idea, although I was actually going to suggest that, once the first apartments are finished that we keep one of them empty, complete with maid service so that we can invite prospective buyers to spend a few days with us. It will provide an ideal opportunity to introduce them to their new lifestyle and, assuming we have selected the other occupants correctly, they will do the selling for us, particularly to the families of those moving in.'

'I move we build both options into our Marketing Plan.'

'It must be good,' observed James, 'You are stroking your chin again Edward.'

Tim rose, 'On that note Chairman, I move we invite you to take us for lunch, perhaps the Services Club and I can take a few bob off you on the billiard table.'

Tim drove them back into town and they parked on Maid Marian Way, before walking the short distance to the Services Club. James had inherited his father's membership courtesy of the president, a member of the Midlands rugby team at the same time as Robert Carrington. They swung open the wrought iron gate and passing through the front door opted to turn right and straight into the communal dining room. Joyce, whose husband was the steward, handed the typed menus and smiled as they all demanded steak and kidney with lots of gravy. Just like boys at school she thought as she returned with the starter, ham and pea soup.

After a pleasant and entertaining lunch, Tim carried out his threat and duly relieved the others of a ten bob note apiece. Thereupon he announced that he really must get down to producing some finished drawings if they were to make any sort of impact at the proposed APP meeting. The others also had work to do and they departed having agreed that dependent upon James's meeting in Bournemouth, further and more detailed discussions would take place.

He walked back into the city and through the Market Square, proud as all Nottinghamians are of this and the majestic Council House designed in 1929 by the distinguished local architect, Cecil Howitt. As he passed the steps at the front of the building he turned, nose twitching into Burton's

Food Hall, heading immediately to the counter that housed the famous game pie, to this he added a selection of delicatessens for his supper and whilst paying for them, decided on impulse that he should get another car, - today!

He made his way along Hockley skirting the edge of the Lace Market until he reached Truman's Motor showrooms at the bottom of Huntington Street.

He did not even have to make a decision as there, centre-stage was an Alvis TD in British racing green. It was every man's dream of a car, the huge curved bonnet flowing into the integrated wings which housed the imposing twin headlights, set one above the other. The chrome was burnished and so was the desire within James to own this thoroughbred masterpiece.

In this mood he was a salesman's dream, they think that the purposeful face is there to haggle, in fact it to disguise the intention that he is not leaving without the object of his intent.

A price was soon agreed and, on James's insistence, the salesman telephoned Charles Lattimer in Birmingham to authorise the cheque. The Manager at Truman's wryly shook his head, he liked to do quick deal himself, but this was something else. Half an hour after entering the showroom a man had been despatched to the vehicle registration office, the atmosphere was blue with fumes as just about every salesman in the building had been co-opted to move cars around, just so that this persuasive character in a Barbarian's tie could drive down to Bournemouth that evening. He had organised all of this and he was a Forest supporter, he didn't even like rugby!

He had the last laugh however as, in the excitement, James had left behind the purchases from Burton's Food Hall, he and his wife were going to have a pleasant supper this evening, as they too were both rather partial to game pie. He hoped she would believe him when he explained how he had come by the repast; hopefully too she would not anticipate a similar treat every time he sold a car.

James meanwhile was euphorically driving along the A453 heading for Birmingham where he planned, out of courtesy and respect for all his help thus far, to confide the new developments to Charles Lattimer.

As he drew nearer to the city, the familiar landmarks etched upon his memory from that first eventful drive to meet the as then unknown Mr Lattimer, were poignant reminders of how far they had come in such a short time. He decided not to dwell on the matter; it was not the time to be getting cold feet. More pleasant by far, to muse about the slim redhead who now so occupied his life. Should the occasion arise, a wryly rude thought crossed his mind; they would have rather more room in this car than the last.

However, back to the present, how to broach the subject?
It would seem best if the idea appeared to come from the Manager as James had no wish to appear to be dropping him, particularly as this was the man whose initial confidence and support had underpinned everything they had achieved thus far. He carefully parked the Alvis, his delight in the magnificent machine confirmed by a passing schoolboy who gave him an appreciative thumbs-up.

His visits to the Bank these days elicited no long delays. He was shown through to Charles Lattimer's office, the attentive smiling face beneath its strategically combed thinning locks looked up enquiringly as he waved James to a seat.

'I will get straight to the point Charles.' He outlined the new proposals in some detail...
'The amount of funding you require James is somewhat over my level of authority, so

much so in fact, that you may well have to consider approaching a Merchant Bank' Inwardly the younger man heaved a sigh of relief, the very reaction he had hoped for. He pursed his lips before politely enquiring,

'Whom would you recommend?'

'Well, you could try Hambros or Hill Samuel, perhaps Rothschild's or APP.

'That is Abercrombie's isn't it.' James interrupted.

The manager nodded.

'As a matter of fact I have got to know one of their chaps, Dickie Jackson, quite well actually. That could be the answer. Thank you Charles, once again you have delivered the goods.'

Leaving the Bank, he was soon heading out of the city along the Stratford Road towards Oxford, his thoughts once again turned to his first visit to the bank and the subsequent brief sojourn in the coffee bar with Kate.

Thinking of the latter prompted yet another U-turn; he would spend the night in Town rather than at the Bear in Woodstock as had been his original intention.

Negotiating the traffic in a heavy and still unfamiliar car at the same time as attempting to read the RAC road map is not easy and not to be recommended. However, he finally managed to change direction to London and was parked outside Claridge's at six thirty.

A hotel of this standing is not impressed by motor cars, nevertheless there lurks a Stirling Moss within most men, and doormen are no exception. The sight of the magnificent dark green Alvis, still with its showroom sheen was sufficient to bring an immediate attendant face to the driver's window. The doorman in top hat and tailcoat opened the door and palmed the ten shilling note in one effortless movement.

James handed over the keys and hoped, as he picked up his hand luggage, that his luck would hold and that this oasis of royalty and privilege would find a room for him. He strode up the steps to the revolving doors and entered the stylish lobby that led to the Foyer Restaurant, to his left he found reception. His good fortune held and minutes later he was in the lift that transported him to an elegant Art Deco bedroom. He deposited his overnight bag and made his way back to reception and the much vaunted cocktail bar.

The walls were a breath taking combination of crystal mirrors set off by art deco lamps depicting 'leaping deer'; to the right through a pillared portico, was the cocktail bar and here on one of the mirrors, was inscribed the name of the man who in 1926 designed and inspired this elegance, Basil Ionides.

Dinner was superb and he luxuriated in the wonderful surrounding of this marvellous hotel which complemented so perfectly the mood of his happiness and anticipation of the next few days, in fact, of the rest of his life.

The following morning James came down at seven fifteen and took full advantage of the marvellously prepared full English breakfast. Foreigners have no idea what they are missing, he thought, as he brushed the toast crumbs off the Times crossword.

He was struggling a little, he usually tussled with the Telegraph but, in this atmosphere redolent of everything that had made Britain one time master of the World, it seemed only appropriate to take the Thunderer, even if most of the writing he had applied to the page was in the form of unsolved anagrams rather than correct answers.

CHAPTER EIGHT

NEW BOND STREET.

He saw the sign as he turned off Oxford Street, and without pausing, walked earnestly past the other jewellers until he reached Asprey's.

He had never been here before but remembered his mother quietly relating to his father how thrilled she had been when he proposed and had produced from his pocket her engagement ring, the case of which bore the Royal crest assigned to Asprey. He had always known that when that special girl came along, that he too would come here, hoping that the eternal love that his parents had known would be his also.

The man in the frock coat approached with a diffident yet at the same time confident air. He had welcomed Princes and notables from all over the world, the more august of course in their own residences.

'May I help you sir?'

'I want a solitaire diamond ring.'

'What sort of price had sir in mind?'

He confided a figure, mentally wincing as he said it, equating as it did to the price of two Alvis's.

The man in the frock coat smiled appreciatively,

'Certainly sir, any particular setting?'

'No, that is why I have come to Asprey's, I would value your advice, this is for a very special lady, but then I expect we all say that.'

'Most gentlemen infer that sir, as to whether they mean it, in view of the number of second hand rings that the ladies leave with us leaves one doubtful.'

Various diamonds were shown, James eventually choosing one he had seen from the first tray.

Pocketing his valuable acquisition and feeling amazingly elated James returned to Claridge's to collect the car.

He weaved his way out of town and finally seeing the first signs for Bournemouth, admitted to a few pangs of concern, not least of which was that Jeremy Palmer would consent to giving his daughter's hand to a young man he had known only a few months. Rather than wait until the evening he drove straight to Jeremy's office.

He was invited up and feeling far more nervous than on any occasion at Twickenham, he shook hands with Jeremy.

'As I don't know how to start, I am going to blurt it out.'

He looked at the older man.

'I want, very much sir, to marry your daughter.'

Jeremy Palmer rose from his desk and picked up the telephone. James watched dry mouthed as he dialled a number. It was finally answered and he heard him say,

'There is a young man here who wants to marry our daughter. Personally I am inclined to say yes, in fact, like you my dear; I am amazed it took him so long.'

'Yes I will tell him just that,' he confided to the voice on the other end of the telephone. He turned towards an excited James; the handshake was firm and welcoming.

'Welcome to the family my boy, I am instructed to invite you to dine with us this evening to celebrate an event that gives both Angela and I a great deal of happiness.'

'We can only hope that Kate says 'yes,' smiled the would-be groom.

'You have a point there, but I am pretty confident,' laughed the lawyer.

'In any case since you and I have gone out on a limb, we deserve to break all the office rules and have a scotch before sundown.'

'I will drink to that.'

His father-in-law to be handed him a Macallan malt.

'Slange.'

'Slange and here's to the start of a very long and happy association, both commercial and family, not necessarily in that order,' James smilingly added.

'Off you go then, we will see you this evening and although I did ask Angela to keep it to herself, I wouldn't leave it too long before you ask her.'

James drove to the house trying, as he got out of the car, not to appear too excited. As it was, Kate was so bowled over by the Alvis that she had no suspicions that anything else could be afoot.

'Care for a spin my lady.'

'Thank you, Carrington,' as usual their humour in accord.

They drove along the familiar path towards Buckler's Hard. On arriving, he again parked opposite the ice cream shop and enquired as to her choice.

'Why a ninety-nine of course, my good man.'

James heaved a sigh of relief and sprinted across to the ice-cream parlour returning with two 'ninety-nines.'

Kate took the cone and licked the soft ice cream that was sliding down the wafer side.

Suddenly she let out a scream, her large eyes transfixed by the single diamond that had been slipped on to the chocolate finger poking out of the cone.

'James, I know you are a cool customer but what are you trying to say to me?'

'That I love you and always will, and want you to make me the happiest man in the whole world by saying that you will marry me.'

'I will, I will, I will,' she cried, her eyes moist with emotion.

They clung to each other, deliriously happy.

'Before the ice-cream totally melts, do you think you could try on this small token of my affection?'

They both watched breathlessly as the single stone, its flawless facets catching the evening sun, gave off flashes of blue and white, almost incandescent light.

'It shines out just like the Fastnet Light,' he remarked.

'Then let it be the beacon that you will always want to return to.' She leaned across and kissed him very tenderly.

They slowly disentangled themselves and set out on the short journey to the waiting Palmers, who had confidently put the Bollinger on ice.

The Palmers insisted on treating them to a family celebration and then hesitated, realising that perhaps the couple would prefer to be alone.

'No, no, not at all,' insisted James, 'this is very much a family occasion.'
Jeremy ordered a taxi, confiding that,
'This might just prove to be one of those occasions when one has the extra tipple.'

At such short notice they decided to eat at a well recommended old friend, The Royal Bath Hotel.

Over many years the Hotel has entertained a plethora of distinguished guests, prime ministers, writers, actors; most of the rich and famous had graced its doors at some time. They were welcomed by Albert, the distinguished Maître de,' who recognised the Palmers as old and cherished customers. They followed him into the cocktail bar where the champagne, Bollinger of course, was on ice and awaiting them.

'This is a very proud moment for Angela and myself, one always hopes, indeed prays that when one's daughter makes a decision to become married that we the parents will approve. James, please believe me, we welcome you into our family most sincerely, particularly after some of the other candidates...' he ducked to avoid the cashew nut thrown by his daughter.

The good humour continued. James was so happy that out of all the girls in the world, fate should have decreed that he would meet Kate. If Osborne had agreed to his request, he would never had made that trip to Birmingham and how much poorer would his life have been?

Albert re-appeared, like all great Maître d's his presence was effortless, a second earlier he was not there and now he was, the timing impeccable.
'Do you know I am feeling quite peckish, it must be the excitement. I have decided on my main course, help me with the starter, Albert.' Angela awaited the expert decision.

It came, appearing tentative, and yet it carried the authority of certainty that went with the pursed lips and shake of forefinger and thumb.

'May I suggest ' Foie Gras de Canard,' it is prepared a la maison, or perhaps...' he paused.

'No no, that will be fine,' both the ladies accepting his recommendation.
'After the champagne, a most excellent choice, mesdames.'
He turned to the men. Both the men opted for smoked salmon.

'Perhaps a Chablis?' ventured Jeremy.

'Impeccable,' confirmed Albert.
Mignon de Boeuf was the choice for all as a main course and the meal continued in fine style. The men concentrating on James's future business plans; Kate and Angela prepossessed with the guest list and, of course, the wedding gown.

The time slipped away as it always does when good friends converge, their host's warning about the extra tipple was just about heeded and everyone was in excellent spirits as they travelled the twenty or so miles back to Cranborne in the Taxi.

A final cognac set the seal on a memorable day.

The following morning James was able to show off the Alvis to Jeremy as they travelled together to his office. On the way in, he outlined the proposal to take four rooms rather than just the one, with a view to converting it into a mews type flat that they could use to entertain prospective clients prior to providing that facility in the finished apartments.

In view of what he proposed, Jeremy hurriedly convened a partners' meeting.

There were no dissenting voices, all of the lawyers sharing the senior partner's mixture of astonishment and admiration that this determined young man could so effortlessly and confidently make these sweeping decisions.

As the rooms all belonged to Jeremy's firm and, as they had originally been part of a domestic dwelling, it would prove a comparatively simple task for the necessary paperwork to be drawn up.

Whilst the lawyers went about their work James telephoned Tim Cooper and arranged for him to come down the following week to do a survey and make a start on drawing up the plans.

Meanwhile he decided to telephone Dickie Jackson and ask him to arrange a visit, preferably for next Monday, to meet Abercrombie Pope & Plummer at their offices in the city.

This is the first time they had spoken since the incident of the bouncing cheque and both men were studiously careful to avoid the subject, concentrating instead on Wednesday's plans for the day at Goodwood races.

CHAPTER NINE

They opened the curtains on Wednesday to a rather heavy sea fret which usually heralded a hot day, they certainly hoped so.

Angela Palmer had discreetly suggested that the love-birds would probably prefer to travel up separately and they agreed to meet in the Richmond Enclosure at one thirty.

They left at ten thirty and drove, in no particular hurry, along the A286 from Midhurst towards Chichester following the RAC signs that proclaimed the whereabouts of the course and as they were early, decided on impulse to go into the town for a drink. They drew up in West Street outside the Dolphin & Anchor and sought refuge in the interior of the bar which was deliciously cool after the brightness of the noonday sun. They slowly cooled down and James was pleased that Jeremy had insisted upon the loan of a panama hat for the occasion, with the cautioning advice that, in the words of that most distinguished doyen of horse trainers, the Hon George Lambton,

'Take this but mind, a gentleman never wears a panama before Goodwood.'

Refreshed, they made their way to the race meeting. The course, its turf a heavy springy tan is never hard and is surely one of the most peculiar and picturesque in the world.

Standing here high up on the Sussex Downs, only Exeter stands higher, they could see the majesty of Chichester Cathedral and beyond, in the English Channel, the faint outline of the Isle of Wight.

James had imagined an oval or round course rather like his memories of York on that day his father and he had been to Yorkshire and so enjoyed that first illicit drink together.

Instead, it resembled a triangle which had lost one of its sides. This eccentric shape was at the behest of its benefactor, The Duke of Richmond, who had contrived with Lord George Bentinck to devise a course that would 'divest racing of its coarse and disgusting accessories.' The hoi polloi – the masses.

They presented the badges kindly provided by Dickie Jackson and were directed to the most expensive area of the course, appropriately called the 'Richmond Enclosure.'

This particular day, the highlight of the meeting, stages the 'Stewards Cup,' which for over a century has been the scene of some of the biggest betting coups in the history of racing. As a handicap it attracts all types and ages of horse, the one thing they have in common is that they have been 'layed out' for this race; the trainers aiming to get them as lightly weighted as possible for a tilt at the ring.

The large field paraded and it was difficult, even for the initiated, to pick out a potential winner. Kate immediately went for a very flashy chestnut with flaxen mane and four white socks, her selection immediately dismissed by the regulars who trotted out the old maxim One white foot buy a horse

Two white feet try a horse

Three white feet, look well about him

Four white feet, do well without him!

'Plus'; James added; Like red hair in humans, chestnuts are regarded as fiery and difficult to control.'

This drew an immediate riposte from Kate.

'Watch it Buster, unless you want me to prove that!'

At which point he rapidly made his exit and headed for the rails, selecting Arthur Snaith as the bookie with whom to go to war.

The excitement was intense as the horses cantered to the start and were finally called into line by the Starter. The tape flew up and about a dozen horses broke ahead of the others as the field began the taxing climb for the first one and a half furlongs.

Standing on tiptoe, James relayed the view from his binoculars to Kate .The sight of the big field as the blazing line of silks crested the skyline before thundering into the dip was totally enthralling and he watched spellbound as, with the course becoming less switchback the leading horses raced into the last furlong.

James was surprised to find himself, arms raised in the air, a jubilant fist waving his betting ticket as the powerful chestnut form of Monet burst into the lead in the final few strides to win narrowly from Deerleap with Hawa only a short head further back in third.

He grabbed Kate excitedly and strode with her towards the rails where Arthur Snaith, whose board proclaimed bookmakers since 1912, was waiting for the announcement which finally came 'The winner is Monet, ridden by Jimmy Lindley and owned by Sir Philip Dunn.'

'Ticket 247, £220 win,' the clerk intoned the bad news to the man with his name above the board.

'I'm in the Monet, I'm in the Monet.' James jubilantly waved the rewards of his twenty to one shot.

'James Carrington, you were always a lucky beggar.'

He turned to see a vaguely familiar face grinning at him from under a panama sporting the Uppingham School colours around the hatband.

'Porky White'

'Just Henry nowadays.'

James turned towards Kate and introduced the large amiable man for whom he had fagged at Brooklands during his early years at Uppingham and who would have dwarfed even Edward Lawson.

'Kate this is 'Henry,' he said emphasising the name and Henry, this is my fiancée, Kate Palmer.'

'You see what I mean,' the big man laughed.

Kate, blushing with pride, at this first public announcement of their engagement, covered her confusion by enquiring as to why this tall, but by no means obese face from the past should be called 'Porky.'

'Porky, Large White,' James explained the porcine schoolboy humour.

Still laughing and waving his handful of fivers, he led them towards the lawn in front of the champagne bar where the others were good naturedly demanding he buy some more bubbly.

Having done so, Jeremy then took centre stage and announced the happy tidings by suggesting that the ladies had better start saving for new hats. Only Rachel looked other than delighted.

The day had been a total success, they had won a few bob on the horses and James had promised his erstwhile ex-school chum to visit him in the near future; the latter, sensing that James was just the sort to get hooked on horse racing, as it would appear to someone of his positive nature that you just bought a horse and it won races.

It was the sort of good fortune that all racing yards need to compensate for all the vagaries of this fickle sport.

The following day James ensconced himself in the summerhouse and made plans for his meeting the following week. He had rehearsed the format endlessly in the time spent in the car but, like most naturally persuasive and apparently off the cuff speakers, he devoted a great deal of time to preparation. He took heart from the fact that the greatest orator of modern times, Sir Winston Churchill, applied a similar attitude to conjuring up the apparent 'bon mot.'

He was excited and yes, nervous, as he had been at Twickenham when seventy thousand stood in the jury to give the verbal thumbs up or down. Thinking of occasions like that always steadied him, he knew that so many in the City would have paid a king's ransom for the skills he had inherited, and that thought always lead him to the man whose life had been so cruelly cut down and the oath he had sworn as they drove out of those gates with the Rising Sun embellishments.

Connie had prepared half a dozen transcripts of the proposals and he was arranging these in his brief case when he was aware of Angela approaching with a tray of glasses behind which lurked assorted fruits, bottles of lemonade and Pimm's Number 2.

'Perfect timing mother-in-law, I hope you are going to keep up this standard after the wedding.'

He flashed her one of his roguish grins.

'I bear tidings from our leader, he requires you to be refreshed and on duty at the golf club at six o'clock.'

'What a nice idea.' James smilingly approved the suggestion.

He spent a further half an hour with his future mother-in-law, confiding to her that, if the old maxim about checking out the bride's mother was true, then he had been most fortunate in that respect.

She accused him of flattery. However the pleasure was far too evident for the accusation to stand and he left for the Ferndown Golf Club in high humour.

Only golfers will know the magic that a summer's evening spent with good friends can conjure up. On days such as this, warm but not sweltering, with a light breeze sweeping away the irritation of midges and other pestilents, when for no apparent reason everyone plays well, when birds sing and hearts soar with them. Such was the mood that no-one was really surprised to see Jeremy hole his tee shot at the first short hole, their delight genuine and unbounded, his more slightly apprehensive, as they gleefully massaged the figures upwards as to how many scotches he would have to buy when they got to the 19th hole.

It was the perfect relaxation for James, the thoughts of next week pushed to one side in the spirit of the moment. He was starting to enjoy his golf again and it had not proved difficult for Jeremy and the others to encourage him to put up for membership. He missed the competitive edge of sport, he needed competition, he would never have the time to achieve the lofty heights of young Mr Allis but a decent low single figure handicap was within his compass.

The scotch cost even more than Jeremy had feared, word of a hole-in-one spreading like bush fire from the course as it is relayed ahead. Consequently most of the members waited around for their ex-Captain to offer congratulations! So many scotches indeed, that he insisted,

'Some of you blighters must have started before I had picked the bally ball out of the hole.'

In view of the merriment and the liquidity that went with it, Angela was telephoned to collect them.

'There is a dark green Alvis car waiting for you Gentlemen.'

A roar of laughter greeted Humphreys, as the club steward relayed on the joke from a knowing member. James's concerned and ashen face at the thought of his future mother–in-law driving his beloved Alvis was a testimony to its telling humour.

The following morning with no particular deadlines to meet, James enjoyed a casual breakfast coping more successfully with the familiar Telegraph crossword.

Finally fully replete, he left the breakfast room and as he had been unable to obtain a response from Dickie's telephone the night before, decided on impulse to deliver the proposals to the Charlton's house en route back home.

He set out at eight thirty and arrived at the Charlton's a little before nine o'clock.

The chiming peals of the bell brought a surprised Rachel to the door where, clad in a pale blue silk negligee, her long black hair cascading across her face she looked like someone from a Hollywood movie and, whereas most women would have been thrown by their less than prepared introduction, Rachel, conscious of her natural complexion and sensuality merely beckoned James to follow her inside.

'I had hoped to catch Dickie', he attempted an explanation.

'He is in Manchester and won't be back until this evening.' She turned and pouted.

'Won't poor little Rachel do.'

'Why yes, I just wanted to drop these,' he held out the drawings.

She leaned across, her arms forcing the large breasts to incur an even greater cleavage.

They were both breathing heavily as she tucked her fingers into his waistband.

'Why don't you drop these instead?'

Without a word she took his hand and led him upstairs. Closing the bedroom door she slid silently out of her clothes and stood staring at him; inviting, knowing the power that she was exerting, as she gazed confidently at his burgeoning groin.

James had never been diffident about going to bed with women but today, the engagement so clear in his mind, made it rather different.

'No one will ever know,' she read his mind.

As if in a trance he kicked off his shoes and felt her long slender fingers release his belt and, still hardly believing it was happening, sank to the bed. The voluptuous body writhed all over him, she oozed sex, never before had he been engulfed by so much lust. He cradled and kissed the great melons that jutted from her body and she thrilled to the feel of his still magnificently hard masculine torso.

Soon the initial apprehension was forgotten as she teased and lured him to heights he had never known, she was like some wild cat, her eyes blazing with the thrill of the hunter but finally even her longing had reached its zenith.

'Now, I will have you my beautiful Jaguar.'

She pulled him down on top of her and the excitement poured from her in great waves as she rapidly climaxed. He was beyond control and felt almost simultaneously the same ecstasy.

They slowly emerged from their exertions and lay, two spent forces, the perspiration streaming in rivulets down their still heaving bodies.

'I have wanted that from the first moment I saw you.'

'If I am honest then I have to admit that I wanted it too,' he confessed to his hidden thoughts.

'I know you are concerned about Kate, but we will be discreet.'

Her comment both facing the truth and denying his rejection of future liaisons.

'You are so handsome and you have such a wonderful body.'

She murmured in his ear as she stroked his thigh, watching the effect it had upon the centre of her desires and, her mission achieved, she slowly rose from beside him and gently lowered herself on top of him.

This time slowly and with infinite affection she took him to even greater heights that had him yelling for mercy.

'I am a very, very, greedy little girl,' her voice came in hoarse sobs as she fell across his writhing body, until finally, even she was satiated...

They lay there exhausted, breathing far too fast to speak until at last she murmured.

'James, that was wonderful, it has never ever been that good before.'

He half believed her and nodded, wondering how the hell he was going to concentrate on driving home; at least the ache in his groin would keep him awake!

He closed the door behind him and walked to the Alvis, thankful that the high hedges secluding the house offered some discreet confidentiality.

CHAPTER TEN

As he turned the key to start the car he decided on impulse, to follow up on his promise to visit Henry White at his training yard in Newmarket.

The roads were fortunately free of heavy traffic and the Alvis purred along as he restrained the powerful three litre engine that was quite capable of booting the car along at around 120 mph.

This was what driving is all about; James luxuriated in the opulence of this last dinosaur of a bygone age of motoring which, depending on your point of view, was the main attraction or drawback to driving a car of this type. The steering in town was both ponderous and heavy, here on the open road it was irrelevant, you took joy in the good taste and pleasure in the coach built body that epitomised everything that was good about Britain.

For some not too obscure reason, the thoughts of chassis' and bodywork took his mind back to Rachel. He still found it difficult to believe it had happened, although he knew from previous innuendoes between them that she was flirting with him, he had not however been prepared for anything as full blown as this.

He must end it now and yet, even as he thought it, he knew he would not, doubted further if she would let him. However, whatever happened, once he had married Kate it must end then.

He was still engrossed in his thoughts as he sped through first Winchester and then Basingstoke. He stayed on the A30 until he reached Staines, where he stopped for petrol to fill up this gas-guzzler that was the new mechanical pride of his life.

The tortuous North Circular brought him around the top of London where he finally met the A1. He was soon picking up on lost time and, just after three o'clock, saw him in Cambridge. He had chosen, for nostalgic reasons, to take this route rather than the more direct A10 link from the A1 to Newmarket. He parked the car in Trumpington Street and walked slowly along The High, his original architectural instincts aroused again by the majesty of King's College, one of the truly great pieces of architecture in England if not the world.

He went as far as St John's and gazed inwards with such longing and with acute disappointment, at the majesty of learning that lay beyond the main gates, this and other privileges that had been so cruelly snatched from him a decade or so ago.

He gazed through the gateway at the other Courts beyond and then, quite suddenly, turned on his heel, breaking the mood and recapturing the positive driving force that had brought him so far so quickly.

One day, he promised himself, he would walk through that gateway with pride and without regret.

He strode out now towards the car, pausing at a coffee bar opposite the old Addenbrooke's Hospital to refresh himself and recapture his good humour.

His mind was on Rachel again as he picked up the A45 and headed towards Newmarket, if Dickie was away on business trips quite often and he could coincide his own business jaunts they could have a lot of fun, at least he could rely on her discretion. He found the prospect excited him.

Newmarket was new territory to him but he followed Henry's half remembered instructions to go down the Bury road.

As he did so, it was difficult at first glance to appreciate the wonders of these old racing empires that lined his route. Stanley House, a place of immense charm and style, founded by the Hon F A Stanley, later the sixteenth Earl of the Derby whose family had endowed upon racing the most famous race in the world, 'The Derby.'

The paintwork here replicates the famous black and white Derby colours. It was the 16th Earl who had appointed the Hon George Lambton as his private trainer at the equally famous Bedford Lodge stables, these were a quarter of a mile along the road from the yard that he planned to build in his own name, Stanley House. This was the same Lambton who had decreed so emphatically when a panama might or not be correctly worn. As the immense wealth of the Edwardian gentry declined, so smaller yards have appeared between the greater establishments and it was in one of these that James finally located Belvoir Lodge Stables. They had been founded, as the name suggests, by a former master of that famous hunt, a wealthy industrialist Sir Leighton Wild.

James inched the car down the narrow entrance road, surprised to see that it opened out into a splendid circular flint walled yard, all the box doors crisply painted in white with dark blue hinges and bolts. A gravel path, neatly raked, surrounded a lawn in the centre of which stood what appeared to be an old buttercross. It was in fact the colours room which, although a famous local folly, was not quite as famous as the crenulated water tower at Bedford House, but had its own charm and quaintness.

James had no sooner cut the engine before a stable lad, accompanied by two Jack Russell's, was in attendance. James explained the impromptu nature of his visit and was directed towards the house. This was built in brick rather than flint and dated from about 1860, the classic proportions were draped in Virginia creeper and he could envisage the dramatic impact they would make as they turned to autumnal red.

An agreeable lady in her fifties greeted him with the news that;
'Captain White was racing in Nottingham but is expected back at around seven thirty.'

James smiled at the irony of it; he was in his friend's home town, whilst the other was paying the reverse compliment.

He accepted the invitation to take tea and was duly shown into the drawing room and whilst awaiting its arrival, he wandered around the room exploring the pictures on the walls, mostly of an equine nature, and came across a large oil depicting a 19th century stallion entitled, MILFORD, with the inscription, 'On the occasion of him winning the Ascot Gold Cup.'

He pondered the strange twist of fate that saw him standing looking at an oil painting, the central figure of which bore the name of his old family home and which hung in a house built by a former master of his local hunt. His reverie was broken by Mrs Williams.

'We have telephoned the racecourse at Nottingham and the Captain has instructed that under no circumstances are you to be allowed to leave. I am to put you in the Brookland room, he thought you would feel most at home there.'

A wry smile crossed his lips; He had been Henry's fag in Brooklands house at Uppingham School, hopefully he would not be yelling at him tonight!

'I should enjoy that very much, I will collect my bag and thank you for your kind consideration.'

Mrs Williams smiled to herself, this one could pull the ducks off the pond.

James ran the hot water into a large cast iron bath in which even his long legs could not quite reach the end, this had obviously been specially built for the 'large White' family.

Thinking of that schoolboy introduction when added to his engagement and the events of earlier today, he almost pinched himself in disbelief; until that is, he noticed his back in the mirror and saw the effects of Rachel's seductive talons, thank goodness he would not see Kate for a few days.

Henry arrived back slightly ahead of time and his effusive greeting left James in no doubt as to the genuine pleasure that his visit evoked...

'Gin and tonic,' without awaiting the reply, he served up three fingers of Gordon's, threw in the ice and lemon and splashed in the tonic.

'Good to see you old boy, bloody marvellous in fact.'

'Now I'm off to have a tub and then we will hit the town, I have booked a table at La Scala, hope you like Italian food.'

James confirmed his approval. 'After that muck we ate at school I can eat anything,'.
They had a marvellous evening, reliving the past and anticipating the future; leaving the restaurant at about ten thirty, in time for Henry to do his evening tour of the stables.

He explained the basic routine to James who, even in his semi-inebriated state, could appreciate the commitment required to succeed in racing. It was, he admitted, a regime too strict for him, but horses for courses he supposed.

'That is original, or have I heard it before.' Henry laughed as his friend winced.

The following morning James woke reasonably early, or he thought six forty-five was early, until he looked through the window to see his host ready with the first lot go out of the drive and on to the Heath. The yard was alive with activity as 'The Captain' issued his instructions.

'Catch up with that bugger, Sandy.'

'They go better forwards,' to a lad whose horse insisted upon going sideways.

Finally he had them all out of the yard and he trotted past them to ensure they used the correct part of Newmarket Heath. No-one, not even Captain Cecil Boyd-Rochfort or any other luminary would dare contravene the allocated piece of the Heath to be used on any particular day. This was decreed by the Jockey Club, whose headquarters reside in the town just off the High Street. They are locally responsible for some 60 Training establishments who in turn house 3,000 horses. Of the 15,000 inhabitants some 3,000 are in way or other involved in the so-called Sport of Kings.

James bathed again in the commodious bath, pleased to see that his battle scars of yesterday were looking a little less pronounced.
He went down to breakfast which he delayed until Henry returned at eight thirty, so instead, after a coffee, he made his way back to the yard where he was met by the Head Lad, an ex-jockey named

Steve Higgins, whose accent at fifty still had the heavy Irish brogue, His Christian name though was in honour of an Englishman, a man who in the late nineteenth century was the doyen of racing, the legendary Steve Archer.

Archer, nicknamed The Tin Man had a racing record second to none, only Sir Gordon Richards could be mentioned in the same breath. He was lionised and adored by trainers and women alike and yet he had powerful enemies, which cost him not only rides but ultimately his life. Sadly this immensely unhappy soul who had gone to enormous expense setting himself up at his Falmouth House yard, named after his principal patron, committed suicide at this house in Newmarket in 1886 aged only twenty nine.

However his legend lives on and ghostly sightings of Archer on a pale grey horse riding across the Heath are claimed by many and have given rise to the verse:-

> *Across the Heath-along the course*
> *'Tis said that now on phantom horse*
> *The greatest jockey of our days*
> *Rides nightly, in the moonlight rays.*

Happily dispensing racing folklore, Higgins took James on a conducted tour of the eighty or so boxes, some of whose occupants were out with 'first lot.' The stables, he explained, were constructed of flint to ensure that the horses were cool in the summer and warm in winter and in the empty ones the clean straw was forked up around the walls to allow the floors to dry.

They moved across the yard to the buttercross-like building in the middle of the lawn, the open door revealing a kaleidoscope of colours; the entire room was a mass of coat pegs from each of which a coat hanger disported the racing silks in the colours of the yard's many owners. Higgins pointed out some famous names, an amused James commenting that he thought Lord Derby could afford to have all black buttons to match the all black silks.

'Well sir,' the Irish tones advised, 'When Sansovino won the Derby in 1924, he not only broke a losing streak going back to 'Sir Peter Teazle' in 1780, he also created a precedent continued to this day. The white silk stock worn by the jockey caught around one of the buttons and the 'white' button has since then been retained as a lucky emblem. These owners are full of superstition he added, and laughing with James beckoned for him to follow.

'Now for the stable star. He is by Nasrullah, a top, top stallion; the governor bought him as a yearling in the USA at the Keenland sales two years ago. He is named Blenheim Palace but we call him Heimy.' Higgins indicated a dark bay head that was gazing through the weaving bars as they approached.

'We are running him this afternoon at Leicester in the three twenty.'

'Will he go out with the others in second lot?'

James was warming to the scene; it had the excitement of competition that appealed to his sporting instincts.

'No sir, as soon as the Captain is back, the travelling Head Lad will box him and the two other runners and set out for the racecourse.'

This information had no sooner been conveyed than they heard the clip-clop of returning hooves. Henry swung into the yard, raised his cap to his enquiring visitor and thought how well his anticipated 'new owner' was settling in.

They returned to the house and demolished the comprehensive full breakfast served up by

Mrs Williams.

'Fancy a trip to Leicester?'

'Depends which Blenheim Palace we are going to see, if it is the equine one then most certainly, I am starting to get the bug for this racing game.'

'Brilliant, I have to be out with the second lot at ten o'clock, have a bath and then we can set off in that fornicatorium of yours and catch up with the box well before we get to Leicester.'

They departed for Leicester at just after midday, the Alvis, or fornicatorium as Henry insisted upon calling it, eating up the miles so swiftly that they adjudged a quick pint and bar snack along the A1 would not inconvenience their arrival. They stopped at Wansford and over lunch at The Haycock, the trainer outlined to the already 'hooked' fish the basic ins and outs of racing, James naturally saw no snags.

On a fine day such as this the racecourse was crowded and those flat Leicestershire vowels were in a preponderance of those who roared Blenheim Palace home in the three o'clock.

The horse had, after his two year campaign been installed as the joint winter favourite for both the Derby and the 2000 Guineas; unfortunately, and James received his first lesson in the vagaries of this sport, he had developed first sore shins and then a virus that meant that he took part in neither of the classics, only coming to hand at the end of June.

It was a good day out and from James's point of view had taken his mind off the events that where to unfurl in London the following week.

They said their goodbyes, Henry to return with the horses to Newmarket, James with the short drive to Nottingham to collect a change of clothes en route for his D-Day.

CHAPTER ELEVEN

Sunday, but with no inclination to have a lie-in, he was up at seven thirty, anxious to set out, to be busy and active, it was the one antidote that calmed his nerves.

James had this time telephoned to make a reservation at Claridge's. The same doorman by chance, observed his arrival in Brook Street and was once again delighted to park the elegant dark green limousine that bore this impressive young man to their door.

Having checked in, James strode across the clinically imposing black and white marbled entrance floor to the magnificent staircase that led upwards to the bedrooms including his own room, number 604, this is where he had stayed on his first impromptu visit prior to his engagement. That had resulted in a successful outcome and he hoped the same magic would prevail as he needed a similar result tomorrow.

In this atmosphere, fuelled by the warmth and elegance of the sparkling chandeliers, it is easy to succumb to its charms: On an impulse, he decided to take afternoon tea in the Reading Room where, under the watchful eye of the portrait of Mrs William Claridge, he speculated again upon tomorrow's assignment

This was the most important day of his life, not only in respect of his business ambitions, but also his ability to provide for Kate and the family they envisaged, plus other more recently construed aspirations. He had instructed Henry to look out for a yearling at the forthcoming autumn sales and so much else.

He was happy here, this was the environment to which he had been born and even had he not, it was a heady mixture that, once tasted, would not easily be denied. He half remembered his mother quoting the Hollywood actor Spencer Tracey who commented;

'Not that I intend to die, but when I do, I don't want to go to Heaven, I want to go to Claridge's.'

He felt inculcated with the same thoughts as he retraced his business propositions; He was happy with the basic content and construction, deciding that if they failed that he would have to re-jig his entire philosophy: He did not believe he could be that wrong.

One final decision, he would do a recce in the morning so that when he arrived on the doorstep of APP he would feel on familiar ground.

No more thoughts of tomorrow, he closed his briefcase and climbed once again the magnificent staircase to his apartment which was still decorated in an art deco style of the 1920's.

He hoped this luxury and the stylish atmosphere would impart to him some of the methodology and originality that his alter ego 'the Bauhaus School of Architecture,' had so wondrously created in that brief fourteen year span between 1919 and 1933. They had evinced so many new ideologies, epitomising the changing concepts concerning the nature and purpose of design in the early twentieth century. All of this of course had been viciously deflowered by the Weimar Republic, which had ironically lasted not the thousand years they had proclaimed but the self-same fourteen years. That one irony is the only point of justice.

He bathed and shaved leisurely, it was difficult not to be relaxed in this stylish atmosphere or not to be amused by 'Hancock's Half Hour' which, with the 'Goons,' was his favourite entertainment and in good humour came down to dinner at 8 o'clock.

As he walked towards the Dining Room he heard the haunting strains of the Hungarian String Quartet entertaining guests in The Foyer, no wonder that this was regarded as probably the finest hotel in the World, everything, simply everything, had an undeniable quality to it.

He entered the Dining Room and was escorted to a table where he ordered a glass of Bollinger as an aperitif. To follow, he started with Salade de Crabe aux Asperges.

As a main course, a simple fillet steak with peppercorn sauce and to accompany this, he indulged himself in a half bottle of Chambertin.

Whatever trifling concerns may have remained when he entered that wonderful restaurant, they disappeared as he soaked up the atmosphere of the room, continuing as it did the splendid art deco of his apartment, this time conceived by the architect Basil Ionides in 1926.

He went to his room at ten thirty, which was very early for him, but he felt so relaxed and ready for the morrow.

He slept well and was down next morning at seven thirty, taking advantage once again of the superb selection of food that lurked beneath the silver lids. These full English breakfasts were becoming habit forming; a trip to the gym must be a priority.

As the appointment with Abercrombie's was not until eleven thirty he decided to go along to the British Library and do a little research on the origins of the Bank, it would help to mentally prepare him.

Abercrombie's Bank he discovered was founded in 1715 making it one of the oldest banks to be set up within the city boundaries. Messrs Coutts & Co claiming the distinction of founding father.

England at that time was very much an agricultural country with a population of around six million. The original Abercrombie had been, like so many other early bankers, either goldsmiths or silversmiths, gradually evolving from keepers of valuables to providers of capital.

To open a bank in 1715 was a very bold action indeed as the Jacobite Rebellion was at its peak and threatened the establishment and all that it stood for. However, William Abercrombie had powerful friends and allies, not least of whom was the Prince of Wales, later to become George the Second. This imposing patronage provided the impetus for the early growth and, as the century progressed, shrewd investments in ideas as diverse as James Watts' steam engine in 1769 and Richard Arkwright's revolutionary advances in cotton spinning thirty years later.

Their plans grew more expansive as they financed the large East Indiaman ships to capture the tea trade, and supported the coal owners in their drive to plunder the fossil fuels from below our land; these and many other commercial enterprises were at odds with many other Merchant Banks who ignored the great revolution in invention that was making this small island the most powerful nation on earth.

Neither did they confine themselves to investing within the British Isles. By the turn of the century, Britain had an empire upon which the sun never set and Abercrombie's had been persuaded by a Swiss consortium to invest in the transport of chocolate from the South America's. The Spanish, with their vast influence in the land of the Aztecs and the Mayas, were the first to be aware of this concoction made from the seeds of the Cacahuaquchtl tree.

The emergence of stable government and a coordinated banking system prompted Parliament to finally rationalise banking procedures with the Banking Charter Act of 1844.

Finally others, such as Coutts, laid aside forever their insular activities as goldsmiths and silversmiths and concentrated on what we now regard as traditional banking.

As the commerce of the country grew, so did the Commercial Department of the Bank. Not only did they pride themselves upon the Aristocracy and Gentry that banked with them, but also the new money that was vested in men like Thomas Telford and Isambard Kingdom Brunel with their visionary feats of civil engineering, and in the emerging publishing houses and the brewing industries.

Along the way Abercrombie had been joined first by his son-in-law, James Pope, and then a hundred years later by Alexander Plummer, the latter having been the senior partner in a smaller bank that merged with Abercrombie's.

Aware of the time, but pleased with his research, James returned the reference books to the librarian. His membership of this august library, a privilege courtesy of his Staincliffe forbears.

He strode briskly in the direction of the Strand and, about half way along that historic thoroughfare, caught his first glimpse of the elegant Regency exterior designed by John Nash in 1817. This was about midway between Nash's other fine buildings in Regent Street built in 1813 and All Souls Church in Langham Place in 1822.

The exterior was of white stone turned grey by the enveloping street fumes and the imposing entrance was gained by climbing the twelve apostles, as the steps were colloquially known within the Bank. The interior of the banking hall was circular, about half of it being accessible to the public and the remainder guarded by heavy mahogany counters behind which sat the tellers. Behind the front line staff was a pierced mahogany screen, the reredos behind the altar of wealth he cogitated, his financial awareness heightened by the pervading fiscal atmosphere.

To the left of the entrance, two messengers liveried in the Bank's navy blue and gold colours looked up as he approached.

'I have an appointment with Mr Stanhope Court who is, I believe, one of your senior investment managers?'

'He is indeed sir, one of the very best and your appointment is for eleven o'clock.'
The messenger confirmed his expected arrival before leading him across the black and white marbled floor to the lift. In the centre of the floor he noticed what appeared to be a pair of palm trees beneath which the inscription 'Floreat Cacahuaquchtl' was beyond his Latin.

They entered the stylish bronze elevator and as the pair of gates closed, he offered up a mental prayer as he prepared to finally make his play for the big time.

They went up to the third floor, alighted and followed a fine Axminster carpet, again bearing the mysterious palm tree motif. Finally they arrived at a mahogany door; the gold inscription invited them to 'please knock'. This elicited a reply from a female voice who turned out to be attractive, efficient and in her mid-twenties, he guessed.

Her telephone call to the adjoining room gained the necessary invitation and James was escorted to a large stylish room with panelled walls and an enormous mahogany desk, its leather top uninhabited except for the silver inkstand and leather blotter case.

'James Carrington, I am delighted to meet you at last, although I do know you a little.'
His guest's puzzled look prompted an explanation.

'I have seen you several times in the white jersey at Twickenham; I can't tell you what a pleasure this is old boy.'

'I bet you oohed with the rest of them when I missed the conversions,' James's innate modesty politely accepting the generous compliment.
'May I offer you some chocolate?'

He smiled seeing James's bemused expression and explained.
'In the early days of the Bank, long before it was popular to do so, the incumbent Abercrombie of the time financed the merchantmen who journeyed to the South Americas to bring this expensive delicacy first to Spain and mainland Europe and then to this country. Most of the aristocracy of Europe had been drinking chocolate since about 1650; the British with their antipathy towards Spain resisted it for several years. However, in the late 17th and early 18th century chocolate or coffee became the normal breakfast drink for the wealthy.

Unfortunately, its popularity was brief and fifty years on, it had been superseded by tea and relegated to a bedtime drink. The chocolate houses closed down and took on other roles, 'White's in St James's, like others, becoming a Gentlemen's Club. You will not be surprised to know that this establishment is patronised by the Directors of Abercrombie's.'
James pursed his lips.

'That will also presumably explain the Palm tree motif and some totally unpronounceable Latin name that you wish to see flourish.
'Cacahuaquchtl translated it means not just the cocoa tree but THE TREE.'
Miles continued.

'Just as in ancient Greece where the Gods ate ambrosia so in Mexico and Guatemala the elixir from these seeds was regarded as not only medicinal but as a drink for the Gods.'
James raised the fine bone china cup.

'Then we are in good company, but I think that the elixir that I shall adopt will be from a small black grape bearing the label of 'Bollinger.'
They laughed and with the preliminaries over proceeded to a large conference table surrounded by a dozen elegant Hepplewhite chairs.

'What I suggest James, if I can be so informal so soon, is that we discuss the outline of your idea and the basic strategy you mean to adopt, then perhaps a spot of lunch, after which I would like to bring in a couple of my chaps to discuss it in more detail.

I hope you will not find this too overpowering, it is just that we chaps in the city here tend to work in droves, it's the only way we can protect our backs!'

James nodded his acquiescence, he had thought about this moment for so long that he was ready for them, no matter how many they muster on the other side. He seized the initiative.

'Miles, if I may also be presumptuous, when your parents retire, die, or whatever, do you intend going back to live in the family home?'

'I hadn't really thought about it old boy, but as I work in town and they live in Northamptonshire, I should say that will be highly unlikely.'

'I take it that the house is too large for their present needs and, even if they are blessed with a long and happy life, they are going to find the upkeep both expensive and also hard work. For your part you haven't really considered the prospect, but you and I are going to have to face up to decisions our parents did not have to make. The eldest son will no longer automatically take over the farm or run the family business. The war has changed the whole nature of things; people will no longer be happy to go into service, they will have their own aspirations, they will be busy looking after their own home, a whole new social order is emerging. For my part, I want to uphold the good legacies from the past; I also intend to be part of the new wave of thinking.'

And then, to lighten the intensity he chided the serious banker opposite.

'You never know one of these damned Grammar School boys might one day become a Director of Abercrombie Pope & Plummer!'

Miles gave him a knowing smile and James resumed his pitch...

'To return to the main thrust of my reasoning; do you not think that a smaller property might not be more suitable and convenient for people of our parent's generation, particularly if it has all the mod-cons that so many houses, imposing though they are from the exterior, do not have.'

The Banker pursed his lips and nodded.

'You make several valid points, particularly with a view to expense and comfort.'
He indicated that James should continue.

'I have a further important proposition which will become apparent when we discuss the plans in more detail and that will revolve around companionship. If people can retire to a decent old age with their own kind around them, it will take the pressure off the likes of you and me who will probably live in a different part of the country altogether.'

The Banker, held up his hand.

'On that optimistic note I propose we adjourn for lunch and let the financial bods examine it in more detail later, I will just let Arabella know we are off to White's.'

The easy relationship that had been established so early in the meeting remained with them as they approached the facade of White's in St James's Street. Built in 1674, it is one of several elegant buildings to have survived in this part of the capital.

Miles leading, they climbed the half dozen stone steps guarded by two large iron lanterns and entered the front hall.

'With all your newly discovered interest in chocolate, I expect you would like to see where it all began.'

'Very much.' His guest's eager agreement leaving Miles in no doubt.

They set out on a whistle stop tour in which the principal memories were the 'Coffee Room' with its wonderful barrel ceiling and the walls which, like the complimentary carpet, were in deep red, creating a very warm and rich atmosphere that seemed entirely appropriate to someone visiting for the first time.

They moved on to the 'Great Subscription Room.' Here, so that the mind should not be diverted from gaming, the walls were traditionally kept free of paintings.

Miles pointed out the gaming table, the bite from its circumference to accommodate the croupier and not, as was maliciously suggested at the time, to facilitate Charles James Fox the corpulent eighteenth century politician.

Onto the 'Dining Room' in which in 1961, a commemorative painting had been unveiled to the nation and dubbed by the Daily Express, 'Top Chaps at their chops and chips.'

This painting, exhibited at the Royal Academy, had been commissioned four years earlier by Lord Camrose and was executed by a White's member, Simon Elwes. His brief had been to depict as many as possible of the luminaries of the day in a scene typical of the club. Randolph Churchill in the foreground has just delivered one of his famously outrageous comments and the other members of this distinguished gathering as diverse as Lord Boothby to Douglas Fairbanks Junior are reacting variously to his assertions.

This room is predominantly red and with its gracious chandeliers is inviting and comfortable. At which table, he wondered, might Sir Malcolm Campbell have discussed in the thirties his dreams of conquering both the land and water speed records in his beloved Bluebirds? Bill Stirling, the man who founded the SAS, had discussed its formation with Evelyn Waugh in this very room. As a result of that meeting, the latter had helped him get his ideas down on paper; they proved so persuasive that Churchill, seeing its merits, overruled his military commanders to ensure the unit was formed.

However, Waugh will be most remembered for the titanic battles of wit he waged with Randolph Churchill for twelve acerbic years. At which point the latter had a lung removed, and peace was declared.

They moved on to the 'Billiard Room,' the memory he carried from here was of the great overhead arched glass ceiling supported by classic Ionic pillars. The whole atmosphere is suitably restrained and dignified with engraved portraits of members, the only sound being the clicking as the balls strike each other, or of backgammon dice being rolled under the great mirror which sits above the fireplace.

'That should have given you a taste of the place, now what about a drink before lunch?'

Miles directed him through a door into a room painted off-white, anything but luxurious, its rather stiff atmosphere so typically English; a small room where men would come together to discourse in small intimate groups as men do. It is surely a hangover or pre-cursor to the public school or university common room.

James felt at ease, he enjoyed the surroundings; he soaked in the atmosphere and wondered how many great men had sat where he now sat. So many momentous decisions would have been taken at White's and Brooks's and the other London Gentlemen's Clubs which have, for centuries, been core to the principles of the British social and political life.

Other countries, America in particular, have sought to copy the atmosphere of the London Club. However, it is only in that small area bounded by Pall Mall and St James's Street that the true uniqueness, born of time and the deeds of its members, is truly found.

The ensuing years, dating from the time of Shakespeare, have seen the membership change from Regency bucks and dandies to the era of Wellington and Pitt, to the moralistic Victorians, and the scandalous Edwardians when 'The Great Smoking Dispute' caused the Prince of Wales to found a rival club.

Throughout the years leading up to the First World War, Britain was the greatest country on earth and London was the hub of that mighty wheel that never ceased to turn.

Since these times, leading politicians and literary figures have graced and disgraced the club. However, White's is the oldest and most senior establishment; it is accepted as special by all other clubs throughout this land and beyond and, until recent years, all British Prime Ministers from Walpole onwards together with most of the nation's military leaders have been members of White's.

Standards have, of course, always been de rigueur, none more so than in the dress code; today's striped suits, rolled umbrellas and bowlers are merely a reflection of what is considered correct in Society. The history of the bowler is quirky, as are so many other things English. The only place for a member of White's to buy his hat was at Lock's. It was more correctly referred to as a 'Coke' in honour of Mr Coke who had bespoken it.

South of the river it was a bowler after Mr Bowler, who manufactured it for Lock's. In the USA, although spelt in the English way it is referred to as a 'Durby' as it was at Derby race meeting the on the Epsom Downs racecourse that they first became aware of it.

Even as late as 1925, when the German Ambassador visited White's, many of the older members still wore their hats in the Coffee Room. An astonished Herr Von Ribbentrop was told by a straight faced member that it was because they were worried about them being stolen by other members. He nodded politely, making no comment.

A few weeks later a German magazine referred to the decadent 'Weiss Klub' in London where members stole each other's hats!

The greatest changes in fashion came at the turn of the century when tall hats and frock coats were increasingly replaced by short coats and three piece suits, often referred to as 'dittoes' because the patterns matched.

An amusing anecdote from Algernon Bourke's History of White's, informs us that some members had even taken to wearing tweeds occasioning the remark from Edward VII to a member so dressed.

'Goin' rattin'?' he had mischievously enquired.

After the potted history lesson and a simple but well-cooked lunch, they returned to the Bank where they were joined by two younger men, probably in their twenties, he thought.

Miles Stanhope Court who was thus far much impressed continued as chairman.

'I suggest James that you run the concept past me once more and give Alastair and Paul here a chance to tune in to your perception and how we might help.'

James handed each of them the critical analysis path that Connie had prepared. He reiterated the need for older people to live in smaller surroundings, complete with all the latest equipment and labour saving devices. The central plank in his platform was that, by making their lives more tolerable, they would become more self-dependent and confidant; in turn they would be less demanding on the younger members of their family.

Each block of apartments would consist of thirty units with a balcony and communal facilities in the form of a lounge area with room enough to play bridge etc. and quiet enough to relax and read. In addition, the ground floor would comprise half a dozen shops; Hairdresser, Newsagent, Butcher, Greengrocer etc. Beneath the entire structure there would be a car park with individual lock up garages.

Paul raised his hand to challenge the necessity for what would be an expensive indulgence.

'I know that it is anticipated that the car population will rise greatly, but don't you think this provision is a trifle anticipatory?'

James nodded.

'I see your point from a budgeting position, but I firmly believe that what is already happening in America will happen here very soon. Also, I go back to my main premise, most of the people we are trying to attract will see the motorcar as vital to maintain their independence. Also rather perversely, this sector of the population are, right now in percentage terms of owning a car, top of the league and have a need that must be catered for. Remember too, that the old and often cherished family saloons are used to living in a garage. The second point regarding the huge increase in car ownership will come from the working class who will see this, along with house ownership, as their inherent post war right. In the future, when this age group are themselves downsizing, a garage will be absolutely essential.' Finally of course this is not a facility that can be added at later date.

He re-opened his briefcase and took out the drawings which Tim Cooper had thoughtfully provided. These coloured three dimensional sketches conveyed to the layman's eye a very clear idea of the proposal. This form of presentation with attractive trees and shrubs gave an exciting portrayal of what might be and drew appreciative comments from the gathered bankers.

Miles pursed his lips.

'What we have seen is an exciting possibility, what we need to be convinced of is that you can organise such a large development and that it will be a profitable exercise for both parties.'

James nodded agreeably.

'If you refer to page twelve gentlemen, you will see the overall costs; these are itemised in more detail on the following two pages. Each block will cost us one hundred and twenty four thousand pounds to build and we intend to market each of the units for five thousand pounds, leaving a gross profit of twenty six thousand. My company can come up with thirty thousand and we have company assets that will underwrite the remainder of the Bank's initial commitment.'

Alistair, notoriously canny when it came to lending was hearing alarm bells, and sought greater reassurance.

'With your previous track record, I am surprised that your own bank will not support you.'

James turned and nodded.

'If we were contemplating a single development then I agree with you. However, we have established the demand and are planning three single developments and then our 'pièce de résistance'; to eventually complete the project, an additional block to form a square, the centre of which will be a sculpture park. We have good advertising contacts in the construction and advertising industries to ensure that this will receive wide coverage. Additionally, we will seek patronage for young British sculptors, the idea being that the work is for sale and will be constantly rotating; this will ensure that the interest in the project will be ongoing.'

He removed the rubber band that restrained a large drawing; watching with pleasure as his inquisitors, keen to see the full effect, rolled out the drawing along the length of the table... they had spent a lot of money on this, having commissioned a very talented artist, Richard Fells, to give them maximum visual effect; the admiring glances suggested he had succeeded.

'I congratulate you on a most imaginative scheme James, no wonder you are reluctant to take it to your chap at Martins. But, we are talking very serious money, your ball park figure, four times one hundred and twenty four thousand is getting very close to half a million pounds.'

'True, but if you examine page eighteen you will see that we have built in a cash flow, this will be generated by the sale of the apartments and of course the capital would be released in stages as the work progresses. We have considered the proposal from three different standpoints, all annotated in the document. We could build one development at a time, but in the final analysis this proposal is the most compelling and the impact on the area would be considerable. The latter is a most important point because, once unveiled, an idea like this will soon become apparent to other developers.'

It also has the merit of continuity which, once the procedures are in place, will reduce costs and improve efficiency. The would-be purchasers will be invited to spend a weekend at a show apartment to sample the mod-cons at first hand and gain some of the flavour of what they can anticipate. The property that will house this is already in place. Having other developing areas of the site to choose from will ensure that expectation stays high.'

'Enough, enough', Miles smilingly held up his hands.

'I am convinced of the concept, however I warn you old boy, it takes a lot to impress the men in the striped suits upstairs.'

He turned to the others for supplementary questions, there were none.

'In that case, needless to say I know you are in a hurry, shall we reconvene on Friday after I have made a presentation to the Board. What time would suit you?'

'Chocolate time,' The impish grin lighting the flushed and excited face.

'Floreat Cacahuaquchtl'. The smiling and immediate riposte from his host.

CHAPTER TWELVE

The following three days seemed an eternity.

He had returned to Nottingham, meeting Edward Lawson and Tim at the office, recounting as accurately as possible the sequence of events, wondering as he did so where he might have improved upon the presentation.

Essentially it had gone well, but he was not so presumptive as to assume success. Initially that lay with Miles Stanhope Court and his ability to convince his Directors that this comparatively new organisation was worthy of the Bank's patronage.

Edward, in his usual quiet way recommended that they consider fall-back positions. The idea was sound, they were all committed to it, however if Abercrombie Pope & Plummer did not deliver the necessary finance he felt they should re-approach Charles Lattimer and build each block as a single development. Tim supported him in this but James, whilst accepting the logic, asked that they defer a decision as he felt that he could best argue their corner with his back to the wall and with no apparent escape route.

With a large backlog of paperwork to demolish he was at his desk before seven thirty the following morning, sticking at it until round six o'clock when, feeling he had achieved quite a lot, he drove to the Services Club for dinner. A few drinks and a game of snooker left him feeling relaxed and at ease with how life was progressing. He would be seeing Kate at the weekend, he was looking forward to that, she really was a beautiful girl, always immaculate and good humoured, he wished they were married and yet at the same time, because he wanted to give her the very best, he would delay that moment for a couple of years until he had established his fortune. When they moved into a family home, no auctioneers gavel would ever again speed his departure. By mid- afternoon on Thursday he was up to date and, wishing to miss the worst of the traffic on his drive to town, he decided to telephone his regular squash sparring partner, Jack Priory, for an impromptu game.

The club like his own apartment was situated in the The Park, an elegant residential area located near the castle in the centre of Nottingham. When the time came for he and Kate to set up home together he would miss living in the Park. It was so handy for the city centre and just around the corner he had not only the Squash Club but also the Nottingham Tennis Club. All this set in the midst of those wonderful Victorian and Edwardian houses designed by architectural luminaries, such as Watson Fothergill. Yes, he would miss these bachelor days; best make the most of them. His mind drifted to Rachel and the steamy episode of last week.

'You look pleased with yourself'.'

The tall athletic figure of Jack Priory, smiling as usual, interrupted his daydream.

All men and possibly most women have a confidant, someone to whom they confide otherwise sacred memories. These two shared that trust; they had had some fairly boisterous times since they had met as teenage county squash players. Athletic though James was, his strength was in the power of his legs and yet those same strong limbs that had brought him such fame on the rugby field were ironically adjudged to be attached to feet that were flat. Thus when their owner had reported for his National Service medical he had been reported as unfit for service.

Jack, with no such problems was the complete sportsman, he played every game to a high standard whether it was tennis or snooker; he had a lightness of touch and a finesse that James envied. They had terrific struggles, always bringing out the best in each other. Paired together as partners in a golf foursome they were at their very best, James with dauntless ambition always going for the big shots, most of the time relieved to see that his anchor man had completed the hole in par to save the day.

At the Nottinghamshire Golf Club's Annual Open fourball at the demanding Hollinwell course last year, Jack had rallied his partner by advising,

'Imagine you are playing against me!'

They had an energetic forty minutes thrashing the yellow spot around, urged on by others on the gallery awaiting the arrival of their own partners. The high on which James was currently living carried the day for a rare victory over his old adversary.

They showered and with the sweat still pumping through their hair sat at the upstairs bar catching up on the latest exploits and antics of mutual pals. Jack, sensing James was up to something, chortled away as his friend related the events in Bournemouth, casually admitting to a little dalliance in Melton Mowbray himself.

James looked at his watch, sensing it was time to make a move.

They walked out together.

'Same time next week?'

'Yes and the best of luck tomorrow.'

The smile and the handshake, equally sincere.

However, pleasurable though the memory was, he decided to press on and as he arrived at Claridge's the sky was still bright but beginning to tinge with red, portending a good day to follow and he prayed that it would be so.

He checked in, enjoying the recognition accorded by the doorman and receptionist, decided on a light meal in The Foyer, where he enjoyed at first hand the Hungarian Quartet and deciding that it would be rather nice to bring his mother here, with Kate, as a celebration... although perhaps best not count one's chickens.

He spent the entire evening without the feeling or the compulsion to speak to anyone other than the waiters. He enjoyed gathering his thoughts, planning and shaping the future, all these dreams and aspirations fuelled by that one persistent thought, that he would one day fulfil the promise he had blurted out as a fourteen year old and had reiterated on the death of his beloved father. He would once again drive back along that long avenue with its imposing gates, this time however he would be heading towards the house, he would be going home.

The clock chimed eleven, the time had sped by, he tilted the brandy glass to extract that last drop that always clings to the bowl and decided to take a stroll around the block before turning in. He walked slowly along Brook Street and around Grosvenor Square trying to imagine the time when the first Abercrombie had put his plate up, then these gracious properties had been private houses. He gained confidence from these thoughts; it was invigorating and challenging to contemplate joining forces with those adventuring spirits. At the junction of Grosvenor Road and Davies Street he turned left and, in a good frame of mind, returned to the hotel.

He slept well and finally it was Friday and ten twenty five saw him rescaling the Twelve Apostles. The messenger smiled his recognition and they retraced Monday's route to Miles Stanhope Court's office. Over chocolate he revealed to James that his proposition had gone upstairs but that he was not party to the decision.

At eleven o'clock, feeling rather like the condemned man, he accompanied Miles along the palm festooned carpet and silently approached the Board Room on the floor above.

Two sharp knocks elicited a single cultured invitation.

'Come.'

The Directors were seated at an oval table at the head of which sat the tall Guards like figure of Sir Julian Abercrombie. The other members of the Board sat two each side of him.

The walls were decorated in original William Morris wallpaper portraying once again the Cacahuaquchtl tree and three-masted schooners intent upon their lucrative trade. Several fine oils caught James's eye, particularly a Turner, in which a large East Indiaman bearing the name Sarah Abercrombie was seen ploughing through mountainous seas off the Cape of Good Hope. Further paintings by Joshua Reynolds and others depicted stern faced chairmen of the past two hundred and fifty years.

Sir Julian rose as they entered and swept his hand around the table.

'You may find this amusing Carrington, five Directors to view a prospective new account.

However my dear boy, it is a principle that has served us well for over two centuries.

We have had very few, in fact remarkably few reasons to regret this procedure.

It may appear to you to be amazingly old fashioned, we however like tradition, it has served us well, what we do know is that when you leave this room Mr Carrington, we will know what makes you tick.'

He glanced around the table before continuing.

'We are, in banking terms, in turbulent times, the war has upset the rhythm of things, the old fashioned precepts that we understood are being swept away, there is a lot of new money about and to be honest and without wishing to be rude, we don't know where it came from and where it is going.'

James could sense the situation slipping away from him. He had invested too much energy and time to be so summarily dismissed. He looked around the room, he knew where his strengths lay, he briefly made eye contact with each of the men around the table, his expression was challenging but not belligerent, it invited a fair trial.

As always he attempted to control the interview by initiating the questions.

'You will have seen my proposal Gentlemen, I believe that the best way that I can convince you of its merits is by justifying both the need and the financial soundness of both the project and, perhaps more importantly, myself.'

Sir Julian nodded.

'Very well my boy, the floor is yours.'

James spoke for half an hour, identifying and agreeing the need, using the drawings and sketches to portray the finished scheme. Questions were raised and answered, objections deflected and countered and it seemed that he was winning when Sir Marcus Partington spoke for the first time.

'The thing is Carrington, you are a personable young man, but what you don't have is any real collateral, nothing that the Bank could fall back upon if one of your grandiose ideas should founder.'

'Here, here, my sentiments too.'

Jonathan Fox-King, sitting next to James, added his concern. Once again he must regain the lost high ground.

'Two points Gentlemen.'

He opened the analysis document.

'If you refer to page twenty three you will see that the offer price of five thousand only purchases a shared equity; that ownership expires on the second death of the original purchasers, or upon sale of the property. So, in either event, the original purchase price is returned to the occupant, but the actual bricks and mortar remain the property of Fordmill Construction.

Secondly, I am here today because I understand calculated risk is what merchant banks are all about, surely this is the very essence of your firm. You are Merchant Adventurers, what has increasingly attracted me to you is that Abercrombie's, even in the early days supported industrial innovation when other Merchant Banks were not prepared to apparently sully their hands. I venture to suggest that if he were around today, William Abercrombie would see the merit in my ideas, he would see that MY bricks and mortar when they return to my full ownership in five or ten or even twenty years will have escalated in value many times. My company will have property worth many millions of pounds. I had hoped to do that in conjunction with APP.'

Sir Julian pursed his lips and held up his hand.

'You put forward powerful arguments Carrington and, had we had known you longer, then I dare say we would have nodded this proposal through. However, as I said earlier, we are looking to stabilise things right now, we feel we owe our commitments to those people whom we have known for some years and who have supported us in the past. I am sorry to have to decline your proposition, which I hope you will not take personally. You have shown us the future and we have, out of courtesy and interest heard you out and I can only repeat, that had we known you longer then we would, as I have indicated given you our support.'

'In that case...'

James paused, before opening his briefcase and extracting from it a large manila envelope, somewhat worn with age. He slid it across the table to Sir Marcus Partington who relayed it on to Sir Julian.

With one eyebrow quizzically raised he undid the red ribbon that held it closed and drew from the envelope several rather yellowing certificates.

'What have we here?'

'Those APP shares you are holding were bought by my Grandfather Sir Albert Staincliffe in 1898 and they have been handed down to me. I have always regarded them as a bit of a nest egg.'

Sir Julian Abercrombie silently pursed his lips, for what to James, seemed an eternity. Finally he rose and without speaking, crossed to the sideboard and removed the stopper from a decanter.

He poured two glasses of Garvey's Fino San Patricio, handing one to James, he remarked.

'Your goose has just laid its golden egg. Welcome to the Club'.

He handed each of the other Directors and Miles a glass of sherry before turning again to James. He raised his glass.

'To your success, Carrington.'

'Aye to that.' Sir Marcus led the others in the chorus of approval.

James gathered up his papers and, still in a daze followed his proposer into the corridor.

'What can I say Miles, except that I am eternally grateful and that I owe you one hell of a favour.'

'That is nice of you to say so, but don't underrate yourself old boy. That is the first time that I can ever remember the Old Man doing a U-turn, you were out until you served him those two last aces.'

'Well whatever, you will not deny me the pleasure of buying you lunch.'

They dumped the paperwork in Arabella's office and walked across the Banking Hall and out into the Strand.

'Simpson's.'

'A splendid choice old boy.'

They walked the short distance to the restaurant and turned in past the hanging baskets and through the glass doors to the entrance hall.

Simpson's, its atmosphere very much in the style of a private club, has been a favourite eating place of the famous and the discerning since 1828. It has built a reputation for serving the 'finest roast beef and lamb in the world' and few will query that claim.

It was Mr Simpson who had in 1848, introduced the 'dinner wagon' so that the joint could be 'carved in front of diners and be served as they liked.' In addition to Scotch beef and English lamb they also offer other traditional and authentic native dishes such as Aylesbury Duck, Boiled Beef and Carrots and of course Steak, Kidney and Mushroom Pudding. They proceeded upstairs where they had a beer in the Lounge Bar, surrounded by sepia photographs of international celebrities before proceeding to the Divan Restaurant where the Maître d', upon spotting Miles, signalled them to a corner table.

'Your usual table, Mr Stanhope Court?'

'Thank you Anton.'

The corner seat with its pew like benches afforded them maximum privacy and, after the frenetic morning, James finally began to unwind. He had enjoyed these visits to town; he felt at home here, it was where he belonged. He was once again reminded of his mother, of her resolute courage when they had lost almost everything, how she must have longed for the past when the Staincliffes would have stayed in town and lunched here at Simpson's. Yes, he must treat her to a long weekend; let her revisit her old haunts. He owed it to her, those old share certificates had, despite his eloquence, been the real key that had opened up this new relationship with APP.

Anton re-approached them, his bald head glistening slightly in the wall lights as he stood with his back to the panelled walls.

James deferred to Miles who chose Potted Trout wrapped in smoked salmon with roast Scotch Beef to follow.

For himself he chose Smoked Chicken and Artichoke Salad followed by the same Scotch Beef...

'A nice full red Anton, what do you suggest?'

'Mr Stanhope Court was, I believe, quite pleased with the Brouilly last week.'

'Indeed I was Anton; in fact, I have recommended it to Sir Julian. He is still rather partial to a fruity and vigorous body.' The knowing aside eliciting a smile from Anton.

'In that case sir, the Chateau Thivin it is.'

They enjoyed the starter but of course the whole point of Simpson's is the arrival of the silver trolley bearing the famous roast.

The chef wheeled his trolley to the table, the removal of the silver lid revealing a copious joint of Scotch beef varying in colour from a brown exterior through a succession of pinks to a deliciously underdone centre.

They enjoyed each other's company and the conversation was easy and relaxed, dwelling more on the past than the future, which had exercised their minds so much of late.

Miles admired the athletic young man who dined with him, he winced as Charles Lattimer had done at that dunderhead Osborne who had turned down his original request, and most of all he envied the athletic skills that had thrilled the nation on the rugby field.

Like most keen and average club players he could not believe that at such a young age, still with the world at his feet, James could turn his back on all that fame.

'What you have to understand Miles is that those skills I inherited from my father, I have used in a way in which I believe he would have approved, to him rugby was a sport, a fun thing and that is how I regard it. Playing for England and the British Lions means nothing compared to achieving my promise to him, that one day the Carrington's will once again be masters of Milford Hall. Your Bank need never worry about my ability to deliver the goods; there is a power far more potent than Sir Julian to whom I must answer.'

They finished the Chateau Thivin with the last mouthful of beef and, like two schoolboys, summoned Anton to bring the famous sweet menu. What is it about grown men, Englishmen in particular, that they inevitably think back to their schooldays when a pudding is offered? James pondered so long that Anton suggested a small portion of both the Spotted Dick and the Treacle Roll. Miles on the other hand, with the advantage of regularly sampling these delights, went unhesitatingly for the Bread and Butter Pudding.

They said their goodbyes and James set out to retrieve his car. It had been quite a day; so much had happened, so much was promised, so much was to be done. James looked at his watch it was three fifteen, Edward and Tim were coming down to Bournemouth for the weekend to be updated. He felt quite guilty at not contacting them; they must be walking on eggs, wanting to know and yet not wanting to know in case the news should be contrary to their hopes.

CHAPTER THIRTEEN

He drove carefully, thinking once again what a good team they were, each with their own strengths, this time James's eloquence and persuasion coupled with the impact and selling skills of Tim's drawings had won the day.

However, he was aware that had the result been different it would have been Edward Lawson, index finger stroking his lips, to whom they would have turned; his carefully thought out fall-back position a bastion from which to re-launch their aspirations.

This was not a one man team, it was a three man outfit, so closely in tune with each other that he could perceive difficulties as the company grew and they would be obliged to appoint other senior people.

The sign for Ringwood, however, diverted his thoughts to other more pressing delights, the thought of Kate and the forthcoming weekend. God she was wonderful.

He arrived at The Cedars at just after seven o'clock spotting Edward's Riley and the dark racing green of Tim's Morgan as he turned into the drive. Seeing them all here slightly and quite irrationally irritated him, it is the same with all great success, once you have achieved it you suffer an anti-climax, you need time with yourself to re-assess privately the achievement. But he had already had that moment he reminded himself.

He tried to compose himself, to keep the smile off his face as walked the short distance to the door, it was opened by Kate, the others standing behind her in the hall.

They looked at him expectantly.

'Bollinger.'

That one word that, was their private victory code.

The next couple of hours were mayhem as the Bollinger flowed and Jeremy Palmer's cellar became ever more depleted.

There was a brief respite when the two cabs arrived to deliver all six of them to 'San Marco' Once they were seated the party atmosphere soon picked up again, this time it was fuelled by Barola that superbly dry but deep flavoured red wine from the region of Turin.

Kate was radiantly happy as she stared at this tall handsome man that could seemingly make anything happen. She remembered that first time when he had visited the Bank in Birmingham, the intense determination that kept him there all day until at last Charles Lattimer had found time to see him. She remembered too the envious looks of the other girls when she confided that he had asked her out. So much had happened and in such a short time.

She looked at him now, he was smiling and responding to the revelry and yet, behind those deeply set eyes, she sensed he was planning further exploits.

As if to confirm how closely in tune they were, he suddenly touched Jeremy on the sleeve.

'I know it is Saturday tomorrow but do you think it possible to organise Anthony Jayes to come to our meeting in the morning?'

The solicitor nodded and walked across the restaurant to the girl on reception, returning after a brief telephone call.

'He is playing in the Saturday Medal at two o'clock so will need to leave by one o'clock at the latest, I fixed the meeting for 10 am at the office.'

'Excellent, in that case, as I know that Edward will need his beauty sleep I suggest we adjourn. Oh, by the way, any one got a few quid? The loan from APP doesn't come on stream until we start digging the footings! He ducked as Edward threatened him with a bread roll.

They returned home, had a quick brandy to round off the evening and turned in, each with his or her own dreams, Kate longing for the day when she could wake in his arms.

He fell asleep, as usual pondering some future conquest. Tonight it was the cheap acquisition of land that occupied his thoughts; they must secure a 'land bank' it would provide them with sites for the future and valuable capital assets to support the balance sheets necessary to continue the patronage of Abercrombie Pope & Plummer.

The following day at Jeremy's office, Anthony Jayes arrived promptly at 10 am politely diffusing the assembled gratitude by acknowledging how important he knew these times to be for the long term success of the company.

James, urging them all to press on, opened the meeting.

'We have all worked hard gentlemen; we are poised to carry out developments that are going to get us noticed. However, we cannot live on this project alone we must, busy though we will be, plan ahead, the ball must be kept rolling forward. The purpose of this meeting is to agree a development plan and a forward looking strategy that will encompass the next five years. I believe we are an innovative company but we must not be relaxed, not for a moment, there are other bright boys out there who, once they see what we are up to will seek to emulate, indeed even improve upon our ideas.

Equally, we must keep our eyes and ears alert to pinching their ideas. Patronise the local Golf clubs etc. and keep an ear to the ground and, as you travel about the country, keep your eyes open for anything interesting, keep a camera in the car and take photographs of idea you consider worth examining. Now, to do this we will need land, preferably bought sooner than later; in this way we can get in before the competition forces the price up. Are you agreed, has anyone any immediate ideas?' Anthony Jayes opened his briefcase and passed a local Ordnance Survey map across the table, attached to it was a large scale map of Bournemouth town centre.

'At our initial meeting James you threw several ideas at me and, I suspect, left me to sink or swim. High on that list was the 'Acquisition of Land'; I believe if you examine the areas circled in red you may well find several suitable sites. You also charged me with compiling a short list of people with the wealth and political clout to finance these developments. I believe that you have already demonstrated in your successful negotiations with APP where the finance will come from, I do however have a list of people with influence in regard to planning etc.'

He handed a typed list of a dozen names to James, whose smiling and approving expression left Jayes in no doubt that he had made a most favourable impression.
Edward grinned.

'I think we are going to get along rather well Anthony, it has taken us years to get up to James's speed, I congratulate you, you seem to have got the drift rather quickly, it all bodes well for the future.'
'Here, here.'

The others acknowledged their approval.

'Time moves on and we must not keep Anthony off the tee. We are all in agreement and the only additional comment I would make is that I too have scoured the town; my own personal brief was to look for shops that were either run down or made derelict by the War. With your agreement, I will stay over for a couple of days and approach the shopkeepers concerned and with Anthony's help, ascertain the owners of the other sites.

In seeking your agreement to do this, I am well aware of the additional strain that this puts upon Edward in particular, who has to cover for me at the office as well as having to organise the day to day construction work and the developments we already have in the pipeline. We should, as a priority, be looking for someone to assist you Edward.

He held up his hand to silence the inevitable protest, pleased to have Tim's support to make Edward see reason, he was too valuable to put at risk through overwork.

'I should of course be consulting with Edward and Tim in private, but Anthony has so much impressed me today with his grasp of how we think and react at Milford that I wish to propose that we invite Mr Anthony Jayes to attend our regular monthly meetings. Would someone like to second that?'

Both Tim and Edward spontaneously raised their hands to affirm unanimous agreement.

'In that case I suggest we reconvene on September the third and let Anthony, lucky fellow, depart for Ferndown. Meanwhile, to cushion your disappointment, my treat to you two is an afternoon's racing at Salisbury.

The three of them returned to The Cedars to collect Kate and then, wasting no time all piled into the Alvis, James handing the road atlas to Kate who immediately transferred the responsibility for finding the racecourse to Edward.

'Head for the town centre and look out for the A3094.'

'I suggest we look out for the RAC signs, we know how good your directions are.'

They all hooted at this, Edward having once gone to Northampton instead of Norwich and spent two hours looking for a prospective site on Cathedral Street. It set the tone for an enjoyable day when good friends are in tune with each other and even the mundane can be amusing.

In the event both directions were correct, the RAC sign sure enough directed them along the A3094; a jubilant Edward convinced that this was a good portent for the afternoon.

They parked the car, James and Kate leading them as they set out for the saddling boxes where

James had arranged to meet Henry White.

Like Goodwood, Salisbury Racecourse is superbly set with a view overlooking the town with its magnificent cathedral that boasts the highest and, courtesy of John Constable's painting, the most famous spire in all the land.

Henry was talking animatedly to a languid figure in a striped suit with trilby and a small fellow whom James recognised as his travelling Head Lad, Dandy Williams. He approached, fascinated by the heady atmosphere of it all, rather like the last few moments on the first tee before it is your turn, when all the surrounding heads will turn and be for a brief moment hushed and interested. He recalled the atmosphere at Leicester, and even more so at Twickenham, when even the oldest heads prayed they would do nothing so elementarily wrong that would bring down upon them that giant groan of disappointment that could whither the soul, just as quickly as the erupting roar of approval could lift one's game to new heights.

Henry White heard them approaching.

'James, Kate, it is wonderful to see you again. May I introduce Nick Carter Brown, what this man doesn't know about the thoroughbred industry is not worth knowing.'

The man in the trilby raised his hat to Kate, modestly deflecting the praise.

'A slight exaggeration to put it mildly, however, as I believe you are contemplating ownership, please ask away as, unlike Jeremy here, I will also tell you some of the downside!'

Kate's jaw dropped at this surprising announcement, James hadn't mentioned even an inkling of this to her; but then she would come to realise that this is what life would be like when she became Mrs Carrington.

The arrival of the other two precluded any discussion as he introduced them.

'Henry and Nick, may I introduce my fellow directors and best friends, Edward Lawson and Tim Cooper.'

The introductions done Henry proposed that, as he did not have a runner in the next two races, they repair to the 'Owner and Trainers' Bar.'

There are several good reasons for racing at Salisbury, it has great tradition, and it also has the oldest racing club in the world, the Bibury which was founded in 1681. However, and this was the reason that Nick and Henry were here today, it is the course where many of the trainers send their improving two year olds to see if they are up to classic consideration. Owning a racehorse is an exciting and thrilling experience, to see it tested and emerge with distinction and go on to Newmarket or York and win one of the premier two year old races is heady stuff. All winter long the dream perpetuates and grows as the racing press anticipate the three year old classic aspirations which fan the flames of glory and expectation. The older hands, however, know just how few of these talking horses will actually achieve these high hopes and aspirations.

This is the real stuff of racing, it makes the blood flow more quickly, and it induces owners to spend again at the yearling sales to try again to capture the dream.

As yet, of course, James knew little of this; he could see only success, the rest he would learn in the painful fullness of time.

In the Owners and Trainers' Bar, Nick Carter Brown ordered champagne, immediately earning brownie points from the Fordmill Board of Directors. The salutations were in full flow and James was finally explaining his recently acquired equine ambitions to Kate when he became aware of the cultured sensual tones of Rachel standing behind him. His reaction was of delight and despair in equal parts, further introductions were effected, more drinks were procured and the party continued unabated.

Henry excused himself as he wanted to supervise the saddling of Nick's colt in the feature race of the afternoon. The others followed ten minutes later and headed for the parade ring. Nick led the way, inviting Kate to join him and the other owners on the lawn in the centre of the ring. As they left the main party, James was aware of the heady smell of Chanel Number 5, a fragrance that was, after the events of the other day, etched firmly on his memory. Rachel wasted no time.
'I have to see you again, we haven't much time.'
She turned to face him, aware of the others around them; he too felt their eyes upon him.
'I will call you, it is too risky here.'
'No, I beg you, I must know.' He tried to reason with her but, as between the sheets, she was not to be denied, 'Dickie has to go to France next week. I am staying with my sister in Stratford upon Avon; surely it would be possible for you to find an excuse to stay over for one night.'
His mind in a turmoil he agreed that he would and Wednesday was decided before he knew quite what he was doing.
Nick's colt, 'The Waggoner', cleverly named by his wife, picking up as it did with all their horses on the family name of Carter, was by 'Donatello' sire of the recent Derby winner, Crepello.
Like its sire, The Waggoner was a powerful heavy topped horse who had shown superb acceleration in winning his maiden race at Newbury in June.
The fascination for James was that Donatello was by 'Blenheim', sire of Henry's stable star, Blenheim Palace. He was quickly grasping the importance of certain sire lines in the breeding of champions. He was just as quickly to realise that being bred in the purple was no guarantee of success as The Waggoner, though starting a hot favourite, trailed in seventh of the eight runners.

Disappointed though he undoubtedly was, Nick Carter Brown showed no outward signs of the anti-climax he must have been feeling, he took this defeat as he took his triumphs, without rancour and without flinching.
They stayed on after the last race to allow the first swell of cars to depart, everyone in good spirits. Rachel discreetly staying in the background, allowing Kate and James to enjoy each other's company, but inwardly squirming at the continual parading of Kate's engagement ring to new and old acquaintances.
They finally departed around 6.30 pm deciding en route home to eat at The Crown in Ringwood, after which they returned to The Cedars in good humour but decidedly short on stamina for any further excesses that day.
They turned in, Kate as ever dreaming of the future and her life with James, he too was dreaming of the future, this time centred on his new found passion; in his dreams, he and Kate were leading in the winner of the Derby.

Sunday was spent relaxing and pouring over the Sunday papers. Angela prepared a light lunch of smoked salmon pate washed down with Chablis, after which they all declared themselves replete and declined her offer of dessert. Tim and Edward said their farewells at around two thirty.
All in all it was a relaxing day, the first for a long time. To make it totally perfect, the Palmers had been invited to play bridge that evening, leaving the couple to their own devices. Kate cooked, they washed up together and then sat in the firelight listening to music and longing for the time when they would be able to do this in the privacy of their own home. They had, on his

insistence, planned to have a two year engagement, this so that he would have the capital to buy the sort of house that she deserved. Now however, sipping brandy, her long fingers caressing the hairs on his arms, she slowly persuaded him that the money left by her grandfather should be used to do this together. Here in the flickering light of the log fire, future dreams laid bare before them, he conceded she was right and his pride was not worth denying themselves a year of extra happiness.

That night as they fell asleep even he was dreaming of the wedding.

CHAPTER FOURTEEN

The following day he cold-called several retailers, extolling the advantages his ideas could offer them and gaining tacit agreement that they would at least consider the proposition seriously. One of these, Donald Kingsley, proved to be a bit of a barrack-room lawyer who, sensing that James needed the agreement of them all appeared to be prepared to hold him to ransom.

James, with no respect whatsoever for this type of blackmail, appeared to overlook it; inwardly, however, he was seething and was scanning his brain for a solution.

That evening he telephoned Rachel at her sister's with the information that he would have to stay over in Bournemouth to sort out the mess caused by Donald Kingsley's attitude, which meant he would not be able to make it to Stratford.

'That little shit, ask him how he came by the money to buy the shop in the first place, better still ask Anthony, he defended him in the Exeter case.'

'What Exeter case?'

His mind suddenly went into overdrive.

'What has Anthony got to do with this?'

'Not Anthony exactly, but his firm, they defended your Mr Kingsley.'

'Rachel, I may owe you a big one for this.'

'Just see that I get one.'

Her laugh at the unintended double-entendre left him with no illusions as to her meaning.

He replaced the telephone, subconsciously and without thinking he dialled Anthony's office and asked for Anthony Jayes.

'I need to see you urgently, say nine o'clock tomorrow morning, it is about a Donald Kingsley, I believe your firm defended him four or five years ago.'

'That is so James, but you must know as well as I do, that the conversation shared between a client and his lawyer is privileged information which I am not at liberty to discuss with you.'

'Nevertheless Anthony, I have to see you tomorrow, it is vitally important.'

'Very well James, but remember I cannot, will not, discuss any more of this case than that which is already in the public domain.'

Anthony Jayes was at his desk immersed in paperwork when his visitor arrived on the stroke of nine the following day.

James outlined his dilemma, receiving sympathy but no positive assistance from the lawyer.

The intercom rang and excusing himself Anthony left the office leaving James gazing impatiently around the room. His eyes abstractly located a manila file upon which the name D.W Kingsley was plainly identified.

Hesitating briefly, he picked up the document and, with pounding heart, read what it was that had been alleged and later validated against Donald Kingsley.

The document was hardly safely restored before the lawyer re-entered the room and once again re-affirmed his professional ethics. So slickly was it done that James could not discern between his official tongue and the apparent opportunity he had afforded.

The following day armed with Anthony Jayes' map he spent most of the morning and early afternoon visiting the prospective sites.

He established within his own mind the potential priority of choice and at ten minutes past three returned to the grocer's shop belonging, according to the sign over the window to A W. Walters.

'Mr Walters.'

The man behind the counter nodded.

'Forgive me turning up like this out of the blue, but I would like to discuss my proposal of the other day in more detail. Is it convenient now, or should I call back later, after you have closed for the day?'

The shopkeeper stared, unsure and clearly undecided.

'I don't know, I have been here a long time.'

'I can understand that Mr Walters, but I can assure you that I will not be wasting your time. I will come back after you have closed, and if your wife can also be here, so much the better.'

He returned at six thirty taking with him the sketches that had so much impressed the Directors of Abercrombie's and was invited through into the living room by Mrs Walters who looked even more bemused than her husband.

Whilst she poured the tea, he unrolled the drawings on to the dining table securing the corners with an assortment of sugar bowls and tea cups.

'I will get straight to the point, I am planning a series of major developments in Bournemouth, I have the planning consents, I have the development sites, what I need are people like you, professional shopkeepers of long standing. Essentially, the offer I am putting on the table is this, when I build the apartments, as you can see from the drawings, I intend to provide the residents with a full choice of amenities literally on their doorstep. Now, I could of course ask if you would consider running the shop for me, however, to do that would be to insult you as you have your own business and I dare say it has been in your family for many years.'

'Forty three, forty four years come November.'

His wife nodded to confirm the facts.

'But we cannot possibly afford to buy the sort of property you have outlined.'

'If I could show you a way, would you then be interested?'

'Not 'arf, but how? It don't seem possible.'

James unrolled a further set of drawings, a few black and white sketches that Tim had done on Saturday morning, he then continued,

'This development is being supported and indeed partially financed by one of the oldest Merchant Banks in the City of London. The local affairs will be handled by Palmer Braithwaite, whom I am sure you will recognise as being a highly reputable local firm of solicitors.

I mention this to underline how above board I wish to be with you and the other shopkeepers. What I am proposing, Archie, if may I call you Archie, and I know this is a fairly radical idea, is to offer to yourself and other high class retailers a brand new shop, fitted out to the highest standards, with a fifty year lease, in exchange for the freehold you own on this site. From your point of view, you will have a captive market of high class clientele within the complex and a further catchment area from a good class neighbourhood in which they will be built. Furthermore I can assure you that there are no greengrocers currently in the area and that you will be a vital part of the local economy. What is your immediate reaction to that?'

'Well, it is a bit out of the blue, sir. I mean, it is not something we have ever thought about. I inherited this shop from my old Dad and I suppose I have always assumed that when I left here it would be in a wooden box.'

'I take your point, and not for a moment did I expect an answer from you today. What I did hope is that my proposal will have whetted your appetite sufficiently to agree to a second meeting, in say a week's time. In the meantime, I shall speak to others retailers, none of whom will clash with your business and you may feel free to discuss with them my proposals, which will be exactly the same to all of you.'

Archie Walters smiled at his wife.

'Why not, gal?'

'Then that is agreed. I will book a room at the Royal Oak for seven o-clock next Monday evening and will bring along a partner from the solicitors to allay any concerns you may have.'

Still slightly bemused by the turn of events and needing to make a telephone call, he stopped at the Romano coffee bar for a cappuccino. Sitting there, he considered the providential opening presented by Anthony Jayes; he had actually done nothing ethically wrong and yet he had presented the opportunity, James was quite certain of that. He was both surprised and impressed, it boded well for the future, a lawyer who would stay within the law and yet know how far the boundaries could be stretched. Even prior to this, his gut reaction to Jayes' performance, given at such short notice last Saturday, had prompted him to request that a Directorship be discussed at this Friday's Board Meeting.

He finished the coffee and spoke to Rachel, advising her that he would be staying at the Lygon Arms in Broadway that evening and that he hoped she might be able to join him!

She complimented him on his choice and left him in no doubt that she would be there. The other retailers he had visited earlier in the day had all agreed to attend the presentation at the Royal Oak. It had been a successful day and feeling content with his progress he set out in leisurely fashion for the Cotswolds.

He drove through Salisbury to the outskirts of Swindon where he picked up the A419 to Cirencester and thence to Stow-On-The-Wold and the charming old Royalist Hotel. He had many happy memories here of visiting the famous horse fair with his father's brother, Richard, and then dining in the evening at what is one of the most historic and charming hotels in Britain. Much of the oak framed building is over a thousand years old and the walls house witches marks and leper holes, pretty frightening stuff for an eight year old, particularly when recounted and embellished by a great storyteller like his Uncle Richard.

He smiled as he remembered he and Louise snuggling together in the Four Poster on the one occasion they had stayed the night, his reassurances did not seem very convincing to a six year old girl with a rather vivid imagination, and daybreak had been a great relief to them both.

He had a ploughman's lunch of local cheese and pickles washed down with a pint of Flowers Ale and continued on his unhurried way. No one can pass through this corner of England and be unmoved by its splendour. The Cotswolds are the highest and widest part of a belt of limestone that stretches from Dorset to the Humber. It was the Anglo-Saxons who first established the region as the finest sheep rearing area in England; indeed, the name itself is derived from the ancient Saxon name for sheepfolds - a Cot, and Wolds meaning high open land. Thus from early times it was an area of great wealth and the churches in the towns of Stow-On-The-Wold, Chipping Campden and others reflect this. Likewise the hostelries that were demanded to service such wealth also abound, none more popular and renowned than the Lygon Arms at Broadway.

The Hotel has stood, set in the very heart of the Cotswolds since 1530, its atmosphere a romantic mix of charming antiques and open log fires. After a splendid dinner, charming bedchambers with black and white ceilings and inviting four posters are waiting to lull you to sleep. He was still conjuring the delights of the latter as he pulled to a halt in the High Street at the front of the hotel.

The Alvis magic worked yet again, no sooner had he stopped than a porter was immediately to hand to assist him with the single suitcase.

James followed the uniformed figure to the reception desk and announced that he had a reservation and that Mrs Carrington would be joining him later. He had toyed with the idea of a nom d'affaire but decided that he would probably end up by shooting himself in the foot; he could only hope that Rachel would remember, but on reflection decided that this was the least of his worries.

He unpacked, had a leisurely bath enjoying the miscellany of Sinatra and Tony Bennett that was playing on the Light programme. He changed into blazer and flannels, a satisfied smile crossing his face as he tied the Uppingham cravat that Henry had presented to him with the salutation, 'Welcome back to the fold old man.'

After a dash of aftershave he headed downstairs, where he settled into a comfortable leather armchair with a glass of Macallan. He picked up the Daily Telegraph but before he opened it he heard the unmistakeable tones of a Jaguar XK150 as it burbled to a halt behind the Alvis.

In his mind he saw Jenkins, the hall porter, setting out to convey greetings to the new arrival and within thirty seconds he heard the reality as Rachel's imperious tones announced her arrival as Mrs Carrington. He left his glass on the counter and attempted to walk leisurely and unconcerned to the entrance hall to welcome her.

'Darling, did you have a good journey.'

She swung round to meet him, every tiny detail was perfection, she looked as if she had stepped off a page from Vogue Magazine. Rachel knew it and everyone watching in the hotel knew it.

'God, what a journey, I need a drink, darling.'

He took her arm and led her into the cocktail bar signalling Pierre to open the Bollinger that was cooling in the ice bucket out of sight beneath the bar.

'You deserve an Oscar for that, how far have you come, four miles?'

'It's how far I am going that I was thinking about.'

They both burst out laughing, collected the ice bucket and proceeded upstairs.

This time with no limitations or need for haste they made love tenderly and with affection, delaying as long as possible that final surge of lust and desire, that left them clinging to each other unwilling to let the moment end. Full requited desire needs no words; it is a moment unique and particular to that moment in time and belongs to those who made it happen.

They slowly relaxed and as he watched her naked form slide out of bed to visit the bathroom he wondered how he could ever give her up, and yet one day he must; meanwhile he would think only of today.

They dressed for dinner, retraced their steps to the cocktail bar, he to continue with the Macallan, Rachel opting for one of Pierre's special cocktails.

The Head Waiter arrived with the menus and then a few minutes later he escorted them to their table in the Great Hall, This magnificent room with its barrel-shaped ceiling and heraldic panels is overlooked by a seventeenth century Minstrels Gallery; It is a most splendid setting for any meal, for a romantic one it is both memorable and superb.

For starters Rachel persuaded him to have a Salad of fresh Mango with a slither of pan fried Foie Gras, her choice proved to be first class.

Skipping the fish they proceeded to the main course, where he insisted she join him with Pot-roasted Squab served with caramelised baby onions, hardly daring to look at her in case he burst out laughing, OR, he relented, as an alternative, Whole poached Scottish Lobster on a bed of spinach pasta.

'You monster, I am starting to tune in to your peculiar humour Mr Carrington but, I confess, you can still fool me.'

He did not seek her advice with the wine and they had the most superb Batard Montrachet, the greatest of all the white Burgundy's, strong, perfumed, dry and yet still luscious.

Occasionally both food and wine hit the same high notes and the result is memorable. This was such an occasion.

'To finish, I fancy a small tart... of plumbs and amaretto,' he quickly added.

'Don't push your luck, mister.'

She pouted indignantly, or was it provocatively; he was more inclined to the latter.

After dinner, over the coffee and the liqueurs, he thanked her for helping with the Kingsley case and wondered whom she knew on the local planning committee. He was amazed when once again she came up trumps.

'Philip Harcross. He is a pal of your friend Nick Carter Brown. They have a stud somewhere in Suffolk; I believe it is where they keep the young stock. I do understand however that Philip has now retired to a house overlooking the coast at Sandbanks, and is apparently less concerned with the bloodstock now that he is heavily involved with local politics. He is very astute but not, I gather, above earning the odd bob or two.'

'Rachel you are brilliant, not only beautiful but the font of all knowledge. Whatever I achieve in the future I will never forget how you have helped me.'

'Of that you may be sure.'

The unspoken implication behind the simple 'Thank you,' she had expressed.

They breakfasted at eight thirty and, as they walked out to the cars he heard himself professing his affection for her, realising as he did so the hole he was digging for himself and yet, he had to admit, she had delivered two aces when he needed them.

A brief husband and wife peck on the cheek and he set off for Nottingham, driving with more urgency than yesterday, anxious to be back at his desk. There was so much to organise and operating from two bases did not help; it was a matter that he must resolve sooner rather than later.

CHAPTER FIFTEEN

On returning to his desk the paperwork was, as he had feared, truly mountainous and the list of telephone messages was not much better. Also, now that he was back, he felt more than a little guilty. He made a firm resolve to address the problem at tomorrow's meeting.

Meanwhile he sorted out the correspondence, attacking the easy ones first and reducing the mountain to more of a hillside by early afternoon.
Connie, who knew that he preferred to be alone to get on with things, left him to his own devices, sensibly deciding that today's queries could wait. They were all so in tune with each other,

'We have been married a long time.' Edward would often quip.

At around five thirty, he knocked on Connie's office door and entered.

'Did you have chance to add the item re Anthony Jayes to tomorrow's agenda?'

'Of course.'

'Will you also add an asterisk to any other business?'

'Any reason why?' she looked inquisitively at him.

'I don't want to forget to say thank you, especially to you.'
He leaned over and pecked her blushing cheek.

'I mean it.'

He returned to his own room and carried on ploughing through the diminishing pile of paperwork. He liked being here alone, with no telephone to interrupt, often arriving at the office at seven thirty or earlier, enjoying his own company before the irritations of the day.

He worked assiduously all day and at nine o'clock in the evening he called it a day and drove back into town, deciding that he had earned a treat and parked on the Poultry, just outside the Flying Horse, yet another of Nottingham's attractive old buildings. It was not as old as the Trip to Jerusalem, set as that is in the Castle rock, it was however more obviously attractive with its five tiled gables over the black carved facade. He walked through the oak doors and marched straight to the dining room. A simple steak with a couple of pints of the local Home Ale was, after the recent culinary excesses, splendidly appetising. It also helped to bring him down to earth, to reflect upon where he was heading and the importance of those around him.

He arrived back at his flat in The Park at ten thirty, reminding himself that he must get back to playing some regular squash again; it would also give him an excuse to catch up on the local scandal with Jack Priory. After the frenzy of last night he slept well.

The following morning was slightly misty, portending a hot summer's day but the air was still cool and invigorating as he emerged from the car, slightly surprised that both Tim and Edward, neither known for their early morning appearances, were already at the office.

He followed the aroma of fresh coffee to see them grinning conspiratorially and already seated in the Boardroom.
'Thought we would get here early and catch up on the gossip before Connie cramps your style.'

They leaned forward and he regaled them with a somewhat embellished version of yesterday's assignation, omitting the concerns he feared re the relationship. It was very much the sort of thing that men chortle over, nothing serious and no harm intended.

He also mentioned something that did concern him regarding Connie and was pleased that they were here early which allowed them time to discuss it.

They all reconvened in the Board Room at ten thirty, as Chairman he called them to order.

'We have several issues to resolve and I suggest that I first of all bring you up to date in regard to the acquisition of potential sites in the Bournemouth area. I have surveyed the proposed areas of redevelopment and have selected two as being potentially the most propitious.'
'What were the main criteria?'

'Principally, Tim, it was the neighbourhood, or lack of it in the case of the second site.

This is a little way out of town; it was heavily blitzed, apparently in error and, apart from the purple colouring provided by the rosebay willowherb, it has a very dreary look about it. To get this site we will have to convince the local council; you will be pleased to hear that I have been given a name to contact.

In respect of site one, I have spoken with all the nine shopkeepers, only one of whom has been openly belligerent and I believe, thanks to some passive help from Anthony Jayes, that I have the ammunition to shoot him down.'

'With regard to Mr. Jayes, I see you have him down as an item for discussion.'

'Quite so Edward, but I believe that it should be a decision for the whole Board to decide upon.'

'In that case James, I propose we now discuss the asterisk item under any other business.'
Edward smiled at Tim and indicated that the proposition be his.

'I propose that, as we are continually stretched these days in terms of day to day decision making, that Constance Elizabeth Cummings be invited to join the Board of Fordmill Construction.'

'I second that, along with a vote of thanks to Miss Cummings for all her hard work and loyalty over many years.'

'No abstentions; may we have your answer Miss Cummings?'
Connie shook her head in disbelief, her cheeks on fire.

'On condition you stop calling me Constance, the answer is yes, I will be honoured to accept.'

The good humoured applause was amended to a cry of 'Bollinger', the libation appearing as if by magic from the cupboard in the bookcase.

'Order, order, may we return to the item headed Jayes. Now that we have ALL the Directors present, I propose we extend a similar invitation to Anthony.'

'I am inclined to agree with James, accepting that we have not known him very long he has very quickly picked up our wavelength and has already made some important decisions, also he is on hand at the centre of operations.'

'Also,' said Connie with a wry smile, 'his law degree will improve the look of the letter headings.'

'Okay, okay, you have rumbled me.' James nodded, once again their humour coinciding.

'One last item, I suggest that, as Tim has to check out the work on the office conversions, he attends Monday's meeting with me. The more professional people we put on stage, the more we will underwrite our good intent. To that end, I have also asked Dickie Charlton to represent Abercrombie's and Anthony to field any financial questions.'

They all agreed James's logic and returned to their own rooms to eliminate any outstanding mail.

He was in a particular hurry as he and Kate were spending the weekend alone, babysitting the Palmer's dogs as Jeremy and Angela were heading off to Paris to celebrate some thirty years of married bliss.

The entire weekend was marvellous, so rapturously so that even James could think only of the time a year ahead when they would have a home of their own.

They had decided upon Rutland, and as they poured over the brochures sent by Strutt & Parker and Savills it all seemed so tangible, so easy to forget that these beautiful houses would look quite different once the antique furniture and paintings were removed.

A germ of an idea was buzzing around in his head when Kate announced that she had found the perfect house. She offered him the brochure which, even in black and white, conveyed a wealth of colour. They could imagine the warm golden stone mirrored in the lake in the foreground and the towering elms and other great trees that appeared to encompass the small estate.

Woolmington Manor the brochure announced; freehold for sale on the instructions of the executors of the late Sir Oliver Cranston.

'You see Kate, I am right, the relatives don't want to take on the old family home, pity we didn't get to the old boy first, these are the very people that we must direct our marketing at.'

'Yes, Yes, but when can we look at it. Oh James, I am so excited.'

'I tell you what; the Carter Browns have invited us to spend a weekend with them, why don't we take them up on that next weekend? Oh to hell with it, let's stay for a long weekend, we will go up on the Friday and return on Sunday.'

'Do it now, telephone them straight away, please darling.'

He went into Jeremy's study, Nick was away racing but Pippa Carter Brown left him in no doubt that they would be made very welcome.

He also telephoned Anthony Jayes and explained that Savills were selling on behalf of the executors of Sir Oliver Cranston.

'See if we can get some of the bigger pieces of furniture included in the sale price, otherwise we are going to be rattling around in the place. Oh there is one other thing, Anthony, but it will wait until Monday, after the meeting with the shopkeepers.'

They made love, with great tenderness, he appreciating the litheness of her body as compared with the overwhelming sexuality of Rachel. It was different, it was beautiful, it was meaningful and afterwards, they lay there luxuriating in each other's company, no words needed to transmit their happiness.

CHAPTER SIXTEEN

MONDAY AUGUST 15th

7 pm

The private function room at the Royal Oak was an excited spot as the hour of seven approached. Copious jugs of ale and a table full of tidbits encouraged the gathered retailers to relax and, wandering around, James overheard several optimistic notes from the gathered assembly. There was however no sign of Donald Kingsley.

Irritated, but realising that they had to proceed; James called the meeting to order and introduced the top table.

'These gentlemen here are professional Bankers, Lawyers and Architects. They are your guarantee of my integrity and of my determination not to let this idea founder because I am unable to answer any queries you may rightly wish to raise. I will run the proposal past you once again.

In return for the freehold on your premises, I will re-site you in a brand new purpose built shop appropriate to your chosen trade. I will also…'

'Make a great deal of money for yourself.'

James turned, outwardly calm inwardly furious, at the interruption from Donald Kingsley who had entered the room with a man in a pinstripe suit.

'Let us hear him out.'

The other traders were not it seemed prepared to be pushed around.

'Thank you. In addition, all the usual legal costs will be borne by my consortium.'

The pinstripe suit rose to his feet.

'I suggest Mr Carrington that you and your associates are trying to acquire land cheaply by offering these inducements.'

A few of those gathered appeared to agree with this viewpoint; the meeting was starting to slip away from him. Anthony Jayes rose to his feet.

'I represent the oldest firm of solicitors in this town. I wish to categorically state that Mr Carrington is completely within the law, indeed if he were to offer my firm a new suite of offices in exchange for ours, I would have no hesitation in accepting.' Donald Kingsley was on his feet again.

'Remember lads, we hold the aces, he needs all of us to support him.'
James rose, appearing to read a faded copy of the Exeter Herald, he opened it carefully so that he appeared to be reading the inside pages, the front page meanwhile was available to anyone who cared to look; one member of the assemble traders was very aware of what it reported. He sat down whilst James carefully folded the newspaper and returned it to his jacket pocket.

'You make several false assumptions Kingsley.'
His voice, despite the apparently friendly demeanour, had a decidedly hard edge to it.
Those who knew him would have recognised the warning signs as he cited:-

I do not need your support, either singly or as a group.
I intend to build the shops whatever the result of this evening's meeting. You should remember that there are plenty of bakers, hairdressers and other assorted tradesmen out there who would give their eye teeth to rent one of my high class shops - particularly when you consider the locations.
If you do not seize this opportunity, and that is what it is, then I suggest that all of you will struggle to remain in business, unless you have the resources to modernise.
Remember that we are entering a new era; the public are going to demand hygiene and standards far in excess of those you currently provide.
The funding for this exercise is from an impeccable source - Abercrombie Pope & Plummer. No tax inspector is going to scrutinise your accounts to see how you can afford such a plum location. He looked directly at Donald Kingsley as he made this point, smoothing the newspaper in his pocket as he did so.
You have, through the luck of the draw, been given first chance, but please make no mistake, be under no illusions, I will not be held over a barrel by anyone. Make no mistake about it, I do not of necessity need you, I can walk away right now as I promise you I will if I sense any mood of blackmail or if there is a split in your ranks. However, if that is the case then I hope the defector will be able to live with the rest of you as you go down one by one. Not I hasten to add, because you are not good at your chosen trade, but because I believe you do not have the funding to modernise and provide the calibre of services the new age will demand.'

He softened his tone and turned again to Donald Kingsley.
'Don here was right to raise his legitimate objections and quite right to say that you can say no. What I am saying to Don is – Will you give it a go?'
'Of course he will, or he will be out on the street.'
The formidable tones of Mabel Kingsley swung the meeting and it was soon back to good neighboured banter.
'Have you ever sold a Times, Charlie? These new punters won't be wanting yer Daily Mirror and yer Park Drive fags. It will be John Player's and Readers Digest from now on.'
'Suits me, it will double the turnover overnight.' Charlie Benson's satisfied response.
And so it continued, the humour interlaced with an assortment of real concerns.
At 9.30 pm James thanked them for their support and announced that the Landlord was instructed to serve them until closing time, at which point the top table left for a few well earned drinks in the comfort of the Royal Bath Hotel.

They sat at a corner table in the Lounge, James glass raised and saluted them.

'Well done and thank you everyone but please, no more talk of shopkeepers tonight!'
Tim, his glass raised, indicated that he wished to speak.

'We do have one more proposal and it is one which, if we get the right response, will have a big and lasting impact upon the company, poised as it is to chart the high seas rather than the backwaters we have trawled thus far. On behalf of the Directors of Fordmill I invite, most cordially, Anthony Peter Jayes to join uson the Board and in the decision making.' A somewhat bemused Anthony, clearly taken aback at this totally unexpected turn of events, soon recovered his poise and left them in no doubt that by accepting he would play a full and positive role in the company's future.

CHAPTER SEVENTEEN

With the anticipation of both a visit to the Carter Browns and viewing Woolmington Manor the week seemed endless. However, finally Friday came around and James collected Kate at two o-clock from Grantham railway station she, having travelled by train from High Wycombe. In high spirits they arrived at Woolmington at two forty.

The man from Savills was there to greet them.

'Good morning Miss Palmer or, as James is an old buddy of mine, perhaps I might call you Kate?'

She looked enquiringly at him.

'We played at the Tigers together, although I was more of a supporting act for the girls, as we forwards always called the backs.'

'Bloody Estate Agents,' laughed James.

'Try to sell you a house and start off by insulting you.' He held his hand out. 'It is good to see you again Andrew.'

The Surveyor resumed his professional mien. 'Where shall we go first?'

'To the front of the house, I want James to see the drawing room for himself, it is marvellous, and just you wait until you see your study.'

Kate babbled on about the various rooms until it finally dawned on him.

'You have been here before.'

She laughed and Andrew Travers joined in.

'Twice, I believe she would have had the decorators in next week if I hadn't stopped her.'

James smiled, it was just what he would have done; they were so much in tune, both in thought and deed. He loved her all the more for it.

They all walked to the front of the house and stood on the stone terrace looking up at the three stone gables that stood guard over the front elevation, the centre one was a scalloped shape, crowned with an acorn finial.

The house, even from the outside had a warmth and friendly feel to it; he knew they must have it for, whilst it was not as big, it took him back to his early childhood at Milford Hall. Kate tugged at his sleeve excitedly.

'Come and look.'

She led him to the low wall that apparently separated the house from the meadow leading to the lake. Instead what he saw now was not a plain grass hollow ha-ha, but a moat which was filled with the overflow of water from the lake and there in front of them, as if part of the sales script, a family of ducks swam past. He shook his head in disbelief.

'How did you manage the 'fly past' or are they anchored to the spot?'

In good humour they followed Andrew into the house where, as predicted, the drawing room was gracious and welcoming, with panelled walls of dark oak, a large Minster style fireplace and above, the ceiling was overhung with interlacing and finely carved oak beams, the intersections of which were decorated with bosses replicating the same family crest that adorned the wall above the mantelpiece.

They trooped from room to room, Andrew Travers confirming which pieces of furniture were to be included in the sale and which might be bought separately.

Amongst the outbuildings was the coach house that James had noted from the catalogue and also a block of eighteen stables forming three sides of a square, the coach house with its arched entrance completing the enclosure. All of these like the house, sound but in need of some renovation. Unlike the tiny cottage that guarded the entrance to the long drive, which was quite derelict.

In all the property comprised 48 acres of which 5 acres were woodland, the rest mostly rolling pastures apart from the 4 acres of parkland immediately surrounding the house and lake.

The terrain being as it was they were pleased to have the guided tour courtesy of the agents Land Rover, prompting Kate to immediately contemplate selling her car and replace it with a similar vehicle plus the de rigueur black Labrador, James joining in and insisting upon an English Pointer.

They finally prised themselves away, but not before James had ascertained how long it had been since the land had been used by horses, appearing pleased to hear that Sir Oliver Cranston, who had been a reluctant rider in his youth, had become even more so after a heavy fall and 'couldn't stand the brutes,' preferring instead to let the land to a neighbouring farmer. That tenancy had, however, fortuitously ceased with his death.

An excited and happy couple drove away from Woolmington, James subconsciously heading the Alvis towards Uppingham and the Falcon Hotel in the High Street. They had tea and cucumber sandwiches, it was all so very English that nothing else seemed appropriate. Afterwards, anxious though James was to see the Carter Browns he could not resist taking Kate for a stroll around the town. It was the first time he had been back since packing his trunk as a dejected fourteen year old, the memories however were still strong.

They strolled in under the tower and into the quad, still as he remembered it, dominated by the great tree situated on School Lawn and facing them the Headmaster's study.

They walked in a little further and he pointed out the chapel tucked away behind the Old School Room. Retreating from the main entrance they made their way down the London Road to the very last of the boarding houses, his old house, Brooklands. He gazed about him, at the warm brickwork punctuated with pointed and arched windows. The memories flooded back quite vividly; His mind flashed to his tie rack at home, every so often when choosing a tie he would glimpse his Brooklands tie with its blue, green and white stripes it was a poignant reminder, that and Milford Hall were the fuel that drove him on.

'One day my sons will take my place at Uppingham.'
Kate turned, hearing the muttered vow; he looked so intense, so lost in himself, that she resisted the impulse to correct him to 'our' sons. Instead she gently took his hand and lightly brushed it against her lips.

Whether it was that or a teenage pupil referring to him as Sir, she was not sure, but the spell was broken and his happy demeanour returned as he swung on his heel in the direction of the car.

It took them about an hour and a half to reach Newmarket but, with so much to discuss, the journey had flashed by; they did agree that in principle she would organise the decorating, subject to overall agreement on colour schemes and furnishings and that he would oversee the external renovations, except for some new and rather more colourful ducks! These, Kate insisted, were to be her speciality.

They drove through the town, James pointing out the location of Henry's yard as they sped down the Bury Road. Across the Heath and its vast acreage of gallops they were soon at Risby, where he took the turn for the Saxhams. Their hosts lived at Old Saxham Priory, midway between the villages of Little and Great Saxham.

Two Lurchers and an English Setter noisily pursued by a miniature wire-haired Dachshund proclaimed their arrival to Nick and Pippa who were enjoying a Pimms on the lawn, shaded from the still warm sun by a magnificent copper beech.
'Good God, was it this weekend?' Nick feigned surprise.
'Lovely to see you, don't listen to him.' Pippa guided them through the dogs to the table whilst Nick prepared the drinks.

Some friendships take off without much lead time, this was one of them. The conversation, with so much to relate, flowed effortlessly, initially about the house and eventually to horses.
Kate related to Nick, James's seemingly knowing remarks about the usage of land for horses.
'I am impressed, hadn't realised you were so informed, but you are absolutely right there is nothing worse than starting a new stud on land that is horse-sick, also from your description of the land it is perfect, nothing better than plenty of hills to go up and down to build muscle and develop a youngster. It will also keep your older horses fit as they are exercising without realising it. You will probably be on limestone as well, nothing better for building good strong bones. I congratulate you James.'
'Well I have to be honest; Kate found it and had almost bought it before I got there. As for the apparent knowledge, I bought a few books on breeding from Allen's Bookshop. Thank goodness all the bits fitted.'
'It was meant for us darling.' She hugged him again excitedly.

'We have two other couples coming over for supper and I expect Kate would like to freshen up. Why don't you take James to look at the horses, but half an hour maximum mark you.'

The two men walked across the lawn to the adjoining paddocks. At this time of the year the mares and foals are brought in twice a day to be checked over and fed and then led out again to enjoy the lush grass. The other advantage of regular handling, Nick confided, is the trust it builds up between human and horse. There is nothing worse than an animal you cannot trust, particularly in a family environment.

As they reached the fence the first enquiring face was introduced as 'The Brougham', a bay mare with chestnut colt at heel, the foal was by the Her Majesty the Queen's stallion, Aureole, second in the 1953 Derby to that excellent racehorse but disappointing stallion Pinza. That particular Derby had of course split the nation, one half hoping that the most popular owner, the newly crowned young Queen would win and the other half willing the recently knighted champion jockey Sir Gordon Richards in what was to be his last Derby. The latter had prevailed and no one had looked more delighted than her Majesty as she sportingly congratulated Sir Gordon on finally achieving the only prize that had escaped him in a truly memorable career.

The second mare, a grey, was 'Diligence.' She was seventeen now and had been rested this year but Nick was optimistic that she would live up to her name and produce him another winner, hopefully as good as her daughter 'Cabriolet', whose fast finishing third in the One Thousand Guineas at Newmarket had been the high spot so far in the Carter Brown's racing career.

Conscious that time was defeating them, Nick quickly pointed out the other two mares with youngsters grazing without concern under the shade of the large trees in the centre of the paddock, 'The chestnut is 'The Haywain' and that foal is by 'Crepello' and the bay with the white blaze is 'The Curricle', her foal is the best of the lot, just look at that backend, he is by 'Acropolis'.'

They walked back to the house, James bombarding Nick with questions and apologising for doing so; this courtesy was waived aside.

'Welcome to the madhouse James, once this gets under your skin you are hooked and the more you learn, the more you realise you don't know. But, they are the most magnificent animals on this earth, and the thrill you will get when you breed a winner is unbelievable. You stand there, all around you the experts are explaining why they tipped the horse, how brilliantly the jockey had timed his run, all congratulating themselves. What you would like to say is, "Excuse me I arranged this, it is my moment, I am the one who poured over the stud books, who against advice opted to use this or that stallion on this mare that they advised me not to buy in the first place. Instead, you listen and modestly thank them for the congratulations. However, old boy, don't ever forget the glory is yours. You selected the mare and the stallion, it was you who anxiously hoped she would get in foal, stay in foal and finally rear a live foal. I tell you it is a bloody miracle when they are born, the magic will never disappoint you, or if it does, it will be time to get out.'

They were back in good time, the others having not yet arrived. James excused himself and shot upstairs to quickly change. Kate was ready, just waiting for that last approving look, which compliment it was easy to pay, she looked stunning in a little black dress that Coco Channel would have approved of.

'I am a lucky beggar, Kate; you look absolutely fantastic in that dress. So fantastic in fact I can't wait to get you back up here to take it off.'

'Really Mr Carrington, what you appear to have overlooked is that you are in the room next door. Ciao.' With a flick of her pert little bottom she was gone.

He looked around the room and it was true, his case was nowhere to be seen.

He retreated next door and had the grace to smile as he tied his bow tie. He could wait, she was well worth it, it made her seem that much more special than having an affair, on which point he decided to close his mind.

He turned onto the landing at the same time as Nick, who indicated that he had something rather delicate to say.

'The sleeping arrangements, kids still on the summer hols and all that, Pippa not quite sure what to do, personally I can't imagine that there is a man on earth who could resist Kate. The thing is, you both have a balcony and you both have a French window - know what I mean, old bean? Say no more, just don't make too much noise!'

He slapped James on the shoulder and they set off down the wide staircase grinning conspiratorially; Pippa was at the bottom of the staircase.

'Surely you are still not talking about horses?'

'I was just giving our guest a few riding tips.'

She shook her head at their schoolboy laughter.

Across the hall Roger and Helen Forster stood in the library doorway waiting to be introduced, the other couple seemed intent upon the photographs on the piano until they turned around to reveal Miles Stanhope Court and his wife Belinda who handed them both a glass of champagne.

'A little late for chocolate, old boy.'

'Of course, you are a Northampton man, I remember you telling me, what a nice surprise.'

'No more surprised than I was when Belinda told me she and Kate were at Cheltenham Ladies' College together.'

Despite the splendour of Claridge's or the efficient perfection of the Savoy Grill, nothing can quite compare with a small intimate dinner party spent in good company, eating well prepared food complemented by fine wines.

The evening ranged over many subjects, too often returning to horses protested the ladies, too often to decorating houses protested the men.

Finally the ladies withdrew to the Drawing Room and the men, to satiate James's appetite, retired with the brandy to the library. Nick had inherited not only a love of racing but also a very extensive equine library from his father. The great names of the past, Eclipse, Gainsborough, Stockwell, Fairway, Hurry On and Swynford were as yet unknown to him. More recent champions such as Ribot, Pinza, Crepello and Aureole were casually lodged within his memory. But, as he gazed around the shelves laden with equine knowledge his heart sank, where on earth did he begin. As if reading his mind, Roger Forster counselled him.

'First thing to do, James, is to decide whether you wish to breed or race, or maybe you want to do both. I will give you some advice I received quite recently from John Hislop and I know that everyone here will affirm just how knowledgeable he is. If you are breeding to sell you must follow the trends and use fashionable stallions and contemporary bloodlines. However, if you are breeding to race you may be more whimsical in your selection of mates.'

Miles, in the act of pouring more brandy, removed the cigar from his lips and interjected, 'You are a lucky chap James, because apart from Johnny Hislop's sound advice you have two fellows here who can help you implement your dreams. My own personal axiom is to remember that it costs no more to feed a good one than a bad one.'

'So when do we start?' He looked enquiringly at the others.

'If you are serious James, and it would appear you are, then I suggest we meet here in September and trawl through the catalogue with Henry White. We will then visit the Houghton Sale at Tattersall's and pick out something that looks as if it will race and that suits your pocket.'

The conversation ranged far and wide, each having their own idea on the ideal racehorse. Mostly they agreed on the merits of the various champions, it was on the breeding that most opinions differed.

'This horse we are looking for, will it be inbred to Donatello.'
This comment brought a howl of laughter from Miles and Roger and a good natured grin from Nick who sought to defend himself.

'You are an apt student James, yes it is true that most of my horses have a large dosage of Donatello, but he has sired one Derby winner in Crepello and figures high up in the pedigrees of Pinza and Aureole, and he sired the best stayer since the war in Alycidon. However, my main reason for rating him so highly is that he was an outstanding racehorse out of a classic winning mare who herself bred seven winners.'

'I agree with your reasoning Nick, particularly in respect of the female tail line and yes, if we are to agree with John Hislop's dictat then you, as an owner breeder can indulge your personal whims and preferences. My own leanings are towards Nasrullah, I can't forgive them for packing him off to the States. The Aga Khan never can resist the opportunity to earn a fast buck and how wrong he has already proved them with Never Say Die winning the Derby and Nathoo winning the Irish equivalent.'

They were interrupted by Pippa.
'Are you coming through, or are we to storm this male stronghold?'
Nick Carter Brown raised an eyebrow.

'If we are to get James off horses we had better join you, my dear.'
They went through and indulged the ladies in small talk, Kate having wrested an invitation from Belinda to join them in the box at Royal Ascot reserved for VIP clients of Abercrombie's.

'Time for everyone to go.'
Helen Forster pointed to Nick who had started to wind the longcase clock that stood in the hall. They laughingly enlightened the newcomers that he did this without thinking once the chimes of midnight had struck; it had over the years been good-naturedly adopted as the time for 'Cinders to leave the ball.'

The Stanhope Courts and Forsters departed; Kate discreetly said good-night before she too went up. James with great sincerity thanked them for a marvellous evening, trying to retain a serious countenance as Nick gave him the thumbs up behind Pippa's back.

He hastened upstairs, changing swiftly into navy silk pyjamas and robe before stepping out through the French window and on to the stone balcony which led to Kate's open window. She had planned to pretend to be asleep but could not keep up the pretence; instead she lay there on top of the covers twitching her hips as he approached in the moonlight.
Their bodies fitted together as only lovers do, and they stroked and caressed knowing they had the whole night ahead of them, wishing to delay as long as possible the frenzy that this was leading up to. Later, when they had made love they fell asleep her red hair cascaded across and intertwining with the hairs on his chest.

The sound of the milkman's float awoke him at six o'clock; he slowly slid his by now numb arm from beneath her and had reached the open window when he heard a mumbled entreaty.

'I love you, see me soon.'

He returned to his room, tossing around in the bed sufficient enough to fool the maid he hoped and then feeling full of beans, had a bath and a shave before trotting down the staircase to meet the day. He and Nick had arranged a fourball with the others last night and the ladies were joining them for lunch.

He followed the appetising smells emanating from the kitchen to find both Nick and Pippa already started on the eggs and bacon. Kate joined them half an hour later also with a healthy appetite. Nick meanwhile sketched out his plans for the day.

'Right, action plan for the day. Men to meet at the Royal Worlington at nine-thirty for eighteen holes, ladies to join us at around one-thirty for the pre-prandials followed by lunch... That suit everyone?'

Pippa saluted. 'Danke mein, General.'

'You will love it James' she added; 'According to the others, it is the best nine hole course in the world.'

Nick saw the slightly disappointed expression on his face at the mention of nine holes. To most keen golfers this is not a 'proper' golf course although in reality it is in some ways better, as you get two chances albeit off different tees, to test yourself against the course and its layout.

'It has a scratch of 6258 yards, which is not long, but I guarantee you will have added another thousand to that by the time we have finished, especially using these clubs I am fixing you up with.'

James laughed; 'That is just what I need, a good excuse.'

The men left in James's car. Nick being anxious to drive and with him at the helm, they headed off back towards Newmarket turning off at Kennett, passing through Freckenham and thence to Worlington. The opposition had assembled and were busy practising on the putting green when they arrived.

'A gentleman never practises,' Nick chided them.

This received an acknowledging wave as the newcomers strode to the locker rooms to change. They proceeded, courtesy of Roger's membership, to the members' changing rooms where, as ever, the act of stripping for action was sufficient for James to get fired up, enquiring of his partner as to the standard of the opposition.

'These boys are pretty keen. Miles got his half blue when he was up at Oxford and I think he still plays off two or three; Roger, on the other hand, is off eight the same as me.'

'That leaves me as the mug off a very bad ten handicap.'

'Come on; think of all the shots you will receive from Miles.'

The Royal Worlington was described by that doyen of golf writers, Leonard Crawley, as;

'Like the old course at St Andrews, a freak of nature. No one knows who designed it and yet, like The Royal and Ancient, also laid out for the old fashioned 'gutta-percha' ball, it still remains a great test of a golfer, despite the apparently obvious advantages of the modern steel shaft and rubber cored ball.

As unprepossessing as it appears at first glance, it has been for nearly a hundred years the home of the Cambridge University Golf Society and is invariably included in the best one hundred golf courses in the world.

With this valedictory firmly in mind they struck off from the first, James playing last and suffering the mortification of seeing his opening tee shot slice out of bounds.

He took another ball and with that immense relief known to all golfers playing three off the tee, saw the second shot soar down the middle. It was to no avail, Miles looking every bit the class player that he was, came very close to birdying the 484 yard first. They were glad to concede the hole without having to cough up the sixpence the birdie would have cost.

The second is regarded as one of the best 'one-shotters' in the country. It follows the same direction as the first, so once again James was under pressure not to slice. However, with a slight following breeze to assist, he smacked a wonderful 4 iron right to the heart of the large 'bowler hat' shaped green, this time the opposition were the ones relieved not to be paying out.

This hole set the tone for the morning. The testing third was tamed by all four, although Miles had to exert all his skills to extricate himself from the ditch that meanders around the green. At the long 500 yard fourth, Roger paid the price of ambition and had to pick out of the deep stream about a hundred yards short of the green. Once again, Miles saved the day and they halved in fives.

The famous fifth hole is one that James will never forget. It is 170 yards played from under the bank of the old railway line with a stream to intimidate the faint hearted, and beyond this a long narrow green elevated several feet above the tee. Still playing first he hit a seven iron right out of the sweet spot. His body arched as the ball flew away and he was left posed and still, the follow through, the feet, everything straight out of the textbook.

They were unable to see the actual hole but the triumphant whoop of delight from those playing in front left them in no doubt that he had achieved his first hole-in-one.

They remained one up until the 'second / eleventh' on the back nine. James and Nick again on with their tee shots, Miles suffering from a rush of blood and wildly over-estimating the slight head wind took a three wood only to see the ball fly high over the green and into Pigeons Wood, a copse which looms ominously not far behind the green. Two up and seven to play. James watched Miles compose himself and with the skill and belief in himself that only the best players have, no longer joined in the banter but slowly began to peg them back until, at the seventeenth when all but he were trapped by the wing bunkers with little chance of making a four, he completely crushed them by holing a long putt for a birdie three.

This was to be the decisive hole; the last was halved by Nick and Miles and they returned to the clubhouse where, as usual, news of the hole-in-one had gone on ahead.

They changed and followed the conquering hero as he made his way into the white painted clubhouse with its distinctive chimneys. Here they were met and welcomed by the captain who, having been a keen rugby player himself, instantly recognised the tall athletic figure.

Unfortunately, the intimate quiet lunch for eight was forgotten in the euphoria, the pints freeing all tongues, as past achievements on the rugby field and on the golf course were related by members, mostly with a degree of embellishment. James and Miles, the two class performers, being noticeably the quietest and most self-effacing.

The ladies retired from the bar to sit outside in the warm sunshine; Belinda raising a smile as she commented,

'At least it got them off the subject of bloody horses!'

CHAPTER EIGHTEEN

The next six weeks were the most hectic that anyone at Fordmill could remember. The meetings were seemingly endless, either in town with the bankers or with the local sub-contractors in Bournemouth. It was essential that everything came on stream together and James had insisted on penalty clauses being included in the terms of the contract with all the sub-contractors.

They had every reason to congratulate themselves on the appointment of the two new directors. It was inspirational in fact, as they kept each of the ends going when the other three were hurtling from one site visit to another.

There were certainly moments when James secretly wondered if they had been right to tackle all four phases in tandem. However, these were private thoughts that he would not admit to anyone, not even Kate. Any captain of industry, any military commander, has to endure these agonies of doubt alone; to those lesser mortals depending on his leadership he must exude unshakeable confidence. But it is draining on the nervous system, calling for understanding and uncomplaining companions and comrades.

James had no opportunity or indeed inclination to see Rachel, he only saw Kate at the weekends, and indeed the last one had seen their first tiff. He was in the midst of some rather detailed calculations when she sought his preference on the choice of curtain fabric for the sitting room and morning room. As always, he made an instant decision which she interpreted as 'saying anything to be rid of me.'

He had tried to reason with her, it had actually been his preference, but yes, although he would not admit it, it did not seem that important, judged in the scale of other things right now.

'Sit down, please. I am sorry if you thought me offhand, it is just that unless I get this right, there will be no point in discussing Woolmington Manor, as we will not be able to afford it.'

Her background, a dynasty of respectable solicitors, had ill-equipped her to understand the pressures of commercial life and her feeble excuses exacerbated rather than healed the situation.

She stormed out and he heard the car engine start and tyres spinning on the tarmac as she left. Feeling low and dejected he picked up the telephone and rang Jack Priory.

'I am totally pissed off, fancy a game of squash?'

'Twenty minutes.' No questions asked; God, it was good to have men friends. On them you could rely.

He strolled round to the Squash Racquets Club, inwardly approving that the Nottingham Park Club still retained the traditional spelling and, in his present frame of mind wondering if he should be leaving the still waters of bachelor life for the tempestuous seas of marriage. He was falling still deeper into this slough when the familiar silver Porsche of Jack Priory hurtled to an equally familiar and violent halt.

'Tell me about it.'

The smiling invitation restored James's mood so that the explanation when delivered as they changed, was embellished with 'man-talk' encouraging Jack to weigh in with his own problems. The highlight of which had been a very long forty minutes crouched in a cupboard on a lady friend's landing; the girl's mother arriving rather unexpectedly to deliver some dressed crab from Whitby!

As he described the hunched figure that had finally crept from the cupboard, unable as he put it, to straighten his back, let alone anything else, the whole of the assembled changing room was in an uproar.

They closed the door of the court behind them, James checking that they were using the slow coloured ball. It was not unknown for Jack to slip in a faster ball enabling him, with his superb timing, to play just about every shot without moving from the 'T.'

The next forty minutes were frenzied, neither of these close friends liked to lose, each shot was competitively played and James, his spirits rekindled, contrived to bring Jack off the 'T' position with some exquisite short drop shots played just above the tin and into the sidewall nick. On the second occasion that Jack had failed to retrieve one of these, a wag on the balcony overlooking the back of the court called out, amidst great guffaws of applause that Jack ought to go back in the cupboard and learn how to bend his back!

All the games went to deuce and, despite playing to the top of his game James had to concede to his old adversary. They collected the spare rackets and towels and went off, the adrenaline still flowing, staving off for the moment any exhaustion but contributing to the sweat that stained both of their shirts and pumped out of the top of the head.

They had a couple of beers and then decided to go on an impromptu walk about town.

The Trip To Jerusalem, The Royal Children, The Flying Horse, The Black Boy and finally, to restore the equilibrium, a meal at Severns in the Lace Market.

It had been fun, but in their cups they both agreed that doing this every night was fairly pointless, the more so because your regular pals fall by the wayside, as they too succumb to feminine wiles.

'Give her another chance and just pray that I will get one when Wendy sees the state of me!'

The taxi dropped James off en route for Radcliffe on Trent and Jack's anticipated warm reception.

James made a scratchy entrance; the key seemed not to want to go in the lock, which was perhaps not too surprising as it was designed to go into the car door. However, he finally made it to the bathroom and had half finished his toilet before he noticed the message spelt out in shaving cream on the medicine cupboard. Sorry -Je t'aime xxx.'

Even in this slightly incoherent state his spirits were immediately uplifted, even more so as he quietly opened the bedroom door. The sleeping figure stirred.

'Hello.'

One word and every bad thought was swept away. He slid in beside her.

'Sleep tight, I love you.'

They curled up together, she curtailing his ineffectual attempts to make love, right now being here was enough.

The following morning, courtesy of several Alka-Seltzers, he emerged relatively unscathed. They had clung to each other, both spontaneously apologising and at the same time suppressing the others regrets and recriminations. They had made love with the intensity and ardour that follows absence or disagreement, that great pouring out of the soul from one to another, re-uniting and re-affirming so that, like a broken limb, it is all the stronger once the healing process has taken place.

Despite the pressures at work he felt compelled to find time to visit Woolmington with her, suggesting to Kate that she meet him at the office at around twelve thirty.
At eight twenty, precisely one hour later than usual, he set out to earn his crust, leaving Kate to contemplate a visit to Griffin & Spalding's department store and as she put it, 'a dummy run up the Derby Road to check out the antique shops.'
　　　　'Don't buy anything,' and then to soften it; 'we must choose it together.'
　　　　'As if I would dare!'
She gave him a pretend pout to be rewarded with a hug and a smack on the bottom.
Kate arrived at the office at exactly twelve thirty collecting James from his room at one o'clock, the interim period spent with Connie discussing the wedding.
They drove out through Tollerton, skirting the Vale of Belvoir, through Melton Mowbray until they reached Barleythorpe on the outskirts of Oakham, where they turned left towards Cottesmore, finally reaching Woolmington at a little after two o'clock.
　　　　'Forty two minutes, give or take a few seconds.'
　　　　'You will have no time to dally in bed,' she cautioned him.
　　　　'In that case I shall have to deal with you the night before.'
They both laughed, blissfully in love, contrition and traumas now forgotten. Although he had been somewhat surprised at how she had suddenly become so unreasonable yesterday, it was a new side to her, one that he fervently hoped he would not see very often.
　　　　They reached the entrance and drove in, James making a mental note to ask Tim to knock out some drawings to renovate the cottage; if he was to keep his brood mares here, they would need to employ a groom. He added a further mental note to ask in the local pub for any decent local builders as Fordmill was too stretched to contemplate taking it on.
　　　　Kate spotted the Land Rover around the back of the house.
'Did you ask Andrew Travers to meet us?' she enquired.
　　　　'No, I haven't spoken to him since last week.'
He turned away quickly so that she would not see the suppressed grin on his face, parked the Alvis and got out.
　　　　'How strange.' Kate walked towards the Land Rover and let out a shriek.
　　　　'James Carrington, you are impossible.'
He joined her and read with her the notice he had left stuck to the inside of the windscreen.
　　　　'With all my love; buy your own Labrador.'
She looked at him, her eyes misted over with gratitude and remorse at yesterday.
　　　　'I am surprised you didn't send it back.'
　　　　'You were lucky, it was Sunday... any road up, as we say in these parts, take me for a spin my good woman.'

They set off to tour the estate, he acting as gate opener, glad of the interludes to escape the vicissitudes of the suspension that left his backbone feeling even more mauled than it had felt after being tackled by the Springboks in South Africa.

They stopped at the Coach House and he elaborated upon his idea to maybe transfer the office here, although at the moment he stressed, it was just an idea. Kate hoped it would stay just an idea; she was anxious not to lose the privacy that such a move would impose.

Once again they examined the stables, he imagining a nodding head gazing from each, and inside and out of sight a foal that would one day win the Derby.

'You really are keen on this breeding lark aren't you?'

'I find it totally absorbing Kate, I can't begin to tell you, I long to move in here and fill my study with books on the subject. Equally I am aware of how little I know and of how important people like Henry and Nick are to me. They can point me in the right direction and save me years of painful and expensive learning.'

'Well I think it is brilliant that you have something other than work to expend your energies on, it will save me worrying about other women.'

'Come on; let's see where we can stable the Land Rover whilst we are away.

He marched into the Coach House, and swung up the eight foot length of timber that secured the two doors together. He hauled them open and they creakily allowed sight of the spacious inner reaches long since unused. As she reversed in, he could not help imagining a galleried landing stretching across joining his office to Edward's.   Actually they had room for two Directors offices each side he mused.

She wagged her finger. 'What are you thinking of now?'

'Nothing important My Lady.'

They took a few measurements inside the house and set off in leisurely fashion, driving across country, admiring the warm golden stone from which so many of the local cottages and houses were built, finally drifting out of Rutland and into Leicestershire and the Vale of Belvoir.

Initially the change is not apparent although eventually they were aware of more brick built properties. Within sight of Belvoir Castle, truly the Monarch of this particular glen, they came into Stilton country, those few villages grouped together, that produce probably the one truly great English cheese.

Colston Bassett, Hose, Long Clawson and Harby, the very names redolent of old England. Here in this small vale set in the midst of what is unquestionably the greatest hunting country in the British Isles, the local farmers concentrate their efforts on producing the rich creamy milk that enables the local dairies to produce the blue veined delicacy that rather perversely takes its name, not from here, but from a village in Huntingdonshire on the nearby A1 highway. For it was from there, in the village of Stilton, that the landlord of the local Inn first established its fame by selling this distinctive cheese to travellers on the Great North Road.

It was seven o'clock, a warm summer's evening and as they approached the Nags Head in Harby, the landlord was opening the doors ready for this evenings business. The omens were too predictable to ignore. He swung the Alvis into the car park at the rear of the pub. They entered the charming black and white building to a cheerful greeting and for him, a pint of his local Home Ales bitter and for Kate a Campari and soda.

They are sociable people in this part of the world and as the regulars drifted in they were drawn into the topics of the day, but eluded the invitation to try their hands at skittles which was played in the bowling alley set in the outbuildings behind the pub. This is a very competitive local sport, none more so than tonight's match, as the Nags Head were playing their arch-rivals from nearby Hose, The Black Horse.

The other conversation in this part of the world revolves around hunting. The great seas of grassland on which the cattle graze, divided as they are by ancient thick hedges, make this a paradise for a foxhunter. The great packs that hunt this 'country', The Belvoir, The Quorn, The South Notts and nearby, The Cottesmore. This is a litany of the sport, an area favoured by not just the wealthy and discerning, but by Royalty itself. The greatest natural steeplechase still run, The Melton Hunt Cup, is organised in rotation with the other Packs, over fences within hailing distance of the Nags Head.

Alas, James and Kate had to admit they did not hunt, although of course his parents had both been keen members of the Belvoir. The painting of his father out with the hounds riding at the head of the field on his grey gelding Claude was destined, thanks to his mother, to take pride of place over the fireplace at Woolmington Manor.

So whilst they would not be mounted they readily accepted the landlord's invitation to be present when the Hunt next met at the Nags Head.

'You will be a racing man then.'

Before he could answer this rhetorical question and put down roots in the low beamed bar, Kate dragged him good humouredly off to the car, insisting that she took the helm. She drove steadily into Nottingham, deciding as they approached to have a curry at the Kohinoor Restaurant on Alfreton Road. This really was one of the very best Indian restaurants in the provinces and one that James visited regularly, a fact not wasted upon the waiters who rapidly found them a table.

'And to think that just twenty four hours ago you didn't love me.'

He pulled a face at her, happy that they had so swiftly recovered the situation.

'Promise me one thing.' She looked deeply into those piercing blue eyes.

'Don't ever go to sleep annoyed with me, talk to me - please.'

'I promise.' He took her left hand and looked at the large single diamond stone.

'I can't afford another ninety nine ice cream to put this on.'

'Do you know something James Carrington; you always hide behind a joke when something gets to you. It is really quite endearing.'

She took his hand and kissed it.

'Take me home and I will pay for my supper.'

CHAPTER NINETEEN

Cranborne Chase, Wednesday September 7th 1960

James woke up seconds before the alarm was due to go off at six o'clock. He leapt from the bed, anxious to confirm yesterday's optimistic weather forecast. The garden at The Cedars was shrouded in a heavy sea fret, the omens were good, and the sun would surely follow. He showered quickly, eager to check the final details, determined that, having come this far, nothing should be left to chance.

Jeremy and Kate clad in dressing gowns were already downstairs sitting in front of a burbling percolator of coffee. Seeing them on edge, seemed to settle him, someone had to assume responsibility and it came naturally to him.

'I propose to go into town and visit the site, make sure the marquees are still up etc. I will also collect Tim and the others from the Royal Bath so should be back by ten thirty at the latest.'

'We are on parade at one o'clock, so will need to be at the Town Hall around twelve.'
James nodded his agreement to Jeremy's summing up, spread a round of toast with honey and took his leave of them.

He drove slowly, savouring the moment, he wanted to be alone: He needed to be alone.

This day when all his efforts would finally come to fruition, when all those lonely and private moments of fears and secret doubts could finally be expunged and be put aside. Later in the day he would bathe with others, in the warm glow of success, but not right now, this was his personal Valhalla.

Many had undeniably played their parts and yet this moment of triumph he zealously sought for himself.

He was the architect of the success, this was a moment from which even his nearest and dearest were excluded; only one person was in his thoughts right now as he savoured his success.

In a few hours' time the congratulations would flow and he would diffidently play down his role and make great store of the supporting roles but, that was for later. Right now : He stopped the car and leaned his head on his hands against the steering wheel and thought of his father, how he wished, what would he have given to have seen him on the dais this afternoon with his mother.

He turned his head towards the sky, reliving that moment when they had departed Milford and remembered for the umpteenth time his muttered and defiant promise.

He saw his father's face, his eyes misted over as he whispered the one word, 'Soon.' And then, just as quickly the mood changed, the melancholia was gone. He mentally gesticulated a 'two fingers' to anyone who might stand in his way and headed for town.

The sun would soon be cracking the pavings; God he felt good.

The arrangements were progressing well; the only cause for concern regarded the food which, because of the way that the temperature was rising, would have to be kept cool for as long as possible. To solve the problem, the caterers had decided to remove a back panel from the marquee so that they could swoop in with the trays of sustenance towards the end of the speeches.

He nodded his approval, pleased to leave such details to the experts, and walked slowly to the front of the development. The large fifty foot sign replicating the sketches prepared by Tim and Richard Fells had been prepared by Simpson's, the Nottingham sign writers, and gave a most impressive idea of how the project would appear in a few months' time and the area below the dais bore the legend **'APP - Financing Success.'** This publicity had been James's idea, Sir Julian Abercrombie and his fellow Directors being somewhat taken aback at the original suggestion. However, younger heads had prevailed, notably Miles Stanhope Court and the more he saw of his new friend, the more impressed he was with his grasp of the coming age.

It had been difficult to decide on the name for the new developments. Edward had wisely erred towards tradition as this would be the prevailing sentiment of the hoped for occupants, and they had finally decided to geographically space out the emotive pull of the names, settling for Blenheim Court, Chatsworth Court, Harewood Court, and finally the 'piece de resistance'; the fourth side, the jewel in their crown, complete with sculpture garden, would be Staincliffe Court.

James had insisted upon this, it would brandish once again to the world the name of Staincliffe, and help repay his mother for the share certificates that had proved so decisively important.

He dragged himself away and collected Connie, Edward and Tim from the Royal Bath Hotel, arriving back five minutes before his ten thirty deadline. The house was starting to fill up, his mother, with his sister Louise and her barrister husband Richard were all kitted out in their finery, although for the latter the tailed coat and striped trousers were merely an extension of his working plumage. The new arrivals shot upstairs to don their party clothes and were soon returned to assist the others plundering the Bollinger that James had insisted that Anthony accept.

The Rolls Royce's, complete with chauffeurs arrived at eleven forty five precisely and they were whisked off to the Town Hall, where His Worship the Lord Mayor and Lady Mayoress received them. Ten minutes later Sir Julian Abercrombie and Sir Marcus Partington representing the Bank arrived with Lord Wimborne, Old Etonian and sometime Ambassador for Her Majesty's Government, whom the former had persuaded to lay the foundation stone.

Also present; and the pre-eminent guest as far as James was concerned, was Sir David Barrington Jones, President of the Royal Institute of British Architects. This compliment, seen in the context of the praiseworthy article in the Architects' Journal magazine, had far reaching and important overtones for the company, not quite Le Corbusier and the world famous apartments of

Marseille but a feather in their caps, particularly Tim Cooper's.

For James and the others, a well built job here would encourage other developers to use their expertise. Yes, as he had silently confided to his father, everything was moving in the right direction.

They moved in a convoy of cars headed by the Lord Mayor to the building site. As they approached, it was gratifying to see the interest that the development had generated to the locals. Obviously the local press and grapevine had been effective.

The two JCB Diggers painted in the Fordmill house colours rather than the familiar yellow, stood with their front buckets raised to form an arch for the guests as they alighted from their cars. From here they would process to the platform directly ahead.

The triumphal arch had been the idea of Joe Bamford whose inventive initials the JCB's bore; despite the change of paint, he knew that the press would pick up on this particular picture, and of course they did.

James was quite happy; he knew that the astute business brain that was building a new Bamford empire, quite separate from the long established family agricultural firm, would use this in his advertising, thus affording Fordmill considerable free publicity both here and abroad.

They were assembled on time and at one o'clock precisely. Sir Julian Abercrombie addressed the press and assembled guests and thanked them for their attendance. He elaborated on the importance of the development and its significance to both to the local area and the economy of the greater Bournemouth area before inviting Lord Wimborne to carry out the honours. His Lordship rose adjusting, as he did so, his half glasses to a more effective angle.

My Lord Mayor, Lords, Ladies and Gentlemen. I was delighted when the Lord Mayor invited me to perform this ceremony. It seemed particularly appropriate as I too, after a career spent in many parts of the world, have also chosen to spend my retirement in this delightful part of England.

I would say to anyone contemplating a move: Do it, and encourage your friends to do likewise. You will have every possible amenity, whether you require active pastimes such as golf or bowls or more passive pleasures such as bridge. Likewise, whatever your taste in scenery you have a landscape that varies from a superb coastline to the glories of the New Forest.

He continued to reminisce before returning to the text of his speech.

We have here assembled on the platform not only the Chairman of one of most respected Merchant Banks, Sir Julian Abercrombie, but also the President of the Royal Institute of British Architects, Sir David Barrington Jones. This underlines, I believe, the prestige of this project, a concept that the architectural press have themselves likened to a renaissance of new standards in British architecture. These ideals are inspired by the glories of the past when all buildings were part of an overall plan and not built in isolation. Here the gardens and statuary will intertwine with the fabric of the building, the part enhancing the whole. The outlook determined for the future and not to be ruined by individuals tampering with their own front gardens as it were.

I congratulate the Lord Mayor of Bournemouth and his Council for the very pro-active and positive role they have played in attracting newcomers to the area and then having got them here providing an interesting and attractive environment.

It has long been a concern of mine that so many museums and libraries have interesting and beautiful treasures packed away in hidden vaults. It is a concern that I have expressed on many occasions at various embassies in which I have served throughout the world. How pleasing it is to see that the City Fathers here are to make available paintings and other objet d'art that would remain otherwise unseen. Not only will this prove pleasing to the eye, it will surely provoke an interest and desire to know more from the residents, many of whom will have time on their hands. At the very least what better environment, one's own personal treasures to live with and your own art gallery in which to relax with your friends. Many future residents will be selling large houses with perhaps large oil paintings too big to be accommodated in their own apartment - why not instead of disposing of them, bring them with you to be hung alongside the museum exhibits.

But I digress; please accept my apologies for expounding so forcefully one of my pet obsessions.
Many people and organisations have played important roles in this concept. However, we must reserve our main congratulations for the Directors of Fordmill who conceived the idea and who now, as it were, stand in the delivery room awaiting the birth of their baby.
With no more ado, I will therefore deliver that baby by cutting the umbilical cord.'

He stepped forward and an extremely pretty young girl of about ten in a lemon summer dress, her blonde hair tied back with a matching ribbon, handed him a pair of gold scissors.

The old diplomat stooped to receive them, clicking the blades appreciatively and smilingly enquired if she would like a haircut. Her bashful reply was captured by the battery of press photographers and would appear in several of the following day's daily newspapers.

He snipped the red and grey striped ribbon to a generous round of applause. Having done so, he turned to shake James by the hand and, at the latter's request, led the assembled dignitaries and guests into the marquee where the results of this morning's preparations lay coolly and deliciously spread before them.

In an adjoining marquee, the builders and other workmen enjoyed their own festivities. Once again Fordmill breaking with tradition by having a pre-celebration party for the men rather than the traditional Topping Out Party at the end of the contract.

Edward went round to join them and was able to report back just how well it had gone down with the men, making them feel part of the job right from the very start.

The last guests dispersed at just after four o'clock, everything had gone well and a genuine air of excitement about the project prevailed both within the company and the local council. The latter beginning to appreciate just how useful to the area this alliance would prove.

However, despite the euphoria, James felt rather flat, his main input into the scheme was now largely over, others would make it happen, he needed a new Everest to climb. With this thought niggling in his mind, he proposed an impromptu Board Meeting at Anthony Jayes' office the following morning.

The following morning prior to the Board Meeting, Tim, Edward and James reconvened at the site. At eight o'clock precisely the JCBs moved into action and the first of the topsoil was cleared to the back of the development area where it would stay until the gardens were laid out at the end of the building phase. All the vehicles, like the signs on site, were painted in the pale grey and red Fordmill livery ensuring that, as they travelled about the town to dispose of rubble and other waste, the painted side boards advertised in visually graphic terms the developments that were taking place.

Today's morning papers had picked up on the enchanting picture of the Diplomat brandishing the scissors to his ten year old assistant. The Daily Express had captioned it 'Hair Majesty's Ambassador', others including most importantly the local press had also played upon this theme.

The most encouraging response, however, had been from the public. The telephone was ringing constantly. So much so that Connie, despite her heavy workload in Nottingham, had felt obliged to stay for a couple of days to arrange appointments and interviews. As a result the Board meeting took place without her.

They sat around the conference table in Jeremy Palmer's office, the euphoria still high, an air of self-congratulation just below the surface. James had no wish to kill this mood but he found it difficult to be complacent. He began by summing up:-

'The reaction from the public has been more than we dared hope and yet it has already provoked a problem, one we had not envisaged. Our success, gentlemen, has caught us unprepared; it is a situation I want resolving today. What cannot be denied is our correctness in building the four sites in tandem, as without those apartments coming on stream we would be turning people away in droves.

As a means of spacing people out and to avoid letting on that we are caught on the hop, I propose that we invite all the applicants to view not only their first choice but also the alternative sites. This way we keep them both interested and satisfied with our sales support and they realise that we are concerned that the decision they make will be, in the long run, best for them.' Anthony Jayes indicated that he wished to speak.

'As you know my father visits the United States on a fairly regular basis these days. He has looked at several potential holiday homes and in each case has been met on site by an attractive girl whose sole job, or so it seemed, was to show him around and arrange lawyers etc. This will be innovative for the U.K, but surely that is what this company is about.'

Edward interrupted

'You make a good point, Anthony; unfortunately, for the moment we don't have an apartment to show them.'

The accountant paused, not wishing to appear rude, particularly to someone he respected,

'This is true, Edward, but we do have a complete suite of newly decorated offices, and all we are waiting for is the furniture.'

James and Tim were immediately convinced by the sound business logic of it and it was not long before Edward was offering to personally interview the 'Dolly-Birds.'

This of course amused them, the conversation soon degenerating into just how short they might decently insist upon the length of the mini-skirt they envisaged being worn.

'You are looking a bit pensive are you planning to pull rank and do the interviews yourself?' James turned to face Edward's curious face.

'Not necessarily, I think the idea is brilliant but, sorry to disappoint you old son, what we need is a slightly different sales lady.'

'So we can forget the mini-skirts.' Now Tim feigned disappointment.

'Afraid so, to make this work perfectly what we need is someone still quite young but poised and elegant, someone old enough to have parents of a similar age to the would-be residents, someone to whom the younger relatives can relate to on a social level, someone with whom they can empathise.'

'What you propose makes good sense, but time is of an essence, where are we going to find this ideal lady at such short notice?'

'In this instance Edward I am going to pull rank, you organise the immediate delivery of the furniture and you Tim, organise the layout. By the end of this week I want this to be the nerve centre of our operation, anyone who steps through that door is going to be knocked out by what they see, no one will leave this office other than excited by what those sketches will convey to them. As for the lady, we will meet here again at four o'clock with a clear cut plan before you leave for Nottingham.'

CHAPTER TWENTY

Before they had a chance to question him further he was gone; they listened to his retreating footsteps as they shot down the stairs and heard the throaty roar as he started the Alvis. He drove hard, deliberately not composing any logical approach, the decision he was convinced would be an emotive one.

He swung into the now familiar gateway and found her at the rear of the house languidly soaking up the sun. Her face lit up as she saw him.

'James, what a wonderful surprise, come and sit beside me.'

'Only sit is it.'

He pretended to be hurt which was sufficient to bring her off the sun bed to stand beside him, he dragged his eyes away from the great cleavage that stared up at him.

'You should be careful in this hot sun; I don't want you burnt so that I can't touch you.' He stroked her shoulder with the edge of his finger.

'Better show me where you keep the sun lotion.'

In an atmosphere charged with static emotion and without a word she took his hand and led him up the long galleried staircase and into her dressing room. She opened the cabinet and, still without speaking, squirted the lotion into the palm of his hand. He turned her around and applied it gently to her shoulders working his way down to the clip that secured the bikini top. She closed her eyes and sighed as he massaged her breasts and shuddered as his hands descended lower until she could stand it no more. She turned to face him, fingers not functioning properly as she sought to take off his shirt and trousers, the latter falling around his ankles and leaving him hogtied and stranded.

He wiped the remaining lotion from his hands on to her trembling thighs and extricated himself from the unwanted bondage. They made love, passionately, he very much the active partner, she anxious to do his every bidding. When the final crescendo was reached in a rush of stilted cries to the Almighty they lay there both having reached heights they had never attained before, this time it was true, she had no need to seek his confirmation.

Conversation was unnecessary; they lay there gently caressing each other, aware that something was stirring that would relaunch their passion. This time they made love with more tenderness that seemed all the sweeter after the earlier frenzy.

'I need to see you more often.' The hot breath whispered in his ear.

'I know and I believe I have found a way in which we can meet regularly and without arousing suspicion.'

'Oh James how, please tell me.' Her optimism emboldened him.

'I have suggested to the others that I ask you to head up our sales drive here.'

'Me, but I have never had a job in my life, how would I cope? I don't believe Dickie would agree to it.'

'Oh he will, I can promise you that.' On this point he felt quite confident.
He resumed his persuasion, gently tracing his fingers along her spine as he did so.

'Please say yes, it is terribly important to me.'

'Will I see you often, you do promise, you do mean it, I need you.'
With every demand he knew he was winning but he did not want her getting petulant. He lifted his hands from the centre of her back and in one quick movement ran his fingers down each side of her body. She let out a scream, the sensation too much for her.

'Do I take that to be a yes?'

'I will think about it.'

'Then I will take that to be a yes.' He held her face, carefully stroking the beautifully etched cheekbones. 'Thank you Rachel, thank you.'

He casually looked at his watch, noting that it was two fifty,

'I must make a move, I have promised to call back at the site to see the foreman Harry Wells, we have a few small wrinkles to iron out.' He dressed as quickly as he casually could, thinking for the first time of Dickie Charlton, in his anxiety to secure Rachel's cooperation he had been careless.

'I will telephone you later after I have reported the good news to the others, maybe I should call round instead to square things with the boss'

'Will you James, he will be back about seven o'clock.'

'Will do, best prepare him in advance, say I called this afternoon to offer you a position you couldn't refuse.'

He dodged the pillow she hurled and still laughing like a schoolboy ran down the stairs and out through the still open kitchen door.

He drove slowly into town, with lots to think about, recruiting Rachel to do this job made a lot of sense; it was something they should have thought of, next time they must give more thought to the back-up systems. However, they were learning quickly and perhaps more importantly they were responding to pressure and finding solutions, that was a sign of the quality of the company's management. On that particular point he was once again appreciative of Anthony Jayes' input; it had been an impulse decision to appoint him, but it had been an inspired one, the more so as he was an outsider, the rest of the team having been together virtually from the start. Connie's promotion on the other hand was overdue; she was so dependable, they must be careful not to take her for granted.

The others had not been idle in his absence; the scene that awaited him took even him by surprise. Yes the furniture would be here tomorrow, having Kate as the Managing Director's PA had ensured that, however, it was in the larger centre office that the surprise awaited him. Edward had enlisted a joiner from the site - at the risk of slowing down production, he laughed. Meanwhile Tim had sorted the sketches and a selection of plans and elevations and these were now displayed around the room giving a most impressive visualisation of the finished project.

James looked at the display, silent for a long time.

'What is it? Surely you must agree it makes quite an impression.' Tim was perplexed.

'That it certainly does, you cannot imagine the effect it has when you see it unexpectedly; ask Anthony and Connie to step in here for a moment.'

Edward went next door to the solicitor's office and returned about ten minutes later with the others, both as intrigued as Tim had been.

He directed them all back into the large office bedecked with the images of the proposed developments. 'Other than an architect's office, where else could you imagine you were?'

They all gazed rather blankly at the walls, no one proffering an answer. He tried a different approach.

'If you were planning to buy a house or apartment where might you go?'

Connie beat them to it.

'God it is so obvious, it looks like an estate agents and I know what you are about to propose James and I second it.'

He smiled at her.

'In that case I propose that Fordmill Properties has just been born and what is more I have today appointed the Manager, only she is only half aware of it at this point in time.'

He outlined the proposal he had made to Rachel, adding that she would need to appoint an assistant to organise the other property sales. Anthony would of course control the conveyancing through his office. Edward interrupted, his cautious instinct wondering where the properties would come from to satisfy the business once the apartments had all been sold... James sighed and put his arm around the big man's shoulders.

'Anthony's firm already do conveyancing for people with houses to sell, it would be quite natural for them to advertise them next door, we are after all still in the same building. However, the main opportunity lies in our own hands. We can sell all those nice juicy properties that our prospective clients have for sale. Work a contract into the deal and, don't forget, many of the younger relatives of the older clients may well be looking to move house. What have we to lose? We have already invested in the offices; we can only gain by this extension of the original concept.'

Tim nodded his head.

'I am in full agreement, the outlay will be minimal and the base of the company will be widened. For myself, I believe that diversification will become increasingly important if the company wishes to grow on a sound and secure base.'

On that positive note they broke up, Tim and Edward to return to Nottingham to wrestle on the morrow with the County Council Architects on a new school they were building to the south of the city and on the following day a new pathology lab they were building for the City Hospital on Hucknall Road.

James went back to the Palmers, explaining over a cup of Earl Grey, the latest development to Angela. She was getting used to his speed of action, but it still came as a continual surprise when he pulled the latest rabbit from the hat.

She looked at the intense face opposite, the ambition scarcely hidden and took his hand.

'I wish you every success James, you know I do but, I ask you one thing, don't ever treat my daughter like one of your businesses, and do not ever add another string to your bow in the case of your marriage.'

His heart missed a beat, did some feminine instinct prompt her to say this or was she just concerned as any mother might be. He prayed it was the latter.

'My marriage to your daughter Angela will be as devout as I am sure yours has been to Jeremy, I will not deceive her.'

He had told her the truth in so much as they were not yet married and he did in any case intend the affair with Rachel to end when that day came. The spell was broken by her husband, who breezed in, enquiring before he had even closed the door.

'Has he told you of the latest saga?'

My God, James, you are unbelievable and I can't believe the effect you have had on young Jayes, he was previously so retiring.'

'And now the chrysalis has developed into a butterfly or, perhaps with his auburn hair, I should say a Red Admiral.'

'Well I just hope he keeps up the good work. I should hate to go into the office one day and see him pinned up as a specimen on the wall.'

Angela looked at him ruefully; she did not wish to see her daughter end up as one of his trophies. However, she joined in the laughter as they imagined the other partners in a similar plight and trying to conjure Latin names for them.

Jeremy reached into the cupboard and brought out the Macallan.

'And another thing Mr Carrington, since you arrived here I seem in danger of turning into an alcoholic.' He handed his guest a dram of that wonderful peaty and most civilised liquor.'

'Slange, I have to go over to see the Charlton's about seven thirty, why don't you come with me and I will treat you all to a curry afterwards at the 'Star of Bombay' and please don't say no because, to be honest, I may need your help to convince Dickie about the suggestion I have made to Rachel.'

In the event it all went amazingly well, Rachel having time to think about it had warmed to the idea and her husband was secretly pleased to think that she might have some personal finance to help fund her dress allowance. The only slight problem with so many diverse opinions had been in deciding which of the fashionable young girls in the area they might approach to act as Rachel's assistant. However, as she was the one who would have to work with the girl, James insisted that the decision be Rachel's.

All in all it had been quite an inspirational day, they were not sitting on their laurels, they were driving forward; once again 'they were travelling and not arriving', it was how he liked it.

'Come on,' James announced, 'I insist you join us at the 'Star of Bombay' and, now that Rachel is a working girl, she can treat us.'

'On my expense account, of course.' Her quick rejoinder.

James winced at the thought of Rachel's idea of expenses, it was something he hadn't thought about, but it was something that he would have to solve diplomatically.

CHAPTER TWENTY ONE

Once the pot starts to boil everything in it is caught up in the swirling vortex, the frenzied activity is contagious and the next three weeks were hectic beyond anything they could have imagined. But they survived and, as the strength of the individual links grew, so even more so did the chain.

Once again their choice of new personnel had proved impeccable, Rachel and her recruit Fiona Jardine proved effortlessly equal to the task. Within twenty four hours she transformed an attractive, although perhaps slightly clinical office, into a welcoming and comfortable sitting room that just happened to have architectural drawings on the walls rather than oil paintings.

The clients felt relaxed with the options open to them, both in terms of location and choice of apartment. The chauffeur driven visits to view the sites particularly impressed them. This and everything else was conducted in the genteel manner to which they had been born and it appeared quite obvious that the two elegant young ladies who arranged everything were ' just trying to be helpful.' How little did they know; Rachel was determined to make a success of this, she had never worked before and for the first time felt fulfilled and independent and grateful to James. On the latter point she would at least be able to demonstrate her gratitude.

With so much to occupy his mind he had not had much time to consider his amorous liaisons with Kate never mind Rachel. However, one thought was always near the surface, the forthcoming sales at Newmarket and the start of his bloodstock empire, for that is how he naively perceived it, unsullied as yet by its vagaries and disappointments.

Prior to the sale he and Kate joined Henry White and the Carter Browns to see the latter's two year old filly, a half- sister to 'Cabriolet' attempt to break her maiden at the first time of asking. The bay filly with no white about her save for a small white star was named 'Droshky', their faith being rewarded as she doggedly refused to be beaten to win by a neck. Immediately of course the conversation turned to next year's Classics and the One Thousand Guineas; this traditionally was the first of the five and, like the Oaks is restricted to 3 year old fillies. The race is run on the broad expanse of Newmarket Heath over the famous Rowley Mile which is named after the man who established the pre-eminence of the town, King Charles II, popularly referred to by his subjects as Old Rowley. This straight stretch of turf is the centrepiece of the July course at Newmarket where not only its undulations but also the vast amount of space can easily make a horse feel lonely, particularly if it is out in front.

Henry White, with the memory of 'Blenheim Palace' and his series of misfortunes still firmly in the forefront of his mind, quietly dampened the conversation although as he acknowledged, it did the stable no harm to be constantly on the front page of the Sporting Life.

James followed the victors as they headed for the winners' enclosure, once again swept up in the excitement of seeing these majestic creatures bearing their multi-hued riders in the drive for the line. The winner would not be denied, resisting all efforts to be headed. The horse's courage made a big impression on the would-be new recruit, the filly was appearing on a racecourse for the first time and yet her instinct had been to win. The others may laugh at Nick's obsession with the Donatello line but they were tough and they were, like their antecedents winners.

He followed the others to the winners' circle to applaud the jockey's efforts, recalling as he did so Nick's comments about all the experts congratulating themselves on why they had backed the horse, on the brilliance of the jockey's timing, on everything except the inspiration that had selected the owner's parents to make this moment possible. He moved over to stand next to Nick and touched his arm.

'I begin to understand what you told me, well done you and well done Donatello.'
As the jockey slipped from her back James joined in the applause, his mostly directed towards the bay filly, her flanks still heaving from her exertions, he wondered what it must feel like to stand beside your champion in any winners' enclosure let alone the most hallowed spot at Headquarters.

After racing, they returned to Belvoir Lodge Stables to clean up and change for dinner. First, however, to placate the newcomer, they repaired to the study for a scotch and a look at the sales catalogue. Henry had markers in several of the pages; choices he felt would suit both James's pocket and his desire to have an early winner. The latter was happy, indeed determined to be guided by the trainer's experience, his only stipulation was that the animal should be a filly. This was contrary to convention, the overwhelming demand was for colts but he was hoping to kill two birds with one stone and have both a racehorse and a future matron for his paddocks. Time, however, was slipping by and the ladies were getting hungry. They packed James off to his room clasping the precious source of all information and met in the drawing room half an hour later. Everyone was in the best possible humour, Nick and Pippa with their exciting new winner, their host still excited by the determination shown by the filly and James and Kate with the whole world at their feet.

Once again they opted for the La Scala, but not before their host had surprised them by the arrival of a most attractive blonde girl. Annabelle Tennant-Brewer was steeped in horseracing, her father Marcus trained just down the Bury Road and, if the press were to be believed, trained the likely favourite for next year's Two Thousand Guineas. Pippa greeted the attractive girl and introduced her around, nodding in Kate's direction.

'Poor Kate she hears nothing but horses and more horses.'

'Well I am here for an evening away from the buggers although, having said that, I will have to leave at around ten to 'do' evening stables.'

'James, have you any idea what you are taking on? '
Kate was genuinely concerned at the commitment required.

'We are going to breed, darling. I presume that unless the mare is due to foal, the day to day management is nothing like the commitment demanded of a trainer.'

'True, but maybe a Scandinavian groom stroke au pair is what you should consider James,

I understand they are brilliant in a close Finnish!' Henry failed to dodge the well aimed cashew nut hurled by Kate.

'Come on everyone into the fornicatorium.' He laughingly led them out to the Alvis.

'What have you been telling him?' an anxious Kate demanded

'Nothing darling, it is all supposition but, looking at you he would think me pretty feeble if we hadn't had a little bit of a cuddle.'

He kissed her affectionately and they squeezed with the others into the elegant dark green motor car and headed off to the Italian Restaurant in the town...

The following morning, after a splendid if somewhat liquid evening, found a few sore heads gathered around the breakfast table however, thanks again to the power of Alka- Seltzer combined with copious black coffee, they were mostly restored by the time the trainer came in after first lot; once again the newcomer seeing at first hand the total commitment demanded by what was on the surface an apparently glamorous living.

They all departed at ten o'clock having thinned down Henry's yearling selection to a dozen that they intended to look at.

'See you under the clock at the railway station, - Nick will explain.'

He watched them drive away, grinning at the bemused look upon both faces.

The following week Nick collected James and set out for the Park Paddocks at Newmarket, the comparatively new home of Tattersalls. Until 1957 they had conducted this sale at the old Glasgow Paddocks in Doncaster. Here the facilities were woeful and the bidders, in an attempt to keep their feet dry, were provided with a few bales of straw spread as a bed as in a fold-yard. The sales ring was equally appalling and the assembled hierarchy of the bloodstock world, many of them members of the aristocracy, would stand wrapped against the cold in an assortment of ancient overcoats and shooting garb, resembling as recounted by the Marchese Mario Incisa. 'As rather more a tramps convention than the gathering of the elite of the racing world.'

Thanks to the driving foresight of Kenneth Watt, the other directors of Tattersalls were finally persuaded to invest in the sort of environment befitting the most prestigious horse sale in Europe. But it would take a long time and now in 1960 the most obvious new facility was the Orangery Dining Room, a copy of a similar Georgian building.

Ken Watt's priority, which had been finished in 1954, antagonised a few but in the main the new facilities were much approved. As they moved towards the ring James spotted the lofty figure of Henry poking above the crowd, he also saw the 'clock on the railway station.' This was the popular and appropriate euphemism for the sales office that stood at the side of the Dining Room and did indeed resemble a suburban railway station.

'Right Gentlemen, to work!' The Captain's authority and serious mien impressed James.

They followed him to Box 103 and watched quietly as he asked for the filly to be brought out. He stood silently looking at her, waiting for her to 'speak' to him, he fondled her long ears and ran his hand down her forequarters and along the length of each leg feeling for any signs of heat or curbs that would signify a problem . He did the same to the hind legs, seemingly satisfied he asked for the animal to be walked up and then trotted. A final 'look' into the horse's soul and they moved on this time to a colt by Crepello. The same routine this time and every time.

'What is he looking for?' James, eager to learn, asked of Nick.

'Firstly he likes to see a kindly eye and a broad intelligent head and when he stands there gazing at them he wants them to 'talk to him,' to somehow communicate a sense of reliability and gameness.'

They spent a busy morning following Henry around the sales boxes. He had a mixture of colts and fillies brought out, trying to match each to an owner's whims and preferences.

They moved back to the ring and watched as a succession of lesser breds, were knocked down to bids in the 1,500 to 2,000 guineas price range. The first lot to attract any real attention was a well grown forward filly by Court Martial out of a winning mare, which finally realised 6,600 guineas.

As is so often the case, once the tempo has been raised, the enthusiasm spread to the other punters and several lots went for over 5,000 guineas.

Finally the one they were waiting for, a bay filly by Pinza that his trainer had, because of its breeding, confidently picked out for his new client.

She was a good sort, well forward in her looks; unfortunately for James the fact that she was a half-sister to both Nasrullah and Drumbeat was not lost on the others who crowded the ringside.

When one is selling, the auctioneers seem to extol the virtues of the offering far too inadequately. Now when they were was bidding, the man on the rostrum, Kenneth Watt, seemed perversely, to have endless qualities with which to regale his audience.

All the big guns were out and James's ceiling of 6,000 was quickly eclipsed, the Duke of Norfolk and Humphrey Cotterill seemingly having it between them. They had however reckoned without William Hill the Bookmaker who, acting on behalf of entrepreneur Charles Clore, had the last say at 15,000 guineas.

Several more lots went through the ring, three of which were on their list; however, despite his client's extreme agitation, Henry refused to bid for any of them. After inspecting them he explained, alarm bells had rung.

Lot 184. A smallish rather backward filly by the stallion Klairon. This was a new bloodline to James but Nick had nodded in agreement when Henry proposed her, confiding to his friend that this was from a very successful French bloodline boasting a host of Classic winners on both sides of the Channel.

The fact that she was rather 'unfurnished' and was in the midst of several cheaper lots meant that some of the big hitters were not in attendance. Nevertheless, her breeding elicited some serious bidding with Ken Watt, at the top of his form after the Pinza filly.

'Are you done Gentlemen?'

The auctioneers gaze traversed the arena, seeking to extract one more bid.

'I intend to sell, don't lose her for a hundred.'

He fixed his stare upon the under bidder, raised the gavel, pausing to allow one last opportunity and then with a quick flourish banged it down.

'Sold to Captain White.'

'Lot 185, a bay colt by...' business carried on as the trainer signed for his purchase. Then, followed excitedly by his new owner they made their way to the sales box where the filly would remain until collected and driven the short distance to Belvoir Lodge.

At the end of the sale 783 yearlings were sold for an aggregate 1,339,037 guineas, James's contribution of 5,800 being about three times the average.

In all the trainer bought twenty six lots, seven of them as yet speculatively bought to pass on to his owners. This was not unusual, many owners will, when visiting the yard, often have a change of heart regarding the coming season particularly as they see the youngsters shed their puberty and acquire that look that marks them out as the aristocrats of the equine world.

One of these seven lots was intended for James, but the new owner was as yet unaware of this, ecstatic as he was with his purchase. Smallish, but with the hardy look about her that was so reminiscent of her Great Grandsire Djebel, who had won, like the little filly's sire Klairon, the French Two Thousand Guineas and continued to race at the highest level for four seasons.

'There was so much to anticipate, so much to do,' he confided to Kate.

'The wedding,' she dreamily suggested.

'I was thinking about what we call her,' his most pressing thought.

'What if we compromise and call her Wedding Belle.'

He thought for a moment, acknowledging the clever and instantaneous play on words.

'Why not, you have been so supportive and it is so appropriate, OK that's it.'

'As for the racing colours,' she began.

'They will be in silver and red to match the Fordmill livery', this time there was to be no discussion.

The following nine months prior to the wedding seemed to race past, most days blurring into each other. They were, however, punctuated by a series of highlights, the first of which was a couple of weeks after the sale.

The October publication of 'Country Life' featured a portrait of Kate.

The photograph captured the beguiling smile that had so enchanted him on their first meeting. And, although in black and white, you could sense the glorious Titian hue to the hair that cascaded across the hand supporting her chin. Through it sparkled 'My beacon of love,' as she still fondly referred to her engagement ring. Beneath the portrait it read:-

> Miss Kate Palmer, only daughter of Mr & Mrs Jeremy Palmer, of The Cedars, Cranborne, Dorset, is to be married in June next year to Mr. James Carrington, only son of the late Mr Robert Carrington and Mrs Elizabeth Carrington of Colston Basset, Nottinghamshire.

CHAPTER TWENTY TWO

In February, the Palmers who were keen skiers persuaded James to join them on their annual pilgrimage to Wengen. Despite the workload, Edward and the others were keen to see him take a break, 'although not your neck!' Connie had added.

It was marvellous, the first time you ski is like no other, the learning curve each day is tremendous. On the fourth day he was gliding around turns that on day one had seemed, even to someone so athletic, to be impossible to negotiate.

He was hooked, and chatting to Jeremy on the balcony of the hotel he declared that he would make this pilgrimage to the snow each and every year, a promise he would not find difficult to keep.

The lawyer leaned back in his chair, sucking contemplatively on his favourite pipe.

He had, by dint of his profession, a fine command of words and his well- modulated tones made him a natural storyteller. James settled back in his seat anticipating with pleasure the bit of social history that would follow.

'My father, a keen mountaineer since his University days, first came here in the late 1880s and was immediately captivated by the place. You can imagine how majestic these mountains must have looked before the hordes of tourists arrived.

Strange though that the man who initially arranged things for the chosen few should be the one responsible for the crowds we have today.

Henry Lunn, a Methodist minister, who hailed initially from Horncastle in Lincolnshire brought a small party to Chamonix in the winter of 1888-89. This was an astute move by a shrewd businessman seeking to find employment for his travel guides during the winter. The major obstacle was that only the wealthy had the inclination or could afford winter holidays. Being British, they regarded with distaste the idea of being organised or sharing a holiday with strangers, even worse to have one's luggage festooned with a Lunn's baggage label.

To avert the stigma and to attract people like my father he formed the 'Public Schools Alpine Sports Club', membership of which was restricted exclusively to those who had attended a public school. As a former grocer's assistant, albeit it a Grammar School boy, he had effectively blackballed himself. However, a mind as canny as his resolved the potential problem by adding the caveat that allowed membership to University graduates; which included himself.

James smiled appreciatively as Jeremy continued.

'To underline the exclusivity he would book complete hotels, ensuring that people could go abroad confident that they would not have to mix socially with foreigners or people of a lower social class.

The original Cup awarded in 1903 was for combined competition in three events, skiing, skating and tobogganing. This continued until 1911 when the Challenge Cup was abandoned in favour of three separate events. This was also the year, when at the age of seven, I made my debut on the slopes, although I do not claim that the two events are linked!' The storyteller admitted disarmingly.

'The skiing trophy was named the 'Roberts of Kandahar ' cup. Why it bears such a name is difficult to comprehend as Lord Roberts never visited the Alps during the winter and, even more perversely, Kandahar is in North Africa which is just about as hot a spot as you will find.

The probability is that Lord Lytton who gave his name to the skating trophy prevailed upon Field Marshall Earl Roberts of Kandahar to give his name to this prestigious and unique trophy.'

He rose from his chair, beckoning James to follow him.

In the hotel lounge he stopped in front of a large sepia photograph depicting a train which comprised an engine attached to a single carriage. A small crowd was gathered on the platform and the third head poking through the open carriage window was identified as Humphrey Palmer, father of Jeremy.

We come back here every year and each year I am drawn to this old photograph. I see my father as he was, in the flower of youth and early manhood, I often long for that age of idealism, realising it is all gone but, thankful nonetheless for the fond memories it always evokes.'

He sighed. 'Little did my father know that this would all disappear as the flower of so many nations would be cut down by the events of 1914-1918.'

James could easily empathise with this and his mind went to a similar sepia photograph in his office, it was one that he often looked at. It was a picture of the Leicester Rugby Club 1st XV, it captured his father in his prime, at his side the stocky figure of Dickie Dickson, both expressions full of hope and expectancy. He was born a year earlier than Jeremy, if only he could have been here now...

'Presumably,' said James to lighten the mood, the train was the only means of going up the mountain.'

'Indeed it was, apart of course from climbing through the new snow. Skiing in those days was damned hard work, old Lunn had probably got it right, you probably needed to have suffered the Spartan upbringing of a public school to even have contemplated it.'

James pondered the thought, 'when did the ski lifts arrive?'

'Not until the 1930s, the skiers remaining content to climb for an hour or more just to taste the exhilaration of a few minutes flashing downwards through the new snow.

Trains however became increasingly more popular in places such as Wengen and I remember very well when the first T-bars were installed in 1935, originally to serve the nursery slopes.'

The older man turned, 'And, if I am going to reach the aforementioned T-bar rather than the Tea-bar tomorrow, it is time I turned in.'

They both went up together, the warmth of the handshake conveying the respect and affection he felt for this man shortly to become his father-in-law.

After two weeks, James returned home, the others staying on for the customary six weeks.

The next high spot, far removed from the cold slopes of the Alps, was the torrid meeting with Rachel to explain that, wonderful though their relationship had been, he was not prepared to compromise his marriage by being unfaithful to Kate.

At first she was silent, seemingly prepared for the news; maybe he thought she had been expecting it.

The hurt expression, the eyes filled with tears, lowered his guard, made him feel sorry for her, she would be ultra-discreet she promised, no one need ever know...

As she continued, his resolute stand became running sand beneath his feet; his determination was melting in the heady charms of Chanel that pervaded his nostrils as she stood beside him. But, her female wiles had gone too far, he hated being manipulated, her tactics backfired and he rounded on her.

The blue eyes blazed with fury as they had done that day at Martins Bank when the incompetence of Osborne, the manager, had sought to deny him. She should have known better, she had seen what he had achieved against all odds.

'Rachel it is no use, I love Kate far too much to begin our marriage on such a footing. Let us stop now, whilst the memories are good. We have enjoyed something unique and memorable, I will never forget it, but a passion born of deceit is inevitably hotter than a day to day relationship with all its common failings. Its soul is too near the surface, we both deserve something deeper than that.'

'Damn you.' She stood up, her brown eyes flashing with rage, at the same time her left hand swept across the mahogany desk sending the photograph of the opening ceremony and the silver ink stand crashing to the floor. The red ink soaking into the cream carpet symbolising the life blood flowing out of this relationship.

She ranted on, accusing him of using her to achieve his ends, how it made her feel little better than a high class tart. She despised him; she would see that Sir Julian and the others would break him, the vitriol poured out endlessly.

'Shut up.' He said it quietly, the voice all the more menacing for it.

'What you have said has destroyed you, now I see you as your husband must see you, a spiteful bitch. If you want to play rough we will both confront Kate with the facts; I warn you though that you will lose.' He would not, he decided, out of respect for Peter Charlton, mention the Jaguar and the bounced cheque, but the question of her position as manager of the sales team was on the line. Furthermore, he spelt it out for her, when it emerged that she was available for 'a bit on the side', it could only provoke plenty of malicious gossip at the Bridge Parties and in the APP box at Royal Ascot. It would almost certainly, sever the last tenuous threads of her marriage.

He stood up, the blue eyes cold and hard.

'You have a choice, you shut up and keep your job or I will destroy you socially and financially.'

It was a side of him rarely seen, but those who really knew him were aware of his obsession to win, his dread of failure; Edward Lawson had once confided to Tim Cooper that he was sure that James had retired from rugby when still in the early days of his prime, rather than ever be regarded as other than the best.

Rachel gathered her coat, striving to regain her dignity.

'You will be back.' The defiant riposte that he denied, but which left him mentally in a turmoil of wondering.

The last highlight prior to the wedding was at Newmarket in the middle of May.
Henry White had two runners in the twelve horse race; James had eyes only for one, the small dark bay filly whose jockey wore the silver with red seams that were his racing colours.

Prior to Derby day, two year olds are restricted to the minimum distance of five furlongs, so a good start is important. Wedding Belle's inexperience probably costing her the race as she dwelt somewhat at the start. Her jockey, the stylish Jimmy Lindley, under orders to give her an easy introduction to the game, carefully wound her up and in a rousing finish the gallant filly was beaten a rapidly diminishing half a length.

It was most encouraging; Wedding Belle would certainly improve with this race under her belt. However, thrilled and excited though he was, he was not prepared for what happened next.

Kate detached herself from him and went to the winners' enclosure beckoning him to follow. As she did so, right on cue, the loud speaker announced.

1st ' Woolmington'; trained by Captain White, owned by Mr. James Carrington.

His open mouth and look of total astonishment brought a cheer from the huddle of race goers who turned around to reveal themselves as the Stanhope Courts , the Coopers, the Palmers, Connie, and the tall figure of Edward Lawson unwinding himself from his crouched position over the rails.

'Happy wedding present, darling.'
'What can I say?'
'How about Bollinger.' Connie's remark rapidly getting the party back on course.

CHAPTER TWENTY THREE

At last the great day arrived, June 8th 1961. How they had waited for this moment and with it the promise of so much for the future. The wedding with the opportunity to see many old friends again, the honeymoon in France and, most of all, returning together as man and wife to Woolmington.

The decorators had finally moved out of the Hall, the whole placed transformed and scarcely recognisable as the sadly neglected house that they had first seen all those long months ago.

To the larger pieces of furniture included in the sale they had added several antiques both inherited and recently acquired on weekend forays to Nottingham, Oakham and elsewhere. Jeremy and Angela Palmer had presented them with a late Georgian longcase clock standing just over eight feet high. Its chapter ring was signed 'John Jefferson ' signalling that it had been made at Driffield in the East Riding of Yorkshire.

It has become something of a superstition that these clocks must stand in the hall and yet, their soothing tones can be a good companion when alone in a room as many people living by themselves will testify; the timeless tick evoking fond memories of loved ones now departed.

However, as they stepped through the front door and set it down it instantly looked right, a great welcoming figure whose measured and rhythmic tones provided a warm invitation to guests as they entered the long oak panelled hall.

His mother had insisted that he take his father's desk for his study. He had accepted with pride tempered by the sadness that his mother would lose this very personal and tangible reminder of his father; she had insisted however 'that the space would be welcome.'

It was a simple task to break it down into its component parts; the side drawers, leather clad top and top drawer all fitting neatly into the Land Rover.

Back at Woolmington he sat behind the re-assembled desk conscious of his past, his resolve firmer than ever to return it one day to its rightful place in the study of Milford Hall.

Above the mantelpiece in the Drawing Room there now hung the oil painting of 'Milford' that Jeremy White had so generously, despite all protestations, insisted on giving them. In his study, the painting above the fireplace was the picture of his father leading the Belvoir Hunt in pursuit of the Master and the hounds.

The evening prior to the great day Kate spent with her parents and close family, he did likewise staying with his entourage at the Royal Bath Hotel.

After a pleasant and sentimental meal he had excused himself, preferring to spend this last evening alone. The others had urged him to stay with them at the hotel rather than in the solitude of the flat adjacent to the office, only his mother understanding his need to be alone. It was a trait that during his life she had seen many times, always when he came to a turning point, always when some new decision had to be taken. She recognised it within herself; perhaps it was a Staincliffe thing, the need to be absolutely sure in one's own mind that the decision was right. She had no fear that he would have doubts about his marriage, only the need to remember the highs and lows thus far. She had done it herself and suspected that the two memories would, in many ways, mirror each other. Elizabeth's thoughts were interrupted by a gentle hand on her arm, it was Louise.

'Pray that he will be as lucky in love as you were.'
The misty eyes nodded back, too full to speak.

The others, aware of the intimate moment, made more noise than was necessary to bid James farewell.

He awoke at six thirty the following morning, an anxious look through the window revealed a misty scene through which he could see only a hazy view of the street below.

A good omen he thought, such a day had started like this prior to the 'opening' ceremony, he hoped fervently for the same glorious weather.
He bathed and dressed casually before striding briskly down the staircase and into the Dining Room. The others had beaten him to it, Louise his sister signalled a waitress.

'A hearty breakfast for the condemned man.'
The others took it up, conviviality the order of the day. At eight thirty the cars arrived to transport them all to the 'Fleur de Lys', the gabled Inn standing in the centre of Cranborne. Fortunately, it was out of sight of 'The Cedars', where Kate was nervously preparing herself.

The Landlord, by now an old friend, warmly ushered them in to the famous hostelry whose many distinguished guests had included the first world war poet, Rupert Brooke. Amongst his many fond memories of England, though less well known than his poem 'The Soldier', and its patriotic references to 'some corner of a foreign field, that is forever England', he had written:

> 'We somewhere missed the faces bright
> The lips and eyes we longed to see
> And love and laughter and delight
> These things are at the Fleur de Lys'

The poignancy of the above was not lost on James and his mother when Edward proposed a toast to 'To absent friends and, not for the last time today, the happy couple.'

A brief respite was called to allow everyone to change into their finery although, in the case of the men, it had been simply a case of sponging and pressing the family morning suit. James had been tempted to buy a new one but, it was still the custom to bring out the old favourite, the survivor of many ' hatchings and scratchings.'

They returned to the bar of the fine old Inn, bonhomie very much the order of the day, all but the faint hearts calling for Bollinger, the others settling for Buck's Fizz.

The most agonising decision for James had been the choice of Best Man. Of the three 'candidates' he had known Tim least long so did not feel too uncomfortable about 'relegating' him to the part of usher. He finally asked Jack Priory to assist Tim, leaving Edward to play the main supporting role.

The wedding was scheduled for eleven o'clock. At ten fifteen the ushers left to begin their ministrations and from the sanctuary of the Inn, the Groom and his Best Man saw the cars arriving, the clock ticking away the minutes to the appointed hour.

Cranborne is an attractive amalgam of colour washed cottages set in narrow streets that lead to the market place and splendid town houses, many of them dating from Georgian times. A few, like The Cedars, are set in large private gardens surrounded by trees. The village itself is set on the edge of Cranborne Chase, one of the great Royal hunting forests favoured by amongst others, King John and James I.

James and Edward with their awareness of architecture enjoyed this sense of history as they made their way to the finest building in Cranborne, the Church of St Mary, St Peter and St Bartholomew. Originally it had been part of a 10th century Benedictine Abbey; the oldest part still remaining is the Norman doorway in the North Porch which had not been demolished when the church was rebuilt in the 13th century.

Prior to entering the church they paused for the obligatory Groom and Best Man photograph. Edward took James's hand in his great paw.
'Be happy old son, you both deserve it.'
'Thank you, for everything. You have looked after me, guarded my back since I was fourteen years old. I owe you so much. I really can't imagine doing anything without you.'
'Well you will have to run your marriage without me.'
The big man's reply concentrating their thoughts on the day's business, but in no way diluting the bond of affection between them.

'Off to the block then.' James led the way through the great oak doorway and into the pleasant coolness of the church, above them the fine barrel roof and ahead the superbly carved oak pulpit.

They reached their pew at the front, nodding and smiling at those guests already seated. James unhooked the kneeler before sinking to his knees to thank God for this day. The silent prayer with its hopes and dreams and thanks to the Almighty came easily and, feeling spiritually uplifted, he resumed his seat.

On such occasions the small talk is all fairly light hearted, interspersed as it is with snippets from the low babble of conversation elsewhere. Why is it, he found himself wondering, that so many people cough when they enter such a sanctuary. To divert himself he looked around at the fine stained glass windows, in particular at the one in the south wall.

It is in commemoration of John Tregonwell who died in 1885. The son of Lewis Tregonwell the man who, on the whim of his wife the wealthy Lady Henrietta, had built a house on the site of what is now the Royal Exeter Hotel. Later he built a group of cottages for summer lettings to visitors. From these small beginnings he built more permanent residences exploiting the health-giving reputation of sea bathing. James had only recently, thanks to several interesting meetings with the vicar the Rev Alan Haycock, come to know and appreciate Tregonwell.

'A good omen, you and he obviously share the gift of vision, although you approach it from different standpoints.'

James was musing the vicar's thoughts when the organist struck up to announce the arrival of the Bride. A quick glance at his watch, one minute late.

He heard the procession as it approached through a corridor of craning necks as the ladies in the congregation sought a glimpse of the Bride.

The altar boys and choir moved from the head of the procession to take their allotted places in the choir stalls. With Edward he followed Canon Haycock to the steps leading to the altar and, as the Vicar turned to face them, he finally turned his head to meet his bride.

What he saw brought a lump to his throat

The beautiful Titian hair was swept up at the back in a French twist interwoven with freesias and other spring flowers that complimented the bouquet now guarded by a bridesmaid. Her face, though still hazily concealed by the veil of Nottingham lace, was stunning.

'You look so beautiful', she read his lips, the loving expression in her eyes conveying back unsaid, the love she felt for him.

'Good morning and welcome to Cranborne on this very happy occasion.'

The vicar's greeting and the loud positive response from the congregation, breaking their reverie.

'Let us begin our worship with the hymn Lord of all Hopefulness, Lord of all Joy.'

The mood of the day was infectious, the choir and congregation striving seemingly to out sing each other.

The happy couple were bathed in the colours of the great rose window as the sun did its best to complement the moment they said their vows. Their pledges made, the singing continued unabated as they celebrated the marriage with Dear Lord and Father of Mankind, Forgive our foolish ways,

At this line they turned to smile at each other.

At the conclusion of the hymn they approached the altar for the blessing before the vicar unleashed the congregation upon the choir with Now Thank we all our God...'

They retired to the vestry to sign the marriage register and finally emerged looking more relaxed, ready like their friends, for the more civil festivities to commence.

As ever the photographers seemed incapable of haste, relying as they always do on the good nature of the wedding group and guests to pose endlessly.

At last they were done and everyone strolled in great humour across to The Cedars where the waitresses plied them with bubbly.

'My Lords, Ladies and Gentlemen.' The Toastmaster called them to order and they descended the steps from the terrace and filed into the large marquee erected on the lawn below. The starter was requested by James in honour of the first meal he had enjoyed as a guest of the Palmers. Terrine of crab and Dublin prawns presented in a sauce of yoghurt and dill; to accompany it, Saint Aubin, a little known close neighbour of the mighty Chassagne–Montrachet,

'A most splendid and so often underrated white Burgundy, strong and yet subtle, an excellent choice, Jeremy.'

Sir Julian Abercrombie conveyed his knowledgeable appreciation to his host.

The meal continued with Aiguillette de canard aux peches, the wine a splendid Saint-Julien.

This time the compliment was from Miles Stanhope Court.

'You are setting new standards for wedding breakfasts, Mr Palmer.'

He raised his glass in salutation, adding that he presumed the duck was in honour of Nottingham and its oft mimicked phrase of 'my duck.'

The meal continued in the same high vein, the guests in continuing good humour.

The cake was cut to the usual cries of "save the top layer."

'How long will it keep?' enquired an apparently apprehensive groom.

Finally Jeremy Palmer rose to his feet. In his cultured lawyer's tones he welcomed the guests, paid tribute to the excellence of the caterers and their help in making this the memorable day that he and Angela had so wanted for their daughter. He recalled his first meeting with James, how Angela had described him as any mother's dream son-in-law.

'He always was a creep,' Tim Cooper's good humoured observation refuting the need for serious memories.

'As a matter of fact,' the host continued, 'He did once remark to me the old adage that,

"He who would the Daughter win; with the mother should first begin."'

'Need I say more,' interjected Tim.

'A wedding,' Jeremy confided, ' Is not unlike buying a car. It is one of those marvellous occasions when a woman leaves home with an older man and trades him in for a young one. In this case Kate, I know you will be more than happy trading in the family saloon for your new sports car.'

'The ancient Greeks said of a true friend,' he continued.

'I have taken bread and salt with him. We have now done that many times. James, I believe that you are more than a son-in law, Angela and I are proud to regard you as a friend.'

He sat down to polite clapping that was underpinned with genuine affection and appreciation.

James rose to his feet, aware of the serried rows of finery that grew attentively quiet at the sound of the Toastmaster's gavel.

He had rehearsed this speech just about every day for the last two months as he travelled to the office. He hoped, no, was confident that the empty silences he had left on the tape would fill with laughter when the great day came. Now it had, he was not so sure, but he need not have worried, on such occasions the corporate goodwill of those present will carry the day.

'Mr. Osborne,' he began, 'I don't even know his first name and yet he is the man responsible for all this expense. The food, the drink, the gifts, it is endless.'

He smiled at his father-in-law; 'I am sure Jeremy, that you would have a case in law to sue him! If he had only acquiesced to my small request, a few quid to launch a modest business venture... However, if Osborne is the joker in the Martins Bank pack then surely Charles Lattimer is the ace. I can never thank you enough Charles for all your support but even you, had you not kept me waiting for hours on that first day, could have saved Jeremy all this expense; as I would never have got to meet his daughter.'

He acknowledged the chuckles, warming to his task.

'Between you however you conspired for me a dream.'

He took a diary from his pocket.

'March 13 1953, met a stunning girl today. Her figure, her face, her hair, everything about her is perfect. I am going to marry her one day, although she does not know that yet.'

He was aware of Kate's blushes and the ooh's and ah's from the ladies present.'

Anthony Jayes summed up the male appreciation, 'Get on with it, you old smoothie.' James resumed, flicking through the pages.

'If I tell you that the only other comments in this diary refer to rugby, golf and squash matches you will realise the impact she had upon me.

A few months ago I asked my father-in-law what his fees as a lawyer were.

"One hundred pounds for three questions." That is rather extortionate isn't it?

"Yes", he replied, "you have one question left."

At which point, as my finances were running low, I asked him for his daughter's hand in marriage and here we are today.

Like all men, I was not familiar with the procedures on such occasions as this. I find that my special task today is to thank the Bridesmaids and that I do. You both look so beautiful and have attended Kate so well that she has had no time to think of changing her mind and escaping.'

'I would also like to use this occasion,' he cleared his throat, 'to thank you all for giving my wife and I such a marvellous occasion and a wonderful memory with which to start our married life.

In thanking you all for the superb and most original wedding presents, I am assuming that toast will never go out of fashion!

In particular I would like to thank Jeremy and Angela for the marvellous coffee percolator and I say that very carefully, unlike a friend of mine who thanked his astonished new in-laws for the perky copulator...'

Howls of laughter reverberated around the marquee as he continued.

'This really was a fairy tale wedding ..... Grimm!!

I would also like to thank my fellow directors who have worked so hard to cover for me at the office whilst I have been mooning about the place dreaming of Kate.

So many of you have done so many things for me and I do thank you all most sincerely.'

At this point he studiously avoided looking at the table where Rachel and Peter Charlton sat.

He continued with a few more anecdotes, thanked his Best Man and warned the assembly to pay no heed to the completely apocryphal rumours of events relating to rugby tours; howls of derision from his male contemporaries leaving the gathering unconvinced and his new wife anxious to know more.

'I will conclude my speech by quoting from Mark Twain. Making a speech he said, is very much like making love; any fool can start, the art is in finishing tidily.

Ladies and Gentlemen will you please raise your glasses; the toast is 'The Bridesmaids.'

They blushed demurely as the toast went around the room and shyly thanked him for the handsome green leather bound copies of 'Browning's Love Poems' that he had presented to them both.

The accompanying friendly clapping was once again interrupted as the gavel was brought down by the MC.

Edward rose, looking seriously at a newspaper cutting, which he held up for the guests to view.

'The love story that James has weaved around the unfortunate Mr. Osborne is delightful, but I can reveal the true story.

This is an advertisement from the Nottingham Evening Post, it reads.
Wanted man with sports car; please send photograph of car...'
He continued in this vein.

'Today has been a most marvellous day. James has seen his beautiful bride come down the aisle and stand beside him in front of the altar. We have all sung, rather well actually, hymns in their honour. He will always carry away with him those three evocative words, Aisle, Altar, Hymn. If I am to believe our other rugby pals who have also trodden this path, Kate will take away with her the same three emotive words but with slightly different spellings; I'll alter him.'

Cheers from the men, even more cheers from the ladies.
He continued the audience eager for more.

'Our hero's sporting achievements are legendary; you will have read about them.

But, not all of them have been reported, until today that is.'
'Never lock a wardrobe,' He counselled Kate.
'Your husband does not like being locked in, as he proved when he found himself thus compromised on the Barbarians Easter tour in Wales a few years ago. The noise it made when falling over brought an astonished manager up to the room where he was greeted by a crab like figure crawling around the floor, the shattered furniture on his back, the astonishment all the greater, when the crustacean complained about the quality of Welsh craftsmanship.

'I thought you players were celibate the night before a match,' the manager observed.
'That is in Wales,' our hero retorted, 'In England we celebrate.'
'Good thinking,' Responded the manager. 'You will not be so happy after the game!'
The Welsh contingent roared their approval, the English winced.
Now in full cry Edward continued.
'Whilst on the subject of rugby, may I say a special welcome to Gareth Morgan, the only Welshman, to my knowledge not to have had a schoolboy trial for Wales.'
The knowing English rugby fraternity, really enjoying this aside at their Welsh counterparts who endlessly, they would have us believe, have been considered as future internationals. Edward continued with his damning prosecution.

'The great thing about playing First class rugby is that incidents like this are reported as 'A disturbance.' On an extra A's tour it will be described as 'Wrecking the place.

However, the greatest of all Rugby tours is when the British Lions visit South Africa, and it is here that James achieved his greatest highlight. The Lions, you will remember, defeated the Springboks by a single point, that victory achieved in the last minute when the toast of the nation, James Carrington, dropped an enormous long goal to clinch a thrilling victory.

You will not be surprised to hear that after the banquet that evening the hero of the hour had, understandably, had a drop more than usual. He remembers little of the event, but every detail of the following morning when he was awakened on the terrace of the hotel to the sound of camera flashbulbs.'

He held aloft a yellowing photograph culled from the Transvaal Herald. It depicted a man in a long blonde wig wearing a pink bikini: Before adding.

'Mind you he has the legs for it.'

'Was that when he had laryngitis?' Jack Priory mischievously enquired.
This was an old joke, told by James, when he was sent to the local hospital for a precautionary check-up prior to an earlier match on that tour.

Edward had decided that perhaps, with ladies present, he should not relate this particular anecdote. However, with his audience in such good humour and crying out for more, he boldly pressed on.

'Two other members of the team also suffering minor ailments accompanied James to the hospital; I shall refer to them as Mac and Seamus. They were lying in three consecutive beds.

The resident reporter from the Times asked Mac what he was suffering from and what he most wanted.

'I am suffering from piles which I treat myself with a brush and ointment. What I most want is to get out of here and play again for The British Lions.'
Seamus when asked replied, 'I am suffering from VD which I treat myself with a brush and ointment. What I most want is to get out of here and play again for the British Lions.'

James's response when asked was, 'I am suffering from Laryngitis which I treat myself with a brush and ointment. My ambition is to get to the brush before the other two!"

Even the frostiest old sticks in the gathering were caught up in Edward's good humour and the whole gathering laughed as James attempted to protest that it was not true.

Undeterred, Edward solemnly reached below the table and produced a plastic bag, from the inner recesses of which he produced a toothbrush.

'My special, personal gift, to my best friend.'
He handed it over to the Groom who, shaking his head with laughter, enquiringly asked.

'Where is the ointment?'
'Your amusement,' Edward continued, 'Reminds me of a quotation from the diary of Samuel Pepys. 'Strange to say what delight married people have to see these poor fools decoyed into our position."

And then, turning to James, 'But I jest.' He looked around the room.

'Gentlemen I see you are already looking at your watches but, this is not a rugby club dinner and whilst side bets on the length of the speech may be allowed, may I remind you, as no less an authority than Lord Birkett observed, the shaking of timepieces is definitely not good form.

I will end this walk down memory lane by thanking you all for coming today and so correctly interpreting the Jewish salutation RSVP, Reply Sending Vedding Present.

I have counted them and they do correctly add up to the number of guests present.

'I would ask you to join me in a toast, not only to James and Kate, but also to their families; Ladies and Gentlemen, the Bride and Groom and their families.'

The gathering joined in the salutation and Edward sat down to a genuine round of appreciative applause and much good humour.

The speeches over, James led Kate from the room to change into their 'going away outfits'.

'We are timing you,' observed a good natured voice from the crowd.

They returned, Kate in an ivory silk suit, James in a more formal chalk stripe and his father's faded Leicester Tigers tie. His mother kissed him on the cheek, whispering 'He would have been so proud of you.'

He squeezed her hand gently.

'I know,' he said hoarsely; 'And he would have been so proud of you, as I am.'

The guests followed them as they walked from the terrace at the rear of the house to the semi-circular gravelled drive at the front. He stopped to briefly kiss her and, at the same time pressed into her hand a key ring.

She slowly looked down wondering what he was up to now.

She saw a red enamelled key ring upon which were emblazoned the initials K.L.C.

Before she had time to ask, they were on the drive at the front of the house.

There to answer the unasked question, standing proudly, was a red Morgan sports car, its hood down, the number plate KLC 1, proclaiming its new owner.

'I don't believe it.' She was lost for words.

'Well, we want to give the Frogs something good to look at, as well as you of course.'

His modest and contented reply, to her obvious pleasure.

In a state of great excitement Kate fired-up the Morgan and to a round of cheers they set off for Sussex, trailing the traditional string of pots and pans.

Here they would spend their first night as man and wife in the sumptuous surroundings of a decent hotel in Brighton, although as yet, she was not privy to all the information.

Tomorrow, he had confided, they planned to take the car to Dover and then the cross-channel ferry to Calais and onwards to Paris, that unrivalled city for lovers. After three days at the Hotel Ritz they would travel to Azay Le Rideau and other as yet undiscovered gems of the Loire Valley such as the chateau of Chenonceaux.

Meanwhile Kate, knowing only that the destination was Brighton, initially drove carefully, but then as she relaxed her confidence grew, certain that she would guess which hotel they were heading for – if you were with her husband it would be either the biggest or the best. In fact it was both, and when she saw it she knew instinctively that this building had his name written all over it so, without waiting for directions, she swung her new pride and joy into the reserved parking area outside the main entrance.

The Grand, which dominates the sea front, is a magnificent example of Victorian Renaissance architecture, which was originally conceived as a watering hole for the upper classes. The gentry of the day, many of whom enjoyed gambling and other excesses of the time, followed in the footsteps of the Prince Regent, later George 1V, whose staggering creation, the Royal Pavilion, was a Must See for the Victorians, many of whom had a voracious appetite for knowledge. This trend was accelerated in 1841 when rail travel to Brighton transformed a small seaside resort into a most fashionable place to be seen.

As she applied the handbrake, he laughingly shook his head.

'This looks quite impressive, perhaps we should see if they have a room for the night.'

'You sound like Joseph speaking to Mary; I can assure you however that I am not with child!'

The man in the frock coat and tall hat opened the door for Kate and with perfect timing one of his minions opened the boot to retrieve the suitcases.

Hand in hand they checked in before accompanying the porter to the lift, or as it was originally described, the 'Vertical Omnibus'. This hydraulic feat of engineering was only the third to be installed in the United Kingdom; the other two were both in the Capital.

They excitedly followed him to a suite, from the balcony of which they had a wonderful panoramic view of both the beach and Brighton's spectacular pier. Their romantic sightseeing was briefly interrupted by a knock on the door. She opened it see, surprise, surprise, a waiter with a champagne bucket containing a bottle of Dom Perignon.

They unpacked, undressed, sipped champagne and made love with the tenderness and desire unique to people deeply in love.

After which they bathed leisurely and dressed for dinner. First though they took a leisurely stroll in the in the still warm evening sun. Neither of them had previously visited the town so, like most visitors, they were impressed by the so called Palace Pier, which is well over a quarter of a mile in length. It houses a fascinating mix of restaurants, children's entertainments and other gaudy attractions – not least that Victorian favourite, What the butler saw!

Noisy it may be, quirky it may be; but it is the quintessential British seaside adornment, which is most certainly not how you would describe the totally unique edifice that is the Royal Pavilion. Formerly a royal residence, this exotic Indian styled structure with its many spires and domes was the inspiration of the architect John Nash. The interior is also heavily influenced by the East; it is the most extravagant example of chinoiserie in the British Isles.

During the First World War, the Pavilion was annexed for use as a military hospital. This at the suggestion of King George V, to encourage potential Indian recruits that their countrymen were well respected and if injured, would receive the best possible treatment. To this effect a series of photographs were produced showing these now grand rooms when they were converted into hospital wards. Few pictures were issued of the former Brighton Workhouse – now the Brighton General Hospital – which housed the majority of the wounded British troops.

Kate and James were, like the vast majority of visitors, hugely impressed by the Pavilion but, as it was now closed for the day, they decided to continue their introduction to Brighton by paying a brief visit to the charming assortment of small streets, known locally as The Lanes.

This area was once the heart of the old fishing town; now it is an extraordinary maze of twisting alleyways which house a fascinating mixture of boutiques, cafes, and galleries, the atmosphere is further enhanced by buskers whose renditions range from jazz to pop music.

Once again this exciting seaside resort had touched a nerve; another good reason to revisit this cosmopolitan town.

It was a wonderful finale and their hearts were light as they retraced their steps to The Grand. The exercise had been good, but after the splendid feast provided by Kate's parents, they both decided upon just a light main course of Poached Wild Salmon. This was accompanied by a very fine Chablis, recommended by the black aproned and knowledgeable Pierre.

It had been a marvellous day and now finally curled up in his arms, Kate could think only of the future, of a life together at Woolmington Manor. He too was anticipating the future but on so many fronts of which Woolmington, although important, was only one. Seeing his mother again today and wearing his father's tie, everything he ever did strengthened his resolve to return to Milford Hall. He had even driven past it last week, had wanted to get out of the car and walk through those great iron gates that still bore the 'rising sun' motif. But as soon as the thought crossed his mind, he had dismissed it. He would never enter those gates again until he could return as master.

'What are you thinking about?'

'Of the future; goodnight God bless my darling, I love you so much and tomorrow it's La Belle France.'

CHAPTER TWENTY FOUR
PART TWO

1968

James Carrington was a rich man, or at least he had the trappings of a rich man. The Bentley Coupe in which he quickly ate up the miles between Bournemouth and Nottingham was evidence of this, so was the imposing house at Woolmington where he now lived with Kate and their two sons, Charles and Edward.

If he could ever liquidate all his assets he would be a very rich man indeed; like many an entrepreneur before him he had cash and assets, but his probing mind was always looking to invest, so liquidity and not over exposing himself financially was always uppermost in his thinking. Sure he earned a big salary, he needed to, the boys now aged almost six and three would soon be off to Prep school and Kate whilst not exactly extravagant had, because of her solid old family background, an instinct to like the better things in life and, to be fair, he hated to deny her.

The original development at Bournemouth had been an unqualified success. They had in fact built a further block of four, again incorporating communal amenities and a sculpture park. However, the real advantage from the developments would come when the occupants died. The shared equity concept required Fordmill to reimburse the full purchase price to the estate of the deceased, the apartments could then be sold at current market prices. In their initial costings they had reckoned on a two year 'no sale' position and then probably a fifteen percent mortality rate each year thereafter. Sadly, from the cash-flow point of view, Rachel and her team had chosen too well or maybe, he ruminated, the tenants were so happy in the environment he had created.

Meanwhile he was en-route to developing a new idea. As in the past, he had not mentioned it as yet to the others, preferring as usual to present them with au fait accompli.

They, however, knew him well enough by now to know that something was in the wind.

The one serious lesson learned from the Bournemouth contract was the impact that time and travelling had on their resources and, in particular, on themselves and their families.

This was why he now found himself turning into a quiet lane in the leafy confines of South Nottinghamshire. He drove slowly and briefly saw his destination, a large brick house with a slate roof and distinctive stone windows, just as suddenly it passed out of sight and disappeared into the woodland that surrounded it.

He finally spotted the open wrought iron gates he was looking for and drove through them for perhaps two hundred yards before the woods surrendered the house to him.

He parked the Bentley, subconsciously thinking how appropriately it sat on the gravelled drive. The large oak front door was accessed by two stone steps and stood under a stone canopy that in design complemented the parapets above the large bay windows on either side of the entrance.

An old brass door- bell eventually elicited a shuffling response from within.

'Good afternoon sir, you must be Mr. Carrington.'
James affirmed this to the old lady who, wiping the flour from her hands on to the white apron, signalled him to follow.

'Madam is expecting you.'
She showed him into the Drawing Room where a lady with a kindly face and of similar age to the other stood up to greet him.

'Mr. Carrington do come in, may I offer you some tea.'
'Why yes, thank you.' He liked her immediately.

'What a lovely place you have, how old is the house?'
Actually he knew the details but, reasoned correctly, that more would be gleaned by listening.

'My Grandfather built the house in 1892, the family have lived here ever since, and it will be a dreadful wrench to leave.'

'I do understand how you feel Mrs Watkin-Downes.'
She looked at him, shaking her head, 'I don't think you do, Mr Carrington.'
He smiled kindly at her.

'I will tell you a secret, and it is one I trust to very few people, almost no one in fact.'
He stood up, with his back to the unlit open fire.

'My Great Grandfather built a house such as this, about fifteen years earlier in fact.
When I was fourteen years of age we were evicted from that house and I saw on my mother's face the anguish you expressed just now.

'I give you my word Mrs Watkin-Downes, I will do nothing to this house that will cause you pain, rather the opposite I hope, as I intend to restore it to its former glory.'

His face alight with a huge grin, he turned to her and laughed.

'What do you think to that?'
The response went unsaid as Alice returned with the tray.

The hostess poured the Earl Grey and turned, the milk jug poised.

'I hope you take milk, I am afraid we can't run to lemons anymore.'
'I prefer it,' he assured her.

'You were telling me about the house,' he prompted her memory.

'Oh yes, when I was a child I lived here with my sister and parents, they were thrilling days, particularly the school hols during the Hunting season. My father was Master of the Quorn for five or six seasons if I remember. They would meet here in March and Ma and Pa always made sure that it coincided with an exeat from school.'

She rose from her seat and stood in front of the large oil painting that graced the end wall of the drawing room. It depicted a group of horsemen and women surrounded by a milling pack of hounds, the scene was animated, and James could easily fancy the baying of the excited dogs, anxious like the Hunt to be away. Mrs Watkin-Downes indicated the scarlet clad figure with black topper at the front of the group.

'This is Pa and this is Ma.'

She drew his attention to a smiling attractive woman sitting side saddle in black hunting coat and skirt, white hunting tie and gloves, all set off by the veil that mysteriously shrouded her face and secured the hunting top hat.

'This was painted just after the First World War, not many women went out before then,' she added.

James studied the assorted group that represented the Quorn all those years ago; the coats in the main red, the children in brown hacking jackets, the few ladies all riding side saddle of course in black, mostly wearing toppers, a few in bowler hats.

'Is that really a yellow coat?'

He pointed to a mounted figure conversing with the Huntsman.

'Why yes, the Earl of Berkeley hunted with us that day and that is the famous 'tawny yellow' coat that the Master and members of the Berkeley hunt staff always wear.

The Gentleman mounted next to him is Lord Lonsdale who was Master when my parents first came here, the horse is one of his famous stud of chestnut thoroughbreds that he always hunted

'And this must be you.'

He pointed to a girl aged about nine or ten mounted on a grey pony.

'Not quite, that is my sister Amelia, this is me.'

She indicated the girl on the matching grey at the other's side.

Her face was alive as she reminisced to him, but just as suddenly it clouded over as she was brought back to reality. He carefully replaced his cup into the saucer and gave her a kindly look that affirmed his understanding and sympathy.

'If you agree to sell me the house, I would very much like you to help me get it back together, just as it was.'

'I do believe you mean that.' She looked at him intently. 'Do you plan to live in it?'

Now it was his turn to take centre stage.

'I want to restore it and bring it back to life. I want to fill it with people who will appreciate its history. I want to convert it into a series of self-contained apartments for retired folk and, I want you to be my first occupant!'

'My goodness, how, what do you mean Mr. Carrington? I am quite lost for words.'

He gave her a reassuring look. 'I came here today Mrs Watkin-Downes to persuade you to sell me this house. Talking to you, I have come to realise just how much it means to you. I had other plans for it, but you have shown me a much better and more appropriate way of developing the property, much more in keeping with its past. I have a secret to tell you; I want my own mother to live here, I know you will get on famously!'

'You are serious; Alice and I really can stay here?'

'Absolutely, you have my hand on it.'

'Well in that case.' She stood up and pressed the bell above the mantelpiece.

The dutiful Alice presented herself, unable to believe her ears as her employer instructed her to bring in the sherry with three glasses!

'I have something amazing to tell you.' She promised the old retainer.

It was not just the sherry that left him with warm feeling; it was the excitement and happiness he had created. He poured them another glass, excusing himself as like most men sherry seems to go straight to the head.

The two old dears showing no such hesitation, or to a third, as he took his farewell with a promise to be in touch shortly.

CHAPTER TWENTY FIVE

He drove away in high spirits; it was ages since he had had a really inspired idea. The very pressures that had been so difficult to cope with at Bournemouth, the distance and supply of building materials etc. would not be an issue here.

I still have to sell it to the others he thought, not to mention the financing, he winced inwardly, he loathed having to justify himself to bankers.

Still conscious of the effects of the single sherry, he drove carefully through the Quorn 'Monday Country.' So called, he now appreciated thanks to Mrs Watkin-Downes, because like all the great packs of Foxhounds, the land over which they hunt is divided into days of the week.

He soon reached the Melton road and, head now cleared, he was anxious to be home to relate to Kate the exciting new concept. On the quiet roads he picked up lost time as the Bentley cruised through Melton and Barleythorpe and on towards Cottesmore, home to yet another famous pack of foxhounds, finally arriving at Woolmington a little before six o'clock.

As he approached the Hall he saw Kate leading the chestnut pony named Oliver, after the previous incumbent Sir Oliver Cranston. Edward the youngest was in the saddle, kicking away urging the pony to go faster, he really did not exhibit any of the fear that most children, including his elder brother, usually displayed when introduced to riding.

After the exciting chat earlier vis-à-vis the Quorn Hunt, it did not take James long to imagine his son in brown hacking jacket soaring over five barred gates, at his side the scarlet clad figure of his father. He was still smiling as he stepped out of the car.

'What are you looking so happy about?'

'Just pleased to be home darling.'

He would save the explanation, not even Kate was ready for that just yet.

Instead he lifted Charles up behind Edward and led them both around to the back of the house where Sue, the stud groom, was leading in a mare and foal for their evening feed.

James had never forgotten Nick Carter Brown's advice about maintaining regular contact with the foals; it really did make life so much easier as they grew bigger and stronger. That early bonding was so much preferable to the brutal enforcement still the norm with lots of old nagsmen.

As always, he made his way to box number three where a brass plate announced the resident as 'Woolmington.' The chestnut filly that Kate had bought for him as a wedding present had proved an inspired choice. She had won five times and been placed on a further three occasions, only once failing to be in the shake-up. Most of all, in addition to her ability she had displayed guts and a tigerish will to win, vital qualities in a brood mare; assets that any athlete, human or equine must possess if they are to be a champion.

'Wedding Belle', the choice of the experts, the subject of endless hours poring over pedigrees, had been moderately successful. She had won her next two races but Henry had found it impossible to keep her sound; one last effort when she trailed in last at nearby Nottingham convincing them that her career lay in the paddocks.

This was the first salutary lesson for her owner, the consolation being that she had enough pedigree to justify breeding with her. She still occupied the number one box at Woolmington Stud, except it had number thirteen on the door - her owner's lucky number.

He thought back to those heady first days, swotting up on pedigrees, constantly demanding advice from his trainer and Nick Carter Brown.

Excited though he had been, his natural business acumen insisted that he check out the possibilities and probabilities of making his passion financially viable.

He had already bought Woolmington, which fortuitously, because of the previous owner's aversion to horses, had been used only for sheep and cattle and was not 'horse-sick.'

It was situated on limestone and the streams that gurgled through its pastures to fill the lake in front of the house would provide the calcium so necessary to strengthen and grow young bones. Once again his luck had held.

Despite the fortune of good advice received from his friends James, he realised that if his venture was to succeed he needed constant ongoing good advice and management.

In the case of horses in training he considered himself fortunate to have met Henry, a fact confirmed by many knowing judges. However, it was on the breeding front, the aspect of racing that fascinated him most, where his knowledge left him most exposed.

If the mares are not correctly fed, if they are not looked after they do not get in foal or if they do it is late in the season. This is not good news as all thoroughbreds in the northern hemisphere are deemed to be born on the first of January; rarely at the sales will a June foal have the size or maturity of one born earlier in the year and is less attractive to most trainers whose clientele are looking for early winners...

There are of course exceptions to every rule and the foal bred by Mr. E.P Taylor at his Windlands Farm in Canada was one such example. That the foal was born at all was fortuitous, his dam being sent to Nearco only because she went lame and was unable to continue her racing career.

Thus was born Northern Dancer, retained and raced by his owner only because he was so small that he failed to reach his reserve at the yearling sales. A horse who, despite his size and immaturity, became the top Canadian two year old and the following year posted notice of his potential by winning two thirds of the American Triple Crown, the American equivalent of our Classic Races for three year olds.

Last year in 1967 the same Eddy Taylor had bred a colt foal by his champion; this one, unlike his sire in stature in that he was big and imposing would change forever the old precepts of racing, based as they were on the assumed superior quality of the European thoroughbred. He would be brought to Europe by the greatest trainer in the world, Vincent O'Brien, he would be named Nijinsky, he would be the first horse since Bahram in 1935 to win the English Triple Crown and he would make his sire, Northern Dancer, the hottest property the world of racing had ever seen.

As yet this was unknown, but James had been persuaded by Henry White to accompany him to the Keenland Sales in July next year, the trainer having some years ago realised that the times clocked by these American breds were impressive. It seemed obvious to him that although they raced mainly on dirt, they would also, as they were in the main descended from European horses, be equally as effective on grass.

At present the Woolmington Stud would not justify a manager, but he had appointed a stud groom who came well recommended by the current Master of the Belvoir Hunt which, after the events of this afternoon in Quorn country, seemed slightly ironic.

She was assisted part-time by June, a horse-mad nanny employed by Kate to help in the house and with the boys.

The financial aspect and his determination to make the stud pay its way were never far from his thoughts, particularly when he was at home. One day, early in June this year accompanied by Kate and the boys, he was sculling idly around the lake in the small dinghy when a chance comment from his wife gave him an idea.

They had both turned to the sound of neighing and the thunder of hooves as the foals galloped off and over the brow of the hill.

'I love seeing them James, more than I ever thought I would, but the colts do seem to cause far more hassle than the fillies, just like teenage boys; particularly when they become yearlings and start acting coltish.'

'Eureka Kate, you have just crystallized something that has been going round and round in my brain for ages.'

He leaned forward to kiss her, his instantaneous gesture very nearly capsizing the dinghy.

'Steady ,' she yelled, the kids screeching with delight as the water came briefly over the side.

He expounded the newly formed wisdom.

'At the sales, for reasons I do not fully understand, the demand is always for colts, so much so that breeders sending up fillies rarely come away satisfied. The vast majority of these expensive blue bloods will not pay their way as, in addition to the purchase price, further outlay is required for training etc. In future, we will sell all the colts no matter how good they appear, either as foals or yearlings. If they are flops, we will already have been paid and if they win the trainers will come back for more and be prepared to pay more.

The fillies we will race, any that are successful we will retain to build up the broodmare band. Yes, I can see it all.'

He picked up the oars and pulled across to the landing stage.

'Anyone for a picnic?'

'Yes, yes,' the delighted response from his crew.

They lay back on the rug, luxuriating as all parents do to the soft skin and prodding of tiny fingers.

Charles, at six the elder of the two, had a marvellously enquiring mind, he saw interest in most things. Edward at three did not as yet show this same aptitude, but the way in which he caught balls and the ease with which he had won his race at the kindergarten suggested that another embryonic star of the rugby field may well have arrived. To see his son in a Leicester Tigers' shirt....... it brought back memories of his first game in the First Fifteen. Quite a baptism it had been, the rugby press heralding the arrival of another Carrington in the famous red, green and white hoops, the opposition determined to bury this upstart from the England youth team. An early clean catch and a long punt into touch soon had the crowd warming to him and the Harlequin's flankers and centres finding him an elusive quarry.

'He's bloody quick.' The enthusiastic aside from a supporter on the terrace to his companion, as James outpaced the whole of the Quins back division before diving over in the corner.

Up in the stands, his old rugby master, Gareth Thomas turned to Dickie Dickson,

'His old man would have been proud of that.'

'Now where are you, what's going on in that head of yours now?'

Kate interrupted his daydream.

'That I love you, so much, that we are so lucky to have all of this.'

'I want to stay here forever.'

Kate's riposte the first time anyone had ever sought to deny him his goal of Milford Hall. He let it pass, she had probably not realised what she had inferred. But she had, and she let it pass too.

'Why don't we leave the boat and walk back through the park?'

'So that you can see your beloved horses.'

She laughed, he was so transparent.

As they strolled, he explained to her how most of the studs were still in the hands of the landed gentry and the aristocracy, the Earls of Derby, Rosebery or foreign bluebloods such as the Aga Khan. Other rich players such as Sir Victor Sassoon, a member of a wealthy banking family, occasionally entered the fray. The one definitive exception to this was a self-made millionaire David Robinson, whose fortune was founded on the rental of radios and more latterly TV sets. Most major high streets had a shop bearing his initials 'DER.'

He had first dipped his toe into the water in the mid-forties, twenty years later he had in excess of one hundred and fifty horses in training. So large had his string grown that he appointed his own salaried trainers in Newmarket, Michael Jarvis and Paul Davey. Their responsibilities did not stop there, they had a budget to work to and their employer, never an easy man to work for, demanded they account for every penny.

James had no aspirations to own such a large string, he had too many other ambitions to fulfil, but he had studied David Robinson's business approach to racing and that, particularly the accountability, did appeal to him. It was a principal he was determined to adhere to.

The greatest difference between them was that Robinson had no interest in breeding; he had the cash to buy success and to do so he was again imaginative - he appointed a group of experts headed by Lord Harrington to plough through the sales catalogues and select his winners for him.

James, however, although somewhat squeamish by nature - he could not, for instance, bear to be at Kate's side when she had the children - had no such qualms if a mare needed help when she was foaling.

Apart from your own children, nothing, if you have not experienced it, compares with the joy and relief of seeing a new born foal after thirty or forty minutes of staggering on wobbly legs finally standing and suckling.

As they neared the stables, the sound of Charles and Edward attracted the dogs who gave up on their investigations in the wood to greet them. Henry, the pointer, named in honour of his predecessor arrived first, followed by Kate's black Labrador, Mac short for Tarmac, and finally a great lolloping black and as yet slightly uncoordinated four month old Irish wolfhound named Vincent after the peerless Irish Trainer, Vincent O'Brien.

They all proceeded into the yard; it being feed time, no welcoming heads poked out of the top doors, which encouraged Vincent to be a little bolder. Last week he had stood on his hind legs and stuck his great head into the box, his curiosity being rewarded by a snap of teeth from the ever protective mother. He had slunk away to hoots of laughter from Sue and June.

James loved being here with his horses, it was the one time when he could put from his mind the thoughts of work, here his dreams were of excitement and not the mundane and today's decision to sell all the colts was a sound one; if they won, he could still share in their success knowing that he was responsible for them being born in the first place.

The breeding continued to dominate his thoughts, he had persisted with the 'Donatello' influence and the filly foal at Wedding Belle's side was by Crepello, the 1957 Derby winner. Assuming she showed ability he would race her and then retire her to join his growing band of brood mares. The recently retired four year old, Royal Palace, the winner of last year's Derby, had been her intended mate in the spring of next year.

With this in mind, he and Nick Carter Brown had visited the Egerton Stud in May this year to discuss with Michael Oswald, the stud manager, the possibility of using Royal Palace. The horse had gone from strength to strength as a four year old winning a further five races for his immensely popular owner Mr Jim Joel. In particular, his victory in the Eclipse when he defeated his old rivals Taj Dewan and this year's exceptionally good Derby winner Sir Ivor. He had also won the King George and Queen Elizabeth Stakes; this, plus the fact that he was an exceptionally good looking horse would mean he would be very popular with mare owners. Securing a nomination was made even more difficult as Mr Joel had decided to form a small rather exclusive partnership with Lord Howard de Walden and Lady Macdonald Buchanan.

Michael Oswald was in an impossible position. The horse was required by the partnership and the other nominations had been filled by an exclusive band of blue-blood mares.

James understood his dilemma; Michael Osborne's natural charm diffusing the disappointment for the would-be nominees. As a keen rugger man it was a regret to him that he was unable to accommodate James whom he had seen on many occasions at Twickenham. Nick Carter Brown and his wife had been friends for several years, this and James's obvious enthusiasm and passion for his new sport did however prompt an invitation to look at the other mares and foals.

The most outstanding foal at Egerton that year was out of a mare named La Paiva. She had an undistinguished racing career, possibly due to blindness in one eye, but was nevertheless well made with particularly good legs; her main attraction, to her owners at least, was that she traced back to Pretty Polly, the most outstanding race mare at the turn of the century. In twenty four starts she was beaten only twice and, in retirement continued her success producing the winner of the Irish Derby but, above all she produced four fillies the direct female line of which produced two Derby winners in successive years in the sixties, St Paddy in 1960 and Psidium the following year.

The foal, the property of John and Jean Hislop, was a beautiful mahogany bay with a small white star. He had an imperious look about him but his nature was kind and generous and he stood calmly as they stroked his muzzle and ears, following them as they walked to another occupant of the paddock as if to let them know he was the star attraction.

Although they did not know it they were looking upon greatness, in the fullness of time the strong bay colt that stood before them would burst upon the racing scene and become recognised as probably the greatest miler of the century. His name would be Brigadier Gerard who, in company with another foal at the moment three thousand miles away in Rokeby, Virginia, would bring an excitement and buzz to racing such as the public on these shores had never experienced before. The name of that other colt would be Mill Reef.

These two champions, following on from the exploits of the mighty Nijinsky the year before, would generate an excitement and desire to get into racing that would stretch beyond the confines of the Jockey Club and bring new owners into the sport. This was the way forward, new blood being vital if the Sport of Kings was to survive the demise of the aristocratic involvement.

Had James known this he would have been, if it were possible, even keener to breed and get on to the gravy train.

At the moment though, save possibly for the Hislop's and Lord Carnarvon whose stallion Queen's Hussar had sired him, no one could suspect what might be.

The icing on the cake so to speak, was Michael and Angela Oswald's invitation join them for tea. Nick encouraging James to pick the brains of their knowledgeable host before returning home disappointed, but understanding of the stud manager's dilemma.

As it would turn out, Royal Palace would prove a disappointment at stud. However, there was bound to be a clamour for his first one or two crops of foals which would sell at premium prices before the bubble burst.

Unfortunately, this was a bonus that James would miss out on, however it only served to make him even more determined to improve his stock so that in future he would secure these prestigious coverings.

Back home, with these memories etched on his mind, he walked slowly around the yard with his family, stroking and feeding carrots and mints to the occupants. He was in no hurry; this was the one place that he felt divorced from the pace of life.

Kate took the kids in for supper whilst he walked up the flight of stone steps on the outside wall of the barn. This converted hay loft was his sanctuary; the walls a mass of framed photographs of his horses and the legendary names of the past, both British and overseas. He sank down in the comfortable chair at the large scroll top desk and opened the form book... to dream the impossible dream...

His reverie was shattered.

'Come on Lord Derby, your supper is ready.'

He heard the laughter in Kate's voice and made his way to the house, smiling at her indulgence, though in fact she was starting to enjoy going racing, particularly when she was able to remind the experts that their original star, Woolmington, had been her choice.

CHAPTER TWENTY SIX

The first Monday of the month was traditionally the occasion for a Board Meeting. He was as usual first at his desk, still relishing those early hours before the telephone rang, as the most productive time of the day. At around eight thirty he heard the others as they exchanged greetings with other members of staff.

At ten thirty the telephone interrupted his concentration. It was Connie.

'All set, ready when you are.'

He joined them, taking his place in thoughtful mood at the head of the long refectory table that had been harvested from a Manor house vacated by one of their Bournemouth tenants. The move to their existing offices, built in such splendid Gothic style by Fothergill Watson, had prompted a U-turn in furnishing and decor.

They looked at him expectantly.

'It occurred to me as I sat at this table that we should be more actively engaged in acquiring antique pieces of furniture, at the moment no one wants them, the prices are scandalously low and whatever happens they can only appreciate in value in the future.'

'Long term, James, I can see the logic of your argument.' Tim's rhetorical response.

'Where on earth do we store them?'

Edward as usual, requiring a reasoned and sound financial appraisal.

James turned to him.

'This brings me rather neatly to the point. We have pioneered a brave new world for retired people but, as we anticipated, the big boys are seeing the commercial logic of it and to maintain our market share we will have to trim our prices to the bone. I believe we have seen the best days; it is time for something new. We should turn the whole idea on its head; we should put retired people back into stately old houses.'

Anthony Jayes raised his gold pen to indicate his concern.

'Lord Birkett you have a question?'

Humour was never far below the surface on these occasions. The others laughed at this legal aside, Lord Birkett Q.C being well known for this gesture.

'Chairman, the whole point about the Bournemouth concept, indeed it's very essence, was that older people no longer wish to live in these cold and draughty old houses that are far too large for any family other than the very rich to maintain.'

'You have, as always Anthony, summed it up completely.'

They all looked at him mystified as he tried to dredge from their minds the concept behind his veiled idea.

'These houses are too big for one family...'

'But not too big for several families.' Connie, as at Bournemouth, the first to realise the potential.

James threw them a copy of the Daily Telegraph.

'Open it at page fourteen.'

He watched the incredulous look on their faces as they read the article in which a Georgian House of the most splendid proportions was now home to hundreds of pigs. Tim Cooper, perhaps not surprisingly in view of his calling in life, the first to speak.

'This is appalling, what sort of swine could do this?'

'Probably Large White'.

Anthony beat them to the punch before the whole gathering, including Tim, collapsed in hoots of laughter.

Finally, tears of laughter still running down his cheeks. Edward suggested.

'They do it Tim because that house, which no one wants, is cheaper than building a piggery - and they don't even use the upstairs!'

Tim fought back with.

'I expect the ladies are keen to use the bored room'.

The Chairman attempted to restore sanity and finally had their attention. Ready once again to set them running, ready to crank up the adrenalin and motivation.

'Where do we start to look? Presumably not on the south coast.'

Anthony the first to state the obvious.

'Wrong,' James's voice rang out. We start by examining the pluses and minuses of the Bournemouth operation, financial as well as logistical.

'Financially it has been a brilliant idea, the only drawback being the short term cash flow because the buggers are so happy they are not dying quickly enough!'

'As ever Edward, your financial acumen is impeccable, however, in the longer term the value of the apartments will rise and at that point our cash flow will be even greater as property prices rise. Convincing the Bank to ride out the storm with us is the key area and one on which I want you to concentrate your mind, Edward, it is important that your meeting next month with Abercrombie's goes well.

The big man nodded, inwardly satisfied at the confidence the other Board members accorded him these days.

'The biggest problem we had, apart from the initial over demand, has been the travelling to and fro. I agree with James, the South coast is not the best option.'

James nodded approvingly at Connie; she was very astute at crystallizing a situation.

'I will put you out of your misery and then take you to Severns for lunch.'

He outlined his meeting with Mrs Watkin-Downes, how she had responded so positively to the prospect of living the rest of her days in a house that not only looked stylish but would, for the first time in many years, be warm and comfortable.

They left the Boardroom excited and switched on, eager to get to grips with the new idea, realising not only the potential to acquire the properties cheaply but also the furniture with which to enhance them. The fact they were to be found in their own environs was also a big plus point, the real downside of Bournemouth for all of them had been the travelling.

'Apart from my trips to meet Kate,' he counselled them, rolling his eyes to signify no further recollections would be appropriate.

The men laughed, Connie looked mystified but decided that now was not the time to enquire.

With lots of new possibilities to discuss they decided unanimously to continue over lunch.

They piled into the Bentley which transported them regally into the heart of this ancient city with its majestic Market Square and stately Council House.

The Bentley Convertible, with its elegant Park Ward body, had a galvanising effect on other motorists, it really did not have to overtake, they simply moved to one side.

The men luxuriated in the sumptuous leather seats, delighted as all their gender are by the power of such a beast, their indulgence interrupted by Connie.

'It really is true,' she exclaimed, her head bent so that her ear was against the dashboard,

'The only thing you can hear at sixty miles an hour is the ticking of the clock!'

'And did you know,' countered the driver, 'That it takes three cows to supply the hide for these seats!'

With these two thoughts on which to ponder they arrived, parking in the Lace Market and walking the short distance to Severns Restaurant.

This was a superb old style restaurant serving traditional foods in a splendid manner.

'First class, this city's answer to Simpson's.'

Edward's observation, half way through his second helping of spotted dick.

Lunch passed very quickly, the conversation animated, everyone seeing the exciting possibilities that the new proposal posed.

'Do you think James that it would be too much to telephone Mrs Watkin-Downes and ask if we could go over there this afternoon? '

'Why not, we could take some bubbly and a few bits from Burtons Foodhall.'

He disappeared behind the reception desk, emerging a few minutes later with his thumb up.

As they retraced his steps of the other day he let slip a few details about the Quorn Hunt, this being 'Monday Country ' etc., much to the amusement of the others.

'You are so easily transported to new delights.'

Tim could hardly contain his amusement at James's enthusiasm for yet another new interest.

'If you never had a dream, you never had a dream come true, to paraphrase South Pacific. Mind you, the prospect of riding hard and leaping these big hedges does give me quite a buzz.'

Before they could tease him further the House came briefly into view, just as quickly retreating into the wood. They turned into the long driveway, the atmosphere in the car one of anticipation.

They were not disappointed and to James, perhaps because he was less apprehensive this time, it seemed even more dignified and stately.

A pull on the doorbell produced Alice, clad not in apron, but in a smart silk paisley blouse with a high ruffled neck and a smart black skirt.

'Mr. Carrington, please do come in, Madam is in the library.'

They followed James, he certain that there was a spring in Alice's step that he had not seen on his previous visit. Their host rose to meet them, her blue eyes twinkling with pleasure, she waved them to sit on the variety of old leather sofas and chairs that dotted the room.

'I haven't slept a wink since we met yesterday.'

'Nor me, I was so worried you might change your mind.'

'But we shook hands.' Her simplistic belief in the old standards of her youth both refreshing and damning of so much of today's sharp business conduct.

Connie produced the hamper with the champagne and nibbles, indicating that the famous Burton's Game pie was intended for later, for the two ladies at suppertime.

Mrs Watkin-Downes rang the bell for Alice, smiling as she did so.

'The old dear's quite beside herself, I have never seen her so alive!'

Alice returned for the champagne toast proposed by Connie,

'To Watkin Hall and all who live in her.'

'Watkin Hall'; the response a chorus of assent.

'And to you all for making an old lady, indeed two old ladies happier than you can ever imagine.'

They left Connie to talk about old times, James leading the others on a tour of inspection. They were not disappointed, the rooms were large and airy, most of them big enough to be reduced in size to accommodate the kitchen and bathroom space that was essential to lift them to the standards provided in the new apartments in Bournemouth.

As they progressed through the house they could not but be impressed by the quality of detail that was everywhere. The house had been built when time was still subservient to perfection, when tradesmen inherently did things correctly to approved standards and, wherever they looked, be it at the ceiling with its ornate plasterwork, or the magnificent staircase with its intricately carved balustrade and newel posts, it did not take much imagination to imagine the days of yesteryear when grand ladies in ball gowns would have swept down to the hall below, or men in scarlet hunting coats would have hastened noisily to relieve the grooms of their mounts. The latter prompted a thought that he mentally filed away for the future.

CHAPTER TWENTY SEVEN

On Thursday, satisfied that everything was now moving forward, he set off with Kate for Yorkshire. In reality, the others at the office, excited by the new idea, needed no prompting; this was a team in unison.

They were accompanying the Stanhope Courts to stay with Gerald and Tiggy Seymour at their family home just above Helmsley on the North Yorkshire moors.

It was a warm day that threatened to be very hot and they drove leisurely, the hood down, allowing them to see from afar the great White Horse above Kilburn, the village now equally well known for its famous oak furniture made by Robert Thompson, each piece bearing his distinctive hallmark, a carved mouse.

They climbed Sutton Bank, admiring from the top the long view over the Vale of York and as they descended towards Helmsley, the superb sight of the Cleveland Hills that he remembered so well from that day, all those years ago, when he and his father had come north to collect the day old chicks and turkey poults. He smiled inwardly, his method of transport today a long way from the Austin pick-up truck of yesteryear.

This is marvellous country and they needed no prompting when Miles suggested lunch in Helmsley. They drew on to the car park in front of the Black Swan - a superb hotel in a superb location and, over the meal, Miles explained to James the basics of grouse shooting which, tomorrow being the ' Glorious Twelfth' of August, marked the first day of the shooting season.

'The word 'grouse' is most probably derived from the old French word 'griesche' meaning speckled or grey. In the past it was often called the moor-fowl or moor-game or even moor-cock. However, back in the reign of Henry VII it was amended to 'grows' - a term originally referring to the blackcock whose mate resembles the grouse, eventually though the expression came to apply exclusively to the red grouse. The latter is unique in that it is the only British bird that is not found in any other country. Its whereabouts here are decided entirely by the source of its main food, heather. It is therefore usually encountered on open moorland, principally in Scotland and Northern England as far down as Yorkshire and Derbyshire, with small pockets in North Wales and Northern Ireland.'

'Grouse moors and the driving of grouse seems to have originated', he continued, 'in the

Barnsley area of Yorkshire when, in the year of Trafalgar, George Fisher the keeper of Cannon Hall, drove the birds, in order to present a better target for the owner Mr Spencer Stanhope and his sons. To disguise their presence the latter hid themselves behind large rocks on the moor. Thirty years later this practice was commonly adopted, holes in the ground replacing the rocks as 'hides.' As the fashion spread to other counties in the North East and Yorkshire larger and larger bags were shot, surpassing those in Scotland which had previously been considered as the best breeding and shooting region.

An unconsidered and advantageous side effect was that the driving put up the older, more canny birds that tended to dominate large territories but which bred less efficiently than several younger cock birds operating in smaller areas of the same ground.'

Kate smiled indulgently as her husband warmed to yet another new pastime, enquiring gently how he was going to fit this in with the racing, breeding, skiing, golf and not to mention hunting; she teased.

'If you want a job doing, ask a busy man,' his smiling rejoinder.

Conscious though he was of the importance of tomorrow in the social calendar to the other house guests, his interest was centred a few days on when on the last day of the famous Ebor meeting on the Knavesmire at York, his two year old filly Fleece out of Woolmington would put her unbeaten record and Guineas potential on the line in the Lowther Stakes. This was a most important test in the racing calendar for next year's aspirant female champions, a good performance would add the all important 'black type' to her pedigree and mark a significant step forward for James's Woolmington Stud.

When her time came to go to the paddocks, his intended choice was 'Petingo' who at this same August meeting last year had turned the Gimcrack, the corresponding race for two year old colts, into a procession with a devastating display of sprinting. This year as a three year old, he had not quite fulfilled his potential but it had taken an exceptional horse, Sir Ivor to lower his colours in the 2000 Guineas. He was also, as Kate had observed, an extremely good looking and athletic horse and, since she had chosen the dam, who could deny that she should choose the mate for Fleece.

On checking his pedigree, James had wryly noted that he was descended from...

'Don't tell me, Donatello?'

'Who else?' He had chided her.

Miles, conscious that James's thoughts were elsewhere, stopped talking and winked at Kate and Belinda, it was several seconds before an embarrassed James re-joined the conversation, the others taking it in good part with Pippa saving the day by confessing that shooting also left her cold.

'No, I would like to give it a go; it's just that I was so useless at fishing that I wonder if I have the eye for it.'

'I don't intend to go out every day so, if you are game we will have a morning together, nothing to lose and you just might enjoy it.'

James happy to agree to Miles's offer and graciously admitting that it was , in any case, something that a Gentleman should at very least be conversant with.

They decided wisely to forego the dessert, Belinda warning them that the Seymour's

'Eve of the Twelfth' dinners were renowned for the copious amounts of food and drink provided by their large amiable host, who would declare, 'Never send a man out onto a grouse moor with an empty stomach, as my dear old Ma was one to confide.'

They all piled into the Bentley, decamping at Strudwick Hall a little after four pm. It was an ancient pile, the tower and adjacent part being the remains of an old priory dating back to 1247. It had survived the reformation when the Seymour's converted to the new religion like many other powerful Catholic families, before returning later to their true faith.

A butler greeted them and ushered them into the large conservatory at the back of the house where their hosts, extricating themselves from a mélange of Lurchers, Labradors, English Setters and a Great Dane named Alfred, rose to meet them.

'Not like you to be first Miles,' Gerry Seymour extended his hand.

'You have James to thank for that.' Nick introduced Kate, her husband needing no introduction as Gerald Seymour had been an England selector when James was first chosen to represent his country. An honour he had himself been accorded whilst still at Oxford.

They moved through the open French doors and onto the terrace, Kate appreciating for the first time the glorious moorland setting for tomorrow's sport.

All moors have a quality unique to themselves, today under a flawless blue sky, the heather in full bloom, the impact was stunning - its effect at the same time both welcoming and forbidding. She gazed out across the bracken, still in full colour, punctuated by large dark boulders sitting in unseen beds of emerald moss. She was lost in the majesty of it.

'I have lived here for thirty years and it still takes my breath away.'
Tiggy Seymour rightly interpreting Kate's silence.

'And yet in winter', she confided, 'it can be a bleak and hostile place, the mists can come down so quickly and those delightful becks you will see tomorrow change to raging torrents.'

They were interrupted by Jenkins, who announced the arrival of Roger and Sarah Laverick and the Hon Robin Baker-Blackwell, universally known as Blackie, and his wife Lady Penelope, 'do call me Pen,' she requested Kate.

The champagne was sent for; it was delivered by the Armstrongs, long time family friends who had intercepted Jenkins in the hallway.

'I think we have a big enough quorum to get started.'
James was charged with the uncorking on the assurance from Miles Stanhope Court that he was a bit of a connoisseur of the product of Rheims.

'Not so, not so, although our tastes do coincide and this, a Grande Année is very special indeed.' His modest assurance to the host, as he twisted the cork from the Bollinger.

'To Strudwick Moor!' The toast from William Armstrong, echoed by the others.
Any natural sportsman will flex his sensual muscles when he is at a sporting event, his competitive instincts naturally aroused, James's mild indifference to shooting rapidly evaporating as he heard the others discussing previous shoots, their exploits as with golf and fishing, more successful with the re-telling.

In the midst of the story telling the final guests arrived, George Stokesley and his wife Abigail, he a tall fair haired man, about the same size as Edward Lawson but, instead of the wide open face of the latter, he wore a sneering expression that remained fixed even when he occasionally laughed. His wife, as one might have anticipated, was a shy creature whose mien matched the colour of her mousy hair.

At six thirty they all adjourned to change, the maids having already unpacked for everyone. In the room Kate stood in front of the open window looking again across Strudwick Moor, James moved next to her closing his arms around her.

'This place has really got to you hasn't it?'

'I can't explain it, but it does exert its influence, quite apart from the shooting I would love to be out there with the dogs, particularly on a wild stormy day.'

'Kathy, Kathy,' he teased, 'Heathcliffe needs you.'

'That's a new name for it.'

She turned to meet the welcoming lips that sought hers.

Her hand slid down to his groin, and they both laughed as she exclaimed.

'My, Heathcliffe is pleased to see me!'

They made love in the capacious surrounds of the ancient four-poster, revelling in the delights of each other.

They lay back exhausted, Kate going into the bathroom first, before, as she put it,

'Mr Heathcliffe gets any further ideas.'

He watched the pert little bottom disappear and remembered when he had first been attracted to it, all those years ago in Birmingham...

'Kathy, Kathy.'

'Tell Heathcliffe he will have to wait.' She laughed and closed the door.

Another great advantage of marriage over affairs, more costly, but the togetherness is unquestionably worth it he decided.

They finally made it downstairs and joined the others in the Library, one wall of which was a magnificent bookcase it's oak shelves filled with mostly leather bound volumes of great English literature. On closer examination he spotted the mouse carved into the end of each row.

He turned to Gerry Seymour. 'Mousey Thompson I imagine.'

'Yes indeed, that chap has done so well, so many great buildings, Ampleforth Abbey and College for instance are full of his work.'

They downed a quick G & T before processing into the Dining Room.

The famous Strudwick dinner promised by Belinda more than lived up to expectations, both in quality and quantity.

For starters the choice was either Smoked Salmon or Salade d'artichaut, a delicious salad of thinly sliced artichoke hearts and seasonal vegetables. To accompany this an excellent dry, yet pungent Gewurztraminer from Alsace; followed by Iced Soup of cucumber and dill with crispy croutons of lobster.

After the heat of the day both courses drew appreciation, summed up by Blackie who with glass raised drew their unanimous approval.

'My dear Tiggy, every year you seem to excel the last and, every year, we cannot believe you can surpass what we are now eating.'

Turning to James he urged.

'My dear chap I recommend this shooting lark, well you know what I mean; if only to book a place at this marvellous table.'

'You don't shoot.'

The comment with its inbuilt sneer from George Stokesley, intruded into the civilised atmosphere, James inwardly seething at this uncalled for rudeness, remained outwardly calm; he turned slowly to face his accuser.

'I hadn't used to play rugby.'

'Touché, old boy.' Miles delighted to see the calm way that Stokesley had been put down.

Gerald Seymour, also delighted that his wife's brother-in-law had received his comeuppance, signalled Jenkins to bring over a decanter of red wine.

'Blackie, give us an opinion.'

The Hon Robin swirled the small measure in his glass, sniffed appreciatively, sipped enough to tantalise his palate, swallowed slowly and pronounced,

'A Medoc, almost certainly a Mouton-Rothschild- 1960 I would say.'

Absolutely bang on', Gerry turned to James.

'Every year I test him and every year he gets it spot on, it's quite uncanny.'

Blackie turned to face them all.

'It is so bloody simple, every year I know you will ask me, so every year I slip Jenkins a couple of quid and he tells me!'

The whole gathering roared with laughter, most of them thinking it was modesty rather than fact but it set the tone and ironed out the crease of rudeness created by George Stokesley. They moved on to the Rack of Lamb with spirits and appetites soaring.

Miles, who also had a reputation as a Bon Viveur, raised his glass to Gerry.

'Surely they cannot deny old Philippe de Rothschild his Premier Cru status for much longer.'

'You would think not. It is what he craves and with this quality year in year out, I agree he must be recognised as a First Growth sooner rather than later.'

Jenkins served the home grown lamb, one from Tiggy's small flock of Jacob's sheep, the meat slightly darker and with a distinctive sweeter taste, cooked to a beautiful pink perfection, so good that all the men without exception requested seconds.

Kate sitting next to Gerald confessed that,

'We came here with our appetites honed, Belinda denying us a pudding at the Black Swan; my goodness she was right, I cannot remember such a splendid meal.'

'Take my word for it Tiggy, that is high praise as my mother-in-law is a very fine cook and my wife too,' James hastily added.

The banquet moved on to a seemingly endless selection of desserts, most of the ladies trying several of them. The men, with the exception of Gerry, settling for cheese, their host 'just sampling' a couple of the sweets, prior to his cheese.

Blackie, his face as ever full of fun, looked across at Gerry before exclaiming,

'You would never believe he was once supposed to be the fastest loose forward in the British Isles.'

'The world surely,' quipped Gerry, conscious of his now somewhat corpulent shape.

More good humoured laughter accompanied the port as it circled the table, the ladies finally withdrawing, leaving the men to listen to Blackie's endless amusing stories.

Thus was James's first introduction to the great 'Eve of the Twelfth' dinner of which he had heard much, all of it living up to expectation. It was a shame about George Stokesley, but it had served a purpose, James was now determined to try his hand at shooting.

They went up, very happy; he felt at home in this environment, it was where he belonged. Heathcliffe went to sleep happy as well!

The following morning the house stirred early, an air of excitement percolating through to the staff who knew from experience that a successful shoot would bring a few welcome extra pounds to each family as they all had someone, sons or husbands who would be beating or assisting in some capacity with the organisation of the day.

From the bedroom window, Kate had drawn James's attention to the beehives near the keeper's cottages. When they came down to breakfast she was delighted to see that the fruits of those industrious creatures were present on the breakfast table. Is any honey as delicious as that produced from heather? They both rather doubted it after tasting some of Mrs Fletcher's 1967 vintage.

The dining room was an active place, the men and those ladies intending to shoot noticeably on edge, all hoping to acquit themselves well. The dress was sombre in colour, most experienced shots believing that bright colours will turn the birds.

Although they were not shooting, both James and Kate had sought advice about what to wear. Miles, knowledgeable in these things had advised a tweed shooting suit, but with thin stockings to accommodate the anticipated August heat, these and the stout brogues which they had worn around the stud for several weeks now. James's experience of blisters from new rugby boots had made him keen to not have blistered feet; the challenge of learning to shoot was quite enough to occupy the mind.

It made them more comfortable; it also made their new owners less self- conscious. In point of fact they melted into the background, the men almost invariably attired in 'plus two's or 'breeks' as they are more often called; the ladies, some in Knickerbockers, the others in divided skirts. This was the option selected by Kate; it reminded her of the P.E skirts at school, an opinion shared by Penny.

CHAPTER TWENTY EIGHT

August the 12th, one of the dates, some would argue THE date on the social calendar sitting as it does with typically English thoroughness, between Royal Ascot and Cowes Week on one side and Henley Regatta on the other and, as Yorkshire folk would argue, just a few days before the Ebor race meeting on the Knavesmire at York.

A blast from a whistle and it was time to move off, a convoy of Land Rovers and men with an assortment of sporting dogs - most of the sportsmen adamant that their choice of breed was best, moved off in the direction of the high moor where the beaters, long since departed awaited them. The task of the men with the dogs would be to pick up and collect the day's bag.

Johnson, a now retired head keeper, drove the Land Rover that towed the trailer fitted with compartments for transporting the guns. Other such vehicles would be pressed into service later in the day to carry the lunch up to the Barn where the guns would eat. But this was a pleasure to be anticipated for later, now the only thought was the first kill, then one would know that your twelfth had finally arrived.

In a Land Rover borrowed from the house, Belinda directed James and Kate to a good vantage point; in the distance they saw a line of beaters probably a mile or so away, waving white flags to signal that the drive had begun.

The weather was as perfect as yesterday and they felt exhilarated to be part of such a scene; Belinda drew their attention to a dark cloud, it was a flock of maybe a hundred or more grouse.

'They will miss the first three or four butts,' she advised knowingly, she was right and they heard the crack of the first gun and then it was pandemonium as successively all the butts came to life, the sky overhead full of white smoke.

Through binoculars they could see the beaters waving their flags from side to side, occasionally disappearing as they descended into the contours of the landscape. Further coveys of birds appeared swerving across the line of the butts, which relentlessly attempted to mow them down. The morning continued in the same vein until Gerry signalled a halt, whereupon everyone, by now very peckish, trudged to the large stone bothy that on a wet day would provide welcome protection from the ravages of the wind and rain. Today it would provide a cool sanctuary in which to eat the splendid lunch provided by the Seymour's.

As house guests, James and Kate were invited to join the guns. The beaters and pickers-up eating their fare al fresco from the backs of the Land Rovers.

Inside the bothy, the walls by now lined with coats of all sorts, the lunch was, in its own appropriate way, every bit as good as last night's dinner.

James walked towards the huge crock of mutton soup, making a point to acknowledge George Stokesley. He received a grunt in return. Smiling to himself he didn't offer a comment, he was beginning to enjoy winding up this big taciturn bully and it was certainly encouraging him to try his hand at the shooting.

The main course was a choice of either cottage pie or steak and kidney pudding, he opted for the latter followed by a helping of the huge Stilton cheese that commanded the centre of the table.

'By God Gerry, I have never seen such a whopping Stilton, bloody good too.'

'I quite agree George, we have James to thank for that, he staggered in with it yesterday, nearly broke the kitchen table.'

Miles and the other house guests enjoying immensely George's further discomfort.

The repast was washed down with the local ale, Gerry being firmly against strong liquor in the shooting field. As a young man, he had witnessed a dreadful accident as a result of one of the guns imbibing too much of the sloe gin made available by the host.

In the afternoon the shooting party returned to the butts, to recommence the ritual warfare that this time of the year demanded, watching them go he was envious and keen to join them.

'Heathcliffe, Heathcliffe,' Kate grinned at him.

'Find me a cave where we can hide away together.'

They set off, Belinda quite content to go back and get a bit of peace and quiet before the men arrived back when the talk would be of little else other than the day's heroics.

They walked hand in hand, very much in love, the silence between them emphasising that love. They felt warm and content, deliriously happy, impossible to define in words. Finally Kate broke the silence.

'I am so proud of you, you were born to this life and yet, unlike all the others here this weekend, it was so cruelly snatched from you. You have achieved so much James, we have a home that anyone would be proud of, we have so many things beyond my wildest ambitions and yet you are not satisfied are you?'

He shook his head, seeing with perfect clarity the picture of his father as he listened kindly to the white lie his son had told him regarding his failure to get in at Cambridge.

She saw the moisture in his eyes and squeezed his hand.

'Milford Hall, is that what drives you, that promise you defiantly blurted out as a small boy - why, when it means so much, have you never taken me there?'

His voice was gruff with emotion as he spoke.

'That is not the promise that drives me, I wish I had never said that, hurting as it must have been for my parents. The promise that drives me is the vow I made to myself when I cycled up that hill on January 13th 1951; the next time I climb that hill and ride down that drive it will be as Master of that house.'

To lighten the mood he turned to her, his eyes exuding kindness and care.

'When I made that vow, I suppose in the back of my schoolboy mind, I imagined I would be married, what I could not have imagined was that my wife would be as beautiful and kind as you. You see, I believed I could, by working hard achieve the former, to have expected the latter would have been too presumptuous.'

'And, if that idiot Osborne had said yes, you would never had made that trip to Birmingham and met me....'

He sat down and drew her down into the bracken.

'One day I will take you to Milford Hall, meanwhile, Heathcliffe has other ideas.'

'Mr. Carrington...' her voice tailed off as she readily succumbed to his loving advances, feeling safe and alone in the anonymity in the vastness of the moor.

They lay back when it was over.

'I have never made love on a battlefield.'

She laughed, aware now of the constant cracking of guns in the distance.

'It is a shotgun affair.' As usual he had a quick rejoinder.

They returned ahead of the shooters, Kate joining the other ladies for tea on the terrace, James investigating Gerald's library where sure enough there was a comprehensive section on thoroughbred horses, the house was after all, hardly a stone's throw from Sledmere and Burton Agnes. These two great names were still regularly the largest consigners of horses to the bloodstock sales, particularly the premier yearling sales held by Tattersalls, nowadays at Newmarket but prior to 1958 they had of course been in Yorkshire at Doncaster.

Immersed though he was, he could not but be aware of the triumphal return of the gladiators as the studded brogues clipped the stone flags in front of the house.

'Scotch ', the rhetorical question as they traipsed through into the library and sank wearily into the assorted leather couches and armchairs.

James put his book down and stood up.

'The least I can do is serve drinks for you heroes.'

'James, that would be bloody marvellous, I am totally knackered.'

Gerry sank back into his favourite chair.

The conversation was animated; the day had been exceptional, particularly for their host who, for all his bulk still had the sportsman's eye. High bird or low, ducker or diver, he would pick them off with the relaxed ease that marked out an accomplished performer at any game. It was the same effortless ease which James had witnessed when he saw Peter Allis swing the golf club at Ferndown.

They were interrupted by Jenkins who confirmed that Johnson had made it to the railway station and that part of today's bag was en route to London, where many of the top hotels would serve grouse from the moors of Yorkshire as the 'chef's' selection that evening.

As three or four scotches slipped down, the shooting exploits rose, it had been a most successful day, even George Stokesley appeared to be on the brink of a smile as they trooped off in Indian file up the great stone staircase where the ladies were already engaged in donning tonight's finery.

At dinner that night, the main course was naturally grouse.

The youngest and most succulent of today's bag had been selected by Mrs Fletcher the cook, the birds were dressed and into each truss she inserted a cut of seasoned rump steak, the breasts were then draped with bacon and roasted to tender perfection for about thirty minutes. Before serving, the steak was removed and would reappear on the table with other cold meats at tomorrow's shooting lunch. The more knowing regular guns certain to be at the head of the queue for this superb delectation.

Finally, the cause of today's frenetic activity made its appearance, it was roasted a golden brown and sat on a bed of croutons surrounded by its own juices.

With a simple dish the emphasis has to be on presentation. Today, Mrs Jenkins had sent up two enormous meat dishes, in the centre of each were four brace at the feet of which she had interlocked game chips to form a scallop which held the hot chestnuts cooked in butter. At the neck end, succulent white grapes added a softer colour whilst the watercress bed at each end of the dish enlivened it. To complete this epicurean feast, a simple bread sauce and copious boats of gravy.

Jenkins brought it over for the hostess to approve.

'Bravo, bravo.' The response from Miles, echoed all around the table.

With young game, it is essential that a host serves his very best red wine and, as anticipated, Gerry did not let them down, a Chateau Margaux 1951.

'Most appropriate,' the knowledgeable affirmation from Blackie.

'Particularly on this most English of days, am I right in believing that the chateau was originally owned by the King of England.'

'You are quite correct James, although it is not a commonly known fact, I salute your erudition.'

'My father was a bit of a wine buff, it is a smidgeon of useless information that has stuck with me.' As usual he tried to pass it off casually, not wishing to be seen as showing off, particularly in such august company - although it is of course August, he mused to himself. He did, however, permit himself to say a few more words. He raised the Margaux.

'Gerry you have known me since I was a young fellow, so it is most appropriate that you should initiate Kate and myself into this most British of occasions, on behalf of us both, I do thank you and Tiggy most sincerely.'

'My dear boy, I have, as you say, known you for some time, I have admired you on the rugby field and off it and it is our pleasure to welcome you here this weekend. Now I expect you will want me to teach you to shoot as well as play rugger!'

That set the tone for a memorable evening which rounded off a truly marvellous day, the sort of day when no adjectives are adequate.

Tomorrow, well tomorrow was another day, and that held much promise also, James Carrington was taking up arms, well a shotgun at least.

With so many thoughts going through their minds, not least their tryst on the moors, Kate and James did not take any rocking off to sleep.

The following morning they watched the others leave, the atmosphere perhaps understandably not quite as high as yesterday, but nevertheless there was still a great feeling of anticipation. James envied them, but at least he was taking his first steps.

He stood at the front of the house waiting nervously for Miles to appear. He heard a scrunching of gravel and a smiling Miles appeared at the wheel of a familiar green Land Rover.

'All set, then pass your gun to Harold in the back.'

They set off for a flat area of grassland about a mile from the house. Harold jumped down and made his way across to the trap that would catapult the clay 'pigeons' for them to shoot.

'First thing to remember old boy is that we all had to start and to be quite honest, I was bloody useless, so do not feel embarrassed if the clays keep sailing by unscathed.'

'Thanks Miles, I do confess to feeling more than a little apprehensive.'

His instructor looked approvingly at the broken gun that his pupil held.

'A Churchill, my word this will have set you back a few bob.'

'Actually no, it was my father's, or grandfather's to be exact. I collected it from mother's last week; she was delighted that it was going to be used again. I have a pair in fact.'

'You would have!' Miles shook his head from side to side with amusement; this man never did anything by halves.

'I am sure your father will have instilled into you the importance of safety, the fact that you had the gun broken is evidence of that. I will only say one more thing, NEVER EVER turn round with an unbroken gun, it is the nightmare we all fear, facing down the barrel of a loaded shotgun. You have a good golf swing James and a good stance. These are the essentials of shooting; the accuracy, as with golf, will improve with practice.'

Miles slipped two cartridges into the 12 bore, he leaned slightly forward, legs splayed with the weight on the left one.

'Pull,' he commanded Harold.

The clay flew out sideways, the head nestling into the stock, remained stock-still. Is that where the expression came from, the onlooker wondered, as he heard the crack of the cartridge and the disintegrating clay seemingly at the same instant. Harold released another 'bird', again the apparently casual attitude; James could see and appreciate the analogy with golf. Once again his thoughts turned to young Mr. Allis at Ferndown Golf Club.

'Your turn and don't forget if you hit that bird it will be a bloody miracle.'

He handed the gun to James.

'Keep the point of the gun higher than the stock, that way you will have a good view of the target before you shoot. Hold it along the length where you feel comfortable, point your forefinger underneath the barrel at the target, that's good.'

He adjusted the stock into the pupil's shoulder.

'That little soft area below your collarbone, that's the spot; it will take any recoil without causing you any discomfort, now for your head.'

He rubbed his finger upwards on James's cheek finding the soft spot below the cheekbone.

'That's the spot, as with the collarbone, you do not want any bone in contact with the gun. Now then, gun down and set yourself again.'

They practised several more times, the student starting to appreciate the balance and timing, he was a gifted games player, instinctively keeping his eye on the target and head still, as when converting a goal or taking a long iron at golf.

Finally, Miles handed him some cartridges, he loaded two of them and the order was given to Harold.

The first clay sailed by, he got a shot off at the second, clipped the fourth and the fifth and then the big moment, blasted the sixth to smithereens. In the next batch of twenty five he scored nine, then fifteen, when they called a halt for lunch he was in high spirits. He could now appreciate the banter of yesterday, as each participant recounted the exploits of the day.

Flushed with pleasure they joined the guns in the bothy, his day complete when Gerald asked him to join them in the butts that afternoon.

After an excellent cold lunch they stomped back to the line of butts, each about forty yards apart. There were twelve in all, of which nine were being used, James the new occupant of number 10.

Gerry laughed, remembering his days as an England rugby selector.

'The last time I put you into a number 10 you did rather well, let's hope it is a good omen.

Accompanied by Harold, James went into the circular butt; it was made of the local stone faced with turf, good and solid, able to withstand the ravages of the weather and the regular assaults of moorland sheep scrambling all over them.

The loader turned to his 'gun'; He liked the enthusiastic young man, unlike so many shooters who are regarded as 'pompous pratts', he had no side or unnecessary airs and graces. It was also obvious that he was keen to learn and succeed.

'Here they come, sir,' the loader had picked up the warning whistle from the neighbouring butt.

After the solitary clay pigeon, a drive of grouse is quite a sight. They came, about forty or fifty of them, swift and silent straight at them; quite awe inspiring the first time a new gun encounters them.

James tried to remain calm, tried to remember all that Miles had taught him, but they were gone. Harold laughed at his shooter's dilemma.

'Bit quicker than you imagined, sir.'

'The one I thought I had, he was coming straight at me and then as I prepared to fire he swerved.'

'They don't want to die,' the sanguine response.

Once again they heard the warning, this time James Carrington with his Churchill 'side by side' 12 bore registered his first kill, it would not be his last, he had enjoyed the day far too much for that.

Finally, Gerry called a halt and they retraced yesterday's footsteps except that he was part of the conquering band that slumped into the comfortable armchairs in the Library. The one similarity was that he resumed his role as waiter.

'You are the youngest and the fittest; I think I am getting too old for this sort of caper.'

Gerry collapsed into his armchair by the window; from here he could see the moor drenched in the red glow of the setting sun that portended another fine day tomorrow.

No one believed him, they all knew he would have to be carried out in a box before he would give up his beloved shooting.

It had been a splendid time, the pleasure of new and reaffirmed friendships easily erasing the irritation of George Stokesley. Both he and Kate felt refreshed and eager to accept the new challenges and opportunities of Watkin Hall.

Thinking of that splendid house and of the new life he would give it excited him, they were going forward again. Work, despite all the pleasures of the chase and the racecourse, still remained the most exciting and vital element in his life.

He looked forward with anticipation to being at his desk again tomorrow.

'You look far away.' Miles interrupted his daydream, 'Thinking about that grouse you got?'

'No, the six hundred I didn't.'

Still laughing he accepted a scotch and resumed the banter of the day reflecting that, as with all sporting occasions, so much of the enjoyment is derived when the game is over. An hour slipped by before they made their way wearily to a much needed hot bath and change before dinner.

What culinary delights did Tiggy have in store this evening? The delicious question on all their lips as they relaxed in their various deep hot tubs, they knew they would not be disappointed and of course they were not.

This time they started with Quenelles of Sole served in a delicious Mornay sauce accompanied by crescents of choux pastry and watercress. It was a delightfully light prelude to the main culinary event of the evening. Roast Beef and of course particularly in this location, large inviting Yorkshire Puddings.

Originally, their host confided, they were cooked under the joint to catch the juices and then served as a starter with thick Yorkshire gravy.

'So the guests didn't eat too much beef,' Blackie coyly observed.

'Aye we watch us pennies up here,' chortled Gerry.

The cut of beef when it arrived surrounded by roast potatoes, lightly cooked baby carrots and broccoli and of course Yorkshire puddings was of the proportions that you only normally see in restaurants such as Simpson's.

The brown exterior revealed wonderful shades of tender pink beef that had been home grown on the estate's Home Farm, all the men demanding encores, much to the delight of their hostess.

James smiled across at Kate, her pleasure was openly apparent; he felt so happy to have introduced her into such a gathering of intelligent and interesting people, all with something to add to the occasion. He applied a liberal portion of horseradish to his last slice of beef when once again George Stokesley's sneering, supercilious tones intruded.

'What do you do for a living Carrington?'

James thought quickly. 'Nothing very special, I am an Estate Agent.' The half- truth he knew would infuriate Stokesley and so did the others, none more so than their host.

'Same job you then George.'

George Stokesley was apoplectic. 'I am not a bloody Estate Agent,' he growled, 'I am a Chartered Surveyor and Auctioneer.'

James could not resist turning the screw a fraction more.

'Actually I am hoping to open some offices in Yorkshire, we love it up here and it is so much more convenient than the South Coast.'

Gerry decided to enter the fun.

'James, remind me to have a word with you tomorrow, you really ought to have a word with Arthur Braithwaite, I believe at some stage he will have to sell up or there will be nothing left of what was once a highly regarded business.'

The whole gathering watched George Stokesley; once again his rudeness had backfired on him.

'Braithwaite's business is not worth a toss,' his guarded and defensive reply.

The mood was restored by the arrival of the dessert course and once again, as Belinda had warned, Tiggy Seymour had eclipsed even yesterday's masterpiece.

This time it was Summer Fruit Cup; individual dishes of raspberry puree, in the centre of which was a scoop of homemade vanilla ice cream on which balanced half a peach and around the rim of the dish, a circle of strawberries.

Alternatively, the men's choice, Apple Lattice Tart with cream or ice cream, or both most of them decided. For those whose appetite's had been conquered by the magnificent banquet their hosts had provided, there was a simple palate cleansing Orange and Pineapple Salad.

The ladies retired, leaving the men to their cheese and port; the centrepiece of which was the remains of the Stilton Cheese provided by James, the very same that George Stokesley had unknowingly approved of yesterday. This time he selected the Wensleydale, adding that it was the one and only great cheese of England.

It had been another splendid meal and not even the cantankerous Stokesley would be allowed to spoil it; his declaration remained uncontested, his invitation next year exceedingly doubtful.

CHAPTER TWENTY NINE

The following morning they said their genuine fond farewells, the Stanhope Courts intending to stay over until the Ebor race meeting at York.

An assignation was arranged and they set out both now anxious to be home, Kate to see the children, he to see the drawings that Tim should have ready for him to approve prior to the planning meeting in Nottingham at the end of the month.

They retraced their steps to Helmsley and this time, despite the intended haste, avoided Sutton Bank, preferring instead to meander through Wass and past the lovely remains of the Cistercian ruins of Byland Abbey. It was here that Edward the Second was resting when The Scots engaged his forces and destroyed them at the Battle of Byland.

Into beautiful Coxwold, with its unique octagonal Church Tower and the splendid Fauconberg Inn; as it was too early to take advantage of this fine old hostelry they continued up the steep main street flanked by its greens and cobbles. Past the fine stone Edwardian Vicarage which stands adjacent to its predecessor, the enchanting Shandy Hall, made famous in the late eighteenth century by a former vicar, Lawrence Sterne, the eccentric author of 'Tristram Shandy'.

They also resisted a visit Kilburn's great White Horse and Mousey Thompson's workshops, instead leaving behind them the warm limestone houses and cottages they crossed the A19 and headed across country towards Boroughbridge and the A1 trunk road that would deliver them home.

Kate exhausted by the events of the last few days, closed her eyes and soon drifted off to sleep. He looked across at her, the complexion and youthful looks in no way diminished by motherhood and he thanked his lucky stars that fate had contrived to make this beautiful woman his wife.

He was pleased she was sleeping, it gave him time to think and he cast his mind back to the lifestyle he had just left; it was so civilised, he felt so at home in this environment and was excited by the new prospect and challenge that shooting now promised. Yorkshire like the Alps would form part of his future calendar.

It was this recollection and the reminder of George Stokesley, coupled with the sign as he entered Brafferton Village that determined his next decision.

The fingerpost invited the traveller to choose between the A1 at Boroughbridge or the turning for York. He chose the latter option deciding on a whim to check out Gerry Seymour's suggestion about Mr Braithwaite and his Miller Braithwaite Estate Agency.

He drove into the centre of the city, parking close to the on the forecourt of the Judges Lodgings, now an interesting hotel. He stopped the engine and quietly removed the ignition key hoping not to disturb his passenger. However it was sufficient to wake Kate, whose first reaction was of surprise that she had slept all the way home. Her second was even more of a shock when she realised that they had travelled only about thirty miles and that they were in the middle of what is probably the most interesting city in the north of England.

York is steeped in relics of both the Vikings and of ancient Rome, not to mention one of the truly great cathedrals of the world York Minster; which in Northern Europe is second in size only to St Peter's in Rome. It also has a famous Public School, ironically called St Peter's, which dates back to AD 627, the second oldest in Britain: Amongst its many famous old boys was a certain Guy Fawkes; the cause of much excitement and expenditure on November the Fifth each year. The School whilst recognising the event not surprisingly allows the fireworks but not any effigy of their former student!

He looked at her coyly; 'Just a hunch darling, I thought it might be interesting to look in and check on Mr Braithwaite.

She shook her head in disbelief but knew it was pointless to argue. 'It will cost you lunch.'

'I know just the place,' he assured her. 'Come on let's find out where they operate from.'

'Somewhere fairly central,' Kate reasoned.

Her judgement vindicated when after a hundred yards or so they spotted the Braithwaite sign on a Georgian brick building close to the Minster.

'What are you going to say?' Kate wondered.

'Best to play it by ear,' he assured her as they climbed the stone steps that led to the front door. To the enquiring receptionist in the tweed suit, he smiled one of his defenceless smiles.

'Would you advise Mr Braithwaite that a friend of Mr Gerald Seymour would very much appreciate a word?'

This eventually elicited an invitation from the inner sanctum where, surrounded by files and deeds wrapped in red ribbons sat, seemingly in a Dickensian time warp, Mr Arthur Braithwaite.

He motioned James to sit and then, seeing Kate for the first time he stood up and collected an extra chair for her.

James quietly seized the initiative to begin a friendly low key discussion.

'Mr Braithwaite, thank you so much for allowing us to intrude on what I can see is a busy working day.'

The surveyor waved at the mound of papers. 'To be quite frank Mr Carrington, I do not, since my dear wife died, have the inclination or the impulse to clear his lot up. If it wasn't for Miss Reed, whom you met on the way in, I think we would go out of business.

Kate heard herself speaking.

'I remember when my grandmother died, my grandfather's law practice went through the same trauma, it was only the consideration and extra work put in by the other partners, in particular a couple of the younger ones that kept the business afloat.

The old man looked at Kate, his expression one of respect.

'You are very kind and you sir are a very lucky man.' James's smile was evidence of his accord.

She continued.

'You are a Yorkshireman and proud of it, you have no doubt lived here all your life, you are lucky. We have only recently, through Gerry Seymour, come to know and love your wonderful landscapes. We do, however, intend to spend more time up here and what better way of doing that than by investing in Yorkshire and providing jobs up here.'

She drew in a deep breath. 'I suppose that was the easiest way, just blurting it out.'

She looked appealingly at him, the reciprocal smile encouraging her to continue.

'As part of our business, we have an Estate Agency, rather high class, such as your own and we would like to make you an offer for your firm.'

The silence seemed interminable. Finally, Arthur Hardcastle leaned forward and rang the small silver bell sitting on his desk. It summoned Miss Reed.

'Would you like some tea for your guests, sir?'

'No Miss Reed, although that may be appropriate in moment. What I want to ask you my dear is would you like to work for Mr and Mrs Carrington?'

Before the startled girl could answer, he turned to Kate.

'I am assuming you do wish to employ Miss Reed?'

It was a rhetorical question but it invited a response; one word was sufficient. From the other side of the desk it came in unison. 'Absolutely.'

With no one quite sure what to do next, Kate again took control.

'Miss Reed why don't you and I go and make the tea, it will give us a chance to get to know each other.'

As the ladies left the room, Arthur Braithwaite reached into the cupboard in his desk and produced two glasses and a bottle of Bell's Black Label whisky from which he poured two generous measures.

'Your very good health, Mr Carrington, your inspiration and your wife's advocacy have resolved several undecided issues for me. You have made me face consequences which I have long been avoiding.'

He tilted his glass, James did likewise before responding.

'The feeling is mutual; I have a very good feeling about today's events.'

Kate reappeared, opening the door for Miss Reed who was bearing a silver tray upon which sat a silver tea pot and jug and the necessary cups and saucers. Her part in the celebrations was however curtailed by the bell in the front announcing a visitor.

She placed the tray on Mr Braithwaite's desk and returned to the front desk.
They heard a now familiar pompous voice.

'Get Braithwaite for me.'

'He has visitors, sir,' Miss Reed politely and firmly informed him.

'This won't take a minute.' They heard Miss Reed protest but, seconds later, the large frame of George Stokesley filled the doorway.

'What the hell are you doing here?' he snarled.

And then, turning on Arthur Braithwaite, with equal venom, he demanded,

'What the bloody hell is going on Braithwaite?'

The recipient of the abuse carefully returned his cup to its saucer and calmly turned to face the bullying face.

'I don't remember inviting you in here Stokesley, so I will be obliged if you will leave.'

'I will leave when you have heard what I came here to say; my offer for this run down business. Do you accept it?'

Arthur Braithwaite leaned forward, gently rubbing his hands in anticipation. As a schoolboy he had been bullied by Stokesley and this was the first time he had ever held the upper hand and he was really enjoying himself. His answer was monosyllabic.

'NO'.

James and Kate were also enjoying it, unlike Stokesley they knew were this was leading.

'What do you mean no?' His face was as puce as the other day in the shooting bothy.

Arthur Braithwaite gave James a knowing look.

'Quite simply I am not empowered to any longer make that decision.'

James intervened. 'Mr Braithwaite has decided to sell the business to me.'

Having let this sink in, he continued,

'As I understand it George, and these are your words not mine, you are an Auctioneer and Valuer and I am an Estate Agent and this is an Estate Agency and I think it quite probable that you have valued these premises with a view to asset stripping them with no heed to the future of Miss Reed or other people we intend to employ in the future, I think that is how it is – yes?'

Stokesley turned on his heel. The invective in his voice not disguised as he pointed a finger at James. 'You will regret this.'

James looked at him and very calmly said, 'Stokesley, I have flattened bigger bullies on the rugby field than you so your ranting holds no terrors for me, do I make myself clear?'

The intruder pointed his finger menacingly at Arthur Braithwaite. 'You will regret this'.

He stormed out, closing the front door so violently that the pictures shook on the wall in Mr Braithwaite's office.

James having taken the reins from Kate continued,

'Our lawyers will contact you tomorrow Arthur.' He hesitated, 'I may call you Arthur?'

The older man took his hand. 'Yes of course and I would like to be as familiar with you and Kate.'

'We will both be delighted,' Kate assured him.

The Surveyor looked enquiringly at James. 'Your visit and Stokesley's sudden interest, it all seems so mysterious, is there a connection?'

'Arthur, to answer a question with a question, just when did Stokesley make you his offer?'

'As a matter of fact it was only yesterday.'

'Something was said at a shoot dinner that triggered both our overtures, the resolution to your conundrum is Gerry Seymour. Speaking for myself and for Kate and, I hope, Miss Reed, I am so delighted to be able to establish a relationship with Yorkshire – it does after all have the best racecourse in the UK and we hope you will join us when our filly is running in the Lowther.

'Indeed I will. You must have a very decent young horse to be running in such a race, it is after all the supposed guideline for next year's One Thousand Guineas. I look forward to it very much, in fact, it is so long since I went out I had forgotten what anticipation means.'

He stood up and proffered his hand. 'Good luck, I am delighted to have met you both, particularly you Kate.' He winked at her; something he had not done since he was a young man.

She blushed disarmingly and they said there adieus, all of them genuinely looking forward to meeting in the Owner & Trainers Bar at the Ebor meeting.

– 'We will leaveyou a badge'; she promised.

They walked with obvious excitement to the front office, where an ecstatic Miss Reed opened the front door for them and watched as they walked hand in hand back to the car.

On reaching it, James turned towards her, unaware that they were being observed by a still apoplectic George Stokesley. He held her with both hands at arm's length, his face full of admiration.

'Where did you learn to negotiate like that?'

Her face still flushed with excitement she confessed, 'I don't know, I just somehow found the right words, a mixture of what I have heard you and Daddy say I suppose.' She shrugged her shoulders and burst out laughing. 'Mind you it's a great feeling; I can see why it gives you such a buzz and why you can't wait for Monday mornings to come round.'

'Well Mrs Carrington, you have proved you can do it and this little venture is going to be your baby; how does that grab you?'

'You mean that don't you?' And without waiting for an answer, she hugged him. 'I will show you Mr Carrington what woman power can do. Meanwhile, what about this lunch you promised me?'

He opened the car door for her. 'Right away, madam.'

In high spirits, they crossed Ousegate Bridge and departed via the medieval exit from the city walls at Micklegate. Heading towards the racecourse they past the many fine Georgian buildings on Blossom Street and the Mount until Kate recognising the Knavesmire entrance on Tadcaster Road also spotted the sign for the historic Chase Hotel.

He parked and chauffeur-like, opened the passenger door and greeted her still smiling face with. 'And this madam, very much like yourself, is where my first commercial enterprise started.'

Hand in hand he led her, his schoolboy memory clicking in unerringly, to the Lounge Bar. Seating her in the same window seat he had sat in as a fourteen year old boy, he repaired to the bar and ordered two halves of John Smith's Bitter shandy. He re-joined her and explained.

'When I was fourteen and my father was restocking with day old chicks, he brought me to Yorkshire for the first time and, with funds saved from my pocket money and odd jobs during the school holidays, I bought some young turkeys which I fattened up for Christmas. So, like you, my first business venture started in this great county.'

The barman arrived with the drinks. He raised his glass.

'This John Smith's Bitter is the official way to toast a new venture up here, or it is at least becoming so in our family. I propose a toast to you Kate darling. To Braithwaite Palmer Ltd.'

'Thank you James; This time I am stuck for words.'

They enjoyed a beef sandwich; 'grown just down the road' the barman had assured them, before they slightly reluctantly returned to the car and continued their journey home.

They headed out of York along the Tadcaster Road before joining the A1 where he was able put his foot down and allow the Bentley to show its paces as they roared south past Doncaster and Grantham until they saw the familiar signs for Belvoir Castle. They turned into the vale and on to Woolmington.

It was much later than he had intended and so stopping only to carry the suitcases in, he set off back to Nottingham.

'Get the maids to unpack please darling and telephone Connie and tell them I will be about fifty minutes.'

'I knew we should have trouble with you, but it is back to reality and I do at least have my own dreams now.'

He laughed and kissed her.

'Love you'. A swirl of gravel and he was gone, heading for the office, really excited at the prospect of being back at work.

CHAPTER THIRTY

They heard him arrive, it was good to have him back; they had all worked hard, they always did, but not at the speed as when he was around - maybe he just thought faster or, more probably, he came to decisions more quickly. Whatever, they all automatically trooped into the Board Room for an update; the air was one of expectancy.

The plans were already pinned to the walls and standing rather diffidently at the side of them a young man of maybe twenty-two or twenty-three whom James had not met before.

He walked over to him, liking the confident open face; it reminded him of himself at that age.

'You must be Giles Moorcroft, which is most appropriate as I have just come back from the Yorkshire Moors. I have heard a lot about you and, since it was Tim Cooper who said it, I have every confidence that you come well recommended.'

'Thank you, sir.'

James looked him and smiled.

'I spent a few days in Yorkshire with all these 'old' men of about forty-five or fifty, I feel young, for God's sake call me James, don't take the illusion away just yet.'

'Peter Pan more like,' Connie's aside, sparing Giles any further blushes.

The young architect studied the faces around the table.

'If you are happy with the concept, Tim will get two or three of our people on to it and we will have the finished drawings ready for the Planning meeting scheduled for October 21st.'

James nodded. 'I like it, everyone agreed?' He looked around the room.

The nodding heads signalling a yes.

'Let's go for it.'

The chairs scraped back, everyone eager to push on with the new project; he raised his hand. 'One further item for the Board to debate,' he announced.

'We have acquired an Estate Agency to add to our Portfolio – in York', he added. There was a long silence before Edward Lawson spoke.

`I cannot believe you are serious James, we are up to our necks in these conversions and, it is in York, which is exactly contrary to your logic for dropping the South Coast and concentrating on our own turf.'

Edward was obviously not best pleased and the others waited for the sales pitch and reasoning from their Chairman. When it came, it took them by surprise; it was an idea that he had been fleshing out on the journey from Woolmington to Nottingham.

The initial germ of the idea, he explained, had been formulated when on the drive up to Strudwick Moor he had been struck by the number of large houses which, on the evidence of their state of repair, appeared to be suffering the same fate as Watkin Hall. They were too large for one family and it would not be long before more of these fine properties became host to pigs or poultry.

Distance and accessibility was not on the scale of Bournemouth - Yorkshire adjoined Nottinghamshire he argued and the A1 trunk road offered a direct link, as did the train service. Nor, he insisted, would the only consideration be full time residential occupancy. Yorkshire had an attractive coastline in and around Scarborough and Whitby; superb countryside on the North Yorkshire Moors and it hosted major sporting events such as racing, shooting and cricket festivals. For all of these occasions, people rented property for one or two weeks or more. And more importantly, he emphasised, lots of these visitors are looking to buy.

They listened but without their usual conviction, even Connie wasn't enthusiastic, going so far as to say he should consult the Board before making such far-reaching decisions. He had not anticipated this; he was not used to having to defend his strategy or changing rational. Looking extremely irritated, he stood up and demanded a vote. This stopped the bickering over the concept, but did not stop Edward challenging the drain on cash flow.

He looked at them and they recognized the signs, he would not give up on an idea if he believed in it. His next statement did, however, take them by surprise.
`Record the proposal in the minutes as overruled,' he instructed Connie.

`Will you also add,' and he looked at them all in turn, 'that the recommendation having been rejected by the Board, Mr and Mrs Carrington will be proceeding with the suggestion in a private capacity, and will be funding it from private resources.'
`James,' Edward appealed to him, 'maybe we can look at it again in a few months.' `No, the matter is closed. Permanently.'

The white flag was rejected with an emphasis that surprised them all. It was the very first chink in the corporate armour. Someone had to move quickly before the situation deteriorated and the company suffered. It was Connie.
`We all need outside interests; Tim for instance has his architecture practice. I propose that we all wish James and Kate well with their project, we can all be certain that James's pride will not let it detract from his enthusiasm here'.

Edward Lawson held out his hand. 'Pax?' James took the proffered palm. 'Pax.'
The day was saved and, although he was loathe to admit it, he had taken them for granted once too often. This was no longer a small family business that could rely on friendship and ties of loyalty; it was a highly successful and diversified company with major institutions such as merchant banks to whom accountability and not personal whims were a pre-requisite.

He left the meeting wondering how he was going to break the news to Kate; just as suddenly he put it to one side, as Connie had rightly presumed it would not intrude on his responsibilities at Fordmill.

The consideration did, however, germinate an interesting thought. The afternoon passed swiftly as he devoured the heap of essential paperwork in his in-tray. Connie or one of the others had dealt with the less essential matters, a far cry from the early days when he had done just about everything including the wages and accounts. Like most people that have started a business from scratch, he had learned through hard experience the basic and fundamental skills of running a company. Now the scales were much greater but the essence was still the same, he had not forgotten them, a fact that dovetailed rather neatly with the other thought he had conceived earlier.

At six thirty he called it a day and set out for Woolmington. As he drove, he pondered again how to present the events of the board meeting. If he recounted verbatim the reaction of the others, he knew Kate would strike a defensive pose that would reconcile her to the majority decision. Since that position had now been totally usurped, he decided to adopt a proactive stance and so his response to her enquiry

'How did your meeting go?'

'it was fine, I explained that we needed a new impetus and that you and I had formed a new company, albeit under the old and established banner of Miller Braithwaite'

'You did what?' Her expression was incredulous.

'It was the least I could do, seeing how you singlehandedly persuaded old Braithwaite to sell us his firm.'

'But James I know nothing about business.'

'You know more than you realise and it will be an exciting challenge now that the boys are away at school.'

'It will also give us an excuse to visit Yorkshire,' she conceded, her initial resistance diluting.

He held her closely; he was excited at the prospect and sensed that she too, now that the surprise had passed, felt the same.

Taking her hand he marched her out of the house and across the yard to the stone steps that led to his office. The evening still being warm he left the top open so that they could enjoy the sunlight that angled in from over the stable roof tops opposite.

He waved Kate to sit at the large conference table. 'At the far end,' he instructed.

'We need a business plan and the first thing we have to decide is the name of the company.'

'Why?' she countered, 'Miller Braithwaite is an established name, although we do need to advise a change of management.'

She pursed her lips and continued thoughtfully.

'We also have Miss Reed to consider - I feel she is integral to the success of the business. We must encourage her to assume responsibility and give her an appropriate title and a salary to match. She will also need an assistant, probably a man who is suitably qualified; in fact, why don't we acquire a similar firm in say Harrogate and kill two birds with one stone.' She continued to list the opportunities that must exist in such a wealthy area of the country, growing evermore excited at the prospect and the challenge. James closed the leather bound ledger in which he kept his meeting notes. 'Apart from the colour of the notepaper, you haven't missed a trick.'

'I suggest cream with dark blue lettering.'

They both laughed at her spontaneous reply, as ever completely in accord. 'Now you know why I suggested you sat at the head of the table, Madam Chair.'

Thus began his business relationship with his wife, his commercial judgement proving to be once again spot-on. Kate was effortlessly in tune with his aspirations and, having been given the opportunity she seized it with both hands.

She was naturally intelligent and inquisitive and not surprisingly, being the product of three generations of lawyers, her thinking was pragmatic. Her financial instincts too were based on a sound bedrock that demanded value for money.

`Are you sure you do not have Yorkshire forebears?' he chided her.

Once she had accepted the responsibility, she needed no encouragement to travel up to York and begin the search for a partner in the Harrogate area. Heeding her own advice, the first person she consulted was Miss Reed who, when asked to confide her Christian name, admitted to Alice. `But please call me Liz, everyone does, Alice makes me feel about eighty.'

Kate laughingly acknowledged her distress and sat her down with a pot of tea and expounded her plans to an increasingly excited and enthusiastic ally.

`The first thing we need to do Mrs Carrington, sorry I mean Kate, is to improve our image. I suspect that your offices are modern and generate an atmosphere of a company that has a future as well as a respectable past.'

Kate nodded; she knew she had chosen well in the determined young woman who sat so confidently across the desk from her. `What should we do first?' she enquired.

`Get rid of all these old dark desks and filing cabinets and remove the screen across the window so that people can look in and be aware that we are changing with the times.'

Her voice was excited and the enthusiasm rubbed off on Kate who joined in,

`Maybe we should take down the wall that separates the reception from Mr Braithwaite's office, have one big workspace, it is certainly what Fordmill are doing for their commercial clients'.

`That will make a big statement to the public and, situated where we are in the city centre with constant footfall on the pavement, word will spread very quickly.'

`You make a very good point,' Kate acknowledged.

`In fact I am certain, having listened to your reasoning, that this should be our priority. Until now I had thought that finding a partner in the Harrogate area so that we can expand was the number one issue.' Liz took up the running again. `If we get this office back on the map it will make it a far more attractive proposition to any would-be partner.'

The ideas flowed endlessly and they had several positive objectives listed in Kate's leather bound ledger. She firmly closed the book at six thirty but not before she had drawn Liz's attention to the inscription inside the font cover.

Miller Braithwaite the North's largest firm of Estate Agents.

`That sounds like Mr Carrington.'

`Can you imagine living with him Liz, he never stops?'

Miss Reed smiled. `It must be exhausting.' What she did not say was `there would be no shortage of applicants if the position became vacant!'

`We have achieved a lot today, so why don't you join me at the hotel for supper and maybe we can start to solve the problem that did not intrude on our discussions today, namely how do we get some clients through the door - ASAP.'

Liz signalled her delight and drove her new MD to the Chase Hotel in her pride and joy, a Citroen 2CV that's red paintwork was adorned with giant ladybirds.

`The firm will of course provide its Partners with a company car,' Kate confided, as she extricated herself from the less than luxurious carriage.

Liz stood open mouthed, slightly dumfounded and querulously managed one word. `Partner?'

Kate took her hand. `Please say you accept, I had meant to save it until this evening when we had a glass of something appropriate in our hands.'

Completely out of character, Liz Reed leaned forward and gave her new boss a peck on the cheek.

`Thank you, I promise you this will be a decision you will never regret.'

The evening lived up to its auspicious start, both women easy in each other's company and fiercely determined to succeed. They had several glasses of champagne and, since there was no Bollinger readily available, they resorted to Taittinger.

`From now on, this will be our tipple, it will define our independence,' an exultant Kate declared.

'To Miller Braithwaite, the largest firm of Estate Agents in the North.'

The equally optimistic and slightly tipsy new Partner happily acknowledged the salutation and also the suggestion that, in view of the liquid celebrations, she should stay the night at the Chase. The following morning they clambered aboard the Citroen and set out for the office anxious to set the ball rolling.

Kate had rejected the idea of asking Fordmill to do the alterations, it was too small and they needed to establish on ongoing relationship with a local builder, this was after all, only the first of many makeovers she planned as the company grew.

She consulted the 'Thompson's Business Directory,' trying to outguess the claims of quality and professionalism that all the advertisements proclaimed. Her first four choices assured her they could make an early start but were unable or unwilling to commit themselves to a contract that would penalize them if they did not complete on time. She turned to what appeared to be smaller firms but here the stumbling block was that they were out working and not at home to answer the phone. By midday her early optimism had turned to exasperation so, needing to clear her head, she decided on a stroll along the banks of the adjacent River Ouse.

On the opposite side of the river, two bricklayers were chopping out a hole in the wall of a warehouse that fronted onto the city of York's main waterfront, presumably to fit the window frame that stood on its end a few feet away.

They were both young, about twenty two or three she decided, and were more than a little surprised when the elegant by-passer greeted them.

She pointed to the name on the small truck, from which hung two donkey jackets presumably belonging to the two men despite the name on the back of each which proclaimed 'Wimpey'.

`Are either of you Mr Wright, or perhaps Mr Wimpey?'

Her infectious smile evoked the answer she had hoped for as the taller of the two denied either title.

`No such luck, we just work for old man Wright, although the way things are going it won't be for much longer.'

`Why not?' Her concern now for them.

`The old man, Dick, he just isn't interested any more, it is sad really, we started together six years ago, it was the best small building firm in York. We did alterations and repairs for all the big landowners and toffs for miles around. Every couple of years Mr Wright would take on two apprentices, he was a perfectionist and unless you started here, he would not employ you.

`We had about forty men until David was killed, and now we do jobs like this,' his mate added. She looked at them quizzically and they took up the story again.

`Mr Wright's son David was killed in a car crash on the A64 near to Malton just over a year ago, it has just about destroyed him and the business is on its last legs. Gary and me, I'm Dave by the way, are the only two left.'

'And we only stay because we feel sorry for him; if the firm closed down completely it would finish him off.' Gary's nod confirming Dave's assessment.

Kate took a business card from her handbag and handed it to Dave.

'Will you two come and see me at my office when you finish here this evening, - say six o'clock?'

They looked enquiringly at her. 'It will be to your advantage,' she assured them.

She hurried away, Liz would be getting anxious and she needed her to hold the fort this afternoon.

'I have to go out, it is to do with the alterations, I will explain later.'

Just what James would have done; the thought gave her confidence.

She walked briskly to the railway station and asked the driver of the black cab that stood at the head of the rank to take her to Shipton on the outskirts of York.

'What address lady?' the driver enquired.

'I don't know exactly, it is a building company called Wright's, they have blue trucks, does that help?' She felt her confidence falter, it sounded rather feeble. The cabbie restored her resolve. 'No problem, Wright's have been around for yonks; mind you, they are not what they were.'

Kate tried to rehearse in her head what she intended to say to Mr Wright, but it was hopeless as the cabbie, like so many of his breed, subjected her to a nonstop barrage of questions on where she was from, why she was up here, what did she do, the latter bit of information eliciting.

'Good timing that, the housing market will be booming soon,' he affirmed confidently. She did not bother asking on what he based his assertions and was spared further by the road sign which announced their arrival in the village. He swung into a lane on the right hand side of the A19 and continued past several houses until, after a few hundred yards they came to a long stone wall, the pair of blue gates in the middle announcing this as the premises of 'R Wright Ltd, Builders since 1883'. She stepped out of the cab and asked him to wait, adding that she did not know for how long. 'No problem lady,' he assured her as he resumed his tortuous attempt at the Mirror crossword.

She opened the wicket gate set in the larger pair of gates and stepped through. Taking a deep breath and remembering James's advice when they had called upon Arthur Hardcastle 'to play it by ear'.

She tugged on the black knob that was set in the stone jamb of the doorway. She heard the old-fashioned bell ring out, presumably in the kitchen.

With heart pounding she waited, but there was no response and she wrestled with her instincts to leave or to ring again and risk the occupants' wrath. Just as she had plucked up courage to try again she was aware of dog standing behind her, tail wagging furiously. Close behind the English Setter, a grey haired man shuffled across the gravel towards her.

'Can I help you?' The voice was tired but not aggressive.

'Mr Wright, I am Kate Carrington, please forgive my intrusion but I would be so grateful if you would spare me a few minutes of your time.' She smiled, her face sympathetic and disarming. He regarded her for a few long seconds before producing a key from the pocket of his cardigan.

He opened the large studded front door, its paintwork heavy and glossy, a testimony to his reputation for quality. He led Kate into a panelled hall from which sprang a similar oak staircase which, like the hallway, was host to several attractive water colours, each one bearing the initials RSW.

She followed him into the kitchen, which whilst not dirty was untidy, with yesterday's dishes washed and stacked on the table together with weeks of newspapers; She recognized the signs of a lonely man bereft of any purpose, meanwhile he lifted the Aga lid and interrupted her thoughts.

'May I offer you a cup of tea?' She nodded, grateful for the time this would allow her to gain his empathy for what she proposed.

'Did you build this house?' She enquired kindly and with genuine interest.

`My father did in 1913, the year before he married, I remember growing up here, I had hoped to see my grandchildren do the same but not now.'
His voice reduced to a trembling hoarse whisper as he reached for the silver framed photograph.

`Now, not only have I lost my son, the firm too is lost and my grandson will not have the chance to carry on the business, I had so looked forward to our centenary year.' The kettle whistled, but he was oblivious to it, lost in his dreams of what should have been.

Kate stood up and gently squeezed his hand. `Let me make the tea.' He nodded and sat down at the large pine table. The vast array of stacked crockery yielded without question, the teapot and cups and saucers; the tea caddy and the sugar bowl stood on the dresser and she rightly assumed that the milk would live in the fridge.

She poured the tea and passed the milk towards him, he poured a very small amount into his tea, added two heaped spoons of sugar and for the first time in a long time, a smile crossed his face. `Proper builders' tea is that, you can stand your spoon up in it.'

`Mr Wright,' she began hesitantly, but then taking, courage in both hands, started again.

`Mr Wright, I have come here today to make a proposal to you. I believe that what you have told me today makes my visit even more worthwhile, as your hopes as well as mine can be at least partially realized.

He looked enquiringly at her.

`Without being unkind my dear, I cannot imagine how that can be.'
She gained in confidence and continued.

`I met two very nice young men today, two very proud young men, they told me they worked for the most respected building company in Yorkshire.'
A gentle affectionate expression crossed his lined face, `Dave and Gary.'
She nodded. `They also told me about the tragic loss of your son and, even though they would soon be out of a job, of the respect they had for you and the pride that being trained by you, meant to them. Everyone will employ a man with that pedigree,' was how they put it.'

`You are very kind Mrs Carrington, but how can we possibly help each other?'

Kate explained to him of her expansion plans for Miller Braithwaite and her inability to secure the services of top class builders to push that programme through. She sought his opinion of the two young builders, `were they manager material, could they run a business?'

`With guidance yes, 1 have no doubt of that. We only ever took on apprentices that we thought could one day be capable of running a contract.'
She looked at him intensely, willing him to say yes.

`Mr Wright, will you offer them that guidance, help them to save this business and safeguard it for your grandson?'
The eyes were misted over and the word was hardly audible but it was `Yes'.
Kate's own eyes were rather clouded as she also replied with a monosyllabic `Thank you'.

They shook hands and she was surprised to hear herself saying.
`I am meeting Dave and Gary at six o'clock; will you come with me to break the good news?'

He was equally amazed to hear himself not only agreeing to her request but also to telling her to dismiss the taxi as he would drive them into York.

With a spring in her step, she retraced her way down the hall and to the reclining cabbie waiting in the lane. She paid him off and took a turn around the garden whilst Dick Wright spruced himself up for the journey into town.

They arrived at the office at five-thirty to relate to an astounded Liz Reed, the solution to their problems and the rebirth of Wright and Son.

The scale of Liz's surprise was, however, very small on the Richter scale compared with that of Dave and Gary who, when invited into the back office, just stared at their boss.

When they did finally speak, it was not to ask what brought him there, it was a simple and concerned, `Mr Wright, how are you?'

`Very much the better for having met Mrs Carrington, she has done more than resurrect my business she has given me the will to live.'

Liz reappeared with a tray of tea, three mugs of builders' brew and two genteel Earl Greys. The atmosphere was light as Kate waved them to sit around the table onto which she rolled out a plan, yellow with age, of the building in which they sat.

`We intend, with your help, to remove the wall between this office and the main reception area.'

`You will need an RSJ – a steel beam,' Gary explained, realizing as he said it that he was not talking to two uninformed ladies, adding disarmingly; `Sorry Ladies.'

`How soon can we do it?' Kate stepped in to save his blushes.

`For you Mrs Carrington, we will come in over the weekend, get the wall down, put the beam in and have it plastered. It will need a few days to dry out before we can paint it, but at least anyone looking through the window will know that things are happening.'

Dick Wright turned the plans around so that he could see them more clearly.
`As regards the shop-fitting, I will come in tomorrow with my tape measure and you can explain what you are planning in the way of permanent fixtures and fittings.'

`Why not ask Roger and Ron to come back? I know they are fed up sitting around at home.' Gary looked at Kate, `R & R' – Rolls Royce was their nickname wasn't it, Mr Wright?'

The old man nodded approvingly; `Good thinking Gary.' And then turning towards her,

`You leave the alterations to us Kate, you ladies meantime can concentrate on finding the next Agency for us to reorganize!'
The easy use of her Christian name and the fact that he was looking forward was as surprising to himself as to the others and they adjourned at seven fifteen in high spirits.

When she reached the hotel, Kate felt totally and utterly exhausted, her only intention to have a hot bath and an early night. James was coming up tomorrow; she had so much to tell him, but most of all she wanted to hold him and, if she was honest, hear his approval. She felt pretty confident about that, she knew how he admired people that made things happen; he was certainly someone who did and, as she lay in the bath thinking of all the things he had done, this consideration struck home properly for the first time. Where did her husband get his seemingly endless source of energy; did he never feel this tired or was his secret never to admit it?

She slept like a log, in fact was woken by the telephone at the side of the bed. It was Liz.

`Kate, Mr Wright is here, I have outlined what we need and told him you had a business meeting so there is no panic, I have called to make sure you haven't changed your ideas.'

`Thanks Liz, I will be about half an hour or so.'
She showered and dressed quickly and forty five minutes later appeared in the Agency doorway with a leather handled wallpaper book in each hand. She winked conspiratorially at her Partner. `I have been looking at wallpapers. I think the Sanderson's are a bit too traditional; this Rasch collection from Germany, on the other hand, is more our cup of tea. Talking of which why don't we have one?'

They went through to the as-yet unmolested office, hardly able to contain themselves.

Dick Wright heard the shrieks of laughter and wondered what on earth could be so amusing about wallpaper.

James Carrington arrived at four twenty, the effect upon Liz Reed as tremulous as when she had first seen him. They sat around the large desk in the back office, James insisting that his wife sit where Mr. Hardcastle had sat. She opened her ledger and read out the points they had so far either resolved or were in the process of doing; the only major item they had not yet addressed was the choice of a business partner in the Harrogate catchment area.

He was impressed and told them so, he had every confidence in his wife's business acumen but was still surprised at the speed at which they had moved. His decision to abrogate his own responsibility and leave them to it was eminently the right thing to have done. He personally would have concentrated on the acquisition of another practice so that they would have had some properties to sell. He decided to tease it out of them. His fears however were unfounded; Kate informed him that they would be closed on Saturday so that Dave and Gary could remove the office wall; she and Liz intended to visit all the Estate Agencies in the Harrogate and Ripon areas to decide which would most closely mesh with their own.

`We are also,' she disappeared briefly into the front office, 'displaying this in the window.' It was an artist's impression of what the new offices would look like.
`Dick, as he insists we now call him, brought it in this afternoon - isn't it brilliant? Mind you, I am not surprised as I saw several very good watercolours in his house, they all bore the initials RSW.'

James shook his head ruefully. 'I am surplus to requirements here.'
Kate took his arm. `I only dare do these things because I know you are there to bale me out if they go wrong.'

She winked to Liz. 'I think that calls for a drink, don't go away.'
She set out for the kitchen, returning shortly with a bottle of Taittinger. He did the honours and she confided that this was the product of Rheims they had chosen to symbolize Miller Braithwaite

`I suppose it will make me appreciate the Bollinger all better when I get home,' he chided them.

CHAPTER THIRTY ONE

The last of the Bournemouth developments were finally drawing to a close and, with new projects occupying his thoughts, James found the site visits increasingly irksome and time consuming. The Nursing home, a stately old building, similar in many respects in style to the Watkin Hall development, was being modernised to provide care for the elderly, and was intended to be the last in this area.

They had been plagued with problems; an excavation to build the footings for a new communal lounge area had revealed 'running sand ' that necessitated expensive shuttering to shore it up. The long and exceptionally cold winter had dragged on, it had been March before they could pour the concrete and then, just when they were set to go, one of the workmen had uncovered a skeleton.

Work ceased immediately to allow first the police and then the local archaeologists to investigate. Fortunately, at least from the Fordmill point of view, the remains were adjudged by the pathologist to have been there only twenty or thirty years and, as nothing else of interest or help was discovered, work resumed one week later.

The prospect of the digging being a Stone Age burial site or similar, demanding years of arduous exploration, made him go cold. The financial implications of one week when added to the other delays occasioned by the weather were serious enough, particularly when the plant and machinery were desperately needed on site in the East Midlands.

The thought of it urged him to be back and he drove swiftly through the Cotswolds. However, even in this black humour he could not but be impressed by the scenery that flashed by. He drove past the Lygon Arms in Broadway, his mind casting back to the halcyon nights spent there with Rachel. He still experienced a surge in his groin when he thought of her, increasingly wondered if he could have continued the liaison after he was married, often ruminated on how they could discreetly pick up the threads.

He had been so confident when he had told her so emphatically that the affair was over, so certain that his love for Kate would satisfy his every need. Those vows made so lovingly in the sight of all their family and friends just ten years ago, he had remained resolutely faithful to, although on occasions such as this he had to admit the temptation.

His mind flicked backwards through the album of memories, recalling so easily every detail. The wedding itself, no expense spared by Jeremy Palmer to make this day complete for his beloved daughter. She had been stunning, breathtakingly so and he remembered the choke in his throat when she joined him at the altar.

His mind drifted on to the honeymoon spent in Paris, at the Ritz of course.
'Where else do celebrities stay?' he had laughed.

They had walked those magical streets as all lovers should, arm in arm, stopping at the bistro's and wayside cafes fascinated by it all, particularly the picturesque atmosphere of Montmartre which was both the literary and artistic centre of this enchanting city. They had climbed the endless steps to view the Baroque splendour of Sacre Coeur, standing as it does so majestically at the top of Montmartre hill and then returning back down in the cable railway.

'Don't you think we should have done that the other way around?' she had teased.

After the exquisite pleasures of the capital they had drifted down to the Loire Valley, a meandering route that his own parents had idled along some thirty years earlier.

If anything could be a prescription for a happy life, then surely this must be it.

This is a corner of France full of gems, architectural and gastronomical; Balzac wrote some glowing testimonies to its charm, for anyone else to attempt the same would be fatuous.

He remembered the drive to Azay-le-Rideau, the excitement Kate's red open-top.

Morgan had created when they arrived in the town. It is a small place sitting on the Indre river; nothing of consequence has shattered it's idyllic calm for centuries and from the Chateau surrounded by its moat, to the parks and woods that encompass its boundaries, it is a perfect spot for lovers to come to know each other. He thought of the photograph on his desk, he had taken it as the roundabout on which they had played like adolescents had brought her back into view. She was smiling and serene, so confident in her love for him and the future.

The other names that still sprang to mind, Villandry, Amboise, Blois, Cheverny and the priceless jewel in the crown, the Chateau of Chenonceau. Not as big as Chambord, but the sight of its classical lines and turrets as it sits aside the river Cher remains with one forever. The memories were bathed in love and expectation.

What had gone wrong? They had been so completely in love, so wrapped up in each other that not even the emerging Fordmill giant could intrude into their private idyll.

The following July his eldest son was born. The Times had proudly announced to the world, 'On July 18th To Kate (née Palmer) and James Carrington, a son Charles Jeremy Robert'.

The following year on November the 21st a similar insertion proclaimed the arrival of Edward Timothy Miles.

He remembered as if yesterday, the immense satisfaction he had felt when he showed to his mother the letter from Uppingham confirming their entries to the school.

'Brooklands House naturally,' he confided.

'Your father would have been so proud.' Elizabeth Carrington brushed away the small tear that was forming in the corner of her right eye.

Where oh where had it all gone wrong, where had the magic gone?

It was not that Kate had lost her figure, she was still extremely elegant, he was proud to be seen with her, but the excitement that had marked her out had gone, she seemed more and more to turn her attention inwards to the boys.

Only last week he had spontaneously pressed some money into her hand.

'Buy yourself a new dress.'

To his acute disappointment she returned from Nottingham with new shoes for the boys. He still felt sad recalling it.

The sound of a milk float and its tinkling cargo returned his thoughts to the present.

He became aware of the scenery changing from the warm yellow Cotswold stone to the olde worlde charm of black and white half-timbered houses of Warwickshire that to many, particularly foreign visitors, represents the quintessential spirit of England, embracing as it does Stratford-upon-Avon and the endless reminders of the Bard.

It was against this rural charm that he saw, unbelievably, two JCB diggers in Fordmill livery, digging out the footings of a large building, nearby stood two lorries each half full of soil, they too were emblazoned 'Fordmill Construction'.

He pulled the car into the next lay-by and walked back to the site. Trying to appear composed and casual he called out to the nearest driver who responded with a cheerful,

'Morning Mr Carrington'.

'Been here long?' The enquiry as low key as he could manage.

'Mr Lawson sent us on Friday evening Boss.'

James was fuming; worse still he was inwardly confused and shaken by the surprise discovery. Rather than show his hand however, he decided to leave.

'Just passing Reg, no need to mention it.'

He returned to the car, all thoughts of Rachel and amorous liaisons erased by the sight of the machines digging behind him. He could not believe it, they were pressed for short term cash, both the major developments at Bournemouth and Derby were, as a result of the hard winter, running behind schedule and yet here, in the midst of nowhere, his equipment and workmen were earning money on the side.

He ate up the few remaining miles to Woolmington, his mood by now extremely dark, snorting out the essential details to Kate and dismissing without consideration her ineffectual attempts to justify what he had seen.

As ever when in a crisis, and needing a good listener, he telephoned Jack Priory.

'He is playing golf at Hollinwell'. Wendy's reply closing this avenue.

He stamped into his study, the slamming of the sturdy oak door helping to relieve the tension that had built up inside him.

He poured a large Macallan and sat there staring at it, wondering how Edward, the cautious saver of every penny, could possibly condone this expenditure, particularly at a time when every cent was so important.

The morning saw him at work at seven thirty. He went immediately to the Accounts Office, opened the safe and took out the Petty Cash book. What he saw confirmed his worst fears, over a period of several months, various sums had been withdrawn in cash, each one initialled E.L.

So it was true, his worst fears confirmed, Edward Lawson had been siphoning off funds for his own project; what else had been misappropriated? How could Edward, whom he had trusted for so long, take money out of business at a time like this when they were so strapped for short-term cash?

James sat there, his head in his hands hardly daring to contemplate what other funds might have disappeared. He had confided everything to the big man for so long; had abdicated all financial decisions to him, relieved to do so, he had been so busy driving the company forward he did not have the time or, to be honest the inclination, to check the minutiae of the day to day finances.

Why had the accountants not picked it up, were they in cahoots with Edward Lawson?

He looked again at the withdrawal dates – they were all in this current financial year so, of course, they would not yet have seen them.

He was brought back to the present by the arrival of the subject of his thoughts, who declared,

'Don't often see you in accounts.'

'Precisely.'

The icy sneer in his voice provoking a surprised response.

'James, what the hell is going on?'

'You tell me?' He proffered the open Petty Cash book and said, this time more quietly,

'Not only are you taking cash out of the business, you even have the audacity to sanction it yourself.'

'James for God's sake, I am the Financial Director of this company, I have been for several years, I am not a junior clerk who has to ask permission to authorise a few quid.'

'Just how much is a few quid and does it stop at a few quid?'

Edward Lawson looked him squarely in the eye.

'I cannot believe I am hearing what you are implying; after all I have done for you. Since you were fourteen years of age, I have watched your back, followed your fanciful dreams, worked my bloody balls off for you and you dare to accuse me of fiddling the books.'

'Well, if there is an explanation, I apologise.' He looked enquiringly at his friend of so many years.

'If I have to give you an explanation, then the bond between us is broken forever.'

The two men stared at each other, the air congealed with willpower as each tried to break the others gaze.

Footsteps in the entrance hall caused them both to turn and see Connie, her cheeks flushed with excitement.

'Has Edward told you?' her voice breathless. James turned to see her smiling enquiringly at him.

'Told me what?' He tried to lighten his voice, but some of the hard edge remained. She appeared not to notice.

'We are engaged.'

'Now I really am on my own.' Even as he said it he regretted it, but it was too late. Edward took Connie by the arm.

'Come on, we are leaving, he can run the bloody company on his own from now on.'

A bewildered Connie was ushered out and he heard the engines start in unison as they left the car park in a shower of gravel.

He sat staring through the window, seeing nothing and regretting everything. He knew he had handled the situation badly, he knew what he should do, but he was too proud, the stubborn streak of the Staincliffes that he inherited from his mother's family would not let him back down.

He did concede to himself that he wo uld talk to them when they came back, listen to their explanations. But they did not come back and the turmoil that followed would cost James Carrington dearly.

CHAPTER THIRTY TWO

The following day he received a letter from Andrew Harker, Senior Partner of Baxter, Grimshaw & Harker in Leicester. This confirmed the verbal resignations of Edward Lawson and Miss Constance Cummings from the board of Fordmill and all subsidiary companies. This was to take effect immediately.

He sought the council of Anthony Jayes; this however fell on deaf ears. As a friend of both parties he politely and sympathetically declined to take sides. Tim Cooper meanwhile had heard the news from a very distraught Connie.

Worse still, Kate was less than supportive, insisting that her husband should suppress his pride and remember just how much he owed his friend, out of loyalty for the past if nothing else.

'I cannot believe Edward would do anything like this and I told you so on Sunday. Once again James you have marched in with your great big feet and it would appear that your luck has run out, because this time you don't have that big, kind man at your elbow to save your bacon.'

'Thank you for your support, I might have known you would take the line of least resistance.'

He slammed the door and stormed out into the stable yard, quickly climbing the open stone steps that led to his office.

The walls were festooned with photographs of horses, but there in the centre was a black and white photograph from which hung a dark blue satin cap proudly embroidered 'ENGLAND v SCOTLAND 1949. It belonged to Edward Lawson.

The self- same picture decorated with James's cap hung in Edward's study. They had exchanged these, after their second match together in the white shirts of England.

Over the years, the memory of that boyhood bond had been kept alight by the sight of these proud symbols.

To the photograph James had pasted a cutting from the Daily Telegraph; it read quite simply, 'Carrington and Lawson, an unstoppable duo'.

He stared into the picture, saw the bright expectation there and compared that with now.

His heart felt like a stone, his whole world was tumbling around him, on all sides he felt condemned and betrayed.

He retraced his steps and crossed to the other side of the stable yard, absentmindedly stroking the assortment of heads that poked enquiringly out,

'Wedding Belle' as usual laid back her ears.

'I might have known you would side against me,' he muttered.

He walked to the barn that housed the cars and slid back the twelve-foot high doors. He slipped into the Bentley and started the engine, glancing as he did so at the clock, six thirty-two he noted. The gesture reminded him vividly of Connie, her ear to the clock as she declared,

'It is true, as Rolls Royce claim, the sound of the clock is louder than the engine.'

This and the excitement as they travelled after a fine lunch at Severns Restaurant, to meet Mrs Watkin-Downes at Watkin Hall, so many wonderful memories...

He switched the engine off, his mind suddenly steeled by the poignancy of these reminders.

'Damn you all, it was me that founded Fordmill, it was me that negotiated with Martins Bank to provide the start-up capital, me that conceived the development at Bournemouth and persuaded a major Merchant Bank to back us and me that found Watkin Hall, and it is me to whom you always turn to point the new way forward.'

He stood there surrounded by the tangible signs of his success. The magnificent house they had so lovingly restored, the stable yard with its growing band of broodmares, the Bentley and all his other earthly treasures, he had come too far, fought too hard to surrender these.

The valedictory vow he had made as a fourteen year old as they left Milford Hall, to one day return as its master would not be quenched.

'Now that is all history, I will form a new team.'

Rather more easily than you will find a new leader, he sought to convince himself.

He needed time to think, to regroup his thoughts, to get away from the local reminders of his current dilemma, he had to get his life back on track and quickly.

The solution came sooner than he expected, the following day in fact as he was clearing his desk and preparing without much enthusiasm to go home, when his private telephone rang.

'Fancy a couple of days at Lytham?'

'When?'

'This weekend.'

'That will be fine, it's a great idea,' he enthused, 'Why don't we go up on Friday -; Shall I collect you about eight o'clock?'

'Fine, that will get us there about eleven and in time for a quick sandwich and then get in eighteen holes.'

He leaned back in his chair and contemplated for the first time in ages, actually enjoying himself and it would also get him from under Kate's feet and the oppressive atmosphere at home.

Friday morning on the dot, he swung the Bentley into Jack Priory's semi-circular gravel drive, almost simultaneously the front door opened and he was greeted by Wendy, the long-suffering wife of his golfing partner.

'Come in James, he won't be a minute.'

Sure enough, before he started to drink his coffee, the athletic figure in question joined them.

'Fancy a bacon sandwich to set us up for the drive?'

The invitation was too good to refuse and the hungry way in which he devoured it alerted Wendy's female wiles to the likelihood that Kate had not bothered to cook his breakfast or see him off this morning. She was right, last night had been like so many of late, fractious and unpleasant; the smallest comment capable of causing resentment and unkind words.

She squeezed his hand. 'Look after yourself and Jack.'

'Have you packed your golf shoes?'

This enquiry prompted by his last golfing holiday in France when he left his shoes at home and had to buy a new pair which blistered his heels and meant he could not play for the two remaining days.

James was privy to what had really happened – Mr Priory enjoying the local French hospitality, courtesy of a private guide in the form of very chic Madame, whose Diplomat husband was busy solving third world debt in North Africa. Blissfully unaware of this, Wendy chattered on about the cost of golf shoes in France compared to the UK.

Assuring his wife that he was fully equipped and with a knowing wink over her shoulder, he helped James load the assortment of suitcases and golf clubs into the boot of the car.

A peck on the cheek for them both from Wendy and they glided out of the driveway in search of the A6 and the hundred or so miles to the Royal Lytham & St Annes Golf Club.

They made good time and, as promised, had a quick sandwich washed down with a pint of the local brew. They changed and made their way to the first tee which, unusually for a championship links course is a par three. Remarkably, there was no-one immediately in front so they played at a good steady pace, most of the holes halved, both reaching the turn in thirty nine shots which is just four over par. Coming back with the wind against, the going got progressively harder, particularly after the fourteenth.

This is the hole that toppled the mighty Jack Nicklaus and on this particular day it destroyed James's card and put Jack 'one up'.

Fortunately, match play is scored on the number of holes won and not the total number of shots taken. However, a really bad hole can so easily destroy a golfer's rhythm and it was with some relief that James hit a good drive at the next. Again at seventeen, they shared the spoils although Jack had a narrow escape with his second shot which very nearly came to rest in the bunker made famous by the legendary Bobby Jones.

They stood on the last tee, James was still one down so played second and had to concede a congratulatory 'Fine shot,' as his opponent unleashed his best drive of the day.

The thought of defeat got his adrenalin pumping and he responded with his best effort, which skipped on a full twenty yards past the first ball.

'Take it easy old boy, it is only a game.' Priory was as ever, the master of gamesmanship.

They walked to their balls, both of which had both landed beyond the clutch of bunkers near the flagpole. As he waited to play, James was subconsciously admiring the red brick clubhouse with its black and white gables which stands behind the eighteenth green. To the left of it lay the putting green and the Dormy House, their lodgings for tonight. A bit like being back at boarding school occurred to him, further reflections were brought to a halt by a cry of, 'Bugger.'

The expletive and the sight of the leaning body imploring the ball to 'Get down', brought him back to golf; the task appearing easier when Jack's ball, despite his pleas, sailed without bouncing into the left hand greenside bunker.

James hit a perfect eight iron to within four feet of the hole; he smiled as he heard the customary, 'well played.' The tone of Jack's voice, as all golfers know, whilst appearing appreciative was disguising with difficulty the disappointment at seeing the opposition so well placed.

He strode on to the green, his step suddenly much lighter.

His opponent meanwhile, after a couple of practice swings in the rough, entered the bunker, shuffled his feet and swung an open faced club at the ball which emerged from a cascade of sand and against all odds, flew straight into the hole to clinch the match.

Jack with a huge grin on his face knocked James's ball away to concede the matching birdie.

'I don't think I could stand the thought of you missing that and taking more of your money.'

The caddies collected the clubs and carried them to be stored in the Professional's shop.

As they paid them, James's caddie observed in a broad Glasgow accent,

'Ya cannie fart agin thunder sir.'

He ruefully agreed with him and arranged to meet again on the first tee at eight thirty the following morning.- we are off at 9.00 clock he advised.

Jack, still highly amused, waited for him at the entrance to the Dormy House.

'See you in the entrance hall at six thirt for a couple of pints before dinner.'

James grimaced.

'As a prelude to relieving me of more money on the snooker table, no doubt?'

They met in the entrance hall, checking the starting sheet for tomorrow's 'Better Ball' charity competition and noting that their partners were down as JBO Hebb and EJ Court.

'With a bit of luck they will be off a decent handicap and not have us searching in the rough after every other shot, and put us off our game.' Jack Priory as ever, looking forward to the challenge.

'Yes and with a bit more luck you will land in a few more bunkers and totally demoralise them!'

They were still laughing as they climbed the stairs and entered the Members Room. Jack, to ease his conscience as he put it, insisted on buying the first round.

They sat near the window that immediately overlooks the eighteenth green, James choosing to sit with his back to it, observing as he did so, 'I can't bear being reminded of your daylight robbery.'

They sank into the big leather armchairs, conscious of the portrait of the immortal Bobby Jones who in 1926, at the height of his golfing powers, played what is generally regarded as the greatest shot of all time.

On the last day of the Open Championship he was two shots down to Al Watrous, but had clawed that back to go level as they played the seventeenth.

This is a demanding hole in which the priority is to stay to the right of the fairway, which

Watrous did, driving safely up to the elbow and leaving himself with a clear shot to the green.

Jones meanwhile appeared to have surrendered the initiative to his adversary when he pulled his drive into a small bunker that lurked in the deep rough.

It was from here, a spot now venerated with a small plaque, that the great man took his 'mashie', the equivalent of today's five iron, and hit a shot from the sand fully 160 yards to land on the green.

He duly got his four but Watrous, staggered by the sheer effrontery of the shot, three putted and was given no further chance to grasp the championship.

Next to the picture of Jones is the very club which he used to make that legendary shot, together with a typically modest letter addressed to the Royal Lytham & St Annes Club. James gazed at the hickory shaft with its leather grip and sought the same inspiration and resolve that had been shown by this unassuming man when all seemed lost.

The steward appeared with the news that the dining room was now open. They followed him in and sat at a table furnished in stiff white Irish linen and gleaming silverware, this time overlooking the Practice Ground.

'You will doubtless be wanting to go out and practice your famous bunker shots.'

'The minute we finish dinner,' Jack promised, adding gleefully, 'can you imagine if I had played with Bobby Jones as my partner!'

'The Royal & Ancient would probably have ordered all bunkers to be filled in, just to give the rest of us ordinary mortals a chance.' James joined in the banter, his old humour reasserting itself, as for the first time in ages he felt relaxed.

Dinner was a simple affair, Ham and Pea soup followed by Lancashire Hotpot, the latter not surprisingly, a speciality of the chef. They concluded with cheese, choosing rather diplomatically they thought both Stilton and Lancashire and washing it all down with a decent house red.

'Rather like being back at school, don't you think?'

'That is what I was thinking when put your second into the bunker at the last and then look what you did to me.'

'And of course, there is still the snooker to come...' Jack left the further financial threat unsaid.

'Well, before you do relieve me of any more cash, what about a brandy with Mr Robert Jones?'

'Good idea, my treat.'

They returned to the same leather armchairs after passing a few pleasantries with members who recognised them from previous visits.

They sipped the cognac, enjoying its smooth texture, Jack briefly disappearing in a cloud of smoke as he lit one of his inevitable cigars.

'How is business?' James enquired of his friend, who ran an old established family company that manufactured furniture in Long Eaton.

'Booming, particularly the kitchen side, which is the area of the house that most people see as the priority in terms of upgrading the house.'

'Why should that be?'

James was immediately interested, his fertile business brain open as ever to new ideas, particularly so in this case, in view of his own family. His grandfather, Albert Staincliffe had after all been knighted at the turn of the century by Edward V11 largely due to hefty donations made from the profits of a highly successful furniture empire.

'New houses have bigger kitchens, people spend more time in them, and they want them to look smarter and that same mood prevails in older properties.'
He drew on his cigar and laughed. 'I actually had someone come in last week and ask me if we could make a kitchen table and cover the top with 'Formica'.
He winced, 'Must be like living in a transport café.' James looked at him pensively,
'Have you been to the States or Sweden or Denmark?'
    'No, where is this leading?'
    'You have obviously seen American films – what do you recall about their kitchens?'
    'Big fridges and freezers,' the puzzled response.
    'What about the kitchen furniture?'
    'It is all fitted units,' his voice tailed off.
    'With Formica tops,' James finished the sentence for him.

Jack Priory stroked his upper lip with his index finger, a sure sign that he was talking finance and talking seriously.
    'I have had enough of building, the weather over here plays havoc with the work schedules and from our experience when refurbishing older properties, the kitchens and bathrooms are I agree top of the improvement agenda.'
    'So, what are you proposing,' he looked enquiringly at James.
    'You and I should work together, we have skills that mesh and complement each other. These are first thoughts, off the top of head, they will need to be fleshed out but, Mr Priory, we are onto something here and it is not going to be an opportunity for much longer. We have to formulate a business plan. Jack, write down these headings and, at the side, your response.'

1.	Premises	We have spare capacity at the moment.
2.	Manufacturing Expertise	Leave that to me.
3.	Finance	Leave until last.
4.	Market research	That is your area of expertise.
5.	Designs	Your design/my manufacturing know how.
6.	Raw Materials	Essentially my department.
7.	Outlets to distribute them	The furniture stores we sell to?
8.	Advertising	Your department again.
9.	Market Sector	You are the property man – what/where?
10.	Timescale	Must develop designs & production in concert.

Jack handed the diary to James; the notes were on the back page. He smiled as he took the black leather book. 'So this is it.'
    'Casanova's Guide to Nottinghamshire: I wouldn't mind seeing the other pages in here!'
    'You would need to know how to break the enigma code to get at that information and if Wendy can't crack it, no one will.'
They did not play snooker that night, more paper was procured and more detailed plans were made.
    This was to be a joint venture with both partners putting up fifty percent of the capital. The units would be made by Jack's company to designs commissioned by James.

The procurement of suitable materials and all manufacturing decisions would also be left to Jack.
The market sectors they decided would fall into two essential categories:

1. Mass market – speculative builders.
2. Up- market - private sales from glossy magazine ads and sales generated in stores.

They were agreed that there was no sense in trying to reinvent the wheel, they would get hold of trade magazines from the USA and Scandinavia and reproduce the best of those designs.

James was to have the responsibility for sales and marketing, which would be very time consuming and require all his energies. It crystallized in his mind something which had been troubling him since Edward and Connie's departure; it would also hopefully help to resolve his finances.

The following day, they walked to the tee, putting behind them the exciting proposals of last night, knowing that the journey home would provide an ideal opportunity to make further plans. Their opponents, rather remarkably were almost neighbours, hailing from Nottingham and both being members of the Beeston Fields Golf Club. This is an attractive parkland course that James and his partner knew quite well, although they had never met Eddie Court or John Hebb.

Fortunately, Jack Priory's fears were groundless; their opponents were both fine strikers of the ball and a very similar pairing in terms of style, with Eddie Court matching James for ambition and John Hebb's technical skill counteracting Jack Priory's dogged and relentless march down the middle of the fairway. Both pairings reached the turn with a Stableford card showing twenty points, a good score but with the menacing back nine waiting for them, they knew they could not be complacent.

As they stood on tee of the tenth hole, James, with the optimism of last night suddenly percolating through, relaxed and began to play with earnestness that he had not shown for a very long time.

He hit a huge drive of around 330 yards that left him with a tiny flick of his sand iron to the green, the resultant tap in birdie earning them three more points and so it continued. Not even the dreaded fifteenth could stop him today and when he had landed his seven iron second shot to within five feet at the seventeenth, Eddie Court tied a white handkerchief to his putter, raised it aloft and called out for mercy; 'Not just for John and myself but for everyone playing here today.'

He was correct; James and Jack finished with forty five points and when, ten minutes later the wind got up and it started to rain, they were in no doubt that they would win the day. Their partners on thirty nine points were also very respectably placed, claiming good naturedly, that they had been intimidated.

The prize giving was at seven pm and shortly after, bearing away inscribed silver salvers, they departed for Nottingham. The trip, with much to discuss, passed swiftly; they divided the workload pretty much as had been their first inclination, James being charged with the initial task of registering the name and agreeing the Memorandum and Articles of Incorporation. However, as he did not wish to disclose his hand at this point it was decided not to use the Fordmill lawyers but Jack Priory's firm in Nottingham.

CHAPTER THIRTY THREE

The Nottingham Architects & Builders Dinner, perhaps not the most salubrious of occasions he thought when the invite came, but every year out of old loyalties he would attend along with others from quite a wide range of professions that included lawyers, accountants and others only tenuously connected with the construction industry.

This year Kate had declined. He had not been surprised and had not tried to reason with her, no-one would be surprised but it would acknowledge what many suspected, his marriage was on the rocks.

There were ten others on his table, all of them couples except for Jack Priory, Wendy having decided out of loyalty to Kate not to attend.

After the dinner and the speeches, the Band struck up and the more energetic took to the dance floor. These were joined by the more reluctant whose wives were invariably the proactive participants. As his table was rapidly emptied by the cajoling MC, he turned to attract a waitress and saw at the next table, the most stunning tall blonde girl; she was leaning back and laughing.

He looked round for help; he found it in the form of Charles Firth, a local solicitor who specialised in contract law.

'Who is that?' he enquired, whilst trying not to look too obviously in her direction.

'Sir Robert Parkinson's daughter, I believe her name is Sally.'

'Thanks Charles, I owe you a drink next time I see you at the squash club.'

He walked slowly across to her table.

'Hello,' he had that defenceless small boy expression that defied rebuff.

'Hello, are you with us?' she enquired sweetly.

'Not quite, I am on the next table actually so, as a good neighbour, I thought I would call and see if you wanted to borrow a cup of sugar or something?'

She smiled coyly, her expression in no way defensive.

And then, taking his courage in both hands and before it deserted him.

'Would you like to dance?'

He took her hand; 'Please don't say no, it will make me look so silly.'

He turned and led her on to the dance floor, conscious that at least two tables were looking rather surprised.

'God, he has got some nerve, her father is the Lord Lieutenant and a big pal of the Duke's,' the guest sitting opposite Jack Priory advised.

'He has got some bloody good taste as well,' sighed his cohort.

Roddy Forsythe on the adjoining table was neither amused nor pleased.

'Who is that?' he demanded of his host, his face now as red as his hair.

'It is James Carrington, I knew his father, neither of us were sadly quite in his league as rugby players, although his old man was very unlucky not to get a cap. I believe he is a property developer.'

'A damned builder, you mean,' he retorted furiously as he watched the elegant couple swaying in complete harmony to the Band's rendition of the Beatles   'All you need is love, love, love…'.

They were far too engrossed in each other to be aware of the irony of this particular tune; it was not however, lost on some of the other guests, two in particular.

'What are you doing here?' he asked her. 'A Builders' Dinner Dance is hardly your scene.'

'Daddy has a party up for the weekend; the Belvoir Hunt are meeting at the house on Saturday and Sir Andrew Farquarson, the guest speaker was at school with Daddy. As he hunts with the Beaufort he has been invited to the meet - we always have a couple of spare horses.'

The words came rushing out. 'Does that make sense?'

'Perfect,' he assured her.

She looked into the deeply set blue eyes and felt quite weak.

'Do you ride?' His tone was interested and she warmed to him.

'Oh rather, I am a total horse freak.'

'Me too, although I am more interested in breeding.'

They both burst out laughing, causing further apoplexy to Roddy Forsythe.

'Actually I would like to learn to ride, I have always fancied riding to hounds - is that the expression?'

'It certainly is, you should try it, although you are going to need a pretty big horse with your long legs.'

'Perhaps you will be my adviser.'

He left it at that, the hook upon which to hang his hat in the future was in place.

He led the girl back to her table and quietly but graciously sat her down.

'Thank you,' he said, and with a smile was gone.

Roddy Forsythe could hardly control himself as he confronted her.

'Enjoy mixing with the working classes?' he sneered.

'He is not working class.' She had defended him before she realised it.

James arrived home just after midnight, stopping his taxi at the bottom of the private lane that led to Woolmington so that he would have more time to think before Kate confronted him.

He strolled without haste, enjoying the cool still March evening and pondered the events of the night. Sally Parkinson had left a big impression, did he take it any further, did he want to and where would it lead and what complications and unhappiness would follow in its wake?

He decided that he would shelve this decision and concentrate on the other conversation he had engineered. He had spotted Edward and Connie, Mr and Mrs Lawson as they now were, sitting about six tables away from the Parkinson's when he had led Sally back to her seat.

Walking across to speak with Sally had taken a bit of nerve; approaching the Lawson's table had been exceedingly difficult but, in the light of the new developments with Jack Priory, it was vital that he made contact with them.

'Edward, Connie, how are you?'

'We are fine, how are Kate and the kids?'

Was this omission of his own wellbeing a deliberate slight? They must after all have seen him dancing with Sally Parkinson, he let it pass.

'Regarding Fordmill we need to talk, can we arrange to meet?'

'Wednesday morning ten am, my office, will that suit you?'

'Fine, see you then.' The voice was still cold and without emotion.

He cleared his head and prepared for Kate, he need not have bothered, she was in bed and thankfully, fast asleep. He undressed as quietly as possible, anxious not to disturb her and fell asleep planning his next encounter with Miss Parkinson.

He awoke on Saturday morning, his first thoughts again of the girl at the Dinner; the reverie was broken by Kate's arrival at the breakfast table.

'Did you see anyone last night?'

He ignored the dumbness of the question. 'No-one in particular although I did speak with Edward.'

'I am surprised he could be bothered.' Her voice was about as warm as had been his former friend's.

He sighed, he was beginning to understand why marriages break down, you did not need to be unfaithful, tedious boredom would eventually take its toll.

'I am off to the golf club'.

'What time will you be back?' she demanded.

Kate asked the same question every week and every time he replied, 'about six o'clock.'

'I suppose that means you will be going to meet your cronies at Welford Road.'

Once again she expressed the boring continuing sameness which required the same needless affirmations.

He collected his clubs from the gun room and walked briskly across the stable yard to the barn, which housed his new toy; a black 911 Porsche Carrera.

'An attempt to rejuvenate my youth,' he had told the salesman at Sytner's showroom, as he handed over the keys to the Bentley.

He drove down the lane but, instead of turning left up the hill towards the golf club, he drove in the opposite direction towards Manston Hall.

He stopped at the first telephone box and called the professional's shop to cancel his time in the Saturday Medal and then, with trembling heart, set out to see her, although quite what he was going to say or do he had no idea.

Manston Hall was a large stone pile approached along an avenue of lime trees. He stopped fifty yards short of the entrance and parked the car on the road side, fervently hoping that some wayward steed would not give it a kick - that would take some explaining, he mused.

Turning up the collar of his Barbour and feeling very conspicuous he walked slowly towards the house wondering how he would explain his presence if challenged. He decided to rely on his wits.

Ahead he heard the call of the hounds and an occasional whinny, these and the noise of the riders and grooms created an air of great excitement, he quickened his pace to see at first-hand what was hidden behind the wall of horseboxes and trailers.

'Good morning,' the greeting from a passing rider.

'Good morning to you,' he responded.

He felt much better, it must be the camouflage afforded by the Barbour jacket, he decided.

He looked at the milling group of riders and saw her immediately as, with a wide smile, she acknowledged the stirrup cup handed up by one of the Manston estate workers.

He also spotted Roddy Forsythe sitting red coated on a grey horse, raising his black hunting topper to a group of lady riders joining the throng.

His mind went back to Watkin Hall and the large oil painting that still hung there, the sight of that had stirred him and he remembered how amused the others had been as he explained that they were in 'Monday Country', the area which, in that instance, the Quorn hunted on Mondays.

He accepted a small whisky from a tray that was offered to the hunt supporters and let his mind drift back to Milford Hall, where the Hunt had met every year in December he recalled his mother saying.

He grew bolder and edged forward, near enough to hear the Huntsman call out. 'Hounds please.'

The excitement was tangible as the huntsman sounded his horn which immediately unleashed a frenzy of anticipation amongst both the hounds and the riders.

As they set off he heard one of the followers advise the assortment of hunt enthusiasts

'They are drawing the spinney at Home Farm.' He watched fascinated, as they fired up the battered assortment of Land Rovers and cars.

The air was blue with smoke and diesel fumes as the convoy set off, headed down the drive by the white pick-up truck belonging to the fence men, whose job it was to repair any damage caused and thus prevent any stock escaping.

He spotted her in the middle of the field and recognised, as a natural sportsman himself, that she was at one with the striking dark brown, almost black horse she rode.

'Well mounted', he recalled the expression, chuckling inwardly at the unintended double entendre.

James Carrington was not a man to whom decisions came slowly so that, before he had reached the car which had fortunately remained intact, he had decided on his next course of action.

He drove to Leicester but instead of going straight to the Rugby Club at Welford Road, he drove into the city. Despite his considerable involvement with horses he knew very little about riding but was aware that Kate bought the children's riding outfits from Harry Hall's, as had his sister before that.

He strode in thinking it best to plead complete ignorance and threw himself at the mercy of a middle-aged lady whom he discovered, was called Susan.

Forty minutes later and he had asked for and acquired all the essentials; Jodhpurs, Stock, Boots, Gloves, Hat, & Black Riding Coat.

In the case of the latter, he had jokingly said to Sue, as he now called her; that he was in fact a landowner and did she think he should have a red coat. She joined in the fun but thought not, 'you must wait until you are awarded your hunt button, a bit like first team colours,' she added!

He took one last look at himself in the changing room mirror, an admiring one if truth be told, this opinion confirmed by the manager. 'You cut quite a dash sir and, if I might be so bold, if you go hunting don't forget to refer to your stock as your hunting tie.' 'Stock,' he continued, 'according to the old Duke of Beaufort who was universally known as Master, was something shopkeepers place on shelves.'

He smiled, shaking his head in bemusement and handed over his cheque.

He carried his bags emblazoned with the proprietor's name and dropped them under the bonnet of the Porsche and with plenty of time to spare before the match, decided on a bar lunch at the Royal Hotel in the city centre.

Finally at just after two pm he turned into the car park at Welford Road. The ground with its two great stands, the finest in England with the exception of Twickenham of course.

It was still nearly an hour before kick-off but quite a crowd was already streaming through the gates.

He was instantly recognised by several members. 'Have you brought your boots?' one enquired.

'They are a bit too quick for me these days.'

He modestly but warmly passed off the compliment, but pleased to be still recognised.

In the bar under the stand his cronies, as Kate referred to them, were gathered and he soon had a pint of Everard's Bitter in his hand.

'Played any decent golf?' Andrew Robertson enquired.

'I haven't dropped a shot today.'

'You must have been shacked up with some woman then.'

'Chance would be a fine thing,' he defused the near truth.

At ten minutes to three they took their seats in the Members' Stand, just in time to applaud the arrival of the 'Tigers', as Leicester are universally known and their opponents, Cardiff.

Any game between these two was virtually an international match and from the first kick-off to the final whistle the pace and the action was hectic. There was never very much between these two great clubs and so it turned out today. Home advantage and the ceaseless encouragement from the local crowd just seeing the Tigers home with a try two minutes from the end.

He returned home and to his wife's enquiries he concentrated his answers on the events at Welford Road.

'You obviously still enjoy it, I suppose the next thing I know, is that you will be playing again.'

'No, actually I am thinking about taking up riding.'

She looked amazed.

'I suppose this notion has been in your head since you discovered Watkin Hall?'

'I guess so.' He was grateful for her suggested escape route. 'I need to keep active.'

'Everything revolves around what you need to do.' Kate was getting quite heated.

'When do we do things together?' She challenged him.

'We go skiing.'

'Yes,' she snapped, 'I go once and then you go on two or three more trips with your cronies.'

She turned to him, really angry.

'I really do not know why you bothered to get married'.

'And neither do I.'

He turned on his heel and headed for the shower. This not at all how he had planned it, he had returned home feeling morally guilty and wanting to make amends to Kate.

What had gone wrong? He tried to reason it out as the hot water cascaded over him.

When he first met her, that fateful day at Martins Bank in Birmingham, she had captivated him.

Her looks and figure, which she still had, her friendly nature that inspired everyone to like her, she had so much going for her. It was the zest for life that was missing, motherhood had eroded her sense of fun.

It was that recognition of motherhood that brought him back to earth. When compared to the two sons she had borne him, Sally Parkinson seemed suddenly not very important.

He heard her come into the bedroom and a minute later the shower door opened. She stepped into his arms.

'Sorry'. One word, that conveys so much.

'Me too,' He drew her to him, it was not difficult, the affection had been dormant of late, but it still existed. They made love tenderly and, when they were finished, slipped into their robes and sat in front of the drawing room fire sipping champagne, for the moment at least, the spark rekindled.

CHAPTER THIRTY FOUR

Lawson Construction Ltd

The red and green lettering on a white background, those same colours they had worn together as rugby team mates at Welford Road. Edward was obviously appealing to whatever contacts he had made over the years.

James had taught him too well, Jack Priory's sardonic first reaction.

He parked and was escorted from reception to the Boardroom where Edward and Connie, together with their Accountant and Solicitor sat in anticipation of James Carrington.

At the sight of Jack, Edward's response was decidedly angry.

'So, he did not have the guts to come himself.'

Jack Priory smiled indulgently.

'Let me explain; I persuaded him not to come. There is too much bad blood between you right now to make any serious commercial decisions.'

'Jack is right.' Connie interrupted, her expression, showing evidence of the stress she felt.

'To be honest I am glad he didn't come, the wounds are too deep.'

The Accountant, Bob Pickard, whom they had all known for several years, suggested they start.

'Very well, I should first tell you that I am now the Financial Director of Fordmill and do, as such, have full authority to act..

'I had that same understanding and look where it landed me.' Edward's acerbic response.

'I know what has happened Edward and I can't say I don't sympathise with your view, but recriminations are not going to resolve this problem.'

Connie took her husband's hand. 'Let it go darling.'

She indicated that Jack should proceed.

He looked enquiringly at Edward and Connie before continuing.

We have taken advice and the valuation you have put on your shares is too high and we assume that this is merely a point from which we can begin to negotiate.'

He waited for their reaction, which wasn't long in coming.

'We strongly disagree, Fordmill had a quiet patch last year but we know the true capital value of the company. We also know you have some large contracts that are just waiting to be signed off, probably as soon as this deal has been done.'

Jack fiddled with his fountain pen, before returning to his point,

'It is never easy to put a value on a private company and, unless we can liquidate a substantial amount of the company's assets, you risk putting us out of business and right now the market is not very buoyant.'

'So you will understand how my clients must feel in respect of the monies owed to them.' Arnold West, the Lawson's solicitor had an unfortunate smug expression, which rarely left his face. Right now, sensing that he was about to draw first blood, he was positively drooling.

'Your internal problems are no longer of interest to my clients and I have to inform you that we are not prepared to negotiate on this matter.'

He looked across at the others, who nodded in unison. The lawyer leaned forward.

'There is also the consideration of defamation of my clients' characters.'

He looked enquiringly at Edward and Connie before continuing.

'We have taken advice and the valuation you have put on your shares is too high and we assume that this is merely a point from which we can begin to negotiate.'

He waited for their reaction, which wasn't long in coming.

'We strongly disagree, Fordmill had a quiet patch last year but we know the true capital value of the company. We also know you have some large contracts that are just waiting to be signed off, probably as soon as this deal has been done.'

Jack fiddled with his fountain pen, before returning to his point,

'It is never easy to put a value on a private company and, unless we can liquidate a substantial amount of the company's assets, you risk putting us out of business and right now the market is not very buoyant.'

'So you will understand how my clients must feel in respect of the monies owed to them.' Arnold West, the Lawson's solicitor had an unfortunate smug expression, which rarely left his face. Right now, sensing that he was about to draw first blood, he was positively drooling.

'Your internal problems are no longer of interest to my clients and I have to inform you that we are not prepared to negotiate on this matter.'

He looked across at the others, who nodded in unison. The lawyer leaned forward.

'There is also the consideration of defamation of my clients' characters.'

Jack's rebuttal was emphatic and unequivocal, he continued on the attack,

'Nonsense, they resigned, they brought the facts into the public domain and as to the value of their shareholding in Fordmill, we are unconcerned that they retain those shares as we still hold a majority and do not need your approval to make company decisions or policy.'

The lawyer attempted to brush this aside.

'I believe you are misleading us in terms of your liquidity.'

Jack looked the solicitor in the eye.

'In what way?'

'Both Bob Pickard and myself have advised our client that, with bank rates currently so high, trading without those funds you owe them will be very costly, that factor also has to be built into the equation and we believe a jury would recognise that.'

'So,' Jack rubbed his index finger across his upper lip, 'you seem to be missing the point or, should I say, avoiding the point. Why should James Carrington be concerned about your financial shortfall?'

He looked across at Connie and Edward Lawson, his expression was understanding.

'I am here to agree how we best move forward because I have to tell you that we do not agree your share valuation.'

'My clients have contracts to fulfil, your prevarications will cost us money and, unless we receive full settlement, we intend to sue.'

'I have no wish to be rude Mr. West, but you are a lawyer, your natural inclination is to go to law, it is how you earn your living. Whatever the outcome you will be paid, your clients on the other hand, whom I have personally known and respected for many years, may well end up as bankrupts with little chance of resurrecting their finances.'

Connie glanced at Edward; Jack saw his reasoning striking home.

He softened his tone, 'We need to negotiate our way out of this impasse. If we go to law, James can afford it, can you? I think not.'

'It is not acceptable, it is too cruel that James Carrington can ruin our lives like this.'

'Connie, it was you and Edward who stormed out.' Jack continued with the soft touch.

He was conscious that he still held the upper hand, but knew that Edward did have a case in law, a top London based QC had left James in no doubt about that. He summed up.

1. You have successfully negotiated contracts which are due to start in 2-3 months' time.
2. In order to fulfil these works you have to purchase considerable plant and equipment.
3. You do not have the funds to finance these works.
4. Going to law may possibly recompense you for loss of income etc. – we think not. Consider too that if your appeal fails, as we are confident it will, then your capital will be considerably eroded.
5. If there is a way to break this impasse and allow you to honour these contracts is that what you really want?

'Why don't I give you ten minutes to discuss my observations,' and then to lighten the moment, 'If I don't get a smoke soon, I will not be able to make any rational decisions anyway.'

Edward rose from his seat at the head of the table and flicking some non-existent dust from his lapel, opened the door to let him out.

He returned to his seat and looked expectantly at the others. 'Who wants to go first?'

Connie took the initiative. 'Do you think he is going to ask us to go back?'

'That is not an option, full stop.' Her husband's reaction angry and clearly not up for discussion.

'I think he is trying to bluff you over our chances in court.' Arnold West sought to defend his advice.

Bob Pickard took a similar professional viewpoint.

Edward looked them both directly in the eye.

'Then if you are so confidant, I take it that you will both represent us on a 'no win, no fee' basis'.'

There was no response other than a shrug of the shoulders, which the Lawson's took as an emphatic no.

The knock on the door brought the fairly indecisive deliberations to a halt and without being asked, Jack again seized the initiative.

'You are adamant that Fordmill Construction, even without its property portfolio, is worth well in excess of the sum for which you are prepared to institute legal proceedings. Our proposal to you is, and I have to have agreement to my proposal today or it will be withdrawn:

1. We will give you full control of the construction side of the business - including all the plant and other working materials owned by that part of the company. You will also agree to take on any other commitments relevant to that division. There have been no new ones implemented since you resigned so you will be aware of these responsibilities.

2. As its assets are in excess of your proposed claim, you will issue loan notes to James Carrington representing the value of his shareholding which is 60% of the company. This will be redeemed in full by five equal annual payments.

3. In return, you will have his word - legally documented – that he will not engage in any similar or allied construction business.

4. Page two of this agreement lists the assets included in the proposal.

5. All the major items are listed and concur with the last balance sheet, also attached.

6. Our proposal includes the Head Office building and those offices and premises usually associated with the plant hire side of the business. These are also as the last company accounts but, in order that there shall be no confusion, they too are also itemised.

7. The property portfolio; viz the Bournemouth developments and Watkin Hall will be transferred to James Carrington's sole name, as will the outstanding liabilities in respect of those properties.'

He placed the proposals on the table and handed a copy to each of them.

'I hope very much that you will find these terms acceptable. I have personally drawn them up and have had to persuade James as I have sought to convince you. This town, this county, just isn't big enough for Lawson and Carrington to lock horns, one of you will go bust and I really don't know which. Either way it would be a great shame. I give you my word, out of respect for you both, that there is no hidden agenda. Anthony Jayes has drafted the document that constitutes the agreement in its final form. I don't need to tell you, because I know you are aware, that he has remained fiercely neutral in these matters and remains as a director of Fordmill. Off the record and strictly 'entre nous', I can advise you that he is willing to continue serving in that capacity, should you so wish.'

He looked deeply into his empty teacup as if hoping he would find some message there. Standing up he observed. 'A lot for you to consider, I will take a stroll around the car park, call me when you are ready.'

They heard him go down the stairs and all started speaking simultaneously. Edward as chairman insisted on addressing each of them, turning first to Connie for her view.

'I personally think this is a great deal. We owe Jack Priory a big vote of thanks.'

'Arnold, how does it sit with you?'

The lawyer pursed his lips, unsuccessfully striving to find a new tact on which to widen the debate.

'I think we should haggle over the size of the loan notes and be certain that the plant and machinery are what you are expecting. Otherwise I am amazed at what he is offering.'

'The value of the loan notes,' Connie looked up to the heavens. 'We insisted on the value, which is now backfiring on us, as it means we have to buy back his shares at the same price, Arnold, as you screwed out of them!'

Edward switched his gaze to Bob Pickard.

The accountant, his hands clasped under his chin, looked very thoughtful; like most of his calling, black and white decisions did not come easily.

'With regard to the value of the shares, I agree that we let wily old Jack manoeuvre us into a corner, but I think that you will have an up and running company with an experienced workforce that more than compensates you. Also if the company is really successful, you can redeem his loan notes early and get him out of the system. I would normally urge you to take your time over what is quite a surprising turn of events, however, I know Anthony Jayes and I do not believe that in a document as concise as this that he can have hidden any elephant traps or, would consider doing so. It is this last point that convinces me to advise you to accept.'

'Mr Chairman.' Connie turned to her husband, wondering if he would see the proposal as a climb down on his part. She knew he was a very proud man, conscious too that he had been in the shadow of James Carrington since he was fourteen years of age. She also knew he was a practical man and a shrewd financial one. She devoutly hoped he would base his decision on commercial logic and not pride.

Edward Lawson was in fact wrestling with the very same thoughts that his wife and long-time confidant had shrewdly imagined. He smiled wryly at them, his demeanour giving nothing away.

'James Carrington is a most unusual man. He used to be my best friend and I thought I knew him well. I have enough respect for him still, to know that he did not chicken out of coming here today. We owe that to Jack Priory; in fact we owe a bloody great deal to Jack. Quite literally a great deal. Connie and I know that business inside out, we know where every pen and pencil are and it is not conceited to say that we will get a great reception from the staff, many of whom we personally employed.

I have no idea what our Mr Carrington is up to, but we have a document promising that he will not cross our path in business terms. If I had to make a guess, I would say he is disenchanted with the construction industry, the only thing you may be sure, is that he has other fish to fry.'

He looked at them in turn, a large smile lighting his great features.

'Get Jack back in here and let's do some business.'

A flushed and ecstatic Connie went in search of their benefactor; she returned triumphant.

'I understand we have a deal.'

Edward took Jack's outstretched hand in his great paw, and put his other arm around his shoulder.

'With one proviso, you can inform Mr. Carrington that we will be tradingas Lawson Fordmill.

Jack winced. 'He won't like it, but I think I can deliver.'

'Let's have a drink.'

He reached into the cupboard and produced a bottle of Talisker Malt.

He poured five generous measures, 'Slange.'

'Slange,' the reply in unison.'

Jack noting mischievously, 'You have even changed your poison.'

'Yes, the Macallan does not leave me with the best of tastes these days!'

CHAPTER THIRTY FIVE

Jack Priory left the meeting at a little after one o'clock, declining lunch, knowing that James never the most patient of men would be getting very agitated at being for once, not at the centre of things.

He parked in the spot where the small sign that had previously indicated Edward Lawson's parking space had been removed, as had Connie's.

He tried to compose his features as he followed his friend into the boardroom.

They sat opposite each other, Jack much the calmer of the two. James did not beat about the bush.

'Well, put me out of my agony, did they buy into my proposal?'

'Yes, but they think the idea was mine which, until the ink is dry on the legal agreement, is how I suggest you let it lie.'

James crossed to the refrigerator that was secreted in the clothes closet. He removed the traditional celebratory Bollinger and two glasses. Before he could open it, Jack interrupted him.

'Before you crack the bubbly, I had to make one concession which you may not like. They intend to trade as Lawson Fordmill and, I suspect, change the company livery to red, white and green.'

A black look crossed James Carrington's face and for a moment Jack thought the deal might be off.

His concern vanished as it was replaced by a satisfied chuckle.

'Good, it will make the break more complete and it will cost them small fortune to repaint the diggers and all the other equipment.'

He turned again to his friend and eased the cork from the champagne bottle.

He poured two glasses and in a voice that was completely sincere faced his old confidant and friend

'I owe you Jack, thank you.' The reply was as ever, light-hearted.

'Don't worry; I won't let you forget it!' He smiled.

'All of a sudden I am everyone's friend, long may it last. I give you a toast, to the future and the success of 'Minster Kitchens'.

James grinned as he considered the name, 'Minster Kitchens. That really is quite clever Mr. Priory and to be honest, I had been trying, rather unsuccessfully to think of a name for our new venture. Your choice is good; it ties it in with the name of your long established 'Priory Furniture', but denotes a new beginning.'

James raised his glass and tipped it to acknowledge the sentiment. 'Minster Kitchens.'

And then, one eyebrow rose.

'Did you insist that they install our kitchens in all future housing developments?'

'No, but it did cross my mind, to be replaced immediately by the thought that you should keep your future plans quiet for the time being.'

It was probably for the first time in his life that James Carrington realized that he had someone on the same commercial wavelength as himself; it was a reassuring feeling that augured well for the future.

Both parties were anxious, for reasons of their own, to conclude the agreement as quickly as possible. The new Fordmill set up, already sporting its intended 'Lawson' prefix, had received considerable press coverage in the business sections of not only the Nottingham Evening Post and the Leicester Mercury but also the Architects' Journal and other trade publications.

Meanwhile, Jack Priory and James had been to the United States and Scandinavia and bought the licence to produce copies of those designs they felt would most appeal to the British public. All of these carried an identifying name that portrayed the dream that the purchaser would most relate to.

Manhattan, San Diego, and Palm Springs were from the US collection and Copenhagen, Norse and Tivoli from the Scandinavian range. To these they added the most popular top of the range numbers from the Priory collection, renaming them appropriately after the great Minsters and Cathedrals of England – York, Canterbury, Westminster and Salisbury.

As soon as the agreement had been witnessed and sealed, James Carrington launched his glossy new brochure on an unsuspecting public. It arrived through the letterboxes of a selected cross-section of the public in the East Midlands; they all lived in desirable residential areas that had been built pre-war when people cooked in the kitchen and ate in the dining room.

The existing kitchens were, with very few exceptions, cold and uncomfortable; what they all had in common was the potential to convert a large space into an attractive and welcoming family room. Also, now that most visitors tended to arrive at the kitchen door rather than the front, it gave the lady of the house an immediate opportunity to show off to her friends and neighbours the stylish new improvements.

James had convinced Jack that the British desire to 'Keep up with the Jones', should play a significant part in their marketing strategy. The brochures therefore depicted before and after kitchens in these self-style homes. All the finished display kitchens had been supplied free of charge; More importantly, they had been delivered on time and been installed on time.

It was on these two tenets that they both knew Minster Kitchens would stand or fall and for this the responsibility was equally divided – Jack would deliver the parts on time, whilst James would guarantee the completion to the client's satisfaction.

With this guarantee very much in mind, he had sought out every good joiner they had ever employed and invited them to an evening meeting at the Nottinghamshire Cricket Club at Trent Bridge.

The format was similar to one he had employed at Bournemouth when he was seeking to convince Donald Kingsley and the other shopkeepers to sell him their premises, in return for a lease in his new development. A select group of fifty joiners turned up, delighted to avail themselves of free beer and the chance of a chat with their mates.

'Not to mention a night out without the wife,' one wag's dry aside.

James, accompanied by Jack Priory, greeted them at the door; the usual derogatory banter that men resort to on these occasions quickly lightened the atmosphere and set the tone for a pleasant evening.

Jack, unlike James, had turned his back on rugby football, preferring to play soccer in the local Midlands Amateur Alliance where his skills had, as with every other sport, won him his county cap. Many of those present had played with him and against him, which provided a further convivial topic on which to embellish their various achievements. The most amusing topic of conversation however, was the very large, about two metres wide Stetson hat, that hung above the raised platform at the far end of the room.

'Normal sized hats no longer big enough Jack?'

'When one has such a mighty brain, one has to have them specially made,' came the easy riposte.

At eight o'clock James went to the platform and tapping on the table, invited them to collect a drink and choose a seat at the tables adjacent to the stage.

Ten minutes later an expectant hush descended as he pointed to the large Stetson swaying slightly above his head.

'You may be wondering at the significance of this and I will explain later. Jack Priory and myself are well known to most, if not all of you. We have either worked together or played sport together. In the case of the former, I have provided the work and you have delivered on time and have always been paid on time. In the case of the latter, as I understand it from Bill Daly, who played with Magdala FC for many years with Jack, you all ran all over the park to win the ball and delivered it to our hero who swept it into the net before running triumphantly back to the centre circle for the restart!'

There was a good-natured chorus of 'Hear, hear' and 'Dead right James's.' Jack refuted the accusation although grinning as he did so. There was an element of truth in the charge as, not for nothing had he been known as Beau Brummel. His languid skills sparing him most of the crashing tackles aimed at him and enabling him to finish most matches with hardly a speck of mud on him.

James held aloft a glossy brochure and invited the assembled tradesmen to open the envelopes on the tables in front of them.

'What do you think?' His gaze wept the floor inviting an honest answer.

'The sort of thing you see on the films.' Bill Shaw ventured, causing Jack to smile, identifying as it did, his own initial reaction.

'I bet they are expensive', this and other similar comments, until finally, 'how does this affect us?'

James pulled a thin cord, not discernible to the audience, a banner fluttered from out of the hat, it read. 'Will all the cowboys leave the room?'
They all laughed at this well-known reference to the fly-by-nights of the building industry, it also heightened their curiosity and they all looked enquiringly at him, wondering where this was leading.

A further string lowered the Stetson out of sight and he leaned on the lectern.
'Over many years I have come to know you and respect you all, both as tradesmen and more importantly as people. You will I am sure, be able to appreciate how these kitchens will transform an old fashioned, weary scullery into a warm and inviting place in the house. This is only the start

because Minster Kitchens will give birth to Minster Bathrooms and Minster Conservatories. If we pledge to support each other, we can for many years be assured of a very good income and a working environment very much more preferable than a wet and windy building site.'

'What about the plumbing and electrical work?'

The enquiry came from Roger Edwards who, along with his son Gary, had worked for James for many years.

'Good point Roger, you will all have guys in other trades who you can rely on - carry on using them; encourage them to pass on kitchen work to you, the only criteria is quality and reliability.'

James looked around the room. 'Any more questions?'

The upturned faces were overwhelmingly contented, so he proceeded.

'I have here,' he indicated the stack of forms on the table, 'this is a pledge: on the one part, the company will guarantee that any future installations or work required at a property previously fitted by you will be automatically assigned to you in future. You in turn will pledge to recommend other products developed by Minster – Bathrooms, Conservatories etc. to your clients

In recognition of this, the company will pledge to allocate 10% of the profits in this venture to those tradesmen who have worked for us in the year in question. The year will run as per the tax year, i.e. April 4th to April 3rd the following year.'

He looked at them expectantly and the reaction was all he could have hoped for; these were men with whom he had worked for years, they respected him, they also had a similar liking for Jack Priory. There was none of the apprehension shown by the shopkeepers in Bournemouth, they sensed immediately that this was much lighter and easier work than that normally found in their trade.

It was also a compliment to their skills and ego and, as the man said, he always paid on time, by no means the norm in the building industry.

'When do we start Mr. Carrington?'

'What I propose, Steve, is that you have your suppers and I hand out the 'Pledges'. You will note that Jack and I have already signed on behalf of the Board of Minster Kitchens.

After you have eaten, we will put all the forms into the dreaded Stetson and Jack will draw them out – the first name will be awarded the first contract, and the jobs will be allocated numerically as we sign the contracts. This way, being down the list is not necessarily a drawback, as you may well be offered a bigger and more expensive job. The only exception to this rule will be any contracts that you personally initiate; they will of course be allocated to you. So, when you are at a house, sell yourselves and get some referrals and I will send round one of our sales team to clinch the sale and negotiate a contract. Is that fair and acceptable?'

His eyes swept the room, the conversation was animated and several thumbs were raised in approval. He signalled the waitresses to bring on the cottage pie and cheese and biscuits, which were rapidly demolished in an atmosphere of delighted anticipation.

When they had finished and all the names had been counted into the Stetson, the draw took place.

Number One	Richard Hodgson
Number Two	Richard Bell
Number Three	Gerald Simmons

A voice piped up from the back of the room. It was Don Hartley, a well- known wag.

'Two dicks and a Gerry; come on Mr. Carrington give us ordinary mortals a chance.'

The others laughed and continued to cheer loudly when their own name came out of the hat, none more so than when Jack finally declared. 'Number Fifty Wilf. Jackson.'

James stood up for the last time.

'Gentlemen, we have had a wonderful evening, one which I am quite confident will prove to be prosperous for us all. This is an appropriate venue, in a city famed for innovation. It was on this very site that the first ever Test Match was played between England and Australia. The city of Nottingham has many other 'firsts' and many great businesses have been founded here – Boots the Chemists, John Player Cigarettes, HP Sauce, Nottingham Lace, Notts. County, the world's oldest football club, Raleigh Cycles, The Salvation Army, the oldest Pub in England – The Trip to Jerusalem. And the mention of that splendid long-lived enterprise and its continuing success seems a good note to end on. Thank you all and good luck.'

He left the room with Jack, having instructed the staff to continue serving; this gesture evoking a spontaneous cry of 'Three Cheers for the Governors. Hip, hip hooray; Hip hip...' The call faded as they left the hallowed shrine of the Long Room at Trent Bridge.

It had been a most successful evening and they both savoured their own thoughts as they walked slowly to the car park at the side of the famous cricket pavilion. Pausing to find the key, James looked across the roof of the Porsche and leaned across the canvas roof, hand outstretched.

'We are on our way partner.'

Jack Priory took it in both hands.

'I have a good feel about this James, but let's make sure we are up-front about everything, we don't want any of the nasty surprises that broke up your last company.'

'You have my hand and my word on that.' His smile was sincere, Jack Priory believed him. They pulled out of the Trent Bridge car park and within ten minutes the Porsche had consumed the few miles to the outskirts of Radcliffe-on-Trent and the Priory residence, amusingly called 'The Cloisters'.

'Coming in for a nightcap'.

James declined his friend's invitation, he had another half an hour's drive to reach Woolmington and his car was a magnet as far as the local traffic cops were concerned. 'I will call you tomorrow, about elevenish, hopefully after I have done the other deal.'

Jack heard the Porsche pick up speed as it left the lane and returned to the open road and pondered what sort of reception his friend would receive when he arrived home. He knew himself what it was like to metamorphose from the excitement of an occasion such as tonight, to the strained and tense atmosphere that pervades an unhappy house. His many affairs had, in the early days, provoked a great deal of the tension that James was returning home to, but they had never seriously threatened his marriage. The bottom line was that he still loved Wendy and she was still totally in love with him and even in the blackest moments, the financial implications had always been enough to focus his canny mind on what he had, and what he would have to give up. He closed the front door, aware that the light was still on in the study.

'Checking up on me, eh?' He leaned over and gave his wife an affectionate peck on the cheek.

Wendy smiled and held his arm; he would never really understand how much these little gestures meant to her.

'You look mighty pleased with yourself; sit down and I will fix you a drink and you can tell me what you and Mr Carrington have done now.'
Jack took the scotch from Wendy and lit a cigar.

'We have signed up the top fifty joiners to work for us on an exclusive two way basis. It really is such a simple concept and yet it takes an exceptionally astute brain to realise it.

I have known James since we played squash for the County as teenagers, it was always obvious he was going places – he has talent, brains, good looks, but most of all an obsession to win. To be completely honest with you Wendy, I find it quite frightening at times.'
She sat next to him on the arm of his chair, enjoying his trust.

'Have you ever discussed this with him?'

'Not in so many words, although I did seek his reassurance this evening and he gave me his promise.'
She stroked his neck absentmindedly and looked at him with a love born of affection for this kind man whom everyone liked. He took a sip of the whisky, tilting the crystal glass towards her and smiled.

'He can't help himself, he just takes control, and I even drink bloody Macallan Malt whisky since I got involved with him. Seriously however, I do believe the split with Edward Lawson and the others has made him more aware of the need to communicate.'

He stood up and took his wife's hand. 'Thanks for listening but it is getting late, let's go up.'

'You carry on; I will clear away the glasses.'
She watched his tall slim figure disappear through the doorway and sighed, why couldn't they share more moments like this. Perhaps they might as he got older, she hoped so.

CHAPTER THIRTY SIX

James drove without haste, in no rush to get home, hoping that Kate would be asleep and that he could sneak into a guest bedroom and get a good night's sleep prior to tomorrow, which promised to be a busy day.

As he came up the lane his heart sank, the lights were on all over the house. He parked and was greeted by the dogs and an open back door, heart pounding he raced in calling her name. There was no reply and he ran from room to room becoming ever more concerned; Thank God the boys were away boarding at prep school.

He went downstairs and tried to gather his thoughts; the cellar, why hadn't he thought of looking there, but it was to no avail. Should he call the police? If he did, it would confirm to everyone his troubles and yet if he did not and anything happened to her, how would he explain to his sons, how would he live with himself?

He concentrated his mind, thinking ironically that the other prevailing thought in his head as he drove home had been a desire not to speak with the law.

He entered the study and without bothering to sit down grabbed the telephone, seeing almost instantaneously her foot protruding from behind the dark green leather Chesterfield.

'Kate, Kate, what have you done?'

He pushed the sofa to one side, lifted her limp form and carried her tenderly into the drawing room where he laid her gently on the biggest of the sofas.

He stroked her face, aware as he did so of the smell of alcohol and, with sinking heart, wondered what else she might have resorted to.

He collected his thoughts, pride and secrecy no longer a priority. He sat at his desk and dialled Dominic Forster, their GP, whose wife and Kate had become good friends. The phone rang interminably but finally responded, the voice heavy with the overtones of sleep.

'This is Dr Forster, would you kindly ring my locum, the number is...'

James interrupted him.

'Dominic, it is James Carrington, I think Kate has taken an overdose of something.'

This time he was cut short.

'James, I am on my way, stay with her and make sure she is lying on her side in case she starts vomiting. In the meantime, check the bathroom cabinet or whichever cupboard you keep medicines in and dig out any white boxes with her name on them; I need to know how many pills are left so that I can check it against those I have prescribed recently.'

The fifteen minutes it took for the Doctor to arrive were the longest he had ever known, he felt numb and confused, angry and sad. Most of all he felt guilty and he was starting to wallow in self-recrimination when Dominic Forster dashed in.
'I have sent for an ambulance, we will need to stomach pump her and she will need to rest after that.'
     He took the proffered selection of pill boxes and looked sympathetically at James, knowing that beneath the confident exterior lurked a very private person.
'I have asked them to take her to the Leicester Royal Infirmary so the locals should not get to know. The main thing is you came home in time and found her.'
James looked at him, his eyes misted over and confessed, 'I very nearly didn't.'
'But you did, just you remember that when you are tormenting yourself.'

They heard the ambulance arrive at the front of the house, the doors slammed and almost immediately the paramedics ran in through the already open front door, he directed them down the hall and into the study where Dominic Forster wasted no time in alerting them to his diagnosis and assessment of what she might have taken.

He followed and watched with a heavy heart as they laid her gently onto the stretcher and covered her slim form with a red blanket; briefly her left hand remained on top of the cover and for a few brief moments he saw her engagement ring sparkling in the light cast by the lamp on his desk.
It took his mind back to those carefree days, to her scream of delight when she saw the ring that he had slipped on to the chocolate flake of the 99 ice cream.
     Where had all the magic gone and what must he do to bring it back?

He followed them to the ambulance with the intention of accompanying her to the hospital.
     'She won't wake up until the morning, James. Time enough then, to make a visit.'
He nodded. 'Thanks Dominic.' The Doctor squeezed his shoulder.
     'Try not to blame yourself; it happens more often than you would think.'

He watched them drive away, hoping that it would have escaped the notice of the locals in the village a mile away, but he doubted it; there was always someone, gamekeepers and the like that were abroad at all hours. However, having seen Kate so close to death, he really did not care and it was in defiant mood that he poured a drink and sat at his desk.
     All around him were family photographs, all depicting special moments and special people and, right now, in the middle of the night, in that darkest hour that precedes the dawn, they seemed doubly important.

He stood up and walked to the shelves that lined one of the walls; without thinking he chose an anthology bound in dark green leather, it was the gift that Jeremy had presented to him on his wedding day. He remembered his father-in-law saying that the lines contained within had sustained Lord Wavell's men in the dark days of the Desert Campaign in World War Two;
     '...it gave them the courage to see things through,

Because like marriage, the cause was good…

James still had a great fondness for both his parents-in-law and breaking tonight's events to them was not something he relished, knowing as he did their devotion to their only child.

He sank into the leather sofa and flicked through the pages, seeking the solace that Jeremy had promised, noticing for the first time a hand written poem at the end of Lord Wavell's introduction. It was Shakespeare's Sonnet number 116. It began;

Let me not to the marriage of true minds
Admit impediments; love is not love
Which alters when it alteration finds
Or bends with the remover to remove
O no, it is an ever fixed mark
That looks on Tempests and is never shaken…

Jeremy had underlined the second and third lines.

James stared at them wondering why; had he too suffered the doubts that faced him now?

He was still pondering 'love is not love', when he fell asleep, his rather crumpled form discovered by June when she arrived to feed and muck out the mares and foals.

'Mr Carrington, what has happened, where is Mrs Carrington?'

He held his hand to his head and tried to focus.

'June, get some coffee on and I will try and explain.'

She retreated to the kitchen, meanwhile he repaired to the bathroom where he cleaned his teeth and slung a couple of Alka-Seltzers into a glass, hoping they would provide some comfort to his throbbing head.

He came down to find coffee and toast awaiting him. He related as accurately as he could remember the events of last night and implored her to provide him with any other relevant details that would explain Kate's behaviour.

'She must have said something June.'

'Nothing that I could put my finger on, the best person to talk to would be Dr Forster's wife, they do spend a lot of time together and of course the kids are all at the same school.'

'Thanks June, I know I don't need to ask you to keep this to yourself, I will have a bath and go over to see her.'

A telephone call elicited the necessary invitation and they arranged to meet at eleven o'clock.

The mention of which time, prompted him to make a further call, to rearrange his visit with Frank Innes, the Estate Agents in Nottingham.

He returned upstairs and changed into some slacks and a blazer before setting out, rather tremulously to meet Liz Forster, with whom he was on scarcely more than a nodding acquaintance.

The house was an old rectory, set in an acre of garden which included a hard tennis court and, over the stone wall that surrounded it, a paddock containing two ponies that he assumed belonged to the Forster boys. She had seen him arrive and hurried out to greet him.

'James, do come in, Dominic won't be a moment, he is speaking with the hospital right now.'

No sooner had she sat him down than her husband appeared, his expression was cheerful.

'No harm done old boy, but she does have rather a bad headache - taking pills with drink does nothing to lessen the pain, rather the reverse I am afraid.'

He saw the tension go from James's face, he sensed the relief was genuine and sincere; the question the inevitable one.

'When can I collect her?'

'I would give it until mid-afternoon; give her a chance to collect herself.'

James nodded and looked at Liz, his expression both fearful and concerned.

'Has she said anything to you Liz, has she indicated she might do this – Is it my fault?'

'I think she has become very lonely since the boys went away to school, and I think she probably finds it more difficult to speak to you nowadays.'

She looked across at her husband. 'It is not unique; we have had a few similar problems.'

Her husband appeared annoyed at this intimate revelation,
'Be fair, you know the pressure I am under at the practice, all the bloody paperwork on top of the medical stuff.' The swiftness of his reply however, seeming to confirm her accusation.

James flashed him a wry smile.

'This is a conversation I know all too well, but at least Liz hasn't resorted to harming herself.'

'Not as yet.' She said it softly, but it carried menace and then to cover the embarrassment of the unintended slip, 'you must both come to supper very soon, we should have done it before.'

'That would be very nice, I am sure Kate will enjoy it.' He stood up and kissed her on the cheek.

'Thank you both, I can't tell you how much and please excuse me for dashing off, but I have to be in Nottingham at one thirty.'

He pushed the top down on the Porsche and slid into the sculptured leather seat and headed for Mapperley Park. This, like The Park area in the city centre was still essentially a very up-market residential area on the edge of the city; the houses and the grounds designed for wealthy men, to whom detail had been important and expense no hindrance in making a statement to their peers and neighbours of their financial and business prowess.

Some of the very large properties had been converted into apartments, a few more into offices and it was at one of these that he had an appointment with the agent from Frank Innes.

He arrived with fifteen minutes to spare and took the opportunity to explore the extensive lawn that sloped away to the rear of the property. As with the house, it had all been done with great detail and forethought, the wonderful great beeches that cast their lengthy shadows across the lawn could only have been imagined by the people who planted them, as they would never live to enjoy them as he did now.

Successive occupants had also, no doubt, made their contributions and it made him angry to see the violation that planners allowed property developers to get away with, as their bulldozers ruthlessly crushed the past in their haste to cram more people per acre into these wonderful settings; he would deny them that ill-gotten pleasure here.

He put his foot on the arm of the wrought iron garden seat and retied his shoelace; from this vantage point beneath the canopy of overhanging branches, he could see the rear elevation and noted with satisfaction the considerable space to each side of the main house that would allow the building to be sympathetically extended and developed should he wish to follow the example of other owners and convert it into a multi-tenancy property. He smiled wryly to himself and wondered if this would contravene the agreement with Lawson Fordmill - he would quite enjoy tussling with them over that.

A tall wavy haired man of about his own age came striding towards him, interrupting his thoughts.

'You have to concede the Victorians knew how to build houses.'

'And gardens,' James added as he turned to take the others hand. 'You must be Neil Hannah.'

'Pleased to meet you Mr Carrington; the last time I saw you was when a group of the Nottingham Rugby Club went to see Leicester play the 'Ba-Ba's' at Welford Road.'

'Those were the days, Neil, mind you we had a price to pay, the game was, as you will remember, always played on Boxing Day, so we had to go a bit easy on the turkey and drinks.'

'I would have given up turkey for life to have swapped shoes, or should I say boots, with you.'

James smiled disarmingly. 'You are very kind and I was very privileged.'

'You are too modest Mr Carrington but I suppose we had better address the job in hand, tempting though it is to spend all afternoon jawing about rugby.'

James nodded his agreement, adding, 'I suppose I have already conceded that I like the gardens so we had better move inside.'

They strolled along a narrow path formed from old bricks laid on edge, it was flanked by rhododendrons, laurels and other shrubs which quite dramatically opened out to reveal a circular enclosure with wooden seats and tables and, around the edges, six small stone headstones on which were recorded the names of the dogs buried there. The oldest were too weathered to read; two of them were just about discernable, they remembered 'Jack'; and another, rather faintly recalled 'Toby', died April 12th 1924, aged 8'.

'This is obviously the Dingly Dell that is referred to in the catalogue.'

'Lovely isn't?' the agent affirmed.

James heard himself agreeing, despite realizing that he was weakening his own bargaining position.

They paused briefly on the terrace at the back of the house to admire once again the sweep of the lawn and the cooling dappled effect of light and shade that the great beeches sprinkled upon it.

He followed as Neil Hannah opened the heavy oak door in the wall to the right of the terrace, its heavy panels weathered silver over the years, the heavy hinges squeaking from disuse as they gained access to the front of the building.

The other side also had a wall, a much shorter one that linked the main building to the coach house, this was currently employed as a garage.

A porch that replicated the heavy black and white gables of the exterior guarded the front door; this led into a hallway of panelled oak, not dissimilar to the offices that he had recently acceded to Edward Lawson. Perhaps it was this similarity, he was not sure, but what he was certain of, was that he must have this splendid Gothic house with its many reception and other rooms, most of which he intended to use as display areas for the Minster range of kitchens. This way any prospective clients could walk around the various options, sit at the breakfast tables and bars, sip a coffee and all the time the atmosphere would be inculcating them with the need to transform their own homes. To underwrite this thought he intended to leave one of the rooms untouched, it would serve as a stark reminder of *before and now.*

Upstairs he planned to introduce a similar range of bathrooms and, on the terrace at the rear and along the longer of the two walls, Minster Conservatories, which he envisaged, furnished and bedecked with plants. Conservatory furniture he mused, making a mental note to source a supplier. Or, maybe Jack could produce them, they must after all be quite simple compared to the high class dining room suites etc. his factories designed and built.

He marched through the house, accompanied by Neil Hannah and so absorbed in his own plans that, apart from the odd grunt or pursed lip as they moved from one room to the next, he had said very little. He seemed to have lost the enthusiasm he had displayed outside; the Agent sensed the sale was drifting away. In an attempt to tease out James's thoughts he suggested,
'Of course the kitchens and bathrooms need some major surgery, but the rest is really a matter of decoration and I suppose the vendor will be prepared to be a little flexible on the price.'
'How flexible?' He looked Neil Hannah in the eye, the latter for the first time seeing not James Carrington rugby player, but James Carrington very successful businessman.

Either way the Estate Agent sensed he was toying with him. 'I think I could persuade him to come down 5%.'
James gave him a knowing smile.
'Neil, this is a large property, far too big to be sold as a private dwelling house for one family. I also know that planning to convert it into flats has been turned down, which is why it has been offered as a commercial property. You will also know that the company I built up, 'Fordmill Construction' builds commercial properties; we pioneered the essence of businesses moving into modern purpose built offices and I also know that this property has been on the market for eight months. I also know that the former occupant, Alfred Barker, left the building and his entire estate to his four nieces and nephews. I am prepared to make you an offer, but my valuation is 25% below the asking price.'

The estate agent shook his head. 'There is no way my clients will accept that.' 'I suggest you put it to them and also remind them that as long as the property is empty, it is slowly gathering dust and damp and that it is already depreciating. Furthermore, my price when divided by four, will not actually make that much difference to them individually.'

He looked at his watch and winced when he saw the time.
'Neil I have enjoyed meeting you, please call me at home or the office as soon as you have a decision.'

CHAPTER THIRTY SEVEN

The pleasure of viewing this lovely house had distracted him from the main purpose of the day, which was of course to collect Kate from hospital and bring her home.

It was not something he was looking forward to, sensing that she would be either very embarrassed or very defensive, it was also going to make work more difficult at a time when he needed to throw all his energies into launching Minster Kitchens.

He had also arranged to meet with Miles Stanhope Court at APP Merchant Bank regarding his new venture with minster kitchens.

He suspected that this would be referred to the main board headed by Sir Julian Abercrombie; the old man was a stickler for family values and morality and if the events of yesterday reached him it would not help James's cause.

He was also greatly concerned as to how Kate's parents would react to the news, sensing that whichever choice he made, either to tell them or not, would be open to criticism.

He decided on impulse to call them, Jeremy Palmer answered the telephone and listened without response as James related the short sequence of events as far as he yet knew them.

'Angela is out at the moment but will be back by four o'clock, we will set out right away, it will take about four hours.'

James interrupted him. 'Jeremy, we all need time to think things through and, to be honest, I don't know how Kate is going to react to me spilling the beans as it were. It would be much more sensible to come up tomorrow.'

'Very well, I will try and keep the lid on things at this end, but please call us when you get her home, otherwise her mother will go round the bend.'

'That is a promise, I must go, I am running out of coins.'

He replaced the receiver, his heart was heavy, the future domestically looked pretty bleak, and it was a dispirited figure that made its way from the telephone booth to Ward Six.

He opened the door, there were four beds, and Kate's was nearest the window.

He took her hand, stroking it gently, tears welling in his eyes; lost for adequate words.

'I see they gave you the best bed.'

'Thank you for the flowers, they are lovely.' She too was bereft of further words as she clung to his arm.

He tried to lighten the mood, grateful that Jeremy had agreed to delay his departure.

'Come on, I am taking you home, although it might be an idea if you were to get dressed first.'

She smiled. 'I hadn't thought of that.'

They walked hand in hand to the car, but there was a distance between them and neither could find the words that would lessen the tension. It was the same in the car and he delayed until they were parked outside the front door, the news that her parents were aware of the situation and would be coming tomorrow, with the intention of staying a few days.

'It will be nice to see them.'

Her response surprised him; it also emphasized how low she was feeling and that her action was more than a cry for help, she would obviously need psychological as well as medical help.

It also irritated him; she could not have chosen a worse time, it was imperative to rebuild his commercial base, as no longer would he receive the big income from Fordmill. He would, of course, receive the loan notes from them for the next five years but these were sums he intended to invest in expanding Minster Kitchens into Minster Bathrooms and Minster Conservatories and whatever other opportunities might excite him.

He made a conscious effort to switch his mind off, seeing in his head the light switch that was his safety valve; he mentally switched it off and immediately felt more relaxed. It was a refuge that he had first employed as a teenager following his father's death. It worked now and he opened the car door for her, determined to concentrate on today and her parent's visit tomorrow.

In a slightly better frame of mind they went inside and he sat Kate downat the long oak kitchen table, the warmth from the Aga making this as usual, a welcoming place to sit and talk.

He lifted the lid and placed the kettle on the hotplate, the still warm water did not take long to boil.

'Let me do that, you go and let the dogs in.'

The normality of her response lifted his spirits and he gladly did as he was bidden, returning in a few seconds with a posse of squealing dogs, all obviously elated to seeing her.

'At least someone is pleased to see me home.'

'So am I.' Those few unnecessary words, dampening his enthusiasm and diluting his resolve.

'Are you James, are you sure?'

'Of course I am pleased to see you.' He incanted the words, seeking solace for himself as much as his wife.

She handed him the cup of tea, her expression was not of someone convinced and he sought to change the subject before she started to probe more deeply.

'We have to speak to your parents, do you want me to call them or will you do it?'

Without answering she walked to the dresser opposite the AGA and dialled the number, when it was answered she spoke brightly, seeking to allay their fears, attempting to deter their visit but eventually conceding it would be nice to see them. This done, her mood evaporated and she turned to face him.

'I know who she is James.' Her voice was calm as she waited for a response.

'You are wrong, there is no one else, and where did you dream up this nonsense.'

His eyes bored into hers, he was speaking the truth, events had been moving so swiftly of late that his aspirations in respect of Sally had been on hold; there had been no liaison of any kind.

'What about Sally Parkinson? I suppose she doesn't exist!'

Her expression was triumphant and smug, so much so that he did not make any further denial.

'Why?' she screamed at him.

'Because you have become so bloody boring,' he yelled back and then more consolingly, 'all I did was dance with her, just once; as I keep telling you, you couldn't be bothered to go to the dinner with me.'

'Flirt with her is how everyone else saw it.'

Once again a triumphal expression challenged his explanation.

'We both need time to think and cool down.'

He turned on his heel and strode into the yard where he slid into the Porsche. For the second time in his life, in a moment of real crisis, he sought the sanctuary of the place that drove him on and fuelled all his dreams and ambitions. He drove hard and aggressively for forty minutes, the car responding to his mood as it snarled in and out of the tight corners and roared along the short straight stretches of road that led to the hill that he had climbed, lungs bursting and head pounding on his Raleigh all those years ago.

He stopped the car, recognizing with complete clarity the spot where he had thrown down his bike before sinking head in hands, on to the small grassy knoll and seen, as he saw now, this great stone house that had stood here for more than three centuries.

There were no tears this time, but his heart was equally heavy as he faced up to the inevitability that he was going to have to choose between his desperate youthful promise to his parents and his responsibility to Kate and the boys. The thought of the latter and their loving, trusting faces brought about for the first time, a tiny chink in his determination to reclaim this great house that represented all that his family had once stood for.

Semper Altiora Speramus, he visualised the Latin inscription above the main entrance and remembered his mother pointing to it and explaining to him as a young boy just off to prep school, 'Ever to aspire to greater things'.

She had kissed him gently on the forehead, the expression on her kind face one of confident trust, sensing with certainty that the Staincliffe blood that coursed through his veins would one day enable her son to fulfil all of these aspirations.

This memory invoked his original objectivity, part of which had always imagined his elder son following him one day as master of this house. His irritation with Kate hardened as he recalled how difficult she sought to make his ambitions, by innuendo constantly aligning her allegiance to Woolmington.

He stood up, his resolve re-awakened, recognising that his life with or without Kate and not this house would determine his future with his sons. Meanwhile there was the not inconsiderable problem of finding the means and persuasion to convincethe current owner to move out.

He drove home more leisurely, determined to calm down the atmosphere prior to tomorrow's visit of Kate's parents. In the event, they struggled through an awkward monosyllabic evening hiding behind newspapers and a feigned interest in television. At eleven o'clock she announced that she was going upstairs to a guest room and would be grateful if she was not disturbed.

James resisted the temptation to assure her that there was no chance of that, instead he held out his hand, which was ignored, and wished her 'God Bless', this too fell on deaf ears and he watched that still small bottom disappear, wondering how his reaction to that part of her anatomy could have altered so much in ten years or, in reality, over the last two or three years as her provincial, professional background exerted itself into a more sedentary way of life than he could ever contemplate. The thought of which brought back thoughts of tomorrow's meeting with the Palmers.

James respected his in-laws, more than that he liked and admired them, tomorrow would be difficult. He crossed to the drinks cupboard, poured a Macallan and took from the drawer of his desk the green leather volume of Other Men's Flowers.

This anthology of poetry first published in the dark days of 1944 by Field Marshall Lord Wavell is a compilation of favourite verse, both his and those who served under him in the Middle East as they staved off first the Germans and then the Japanese.

As his father-in-law had remarked at the time of presenting him with this handsome book,

'It brought great comfort to them and it has brought hope to me and I can think of nothing more appropriate than the words of the French Renaissance writer Montaigne whose observation, 'I have gathered a posy of other men's flowers' was included as an introduction.'

Jeremy had also appended a foot note.

P.S He was also famous for introducing way back in the sixteenth century, the expression

'Que sais-je' - What do I know!! - Which you may well be thinking when you read this? He turned again to Jeremy's hand written sonnet 116 and dwelt on lines two and three and wondered again why his father in law had underlined them.

> …Admit impediments; love is not love
> Which alters when it alteration finds…

Once again he pondered what doubts he too might have entertained, indeed what all marriages must at some time face. Can marriage be a transitory friendship? Until now he would have thought not, but people change and unless there is give and take sooner or later things will come to a head. If he was honest, whilst he paid lip service to this creed, his very positive approach to everything meant there was very little 'give' from his side and matters had rapidly deteriorated with Kate since his fall out with Edward Lawson.

In the ensuing turmoil, both commercial and domestic, he knew he had not been rational, but he had been under considerable stress, financial and otherwise. She was only partially aware of this, she could not have coped with these extra worries, he would not have expected her to and so trying to explain all those financial withdrawals, initialled E.L. without any form of explanation from Edward, had wounded him far more deeply than any of them knew.

Glancing down at the handwritten poem he suddenly realized that this applied to Kate as much as himself.

He sighed, he was tired and lonely, his head was aching and the prospect of people pointing accusing fingers made him angry and he determined to take them on.

In this mood, scarcely prepared for sleep he deliberately left the open book on the sofa for Kate to ponder tomorrow and went upstairs, in hope rather than expectation of sleep.

He threw himself down on the large four-poster bed and stared up at its oak panelled top, the memories of better times finally calming his churning mind but not his throbbing head. He went into their bathroom and whilst he waited for the Paracetamol to kick in, the familiar odour of the Cartier she wore softened his mood and he re-traced his steps to the study and removed the book from view, whatever may have once been the Palmer's problem did not need to become known to their daughter now, she had enough concerns.

James returned to his bed, the small cathartic act sufficient to send him to sleep and awake him as usual at six thirty. He showered and still in his robe came down to find that Kate was ahead of him, the dogs were out and the coffee was busily percolating as he entered the kitchen. She attempted a smile, a little awkwardly maybe, and he returned it, squeezing her shoulder affectionately to help ease the tension of what threatened to be a difficult day.

Jack Priory was aware of what was going on and, from past experience, sympathetic to James's plight, part of which concern had been to order his friend not to contemplate coming to the office.

He tried to help at home but was more of a hindrance really and was quite relieved when the Palmers, due at around midday, not unexpectedly arrived at twenty minutes past eleven. Their concerns were visibly lowered when they saw their daughter dressed and, on the surface at least, appearing to be in control of herself.

Coffee was served and the attempt at pleasantries gained them an hour or so but, situations like this are always difficult, recrimination is rarely far below the surface and it was Angela, perhaps not unexpectedly, who pointedly asked James how he had let this happen to her daughter.

'Angela, if I had seen it coming I would not have let it happen.'
'Perhaps you should alter your priorities and pay more attention to your family and less to your business. And your friend Edward, did he not guess what was going on?'
Kate piled in with. 'The fact is Mummy, he has let Edward down as well.'

Before James could respond, Jeremy's professional training sought to restore fairness.
'We are aware that the company has been demerged and that James and Edward have chosen to take their own paths. Personally, I think it a great shame because I liked Edward a lot but.' He held his hand up to rebut any comments and continued, 'I admire my son-in-law a great deal more and I will not hear his business acumen questioned. As to the friendship between them, to have destroyed that, whatever it was, must have been a very serious difference of opinion which only they can possibly fully understand. Unless it is pertinent to this sad affair, I suggest we steer clear of that subject.'

James's attempt to thank Jeremy was cut short by another broadside from Kate.
'Daddy, you are making it too easy for him, he listens to no-one.' She saw his hackles rise.
'You are so wrong Kate, I always take heed of good advice, Your Father, Miles Stanhope Court, Tim Cooper, Henry White, Sir Julian, there are many more, but you are correct to assume that unless I see the merit of advice, I do not heed it. And, before you can say any more, I have always listened and deferred to what you have to say about the children and matters relating to the house etc.'

'But not anymore,' she snapped back.
'I wonder why,' he said quietly.

Angela looked at her husband, seeking support for their daughter. He held up his hands.
'I had no idea things were this bad, why don't we all take a break to cool down?'

He signalled James to follow him into the study. Closing the panelled oak door firmly behind them he turned to face James, the following confession being the last thing in the world that the younger man expected to hear.

'Before Kate was born, Angela had an affair; she nearly left me for another man, someone whom I had met at Oxford. It was my fault, I was working so hard carving a name for myself, I lost track of what was important.'

'I guessed,' said James.
The solicitor's intelligent face looked at him quizzically?
'The sonnet'.
Jeremy nodded, 'You are a bright chap, and I can only pray that you draw the same inspiration from it that I did.'

'Does Kate know?'
'Not unless Angela spills the beans today, but if you think it will help I will happily tell her myself.'
James shook his head. 'When Kate accuses me of not listening, she is never more wrong than in your case, I respected you from the start; I have come to hold you in great admiration, never more than today.' He held out his hand. 'Whatever happens I will always value your friendship.'

'And I will always value yours.'
The lawyer grasped his son-in-law's hand and turned away to hide the moistness in his eyes.

They rejoined the others, Kate's previous comparatively bright mood had dissipated, there was a distinct air of gloom, no one sure of the next step. James grasped the nettle.

'Kate darling you are all stressed out, things seem more confused than they really are and I must take my share of the blame for that; I am genuinely sorry for not noticing you were so unhappy. However, on the central issue of this unhappiness, I give you my word, an oath on the thing I hold dearest to me along with you, the happiness of my two sons; there is no affair with Sally Parkinson. I met her at that dinner in Nottingham, an occasion you deliberately chose to avoid and I danced with her, something that I now regret in view of the effect it has had on you. Maybe I was showing off, making a futile gesture to Edward and Connie Lawson because yes, excuse me Angela; I was well and truly pissed off. But, I am not going to repeat this again, I HAVE NOT SEEN HER SINCE and if these accusations continue then we will definitely have no marriage.'

In despair he looked at them, hoping for support, it came from the most expected source, the ever understanding Jeremy.

His voice was soft and kind. 'I believe you James, I think we should all trust you and try and move on.' He turned toward his wife and sought her agreement. 'Angela?'
'I want to believe you James.'

'Well I don't.' The hostility in Kate's voice seemed unreasonable even to her mother, whose suggestion that she spent a little time with them in Bournemouth was also savagely rejected.
'Why s hould I move out and leave the stage clear for him to see her.'

'Then I suggest I stay here with you.' She looked enquiringly at James, who gratefully nodded his acquiescence. The years slipped away as she assumed her mother role, the resistance from her daughter completely melted as she asked James to arrange for them to see Dominic Forster so that an early appointment could be made to see a Consultant Psychiatrist. She stood up and gently took her daughter's arm.

'Come on dear you need a little rest?'
The men slumped in their chairs, drained by the events as they heard Kate and her mother climb the stairs.
James looked across. 'Fancy a coffee?'
Jeremy's forlorn and weary expression, a firm indication of his own plight and inclination.
'Let's take it outside; we need to have a change of air.'

The lawyer stood up slowly, for the first time since James had known him, he looked his age and seeming to sense the other's concern, gave his son-in-law an intuitive wry smile before disappearing through the French doors and out onto the stone flagged terrace.
Angela had joined him by the time James returned with the pot of coffee, the atmosphere was difficult, not with embarrassment, but with the sad foreboding that Kate was going to take time to recover and that its effect on them all, including the boys, was likely to make life difficult for all of them.

Their somewhat muted conversation was interrupted by June who advised that Doctor Forster was on the telephone. James returned with the news that Dominic had pre-empted their earlier decision and had pencilled in an appointment for Kate after tomorrow's morning surgery. An hour later, almost to the minute, Kate joined them professing to feel much better.
She received the news from Dominic by kissing her husband lightly on the cheek and whispering 'thank you'.
The conversation was light, with everyone trying to make Kate feel relaxed and welcome, the unspoken concern was the Jekyll and Hyde personality she had exhibited; it did not bode well for the future.

CHAPTER THIRTY EIGHT

The following morning James was at the office by seven thirty. He cleared his in-tray, had a brief update from Jack Priory on the new 'Chicago' range of kitchens and left a five o'clock deadline on the Mapperley Park property for Neil Hannah at Frank Innes.

The feeling that he was getting back into harness improved his humour and Jack, watching him from his upstairs office, smiled as he saw him chatting easily to three of the workers from the production line before taking the top off the 911 and sweeping out of the brick archway in the direction of Nottingham.

He returned home to accompany his wife to her appointment, his mood swinging back towards despair as he saw Angela's unhappy expression.

'She will only go to see Dominic if I take her. I am sorry James but she feels you will try to manipulate him, I think it best to agree otherwise she is going to retreat even further into her shell.'

He made no attempt to disguise his annoyance.

'Whatever.' His response both cryptic and empty.

Jeremy appeared with his daughter and they watched him jump back into the Porsche and disappear in a flurry of flying gravel. His mood as black as the car and his mind moving at the same impetuous speed, he once again hurtled towards Milford Hall. This time he was not looking for solace or inspiration he was seeking his destiny.

As he drove he remembered his cherished red MG sports car and his defiant trip to Birmingham after Osborne the manager at Martins Bank, had sought to deny him his first commercial enterprise. The apparent impasse that was Charles Lattimer's busy diary – no possible chance that he could spare him a few minutes… he remembered sitting in the banking hall, reading and re-reading every magazine until finally his siege tactics had paid off and the Manager's intrigue provided him with the window of opportunity that he craved.

The even tougher opposition that he had encountered at APP and how he had at the twelfth hour not only persuaded the tough old ex-Guards officer, Sir Julian Abercrombie to support him, but also earned the respect of the other Directors as they saw him succeed, as very few of their 'would-be' new clients ever did.

On a more mundane level, he had won over the suspicious retailers of Bournemouth; the nervous old ladies at Watkin Hall to whom, like Mr. Braithwaite in York, he had given not only financial help, but also a new purpose in life.

With Jack Priory's help he had introduced a brand new business concept which was already making many of the rough tough plumbers and joiners of Nottingham far more successful than they had ever imagined and likewise, with this same friend, he had outmanoeuvred Edward Lawson.

This was a pyrrhic victory that still saddened him, not that he would ever admit it; that the schoolboy rugby photograph, including Edwards's international cap, still remained in his office was clear evidence of that.

Of course, had his family not left Milford Hall he would not have changed schools and he would probably not have met the fair haired giant. We could still have been in the same England team, he mused defiantly…

His reverie was interrupted by the sight of the great iron gates with their well- remembered Rising Sun motif and for a moment he almost faltered, but the view from the back seat of the Rover re-asserted itself; as did his father's distressed face, captured in the rear view mirror. He heard with even greater clarity the youthful oath he had defiantly declared, 'One day we will move back into our home.'

That day and even worse, the day he had returned home from school in triumph with news of his place at Cambridge, only to hear against a background of the haunting sound of Mendelssohn, the whispered conversation between his mother and her sister, the sad acceptance that his father's life was to be taken away.

The unjustness of it had never left him, it was not fair and there was so much he could have shared with his father. He knew he could not have him back but he would deliver his youthful promise.

The left hand gate was open, he cautiously drove through, parking the car outside the stone lodge; almost in sequence the front door opened and an older version of a face he remembered, looked shrewdly at him.

'Is that you Master. James?' The cautious voice ventured.

'Hello Mrs. Price,' his smile lighting up the old lady's face as she took his hands.
He leaned forward and kissed her cheek, her pleasure at seeing him again was obvious. 'My you have grown.' She laughed at the innateness of her own comment.

'Is Mr Price still running the shoots?'
'We have a new gamekeeper now, although Arthur helps when he can, he has had a new hip you know - but there is still no one better at raising pheasants,' she declared with obvious pride and then realizing they were still on the doorstep.

'Come in, come in, you will have a cup of tea.' His response to the rhetorical question was to ask if that included a piece of her cherry and raisin cake.

She went to the glass-fronted cupboard that housed her best china and took out the Royal Albert, admiring the Country Roses design that she and Arthur had collected in the early years of their marriage.

'Fancy you remembering that, how many years is it?'

'Twenty three.' She detected the sadness in his voice and watched carefully as he sought the right words; finally she pre-empted him.

'Is that what brings you back?' He nodded and waited for her to continue.

'The people around here missed your family, although I have to be fair and say that Mr Gilbert treats us well enough, but it's only the shooting he is interested in. We all thought young Stephen would take on the cattle and the farm, but he went off to Australia so the place seems empty most of the time. But don't listen to me harping on, as long as the two of us can stay here, that is all we really worry about.

She continued in full flow, barely letting him get a word in unless he was answering questions about his mother and sister.

'Mr Robert,' she began and then faltered as she saw the effect it had on him, the awkward moment fortunately spared by the sound of a large car heading towards the house. She peeped through the window and confirmed it was Mr Gilbert and he knew the moment was nigh, the old lady sensed it too and although she didn't comment, he guessed that she had an inkling as to what his visit might be about.

He stood up, his face serious, with the passage of time his features bore an eerie likeness to Robert Carrington, but she refrained from comment, instead she put the remains of the cherry cake into a Tupperware box and handed it to him.

'Bring the box back the next time you come.'

He laughed, 'It has been lovely to see you again Mrs. Price, please give my regards to your husband'.

She let him out, wondering quite what he was up to at the big house, she sensed it was important but was surprised when he left the car and made his way on foot.

James tried to collect his thoughts but nothing logical was in his head, he would have to play it by ear or turn back; the latter was not an option.

He found himself standing under the great stone tower, where in the early days carriages and then later motor cars would have decanted their passengers here to be received by the butler, in his mother's day he remembered it had been Wilson, or Mr Wilson to himself and his sister Louise.

He steeled himself, pulled the bell handle and waited; finally he heard the click of leather heels, a large key was turned in the brass lock and finally the heavy door swung open to reveal a grey haired man in his mid-fifties. His face was serious but not harsh and a smile appeared as he said.

'J R Carrington, Leicester and England number ten.'

He saw the surprise on his guest's face and enlightened him.

'I saw the number plate on the Porsche; it was a number I had seen many times at the Leicester Tigers' training ground.'

'My son,' he explained, 'got a couple of schoolboy caps, also at fly-half

'Steve Gilbert,' Mrs. Price's information and the father's explanation providing the clues.

'He showed a lot of promise, whatever happened to him?'

'He became disenchanted with England and emigrated to Australia; sadly, I don't see much of him these days.'

The irony was not lost on James who was here today largely because fate had taken his father away and here he was discussing with a father, the decision of his son to transfer himself to the other side of the world and effectively out of his father's life.

'I was quite a fan of yours, I dared to hope Steve would follow in your footsteps at the Tigers and maybe even England, and then he flew off into the far beyond and you retired.'

'He would definitely have got my place in the Leicester team and he had the skill to go even further - I could never tackle like he did.'

'You didn't need to, but it is nice to know he is remembered with regard.'

James's understanding smile, prompted Mr. Gilbert to formally introduce himself and extend an invitation.

'Forgive me James,' he held out his hand, 'David Gilbert, please do come in.'

He stepped into the porch and through the inner half glazed doors into the imposing great hall with its wonderful semi-circular staircase, its oak steps and balustrading which lead to either side of the galleried landing above.

'Why don't you go through to the study, I will organise a spot of lunch - you will stay?'

His voice suggested disappointment if the answer had been negative, which of course it was not.

In a daze from the rapid turn of events, James opened the panelled door on the far right hand side of the hall and accessed the short corridor that led to the study. His heart was pounding; he felt quite overcome as he pushed open the door to reveal so many remembered treasures from his childhood.

There was a different desk, his father's now had pride of place in his own study, but the rows of imposing leather bound books still lined the walls, the fireplace with its brass club seat still surrounded the fireplace and the carpets too with their red Turkish design still provided familiar warmth.

He didn't hear David Gilbert enter, and his educated Leicestershire voice, so similar to his father's had quite an effect on him. He was ashen faced as he turned to his host, on whom the effect was not lost.

'My dear boy, I am sorry to have crept up on you, why don't you sit down whilst I get you a drink.' He waved towards the large leather easy chairs and moved to the bookcase. James recovered in time to say.

'War and Peace.'

David Gilbert laughed and pressed the well-worn spine of what appeared to be a row of books, the action prompted a panel of books to swing open revealing the 'Butler's Pantry'.

He knowingly handed James a large Macallan, enjoying the pleasant astonishment as his guest accepted.

A couple of days after I moved in your father kindly sent me a case, along with this note; from the top shelf of the cupboard he retrieved an envelope it read, in handwriting he immediately recognized as his father's, David Gilbert Esq.

'Open it,' he said kindly.

With trembling fingers James slid the notepaper from the cream envelope and read in the same firm sloping hand.

> *Welcome to Milford Hall, - look after it well,*
> *I have a feeling my son might want it back one day!*
> *Sincerely,*
> *Robert Carrington.*

James was dumbfounded, he stared at the note and with some embarrassment at David Gilbert, he was quite unable to think coherently. The situation was rescued as the housekeeper tapped on the door and brought in a trolley on which she had prepared game soup and beef sandwiches.

The two men looked at each other with understanding, the host again taking the initiative.

'Since Steve went to Australia, I have been expecting, even hoping you would call; it is why you came isn't it?'

He looked enquiringly at James who was at last regaining some colour to his cheeks,

'Do you want to sell, David?'

'I hadn't used to, but I miss Stephen so much and this is a bloody great house to rattle around in on one's own. But I am not in any rush.'

James looked at him trustingly, their relationship had come a long way in the past half an hour or so. He gave David Gilbert a synopsis of his life, his dreams and ambitions and with sadness his present difficulties with Kate. He had come here today he confided, without any plans but in desperation, hoping that somehow this house which was the centre of his families fortunes, both good and bad, would somehow guide him forward.

'It will evoke even more memories when you go round it,' David assured him.

'As you probably know the sale of the house included all the big pieces of furniture, they were after all made for the house and your parents more or less insisted that it should remain whole. They were right, but it was an extraordinarily kind gesture as I knew they had gone through a bad patch financially and they could have raised quite a lot by selling them at one of the big auction houses in London'. He smiled, an understanding expression on his face, before continuing:

' When you buy the house they will all be included, together with the large Staincliffe portraits and hunting scenes which are all set in the Belvoir Hunt Saturday Country.'

James Carrington had never found decisions difficult, quite the reverse when his track record was examined; he was nevertheless at a loss for meaningful words.

'What sort of price do you have in mind David?'

Now the older man confessed his uncertainty.

'Until I met you today, I had toyed with the idea of selling so that I could, as I told you, spend more time with my son. However, he doesn't know that, so I may well have to convince him of my decision. You have your life to sort out so I suggest we keep in touch and when the time comes, we will both seek advice from reputable agents and agree a price. There will be no need to put the house on the market. I think in the brief space of time I have known you and the confidence I hope you have in me, will mean we can do this as gentlemen.'

James stood up, his eyes decidedly moist; he offered his hand, which was firmly received by his host.

'Next time I will bring the drink.'

'I should damn well think so!'

Smiling, they retraced their steps to the front door, James declining a full tour of the house until his next visit which, he hoped, would be sooner rather than later.

Still in a dream he set off down the drive aware of the amusement in David Gilbert's voice as he called after him. 'You can drive up here next time.'

He reached his car, praying that Mrs. Price would not intercept him and spoil the day with any unintended banal chatter. Sliding into the seat, he swung the car around and was gone. This time he drove slowly, deferring the moment when he must explain his absence and face the reality of Kate's illness. Then reality kicked in and the euphoria vanished, how on earth was he going to convince her and fulfil his promise to David Gilbert?

CHAPTER THIRTY NINE

They were all on the terrace talking quietly with Kate seemingly holding centre stage. He steeled himself and walked up to her, casually giving her a peck on the cheek and declining a drink from Jeremy until he had listened to Dominic's prognosis.

Glancing at her daughter, Angela hesitatingly took over,

'Kate's Hb blood levels are low, which explains her lethargy. He has prescribed,' she perched her glasses on the end of her nose and read the label on the white box, Ferrous Sulphate tablets, to help increase her iron levels.'

She continued, 'the Psychiatrist's report has concluded that mentally there is nothing basically wrong, but she is very stressed and he suggests she should take a short break, a change of scene, somewhere away from here, or Bournemouth,' she added quickly.

'Mummy is taking me to Harrogate.'

'I hope you don't mind James; I thought a week's cosseting would be just what the doctor ordered, or at least it was what his wife ordered. She suggested we go to a health spa which is, as Kate has mentioned, quite close to Harrogate.

She looked at James for approval.

He squinted and grimaced. 'I hope the spa water tastes better than the stuff I had to drink in Bath.'

'Speaking of which,' Jeremy disappeared, emerging with a bottle of Roederer Crystal Champagne. 'Nothing but the best, to get my daughter back on her feet.'

James nodded approvingly, 'as with women, Jeremy, you associate only with the best.'

They sipped the champagne and finally Kate asked the question on all their lips.

'How was your day James?'

'Well, I spent a lot of it feeling pretty sorry for myself and, to be honest, dreading coming home. Had I anticipated this, I would have been here hours ago. Why don't I treat you all to a nice meal out - what about the Falcon in Uppingham? We could point out the house that the boy's will be going into - Brooklands, my old Alma Mater, or it was until the world turned upside down, which is not going to happen to my sons, our sons.' He swiftly corrected himself.

The looks he exchanged with Kate suggested they both remembered the same slip of the tongue he had made on their last visit to the school. Perhaps Angela picked up on something because she diplomatically suggested The Peacock, their local hostelry. 'It will save us having to drive so far – after all we only normally drink Bollinger.'

This aside at James's usual tipple restored their good humour, although he was still protesting when they set out for the Peacock. With spirits restored, the evening passed pleasantly without James having to explain his whereabouts or the remarkable events of the day.

The following morning the atmosphere was still light and friendly, the ladies were packed by nine thirty, cases standing neatly at the top of the stairs and they were laughingly demanding the hall porter. James hearing them, quickly grabbed his morning coat from the dressing room and tails flapping, hurtled along the landing to the head of the stairs, loudly apologising for the delay.
He put their bags into the somewhat limited confines of Kate's Triumph Stag. She still had the bright red Morgan he had bought as her wedding present, but these days it was reserved for short journeys when the weather was guaranteed to stay fine. It is gaining value every day, he assured her.

He fastened the hood down and, as he helped Angela into the passenger seat, was conscious of the long slim legs opposite; she was still so attractive, did he really want to risk losing her? In the same breath he wondered if she was prepared to change or risk losing him.

'Yorkshire here we come,' she revved the engine, adjusted her sunglasses and in a cloud of dust, which scattered the dogs, the smart little car headed north.

Jeremy too was packed, his mode of transport a more stately Jaguar.

'I will let the dust settle and then I will be off. Look after yourself James, I have a feeling everything is going to be okay, but it will take time.'

He looked his son-in-law in the eye, 'She is worth it James, you can get over these hiccups, as I did.'

James took his hand, unable to conjure up the right words. He stood watching until the car was out of sight and suddenly feeling very much alone went into house accompanied by Vincent and the other dogs.

On an impulse he went into the study and sat at his father's desk, wondering when and how he was going to return it to its rightful place at Milford. He thought of his mother, he wanted to let her hear the news but just as quickly dismissed the thought, he had long since planned his mother's return to Milford; she would be at his side as they returned down that long drive to their home.

This last thought, stiffened his resolve with regard to Kate, either she came willingly or not at all. This house had been his impetus for nearly a quarter of a century; he wanted it not just for himself but also for his sons, as his parents had wanted it for him.

The thought of Charles and Edward decided him on his next course of action. Tomorrow was Saturday, he opened the top drawer of his desk and took out this term's calendar, he scanned the dates, both the under 10's and the under 9's were at home to Nottingham High School Prep. He knew from personal experience that they would be well coached and very well organized; the head of games in the main school was the England coach 'Chalky White', whom James knew because of his Leicester connections, he knew his influence would have filtered down to the junior teams.

He was excited about tomorrow; he was interested to see if the boys were showing any aptitude for rugby. His stargazing was interrupted by the telephone, it was Jack Priory with the good news that the agents had confirmed their clients' acceptance of James's offer for the property in Mapperley Park - 'your Dracula house', as his partner irreverently described it.

'Philistine.' James's first response and then thoughtfully, 'I was just about to come to the office, why don't we have a proper look round this afternoon? I will get the keys on my way in.'

Jack agreed, secretly looking forward to seeing what plans James had for the place; his track record at spotting and renovating properties was, after all, impeccable.

Jack was already there when he arrived; he had, as James had done on his first visit, filled in the time by exploring the garden, he had been similarly captivated by the detail not only in the grounds but the external statement that this wonderful property inspired.

He heard the Porsche snarl to a halt and joined his co-director in the black and white gabled entrance porch.

'Good eh?' James challenged him.

'Superb,' Jack conceded, 'for a Dracula house that is!'

Nevertheless, he quickly warmed to his friend's ideas in terms of converting the various downstairs rooms into kitchen showrooms and the upstairs into bathrooms.

These would be interspersed with a coffee bar and sales area where, Mr Priory suggested, 'Very attractive girls in mini-skirts would effortlessly persuade prospective clients to part with their money.'

'Exactly, just like we did in Bournemouth with Rachel and Fiona.'

'Maybe, they would come and work up here.'

'They probably would, but those are wonderful memories that I would prefer to remain as memories if I am to retain my sanity let alone my concentration.'

He signalled Jack to come outside, 'these garden walls that face the lawns will be absolutely perfect to set our conservatories against.'

Jack was beginning to understand very clearly why this man had become so successful. He also recognised the potential it offered not only to their new company, but also his existing one, the investments he had already made in machinery and production space could be maximized by working round the clock, in shifts if necessary.

They were also 'in on the ground floor', they were just slightly ahead of their time. The property improvements they planned to introduce would in the future be inherent in every new building, meanwhile hundreds of thousands of older properties were crying out for development; improvements that banks and building societies would lend money on.

Jack signalled to James. 'Who do we know in the local building societies, banks etc. who would extend mortgages against these proposals? We need to establish lines of credit and make it easy for people.'

'That is a brilliant thought, in fact why don't we encourage them to have someone in-house, their own sales desk in our building at the week end?'

Jack Priory was rubbing his index finger against his upper lip, a sure indication that in matters financial, he was giving it very serious thought.

'I like it James, I can see my retirement yacht on the horizon.'

'Wait I haven't finished yet. The garden area, the 'Dingly Dell' where the dogs are buried, the shady areas under the beech trees, we can sell garden furniture, franchise it for the time being, that way we don't have to re-invent the wheel, we can pick up later on the best ideas.'

Jack Priory was constantly amazed at this fertile mind that could conceive one idea after another and then seamlessly turn them into a logical and coherent business plan.

He had first met James when, as juniors, they had represented the County at squash, they had respected the other's skills; he knew that his association with Edward Lawson had also been forged on the playing field before that understanding had been harnessed into founding the highly successful Fordmill Construction empire.

He recalled the night they had launched Minster Kitchens and, at the end of that momentous evening, the handshake across the roof of the Porsche in the Trent Bridge car park.

He had made it clear to James that they must always be upfront with each other. He had received his assurance on this and hoped, fervently, that his friend would always take him seriously.

Unlike Edward, whom James had launched into business, Jack was the third generation of his family to run an ever more profitable company, one that had repelled several takeover attempts, in their determination to remain in charge of their own commercial destiny.

'You are quite something Mr Carrington, I feel exhausted listening to you.'

A broad smile lit his face, 'But I am very happy to be doing business together.'

There was just a hint of emphasis on the last word - James smiled wryly at him, nothing said, but message clearly understood.

CHAPTER FORTY

Meanwhile in Yorkshire, Kate and her mother were having their last 'proper food', albeit a simple plate of smoked salmon washed down by a glass of Sancerre, at the Harewood Arms, half way between Leeds and Harrogate.

The atmosphere like the lunch was light, but pleasant though it had been, they did not delay returning to the car as they were both keen to check out the credentials of the spa which had been so highly recommended by Liz Forster.

They drove as quickly as the traffic would allow, Kate to her mother's consternation, booting the Stag up the hill on Leeds Road and then resuming the more pedestrian pace as they entered the town.

It had been many years since her parents had visited this elegant Spa town famous for its Baths and efficacious water. Angela did, however, remember the vast green space that was the Stray.

'It must have been around Easter, there was a most amazing display of crocus or should that be crocuses or whatever is the Latin plural for it?'
Angela paused, thoroughly enjoying the memories of her youth, her daughter meanwhile admitted she was unsure of the answer.

'I think it is croci, but best ask Daddy, he is brilliant on things like that.'
'We stayed at the Majestic.' Angela declared. 'It was an enormous hotel, and there it is.'
She pointed with delight to the imperious building that did indeed stand majestically high at the end of the town.

The traffic started to speed up and spotting the signs for Skipton they headed for the Dales which, with the equally impressive Yorkshire Moors and its adjoining coastline, surely offers as diverse a scenery as can be found anywhere in Great Britain.

Angela studied the green leather AA Road Atlas, trying to identify their position.
'Menwith Hill is on our right.'
Kate identified the great 'golf balls' that housed the American radar tracking network that reputably intercepts messages from all over the globe. These are supposedly analysed at this

intelligence base, much to the chagrin of the various Peace movements who regularly organise mass protests here, as illustrated by the collection of caravans and placards here today.

'How far to Bolton Abbey?' And then as her mother lowered her head to look, 'don't bother, I have just seen the sign, put the book away dear.'

Her mother sighed with relief, 'You are worse than your father, he is such an understanding man, but in a car he is a different person.'

'We are looking for a sign,' her daughter continued, 'According to the brochure it should be dark blue with gold lettering, it will say Nidderdale House.'

The Stag roared down the hill into Bolton Abbey, crossed the ancient stone bridge and was picking up speed on the other side when the co-pilot's excited voice proclaimed that their destination was, according to the sign, 200 yards on the left.

Kate went through the gears and they emerged reasonably sedately from the avenue of trees that led to the house and saw the fine Yorkshire building that had, according to the brochure, once been part of the Devonshire Estate.

A few guests were sitting under umbrellas on the terrace and one person in particular noticed the auburn haired slim figure that jumped out of the driving seat.

He strolled casually across; his smile both warm and welcoming. 'Allow me.'

Kate turned to the tall good-looking man in a cream linen jacket and navy slacks.

'Thank you so much, it is a difficult car to unload.'

He smiled and directed the porter to take the cases to reception, effected a mock bow.

'I hope that you and your sister have an enjoyable stay.'

Angela laughed, 'I can see why you wanted to come to Yorkshire.'

At reception they were allocated adjoining rooms and, having unpacked, attended a five o'clock meeting to hear what fitness routine was planned for them and the other new guests, about eighty per cent of whom were women.

The men were definitely in need of treatment, the women were divided into large ladies who like the men needed an eating regime and others, varying from mature types like Angela still blessed with a good figure, to the younger ones like Kate who were merely indulging themselves in a little TLC or escaping from the chores of motherhood.

After the introduction they availed themselves of a bicycle and rode along the trails that meandered through the spacious grounds of this fine estate. Except that the paddocks housed cattle instead of horses, Kate felt that she could have been at her beloved Woolmington.

Her mother sensing that her daughter was mentally somewhere else left her to her own thoughts.

She too had memories of the stress bought on by a marriage under siege; in her case, she had caused that anguish. Looking back she remembered with sadness the grief she must have inflicted on her husband and yet Jeremy, as quietly proud as ever, had never let on. For once he forgot his professional reasoning and pretended it wasn't happening, hoping it would go eventually go away. He threw himself into his work, concentrating on what he was good at and had the satisfaction of seeing the practice grow until it was the largest in the county.

The affair had been brief, it had been exciting, but not without its anxious moments, particularly the afternoon at Brighton when she came down the staircase at the Grand Hotel, to be confronted by Jeremy's sister who emerged from the lift.

She thought that Pamela guessed, but she appeared to accept her comment that she had climbed the staircase to 'admire its wonderful cast iron details'. It had never again been mentioned and she split with Roger shortly afterwards when he was offered a job as a Don at his old college.

Her husband knew instinctively that it was over, but they had never discussed it and ten months later Kate was born and she sank back into respectability.

No, life had been good to her, she had a devoted, much respected husband, but she had in the early days wondered occasionally what life would have been like at Oxford.

She had since seen him only once, at a Balliol College re-union, when she had tremulously accompanied Jeremy who had been asked to propose a toast to the retiring Dean.

They had both carried it off rather well, although the conversation had the stilted forced politeness that such meetings inevitably have.

'Angela how lovely to see you again, how long must it be?'

'Fourteen years,' she had responded far too quickly.

'Can you imagine that old boy; she has quite a memory your dear wife.'

'She is a remarkable woman; I cannot imagine life without her. Have you never thought of getting hitched?'

'Good Heavens no, far too many pretty girls in Oxford to make a commitment like that.'

The cruel remark had remained with Angela, sensing she would have been dumped when his eye had fallen on a new target. If she was honest the clandestine side of the affair had been exciting, it had for a while certainly spiced up her life but once passion has run its course, lovers without love and an enjoyment of each other soon become resentful and sad. In that period before the war, unfaithful women were ostracised by their circle of friends, the other women fearful of what influence such a woman might have on their husbands.

The pain it causes and even worse the inadequacy, particularly the sexual side of it to a sensitive person like Jeremy Palmer, could so easily have ruined her husband's life and career.

She understood what might be going through her son-in-law's mind and hoped that Kate would have her father's resilience and resolve to see it through.

They arrived back at the cycle shed, parked the front wheels in the slots allocated to them and made their way back to their adjoining rooms.

Kate suggested meeting at seven thirty, declaring she was, 'famished after all that exercise.' Back in her room, Angela sorted through her large shoulder bag.

'It's just as well I sneaked in a few biscuits!'

Kate did not sleep well, tossing and turning until nearly three, almost getting up and leaving at one point. She knew that the accusations against James were not substantiated and knew well enough that if anyone sought to question or deny him further, he would push them out of his life without remorse or without heed to others. The events with Edward Lawson had clearly depicted the ruthless side of her husband, not only did he get rid of his friend to whom he owed so much, he had also disposed of the company although not the respect for his former directors.

The trouble with living with someone like James Carrington is that they subsume your character until you have to consciously make a decision or it is made for you. Conversely, he would say that she should make her own mind up as he was too busy to be bothered with trivia.

Why, she asked herself, do I put up with it?

She knew why, because whilst at times she hated him, she still deep down loved him, even more she was terrified that anyone else should have him.

She longed for the stable loving relationship that her parents had.

She finally drifted off and not feeling very energetic joined her mother for breakfast, which to their surprise was a plentiful selection of healthy fruits and juices, with no limit on portions as the plates of the gentlemen opposite indicated.

From here, dressed in the white robes provided by Nidderdale, they proceeded to the dietician to be weighed and after exercising, have their pulse rates checked to compare the readings before and after the workout. A computer clicked into action and they were handed a printout designed to meet their demands from the course based on those readings.

Both were complimented on their general fitness levels and shown to the next room where, to their immense surprise the man dressed in the white suit was none other than Sir Galahad from the car-park.

He stood up smiling and introduced himself as Jonathan Mortimer.

'Don't be concerned, I am filling in for my mother, all I do is give you a list of treatments and activities. We can, for instance, wrap you in seaweed from Whitby, cover you in mud from Ilkley Moor, or perhaps you might prefer aromatherapy or a complete body massage. Personally I prefer the tennis or using the gym equipment.'

He handed them a health spa brochure which enticed them with a long list of facilities. All designed he assured them, 'to make your stay as welcome as possible, as we very much want you to come back.' There was a slight twinkle in his eye as he said this and Kate found herself adjusting her robe to hide the slight blush that had crossed her cheeks. They stood up, Kate thanked him and advised, 'I think my 'sister' and I will try the aerobics in the pool.' He was still laughing as they closed the door.

'I think you have a new admirer dear.'

'Mummy how could you.' Her daughter feigned surprise but she thought so too.

They opted for the indoor pool, joining four other women and two men in a few fairly elementary exercises, the time passed quite quickly and they were surprised at the end of the session to find it was lunchtime.

On the way to the dining room they called at reception to book a four o'clock massage. 'We are here to pamper ourselves,' Angela confidently assured her.

The buffet lunch, like breakfast, was an impressive spread, this time it was various salads with a large selection of fish, cold meats, fruit juices and numerous vegetarian options.

They tried not to be greedy but the food was very good, 'and we can work it off afterwards,' said the lady sitting opposite, although her appearance denied that claim.

Angela, however, nodded her agreement, assuring Kate,

'We are not going to starve after all, in fact I need a nice rest before I allow anyone to start pummelling my body, you don't have to join me, you never were any good at sitting still and besides you need time on your own.'

Her daughter smiled back. 'You mean I will keep interrupting when you are trying to do the crossword. Still the weather is rather nice, I think I might go and explore the park.'

She enjoyed her own company, she felt more relaxed than she had for a long time, it must be the Yorkshire air she thought and, probing her subconscious had what she thought was a brilliant idea, the more she considered it the better it became.

She sat on a rustic bench beneath one of the many oak trees, their branches all trimmed by the generations of cattle that had grazed beneath them, their judicious munching allowing a fine view of the park wherever you chose to sit. She was lost in her own thoughts when she became conscious of someone standing a few yards away, it was Jonathan Mortimer.

He was dressed in running vest and shorts; she subconsciously admired the long tanned legs and looked up to see him looking at her, his expression kind and warm.

'As you can see my sister has let me out on my own.'

He laughed sympathetically. 'I know how possessive mothers can be.'

Now it was her turn to empathise. 'It must be quite difficult if you work together.'

He gave her an amused look.

'I just help out, this is mother's place, I am afraid I have to confess to being an Estate Agent, please say you forgive me.'

She burst out laughing, 'So am I, well sort of, you are no doubt a chartered surveyor and I am just learning the ropes.'

He looked at her enquiringly, 'I know from your registration that you come from Rutland, is that where you have your branches?'

'On the contrary, we have three on the South Coast and have recently acquired one in York.'

He raised his eyebrows, 'Not Braithwaite's?'

'I am afraid so.'

'So it is you who are responsible for making the rest of us look like we are still in the stone ages. I have to compliment you on what you have achieved in getting old Braithwaite to sell; just about every firm in the county, including ourselves and even Stokesley's, who are the biggest, have cut no ice with him at all. How on earth did you manage it?'

'Are you sure you want me to bore you with this?'

He nodded, 'Anyone who has put one over on George Stokesley has a good tale to tell.'

He listened intently as she gave him a potted version of the events, including the wrong footing of Stokesley and told him that Liz Reed was in chargeon a day to day basis but that she intended to get more closely involved from now on.

'In fact, when you came over and I was looking a bit distant, that was the decision I had just reached.'

'Strange,' he said, 'I would love to give up the control, I have seen what Mother has achieved here and I think these retreats are going to become ever more popular. Four years ago this was my family home, as it had been my parents and grandparents. Now it is far too large for one family.'

She thought of her beloved Woolmington and James's obsession with buying back

Milford Hall, a place that dwarfed Nidderdale House.

As she perused her thoughts she heard him say softly. 'Presumably you are married and, looking at that magnificent engagement ring, to a pretty wealthy guy.'

'I am at the moment,' she heard herself saying, realising as she did so that this was the first chink in their marriage that she had ever admitted publicly, and this to someone whom she had only just met. She looked into his grey blue eyes.

'And you must be married with a couple of kids and all the trimmings.'
His eyes looked vacantly into the distance. 'Not any more'. His voice was empty as he turned to face her, 'Madeleine, she was French,' he stopped, summoning enough control to go on.

'She and our two daughters were killed in a motorway pile-up in the French Alps in March three years ago; they had been skiing with Madeline's parents.'
He looked drained of all life and as he sat down beside her he whispered, 'I don't often talk about it, it is too painful.'

She rested her hand on his. 'Everyone needs someone to confide in and if it helps I have never confided my doubts to anyone other than my parents.'

He drew a deep breath before checking his watch.

'We have some new guests arriving at five, and I must go and prepare for them.'
He stood up, once again she was aware of the long tanned legs and then he sat down again.

'Kate would you come for a drink this evening, at the Devonshire Arms just down the road?'

Before she could reply, he continued, 'it is allowed, ve do not lock you in zee bunkers.'
'Yah, I vill, danke.'

'At 7.30 Uhrs in ze auto park.'
And he was off, laughing as she was at the nonsense German that had so successfully broken the despondent mood.

CHAPTER FORTY ONE

Angela finishing her crossword in the conservatory, saw first Jonathan and then shortly afterwards her daughter, both seemed happy. Kate more so than she had seen her in a very long time; maybe this break was proving a good investment, she hoped so.

To her mother's chagrin they went in separate rooms for their body massage so she was denied, for the time being, an update on the afternoon's walk in the park.

Kate alone with her thoughts was amazed that she felt no remorse at agreeing to Johnnie's invitation; in fact she was genuinely looking forward to meeting him again. James had after all 'only' danced with Sally Parkinson; she was 'only' going to have a friendly drink with someone.

Her thoughts returned to the ideas running through her head when he had joined her in the park, these had been strengthened by what he confided regarding his own preferred future.

James would be impressed with her plans; it was what he would do.
She stopped, annoyed with herself, she was not looking for his approval. Damn him, he had told her that she was in charge and that is how she intended it to be from now on.

She was so lost in her thoughts that she did not hear the masseuse inviting her to turn over and when she did was slightly irritated at having to lie here doing nothing; she had plans, she needed to develop a strategy and she needed to arrange a meeting with Liz Reed.

The soothing hands eventually calmed her racing thoughts and at the end of the session she was thinking more logically. Her mother meanwhile had succumbed to the various oils and potions but, once they had reached the resident's lounge, was agog to know what Kate had been up to.

'Up to, mother!' Kate adopted an air of astonishment.

'I know you too well, you don't often come out of your shell and I suspect that Mr Mortimer has something to do with the spring in your step.'
Angela was not, however, expecting the next announcement.

'Actually Johnnie has invited me out for a drink this evening, I hope you don't mind.'

'Is that wise?' her mother was about to say, amending it to, 'my, my, he must have made quite an impression!'

She settled back expectantly and listened with a little concern about Kate's business plans.

'We came here Kate for you to relax not to exhaust yourself planning to run a business.'

'No, you brought me here to lift me out of the depression I had fallen into, to give my life some purpose.'

'But what will James say?'

'What can he say? He told me it was my company, I have seen him in action, he threw me in at the deep end with Mr. Braithwaite and, in Johnnie Mortimer's words, I pulled off what apparently every estate agent in Yorkshire had failed to do, persuaded him sell the business and, what's more, I gave him back a purpose in life.'

'Which is what perhaps, you hope to achieve with Mr. Mortimer.'

'Possibly, although my priority is the business, the other depends on James; I am not going to be dominated by him again.'

'Wow, this Yorkshire air really is good for you, you had better go and get ready, I had said we would have dinner with those people from Bakewell; you remember they were on our table at lunchtime?'

Kate kissed her mother on the cheek, 'You are a sport.'
As she walked away she heard Angela call out, 'put that lemon dress on, it shows off your figure.'

She returned to her room and telephoned the Braithwaite office in York, hoping since it was past closing time that she would still find Liz at the office. She did, the simple impromptu call a testimony to her commitment and determination to reward the faith that Kate had vested in her.

'Liz, hi it's Kate, how are you?'

'I'm fine, business is really good, I saw James last week, he probably told you.'

'No he didn't actually, which is partially why I am calling. As you know I am the MD and I have some big plans for Braithwaite's and those ideas involve you and me, Liz. He has other fish to fry. Can we arrange to meet tomorrow evening at the Devonshire Arms in Bolton Abbey? Bring an overnight bag as we have a lot to discuss and we are going to need a few glasses of shampoo.'

Liz chuckled at their code word for Taittinger. 'You're the boss, I will be there.'

'Before I ring off and forget, will you bring me a large notebook and a calculator?'

'You sound just like the Kate that swept Mr. Braithwaite and me off our feet a few months ago, not to mention the demolition job you did on George Stokesley.'

'To be fair, I think the latter was really down to James,' she admitted.

They chattered on about life 'Would she be coming up to York next week for the races?' 'You bet,' the enthusiastic reply.

Kate eventually rang off, almost mentioning that she had to get ready to go out, but that was a secret she intended to share only with her mother, at least for the time being.

She looked at her watch, it was a quarter to six and dinner was at six thirty, she showered quickly and dried her hair, not at all happy at how it fell across her shoulders, she would tell 'the manager' he needed to get a better class of hair-dryer she decided.

Taking the lemon dress from the wardrobe, she put it on and admitted to herself that Angela had been right; it did show off her figure. However, she hoped that she would not sit on a fly as she had done the first time it was worn, the squashed insect on her bottom had not exactly enhanced the impression she had set out to make.

With two minutes to spare she arrived at the dining room, less than inconspicuous amongst the track suits and casual wear of her fellow guests, most of whom turned to watch her entrance; A low wolf whistle from one of the men followed by a small curtsy from Kate providing a laugh and a dramatic indication of the increase in her self-esteem that was suddenly evident in her smiling demeanour. This positive reaction would have been quite impossible a week ago.

She tried to appear normal and chatty but was constantly looking at her watch, willing it to go faster, finally it was twenty five minutes past seven and she excused herself, advising she had to attend a business meeting.

She reached the car park with one minute to spare, he was already there leaning casually on the passenger door of a silver and azure blue Austin Healey; he too had made the effort, wearing corn coloured cords and a green check tweed jacket.

'You look stunning.' There was no flattery, and she knew that she did.

'And you look very handsome.'

'Made for each other,' he quipped and then turning the door handle swept his hand in the direction of the dark blue leather seats.

The Healey roared and snarled as he drove it, mostly one handed, the short distance to the Devonshire Arms. He parked near the hotel entrance, their arrival at the desk eliciting a warm welcome from the girls on reception. He asked them to advise the restaurant of their arrival and they continued into the cocktail bar; once again the reception was inviting.

'They all seem to know you,' Kate observed.

'They are all probably shocked at my dazzling guest; I normally come here for Sunday lunch with Mother.' He smiled coyly, his pleasure in her company evident.

They were interrupted by Robert, the head waiter.

'Mr. Mortimer, Madam, good evening, perhaps I might leave the menus with you and ask Alan to bring you a drink from the bar.'

He inclined his head towards Kate. 'A gin and tonic please.'

'And for you sir? A pint of Theakston's I imagine.'

'Your imagination is spot on as usual Robert, although one of these days I am going to change my poison if only to keep you on your toes!'

The mood was light and like the wine, the atmosphere was good and a little intoxicating, so much so that the evening simply slipped away, only the lack of other guests alerting them to the fact that it was close to midnight and as he put it, 'time to go before I turn back into a frog.'

They returned to the car, each happy with their own thoughts; overhead the moon pierced the leaves of the great trees and dappled the car park, giving it the appearance of a giant camouflage net. Fingers entwined they enjoyed its refuge, its sanctity. Delaying tomorrow, enjoying a spiritual peace neither of them had known for some time.

She broke the silence.

'I suppose this is where you offer to take me back to your place.'

He grinned as he opened the car door.

'I guess so.'

Five minutes later they were back at Nidderdale House. He walked her to the bottom of the stairs, sensing rightly, that she was not ready for any expansive romantic gestures. He squeezed her hand gently and brushed his lips across her cheek.

She returned the squeeze.

'Thank you Johnnie for a wonderful evening, I do believe you have given me back my life.'

She floated back to her room, quietly opening and closing the door so as not to risk waking her mother and having to relate events that she had not yet deciphered for herself.

She slipped into bed, the excitement refusing to release her to slumber as events tumbled over and over in her head. Finally, she did succumb and slept more soundly than she had for a long time, so deeply that Angela had returned from breakfast before she emerged from the arms of Morpheus.

Her mother was insatiable in her quest for knowledge of last night's supper. Kate meanwhile was anxious for the day to fly by so that she could meet Liz Reed and start work on her new business plan. Her mind had drifted away from the present when she heard Angela announce that the lady from Bakewell had invited them to join her for clandestine supper at the Box Tree restaurant in Ilkley. 'Don't tell the management,' she had murmured.

She swiftly composed herself.

'Mother, I am so sorry, I have arranged to see Liz Reed tonight – you remember the girl who runs our York office. You must go, of course, and please forgive me for being so selfish.'

'I suppose I must, even though I had hoped it would be a good chance to spend some time together.'

Her mother's reply understandably a little peeved.

Suddenly Kate felt the magic drifting away, no-one allowed her to do her own thing even though they kept telling her to do so.

'Kate darling.' Her mother's voice was sympathetic and concerned.

'I encouraged you to come up here to Yorkshire to rediscover yourself and it appears you have, but I had not expected such a quick transformation.'

Kate looked into her mother's kind face, seeing both concern and affection and above all the love that only mothers can ever know for the child that they brought into the world.

'Sorry mummy.'

'It is me who should apologise; of course you must see Liz. I am beginning to see how making a success of your new business will give you the purpose in life that I saw in your father when he was building up the practice.'

Kate felt the mood lighten and yes, she was going to throw herself into making a success of Braithwaite's and she was not going to change the name to be part of James's empire. That, she decided, would be the second decision to be written into the ledger that Liz was bringing to this evening's meeting.

The atmosphere lightened and even more so, as Kate gave her mother a potted version of the evening out with Johnnie Mortimer.

'He seems to have made quite an impression on you, but surely he must have a family and responsibilities of his own.'

Kate related the sad details of his wife and children and that good looking though he was, it had taken a lot mental courage to ask Kate out.

The day passed slowly, Kate becoming ever more frustrated at the tedious routine of face packs, aerobics, face massage, pedicure; all of this suddenly seemed to be a waste of money and even worse a waste of time. She tried not to let her frustration show, after all two days ago she had happily agreed to spending a few days with her mother, neither of them had anticipated her meeting anyone who could help get her life back on track.

Even if James had been lying about not having an affair with Sally Parkinson, he was still alive; they could still put their lives back together, whereas Johnnie Mortimer apparently could not.

Thinking about him, she allowed her mind to drift, maybe they could work together, he was after all a qualified chartered surveyor who could bring a lot to the business not to mention the four offices they had in North Yorkshire – she must quiz Liz on what sort of reputation they had. She felt more and more that the fall out with James had been for a purpose and not knowing where it was taking her, made her excited, maybe she did have her father's business skills after all.

Finally even Angela signalled that she had been pampered enough and that she was going to have a hot bath and change in readiness for sneaking out of Nidderdale for her liaison with Phyllis Nicholson, as the lady from Buxton was called.

She gave Kate a fond kiss.

'Have a nice evening with Liz and don't spend all your time talking about work.'

CHAPTER FORTY TWO

On arriving at the Devonshire Arms, Kate checked that Liz had checked in before heading for her own room from whence she called her.

'Liz, hi, good to see you got here nice and early, which is a definite must for all of our future meetings. My room is a suite so we can use the sitting room as our conference room. I need to settle in so shall we say thirty minutes? It is room 18 by the way. Bye, see you soon, oh and no business suits, we are also going to enjoy this evening!'

At six forty-five precisely came the knock on the door.
They gave each other a brief hug, each aware of the other's contained excitement. Liz began, 'I have brought you the ledger and calculator you wanted and also a notepad for both of us, as we are sure to need reminding of things we have to do.'

'Brilliant Liz, as ever you are thinking ahead. Now I suggest we have a brainstorming session, where we mention anything that is in our heads. Nothing will be pooh-poohed without explanation. I suggest an hour of this aided by...'

There was a knock on the door. She opened it to reveal a young man of about twenty in a black apron.

'I was about to say shampoo and here is our favourite, Taittinger.'
She indicated that he should pour two glasses, whereupon she offered a toast.

'To Braithwaite's.'

'To Braithwaite's.' Liz echoed the sentiment.

Kate opened the Ledger and wrote in the margin Thursday August 17th. At the side she added:

Item One – Invite Liz Reed to become the Marketing Director of Braithwaite's. She looked at the bemused face opposite. 'Please say yes.'

'Well of course, yes, I just wasn't expecting it, what will James say?'
The reply was immediate.

'This is my company; he has plenty of other matters to concern him.'

Item Two – this company will remain independent of other Carrington companies.

Item Three - we may, however, consider amalgamating with other agencies in order to broaden our base and/or opening new branches.

Item Four –Which prime areas should we consider in respect of item three?

Kate gave her new director a quizzical look. 'Your suggestions would be?'

The answer was immediate as she fired back with, 'Leeds, Harrogate, Skipton, perhaps Wetherby, or maybe Doncaster, no delete that.'

Kate looked intently at her, 'Why the choice?'

Leeds - because it is growing in stature, and is expected to take over as the financial power base of the North of England.

Harrogate - because of the sheer quality of the housing and the huge demand to live there.

Skipton – it advertises itself as the Gateway to the Dales and the demand for second homes is surely the next phenomena to hit the property market.

Wetherby - it is the final piece in the puzzle that forms the so called Golden Triangle, the other pieces being Harrogate and Leeds. Like Skipton, it opens up access to a lot of very smart villages.

'Wow, Miss Reed, I am glad we are on the same side. How long have you been mulling this over?'

'All the time I was working with Mr. Braithwaite I could see opportunities but, of course, he was not interested in progress, but I knew you would be and that is why I was keen to work for you.'

'Work with me' Kate smilingly corrected her, 'this going to be a partnership.'

Item Five – 'How do we achieve this growth and do it quickly, any ideas on that from the Marketing Department?'

'Off the top of my head,' Liz pursed her lips and responded with:

A – By gradual steady growth adding one of the above areas each year.

B – As our finances grow, acquire other agencies already in situ with a similar outlook to ours; it is important however, to attract staff who are receptive to our business philosophy.

C – Go into a partnership with a company already well positioned in these key market places.

Kate looked at the intent, slightly flushed face sitting opposite, champagne untouched, like her own since the initial toast.

'If I said I knew just such a firm as your option 'C', what would you say?'

'Mortimer, Walpole & Scott,' came back the confident reply.

'You are quite a surprise Miss Reed, but what if I told you an even bigger surprise?'

Kate sipped her champagne, was she being too hasty in imparting last night's events to Liz so soon after what had only been an off the cuff remark that had been dismissed as soon as said. She decided to blur the truth slightly.

'I had supper with Johnnie Mortimer last night.'

This time it was Liz whose mouth dropped open.

'But everyone knows he is the most eligible bachelor in Yorkshire and he never goes socialising, everyone has tried. He is handsome, wealthy and charming but, since the tragic accident to his wife and children, he is no longer on the County Set invitation list; he always declines.'

'Is that so Miss Reed, then let me tell you, he invited me out!'

And then glancing at her watch, she closed the ledger.

'Enough for now, let's go and eat and see what other gems we can unearth.'

They crossed the reception area and were met at the entrance to the dining room by Robert; he greeted them with a slight bow of the head.

'A very great pleasure to see you again Mrs Carrington, will you both be dining with us.'

'We will indeed Robert and would be grateful if could put us in a corner. Liz and I have a lot to catch up on.'

'Certainly and may I say what a pleasure it is to have such attractive company.' He looked at them enquiringly.

'Are you ready to eat, or would you prefer to have a drink first?'

'We will start with a drink but perhaps we could go to our table.'

'Most certainly, is it perhaps a gin and tonic?'

Kate nodded her approval and he ventured to Liz.

'And for you madam?'

'I will have the same, thank you.'

'Merci, may I suggest the table in the far corner as being the most discreet?' They nodded their approval.

'Follow me please.'

He seated them and relayed their choice, apparently without movement, to a waiter hovering close at hand.

Kate smiled at her new business partner; she had a warm glow about this evening's turn of events.

'You must have been to the Devonshire Arms before.'

'Several times, once as a guest of Jonathan Mortimer.'

Liz enjoyed seeing the shock on Kate's face and sensed she was dying to know why; her assumption was right.

'You dark horse, you mean you were dating Johnnie Mortimer?'

'Sadly no, he tried very hard to persuade Mr. Braithwaite to sell him the agency and was hoping I could help convince him of the logic of us joining forces, if only to keep that horrible man George Stokesley at bay. Our location,' she emphasised the first word, 'is the most prime position in York, even more so now that you have carried out the renovations.'

Kate considered this latest piece of news, no wonder Johnnie had suggested - even though it had seemed quite flippant - that they could work together.

'So Liz let's put this in perspective, as it is the third of your options that most appeals to me. Give me the background and who is what in the company.'

'Mortimer, Walpole & Scott or 'MWS' as they known in the trade, is the result of the original Mr Mortimer, that is Johnnie's father - you have already got me using familiar terms – starting the business after he came back from the war in 1918. Until then they had been gentlemen farmers and landowners. He was then in his mid- twenties; the family was still pretty wealthy and it is about this time that his grandfather bought Nidderdale House from the Duke. Even the aristocracy was downsizing, although of course the Devonshire's were hardly strapped for cash. They still lived in some considerable style at Chatsworth and their other great houses in Yorkshire and Ireland etc. Like most of the great aristocratic families, the Devonshire's have been very astute and their timing for diversification has been spot on.'

'This hotel,' she continued, 'was taken over by the family in the early 1980s and the Duchess has used not only her own great taste, but also furniture and paintings from their own collections to make guests feel at home whether they be here for the shooting or the racing, or on business as we are…' Her voice trailed away as she sensed that Kate's mind was elsewhere, probably thinking about James she surmised.

She had touched a raw nerve; the mention of the grouse shooting and the racing in York brought back to Kate memories of those sublime days, when they had made love in the heather and she was still bewitched by James and he by her.

Kate collected herself.

'Sorry Liz I missed that last bit; you were saying that this building was used as a residence during the shooting and racing calendar.'

'Jonathan's father'; they both smiled at her correctness in using Johnnie's name.

'Rupert Mortimer had an aptitude for business and obviously a very astute business brain, because between the wars his company became the most prestigious in Yorkshire and, in addition to selling properties, they acted for and managed several of the small to medium sized estates. They did not however, unlike you, branch out into other towns.

After leaving Sedbergh, Jonathan went up to Cambridge and, after doing his stint in the army, set about expanding the business. I know all of this because he told me so when he was trying to co-opt me to influence Mr. Braithwaite.'

'Do go on, it is fascinating.'

'Walpole's were a progressive company that was very well entrenched in Harrogate and Ilkley, which is another potential venue for us. I believe there is also a distant family relationship, so they also had some common ground although it was very faint.'

She paused to sip her G & T.

'Scotts. on the other hand were introduced by Jonathan, but not without a fight. They were regarded by his father and Roger Walpole as being a little downmarket and very strange bed fellows; they had and still do have that reputation of being a little bit 'fly by night'.

They are still a bit hardnosed, but they had agencies in Skipton, Ilkley, Knaresborough, Northallerton and also three or four in South Yorkshire. Although a rather eclectic mix they did bring something different to the party and if you get to meet Roger Scott you will see what I mean.' Kate lifted her glass.

'To you Liz, you are a nonstop revelation. I am only just beginning to understand just how fortunate I am to have met you.'

'Likewise you Kate,' she managed to get out, seconds before the arrival of the starters.

They had both chosen a simple Avocado with Crab to begin and in Kate's case a Crispy Duck and for Liz it was Coq au Vin with a very nice Mouton to complement their choices.

'Rather more calories than Johnnie will be serving up at Nidderdale House.'

'Rather, and much better company,' agreed Kate, tilting her glass before continuing.

'Now that we are replete, let's see if the food has charged up your battery Miss Reed. It would seem to me as a newcomer to the world of property sales that Mortimer's business would sit very comfortably with Braithwaite's.'

'Do you mean in its entirety or perhaps certain parts, the Mortimer and Walpole elements perhaps?'

Kate gazed around the dining room as Liz waited for her observation, it was unexpected.

'It is Scott's that I find most interesting. I can foresee a huge upsurge in the mortgage industry, I know from James's experience with the kitchen and bathroom business that more and more couples of the thirty to forty year old generation are borrowing money to improve their properties; the children of this generation are going to want new houses with all the trimmings; they have grown up with or at very least have older houses that they can modernize and DIY is growing ever more popular.'

Liz interrupted, 'I can appreciate that, but why the Scott's side of the business, they have more branches but they are in smaller locations?'

'Which is where these potential customers live.' Kate's expression encouraging Liz to draw the obvious conclusion, which she was quick to do.

'In other words they want somewhere on their doorstep and they want to be helped by someone of their own background and not by some 'toff' like Jonathan Mortimer, nice and genuine though he is.'

'Precisely Liz, and before we meet again next week we have to consider if this is the route we want to take and I have also got to figure out how we finance it.'

'This has been a momentous evening Kate, I am so thrilled that you have so much confidence in me. You may be sure that I will not let you down.'

Kate folded her napkin, smoothing it as she placed it meticulously on the table; she smiled inwardly remembering her Prep. School, the Nuns would have been proud of her.

'Sleep well Liz, I will see you next Wednesday at York, we will lunch at the Chase Hotel, it is probably the most convenient for the racecourse; shall we say twelve thirty and would you please book a table for two? We can have a chat and meet up with the others before racing begins.'

They stood up, exchanged a brief goodnight kiss and climbed the stairs, both excited at how things were moving forward.

The following morning Kate, dressed in a simple but striking pale blue dress, dropped her bag into the boot of the Stag and was at Nidderdale in time for breakfast with her mother; she knew this would please her.

Jonathan Mortimer was chatting with a group of ladies on the terrace when he heard the now familiar tone of the Triumph Stag. A few seconds later the car emerged from the avenue of trees, her long auburn hair swept back by the early morning breeze. He was rooted to the spot, dare he approach her in front of all these guests?

Kate saw him too, effortlessly moving among his clients, she hoped he might come over, at the same time she was uncertain where this might leave her. The moment passed as he moved with the guests into the dining room, she followed and seeing an empty table sat down hoping that her mother would soon join her.

She did not have to wait long before Angela appeared, busily chatting to the lady from Bakewell. They both appeared happy and evidently good friends, glancing around the dining room they quickly spotted Kate and were hardly seated before Mrs Nicholson muddied the waters.

'You have the most stunning daughter, I hope her husband realises how lucky he is.'

Angela's quick response sparing Kate any explanation, 'he does and they have two lovely boys, Charles and Edward, who are wonderful, but so full of life, they leave me feeling quite exhausted most of the time.'

Kate, her expression caring, smiled at Mrs Nicholson.

'Thank you for taking care of mother for me, I apologise for not joining you last night although it would seem you must have enjoyed yourselves at the Box Tree; do they still have a pianist?'

'Yes they do and it provides such a lovely background to the evening. You obviously know it well.'

'No, to be truthful, but James and I had supper there, just the once when he came up here to play rugby, but we enjoyed it very much.'

Phyllis Nicholson leaned over and took Kate's hand.

'It is lovely that you let me have your mother's company last night, I get a little lonely at times since my dear David passed away last year.' Her eyes seemed bereft of hope; Kate could sense the sadness she was trying to hide.

'How old are you dear?'

'Thirty two.'

'And James?'

'Thirty seven.'

'Make the most of your time together, the years soon fly away.'
Just as suddenly, her expression more animated, she turned again to Kate.

'You said he played rugby, is he the James Carrington of England fame?'
Angela proudly confirmed that he was indeed the very same.

'David was very keen on his rugby, although I can't pretend that he was anything like in the same class as James, who I well remember David telling me, was the star of the British Lion's tour of South Africa a few years ago. You must have been very proud and I expect you are hoping the boys will take after him.'

'Yes that would be nice.' Kate tried to appear enthusiastic, even though right now she did not want them to be anything at all like him.

Angela interrupted Kate's thoughts.

'This is our last day so let's make the most of it. What do you fancy Kate darling?'

Before she could answer Phyllis advised that she and Angela proposed to attempt some aerobics in the pool followed by a foot massage, 'it is so relaxing,' she assured her.

'Yes, you must try it Kate.'

'Perhaps on another occasion, I was looking forward to cycling in the park; it will give me some space to get my head together.'
The ladies heard the sub-text and understood.

'Well we can't do much chatting in the pool.'
Her mother's response was kind and understanding. It was interrupted by the tinkling of a small

hand bell brandished by a smiling Johnnie Mortimer.

'Ladies and gentlemen, enough of this relaxation, we are here to punish your bodies, so please report to your chosen torture chambers.'

His easy charm elicited smiles and good natured banter from the breakfast room, encouraged by one of the more generously built gentlemen who threw a Nazi salute followed by 'Jawohl mein Führer.'

They rose to their feet and the room swiftly emptied save for Kate and the bell ringer. She poured herself another coffee.

He approached, his face kind and strong, unlike his mind which was in turmoil.

'May I join you?'

'Yes, please do,' her voice kind and inviting.

'What are you proposing to do today?'

'Mother has arranged a foot massage this afternoon and I thought I would borrow a bike and go for a ride in the grounds, I have convinced myself that I need some outdoor exercise.'

He nodded and, summoning up his courage, quietly asked, 'would you mind very much if I joined you?'

She looked at the intense face, so different to the casual and relaxed man who had invited the guests to their torture chambers.

'I was hoping you would – I need a guided tour.'

'Half an hour - I will see you behind the bike shed.' The humour once again evident.

She floated to her room and changed her dress for white shorts that showed off her still brown legs, and a lemon coloured Fred Perry tee shirt. She laced up her trainers – white with yellow trim. 'Miss Matchem,' she heard James's laughter, he always teased her about her passion for coordinating colours.

The reminder sobered her mood, she picked up the phone and started to call Johnnie's number and then as suddenly replaced the receiver; she had to be her own person and besides it was James who had hurt her, it was not fair to pass on that wound to another, he had already suffered more than enough.

She was two minutes late arriving, 'a woman's privilege', although she was usually the best of timekeepers.

He was there, the long tanned legs astride a bright red Raleigh, a small hamper strapped behind the saddle.

Her bike was unbelievably yellow in colour.

'I chose it because you looked so fabulous in your lemon dress the other night.'

She smiled but resisted the temptation to relate the 'Miss Matchem' story.

They rode slowly, there were three hours until lunch so they had no need for haste and so much to discuss and yet how to begin.

CHAPTER FORTY THREE

'Yorkshire here we come.'

He remembered her adjusting her sunglasses and leaving in a cloud of dust and gravel.
Jeremy stayed for half an hour, having coffee with James then he too set off although rather more sedately.
He remembered her father's kind and encouraging words.

'See you on Saturday James; She is worth it, and you can get over these hiccups as I did, but you will both have to be gentle and understanding; I thank God I found the will and determination to forgive Angela – but it was not easy, not at the beginning.'
They shook hands and he returned to the house, the dogs now quiet, seemingly aware that something was amiss.

He opened the study door and sat at his father's desk, indeed his great-grandfathers desk. It energised him; he would somehow return this desk to its rightful place in the study at Milford Hall.

He mulled over the problems and solutions and set about it in the same methodical question and answer fashion that he had passed on to Kate.

- **David Gilbert was prepared to sell.** *But at what price?*
- **How did he gauge the price without alerting anyone?** *He would ask Lazzard's and a couple of other top agencies to send details of other such properties, to gauge the price bracket it might fall into.*
- **How did he fund the move?** *He would get his brokers to assess his assets and advise which of them could be most easily accessed and with least penalty.*

He called Lazzard's at their Stamford office, hoping this would allow him the anonymity that the Nottingham or Leicester offices might not.
He asked for, and was put through to Andrew Travers

'James Carrington, what a nice surprise, I thought you were out of the property business these days.'

'Andrew, hello. As you say, long time no see, I need a favour.'

'Okay, but I will need to know if that little filly of yours is going to win The Lowther at York next week.'

'We think she will be in the frame, so have twenty each way.'

'Right, I will do just that, now down to business.'

'Andrew, you remember that you sold me Sir Oliver Cranston's old place at Woolmington? Well the thing is, I need to know what it might fetch as I have somewhere else in mind and I might need to move pretty quickly.'

'James, you were just about as fast as anyone on the rugby pitch so I would not expect you to move at any other pace in business. I also know that you wouldn't call me personally unless it really was urgent, so give me half an hour to rearrange my diary and I will call you back.'

'Thanks Andy, I do appreciate it.'

Andrew Travers was back in twenty minutes with the news that he would meet James on site at Woolmington at one thirty sharp.

He was as good as his word and, by the expression on his face when he stepped out of his Range Rover, was rather impressed by what he saw.

'James, this is superb, it is scarcely recognizable from the rather tired old house I sold you in,' he referred to the file, '1961.'

'Thanks, please do come inside.'

They strode in together, James sensing from the stream of complimentary adjectives that the interior was also making quite an impact on the surveyor. He followed James into the study and was waved into an armchair facing his host who produced a thermos jug of coffee, smiling as he did so.

'The thermos must look a little incongruous in these surrounding, you were probably hoping for a pert little French maid.'

His guest smiled. 'Or a butler at the very least'.

And then, his body language both inquisitive and understanding, he delved below the surface.

'James, we are both guys who have been around a bit, so please don't think me impertinent if I suspect that your marriage has something to do with your proposal to put this house on the market.'

'Your assumption is reasonable, but not entirely correct, although that may well turn out to be the case.'

'James we have been friends since we were at the Tigers together; what is it, twenty years since we first met?'

He continued, the blue grey eyes conceding nothing as they followed him from the other side of the desk.

'I guess I have got ahead of the story, so please forgive an old mate, if I have jumped to a wrong conclusion, could we start again with you taking the lead.'

'You may well be right, but it is complicated and I need your discretion in valuing another property and that too has a Leicester Tigers connection.'

James shook his head ruefully as if to clear his brain.

'Do you remember Steve Gilbert; he was also a stand-off, six or seven years younger than us?'

Guy nodded, 'he was pushing for your place, might even have got it when you retired except that he buggered off to New Zealand, or was it South Africa.'

'You were closer first time, it was Australia and yes, he had a lot of potential, which is what

I told his father. Which brings us neatly round to the reason for your visit.'
He inhaled and paused for a few seconds, seemingly searching for the courage to continue.

'This is not easy and it is a long time since I related what I am about to tell you. In fact, you are only the third person I have ever made privy to what I am about to reveal.

When I was fourteen, my family's fortunes hit the rocks and we had to sell our home, a house that my great-grandfather had re-built around a hundred years ago. It devastated my parents, in particular my father, who blamed himself for the disaster. This was most unfair as when he married my mother he was more or less obliged to give up the life of a fairly prosperous farmer to become an executive in the furniture industry.

Staincliffes, my mother's family, were at one time the biggest manufacturer of furniture in the UK and possibly in Europe. My great-grandfather was made a baronet, so you can imagine my mother had been brought up to expect success and a pretty pleasant way of life. This all ended when my father was at the helm of the company and, incorrectly in my view, was blamed for the company crashing. When I got older I asked my mother why the blame was never apportioned to the other directors, but it seems they were all city types who clung together.

Andrew, I am sorry for rattling on about this, but you need to know me and what drives me to understand why I need to consider selling this house, a property in which Kate and I have invested a lot of time and energy as well as cash.'
His guest held up his hand.

'I feel privileged that you should confide in me, you have my word it will go no further.'
James acknowledged his promise and continued.

'At the time of the crash I was, as I have mentioned just fourteen, it meant I was taken away from Uppingham and sent to the local Grammar School. This is where I first met Edward Lawson; an event that would have a considerable influence on my life, initially on the sports field and later in the world of business.
We complemented each other so well, he was my best friend and I do not expect to find another to whom I will accord such respect.'

He pointed to the black and white team photograph hanging on the wall adjacent to the mantelpiece.

'That was our first game for England as schoolboys; the satin cap hanging there is his second cap - we both kept the first one. He has mine or at least he did have – who knows what he may have done with it now.'
The surveyor, who had walked over to examine the photograph in more detail returned to his seat, he saw the anguish in his friend's eyes as James continued with his explanation.

'You must wonder how we came to fall out so badly and go our separate ways.'
The agent looked genuinely perplexed.
'I have never heard an explanation, although it was certainly big news at the time, not just the business press but in all the sports columns as well. The Leicester Mercury described it as Rolls without Royce, but please continue.'

'Apart from our wives and Jack Priory no-one ever will know; we still have that respect for each other, but there is something I cannot forgive and besides which, the damage is now done.'
James paused and then continued,

'As our car drove through those great iron gates of Milford Hall for the last time, I blurted out a promise to myself and my parents that I would one day reclaim that house and now, rather neatly, it is Steve Gilbert's father, who ironically played in the back row for Northampton at the same time as my father was playing for the Tigers, who now has it in his remit to make that dream become reality. However, to bring this saga to an end; life was to deal me one more blow, an even worse one.'

He collected himself again.

'At eighteen I came home to share with my parents the wonderful news that I had been offered a place at St John's College. However, before I could even share my joy of going up to Cambridge, I heard my mother and her sister Margaret discussing in hushed tones that my father had cancer and had very little time left. Mortified at the news, unable to think coherently, I jumped on my bike and rode the ten miles or so to Milford Hall. I flung my bike to the ground and stood, tears streaming down my cheeks as I looked again through the wrought iron gates at this great house that has driven all my dreams since I was fourteen years old. - I vowed once again that one day it would be mine.'

He grimaced and looked up to see his property advisor looking somewhat stunned by this unexpected list of consequences before continuing, 'Sadly my wife refuses to even contemplate such a move. But I cannot give up on that dream, so it looks as if I am going to lose my other best friend.'

Now it was the surveyor's turn to scratch his head and purse his lips.

'You were always nifty on your feet James, but this sounds like you have the whole of the Welsh team bearing down on you and without your mate around to shield you.

Right, we need an action plan but if you want a figure for this place.'

He paused reflectively.

'Off the top of my head, we are talking £1.5 to £2 million and the ideal buyer would be seriously into the equestrian world, so we need to contact our offices in the Newmarket, Berkshire, Epsom areas. Middleham and Malton will be covered by York.'

As he spoke he saw the wheels turning in James's head. His reaction was immediate.

'Maybe set it up as a racing yard, it has the ideal topology.' We have plenty of uphill gallops to get the horses working on the collar and flat areas that we could easily set up some turns – our own Tattenham Corner, just as Vincent has done in Ireland. What do you think, jumps or flat racing?'

Before Andrew Travers could reply he had another suggestion.

'On the other hand find some rich chap interested in breeding as I am, as it has everything already in place. Or, what about a Hunting set-up, no question it is the best country in England for that; The Quorn, The Belvoir, The Beaufort, they are all here on the doorstep.'

The man from Lazzard's watched as Jack Priory and Edward Lawson had done in the past, the agile mind of James Carrington entrepreneur. Like them he was impressed at the man's mental agility.

This time he was reflective.

'Do you think David Gilbert would be interested in downsizing, maybe doing an exchange with a cash adjustment?'

'It is a nice thought, and I will mention it, but he seems pretty set on joining his son in Australia. In any case, Kate would regard that as even more of a sly move on my part.

For starters, I would like to get David Gilbert's permission for you to make contact. This will give you the opportunity to establish the sort of money he is talking.

I will let you into my confidence Guy, he wants me to have the property and at a fair price. My father you see was exceedingly thoughtful and kind when David Gilbert bought the house. Although short of cash, he insisted on all the big purpose made pieces of furniture that matched

261

the mantelpieces etc. be included in the sale price.'

He suddenly found himself speaking his thoughts out loud.

'Which is why he never should have been forced into the MD's job at Staincliffes.'

He turned, embarrassed, to have off-loaded such an intimate thought to someone he had not seen in a decade. Andrew Travers stood up.

'I hope that I will have such fond memories of my father. Thank you for contacting me James, it is refreshing to have such a truthful brief from a client. I will bring this one home for you with honesty on both sides.'

He gave his ex-team mate an understanding look.

'Did you ever expect an estate agent to really mean such a conflicting statement.'

They were still laughing as James led him out to the Range Rover.

Once back inside he telephoned David Gilbert and elicited his permission for Lazzard's to make contact. It was good to have heard from him so soon he had been assured.

He passed this news on for Andrew's attention and let his thoughts drift to Kate.

Did he really want to lose her, was the possibility of meeting up with Sally Parkinson what he really wanted; what would his mother think – had she any inkling of what had really caused Kate's breakdown? And the boys, how could he even contemplate hurting them.

He was aware that he had not eaten and drifted into the kitchen, decided on a ham sandwich only to find no ham. He opened a tin of baked beans, this time no bread, he settled for cold baked beans which he took back into the study where he somewhat disconsolately, idly fed them into his mouth.

His thoughts returned to Charles and Edward; he remembered hearing the dreadful news of his father's impending death, of how that tragedy had changed his life forever and had driven him, had been his very raison d'être for today's meeting with Guy.

He had related the effect upon him to someone with whom he had merely shared the camaraderie of sport, had expected him to understand, he most assuredly could not expect this of two young boys.

He looked at the can of Heinz Beans and the prospect of what life held for him; would he willingly sacrifice those two children, his children, to a life without a father? No, he would not; but could he have them and Milford Hall?

He sat with his head in his hands, looking down at the embossed green leather top to his desk, at the little 'bird' that a stray nib of yesteryear had carved out of the leather. Dear God, how could he persuade Kate to grant him this wish, why was she so obstinately against it, what was she so afraid of?

He looked in his diary and called the Health Farm.

'Nidderdale House,' the response immediate.

'May I have a word with Mrs Carrington please?'

'One moment.'

He waited, composed himself; he was looking forward to speaking with her.

'We think she is cycling in the park sir.'

'What, with her mother!'

'No sir, we think Mr Mortimer is showing her around, shall I say who called?'

'No need.' He tried to make it sound light, but doubted it.

Who the hell was Mr Mortimer? He crumpled the Heinz Bean can and hurled it into the wastepaper bin. His previous compassionate thoughts towards Kate were irrationally in the bin with the beans.

He sat there his mind numb, unable to think coherently, consumed with jealousy, who did this Mister Mortimer think he was, had this little excursion to Yorkshire been planned with him in mind?

He slowly became more rational; logically he knew that Kate's breakdown and the visit to the health spa had been initiated by her mother's suggestion to take a short break in Yorkshire and she would certainly not allow any impropriety. Or would she?

She had after all, played fast and loose with her husband's affections; if this was the case, could he sit back as Jeremy had done and wait until the flames went out?

He stood up, no he could not, but he must be careful or he would be facing the choice of his children or Milford Hall or neither. He decided to take a walk and then, completely out of character, drove into the village to collect some bread. On the way he stopped and gazed down the lane he had taken when he went to see the hunt meet at Sally Parkinson's home. The memory as he sat there was still very fresh, he remembered as if yesterday, the way she sat astride the superb brown gelding, from its elegant appearance he knew it would have a lot of pedigree blood, rather like its partner.

He also recalled the visit to Harry Halls and choosing the jodhpurs and jacket and the 'Hunting Tie – Stock is what grocers have on shelves' the manager had regaled him with the Duke of Badminton's insistence on correctness.

The thought of grocer's stock alerted him to the time, the village shop closed at five pm and that was half an hour ago.

He drove into Nottingham instead and had a lonely supper at the Flying Horse Hotel pondering most of the time on Kate's return tomorrow and seeing Jeremy again. He wished he was here right now, he could do with his kind advice, he also wanted to let him know that he was going to fight to regain his wife's affection, because he loved her and not as a means to move to Milford Hall.

He took the top off the Porsche hoping the wind would clear his head and enable him to enjoy the weekend with Kate and her family. He would check his diary and if they were all home around lunchtime he proposed going to see the boys, he knew for certain that would be greeted with approval.

Turning into the drive leading up to the house he noticed that June, who now lived in the previously derelict cottage, had left the door open.

He knocked and was met by Keith, her new husband.

'Have you a couple of slices of bread you could lend a neighbour?'

'Come in James, I am sure we can manage that. Fancy a beer?'

'If you are sure I am not intruding.'

He liked Keith, he was cheerful and since marrying June, he had been employed by James to help her with the horses and the other livestock. He must, in the event of selling the house, ensure that they were both retained here or better still move to Milford with him.

Keith returned with both the beers and his wife who as usual was not short of conversation.

'Is Kate back tomorrow?'

'She sure is and I can't wait to see her.' The reply was immediate and sincere.

June smiled. 'She needs you James and you need her.'

'I know and I also know what a great support you have been to her, please help me convince her that I need her back in my life.'

Keith, a little embarrassed by these intimate thoughts, handed him another Ruddles.

'The last one seemed to have slipped down rather well.'

They discussed the horses, next year's coverings, the September Sales at Doncaster and the more important one in October at Newmarket when they had high hopes for Wedding Belle's colt by Habitat. This was a speedy young stallion who had been the champion miler of Europe and one that James had been very keen to breed to, even though this had cost him three grand to back his beliefs. The horse had been born the year before Nijinsky and was owned by the same lucky owner. As a yearling he had cost 105,000 dollars which was some 20,000 dollars more than the mighty son of the legendary Northern Dancer; like him he was an immediate success at stud.

Next week's Lowther Stakes at York would influence the price, as the filly they were running was a full sister to the colt they were selling at the Tattersalls October Sales.

The conversation and the Ruddles bitter flowed, they were all horse mad and could talk pedigrees all night. Even Kate had caught the bug and she was acknowledged as the expert when it came to finding appropriate names for ones they kept to race.

Wedding Belle had been her wedding present to James and despite a fairly ordinary race record she had foaled some top class runners including the filly they were running at York next week. At ten minutes past twelve June called a halt.

'We have to work in the morning, I hope the boss will be understanding if we are not quite so bright as usual.'

James smiled. 'He is such a nice chap, I am sure he will be, assuming of course he gets a couple of slices of bread which is where this bacchanalia started.'

Keith handed over half a loaf.

'This should make him very happy, I am sure he has his own caviar.'

'Thanks both of you, I think I will leave the car.'

He set out to walk the four hundred yards to the house feeling at peace with the world and in the right frame of mind to make Kate happy; he prayed that she would feel the same.

CHAPTER FORTY FOUR

Unusually for James Carrington he did not sleep well and as he tossed and turned and the hours eked slowly away, his resolve to repair his marriage slowly disintegrated. The earlier compassion turned from sadness to irritation and then to anger at the way Kate had manipulated both him and her parents. He was not the guilty party, he had not had an affair but now he was wishing he had and yes, he was determined he would see Sally Parkinson again.

He endured this inner turmoil until six thirty when his feelings towards Kate were completely the reverse to the positive ones fuelled by the alcohol the previous evening. He made some toast with last night's gift before walking around the stable yard hoping that the sight of this year's foals might raise his spirits, but it did not.

June, who had just emerged from the feed room with two buckets of bruised oats, stifled the impulse to pass the time of day sensing correctly from the expression on his face that it was best to leave him to his own thoughts, and she was right. All he saw was a long dark tunnel and it was not a journey he wanted to embark on, strewn as it would be with slander and recrimination.

He returned to the house collected the car keys and walked up the lane to collect the car he had abandoned last night. The hood was still down and he left it that way hoping that the already warm sun would raise his spirits. As the Porsche burst into life he turned on Radio 2, hosted as usual by Jimmy Young, whose nonsensical banter when he handed over to Terry Wogan, was the highlight of the day for most commuters. The cocktail of humour and music slowly assuaged his depressive mood and he found himself subconsciously singing along with the Diana Ross recording of 'It's My Turn'.

For the first time, he consciously listened to the lyrics.

'It's my time to see what I must see...'

The words were so appropriate, it was time to sort out his life which, gilded though it had been in many ways be it work or otherwise, had always demanded that he take responsibility for others.

The words gave him a mental signpost, a clear indication of his future and he shortly found himself turning into the lane that led to Sally Parkinson's family home. He knew he should turn around, this was madness but he no longer cared, he would not be mentally bullied by anyone - he was not Jeremy Palmer.

'I hope you'll understand, this time's just for me
Because it's my turn, to turn and say goodbye...
He was mesmerised by the appropriateness of the words; His spirits instantly rejuvenated but, as he stopped the car within sight of the large stone house at the end of the beech avenue, he equally wondered how he could possibly explain his presence here at eight o'clock in the morning.

He fired up the engine as reality took control and with a clearer head than earlier, sped off in the direction of Nottingham where Tim Cooper and Jack Priory would be waiting to discuss the extensions to the Minster Furniture offices.

He crossed Trent Bridge and followed the crawling traffic down Carrington Street and as he turned into Station Street his eye caught the headline written on the news seller's billboard in front of the station.

'England Rugby Legend killed in A1 smash'.

He swung the car round and pulled into the small parking area at the entrance to the station. He knew instantly what the dread news would reveal and the front page confirmed his fears.

Edward Lawson, the hero of England and the British Lions rugby team has been killed in a head on crash with a high sided truck. The driver believed to be Italian, had careered across the double white lines in the centre of the A1 road at the Stamford turn.'

He abandoned the car and with gulping breaths ran the few hundred yards to the Services Club. He prayed that no one would be about at this time and went through to the Billiard Room and sank into the nearest leather armchair.

Here he remained for the next thirty minutes, head buried in his hands, as devastated as that fateful day when he heard his mother confirming his father's fate to her sister. The wonderful days of their youth flashed before him; how could they have possibly fallen out. Edward Lawson, the gentle giant who had been so central to his life, yet always content to live in his shadow both on the rugby field and off. Until that fateful day that his friend had doubted him, would not even listen to an explanation, even though those closest to James had begged him to at least hear Edward's side of the story.

Not only had he lost his best friend, he had lost Connie who, like her husband, had been with him since the business had started and had been for so long a vital and essential part of Fordmill Construction.

He slowly collected his thoughts, he must call Connie but then so many real friends would be seeking to do that and his was the last voice she would wish to hear.
A broken man wearing sunglasses to hide the puffy red eyes finally emerged onto Friar Lane and walked slowly to Tim Cooper's office seeking friendship not a discussion about office buildings.

As a regular visitor, he did not need any invitation to go straight through to the architect's office and when the two friends met neither was capable of any conversation.

They clasped hands for several seconds before Tim waved him to a seat, clearly as badly affected by the trauma as James.
For several minutes neither could say anything coherent; James finally made the effort.

'What can I do Tim, how can I approach Connie?'

'I will speak to her James and I will let her know how devastated you are; now is not the time for rancour or harsh words although we both know that is not Connie's way.'

'Thank you Tim; you must take charge. Edward Lawson was a much respected and much admired man and you will need a big church as there will be a lot of important people from the rugby and business fraternities who will want to pay their respects to this great guy...' he waved his hands unable to speak.

He trudged back to the Railway Station and closed the hood before sliding into the car, desperately seeking the privacy it afforded. He set off for home knowing that Jack Priory would have heard the news and would not be expecting him to be at his desk. Even the weather was in tune with his mood as the early sunshine disappeared to be replaced by huge spots of rain. He switched on the wipers and saw the remains of a parking ticket flutter into Arkwright Street; not that he cared a jot.

Unconscious of what he was doing, he found old habits taking him back to the scene of his life's defining events. This time it was not Milford Hall but the Grammar School where he had first met Edward Lawson.

He parked a hundred yards or so from the school and slowly made his way to the wrought iron entrance gates. Peering through the iron railings he remembered with great clarity how nervous he had been, everything had seemed so different to boarding school and, unlike Uppingham where he had many friends, he knew no-one and his brand new uniform screamed out new boy and all the potentially awkward questions that could pose.

He recalled parking his bike – a dark blue Raleigh – in the bike shed next to the great mounds of coke that fuelled the school boilers. He remembered pulling his trousers out of his socks and being conscious of a large shadow falling over him and then the relief as this genial giant had introduced himself as Edward Lawson and escorted him to their form room which he still remembered as IVA.

He recalled too that first games afternoon and his moment of hesitation as, apprehensive of being seen to be showing off, he had taken a second too long in picking up the ball only to be swamped and clattered to the ground by his new friend.

A few months later he remembered, as if it were yesterday, the Headmaster Dr Stanley, calling them to the front of the entire school and announcing,
'Because of these two boys, the match with Oakham on March 25th is cancelled. Instead the school will be organising a trip to Twickenham to support them in their determination to beat Wales.'
The whole school, six hundred boys and all the members of staff had loudly applauded them.

He remembered too, with great clarity, arriving at the HQ of English Rugby with Edward and passing together through the dark green door that bore the legend Players' Entrance.

Of the pride they both felt and of how all the other England players had looked to them, along with their scrum half John Murray, to provide the momentum and the axis that would fashion a win in what appeared a finely balanced conflict.
And then the supreme moment when he and Edward had fashioned the dramatic try in the dying seconds when James had released the final pass to the blonde giant on his shoulder and seeing from the ground this unstoppable athlete with three red Welsh shirts clinging to his back, crash over under the posts to give his best friend the simplest of opportunities to score the point that would win the game.
And now fate had again taken from him another man to whom he owed so much and much worse, one whose trust and friendship he had needlessly and stupidly rejected.

He cleared his head and returned to the car and still in a haze, drove towards Stamford and the turning on the A1 where Edward's life had been so savagely ended. The scene was cordoned off and the police were directing the traffic through the remaining single carriageway.

The cars in front started to move and he put his sunglasses back on as being recognised was not an option he wanted to contemplate.

Instead he followed the detour into Stamford and pulled into the car park at the rear of the George Hotel where he hoped the familiar territory would help unravel the contortions within his head. He retreated to a corner seat in the spacious lounge bar and was too engrossed to realise that someone was standing over him.

'James,' she began, 'please excuse me interrupting but I just had to say how sorry I was to hear about this appalling accident.'

He looked up, recognising the cultured tones and the incredible serendipity that had brought them together.

'Sally Parkinson.'

She sat beside him and let her hand rest on his.

Neither knew how to begin but they both realised that somehow fate had contrived this meeting.

'Shall I leave you to your thoughts?'

'No, but if you find me somewhat inattentive this is not how I really feel about you.'

He managed a wry smile which was warmly returned. He looked at her again.

'How did you know I was here?'

'I saw a black car which was parked with its headlights still on, the car park attendant described you and when I saw the number plate JRC 10 I realised it must be you.'

'Well, I can't tell you how glad I am Miss Marple that your powers of deduction are so good. Is it possible for you to give me your number and I will contact you – if that is okay – or is your red haired boyfriend still on the scene?'

'Would it worry you if he was?'

'No.' The answer was very emphatic and it gave her the courage to ask the question she feared.

'What about your auburn haired wife whom everyone describes as so beautiful?'

'Things are not good and since that night at the dinner dance I have thought about you a great deal.' He turned those intense blue eyes on her and smiled.

'Can you believe it, I actually went to Harry Hall's shop in Leicester and kitted myself out for riding – the full works, although I stopped short of Hunting Buttons; the guy in the shop advised me that I had to earn those! So you see how impetuous I am.'

She smiled mischievously.

'So have you sat on a horse yet?'

'Yes, June who looks after the horses for me found a retired cavalry horse from her husband's old regiment. He is more or less bombproof and I can just about stagger around on him. I am however some way off 'Hailing a Cab'.

She laughed at this referral to a hunting expression, in which the rider clears a fence one handed with the other arm raised in the air. The reality of the moment returned and they both returned to earth, each with problems of the heart and he with this massive loss hanging over him.

Sally knew that now was not the time and that there was no easy way out of today's impasse. She stood up, her lips briefly touching his cheek and from her handbag produced a small notepad on which she scribbled her telephone number.

'Call me when you are ready.'

He nodded. 'Take care, I promise I will be in touch.'

And she was gone as quickly as she had arrived.

He gathered his thoughts, remembering that he had to let Kate know before others did, although she would most likely have seen it in the press; it had after all been on the front page of the Times and the Telegraph and no doubt all of the other serious newspapers.

He called the Health Farm to learn that Mrs Carrington had already left for home so it was with a heavy heart that he set out for Woolmington.

CHAPTER FORTY FIVE

As anticipated Kate was home first and so was Jeremy Palmer.

Kate launched in first.

'Where have you been? We have been phoning all round to try and find you.'

His father-in-law, ever the diplomat came to James's aid.

'What Kate means is that we have all been so worried about how this awful news will have affected you James. I cannot imagine the turmoil you must be experiencing.'

He looked at them, attempting a half smile but all he could say was,

'Why did this great man, to whom I owe so much, have to be taken away and please do not remind me of how I must feel; You really have no idea.'

He went past them into his study and sat there with an untouched glass of Macallan in one hand and in the other, the team photograph of them both as England Schoolboy Internationals.

After about half an hour, his old ally Jeremy tapped on the door and, without a word, sat in the armchair next to the fireplace. He knew his son-in-law would speak when he was ready.

James looked up and indicated the bottle of Macallan.

'Will you join me; I just can't fancy it on my own.'

The older man nodded squeezing his shoulder as he leaned across the desk.

'Have you been in touch with Connie or would you like me to speak with her to see if there is anything or any way in which we can help?'

'I really would like to speak to her myself Jeremy, but I do not want to put her through any more pain and sadly she has better friends than me to whom I am sure she would rather turn. But yes, you are the one person to whom I can turn for help and we do have to make contact. Please tell her that I cannot find any words worthy enough, but that my heart cries out for her.'

His father-in-law nodded and with some trepidation went to the telephone in the drawing room. A voice he did not recognise picked up the phone at the other end and, after a brief pause, said she would ask Connie if she would take the call.

After a very long two minutes he heard someone pick up the receiver.

'Hello, this is Connie Lawson.'

'You may remember me, Jeremy Palmer, I am.' He was interrupted.

'Of course I remember you, and I hope we are still friends, despite all that has happened.' He heard her voice begin to falter and quiver.

'Connie, James is distraught and feels that whilst he wants to speak to you it would prove too painful, for both of you, particularly for you.'

'Jeremy, please tell James that I think I understand how he must feel and that he must be at the funeral or I will feel that he has let Edward down and if nothing else, please God, let this awful event bring them back together...'

He heard her voice growing ever fainter as she tried to continue; finally he heard a click as she replaced the phone.

In tears himself he dropped onto the sofa trying to compose himself before confiding Connie's brave message.

A tap on the door and a slouched figure moved into the armchair opposite, his eyes had no expression, he was a man condemned by his own grief and it was several minutes before Jeremy Palmer could compose himself and pass on Connie's plea.

'I cannot believe she wants to see me after all I have done to her.'

'James without you she would never have met that wonderful man and you have to be there because Edward Lawson would want it.'

And he continued.

'If it had been the other way round, I believe it is what you would have wanted.'

He looked up, not for the first time portraying his lawyer's gift for logic and assessment, his quizzical gaze was met by his son-in-law who, still unable to speak coherently, nodded his acquiescence.

Jeremy's appraisal helped James to compose himself and he started to think logically.

'I think the most appropriate church is probably either the cathedral in Nottingham which probably won't suit the people in Leicester, or the church at Long Bennington which is central to where most of his friends live and is also the one favoured by the Dukes of Rutland, so is used to important occasions – from memory I think it is called St Mary's.'

'I will call Connie tomorrow and let her have your suggestions; meanwhile I think we should join Kate and her mother.'

They trooped into the kitchen and he managed a wry smile to his wife, who responded with a bland look that conveyed very little sorrow or understanding of his plight.

Supper, which no-one really needed was a very low key affair, conspicuous by the politely quiet undertones and unspoken determination by three of them at least to repair bridges and create, at least in the short term, as much harmony as possible.

Angela passed the pepper mill to her son-in-law before asking if he knew where the funeral would be.

Kate, hardly able to control herself during the journey back from Yorkshire, launched into her husband.

'I really don't think it is anything to do with James, in fact I am amazed that he should even contemplate attending.'

James looked at her, unable to comprehend her rage; surely she must know the agony and despair he felt at this time. Her parents were also visibly shocked at her disregard for his feelings; they understood the mental agony and torture he must be experiencing and Jeremy had tried to explain that it was Connie's fervent wish that James should use this awful event to heal the wounds that could have been mended if either one of them had held out an olive branch.

But fate had denied them that and so Connie was right, James must be there to show the world just how much he had loved and admired this wonderful man who had been his friend and soul mate for thirty years. He with Connie must together celebrate the life of someone whose sporting exploits had enriched the lives of thousands of people on the terraces of so many countries. He was what every one of them wanted to be, both a colossus and yet always the most modest of men, always seeking to defray his own exploits.

James held up his hand seeking to stem the storm of vitriol and looked her firmly in the eye.

'Is this you or Mr Mortimer speaking?'

This time it was Kate who was momentarily stunned, but only for a moment.

'Don't you dare bring Johnnie into this.'

'I had no idea you were so close, I assumed he was just a cycling instructor!'

Angela sought to redeem the situation

'James, you are reading too much into this.'

'Just as you all read too much into me having one dance with Sally Parkinson.'

He got to his feet before unleashing a parting shot...

'Right now I wish I had kept on dancing.'

The others remained in their seats. All of them bereft of words.

Finally Kate, looking visibly shell shocked but trying to put on a brave front, went across to the Aga.

'This is where we are supposed to have a cup of tea.'

'You are being remarkably strong darling.'

'The trip to Yorkshire, mother, and the plans I have made with Liz regarding the estate agency have made me realise that I do not have to be content to play the little wife. I think I have inherited Daddy's business acumen and I am no longer going to play second fiddle and be a trophy on James's arm, I have my own plans and that may not include him!'

The kettle whistled as if to end the match, which right now looked ominously likely.

In the boot room next to the kitchen, James heard part of their muted conversation about the estate agency and was genuinely surprised and relieved to hear Kate's affirmation and her determination to make a real fist of her new career, but he still could not but be irked by her aggressive defence of Mr Mortimer, aka Johnnie, it would seem.

He pulled his boots on, summoning Murphy to join him. As they walked, he rubbed the large noble head that was waist high. 'If only my life was as simple as yours.'

The dog looked up at him, blissfully unaware of the mayhem that humans can create and the circumstances that flow from these events.

He followed his master into the paddock behind the stable block, the mares were used to him and two of the foals were similarly unimpressed. The one exception was a strong looking bay foal with no trace of white about him which, for a yearling going to the sales, is what many trainers prefer, as they tend to judge white markings as a weakness.

There are of course many exceptions to this theory, the mighty Northern Dancer had a pronounced white blaze and he also had three white socks which is the white marking most objected too. However, if you are breeding to race rather than sell this is irrelevant as the yearlings are not going to auction.

James was of course aiming to do both; he generally sold the colts and retained the fillies to race and hopefully, if they were good enough, to breed from them.

The bay colt immediately threw up his head, whinnied and galloped off to the far side of this ten acre paddock. Whereupon he reared up and started calling the others to join him. They needed no second invitation, both the mares and other foals now infected by this enthusiasm also set off at high speed to join the miscreant. Rebel, as he was already referred to, was the pick of the colts and he would definitely attract some attention when he made an appearance at the Newmarket Sales.

James loved to see them run and having them in small groups like this encouraged them to stretch their legs. Many a good horse has been picked out of a group of yearlings on the basis of his paddock performance. It is no guarantee of course, but someone like Vincent O'Brien has this wonderful eye for spotting potential as he did that day when he went to Canada at the behest of platinum magnate Charles Engelhard.

He dismissed the colt he was sent to see and advised his owner to buy the big bay colt instead. This colt would be named Nijinsky and become the first horse in over thirty years to win the mythical triple crown – 2000 Guineas; The Derby; and the St Ledger; the three races over progressive distances that determine the super star. Ironically, his sire was the comparatively small Northern Dancer, the horse with all that white about him.

Lost in his thoughts, he was unaware of Kate standing at his side, the ferocious wagging of Murphy's tale gave the game away.

'What has happened to us James?'
She was calmer now; more like the girl he had loved so much.
'I don't know Kate; the magic seems to have gone. Not much more than a week ago, your mother rushed you off to Yorkshire for some TLC and you have come back wanting to rule the world. Your Mr Mortimer must be some practitioner!'

They gazed at each other, neither able to communicate anything useful and neither wishing to inflame the situation further. She turned on her heels.
'I will leave you with your precious horses.'
He was pleased to be alone and was soon pondering how he could transfer his stud to Milford Hall; apart from the lodge where Mr and Mrs Price lived, there was no separate accommodation for Keith and June – maybe they could occupy a wing of the house or at least part of it, there was after all plenty of room in the space that had formerly housed the staff that had lived in during his

grandfather's time.

And then, just as suddenly, he put his thoughts on hold. There were so many bridges to cross, by far the most important being his two sons who were unaware of the crisis that hung over their parents. The thought of explaining to them the drama that was unfolding left him feeling lost and bereft.

He leaned on the gate and for the first time considered the reality of moving lock, stock and barrel to satisfy a youthful boast. The material aspects he could face but the emotional toll, could he handle that and even more important could his two son's at this formative stage of their young lives? How could he do this to them and yet, he consoled himself, it need not be the drama that was brewing up; why could not Kate agree to the move, knowing how much this house had fuelled his dreams since he had been fourteen years old.

He walked slowly back to the house, removed his Barbour and put his boot in the cast iron boot pull and, leaning forward, could faintly hear his wife explaining to her parents of her plans for the business. He paused and sitting on the window seat waited for more, he was not disappointed.

'Liz and I have given a great deal of time to formulating a positive business plan and we are determined not to be side tracked by James or anyone else.'

'I am sure you have some capital of your own Kate, your grandfather was after all very generous to you, but are those, or other funds, realisable if needs be? How long have you been planning all of this and surely James will have to agree as whilst you may be running the York office I presume it is still part of his company?'

'Daddy you are speaking to me as if I was a client, I am your daughter for heaven's sake.'

'Kate, you have lived with James for the past twelve years and during that time many of his ideas and indeed much of his thinking will have rubbed off, but you are about to jump into the water with a load of sharks. Therefore, I must talk to you as a client because you need legal advice and I also think you need financial advice.'

She held her hand up.

'Okay, I am not stupid. I have had both financial and legal advice from Johnnie Mortimer and his lawyers. Apart from owning the health spa, his family have a very well connected and established company right up there with the top agencies such as Savills. If things go as we imagine, then we propose to merge the two companies so that we will be the largest in the whole of Yorkshire. I am also contemplating moving to North Yorkshire.'

Angela interrupted.

'What about the boys? It is so handy down here, you can be at Uppingham in half an hour or so.'

This time she was stopped in her tracks.

'I am going to Sedbergh next week to see the Headmaster and if it is as good as they say, then it would make more sense to send the boys there instead of Uppingham.'

The kitchen door crashed open.

'Over my dead body you conniving bitch, first you deny me my home and now you intend to deny my sons their right to go to Uppingham, these two dreams that have been central to my whole life. Well you can have your share of Woolmington, but...'

This time her reply came like a bolt out of the blue.

Well I am definitely moving to North Yorkshire as I cannot commute from Rutland and so yes, if Uppingham is that important to you, then perhaps it is best if the boys do stay there. Now are you satisfied?'

The stunned silence was finally interrupted by the telephone.

James wearily picked up the receiver.

'Woolmington Hall, James Carrington speaking.'

He remained quiet, they all did, his demeanour not betraying who was on the other end of the line.

'I will come over straight away, thank you for calling me.'

He returned the telephone to its receiver before advising them. 'I have to go out.'

CHAPTER FORTY SIX

He went upstairs and returned in his corn coloured cords and blazer. They heard the car fire up and gurgle its way down the drive. It stopped at the lane end and then with a throaty roar it was gone.

The sitting room at Woolmington was suddenly very quiet. No one knew quite how to break the silence.

They all stared at the fire willing someone to break the ice; Jeremy cracked first.

'In all of my life,' he appeared to be talking to himself, 'I have never experienced a family situation like this. One minute my daughter is on the verge of a breakdown, the next she is ready to conquer the world. What in God's name is going on?'

He looked up, shrugged his shoulders and waited.

Finally Kate spoke.

'I did not mean to go as far as I did. It is just that this last week, talking with Liz and yes, talking to Johnnie I have suddenly felt like a free spirit. I wanted to see James again and discuss the future, to seek reassurance that he really wanted me and not Sally Parkinson and yet, when he was out with the horses, I sensed that he had his own plans and so I thought I would state my terms first. Yes, he can have his bloody Milford and he had better not stop me seeing Charles or Edward.'

'Kate darling, James is not a monster and if only you could see it, you are driving him away. I believed him the other day when he said he had not seen this woman again and, to be perfectly fair, you did see an awful lot of Johnnie Mortimer and on a daily basis, not just one night across a crowded room as it were.'

'So what are you both saying to me?'

'I think darling; it is what you are trying to say to us. Who is it that you really want and where do you want to live and how important is this business venture. In which order would you put them?'

'Right, in terms of feeling my life meant something:

One   The Business
Two   I need to live in Yorkshire to run that business

Three If I am living there, then I will not be able to resist seeing Johnnie
Mortimer. He is a very kind person who has suffered a great deal and I
feel it very easy to relate to him. This is probably going to hurt James, his
pride at least, but you know how tough he is, he will not stay down for
long.'

'I am very saddened by your list of priorities Kate, particularly in that you have not even included
the boys, my grandchildren whom I love dearly; they are not even on your list. And as for James
being so tough, I have seen him these past few days and Edward Lawson's death has hurt him more
than anyone can tell. Only Connie, who is the one hurt most of all, has shown him the kindness and
compassion that he desperately needs and your attack on him earlier was shameful.'

Jeremy left the room and went to James's study. He scanned the shelves until he saw the title Other
Men's Flowers; that anthology of English Poetry compiled by Lord Wavell during the darkest days
of World War Two.

He took the green leather bound book from the shelf and sat at James's desk. He
remembered giving it to his son-in-law on the day of his marriage to Kate and, he opened it and
turned to the sonnet, number 116 that was pasted inside the front cover. His mind went back to
that awful day thirty years ago when he realised that Angela had betrayed his love with a friend of
his from his time at Oxford. Five lines in particular had helped him through that bleak period of his
life.

> *...Admit impediments; love is not love*
> *Which alters when it alteration finds*
> *Or bends with the remover to remove*
> *O no, it is an ever-fixed mark*
> *That looks on tempests and is never shaken...*

He had remained stoic and brave until the affair was over, firm in his belief that she would come
back to him and when she did there was no recrimination, the episode was never mentioned and his
life and Angela's had been extremely happy. Would his daughter, could his daughter, put the love of
her family above her sudden personal ambitions?

He sighed; he was too old for this drama, his view on life and morality and decency were
of another time, he would like to walk away and leave them to sort things out, but he knew he could
not.

He sat there, head in his hands and was unaware that his daughter had entered the room and
had picked up the book. She read the words in her soft cultured voice and he turned to her, tears
streaming down his cheeks.

'I am so sorry Daddy but I am so confused and unhappy, though I don't know why I
should be.

When I am here it seems worse, last week in Yorkshire I felt so full of life and ideas and
yes I did meet someone very special who is on the same wavelength as me and with no disrespect
to James I feel subjugated; he makes all the decisions, he thinks so quickly that everything is decided
before I can say a word. I know he means well, but I don't want to feel second class anymore.

The business in York is going well, very well in fact, but I can't run it from here in Rutland. Will you come with me and meet Johnnie Mortimer and make your mind up when you have seen what I am doing up there?'

'Very well I will do that, although I intend to tell James where I am going, do you agree to that?'
'Yes, but perhaps there is no need to mention this to Johnnie, not right now, although I do want you to meet him.'
'Very well Kate, but no more mention of this until the funeral is over.'

James drove hard, his head still reeling from Kate's verbal onslaught; he had expected a much more protracted argument. However, it did have financial implications as his share of the equity was a substantial part of the purchase price of Milford and being Kate's business partner was after today's outburst a definite no-no.

He put this to one side, he needed to sit down in front of his computer and crunch a few numbers, probably quite a lot of numbers. Next week's 'Musidora Stakes' for the leading two year old fillies on the Knavesmire at York could, if the filly ran really well, collect a handsome sum for winning and boost the prospects of Rebel, when he went through the ring at Tattersalls October sale. His sire's first crop had averaged just under 12,000 guineas, and a good looker like Rebel, who had not inherited his father's weak knees, could well make up to thirty thousand guineas. He was still deep in thought as he turned in to the market place in Uppingham and seeing a space parked in front of the Falcon Hotel.

She was already in the cocktail bar, dressed in a stunning blue dress that accentuated the blue eyes which smiled at him beneath her long blonde hair.

'Fancy bumping into you.'
'I am so pleased to see you; I was terrified that Kate would answer the phone.'
'Normally that might have been a bit tricky, but today was anything but normal, so let me get you a drink and I will update you with my news. What pray is your pleasure?'
She gave him a very coy look.
'I think that may have to wait until another day, meanwhile a G&T – Tanqueray please.'
He returned from the bar smiling and relaxed.
'You look happy.'
'I have such good memories of this place, when my parents came up to school we always seemed to come here for lunch. Yes it has very happy memories, although of course I was not allowed to drink pints!'
Now it was his turn to check on her family background.
'Your mother like my mother was shipped off to Cheltenham Ladies College so I imagine it was most probably your Alma mater?'
'Yes it certainly was and I have to confess that my days there were very happy.'
'I bet you excelled at sport?'
'Yes, I played lacrosse in the winter term and tennis in the summer. I also dabbled with rowing, but as you might guess my passion was show jumping. I had two ponies; Albi, a grey, who was a brilliantly gymkhana pony as he was very fast and could stop on a sixpence. My favourite however was Oliver, a very dark bay Welsh Section B pony, he was 13 hands and looked like a miniature thoroughbred, if you were brave he would jump anything. I was devastated when I outgrew him but at least he went

to my best friend who was not as tall as me, in fact when she left school, Oliver went back home with her. The last time I heard he was twenty three and teaching her children to ride.

After that I graduated to hunters and adult competitions but my main passion these days is, as you might guess.....

'As an educated guess I would venture that might be hunting.'

'Top of the class Mr Carrington, and it is a pastime that I very much look forward to introducing to you.'

'As long as I can wear a red coat,' he mused.

That will depend on how well you do, but at least you start with the advantage of being a landowner!'

He reached over and held her hand, no need for words, they both knew how happy the other was and they both knew that the road ahead was going to be rocky and that in three days' time there loomed the dreadful prospect of Edward Lawson's funeral.

They were both quiet, neither knowing how best to go forward, holding hands did at least mean holding on.

'I heard that you and Roddy Forsythe were no longer an item.'

His gaze was pensive and hopeful.

'It's true; we never did have a lot in common, apart from hunting I suppose. Now you tell me about you and Kate. I know her father is a lawyer and that her parents live in or near to Bournemouth.'

He smiled; his face was warm and appreciative.

'We are so alike, if I want something I always do my research be it work or play and I know that you are thirty four and I am a child of thirty three.'

'Fibber, you are thirty seven, although I admit you have worn well but, as you now know I also do my research, no more porkies.'

'I promise. I have been married for twelve years and for the first ten years I was really happy and then, very slowly, Kate started to turn inward and the children seemed to be her only focus and whilst I still care about her, the magic has gone. You will be well aware that Edward Lawson and I had a fall out shortly before the Architects and Builders Dinner, what you will not know is that we also had a disagreement over a business decision I made on behalf of my wife. The estate agencies we have on the south coast are very successful, but not easily accessed and to stray from the point for a moment, you have just inspired a great idea, which will be very much to our benefit.

As I was saying, Edward disagreed and so I removed that part of the business portfolio out of the Fordmill group and into my ownership. When I explained this to Kate, she immediately took sides with Edward and the others and yet, when I suggested that she ran the business together with Liz Reed, who in effect was already in charge, she astounded me by agreeing to this suggestion. She has since spent time in Yorkshire and is making a success of it. Shortly after this came the big bust up with Edward Lawson; sometime in the future I will tell you how two men who had done everything together at work and at play since they were fourteen years old were so pig-headed that, despite pleas from all their friends, neither would back down and now because of this awful tragedy they never will, at least not on this earth.'

His eyes began to cloud over, the grief evidently only just below the surface.

Feeling completely helpless she put her hand on his knee and patted it.

His voice was a husky and the words came slowly as he tried to compose himself.

'The magic that Kate and I once had has gone and until yesterday, she still sought to deny me what my whole business life has been about, how to reclaim all that my family lost and the wonderful house that is central to everything I have ever done. It is very early in our relationship, but I feel that I have to tell you from the very start what drives me, because without you understanding that, you will not know the real me.'

He stood up. 'I bet this is more than you bargained for?'

'I suppose it is, but I have spent so many days and not a few nights wondering about you and I don't want us to have any secrets.'

'Then I will top up our glasses, same again?'

She nodded, happy that he was prepared to share such private and precious thoughts so soon.

He returned with the drinks and related to her the trauma his family had endured when they had to sell Milford Hall and his youthful oath to one day return to that house. He explained why he wanted his sons to be educated at Uppingham, where he had been so happy, although he conceded that but for leaving and going instead to the local grammar school, he would never had met his best friend... His voice had tailed off again and she knew instinctively what he was thinking, that but for that meeting, Edward Lawson may well be alive.

'Edward decided to leave you; he was every bit as irresponsible as you for not patching things up.'

'I suppose so; it would certainly have been easier if only Kate had taken such a fair minded view.'

'So what other secrets have you to tell me, how many affairs has she found out about?'

'None, there are no other secrets; I promised Kate's mother I would remain loyal to her daughter and so I have.'

She smiled at him, her eyes expressing affection and admiration.

'So all I have to worry about is living in a big house and visits to Uppingham to see your sons. Most women would regard that as Heaven not Hell and then there is the awful prospect of going to the races with you, helping with the horses, and skiing together. You silly boy, I have just recited all of the things I most want to do and I haven't mentioned showing you off to my parents, they never could relate to Roddy – 'far too pompous and not very tall', was how my mother described him to Granny Parkinson. Very modest and tall and amazingly handsome is how she is going to describe you.'

He shook his head, clearly relieved to have got all his perceived baggage off his chest.

'I am so glad that I told you about my demons, it makes it so much easier to stand by my resolve, I will not concede anymore on these issues, both she and her Mr Mortimer can make their beds and lie in them, quite literally.'

Sally looked quite shocked.

'Kate has a boyfriend?'

'Well I am not quite sure what the position is, but she has returned from spending a week with her mother at a health spa in the Yorkshire Dales and Mr Mortimer has obviously had a profound effect on her. She has suddenly agreed that the boys can after all stay at Uppingham and that she proposes to live in North Yorkshire. Even more astounding she has suggested that we can sell Woolmington Manor. So Mr Mortimer, aka Johnnie, has achieved in one week what I have failed to do in twelve years, persuade her to move house.'

'What are you planning to do?'

'First of all I have to survive the ordeal of Edward's funeral; it is only because Connie is so insistent that I feel I can go.'

'She is right James, you of all people must pay homage to your friend and comfort as best you can his wife and children. You must remember that you did not cause his death, an Italian truck driver did that because, according to the newspapers, he probably fell asleep at the wheel.'

He nodded his head and attempted a smile.

'When I dreamed of seeing you again I never imagined it would be in such sad circumstances. Will you come to the funeral?'

'No James, I think you have enough on your plate without having to explain my presence.'

'Sally, I need time to think and I need you to help me, will you come away with me for a few days so that we can get to know each other properly?'

'Well yes, but I will need to check my diary with our estate manager, but I don't see any reasons why not.'

'I will take you somewhere special; all I am going to tell you is that you will need your passport.'

He stood up and gazed down at the faultless face framed in blonde hair.

'I am not sure when the funeral is, but I will let you know and we will go later that week?'

She clung to him, no reply needed.

They left the Falcon by separate exits and as he sat in the car and thought of returning home, he felt all of the energy drain out of him. He looked in the rear view mirror and the face that looked back at him had burnt all his boats, there was nowhere to hide and the only person he worried about was Jeremy Palmer, once again he was going to be caught up in infidelity and once again it was very close to home. The thought of home triggered another thought, of another home.

He went back into the hotel and entered the public telephone box, he gave the operator the number and waited for the phone to ring which after a few seconds it did and almost immediately a refined ladies voice announced 'Elizabeth Carrington, who is that please.'

'Hello mother, it's James, I was thinking of dropping in to see you.'

He heard the pleasure in her voice.

'That would be lovely darling, will you stay for supper?'

'I would like to stay for the night, if that is okay?'

'How did you guess I was having steak and kidney pie tonight?'

'I didn't, but it sounds wonderful, I will be about forty minutes.'

He rang off knowing how much it would mean to her to see him and he felt guilty that he was not more attentive. He should try harder in future.

As he anticipated, his call had lifted his mother's spirits and she quickly laid an extra place at the kitchen table and by the time he had arrived, there was a bottle of Merlot opened and ready.

Elizabeth had moved just once more since Robert's death, this time willingly, to a ground floor apartment in the property that James had bought from Mrs Watkin-Downes.

The incoming new client, in this case Elizabeth Carrington had, not surprisingly, managed to negotiate a very attractive sale price from Fordmill.

'Just to make sure that not too much of James's inheritance was squandered!'

Edward had suggested much to everyone's amusement.

Angus, the little West Highland White, ears pricked, jumped off the sofa and by the time his mother had reached the hallway the Porsche was parked outside the front door.

He extracted his long legs and levered himself out of the front seat and then immediately disappeared back into the car, to grab a bunch of roses from the passenger side and skipped up the stone steps to the enormous front door.

'For my favourite lady.'

'From my favourite son; not that either of us has any competition. It is lovely to see you darling, but do come on in, Angus is going berserk.'

He stepped into the hall, admiring as he always did the ornate plasterwork and the magnificent staircase with its intricate carving and magnificent newel posts and balustrading.

She led him into the sitting room where he almost tripped over the white terrier that was spinning around his ankles. He scooped him up and sat with him on the sofa in the hope that it might quieten him down, it seemed to do the trick and he turned round to find a glass of Macallan poured and ready.

'Wonderful, I need this.'

Something in his voice alerted her female wiles; she sensed that something was afoot.

'So, what brings you into Monday Country, are you still thinking about hunting?'

The amusement in her voice, alluding to the day of the week that the Quorn pack traditionally hunts in this area. Her son had displayed such enthusiasm about learning to ride and become part of this traditional English sport when Fordmill first bought the property.

'Well I might just do that, although if I do, it will be with the Belvoir.'

'That would bring back some happy memories, I remember so well the Christmas meets at Milford Hall, so many horses milling around in front of the house, with Mr Wilson helped by Mr and Mrs Price and a few girls from the village handing up the stirrup cups.

Her eyes had a distinctly faraway look and he saw in her moist eyes the wonderful memories that she had conjured up; she turned to him.

'Do you remember seeing your father and me, he always had a grey horse and he was never far from the front of the field. Those were happy days, I still think about that house but without any real regret, your father was never happier than those last four years he had at 'Moors Meadow' running the poultry farm. It was a far cry from his family farm, but he was such a modest man that the thought would never have occurred to him. I do so miss his kind face and the laughter that was never far below the surface; it is such a blow when you lose not only your husband but also your best friend.'

For a moment he expected tears but instead she took his hand and directed him to the kitchen table, indicating that he should pour the wine whilst she nipped back into the sitting room. She returned carrying a braided leather riding crop.

'This belonged to your great grandfather; if you look on the silver collar you will see his initials AJS 1891, just above the leopard's head hallmark, which from memory I believe is London. It has been languishing in a drawer so I am afraid it will need a good polish before you use it.'

He looked closely at the hunting whip with its stag horn handle for opening gates and at the other end of the leather covered shaft a leather loop for closing them.

'Mother, I will really treasure this; just the thought that this was held by Albert Staincliffe, the man who built Milford Hall, wow I am lost for words.'

'It was also carried by your father; it was a gift from my father to welcome him into the family and the middle initial stands for James, which is where your name came from – we thought that Albert might be just a little too much to lumber you with!'

He wanted to say that this riding whip would soon be returning home to Milford but that could wait for another day when he intended to also return his mother to the house that owned his soul.

She took the steak and kidney from the bottom oven and turned to him, her maternal antennae probing for the reason for this unexpected visit.

'Is everything well at home?'

He paused, the hesitation confirming her concern.

'Things have been rather difficult of late and Kate announced earlier today that she intends to move to North Yorkshire and take a serious business interest in the estate agency we have in York.

As you know she has been to a health spa up there and apparently fallen under the spell of someone called Johnnie Mortimer. His family owns the spa and he is, apparently, a chartered surveyor, so property interests are I imagine the common ground.'

All the joy that her memories of Milford Hall had conjured up was immediately dissipated and her expression was a confusion of concern and grief.

'How do you feel about it; what about the boys; where will you live; surely you won't let this happen; Do you want me to speak to Kate?'

He held her hand, unable to know where to begin.

As you are aware Angela and Kate went, at her mother's suggestion, to Nidderdale Spa for a week of cosseting. The reason she went was to clear her head and to try and restore her confidence. I was more than happy to let her go, as quite honestly, I needed some space to collect my own thoughts. Her behaviour has for some time been neurotic; she has a phobia about a girl called Sally Parkinson with whom I danced – just once – at the Nottingham Architects and Builders annual dinner. Despite my assurances to the contrary, she will not accept that I have not seen Sally again. That is until two days ago, when I bumped into her at the George Hotel in Stamford. This meeting was entirely fortuitous, the only reason that I was in the area was my need to see where my best friend had died. I have to be quite honest with you mother, although I had not seen Sally, I had thought about her a great deal and the more accusations that Kate threw at me, the more I wanted to see her, although I had no idea how I would break that news to her or the boys.'

Elizabeth looked intently at her son.

'So she has given you a way out, but what about Charles and Edward? They are too young and innocent to be hurt like this; they need two parents, two loving parents.'

'I know but I also want them to be brought up in a loving environment and not in an atmosphere of bickering and discontent. Also for long periods they are away at boarding school and I am sure that there will not be any reluctance from either of us to having access to them.'

'My word James, you really have been giving this some serious thought.'

'Since Kate came out with that bombshell about moving to North Yorkshire I have thought of little else.'

He lifted his head and saw in his mother's eyes the same kind concern he had seen when they had driven away from Milford Hall, he also felt the same despair.

'Mother, it is early days and maybe things will sort themselves out but one thing is certain, I am not moving to Harrogate or wherever she has in mind.'

'Let's have a nightcap darling, why don't you do the honours, whilst I get rid of the pots and pans.'

'Good idea, a drop of Remy as usual?'

It was a rhetorical question but he heard the amusement in her voice as she asked, 'Does the Pope have a balcony?'

They spent an hour chatting before he called it a night, his bed was already turned down and he felt quite young again, he should confide in his mother more often.

CHAPTER FORTY SEVEN

He slept well, so well in fact that Elizabeth woke him at seven thirty concerned that he would be late for the office.

'Mother!' He had chided her; nevertheless he had a busy day with lots to do and had somehow to make a very difficult telephone call.

From the bathroom he could smell the bacon and eggs and sure enough his mother had somehow conjured up a full English breakfast.

'You obviously know how to look after yourself, this is quite a feast.'

'I always have some bacon and sausages in the freezer and the eggs and tomatoes are part of my usual diet but you did get lucky with the mushrooms as I dropped them into my trolley as a last minute treat when I was in Burton's Food Hall.'

'So tell me what your plans are for today, will I have the pleasure of your company tonight?'

'No mother, I am not running away from my responsibilities, in fact I have decided to call Connie and ask if there is any way that I can help her through the next few days.'

'I think you are right dear, just remember that you were not responsible for Edward's death and Connie has already said that she wants you to attend the funeral. Go and call her right now before you lose the courage and talk yourself out of it.'

He nodded and slowly got to his feet. He kissed his mother gently on the forehead and walked with heavy steps to the sitting room. Elizabeth heard him quietly close the door, she did not envy him but below the urbane and confident exterior he was a caring person and she knew that he would manage to say the right thing. It was apparent to anyone that his remorse was genuine and that after Connie and the immediate family, he would be the one who was suffering the most grief.

He sat with the phone in his hand for several seconds but finally steeled himself to dial the number.

'Hello, this is Willow House.' It was Connie, he was unable to answer.

'Hello, this is Connie Lawson, who is it please?'

Finally, in a very quiet voice he summoned up the courage to speak.

'Connie, it is me James, can I come and see you?'

Now it was her turn to remain silent.

'Connie I am sorry if I have upset you, I never should have called.'

'No, I am sorry James and yes I would like to see you, I really would. Why don't you come this afternoon, say about three? We are about a hundred yards past the pub if you are coming from Melton Mowbray.'

'Thank you Connie I will be with you about three o'clock.'

He replaced the phone on the receiver and wondered how on earth he could be speaking with Connie as if they were strangers, they had shared so many moments of triumph and happiness but of course Edward, the link in this chain of success and bonhomie was missing.

He remained seated, head in his hands, with tears streaming down his cheeks and through his fingers. Finally he regained some composure and after another ten minutes or so was able to rejoin his mother in the kitchen. She saw in his puffed red eyes the pain and loss that she had endured when Robert was snatched from her at much the same age .Without speaking she placed a cup of tea in front of him, the recommended panacea in all such crises. He nodded his thanks.

They had a bowl of soup for lunch and at two fifteen he kissed her cheek.

'Wish me luck.'

She squeezed his hand.

'Drive carefully and leave your hunting crop with me, I will get it cleaned up for you, it will be a good excuse for you to come and see me again.'

She went to the door with him and watched the forlorn face sit behind the wheel and bring the engine to life. He drove away wrapped up his grief and totally unsure of what he might say to Connie.

As he approached the village he was running a little early; But Connie would not be surprised by that, she knew him far too well. Somehow that little bit of intuition helped to calm him down, he tried to concentrate on their long friendship. On the support they had always given each other, it helped to make today's visit seem necessary and it gave him strength.

He knew the house, although he had never been inside. His innate curiosity had prompted him to drive past on his way back from Stamford soon after Edward had agreed to buy Fordmill Construction.

He turned into a gravel drive screened on both sides by a beech hedge, which after about fifty yards revealed an attractive stone house, probably Edwardian he thought. That guess sadly reminding him of why he was here. Fortunately, Connie had heard him approach and seeing her broke the spell, for the moment anyway.

She came to the car to meet him. Neither could say a word, but no words could have conveyed their feelings more eloquently. She took his hand and led him through the front door and the panelled hallway into the sitting room.

He sat on the larger of the two sofas, Connie sat facing him both of them trying to conjure the right words. She spoke first.

'James, this is a meeting we should have had a long time ago.'

He tried to find the right words but she put a finger to her lips.

'There is something you need to know, but first you must tell me why two stubborn men, who had been devoted boyhood friends refused to give each other an explanation of the grievance that has delivered such a terrible blow.' She paused, hoping he might explain, but clearly devastated, he merely shook his head. Connie tried again to encourage an explanation.

'James, the ramifications of this fallout affected not only the two of you but also those involved in the company, a business that we had together made into such a successful giant.'

She looked searchingly at him, demanding an end to this nonsense that had disrupted so many lives.

Her composure and common sense, which he had so relied on in the past, served to compose him.

'Connie, please believe me when I say that nothing could ever justify what has happened to this wonderful man. A man to whom, you so rightly say, I owed so much. However at the time, we were under a lot of pressure from our bankers APP. Our borrowings had escalated due to the delays caused by the totally unforeseen archaeological excavations that brought the developments in Bournemouth to a standstill.'

He paused, seeking to remember clearly the sequence of events that had had wrought such havoc and caused so much pain to all those central to the company.

He paused to gather his thoughts.

'On the way back from a site meeting in Bournemouth I drove through the Cotswolds and saw two Fordmill JCBs digging out the footings for a building. There were also two other guys on site, plus two trucks to cart away the spoil from the excavations. I was angry that we were wasting time and money on a project that Edward was authorising and to which I had been given no knowledge. If he had wanted to invest in some private venture then he should have put it before the board and discussed it, as I had done with the estate agency in York. The other directors would have looked at it and accepted or rejected it, as they did in the case of my Yorkshire project.'

Her eyes bored into him but instead of refuting his argument, she took his hand.

'But you fell out with Edward without even giving him a fair hearing.'

'That is not quite true, Connie; he refused to explain why he had been apparently siphoning funds into this development in the Cotswolds.'

'I am glad that you used the expression apparently because that is what it was, and he quite rightly felt that as Financial Director he had the authority to sanction fiscal decisions, just as you have on many occasions – the Watkin Hall development for instance.'

'But I did discuss it with all of you; if you remember, we all went over to check it out.'

'Yes, but you had already promised the client that we would proceed, prior to discussing it with the other Directors. Maybe Edward should have mentioned it, but if you remember you were somewhat stressed out with these delays.'

'Connie, I have regretted that decision so many times, but it was seeing his initials against those withdrawals, it was quite a lot of money.'

She nodded, beginning to understand for the first time, the sequence of events that had triggered such anger and tragedy.

'James, who was the first man to believe in you and provide the finance that enabled Fordmill to grow from a small company, building a row of cottages out in the sticks, to what they eventually became?'

'Charles Lattimer.'

'And what was his wife's name?'

'Elizabeth.'

'When she died of cancer what did you promise to do?'

'I promised to help fund a respite centre in her name. But where is this leading?'

She shook her head.

'For such an intelligent man you can sometimes be so naive, if only you had asked Edward and if only he had answered your question, insulting though he believed it to be.'

Her voice quavered.

'What were her initials?'

His face was suddenly ashen. He looked at her in dismay as the truth dawned on him.

'You mean that the initials EL stood for Elizabeth Lattimer and not Edward Lawson?'

'Yes, and when we took over Fordmill, Edward personally funded the respite centre that bore her name.'

Connie was the stronger of the two and she continued to be in charge of the unfolding events.

'In order that the company should not be jeopardised by the ongoing building costs, Edward was monitoring the cash flow on a day to day basis, which is why we never defaulted with the bank.'

He sat gazing at the ceiling, totally bereft of all feelings until slowly and emotionally the words trickled out.

'Connie, how can you ever forgive me?'

'Life is too short James to bear grudges as you now know only too well. You will never be able to say sorry to Edward and your best friend will never be able to forgive you, but I can and I do, and I pray that you will feel the same.'

He nodded his head and his voice was hoarse as he came out with that one word that can heal all emotional conflicts.

'Sorry; I am so very sorry and ashamed. If only there was some way that I could put things right.'

'Perhaps you can James, but for now we need to support each other through the next few days.'

'Will you perhaps speak with the vicar at St Mary's Church in Bottesford?'

She smiled; her expression was kind and understanding.

'You see, I did take on board the advice that you asked Jeremy to pass on to me.'

He returned her smile. 'Yes of course I will, do you know which day the service will take place?'

'Because of the accident enquiry it will now be next Tuesday, one week today in fact.'

He stood up automatically plumping up the cushions as he did so.

She shook her head. 'Ever the perfectionist; that was one trait of yours that Edward never did acquire. Come with me, there is something that I want you to see.'

He followed her out of the sitting room and into the room at the far end of the hall, which turned out to be the study.

James sank into the dark red leather chair and there on the wall facing the desk was the black and white photograph with the faded Daily Telegraph cutting announcing Carrington & Lawson, the unstoppable duo. Hanging from the frame was a dark blue international cap; emblazoned below the crest was the legend England v Scotland.

'I so hoped that despite how I had treated him that this would still be in his study.'

He lifted the cap, 'This is my second cap; I have Edward's hung like this in my own study. You see, like him, I never ever wanted to break the bond that we shared. This means so much to me and, Connie; it is so kind of you to let me know that he did not want to extinguish me entirely from his life.'

She kissed the top of his head.

'This means a lot to me as well, please give my love to Kate and ask her to keep in touch.' He squeezed her hand unable to speak, and she watched him shuffle out of the house for once devoid of his usual athletic stride.

He reached the sanctity of the car and sat for several minutes trying to compose himself, seeking to come to terms with the enormity of the stupid pride that had cost him and Edward their friendship. He was grateful that Connie had given him the opportunity to assuage if not heal those wounds.

She saw him sitting there, well aware having known him for so many years, that beneath that unflappable exterior lurked a kind and generous man with a very sensitive side that was rarely revealed.

He finally gathered himself and, with a task to do, his head soon cleared and he decided that he would make an impromptu visit on the vicar of St Mary the Virgin, the parish church of Bottesford.

As someone who lived in the Vale of Belvoir, he had many times driven past this fine building which is known locally as the Lady of the Vale. Even without knowing its precise location, it is easily found as its tall and elegant spire, the fourth highest in England, can be seen for many miles around.

The chancel walls date back to Norman times and it is situated on the outskirts of the village on the banks of the river Devon. Within a few minutes he arrived and inside he could hear someone practising on the organ and so, not knowing the whereabouts of the Vicarage, he decided to seek directions from the organist.

He turned the handle of the porch that led into the nave of the church and was greeted by an array of monuments that must surely raise the eyes of anyone who has ever entered this most stylish and sumptuous church. Much of this magnificence is due to the Roos family and the Earls of Rutland, several of whom are buried here.

As fortune would have it, the vicar too was inside the church, busily tidying up the carelessly stacked piles of hymn books. He turned when he heard the latch opening, his smile warm and kindly, he looked like a vicar, was James's immediate reaction.

'James Carrington, I presume, I am Humphrey Bartlett. You are most welcome and I do of course know that sadly your visit is because of the tragedy that has befallen your great friend of many years. Mrs Lawson telephoned to say you were on your way, so why don't we go through into the vestry and I will make a few notes and discuss with you the order of service and choice of hymns etc.'

'Thank you vicar you are most kind and we will be grateful for any helpful advice. Edward Lawson was an exceptional person and the most considerate of men. He was also, as many rugby players from across the globe will testify, a most formidable opponent. In addition, he was highly respected in the business community and, most of all; he was a wonderful husband and friend. His deeds in business and on the rugby field mean that a great many people will wish to pay their last respects and this magnificent church is a fitting place to pay tribute to this much loved man.'

James followed the vicar into the vestry where he was waved into a chair facing the long table that served as a desk come committee table.

'Do you have any preferences with regard to hymns?'

'Not off the top of my head, vicar.'

'Humphrey please, it is not as if I don't know you.'.

He saw the look of surprise on his guest's face.

'I am a great rugby fan and have seen you and Edward Lawson in action on many occasions both for England and for Leicester, they were quite often painful experiences as I hail from Northampton and have been a Saint's supporter since I was a boy.'

James grinned at the last comment.

'I suppose being a vicar they are a very appropriate side for you to support.'

'Touché, now what thoughts do you have on how we celebrate the life of Edward Lawson.'

'In terms of hymns I personally like 'Dear Lord and Father of mankind and 'Lord of all hopefulness, Lord of all Joy, and I know that Edwards favourite was I vow to thee my country but I don't know if those are the right choices for such an occasion and we would welcome your suggestions.'

'No, I think those are very good choices as most people are familiar with them and Edward's is particularly appropriate given the service he gave to his country on the rugby field.'

'I think they will be perfect but I must of course consult Connie Lawson. As to the prayers and readings, do you have any suggestions?'

'I usually start with a few Scriptural Sentences of Comfort followed by the first hymn and then we need a reading from the Gospels, perhaps St John 14 v 1-7 .and, of course, an address or a tribute followed by the second and third hymns between which we have a prayer.'

He looked at James enquiringly.

'The tribute is possibly something you should do?'

'Perhaps, but I think that I must consult with Connie and get back to you tomorrow.'

'Yes of course and if there is any way that I can be of help, don't hesitate to ask.'

'There is one thing Humphrey, there will be a very large congregation, many of whom will end up standing outside but if you could arrange for extra seating in the aisles etc. it would be helpful.'

'You are just slightly ahead of me James, but don't worry, this church has hosted many important funeral services and we do have contingency plans, all will be well.'

James stood up, he was confident that Bottesford would provide a fitting place to commemorate Edward Lawson, but could he, should he, offer to give the Tribute to his friend, how would others perceive this, it was best to ask Connie to select an appropriate person.

He drove away, his mind in less of a turmoil than when he had arrived and he was so pleased that he had spoken with Connie. The vicar had been very helpful and the church was exceptional, it was a worthy place for a very worthy man to say his goodbyes to his many friends and admirers.

In fifteen minutes he was back at Willow House. He tugged on the bell handle but after two or three minutes not having received a reply, he decided to check the garden to see if Connie was outside. He found a sturdy gate set in the stone garden wall which led him to a large flagged terrace and there in a swing seat, he found her staring at her wedding album.

From her face and the streaked make-up he could tell that she had been weeping for some time.

'This was the only big occasion that you never shared...' Her voice faltered before she managed to bring her grief under control.

'Thank you for coming back to support me James, I have somehow managed to stay strong but it has been too much, I feel so weak and lonely; I don't know how I would have coped if you had not been in touch.'

He joined her on the seat and put his arm around her, they sat there for several minutes as they both strove to control the emotions that starved them of coherent thought. Finally he managed to speak.

'The vicar is Humphrey Bartlett and he is a really nice guy who remembers Edward's exploits on the rugby field. The church is quite magnificent and they are used to conducting services for the great and the good. I have a list of hymns for you to approve and we need someone to pay tribute to Edward's life and achievements.'

She interrupted him.

'That someone James, is you.'

'Are you sure about this Connie, so many people know about our bust up and the traumas that ensued.'

'James Carrington; only you can talk about the life of Edward Lawson, you were like brothers and the only possible dram of comfort that I can draw from this tragedy is that you are united again and that only good thoughts remain and that we are friends once more.'

He squeezed her hand.

'Thank you but I really don't know how I will get through it without breaking down.'

'Just imagine you were at Twickenham converting a try that he had just scored.'

He smiled. 'I first did that when we were sixteen and he had crashed over the try line with three red Welsh jerseys clinging to his back like limpets; if all fifteen of them had been in his way it would not have made a difference, he could be unstoppable when he scented victory. I dare not let him down then and I won't let him down now.'

She didn't say anything; the pride in her face was answer enough,

'Right then I will organise the hymn sheets and let people know the date etc. and of course liaise with Humphrey Bartlett. I will keep you fully informed Connie but, in the meantime, I had better report back to Woolmington.'

She walked with him back to his car and he promised that Kate would be in touch, it seemed easier than disturbing her with his own problems.

The drive home and the anticipated interrogation was as daunting a prospect as the reception he had expected to receive from Connie; in reality it was cordial and polite, particularly after he had explained the events of the day at Bottesford; even Kate was conciliatory.

'I apologise for suggesting you should not attend the funeral James. Of course you must, you are the only person who can fully appreciate and pay tribute to such an outstanding man; without his help and friendship you would not have achieved what you have, in business or on the playing field.'

'Thank you Kate and thank you all in advance for the support I am going to need, especially from you Jeremy, I will need your ordered legal mind to help me find the right words for my ordeal.'

The response was immediate and sincere. 'I will of course be only too pleased to help.'

They were interrupted by the telephone, it was for Kate. She excused herself and took the call in the kitchen. It was Johnnie Mortimer.

'Kate, how are you coping?'

'It is difficult; everyone is being so polite and with the funeral next Tuesday there is an air of unreality as we all try not to upset each other. James seems in a trance and I have not had an opportunity to discuss our plans for the business partnership.'

'Kate I do understand, I remember with total clarity how I felt when I was told about Madeline and my daughters.'

She heard the tremor in his voice.

'Johnnie, I will come up to Yorkshire next Friday, my parents will be going home and I don't want to stay down here and end up arguing with James.'

'I imagined you would be going to see your filly run in the 'Gilling Stakes' at Newmarket on Friday, it is a Group 2 race and a win would make her a valuable brood mare and selfishly, I was hoping we might make a weekend of it by spending a couple of nights in Cambridge. I could show you round my old college and we can make more plans for the future. If I come down by train, you could drive us back to Yorkshire?'

There was a silence, these conversations are never easy. Finally she broke the silence.

'Johnnie I think I had better go and if I can get to Newmarket I will let you know. Otherwise I can't wait for next Friday to come round.'

She returned to the drawing room, flushed with excitement, but uncertain of what to say as the expectant faces turned towards her.

'It was Liz, she wanted to know if we were going to Newmarket next week; I said that it was very doubtful, although maybe James, a little diversion from your grief might be a good idea.' He shook his head.

'It is only a horse race, although I remember so well that day at Newmarket with Edward and Connie when Woolmington so gallantly refused to be beaten and won her maiden. You bought her for me, as a surprise, and all our friends were there; everything seemed so perfect then.'

He stopped himself, reminiscing was not going to help. Instead he excused himself.

'I had better make a start on Edward's tribute, although God alone knows what I am going to say.'

He turned on his heel and headed for his study.

Words had always come easily to James Carrington but right now his mind was devoid of any coherent thought and, as the minutes ticked away, the screen of his computer remained obstinately empty.

He stared at the orange cursor on the black page and willed it to provoke a theme around which he could pay a fitting tribute to his friend of so many years.

His thoughts returned to Connie and her insistence that only he could summarise the life of her husband and he decided to begin at the beginning and prayed that he would be able to deliver these thoughts when the time came, although he knew in an emotive situation it would not be easy.

He slowly eked out the words and, as his mind concentrated on the many happy memories, the words began to flow, bringing with them warmth and sorrow in equal measure.

Finally it was finished and he decided to seek approval from Jeremy; he scanned the computer screen for a final time before hitting the print button and collecting the ensuing draft before seeking out his father-in-law.

His first guess was correct, he found him alone in the kitchen sitting next to a pot of coffee and a half completed Times crossword.

'Unlike you to be struggling with the Thunderer, twenty minutes or so is how long it usually takes you.'

Jeremy looked agitated.

'My mind is not really switched on I am afraid.'

'You obviously need something else to exercise your literary skills.'

He placed the draft speech in front of Jeremy, helped himself to a coffee and watched, slightly nervously as the lawyer scanned the page line by line before turning a sympathetic face to his son-in-law.

'As ever James you understate your own achievements, in this instance quite rightly so. Connie will I am sure, be proud to hear this tribute to her husband.'

CHAPTER FORTY EIGHT

He met Sally the following day, she exuded confidence and seemed full of mischief. He was not therefore surprised to find that she had everything planned and in a business-like manner that he had not yet come to know, she took control.

'Now then James, if we are to take you hunting we had better set about finding you a horse and having a few lessons before the season starts really kicks off in November.'

'Well I was rather hoping that dear old Asprey would be looking after me.'

'Oh yes I had forgotten about the old charger from the Light Brigade. Okay, let's see how he goes across country.'

'Keith has been out on him a few times recently and he was very pleased with him.'

'I suppose he would, they are both from the same regiment, but yes, let's go with him for now. What I propose is that we go and see Maggie Wilkinson, if anyone can sort you out it is her. I also think that it would be a good idea to keep Asprey at her livery yard so that you can pop over there whenever you feel inclined without having to hook the trailer on and load him etc.'

They drove out through Belvoir before turning towards Waltham on the Wolds. The conversation was light, disguising James's apprehension of having to display his rather, as yet inept skills in the saddle.

She pointed out various tracts of grassland all with hedges that needed to be jumped, he tried hard not to examine them too closely as from the roadside they all looked like Beecher's Brook at Aintree. But her enthusiasm was catching and he tried to calm his apprehension by equating the challenge to tackling an All Black open side forward charging toward him with the try line in sight; Right now he fancied taking on the Maori, tattoo's and all.

She was still in full flow.

'This is what you have to anticipate James; some of the greatest hunting country in the UK.'

Finally he spotted the sign and they turned into The Vale Livery Yard.

They were met by Miss Wilkinson, a woman of forty something he guessed, and with a bustling personality that broached no nonsense.

'So Sally this is your friend that has horses but doesn't ride them.'

'Well to be fair Maggie, they are racehorses.'

'Flat bred I'll guess?'

He nodded, guessing where she was coming from; most country people prefer steeplechasing to flat racing as its roots sprang from racing across the open countryside.

The finishing post needed to be the most conspicuous landmark in the area, which in those days, was the tops or points of church steeples, hence the name of the sport, steeplechasing.

The first recorded reference is a print in The Sporting Magazine dated 1793, which depicts The Honourable Mr O'Hea and Captain Magrath being cheered on by a sizeable crowd of spectators on the outskirts of Galloway.

Nowadays, as James was of course well aware, hunts throughout the UK organise their own races which are known as Point to Points. The term Steeplechasing refers to National Hunt Racing which is run over prepared racecourses with fences and water jumps; the most famous venues are of course Cheltenham and Aintree which hosts the most famous steeplechase in the world, The Grand National.

However, such events were not even on James's radar, staying on a horse and controlling it were the limit of his current ambitions.

His thoughts were interrupted by the familiar sound of a horse approaching; he turned to see one of Maggie's grooms holding a bay horse with a distinctive white blaze that she identified as Montgomery.

He seemed friendly enough and was about the same size as Asprey.

'Right James, let's sort out the leathers; put the stirrup under your arm and hold your arm straight out until you can comfortably touch the saddle. Good, so now we know how long you should ride.

You are fortunate to have long legs so that should help this first part of the operation. Now, face the back of the horse, reins in your left hand; with the same hand grab the pommel at the front of the saddle, put your foot in the stirrup and grab the cantle, that's the back of the saddle, and swing your right leg over. That's good; you have obviously done this before.'

'Yes, but not very often.'

His response did not encourage any false optimism of his ability. He was like all occasional riders, immediately aware that he felt he was a long way off the ground; his concern was interrupted by his instructor.

'We are ready to move off.' She barked out her instructions.

'Heels down, knees in, toes forward; straighten your back James and keep your bloody elbows in. Don't look down or that is where you will end up.'

She allowed him to go on a few paces; hopefully he would relax although sadly few novices ever did.

'How do you feel?'

'Fine,' he lied.

'I think we will take the stirrups up a hole.' She pushed her hand under his thigh to shorten the leathers. To make it easier, he took his foot out of the stirrup. This immediately caused her displeasure.

'Never ever take your foot out of the irons, getting them back in if your horse moves off is not easy and you have lost control.'

Maggie grinned at him. 'Are you beginning to regret ever wanting to do this?'

'No.' He lied again.

She led him into the indoor school and handed over control.

'Do you want me to put him on the lunge or are you happy to walk him round a couple of times?'

'Yes, let's go.'

He squeezed his knees against Montgomery's ribs and the horse, reluctantly it seemed, ambled slowly forward. Behind him he heard Maggie yelling 'Keep your back straight and your heels down.'

He completed his two circuits and she sensed that he was finding this too boring. She knew of his reputation as a former rugby player, indeed she had seen him play for Leicester one Boxing Day in the traditional match against The Barbarians. Maggie also suspected that as a natural games player he wanted to pushon; he hasn't fallen off yet so maybe his confidence was a little unrealistic. She decided to push on a little.

'Right James, now we are going to trot, so ask him to quicken.'

James gave Monty, as he now called him, a good dig in the ribs and not entirely prepared for it forgot to rise in the saddle. The experience, particularly for men, because of their anatomy proved very uncomfortable and he very quickly reined his mount to a halt.

Maggie was anxious not to lose her new pupil; she knew the girls in the yard would never forgive her, so she quickly proffered some useful advice,

'Now then James, press down with your feet and raise you bottom out of the saddle, if you feel insecure hold on to the neck strap or the bottom of his mane.

After about five minutes he started to get the rhythm and his rear end and the saddle were starting to move in the same direction and suddenly he started to enjoy it. Three more circuits and he was already seeing himself hurtling across open country with Sally at his heels and then whoosh, he was on the floor and the girls were all laughing. He dusted the sand from his clothes and led Monty over to his audience.

'I was just going to ask you to dismount.' Maggie observed, which evoked further laughter as the girls recommended coming to a halt and swinging the right leg over the saddle in future.

He laughed with them. 'I will try the traditional dismount tomorrow and in the meantime, I will ask Sue or Keith to bring Asprey and his tack over in the morning.'

The lesson over if only partially learned, he changed from his jodhs and into his cords and hobbled over to Sally's Land Rover. He sat in the passenger seat and through the open window he could hear Maggie and her grooms having a good laugh, encouraged it seemed by Miss Parkinson who finally decided to join him.

He tried to appear offended but she was having none of that, insisting instead that she take him for lunch.

'Only if they have a very comfortable sofa.'

'I was only thinking about eating!'

Her mood was infectious and he felt so comfortable being with her, to any observer it was obvious that they were in love - and probably not married!

The short journey was fun and they found they had the same choices in music, in places and so many things.

'We have so much in common.'

'I hardly regard you as common Mr Carrington, as I told the irritating Roddy the very first time I saw you.'

'Did you indeed and how do you think I felt about you? I will admit it kept me awake all night.'

'Really, well that is just what I intend to do in the not too distant future.'

The compliments were brought to a halt as they arrived in the pub car park.

They walked hand in hand into the White Horse in Empingham and the first person they saw as they made their way into the bar was a dark haired attractive woman of about Sally's age. Her affectionate greeting left him in no doubt that they were old friends, the laughter if not ribald was suggestive.

'James Carrington this is Louise Acton, we were at school together.'

'Ah yes, that school in Cheltenham where they let you ride horses if you don't like lessons!' She smiled mischievously.

'My, you do know a lot about her and she has been so very discreet about you.'

He wiped his brow. 'Thank goodness for that.'

Sally interrupted and led him away. 'He is mine.'

They opened the door into the bar as Louise called after them, 'Keep me informed.'

Over a lunch of lobster salad the conversation remained easy and light, both anxious to make the most of the time together but conscious that these lovers' trysts do have a window of time after which one or both have to return to the problems at home. In Sally's case she was not married and Roddy Forsythe was already on the back burner so she had no ties in that sense; her concern was that James might, because of his children, decide to ride out the storm at home; she fervently hoped that would not be the case.

It was two thirty and the landlord had begun making discreet references to closing time, so they reluctantly returned to the Land Rover.

They sat in the front seats, this was their first proper date and neither knew how to suggest the next meeting. Sally tested the waters by asking him to confirm the funeral arrangements.

'It is on Tuesday at half past two. Connie is putting on a brave face and everyone, even Kate, is trying to be supportive.'

He saw the concern on her face and quickly sought to reassure her.

'When I said supportive I really should have said understanding; the atmosphere is most uncomfortable, her mother has suddenly become a mother hen figure, fussing around but not exuding any real warmth. Her father on the other hand is the epitome of fairness and has long become my surrogate father. He understands my dilemma and is giving me support rather than advice. Whilst I have told him about my concerns, he merely, in his kind way, offers a shoulder to lean on. I really shouldn't tell you this, but he was once in my position but, because he is so much nicer than me, he pretended it wasn't happening and eventually his wife came back to him.'

He looked at Sally, what must she be thinking; he sought to console her.

'My wife has made it clear that she has found someone else. I am not Jeremy Palmer, I cannot forgive her but, for sake of our two sons, I do not want any public falling out. In point of fact I genuinely do hope that she and Jonathan Mortimer will be very happy together. This is also what I crave for us, so that we can be together and plan our future. I love you Miss Parkinson and I want you to become Mrs Carrington as soon as possible.'

She leaned across and kissed him tenderly.

'I love you too Mr Carrington and I want with all my heart to be your wife.'
'Love, honour and obey.' He emphasised the last word and the humour returned.
'Just watch it buster!'

The atmosphere was once again light and the two romantics returned to collect James's car. If they did not have the opportunity to meet again before the funeral then they would meet on Thursday morning at ten forty am to catch the London train and thence on to a trial honeymoon as he put it. She merely laughed. 'I'll give you trial Mr Carrington.'
He gave her a final peck on the cheek and then more seriously,
'Despite what we said before, I would like you to come to the funeral; it will give me the strength to pay homage to my friend.'

She nodded and he squeezed her knee gently. 'Don't forget your passport.'

They drove off in opposite directions, he slightly more tremulous than she as the weight of Tuesday's duties once again settled on his shoulders. Sally meanwhile was bursting to tell her parents of the exciting days ahead and inviting James to meet them.

'He might have an important question to ask you' is what she wanted to say, but realised that this would appear rather presumptive, particularly as they had not yet met.

CHAPTER FORTY NINE

Tuesday October 23rd, a day that filled him with trepidation knowing the role he had to play. He took some comfort from the knowledge that no one envied him the task and he was confident they would all be hoping that he could carry it off.

The cars arrived to collect them at one o'clock and they proceeded to Willow House where Connie was also putting on a brave face, dreading the moment when she must release Edward's body and yet wishing it was all over. Tim Cooper and Anthony Jayes had relieved Connie of any organisational responsibilities their roles having been greatly helped by Humphrey Bartlett.

At one forty the cortege set out on its short journey arriving at the beautiful parish church which was, as they had anticipated, full to overflowing, with many more content to pay their respects from the churchyard where loudspeakers would transmit the service from within.

James supported Connie to her seat at the front and nodded acknowledgement to the muttered kindnesses that were offered on all sides. Sitting at the back of the church, accompanied by her father, he noticed a very demure Sally Parkinson in a black fitted coat, her long blonde hair hidden under a black veiled hat.

He sat silently with Connie and Kate, all of them devoid of conversation. Finally the organist started to play and the vicar approached the altar preceding the pallbearers; all six tall figures instantly recognised by the congregation. Each of them had played with or against Edward Lawson and they came from each of the four British Rugby Unions plus one each from France and South Africa. They swung the heavy oak coffin slickly from their shoulders as if determined that it would be the best lineout of their lives and, as they retreated to the back of the church, Humphrey Bartlett offered a prayer and a few scriptural words of comfort.

The hymns proved to be a good choice; they were all recognisable, even to those who rarely attended church and the size of the congregation in this stunning setting created a memorable and worthy memory to this sporting hero.

Not that James was consciously too aware of this, as he silently rehearsed the tribute that he would shortly be called upon to present; he prayed he would not let his friend down.

At the end of the first hymn and a reading from gospel of St. John, he heard the vicar announce that a tribute to Edward Lawson would be given by James Carrington. Connie squeezed his hand and whispered 'Remember Twickenham.' He returned her squeeze and let his mind fall

into the mind zone that had carried him through those moments when the stadium became hushed as he strode up to convert a penalty. This time he knew with certainty that every one of those rugby greats in the audience wanted a successful 'conversion'; there were no patriotic barriers today.
He climbed the steps into the pulpit his confidence feeding on Connie's reminder.

'As many of you will know, I first met Edward Lawson when as a 14 year old; I transferred to the local Grammar School where he was already a pupil. Attending a new school, particularly in the middle of term is not easy and, as I parked my Raleigh with the others in the bike shed, the sunlight was suddenly extinguished by a tall shadow and I feared the worst. However, my apprehension was soon dissolved by the friendly greeting extended by this tall blonde giant. The following day on the rugby field I was not so favourably treated as we were now on opposite sides and within minutes my new best friend had clattered me to the ground and was giving me as hard a time as I was to ever face on the rugby pitch.

Fortunately from then on, we played as team mates and, as one of the 'girls' as rugby forwards like to describe those who play behind the scrum, I received his personal protection.

After school we joined forces and founded 'Fordmill Construction.' Once again his enormous strength was a great asset in encouraging others to work and also served as a deterrent to any backsliders if there was hard work to be done.

As the company grew in stature so did Edward Lawson and major corporate bankers became equally impressed with his effortless grasp of economic and corporate financing and law. At the same time we were both playing rugby for Leicester and eventually for England and the British Lions. The gathering today of
so many great players of yesteryear is testimony to the regard and respect in which he will always be held.

I remember in South Africa how guys from Cardiff and Harlequins; Glasgow and Coventry; Leicester and Leinster; every one of them fierce club rivals were now bonded by a common cause. All of them, even the other number eights, who knew that their test chances would be few, proud to be on the same team as Edward Lawson; club loyalties for the time being forgotten. We were now the British Lions and how proud we all were and still are to this day. Supporting each other was the key element in our successful campaign and today that comradeship still counts; today's turn out is clear evidence of that.

After retiring, Edward and I and Connie Cummings, as she was then, were a team in complete accord as we grew the business until it became the company it is now. And I say 'as it is now', because it is fairly common knowledge that I resigned my directorship of that company to make a new start in an entirely different industry. Only three people know why we split up and I only found out in the past few days that my decision to leave was a great error of judgment on my part and unfortunately, I will never be able to say sorry, not in this world anyway, to the finest person and the very best friend anyone ever had.

His voice faltered slightly but, remembering Connie's advice 'Think about Twickenham he swiftly recovered...

Apart from his sporting and commercial skills Edward Lawson enjoyed a laugh and, as some of you here today will vouch, I was often the butt of his humour. In South Africa after our narrow victory in the final test he persuaded me to have a drink every time he had one, the end result, as evidenced in most sports pages, was yours truly snoring away in a deck chair wearing a bikini top - what is worse the rest of them, supposedly my mates, left me out on the veranda of the hotel whilst they all trooped off to bed.

Speaking to other friends and acquaintances, the other qualities they admired included, loyalty, honesty, kindness and reliability and just a great bloke... the sort of epitaph that we would all crave.

I have chosen the final hymn, as it was Edward's favourite when we were at school and it somehow seems to summarise how he played his sport and how he lived his life which was patriotic, but not racist, hard but always fair and ever loyal.'

'I vow to thee my country, all earthly things above.
I vow to thee my country the service of my love...'

The congregation boosted by such a great army of men, many of them Welsh, sang the hymn with a passion such as Humphrey Bartlett and the congregation had never heard before; James Carrington moved his lips in token gesture but no words would come out and the tears ran unashamedly down his face.

The vicar led them through the final prayer and invited all old friends to join Connie and James at Woolmington Manor for refreshments and an opportunity to meet and remember their dearly departed friend and share again those memorable times spent together.

CHAPTER FIFTY

Connie had been only too pleased to accept Kate and James's suggestion, that they take responsibility for organising the drinks and refreshments after the service and she accompanied them back to Woolmington, a silent and solitary figure despite the warmth and affection that surrounded her.

On such an occasion most families are pleased to share stories and anecdotes which involved the departed and this would turn out to be such an occasion. There was not a single person with any comment that was not favourable and the laughter as old yarns and antics, by now many times embellished, gave Edward the send-off that he would have planned himself.

People age differently but personalities remain and a tap on the shoulder brought James face to face with a great reminder of the past. A faint Birmingham accent accompanied by a broad smile and he was shaking hands with one of the great storytellers and a brilliant schoolboy international who had been the essential link between Edward and James in those early days of fame. It was John Murray, who had played scrum half on that memorable first visit to Twickenham; his was the pass to James that had unlocked the Welsh defence and given Edward the opportunity that only he could have taken as he battered his path through the phalanx of red shirts to score the winning try. His reverie was interrupted by Jeremy who signalled that he was needed on the telephone. It was Andrew Travers.

'Now is not the time James, but I have been speaking with David Gilbert about Milford Hall and it looks as if things are being put in place for him to join his son in Australia. Give me a call in about seven days and we should be able to start putting a proposal together.'

'That sounds okay Andrew, as I am planning to be away for a few days to get my head together and sort out my life.'

'I won't interrupt you any longer, except to say that I was at the service and it was a very moving tribute you gave your old mate and the compliments were not lost on any of the other guys there; we were all as welled up as you, in fact I don't know how you got through it.'

'That is very kind of you Andrew, but he was such a great guy that the compliments came easily.'

He replaced the phone and worked his way through the mingling guests, all of them transported back to the glories of their youth; the camaraderie of sport unbroken by the passage of time, if anything it was greater, rather like the size of many of the former athletic bodies of yesteryear.

As 'Jinker' Davies observed; 'The six packs are now more like 'crates' of muscle.'

A large figure with cauliflower ears shuffled over; 'As James mentioned in his tribute, that's just the sort of comment that we who did all the grafting might expect from one of the girls.'

James left the five foot seven inch Welsh centre trying to jink his way out of the huge group of British Lion's forwards, most of them almost a foot taller than the elusive little man in their midst.

Apart from the sporting luminaries, senior directors of merchant banks and law firms were also prominent; all of them fulsome in their praise of Edward and the impressive send-off that his best friend had afforded him.

James sought out Connie and found her sitting silently on her own in his study; she had his photograph from which hung Edward's schoolboy international cap, the very same picture that he had found in the study at Willow House.

'Thank you for what you did today James, I could never have managed it on my own, even now I still cannot believe what has happened in the past few days.'

Her empty gaze portraying the evidence of her grief whist her forlorn voice emphasised her loss.

'Please promise me that you and Kate will stay in touch.'

He skirted the reference to Kate and assured her would never be more than a phone call away and then, remembering his proposed visit overseas with Sally; insisted that Tim Cooper or Anthony Jayes would similarly always be on hand.

Her next comment did however cause him some consternation.

'James, would you consider coming back to Fordmill? With all due respect to Anthony, he is a great adviser and counsellor, but not the dynamic force that defined you and Edward and gave the banks so much confidence and the company the objective steering that it needs.'

He was non-plussed but promised that he would think about it and let her know in the next couple of weeks, further commitment was avoided by the appearance of Edward's mother, a tall elegant lady with the quiet dignity that had been so evident in her son.

'James, I cannot imagine what drove you two apart but, whatever it was, clearly no longer exists and I am so happy for that, as I know is your own mother. Incidentally, she is coming over to lunch with me at the golf club next week. For bridge not golf,' she quickly added; her brief smile so reminiscent of the one that had so often defined her son's face.

'Thank you Sarah, mother really should exercise her mind more often; she used to derive a lot of pleasure from bridge and the conversation, or should I say gossip that inevitably accompanies it.'

'I will be only too pleased to see her again as I am afraid that I too have been a bit of a recluse of late. However, I really came in here to let you know that Taffy someone, was asking where you had disappeared too.'

He gave her a resigned grin. 'Some well- remembered old nugget about the one time that Cardiff thrashed Leicester; he reminds me about it every time I see him and I remind him that he we were down to fourteen men for most of the second half; but I had better go and remind him again.'

By five o'clock even the diehard drinkers had left and when soon after, Connie and her family had departed, the house seemed very quiet. The effect was not lost on James and Kate or her parents, all of them suddenly conscious that if the fates had decided otherwise it could have been them left mourning their loss. Jeremy voiced what they were all thinking, or at least what he assumed exercised their thoughts.

'Moments like this make one so aware of how fortunate we are to have our loved ones still in our midst.'

His sentiment was rudely destroyed by his daughter.

'I can't imagine for a moment that is how James would be thinking.'

Her parents saw the look of disbelief on James's face, saw him battling to control his distress and striving to comprehend that anyone could be so insensitive on today of all days. Finally he blurted out that he needed some fresh air. He looked so lonely and yet Jeremy sensed from his own experience, that solitude was his best companion.

James, shoulders slumped, wound his familiar route to the stables and sought his strength from these noble creatures who would in the main, put their heads down and battle on for no reason other than not to accept defeat.

Should he battle on or should he shoulder arms? The latter was becoming ever more the better option. He walked across the grass quad that lay in the centre of the stable yard and his heart lightening as he skipped up the stone steps to his office. This was his sanctum, in here his thoughts were his own and today, one of them was crystallising and another was germinating.

He unlocked his desk and pulled out his journal; opening at the next new page and in an attempt to unravel his thoughts he decided to write them down :-

Fact - Kate has determined my plans for the future, at least domestically.

The second idea was still very scratchy; it was completely left field, but Connie's suggestion that he assume control at Fordmill, had the possibility to solve the fiscal solution to plan number one.

However, he had to discuss this with Jack Priory and with his intended holiday with Sally very imminent it needed to be put on the table straight way. He checked his watch, Jack should be home by now; he dialled the ex-directory number which was swiftly answered.

'Wendy Priory; who is that please?'

'Hi Wendy, it's James, I am sorry to call you but is Jack around?'

'I think he is feeding his beloved Koi Carp.'

He heard the amusement in her voice, this was a new fad of her husband's: He had even suggested to James that designing fish ponds could be added to the range of Minster Garden Furniture. Just for once the Carrington brain had not started whirring with ideas; he suggested more research was done and imagined that was the end of the idea. Not so it seemed. He heard the phone being lifted and spoke first.

'I thought that St. Peter and not St John was patron saint of fishermen.'

He heard the amused chuckle and back came the reply.

'And I thought that St James was a tax man.'

'Well yes he was and that is why I need to speak with you.'

'Now what can you on today of all days, have come up with?'

James outlined Connie's suggestion and assured Jack that this was not a route that he had ever envisaged but it needed to be discussed, it might seriously impair the capital he had expected to receive as part of his loan note repayments. If Anthony Jayes was available to discuss this tomorrow would Jack be able to attend the meeting with him so that everything was open and above board?

'Okay, but try and make it late morning or after lunch and I suggest that as Tim Cooper's wife also has a financial interest that we include him. Also my office would probably be more discreet than Fordmill Construction, where the sight of James Carrington would generate more than

a little conjecture and rumour.
I am presuming that Connie will not wish to attend but we should advise her of these discussions and also stress that the talks are exploratory and that no decisions will be contemplated without her full knowledge and agreement.'

'Jack, as ever you have seen the strategic potential of such an alliance but my interest is short term, primarily to help Connie, but also to secure the future for the Fordmill staff many of whom have been with the company from its inception. I will telephone Anthony and ask him to set it up and I will also speak with Connie and then report back to you.'

For the first time in the past two weeks James Carrington was alive and buzzing and, once he had spoken with Anthony Jayes, was convinced that Connie's request had been astute as well as protective. Anthony's reaction had been very positive; indeed he wondered if it had been his sharp lawyer's brain that had formulated the idea to Connie.

With the spring back in his step he returned to the house unobserved by the others, all of whom, from the sound of the television, he presumed to be in the drawing room.

He went up to his dressing room and changed into navy slacks and a blue striped shirt and his favourite suede boots before returning downstairs, where he poked his head around the door to find Jeremy nodded off to sleep and Kate and her mother watching which ever soap it was – Coronation Street, he thought.

'I am going out for a couple of hours.'
'To see her no doubt.' Kate's reply was instant and spiteful.
He did not bother to deny it and a few moments later they heard the Porsche snarl into life and disappear down the lane.

Angela gave her daughter a sympathetic glance.
'It would seem you are right dear and what's good for the gander is good for the goose.'
'You are quite possibly jumping to conclusions.'
From beneath closed eyelids Jeremy urged discretion, but his daughter and wife were in no mood for compassion, they knew where he was heading; to see her.
With this conviction firmly established they both decamped to the kitchen where over a cup of Earl Grey, battle lines were drawn to establish Kate's freedom and future, which firmly included Jonathan Mortimer and definitely excluded her two-timing husband.

Meanwhile James was heading back to Willow House to convey to Connie the arrangements he had put in place for tomorrow.

She had initially been surprised to hear from him so quickly but then she remembered that was historically, how James Carrington had always acted. She was remembering the past and checking her make-up when she heard his car scrunching to a halt at the front of the house. He tapped on the door and came through into the living room.

'You never did hang about but I am pleased to see you, it is just like...'
Her voice faltered as she was suddenly, once again confronted by the realisation that the old times would never again exist. He seized the initiative knowing he must keep her focused or the meeting would serve no purpose.

'Why don't we have a cup of tea and see if we can start to sort things out.'
She nodded. 'Let's go into the Kitchen.'
He followed her to the long kitchen table and whilst she put the kettle on, he outlined the phone calls he had generated earlier this evening,

'Connie, further to what you said this afternoon, I am not sure how I can help, but I give you my word that I will endeavour to do everything that I can to assist you and all the people at Fordmill. So, I have spoken with Jack Priory and Anthony Jayes and he is contacting Tim Cooper with a view to meeting at Tim's office tomorrow. At this stage I am sure that none of us have any clear thoughts but hopefully, we will be able to prompt each other and formulate a plan which will benefit not only yourself but also the staff at Fordmill.

She looked at him, suddenly devoid of the courage that had initiated her request this afternoon. His radar recognised the dilemma and solved his first question.

'Connie, if tomorrow is too soon for you to contemplate the future, then you must let the rest of us, all close friends, all with your interests at heart, figure out a way forward.

Please be assured that no decisions will be made without your approval, indeed I don't believe that we would have that authority as you and Edward are presumably still the major shareholders.'

He paused, anxious not to rush her. 'Are you happy to let us help you find a way forward?'

'Of course, it is not that I don't trust you all implicitly, it is just that I am lost without him...'

Once again the unfairness of her loss overwhelmed her and for the very first time he saw Connie devoid of fight; he remembered his mother's despairing words when discussing his father's tragic and fatal illness and questioned whether he was wrong to have arranged tomorrow's meeting so soon after the funeral. Just as suddenly, she swept back her auburn locks and the green eyes flashed.

'James I want tomorrow's meeting to go ahead, but I think you will be able to think more constructively if I am not present and I know that Edward would want me to trust you and take your advice.'

He heard the sound of a car and shortly afterwards Edward's mother appeared.

'I haven't seen you for years and now twice in one day.'

He smiled and wondered where they were both finding the strength from, the older woman had, like his own mother, known the loneliness of early widowhood; he prayed that Connie would meet someone else. He also realised the cruel irony that two people in love should have been wrenched apart whilst he and Kate were busily destroying their relationship. But it was time to go; he could do nothing further at this time to help their grieving.

He returned home, his spirits low but resurrected, by Kate's spiteful aside.

'She chucked you out then, oh dear she is learning very quickly just what a callous swine you really are!'

Her parents looked aghast.

James turned slowly towards her.

'As a matter of fact, I went to see Connie, she asked me to arrange a meeting tomorrow with Tim and Anthony. There were a couple of details I needed to know and then, as she is totally exhausted, I left so that she could try and get some sleep. As to thinking me a callous swine, you should ask her yourself. Goodnight.'

As he climbed the stairs he heard her parent's disgusted reaction to their daughter's behaviour.

CHAPTER FIFTY ONE

The following morning they convened at eleven thirty, the atmosphere subdued; the usual banter of good friends far from their thoughts as they made their way through to the architect's conference room.

This room, like the corridor they had just walked down, was decorated with tasteful original modern art as well as prints by David Hockney and Andy Warhol.

He remembered Edward, obviously not very impressed by the latter, thanking Tim for his choice of Marilyn Monroe rather than a can of Heinz Beans.

'Philistine' had been the architect's laughing riposte.

James quickly put those memories to the back of his mind and through force of habit, assumed the chair and initiated the discussion.

'During the course of yesterday afternoon's gathering, Connie drew me to one side and made a totally unexpected request that I rejoin the company. I am certain that this does not mean that she has any doubts about any member of her existing management team; it is, I am sure, because she suddenly very feels lonely and probably very isolated. That she wishes to confide in me is because the two of us with Edward, founded the company and the relationship is, despite the recent hiccup, still very personal. I assume she has the authority to make this request, as I am presuming she will stand to inherit Edward's shareholding, which will make her by far the largest stake holder in the company?'

He looked across at Anthony who was sitting opposite, fingers firmly clasped as if to hold onto what he had.

'I was going to ask you how the other shareholdings stack up, but you really do not have to make me party to that unless you feel it will be helpful and I do, of course, give you my assurance that it will remain completely confidential.'

'Likewise.' Jack Priory confirmed his discretion.

Anthony Jayes shrugged. 'I don't have any problems with you having that information. My holding is the 10% you gave me on the first anniversary of me joining the company. Tim has a 5% stake which, for professional reasons is in his wife's name. So Connie presumably has, subject to Edward's will, the remaining 85%. These holdings are of course merely a notional figure as you James still have loan notes for what was originally 60% of the company's stock. The first of those notes is due for payment in six weeks, so it is not quite a black and white picture. However, I will of course be able to clarify the position in the next couple of weeks or so.'

'Okay, so back to Connie's request that I resume an active role in planning Fordmill's future. First, you should know that whilst my instinct is to say yes, I do not wish to tread on anyone's toes, particularly yours Anthony, as it might be seen that I was in some way usurping your authority. Also, my first loyalty is, of course, to Jack Priory and the Minster Group of companies that I am now a director of. In fact, the more we discuss this, the more complicated it is becoming.'

His gaze shifted to the far end of the table where Jack was brushing his forefinger against his upper lip, the tell-tale sign in matters financial, that relevant and pertinent observations were revolving in his astute business brain.
'Mr Priory you are obviously about to unravel this dilemma?'

Jack Priory walked over to the whiteboard and selected a green felt tip marker pen. He gave the board an unnecessary extra wipe whilst he considered his next move and then wrote the number one at the top of the of the clean surface followed by a series of bullet point options.

- I assume that Connie is thinking that without Edward, the most obvious person to have at the helm is James.
- She is also probably thinking that without her husband she no longer has the motivation to continue in her role of Marketing Director, but she also realizes that fiscal matters have to be resolved in order to safeguard her future financially.
- Fordmill has had several suitors in the past and the company is still highly profitable and an attractive bolt-on to another construction company with similar synergy.
- It is also an attractive proposition for an aggressive predator wishing to diversify and broaden its area of operations, as it would gain an immediate foothold in what is seen as a growth sector of the market.
- Fordmill's track record and commercially recognized flair for innovation would give the buyer an immediate footprint that would take years to imitate.
- Likewise to an overseas competitor who could secure an immediate UK foothold.

He placed the green marker pen back on the shelf and selected a red one. His expression was serious; they knew that a sobering thought was about to be unleashed. He turned to Anthony Jayes.
'Off the top of your head, name me a blue chip family-owned British company?'
The reply was immediate, 'One not that far from here – JCB Engineering.'
Jack turned to Tim Cooper. 'Same question Tim?'
Once again the architect's response was quick and referred to a pertinent business sector, architecture.
'Norman Foster & Partners, or the Richard Rogers Partnership.'
They all looked quizzically back at him; his expression willing them to connect.
He helped them along the way.
'We have JCB, a company that is regarded as the benchmark for diggers and other

earthmoving equipment and two world class firms of architects. They all have one thing in common, a CEO who defines the company.'
Finally the penny dropped.

He now selected a blue marker pen and wrote two more observations on the white board.

- The value of a company does not lie wholly in its balance sheet; part of its attraction is the CEO who drives that company.
- If someone bought Fordmill with James Carrington at its helm then they would expect him to commit to working with them – because HE is the company!!

He replaced the pen and looked enquiringly at them.

'How do we solve the conundrum gentlemen?'
They looked at each other expectantly and it was James who predictably offered a solution.

'I could as it were be an external consultant, with Anthony as CEO augmenting the agreed strategies. But, all of this would have to be closely monitored so as not to leave a paper or electronic trail.'

The accountancy side of Anthony's mind was also working, but along immediate accountancy checks and balances, rather than first solving the market conception of James Carrington. He posed them a question.

'James would have to devote a great deal of time and energy to such an undertaking; how would he be remunerated for this?'

Even Jack Priory did not have an answer. As he wryly put it, 'I only set the hares running; I don't necessarily know how to catch them.'

James stepped in, once again underlining why Connie had been so right to seek his help. She clearly recognised that Fordmill had become the powerhouse it was because of the two men who had created it; others such as Anthony were expert administrators but they did not always think outside the box.

'It is fairly obvious really, I will work directly with Anthony and if our meetings have to be clandestine, then so be it. I will not be paid, but the fees I should be receiving will be paid instead to the Minster Group of companies. This as payment in lieu of the debt we owe Jack for once again being the conduit that directs our thinking into the right channels. Does this stand up to scrutiny?'

Jack and Anthony seemed in accord, although the latter's legal brain insisted that he checked the statutes that might have concerns about such a deal, or he suggested.
'Perhaps in Edward's absence, Jack might become a non-executive director and the fees be paid to him personally?'

They requested that he investigate the most appropriate way forward. Meanwhile, they were inwardly trying to assess how this proposed development might affect them personally.

Tim Cooper's architect's practice had blossomed with the growth of the Fordmill empire. He knew that the opportunities presented by James Carrington had been instrumental in his early recognition by the Royal Institute of British Architects and the professional guardian of that profession, the Architects' Journal.
This publication had enabled his name to become widely recognized; not in quite the same vein as the legendary firms he had cited in response to Jack Priory's question, but his success was certainly not due to hanging on to Fordmill's coat tails.

However, a new owner may have his own preferred firm of architects, so the large staff he now employed would have to be even more innovative. He closed the conjecture in his own mind by trusting in his own ability and saw both options as an opportunity – just as he knew James would expect him to.

Anthony on the other hand was seeing the opportunity of being appointed CEO of Fordmill and having the opportunity to work so closely with James. He did not have the other's flare, but he was a quick learner and was very familiar with Management Speak. The sort of talk that CEO's of potential buyers would expect to hear. His versatility had been tested in the early years; he was here today because like Tim, he had always produced the goods. Now he was to receive a master class, one on one, and he did not intend to fail; he would demand explanation from his mentor for each and every new idea and would subject them all to due diligence. In fact he was really up for this, it would be his defining moment; he couldn't wait for this evening when he would explain over supper to Patricia the fantastic news that JC as she always called him, was back in town. He also supposed that he should warn her that the heady news came with a caveat – supper would now become a moveable feast!

Jack Priory was also pleased with the outcome; he had played his part of devil's advocate and secured a good deal for Fordmill and, thanks to James, secured remuneration for his own company. The latter bonus once again illustrating his friend Mr. Carrington's ability to see over the top of any commercial maze and lead all the undecided people out safely, without destroying the illusion that they had been part of the decision making.

It was four thirty, much progress had been made and it was left to Jack to summarise the tacit agreements that had been formulated. He knew of James's plans to take a short break with Sally Parkinson, which he did not intend to share with the others, and so suggested that if Anthony could summarise the Fordmill picture in time they should reconvene in two weeks.

The Financial Director gave this assurance and the meeting, no minutes of which had been taken, was adjourned with Tim given the responsibility of reporting back to Connie.

James excused himself and said his farewells; the drive home was not carefree as he had not mentioned to Kate or her parents that he intended being away for the next few days. He tussled with the options, not sure how to best deal with what he knew would inevitably be a tricky situation. Confront them with the truth or sneak away; the latter was immediately dismissed, whatever they might want to think about him, appearing to be a coward was not an option. No, he would choose the moment and attempt to discuss the present and the future in as dignified a manner as possible.

As it turned out, Kate paved the way for him by announcing that she was off to North Yorkshire for a few days to sort out various loose ends with Liz Reed.
He resisted adding 'and Mr. Mortimer.'
Instead he shrugged and decided to keep his own plans to himself, at least until in the morning.
Supper was once again a low key affair albeit a very polite one. The Palmers had also decided to leave the after breakfast, so in the event, his biggest problem was to assure them that he would be able to cope on his own. This drew the only acerbic comment; predictably it was from

Kate.

'This will afford you plenty of time to see your friend.'

Once again he refused to be drawn, deciding instead to go seek the sanctuary of his study. On impulse he asked Jeremy if he would care to join him for a Macallan; his father-in-law's understanding expression was a mixture of uncertainty and pleasure.

Jeremy sank into one of the green padded leather armchairs, whilst James poured two drinks. He sat on the matching green leather club seat that surrounded the stone fireplace. For several long seconds neither could conjure the right words, they both knew this was a pivotal moment in their relationship; most probably they would never again share this covenant of parent and son-in-law and because of the special bond they had always shared, neither wanted to let it go.

Forces were now seemingly beyond their control; once they admitted this then the esteem forged out of mutual respect and admiration would have to take on a different guise, as Kate and Angela's feminine take on their friendship would not condone their close regard for each other. Jeremy attempted to break the ice.

'We are sailing through turbulent seas James but one day, soon I hope, you and Kate will find less troubled waters and I pray that you will, not only for the sake of your children, but also for the affection and regard you once had for each other, remain friends and remember the good times.'

James leaned across and clasped his friend's hand. 'I give you my word that I will do that; there is still an awful lot of respect and regard that I still have for Kate.'

CHAPTER FIFTY TWO

Six o'clock, he was awake before the alarm, his mind immediately focused on today's momentous plans. As his brain jostled with today's schedule his ears tuned in to the sounds coming from the master bedroom; wardrobe doors were opening and closing and, no doubt, suitcases were being loaded. He slipped on his dressing gown, sadly reflecting that this was a birthday present she had given him only a few months earlier. Had things really degenerated so quickly? Just as suddenly he pushed this to the back of his mind: Yes they had.

He tapped on the bedroom door and went in, she looked flustered but, as was her won't these days, her single word of greeting signalled her consistent hostile attitude.
'What?'
    'I was simply going to ask if you wanted any help.'
His forlorn look appeared to deflect any further rebukes and her reply was almost apologetic.
    'You could carry my case into the hall; I need to be on my way, the A1 as you know is always busy unless you can get to Doncaster before seven thirty.'
    He pursed his lips and nodded his agreement and without further ado carried the case downstairs. He collected her car keys and brought the Stag around to the front of the house and parked near to the door. Extracting himself from the driver's seat he noticed a familiar airline ticket envelope in the door pocket and a few moments later the contents proved to be two tickets to Dublin.
    He swiftly returned them and retrieved the suitcase from the hallway and deposited it in the boot. He was back in the house just as she stepped off the stairs.
Without thinking he adopted the humour that had previously always been so much a part of their lives.
'Case in the boot ma'am; engine running and ready to go.'
    She responded as of old. 'Thank you James.'

It was still only six twenty five so, not surprisingly, no one else was stirring as yet. He returned upstairs to finish his own packing which he then installed in the back of the Land Rover. Still no sign of human life until June appeared in the kitchen at seven o'clock, by which time he had brewed some coffee and eaten a couple of rounds of toast, pondering as he did so the discovery of the two airline tickets to Dublin.

The arrival of Sue put an end to further consideration as she talked excitedly about last week's victory in the Gilling Stakes at Newmarket; 'Two lengths going away', was how the Sporting Life had described it in its feature column. Already she was being touted as a potential favourite for next year's One Thousand Guineas, the ultimate tribute to a two year old filly and yet, unbelievably, James Carrington was too pre-occupied by other matters.

Sue was staggered, not only was this first potential classic a possibility, he also had the yearling they had nicknamed Rebel who was a full brother to this filly. If he stayed sound he would certainly be on the viewing list of the leading trainers at the Newmarket October Sales.

As she closed the kitchen door, he suddenly realised that she was unaware of his impending absence. He dashed after her and spotted her going into the feed room.

'Sue, I forgot to mention I will be away for a few days.'

She gave him an old fashioned look.

'Right then, see you when you get back.'

'Kate has gone up to Yorkshire.'

'Yes I know.'

Whereupon she turned on her heel and was gone; quite obviously not surprised to hear of Kate's plans.

He dismissed it, he had after all kept Jack Priory privy to his plans and whatever it was that she was up to only helped to assuage his own conscience in respect of his liaison with Sally. He checked his watch, hoping fervently that Jeremy and Angela would soon make an appearance, although the prospect of confronting the latter was rather daunting.

His apprehension was merited; the sideways glance she gave him was hostile, inviting an explanation that she had already decided was selfish and unfair to her daughter. Nevertheless he attempted a conversation.

'Good morning Angela, Kate has already left I am afraid.'

'Afraid; you should be bloody afraid, treating my daughter like this. You have wrecked her life as I was always concerned that you would. Do you remember before you were married, when you promised me that you would never be unfaithful to my daughter?'

She glared at him but he remained calm; facing bullies had never fazed him.

'I have told you, on oath, that the one meeting I had with Sally Parkinson amounted to a single dance, I told you then that I did not intend refuting that argument ever again. So if you don't believe me, I no longer care because the high regard I once had for you I no longer have. That respect, however, still applies to your husband for whom I still have a great respect.

She attempted to interrupt but he would have none of it.

'Your daughter has spent quite a lot of time with her Mr Mortimer and, far from condemning it you have actively condoned it, but then again, you are a woman with double standards of your own.'

He saw the barb strike home, she was on the back foot now and his reputation for not taking prisoners was too much, her posturing collapsed and she hastened out of the room.

Jeremy appeared, it was obvious that he had heard the accusations; his expression was weary but understanding. He appeared older and more fragile but the dignity remained.

'This probably means goodbye James, I sincerely hope that you both find happiness.'
His eyes were moist and so were James's.

'Please don't think that, things will quieten down and we still have the boys to share.'
He took the proffered hand.

'I am going now, please don't rush away and have a safe journey home.'

He walked briskly to the Land Rover, thankful that his suitcase was already on board, he set off for Grantham, leaving much earlier than planned but he needed time, plenty of time to gather his thoughts.

Unusually for him he drove steadily and as he neared Grantham, his composure was regained and instead the excitement of seeing Sally had taken over. The anticipation heightened and he leaned over to the passenger seat and checked the inside pocket of the blazer that was folded on the seat.

Moment of anxiety over; he saw the self- same British Airways envelope that he had discovered in Kate's Triumph Stag, this time the tickets were destined to Munich rather than Dublin.

He quickly re-gathered his thoughts; his early departure meant that he had a couple of hours to waste before he need be at the railway station. Ignoring the signs for the A1, he drove instead towards Grantham town centre and made for the High Street. It was in the centre of this usually busy market town but, with little traffic about at this still quite early hour, he was able to park outside the George Hotel. This hostelry was described by Charles Dickens in his novel Nicholas Nickleby, as one of the best Inns in Britain. He was not able to vouch for its accommodation, but the full English breakfast they served up was most agreeable.

He checked his watch, the train was due at ten forty and he first of all had to take the Land Rover in for a service at the local dealership which also solved the problem of parking whilst he was away. He paid for his breakfast and extricated the vehicle from the now busy row of cars outside the hotel before driving the short distance to the edge of town where the manager, a long time Leicester Tiger's supporter and Carrington fan, came out to meet him. The offer of a coffee was accepted and for twenty minutes he was quizzed on the likely outcome of next year's five nation's rugby internationals, naturally they were both optimistic that several Leicester players would feature.

Another surreptitious glance at his swatch was spotted by the manager.

'Time to make a move James?'

'Yes please Roger.'

'Let Ken know what time we have to collect you from the station on your return.'

'I will and thanks for the coffee; I will send you a couple of tickets for the Welsh game.'
The short trip to the railway station provoked yet more questions, this time from Ken . These were cut short by their arrival and the site of a dark blue Bentley convertible sitting near to the car park. Two elegant ladies, clearly mother and daughter, were standing next to the open boot.

'That's what you call class Mr Carrington and the car as well!'
The mechanic grinned at James, who gave a nod of approval as he jumped out of the Land Rover and pulled his luggage out of the back door.

'See you in a few days, I will call and let you know which train I will be on so that you can collect me.'

He slipped Ken a pound note which elicited, 'Cheers Mr Carrington' before driving away, suspiciously slowly, James thought, as he wandered over to Sally and the other lady who was clearly her mother.

Heart pounding he heard himself saying, 'I'm the resident porter, may I help you with your luggage ladies.'

The mother figure gave him an appraising look.

'Not bad, certainly a better class of porter than we usually get at Grantham.'

Sally pecked him on the cheek. 'I think she likes you and her name is Camilla.'

'I can speak for myself dear and yes, I have to agree that on first sight you appear to be a very nice chap James and the proof of that will come next February when we need tickets for Twickenham. But before then I hope that Robert and I will have the pleasure of your company at Manston. However, we don't have time for chit-chat you two need to be on your way to wherever it is that you are taking my daughter.'

He took Camilla's hand and whispered. 'We are going to the Alps.'

She looked at her daughter fondly.

'You are a lucky girl, but you deserve it, bring him for lunch when you get back, in fact bring his mother as well, we were good friends a long time ago; although she will probably remember me better as Milly Worthington.'

With that parting shot she slid back into the Bentley and was gone.

He handed her the train tickets and picked up the suitcases.

'Let's hit the trail pardner.'

For them both, as for any couple, a long awaited first date is a heady mixture of relief and excitement with neither knowing quite how to express their feelings adequately. Their facial expressions would, however, have expressed to any observer just how excited they really were.

As they stood there watching the station clock tick away the last four minutes before their adventure began, his mind briefly turned to Dublin. He fervently hoped that Kate and Johnnie Mortimer would be experiencing the same emotions.

The arrival of the train brought his thoughts back to the excitement of his own adventure with Sally. His frequent visits to the capital meant he was standing in exactly the right spot to board the first class carriage as the train came to a halt. The Grantham bound passengers were disgorged and before he could stop her she had grabbed her case and was stowing it on the baggage shelf and he heard himself protesting that he would have carried her luggage on board.

'I know, I know, but as you will soon come to realise, I am not some poor little weakling, I muck my own horses out and that and the riding have made me a pretty tough cookie.'

His expression was approving; she was already proving to be less demanding than Kate and certainly more inquisitive.

'So Mr. Carrington, having disclosed the venue to my mother, when are you are you going to share the secret with me?'

'At Heathrow and then you will have to see which gate we go to.'

'Surely we are going by private jet?' she quipped.

'Not quite but it is on a very special jet.'

She looked at him, her expression hopeful.

'Please say it is Concorde.'

He tried to imitate her voice. 'It is Concorde.'

She had a grin from ear to ear, it was obviously a dream come true.

'We must be going to New York?'

'I am afraid not, all I will tell you is somewhere in Europe and it is somewhere I have not been with Kate or anyone else. I want this to be our special place.'

The train hurtled on with stops only at Peterborough and Stevenage and, as at this time of day it was neither breakfast nor lunchtime, they settled for a free coffee which was interspersed with Sally's guesses as to their destination. Her first attempt was Paris, then Rome followed by Berne and after some further consideration she opted for Barcelona and then Salzburg, which was a very near miss. Finally the train started to slow down and as a diversion he pointed out the Arsenal football ground at Highbury; she leaned over and kissed him tenderly on the cheek.

'I am so excited, I have never met a real romantic like you, promise me you will never change.'

'I won't because I simply can't change, I do so love surprises, the anticipation of the pleasure someone will get keeps me on a high for weeks. Any road up, as they say in Nottingham, the train arriving at platform four is the romantic special from the Vale of Belvoir. I am afraid that due to time constraints we will not be taking afternoon tea at Claridge's but I do promise you a bun at Heathrow.'

As he said it they both burst out laughing and with tears in her eyes she advised him that she had no plans for a bun, not yet anyway!

They edged through the throng of fellow passengers until they reached the taxi queue which at this time was relatively short. This black cab turned out to be red and like an excited teenager she beat him to it, much to the driver's delight as the blonde hair and cleavage leaning over his passenger front window, advised him that they were heading to Heathrow.

They jumped into the back, the cabby smiling to himself as he contemplated the big tip that from experience, these thirty something lovebirds generally stumped up. He wondered if the guy's wife knew about this trip; not his concern of course but the girl in the back was something a bit special, so the guy must obviously be worth a few bob. He left them to their joy and set out on the forty five minute trip to the airport; with a bit of luck there might be a few holdups to keep the clock ticking.

The traffic was light but the tip was even better than he had hoped for and he even offered to get them a trolley, which in James's long experience of taxi drivers was unique. He was, however, mindful that his stunning companion was the catalyst for this gallantry, an assumption confirmed by the knowing wink he received from the driver as he got back into his cab.

Sally insisted on pushing the luggage trolley and they made their way to the British Airways' Concorde Desk. The luggage was sent on its way and the secret was out, they were going to Munich in the most beautiful airplane that had ever been built, a machine so graceful that it turned the heads of everyone who saw it and that included all the passengers of incoming and outgoing flights as they craned their necks to catch a glance.

They walked hand in hand to the Concorde lounge to join the other ninety eight passengers on this promotional trip to this beautiful city which sits in the stunning Bavarian countryside, alongside the majestic Alps. It was three o'clock as they sank into the dark blue leather sofa and two minutes later they were sipping champagne, what else on such an occasion and, of course, canapés all beautifully presented with an array of savoury nibbles.

'James Carrington, I cannot believe how my life has altered, I used to think about you, even dared to hope we might meet again, but I never imagined the romance of this and starting off by flying in Concorde; I can't wait to tell everyone. But most of all I just want to be with you for the rest of my life.'

'And I can't wait to spend the rest of my life with you and that starts now.'
Two replacement glasses of champagne arrived right on cue.

Finally they were on board walking down the aisle between the dark blue leather seats which were arranged in pairs along a central isle; their seats were 6A and 6B and on each seat was a complimentary wallet containing information about the city of Munich. James was delighted to see the reference to the Kempinski Hotel as this was the setting for their first date.

'Your residence this evening Miss Parkinson.'
She took the leaflet from him and responded in her poshest voice.

'Thank you Carrington, this will do nicely and I have something for you.'
She snuggled into his arm and kissed him tenderly. Happiness radiated from them both.

Finally they took off; the take- off speed according to the data was 250 mph. Today as they were on a short flight over Europe, the flight would not be the supersonic cruising speed of 1320 mph that the aircraft achieved on the Transatlantic flights.
This suited today's passengers, none of whom was in any hurry to leave the aircraft.
The atmosphere in the cabin remained relaxed and cheerful thanks to the six cabin crew who were kept busy serving more champagne and nibbles.

Sally was scrutinizing the hotel details; it looked very stylish rather like her new young man, as her grandmother had described James.

They touched down at the Munich Reim Airport and proceeded from the baggage carousel to the airport taxi rank, arriving at the classical colonnades of the Kempinski Hotel at six fifteen European time.

Miss Parkinson was not disappointed; in fact when they stepped out of the elevator and into the suite he had reserved, she was exceedingly pleased. Falling back on to the sumptuous king size bed she declared,

'You are setting very high standards James, but you really should come and see things from my point of view.'

He needed no second bidding and kicking off his shoes flopped down beside her and for the first time was able to kiss her properly. The output of this emotion after all the trials of late inevitably led to making love when they each saw for the first time, the fit and lithe bodies nestling together so perfectly.
They made love passionately but with consideration for the other although this was forgotten in the frenzied finale. Afterwards they both lay back exhausted; Sally turned towards him her eyes brimming with affection.

'James Carrington, what have you done to me, I have never really known what love was before. I am still…'

He put his finger on her lips and let his eyes wander over the beautiful body that clung to him.

'Well I promise to keep on reminding you!'

They both lay there revelling in the happiness of being together, he once again praying that Kate and Johnnie were experiencing the same happiness. Sally meanwhile was having the same thoughts, frightened that Kate would want him back, unable to believe that any woman would not want such a good looking and exciting man. But she had him now and she determined that she would not lose him. She slid out of bed, conscious that the sight of her nude body was having an effect on him.

'Two minutes.'

She promised, and well within the time span she returned to find him feigning sleep. Lifting the sheet that covered him she muttered in his ear.

'My word it looks as if Roger is looking forward to seeing me.'

'Well you had better look after him as I can't possibly go down to dinner like this!'

They did finally make it downstairs and made for the fashionably chic bar and ordered a bottle of 1973 Bollinger, which he confessed, was his current favourite.

'I do hope you like shampoo. Whenever something special happens I always turn to Monsieur Bollinger and today is so special I feel like ordering a Jeroboam but then I don't want to get tiddly as I want to enjoy every moment with you and see as much of you as possible.'

'I think you have already done that!' The succinct reply

The champagne arrived before he could answer and instead he proposed a toast.

'To the most beautiful woman, with whom I want to spend the rest of my life.'

She raised the flute of champagne.

'To the man I am definitely going to spend the rest of my life with.'

The champagne fuelled their dreams and they strolled through into the Maximilian Restaurant and were given a window seat from where they had an excellent view of the stylish pine panelled walls and candle lit tables.

The Maître d' approached and handed the unpriced version to Sally and to James the copy bearing the bad news. The excitement and their antics upstairs had sharpened both appetites and so for starters Sally went for Paupiettes of Smoked Salmon filled with crème fraiche and James decided on Cream glazed fresh Lobster bisque. To accompany this in deference to his surroundings he pointed to wine on the list and ordered a half bottle of dry white wine.

The amused expression on his face prompted Sally to enquire why he was laughing.

'I have chosen a wine that I think suits you admirably, or will do by the time we get home; it is from a vineyard in Berncastel and is called Friedrich Wilhelm Gymnasium.

She joined in the laughter.

'I'll give you gymnasium!'

'That is just what I was hoping, make sure you don't leave any!'

After indulging the Germans with the choice of the wine for the first course, he adopted a more familiar route with the main course. A bottle of Chateau La Tour Pauillac; the most consistently great wine of Bordeaux with a rich and intense flavour, ideal for their main course choices.

Sally's choice was Aiguillette de Canard aux peches; superbly cooked slices of pink breast of duck in a sauce of fresh peaches.

James went for a heavier option; Filet de Boeuf grille béarnaise. This too was rare and appetizing.

'I must say Carrington, you do know how to treat a girl.'

'Only the best, for the best.' He assured her.

The evening was perfect; they were both so happy, immersed in their thoughts for the future. The conversation flowed and any brief silences were when they were pinching themselves to make sure it was true.

Desert arrived; for Sally it was Chocolate Mousse with zest of orange and for him a selection of cheeses which included a Stilton from Long Clawson in their own stomping ground, the Vale of Belvoir.

Coffee was declined but a couple of Cognacs rounded off a memorable day, although thoughts of Dublin did once again cross his mind.

They retired from the dining room and fingers entwined climbed the impressive staircase to Suite One; both looking forward to the morrow, the venue for which was still a mystery for Sally. However, his ability to conjure surprise after surprise had left her in even more anticipation than if she had known the destination.

They both slept well, still stunned by the speed of events.

CHAPTER FIFTY THREE

The following morning after the feast of last night, they both chose a simple breakfast of cold meats and fruit plus the most delicious yoghurt, which brought back thoughts of skiing holidays in Wengen, a memory he swiftly consigned to the back of his head.

Later, as all visitors to the Bavarian capital do, they wandered down to the old town and into Marienplatz, the central square where they joined the other tourists who crowded in expectation outside the Town Hall or Rathaus, as the locals say, confided Sally.

'Very good, or should I say sehr gut,' he quipped back, but then just as quickly, 'let's keep the sprechen in English, as apart from ordering food and drink on ski hols I have pretty much exhausted my knowledge of German.'

Further discussion was halted by the arrival of the mechanical figures which are housed on a balcony halfway up the magnificent clock tower that soars high above the market place. With others in the crowded square, they craned their necks as the colourful iron figures came into view and struck the hours that announced the arrival of midday.

Once the show was over, they drifted in and out of the neighbouring streets until they lit upon a magnificent baroque building with great arched windows and turreted façade. This was the Hofbrauhaus, famous the world over for its rowdy atmosphere and great steins of beer.

They entered the huge bar area with its row after row of long tables and bench seats, most of which were filled with enthusiastic patrons all swigging foaming beer from large flagons. The music too was hypnotic, the whole place was rocking to renditions
of drinking songs; Ein, Zwei, Drei, Vier – Raise your stein and drink your beer. Recollections from the Mario Lanza film The Student Prince, resonated in their heads and they found themselves carried away by the atmosphere.

'It is a pity the Germans don't play rugby, this would be a great place to come to on an Easter tour.'

Sally raised her glass in salute. 'With wives of course!!'

He shook his head vigorously and she read his lips, the message read, 'Silly Girl.'

Further explanation was spared by the arrival of a waitress dressed in the typical Bavarian costume of green skirt and low cut white blouse. She was bearing huge menus from which they both chose Gulaschsuppe, which even James's German was able to interpret as Goulash Soup.

After this sustenance plus another small stein of beer they finally bade their farewell and began the tricky task of finding their way back to Maximilianstrasse and the hotel Kempinski whose elegantly colonnaded façade was so neatly the reverse of the Hofbrauhaus.

Munich had proved to be an exciting first date and despite her pleadings he would not divulge what tomorrow promised, except to say that they had to collect a hire car in the morning.

The arrival of the lift stemmed the flow of her inquisitive questions and they travelled smoothly from the hotel lobby to their suite. This was lavishly furnished in a style inspired by the era of Maximilian the Second in whose reign the hotel had been built.

The bed had already been turned down which, he suggested, meant it was time to take a nap.

She raised her eyes 'I don't really feel like going to sleep.'

'That was just a cunning ploy to make you take your clothes off.'

She sidled up to him. 'I need some help.'

Help was soon at hand and seconds later it was yesterday all over again except that this time they had no inhibitions and Roger was able to take her to even greater heights. Afterwards they both snoozed off and when he awoke she lay propped up in bed confident in her nakedness and even more confident in her love for him.

'Hello, how did you get here? I was just dreaming about this beautiful girl in a black hunting coat moving off with the hunt and wondering how I could get to meet her and here you are.'

She snuggled up to him, when you are this much in love, words are not always necessary.

They eventually made it downstairs and retraced their steps to Marienplatz and the Hofbrauhaus which was even more noisy than it had been at lunchtime. It was great fun but a little too loud for conversation and so he suggested finding a small restaurant in the Centrum. She shook her head in amusement as once again he had been unable to resist lapsing into schoolboy German. It was much warmer here than back home and along with others, many of them in short sleeves, they sat outside under a typically Bavarian blue umbrella and enjoyed a simple Weinerschitzel and Pasta washed down by the local beer.

'We should leave about ten o'clock in the morning as we have to drive to Rome.'

He held his hand to his mouth.

'I don't believe it, my secret is out.'

She looked at him for a moment, a smile emerging on her face.

'I already know you too well Mr. Carrington; if we had been going to Rome we would have gone by air, first class.'

He tried to protest but she would have none of it, but neither would he divulge where they were heading, even though she threatened withdrawing conjugal rights.

He raised his eyebrows. 'So as we are not yet married, that won't be for the time being then. Meanwhile I will have to find a way of striking a deal to break this impasse; I will talk to Roger about it.'

'It was only a threat and I am very easily persuaded.'

She strode off, presumably heading for the powder room and returned smiling three or four minutes later.

'I will get Der Rechnung.'

'Too late, I have paid it. After all if there are no conjugals it is only fair that I pay my way.'
He burst out laughing and gave her bottom a friendly pat.

'Don't touch what you can't afford.' Her hilarious retort.

In high spirits they marched hand in hand back to the hotel cocktail bar and ordered two glasses of champagne. She raised her glass; 'I forgive you.'

He burst out laughing. 'You are something else Miss Parkinson and I forgive you too; meanwhile, we should turn in as we have another exciting day tomorrow.'

CHAPTER FIFTY FOUR

The following morning after another continental breakfast of cold meats, delicious pastries and fruit juice, James pressed a ten mark note into her hand and asked Sally to arrange for the luggage to be brought down whilst he collected the hire car.

Twenty minutes later he was back in the lobby and directing the porter towards a bright red drop-head Porsche Targa.

'You didn't get this from Avis.'

'No, fortunately I do have a pal who lives in Kitzbuhel who owes me a favour and he insisted that we borrow his car, or one of them I guess.'

'I am slowly starting to get to know you Mr. Carrington and you know what; I like it – a lot.'

The porter stowed his bags under the bonnet but Sally's vast valise, as he had named it, had to be stored in the back behind the front seats.

They travelled south on the E11 following the signs for Salzburg, the weather was perfect and she sat quietly absorbing the wonderful scenery that flashed by. This was an area that had always enchanted her and her time at finishing school in Austria had enabled her to acquire a reasonable proficiency in both French and German. The nearby ski resorts of Garmisch, Partenkirchen and Kitzbuhel were also places she had skied many times, however, at that time of the year the area had naturally always been covered in snow, the Alps in its summer mantle was even more attractive, – or perhaps it was the present company that made it seem so?

She rested her hand on his thigh and gave it a gentle squeeze, he turned and smiled.

'Happy?' The ecstatic look on her face was all the evidence he needed.

As they approached Rosenheim he turned off to the right on the E17, she saw the signs for Innsbruck and assumed this is where they were heading and was therefore surprised when they turned right again, this time along a narrow road which almost immediately brought them into the small but attractive Alpine village of Oberaudorf.

He pulled into the main square and parked outside a typical Bavarian hotel, each balcony sporting red geranium window boxes made even more attractive by the yellow painted exterior.

'This is where all the crowned heads of Europe dine when they are in this region of the

Alps,' he quipped.

He jumped out of the car and opened her door; she looked slightly bemused; his face was radiant as he pointed to the mountain behind them.

'This is my special place on earth, you are the first person I have ever brought here and I want to share it with you. But first we have to take a small journey, but I promise it is one that you will enjoy.'

He took her hand and they walked the short distance to the edge of the village where she saw a familiar sign; Sesselbahn. This was the chairlift that in winter led upwards to the snow lined piste. He paid the man in the kiosk and returned to hold the chair as she sat in it; before snapping the safety bar shut and wishing her bon voyage.

'This is the start of 'my experience'; you will be all on your own for a few minutes to think about spending the rest of your life with me.'

He cupped her face in his hands and gently brushed his lips against hers and then was gone as the next chair arrived. He fastened himself in and as the chair creaked its way past the ski-jump, he sat back to review his own life.

Cocooned in the solitude that this snail pace of transport affords, he remembered his previous visits. He had been to this mountain a few times in the past, but always alone and always when he had to make a decision. It had for instance enabled him to resolve how best to approach Abercrombie Pope & Plummer to secure the necessary and important finances that would launch Fordmill Construction into the big time.

It had given him the resolve to purchase Woolmington Hall and, not so very long ago, after he had split with Edward Lawson and the euphoria of the golf at the Royal Lytham Golf Club had subsided, it was on this mountain that he resolved to build a new career in tandem with Jack Priory.

Finally he reached his journey's end and there, huge grin on her face was Sally. He sprang out of the chairlift and taking her hand led her up the short climb to the restaurant that was perched on the mountain side. They threaded their way past a small herd of miniature mountain goats and through the gate that opened onto the terrace of the restaurant. They chose a table under one of the parasols and he pointed out The Kaiser which rose above a huge swathe of the Alps directly in front of them, the snow ever present on the summits of these peaks that stood watchful over the small villages that dotted the Alpine slopes.

Standing up here, isolated from the rest of the world and apparently lord of all you survey, he understood how Hitler must have felt; it was so easy to imagine that you were master of the world.

His reverie was interrupted by a slim blonde girl dressed in a traditional Dirndl, the same costume they had seen in the Hofbrauhaus in Munich.

She smiled at Sally and enquired, 'Bitte.'

'Zwei bier und der Speisenkarte bitte.'

Sally pushed her sunglasses up into her equally blonde hair.

'I assume that is what you were planning.'

He nodded, he felt so relaxed as he gazed around the towering skyline and for the first time counted the mountain peaks, unbelievably there were thirteen; His heart soared, it was his lucky number, surely an approval from on high that this beautiful woman he had with him was his destiny.

The beauty of it all affected Sally too and they sat with their own thoughts subconsciously aware of the alternate red and blue chairs of the Sesselbahn as it proceeded on its endless journey up and down the mountain.

In these idyllic surroundings the cares and concerns of everyday life are mentally massaged away and the prospect of spending the rest of his life with this beautiful woman in his beloved Milford Hall was consuming him.

She took his hand as they sat under the coloured umbrella which bore the name of the local Rosenheim Brewery, Auer Brau.

'When we are married, can we come here in the winter and then I can take you to my favourite ski hotel which is just down the road in Kitzbuhel?'

'I thought you would never ask.' Their spontaneous laughter was interrupted by the arrival of the beers and menus.

It was enough to launch him into his schoolboy German. 'Danke fraulein'

They had a light lunch and after a further two hours of relaxing and basking in each other's company he reluctantly called an end to their visit.

'Come on mein leibling, I have yet more treats in store for you.'

They bid the waitress Auf Wiedersehen and retraced their footsteps to the chairlift, saying farewell also to the cute miniature goats that followed them. Once on board, they had further time to reflect on how far their feelings towards each other had developed in such a short space of time. He even had time to think about Kate and Johnnie Mortimer; hopefully that romance was also accelerating at the same pace.

They retraced their steps towards Rosenheim and re-joined the E11, this time heading towards Salzburg. They jostled for position with the streams of home going traffic and, more by luck than judgement, emerged on the other side desperately hoping to see directions to Bad Ischl.

Sally spotted the sign and relaxation was resumed although she was relentless in her demand to know where he was taking her.

Surprises and treats are fundamental to James Carrington's sense of enjoyment and his emphatic, 'Won't tell you'; finally called a halt to her questions, by which time they were in the outskirts of their destination, St. Wolfgang.

He drove carefully through the narrow streets and briefly glimpsed the hotel balconies which overlooked the Lake; they drove past the Im Weisses Rossl Hotel made famous by the musical White Horse Inn, whose name it borrowed and in two minutes he had turned into the car park of the Landhaus zu Appesbach.

They sat hand in hand as he explained that this romantic idyll had once been a favourite trysting place for amongst others, Edward the Eighth when he was Duke of Windsor and the woman for whom he would give up everything, including the crown, Mrs Wallis Simpson.

Sally turned towards him, radiating love and affection.

'James, how do you do it? All these wonderful surprises. I have never known anyone remotely as romantic and I can't really believe it is happening to me.'

'Well we had better go inside, before the evil witch waves it all away.'

He took her hand and they walked blissfully towards the large white portico which stood out from the soft yellow walls of the hotel. Before they could start to climb the steps to the front door they were intercepted by a porter who directed them to the reception desk and volunteered to collect their bags and park the car. James suggesting to Sally that he probably just wanted to drive the Porsche. Inside they were welcomed by the manager who looked remarkably like Peter Sellers and whose name ironically, according to his badge, was indeed Peter. He in turn swept them through the salon with its back to back grand piano's and led them onto the terrace where his suggestion of champagne was approvingly accepted.

They sat under the yellow umbrellas and gazed over the crystal clear lake to the mountain peaks on the other side; apart from the birds it was so still and they were both held in the same silent spell, each with their own thoughts, both of which centred on the same two people.

A waitress in the now familiar Dirndl brought over the champagne and a selection of nibbles; Sally tilted her glass.

'To us and to my mountain, I am appointing that pointed one over there, as Mont Sally.'

'That is just the sort of salutation I was thinking of.'

'Naughty boy, you will have to wait until I have drunk this.'

'And I shall re-name the Kaiser as my mountain, Mont James. So we now have a secret code for hanky-panky.'

Sally chuckled. 'It won't take MI6 to work that one out!'

'Nevertheless, I think we should go to our room before anyone listens in to our conversation.'

She attempted to pout but the joy in her eyes told a different story as she grabbed his hand and led him back through the drawing room and up the gracious staircase to their room on the second floor. From the balcony, they could see people swimming in the lake.

She went through into the separate sitting room and pointed out of the window.

'Regarde Mont Sally.'

Before she could move, he was standing behind her and she felt the zip on her dress slowly sliding down and his hands cupping her breasts. She stepped out of the dress and led him into the bathroom.

'Take all of your clothes off; I am going to examine you very closely.'

He did not need a second invitation and in the few seconds it took him to shed his clothing she was in the shower with foam camouflaging her obvious charms. It would have taken a lot of foam to disguise his pleasure although he encouraged her to try. Meanwhile he gently removed her disguise until finally neither of them could delay their desires any longer and wrapping her in a huge bath towel he carried her gently to the king sized bed and snuggled up to her, revelling in the lithe body with its generous breasts.

'I am a very lucky man, I have one Mont Sally outside and two even better ones in here with me.'

She too was happy with what she saw, he was still in top class shape with a well- defined physique that he obviously looked after and he had already proved to be an exciting and yet considerate lover. This time too he teased and tempted her, revelling in her responses trying to delay as long as possible the shuddering climax that kept approaching. Finally they could wait no longer and they both trembled to a mutual moment of breathless satisfaction.

'Miss Parkinson, you are wonderful and I love being in bed with you, in fact I love being with you all the time.'

'And I adore you Mr Carrington; in fact, I want to spend the rest of my life with you.'

After a brief nap they dressed for dinner, calling en route at the cocktail bar, before returning to the terrace for supper under the stars.

He looked at her enquiringly. 'Why did you never marry, you must have had plenty of offers?'

'I was engaged to a really nice guy named Hugo Villiers, he was the son of Daddy's best friend Monty Villiers, the racehorse trainer; we sort of grew up together and everyone more or less assumed we would be married.'

'So, what happened?'

She hesitated, reliving the pain. When she replied her voice was very quiet, the memory clearly distressing.

'He dropped me... for a fellow officer in his regiment. They were overseas, maybe it was the heat; maybe it was me.'

She attempted a rueful smile and looking into his eyes saw the concern; she knew with certainty that he would never let her down.

'I will never ever leave ....' She put her finger on his lips. 'I know.'

That positivity restarted the party mood and the conversation centred on how to spend the next three days. He suggested Berchtesgaden; the site of the Eagle's Nest, a remarkable building perched precariously on top of the mountain. It was commissioned by Martin Bormann as a 50th birthday present for Adolf Hitler; it was however a gift that somewhat backfired as Hitler rarely visited it because of his fear of heights. This they agreed would be tomorrow's day out.

The second day she pleaded was to be her treat and she would like to buy lunch in Kitzbuhel at her favourite hotel. He agreed and so on the last day they would explore the area around St Wolfgang and visit Mont Sally!

The evening slipped away, the conversation never ebbing as they spoke about their past and dreams for the future.

'I have never found it so easy to speak with anyone,' she confessed.

'Could just be the alcohol!' He chortled.

The laughter and anecdotes continued until they became aware that they were alone on the terrace and, with a big day planned for tomorrow, they too decided to call it a night, 'well downstairs anyway,' he suggested.

CHAPTER FIFTY FIVE

They were both awake at about seven thirty and Sally was the first out onto the balcony.

'I can't see an awful lot, go and demand our money back.'

He smacked her bottom.

'Idiot! It is just a little sea fret, as they say in East Anglia, by eleven the sun will be cracking the pavements.'

And so it turned out, in fact by the time they left the car park at half past nine they had the sun roof down and were in short sleeve order. There are no quick routes in the Alps, the mountains may be very beautiful but they do not countenance shortcuts so it was back to Salzburg, which they elected to give a miss and so instead, following the line of the border between Austria and Germany, they eventually happened on the sign for Berchtesgarten.

Kate spotted the Centrum sign and just around the next corner the central car park. Being in its homeland so to speak, a red Porsche with its top down does not provoke the same excitement as it might in London or Nottingham. However, blondes in sports cars always demand a look and in any country Sally Parkinson would turn the heads of onlookers. She was aware of this and so was her driver.

'Would you like me to wear my chauffeur's cap, madam?'

'Thank you James; that would seem most appropriate.'

As at their first meeting, spontaneity and humour were always just below the surface. They parked the car and strolled leisurely through this delightful Bavarian village, along its winding streets and into the medieval market place where they opted for a coffee and a pastry from the many that were on offer.

Sally excused herself and went off to the ladies room.

With a small window of time in which to think, James cast his mind back to this time last week when his life was upside down, the emotions of Edward's funeral, and the hostility from Kate and her mother.

Now in this, his special part of the world, he was once again able to immediately throw off worldly day to day worries and recharge his battery. The fact that he was with this stunningly good looking girl was of course also part of his rejuvenation. On the drive here this morning his stolen glances had revealed her happiness; she was so ecstatic and he was so pleased for her. She had obviously suffered, probably more so than he or Kate: In fact being rejected as a woman for another man must be just about as bad as it gets.

This brought him full circle back to Kate; they too had shared many good times but they had drifted apart and, like many marriages, the original tiny cracks became fissures that eventually split the relationship apart and, unfortunately, there is no super glue that can weld the partnership back together. Nevertheless, he still cared for her and wanted her to be happy again; he hoped that she would find that happiness with Johnnie Mortimer.

Sally's return to the table refocused him and he immediately got things back on track by testing her German vocabulary. He resorted to his pigeon schoolboy grammar

'Achtung mein leibling; vot do you think Kehlsteinhaus means?'
She gave it some consideration.

'Eagle's House or probably Eagle's Nest, Jah?'
'Damn, you are absolutely spot on, how did you work that out?'
'We learned how to cook Eagle Burgers at my finishing school.'
'That certainly was an impressive curriculum.'
Still smiling he led the way out of the cafe unaware that she was almost doubled over with laughter; she would explain later about the poster on the wall which translated into English the 'must see' sights in the town.

They made their way up to the Eagle's Nest and it was well worth the effort, the restaurant sits on the very top of the mountain and the view as they drank a beer on the adjoining terrace was truly breath-taking. Sally was waxing lyrical about the setting and wondering if they would see any Kehlsteins flying about, when he suddenly spotted a copy of the same poster she had seen in the market place; no wonder she had been able to translate Eagle's Nest into German!

'You rat.'
She looked behind her and saw the poster and was immediately once again creased with laughter, as was he, confessing it was the sort of stunt he would have tried himself.

He went to the bar and ordered two more beers; she was still beside herself when he got back.

They eventually retraced the route back to the car and took a scenic route back along the small country roads via Bad Ischl. This is Austria's oldest saltwater spa, the original treatments dating back to 1823.

However the 'Konditorei-Kaffee is also steeped in history so a visit was demanded by Lady Parkinson as she felt that chocolate cakes were more suitable for the complexion than salt; Mr Carrington agreed.

Their spirits were high as they returned to Appesbach, so much so that Sally insisted on buying champagne for the chauffeur, coyly adding that he would pay for it later!

She turned again to view Mont Sally across the lake and he took the opportunity to take a small book out of his pocket, he flicked through the pages, put the book back and confidently asserted.

'Ich verde.'

'You will – my word the mention of sex does seem to have re-awaked your knowledge of the German language.'

He smirked back at her as he leaned on the handrail and put his arm around her waist.

'Thank goodness you are not Polish; I might not have been able to get a Worterbuch to impress you.'

'James Carrington, when did you sneak away to get a dictionary?'

'I brought it with me, so that I could impress you – how was I to know you had finished your education over here?'

As usual they both enjoyed the humour; Sally beginning to understand that attention to detail lay just beneath the affable surface. She loved him all the more for it. He re-opened the dictionary and raised his eyebrows.

'Getranke and then you can tell me where we are going tomorrow.'

'Yes we will have another drink but no I will not tell you where we are going until we get there.'

Despite his pleadings she remained resolute – it was now his turn to be in the dark; although she did reward him with her promised treat.

CHAPTER FIFTY SIX

Meanwhile, whereas he had not yet started his romantic journey by driving to Grantham. Kate had leapt into the stag, anxious to be on her way; she had told James that she wanted to leave early so as to miss the heavy traffic that office workers generated on the A1 between eight and nine. The reality was that she wanted to avoid any further interrogation by her parents.

Her father she knew had very mixed feelings because of his respect and admiration for James; her mother on the other hand, had become a tigress in defence of her young and she did not want today to start with further recriminations and character assassinations, she still had too much latent respect for her husband for that, although love was a thing of the past.

However, the most important concern was to preserve an atmosphere of affection so that Charles and Edward would accept that their lives would be different but still loving and caring. Hopefully when they met Johnnie and, she found it difficult to say her name; Sally Parkinson, they would accept this change in their lives. Fortunately being away at school would mean that the majority of the time would be spent with their friends and the environment would remain the same; she prayed that this would be a help to them and make it easier to reconcile the difference it would make to their lives.

She started to relax, this was a new start to her life and at least she did not have to worry about a jealous husband. She saw the sign for the A52 and was soon heading towards Nottingham and the outer ring road that would take her to East Midlands' airport. She checked the time as she approached Clifton and started to relax as she drove past the quaintly named villages of Barton in Fabis and Thrumpton; names that evoked memories of reading stories to the kids about Postman Pat and his friends.

A car hooting behind her brought her back to earth and she picked up speed again, the die had been cast, she had to come to terms with it.

Regaining her former resolve, she accelerated away from the hooter and twenty minutes later was in the car park at the airport. She grabbed her case from the boot and unavailingly attempted to spot his car. As she reached for the tickets in the driver's door pocket her heart briefly sank - James must have noticed them when he brought the car round from the garage but, just as quickly, her resolve to build a new life returned and this was further strengthened by the sight of Johnnie waiting for her at the entrance to the terminal.

His face was beaming as he held her tightly, so was Kate's as they strode hand in hand to the check-in desk, she was so happy and she didn't care who knew it and there must be someone here who knew them. There was; it was Andrew Travers.

He too was travelling to Dublin, to a chartered surveyors' conference at the Shelbourne Hotel; he naturally wanted to avoid any embarrassment and hoped they would be a few seats apart. They were, but since they were all travelling in the small confines of first class it would seem impossible to ignore each other, although of course she may not recognise him as, until last week at Edward Lawson's funeral, it had been fifteen years since he had shown the excited young couple around their future home at Woolmington.

He had been a few pounds lighter then and still had a full head of hair. But no point in worrying, it was not his problem and she probably had not noticed him at the funeral and in any case, would be unlikely to be aware of his recent meeting with James or its agenda.

On the positive side, he would at least be able to describe to James what her new man looked like which, to be fair, was pretty impressive. However, since James had swapped one beauty for another, you could hardly expect Kate to be escorted by anyone who was not presentable.

The plane started to taxi forward to the runway and the surveyor turned his mind to matters more professional, or to be precise, the presentation he was due to make to the conference.

Kate had seen Andrew Travers, but rather than spoil her day, she drew strength from this 'outing', it signalled that she was going forward, she was not staying at home moping, no she was getting on with a new life and if Andrew chose to talk to James about it, so be it.

She nestled up to Johnnie, he was now her life and James Carrington was essentially history. As someone had once advised her, never go back to a firework that has been lit – just leave it to go out.

They finally had no alternative but to acknowledge each other, as they all boarded the small hospitality bus that would take them from the airport to the Shelbourne Hotel. Andrew took the initiative but stuck to safe ground

'It is Kate isn't it?'

'Andrew Travers, quite a surprise seeing you after all these years. By the way, let me introduce you to Johnnie Mortimer who is coincidentally in the same line of business as you, except that he hails from Harrogate.'

They shook hands, the atmosphere remaining cordial.

'Johnnie Mortimer; then you must be part of MWS and of course I know of you. You are a very well established firm with a fine reputation; it is a pleasure to meet you. Are you by any chance over here for the RICS conference?'

'Not exactly; although we are weighing up one or two property options.'

Kate interrupted them.

'No more talk of work, we are here to enjoy this beautiful city and, unless I am mistaken, this is St Stephen's Square and that superb Georgian building with the wrought iron entrance is the Shelbourne Hotel.'

She was correct and as the small group made their way into the entrance lobby they became detached. She left Johnnie to sign the register whilst she sat quietly contemplating the bizarre coincidence of meeting Andrew Travers, whom she had last spoken with when they bought Woolmington Manor. What a coincidence they had arrived on the same flight, or had James sent him to Dublin to spy on them?

She dismissed this thought; not even her husband had that sort of authority.

Her thoughts were interrupted by a pair of long legs dressed in corn yellow corduroy trousers, she lifted her eyes to see a kind, handsome face looking down at her; the affection was self- evident and she sprang to her feet.

'So, are we Mr and Mrs Smith?'
He chuckled, their humour, as it had been in Yorkshire, was very much in tune.
'No, I thought that was too obvious; we are Mr and Mrs Jones.'
'Well Mr Jones, take me to your locker, I need to lie down after this long journey.'

They declined to use the elevator, choosing instead to climb the magnificent staircase which sprang from a huge carved newel post which in turn supported a great bronze lantern.
He grinned. 'I had it switched on especially for us.'
'Now everyone else will want to do that – keeping up with the Jones's, eh what, boyo!'
They finally reached their room, which turned out to be a sumptuously comfortable suite. He looked pleased, perhaps even relieved that she liked it; in fact he was ecstatic, as it was obvious that style and class were inherent in her make-up and he did not want any unfavourable comparisons drawn with the past. No, everything he did for this woman was going to be perfect. He sensed it had to be.

Kate bounced up and down on the end of the bed; she proffered her hand which he took expecting to lift her to her feet, instead he found himself lying beside her. Her blue eyes bored into his.
'Johnnie Mortimer, we have not known each other long but I do believe I love you.'
He kissed her gently.
'Kate Carrington, I definitely know I love you and I hope in the near future to change your name.'
'Johnnie, I am sorry, but I could never become Mrs Jones, there are far too many of those about!'
He kissed her gently, his hand stroking her neck, wondering how far he might go. She was so much everything he wanted, he did not want to upset her, but neither did he want her to think that he did not find her attractive.
She sensed how he was feeling.
'Kiss me.'
He did not need any further encouragement and although both of them had déjà vu moments, they

were both swept away by each other and the lovemaking seemed so natural.

They finally came back to earth and after an equally memorable shower together they literally came down to earth, this time in the elevator. He led her into the Horse Shoe Bar, so well known to the legions of racing people who visit this equine Holy Grail. He ordered of course, two glasses of Guinness. They sat at the bar awaiting the black stuff which was served with, of course, a shamrock inscribed into the foaming white head. She sipped it apprehensively and then, to his complete surprise, knocked it back in one go.

To his great amusement, she surprised even herself, by turning to the barman and instructing him.

'To be sure Patrick, hadn't we better be having two more of the same, begorra?'

The mood was set as they both immediately fell back into the happiness zone that they had captured on that very first date at the Devonshire Arms in Yorkshire. New love is captivating; and freed from the domestic drama and fear of the future, Kate was looking forward and the thought that James was also no doubt planning a new life without her. This was now suddenly acceptable as she too now had a future with a man who deserved a new tomorrow. She didn't know him that well as yet, but she sensed that life would be more of a two way discussion, so that her role in their lives would play a more important part; she would be part of the decision making.

This idea appealed to her, it was part of her new persona and as they strolled hand in hand out into St Stephen's Square, he sprang his first surprise.

'Your carriage awaits Madam.'

And there by the entrance arch facing Grafton Street, was a horse drawn carriage with the door open and the cabby ready to hand her aboard. She hugged him with excitement; maybe having someone else provide the surprises was not so bad after all. The driver shook the reins and the dark bay horse broke into an even slow trot around the square.

St Stephen's Green is the oldest park in Ireland and Dublin's love affair with the area dates back to medieval times when it was marshland set on the outskirts of the city. In 1664, in order to raise revenue, the central area was walled and the immediate land around it sold as building plots. One hundred and fifty years later the city needed to raise further capital and, as a means towards doing this, keys were sold to the owners of the splendid Georgian houses around its perimeter giving them sole right of access.

Sixty years later, Lord Ardilaun the then chairman of the Guinness Brewery, philanthropically bought out all the key holders and then spent three years landscaping the area before opening it to the general public as the forerunner to the splendid municipal facility that it is today.

All of this was explained by the carriage driver, although he doubted if the lovebirds in the back were taking much notice. A view further reinforced when he heard the sound of a champagne cork being popped and the clink of two glasses. The happy couple were navigated around the square which swarmed with pedestrians, joggers, and lovers like themselves, all seemingly intoxicated by this romantic setting.

Many of the happy throng were relaxing with picnics set out on tartan rugs; others lounged by the lake or just used the park as a shortcut to the other side of the city. On hot days the crowd are loathe to leave but, just before sunset, the sound of the bell-ringer doing his rounds finally sends them home.

However that time was hours away and realising they were in no haste, the cabby slowed the horse down to a slow walk and they clip-clopped back to Grafton Street, two more visitors entranced by this magical city.

Before paying the cabbie Johnnie presented him with the champagne flutes plus £30 so that he could treat his wife to a glass this evening.

Determined to see more they strolled with fingers linked into Kildare Street before turning left which took them past Ireland's most prestigious seat of learning, Trinity College. From here they crossed the bridge over the Liffey, a river that is credited for the unique qualities of the quintessential Irish drink that is Guinness; a beverage that is drunk in more bars than any drink in the world; or so the Irish insist and, when you are here, it is difficult to deny them.

They made their way back in a leisurely fashion to the Shelbourne and whilst Johnnie retrieved the room keys Kate stared abstractly at the 'events board' which featured tomorrow's seminar entitled 'Re–Addressing your Family Estate', the principal lecture of which was to be given by Andrew Travers FRICS. There followed a synopsis which outlined the opportunities to redefine the future usage of the now outdated large country house.

A voice in her ear summed up the thoughts that she was trying to organise in her head.

'Woolmington could be as successful an investment as Nidderdale House.'

'Which is just what I was thinking and do you know what; I think we should use this opportunity to speak to James's pal Andrew Travers, as James will listen to him far more attentively than he would to you or me.'

'We had better reserve ourselves a couple of tickets or, better still ask Andrew to arrange them – start the ball rolling as it were.'

'Brilliant, I will call him right now.'

And with that, Johnnie disappeared in the direction of reception.

'See you back in the room.' She called after him.

Ten minutes later he re-joined her, by which time she had organised the desk with complementary hotel notepaper and ballpoint pens and was sitting in a comfortable upright chair facing the desk.

'As you have the desk you can take the minutes of this, the first board meeting of 'Wooldale Leisure.'

He smiled, impressed as he had been at their first encounter by her decisive and organised mind.

'I can see you are a lawyer's daughter and I can also see that you have beaten me to the punch by choosing a name for our Leisure Group; so to work - how do you wish to proceed?'

She fell back into the routine that James had instilled in her.

'Just bullet point notes that we can embellish after we have heard Andrew's presentation.'

He wrote in a very fine hand that verged on calligraphy.

Wooldale Leisure
* A partnership between Kate Carrington and Jonathan Mortimer
* Share ownership to be decided at a later date
* Initially one property – Nidderdale House

- Consideration to be given to including Woolmington Manor as a second property, subject to availability and price
- Location of further properties is paramount as guest expectations fuelled by the standards of Nidderdale House and other venues under the same management will encourage further visits.

They were both so engrossed with the exciting prospect of working together that time just slipped away until finally Johnnie announced that his stomach was sending out a clear distress signal.

'Okay, I have to admit that I am receiving similar warnings, it must be all that exercise we had this morning.'

'Was that the horizontal or the perpendicular exertions you were thinking about?'
The cheeky grin on her face suggested that it was not the former that she objected to.

The dining room was almost full but he had arranged for a window seat which provided a further view of the park they had viewed from their horse drawn conveyance.

They were both eager to try the locally produced food and so started with Quails' Eggs in a Basket. The choux pastry was lined with parmesan cheese on top of which rested two beautifully presented eggs that had been soft boiled and opened out into a fan sprinkled with paprika.

As a main course, he persuaded Kate to join him with the Crown Rack of Lamb. When it arrived she knew it had been a good decision; each cutlet came with its distinctive frilly hat that formed the crown which was filled with watercress. The serving dish was decorated around the base with new potatoes, broccoli, green beans and sprigs of tarragon; to complete the course a rich and delicious boat of gravy.

The final complement was a gloriously rich dry white, Puligny-Montrachet.

They ate slowly, the conversation easy and gentle as they both bathed in the warmth of each other's company; they both saw a new future which had seemed so unlikely only a few weeks ago.

The waiter approached and suggested Irish Apple Cake as a desert, but whether he was serious was difficult to tell as, despite being French, he seemed to have acquired the gift of the blarney.

Kate pulled rank and chose the dessert which he initially declined, but the prospect of her having a Crème Brulee Avec Cerises on her own was too much. He did a swift volte face.

It was a decision he did not regret when he cracked open the caramel topping to reveal a layer of dark cherries bathing in the kirsch just below the surface. To accompany this, the wine waiter recommended a glass of fine Madeira, a choice that proved the perfect finale to the dinner.

This had been the most wonderful day, not only did they have a new life to look forward to, they also had the added excitement of a new business. Hopefully this would be centred on the two special buildings that were central to their lives; Woolmington Manor and Nidderdale House. The hundred or so miles between them would surely be an appealing alternative prospect to the existing clients of Nidderdale who would be swopping one idyllic parkland setting for another and likewise to the as yet unknown visitors to Woolmington.

'Just one small brandy and then we should call it a day.'
Kate agreed; it was important to be at their most perceptive tomorrow; Andrew Travers' presentation

might well have a massive influence on the rest of their lives and in Jonathan's words;

'How we play this fish and how we land him will test our skills to the utmost, particularly if someone else, namely James Carrington muddies the water.'

He stood up and took her chair, letting his hand linger on her shoulder for just a moment. It was a brief encounter, but it signalled a beginning with a long future and they both slept soundly with that fond belief ingrained in their dreams.

CHAPTER FIFTY SEVEN

The lecture was scheduled for 10:30 am so they had a leisurely Irish breakfast and a walk around St Stephen's Green, which seemed even more fascinating and attractive on foot, it also made Dublin their own special place, somewhere they had already intended to return to each to year.

'Have you been here before?'
He held her gaze, his eyes misty with love.

'No, I have been saving this place just for you. What about you, is this your first visit?'
'Yes.'

She decided that a little white lie was in order. In fact she had been here a few years ago to watch James play for England against Ireland at Lansdowne Road, but his spectre was not going to be allowed to spoil this feast, it was far too special for that, particularly with the potential positive consequences of the lecture they were due to attend in fifteen minutes time.

Hand in hand and looking conspicuously most un-business like, they made their way into the lecture room and after taking advantage of the coffee that was offered, chose two of the few seats that were left. Andrew Travers spotted them from the rostrum; he presumed that the two estate agencies were planning to buy a city centre property and open a branch in Dublin.

At ten thirty precisely, the chairman of the Irish Society of Chartered Surveyors called them to order and introduced the guest speaker who clicked a wand which brought up the title of the lecture on the screen.

Re-addressing your family home
He looked around the audience before posing the question.
- Do you think that your sons and daughters will want to follow you and take on the family seat?
- How many of you have already departed to pastures new?
- Many of these properties are in rural locations and many of our children prefer to live and work in the city, whether that be London or Dublin, so retaining the family home will be counter beneficial and unnecessarily tie up capital.

Why are these large properties so undesirable?

- Help in the house is not easy to find, maids and gardeners are a thing of the past – people have higher aspirations and because mortgages make such big inroads into the family budget, DIY has become the norm, people are busy renovating their own properties so they do not have the time or inclination to do odd jobs for others, certainly not on a regular basis.
- As we get older maintaining the grounds and paddocks is difficult without help.
- The cost of heating and maintenance continues to escalate.

Moving to a smaller house with all mod-cons is very attractive

- The basic running costs are lower – therefore more surplus income.
- It is so much easier to lock up the house and go away on holiday.
- By making our lives more tolerable we will be less dependent on the younger members of our family. Which is very good news for them!

What are the options if I move?

- Purpose built communities with communal facilities such as lounge areas and shops.
- A very good example of this is the Fordmill Construction development in Bournemouth. This has four blocks of thirty apartments with a recreation area; underground car parking and small modern shops such as newsagents, grocers, hairdressers and butchers which are a great convenience, particularly if you are not keen on driving.
- In addition the central garden area is being developed as an attractive sculpture park.
- This development also has a show apartment to allow you to sample the facilities.
- It also has a waiting list which emphasises its success.
- Other options include:-
- Gated Communities which in rural areas can include a golf course and swimming pool.
- In urban areas such as city centres this gated enclosure affords greater security.

Andrew switched off the projector and scanned his audience.

'No one asleep as yet.'

This observation was greeted with muttering of wry amusement. He leaned on the lectern and continued.

'I hope I might have encouraged a little lateral thinking, one negative thought might be - if large houses are now unpopular and too expensive to run, how on earth do I sell my property?'

'This is where your apparent predicament becomes more encouraging because companies such as the afore mentioned Fordmill Construction, who were the trail blazers in this market place, are keen to purchase and develop these large properties, in fact the larger the better.'

He leaned forward.

'If I might be allowed a pun, your family seat is quite possibly sitting on a fortune!'

A chuckle rippled through the audience and he sensed that they had questions for him. A chalk stripe suit in the second row was first on his feet.

'Presumably the properties to which you refer also have commercial opportunities for use as offices for instance? How are the local council planning authorities inclined to these developments?'

'You have a very good point and from my own experience I can categorically inform you that in urban areas, all the local councils are very keen on attracting companies into their region. They see the income stream from rates and the creation of jobs as a means of generating spending in the local shops, restaurants and so on.'

A man in a tweed jacket towards the back of the hall was waving his newspaper. Andrew acknowledged him suspecting that we were now going down the opposite track, he was right.

'I live in a rural area of outstanding natural beauty; surely my opportunities are very much more limited?'

'Yes and no. You are unlikely to be allowed to demolish your property and build a supermarket but converting it into a private hospital or nursing home or indeed into retirement apartments, as long as you maintain the external appearance, should not be present any great obstacles. You will however need to obtain a Change of Use Permit.'

The tweed jacket sat down apparently satisfied with the prognosis.

Andrew fielded several other questions, all of the enquirers seemingly genuinely interested. He was aware that Jonathan Mortimer, who had already gone down this route, was not prepared to give anything away by floating the idea of health farms as a potential change of use. He decided it would be judicious to skirt around this one so conclude the meeting with a summary.

'I have prepared a synopsis of today's ideas and this includes the addresses and telephone numbers of both the Chartered Surveyors' and Architects' institutional head offices in the UK and of course in Ireland. They will give you a list of their members in your areas and I have also given you the addresses of several developments across the UK that have received awards for the integrity of their change of use. In conclusion, I urge you to Address the situation and Re-address your family home. Elphin House will still be Elphin House if it becomes a solicitor's office or indeed a private clinic and think how many more people can enjoy your family history. Thank you for your time and interest, if any of you want a private discussion I will be available this afternoon, in the meantime make the most of your time in this enchanting city.'

A few of the audience gathered around Andrew's lectern whilst Kate and Johnnie joined the general exodus heading towards the free cocktails in the Horse Shoe Bar.
As they sipped the complimentary champagne, he became aware of the puzzled expression on Kate's face; a sure sign that something was going on in her active brain.

'A penny for them.'
She looked bemused not knowing where to start.

'I found the lecture quite enlightening and it might well be a way of solving my dilemma over Woolmington Manor.'

This time it was his face that had the quizzical expression; it also reflected an intense endearment that emboldened her.

'We both have to think aloud so that we both appreciate what is really going on in the other's head. Some of our musings may be fact, others may be presumptuous or wildly romantic because it is difficult not to get carried away in this romantic setting.'

He raised his eyebrows. 'Why don't we take a stroll in St Stephen's Square?'

She nodded and took his hand and they walked silently out of the hotel, neither of them speaking until he directed her to an unoccupied park bench. Kate was first to break the silence.

'As you know I have always refused to even consider moving from Woolmington. However, just as you have transformed your home and given it a new life I can see a similar makeover working at my home. But how much longer will I be allowed to live there? James is a very devious character and he has always had this determination to move back to Milford Hall which would mean selling Woolmington to help finance his dream. My dream on the other hand is to stay where I am.'

He saw the distress in her eyes and for the first time he sensed her concern about the future. He understood her fears; after losing Madeleine and his two daughters he had faced into an empty chasm, he must pull her back from the edge.

'Let's talk about what you want to do and not what you don't want to do – agreed?'
Her face came back to life.

'I'm sorry, I haven't felt like that for ages, not since I met you in fact. But, how do we resolve this?'

'Believe me Kate, there is a solution and this afternoon we are going to find the answer. Does James own Woolmington or is it in joint names, not that it really matters as after fourteen years of marriage any court in the land would award you a half share.'

'But that would still mean me having to sell my beloved home.'
He gave her an encouraging smile and followed up with a stunning suggestion.

'You are seeking to expand your estate agency business in Yorkshire. Why not bring your Braithwaite business into the MWS Group, something I had always wanted to do, but of course old Braithwaite wouldn't contemplate selling; that is until you came along and sweet talked him into seeing the light.'

He sensed what she was thinking and pre-empted her concern.

'I want to back out of the business and Ian Jackson my number two is retiring next year. So Liz Reed who I rate very highly, could step into his shoes and you can take over from me and breathe some new ideas and ambition into the company.'

'Don't you think the other managers might be somewhat averse to a stranger holding the tiller, after all you once told me that you only stayed with the firm because it was always a Mortimer who ran the company?'

The response was immediate. 'And so it would be.'
He watched her expression change from bewilderment to jaw dropping as he added, 'it would be Mrs Mortimer!'

'Johnnie, what are you trying to tell me?'
He slid off the bench and on one knee he uttered the four most romantic words.

'Will you marry me?' She responded with equal gusto
'Yes, yes, yes.'

They were oblivious to everything until the sound of someone clapping brought them down to earth. Looking over his stooped shoulder she saw, just ten yards away, a middle aged lady with her wire-haired dachshund who had obviously witnessed the proposal.

A lilting Irish voice drifted over to them.

'Good luck to you both, to be sure you were made for each other.'

Still shaking all over with excitement she coyly enquired, 'how long have you been thinking about this?'

'Ever since I lifted your suitcase out of the car at Nidderdale.'
He clung to her.

'I have been terrified about asking you, but these last three days have been so perfect and I was just waiting for the right moment; not that I imagined it would be on a park bench in Dublin.'
Emboldened by the last few minutes she now took over.

'But we still have to solve the Woolmington problem.'

'That is easy, I will buy James's half share and we will convert part of it into an apartment for us and the rest of it into a health farm, based on the model that is working so successfully at Nidderdale Hall.'

'But what if James won't sell because the present owners of Milford Hall have no wish to sell?'

'Kate darling, if James is half as determined as you say he is, then we must leave that to him. What we really have to hope is that he comes back from wherever he has been as much in love as we are and just as determined to kick start his new life.'
She nodded, although briefly she felt the pain of someone else having him. However, one glance at the kind and sympathetic man next to her was enough to reassure her inner belief and just as quickly the agony of telling Charles and Edward loomed over her.

Johnnie sensed that she was having problems.

'Is it the boys?'
The tears welling in her eyes confirmed his concern, 'I don't know if I can do it.'

'Kate darling you have to remember that divorce is not the unusual event that it used to be. Several of their friends at school will have divorced parents and kids can generally cope better than adults. However, this is going to come as an awful shock and both Sally Parkinson and me are going to have to let them know that we care for them and that we are never going to come between their parents. So, I have no grudges against James and I think you have to get used to calling her Sally and not 'That woman.'

She tried to regain her composure, humour as usual proving the best weapon.
'Have you ever thought of becoming an agony uncle?'
'I am afraid not, but I have had nearly four years of being alone and it's not nice and I don't recommend it. Now, this is our last night in Dublin and we have a lot to celebrate.'

CHAPTER FIFTY EIGHT

Meanwhile, back in Nottingham, Anthony Jayes was juggling the demands of selling Fordmill and the realities of balancing the books after paying off the loan notes due to James.

The existing agreement had already transferred the valuable property portfolio to James Carrington and the 'Get Out' value of his shareholding reflected that arrangement. The remainder of this shareholding was to be paid off in five annual payments, the first of which was due at the end of next month.

In the period since he resigned, the company under Edward's leadership had continued to prosper and Anthony himself had been an active participant in that success, so much so that they would have no problem meeting that commitment.

In the event of a takeover it had also been agreed that any outstanding annual payments would be paid in full; the residue would then be distributed amongst the remaining shareholders or re-invested as part of the capital of the new ownership. Personally, Anthony preferred the latter as its value would be enhanced if the company continued to be successful and it also displayed a confident and optimistic note to the new owners.

The challenging role that Anthony had to orchestrate was to continue running Fordmill as a highly successful and profitable company and, in the event of a sale, negotiate if possible, a better valuation for the company than had been agreed in reaching the settlement with James.

This would demonstrate to any would-be purchasers that Fordmill was in capable hands. The fact that James would be helping him achieve this was ironic, or potentially rather perverse, if they failed to wrangle as good a price as the one that Jack Priory had agreed with Edward Lawson.

The idea of having James advising him, albeit unofficially, was reassuring. But then just as quickly he thrust that thought away, this was Carpe Diem, his opportunity to seize the day and assert himself. The resulting esteem would be both financially rewarding and a significant addition to his Curriculum Vitae, it would also influence the board of directors that sought to acquire Fordmill Construction, as all companies are keen to head hunt people of outstanding ability. YES, he would seize the day. He would use the aphorism first phrased in the odes by the Latin poet Horace. Its relevance as true today as when it was written in 23 BC.

In this very positive mode he went to the computer and in the presentational style that James had inculcated he started to type:

1970 Current valuation of Fordmill Construction.

In the past five years we have consistently recorded profits of £600,000 plus, so on the basis of multiplying our last annual profit by a traditional factor of five the valuation is:-

£662,000 x 5 = £ 3,310,000

Less agreed loan notes due to James Carrington total value £ 1,000.000

Net current value of remaining shares = **£ 2,310,000**

The revised individual shareholdings are:-

	Previous	Amended	Potential Value
James Carrington	60.0 %	Nil	Nil
Edward Lawson	30.0 %	65 %	£1,478,400
Connie Lawson **7.5 %		18 %	£415,800
Anthony Jayes	5.0 %	12%	£277,200
Tim Cooper	2.5%	5%	£138,600

This year's projected profit will be in excess of the figure used in the above calculations, even after the first instalment of the of £1,000,000 sum agreed with James Carrington as full payment for the shares he held in the company at the time of his resignation.

The first payment of £200,000 would be made on the 28th of next month leaving a further £800,000 due; this to be paid in four equal annual payments or in total on the sale of the company.

Any potential buyer of Fordmill will expect this to be made prior to them taking over ownership and this provision has been agreed with our bankers Abercrombie Pope & Plummer.

This is an internal document and should not be circulated as the estimated value of shareholders' stock is simply a projection based on the last audited figures for 1969.

However, until the sale of the company and due diligence of the company's assets and financial standing has been completed by any prospective buyers, the directors should view the above valuation of their shareholding as an estimate only.

**

Note

In respect of Edward Lawson's holding, which represents nearly two thirds of this valuation, I have assumed that these have been willed to Connie or their children and, if that is the case, then her request that James Carrington assists and advises us to find a suitor to purchase the company is acceptable.

Furthermore, no fees will be paid directly to him as the contract is with Minster Marketing headed up by Jack Priory.

In recommending this I would also like to recommend to the Board that we draw up a battle plan and aim to bring on board a company with the same dynamic and vision that has won us so much acclaim in the past. We must go into the future carrying the baton that so identified the two founding directors.

My final recommendation is that we appoint our bankers, APP, to find us a company with that synergy.

Anthony re-read the manuscript a couple of times; he was pleased with the format and the mathematics which he found very interesting. His original intention had been inclined to accountancy but the family's legal background had ushered him into the law; the unforeseen events of the past eighteen months had propelled him into a position he had never envisaged.

The boots he had to fill were large, but he now believed he could make a good fist of it – Carpe Diem. Yes this was indeed an opportunity he would grasp, the very thought of it stirred his imagination and ambition as never before.

He picked up the telephone and asked for Jack Priory. In a few moments he heard the familiar voice. His message was brief.

'We are all set to go.'

Jack chuckled,

'It sounds as if you are up for it.'

Anthony's reply had the resonance of a man who was certainly ready to go to war.

'Never more so in my life.'

'In that case, I suggest next Monday at Minster Marketing, say 3 pm; I will advise the others including Connie and thank you Anthony for your enthusiasm, it bodes well for Fordmill Construction. I look forward to your recommendations.'

'And thank you Jack for your support. I will courier across a copy of my synopsis.'

Jack replaced his telephone in its cradle, his expression was enquiring; the brief conversation with Anthony Jayes had surprised him, the quiet, slightly retiring man in the shadow of both James and Edward was apparently ready to step into the breach as young officers have to do on the real battlefields. He would be tested, of that there was no doubt. Jack also sensed that he was manoeuvring to secure his own future with the eventual buyer. In the meantime, he concluded, the company was in a safe pair of hands.

CHAPTER FIFTY NINE

Tomorrow evening they would be returning home, but today was Sally's treat and in high expectation James drove them to Kitzbuhel, a very attractive Tyrolean town in the heart of the Kitzbuheler Alps. They drove through the cobbled streets; all were bedecked with predominantly blue umbrellas advertising the local Bavarian beers. It was a hive of activity and made him realise yet again how rejuvenated he always felt in this part of the world.

He tuned in again to Sally as she related the history of this ancient town and Her hotel that dated back to 1582.

'As a family we have been coming here twice a year during the ski season and I am sure you will just adore the elegance and style...'
As she was describing the annual ski trip his mind drifted back to his first ski holiday in Wengen with the Palmers; he remembered with such clarity looking at the sepia photograph hanging on the wall of their hotel. It showed an old steam train, its single carriage full of skiers which it would take to the top of the slopes; one of these was pointed out by Jeremy and identified as his father.

The thought of Jeremy made his eyes go moist; he was such a wonderful man, he epitomised the concept of a gentleman; he had become his father figure and he did hope that when things settled down that they might re-engage that friendship.

He came back to the present and tuned in again to Sally.

'....when it came to choosing a place to go to finishing school it just seemed so obvious that Kitzbuhel was ideal, as not only would I learn how to cook and get out of a car without showing my knickers, I would also be able to learn both French and German.'

He pulled himself together, now was not the time to be maudlin. He chipped in with,

'so that one day you might be able to translate posters depicting an advert for Eagle's Nest, ja?'

'Ja,' she replied and then paused before giving him a searching look, 'I am saying too much, I feel that I just lost you.'
'You did very briefly because I was thinking of my father and how he might have brought me here

to ski, as he did every year with my mother; it was their special treat and, unfortunately, my sister and I were not included. But it meant so much to them to be together that I can only love them all the more for that. Those moments I never had is the demon that drives me, but please believe me you will never lose me.'

She blew him a kiss, her face was triumphant, she knew he would enjoy the hotel.
And he did and his attempt to be cool and unimpressed was very transparent and finally, as they entered the very stylish marble-walled cocktail bar, he could not contain himself any longer.

'It is superb, as I knew it would be; I didn't imagine for one moment that the Parkinson's would settle for anything less.'
They crossed over to the bar on which sat a silver ice bucket containing a bottle of Crystal Roederer, at its side two crystal flute glasses and, as if by magic, a waiter with a French accent appeared.

'Shall I open the bottle Miss Parkinson?'
'Naturellement.'
He joined in with.

'Merci Phillipe.'
'You know Phillipe.'
'No, but my French is good enough to read his name badge.'
She shook her head. 'Imbecile.'

They sat down and he congratulated her on the most wonderful bottle from one of the very best champagne houses and, after an excellent lunch, it was her turn to take him up a mountain, this time in the gondola from which they could see the route of probably the most famous classic ski-race of them all, the Hahnenkamn which, even in its summer garb looked terrifying.

From the main ski area Sally pointed out the numerous chairlifts that in winter lead to the many ski-runs of varying difficulties. This and the fact that the snowfall is so reliable have earned Kitzbuhel the mantle of Tyrol's City of Sport. In addition, hotels such as the Hotel Weisses Rossl have ensured its reputation as a playground for the rich.

'You seem remarkably quiet Mr Carrington.'
'If I am, it is because I am absorbing this wonderful mountain air. As soon as we get back home I shall be angling for a chance to join the Parkinson's on next year's foray to Kitzbuhel.'
She gave him a peck on the cheek.

'I know them quite well; I will see what I can arrange.'
Meanwhile lets go down and have a closer look at the town, I feel quite thirsty'.

They found an attractive bistro and sat under the loggia, its three open sides giving them a real flavour of the area. As the afternoon drifted by once again their thoughts were drawn inevitably to the future; as he was the one with the awkward decisions, Sally sensibly determined to let him set the pace.

'When we get home things will have changed forever, we must both be resolute and I have to discuss with Kate how we can best move forward and this will mean talking to the boys, and God knows how we will manage that. Then, when they have come to terms with these changes, I want them to meet you and see that you are not some awful witch and Kate will also have to introduce them to Mr Mortimer.'

Sally gently touched his arm and interrupted him, her face conveying her compassion,

'James, when you refer to him as Mr Mortimer it sounds as if you resent him, when in fact you must come to terms with him as Johnnie. He is as a big a piece in the jigsaw puzzle as I am and when I do meet Kate, I hope that we can eventually be friends. I sincerely hope this, as I am sure that any hostility will make it more difficult for the boys to come to terms with two new people in their lives.'

'They will love you.'

'Well I do hope so, but I do realise that we have to proceed slowly; I would move in with you tomorrow, but where we choose to live is also a big decision as I clearly would prefer not to move into Woolmington Manor as it will have too many happy memories for you.'

James looked down into the remains of his stein of beer; she could see the cogs grinding in his head. He drew in a deep breath, 'Right; Milford Hall is where we are going to live; I have already started the ball rolling, both with the owner David Gilbert and the estate agent Andrew Travers and from now on I want you to be party to the negotiations.'

He suddenly appeared more relaxed; and continued,

'I have revisited the house and had a very convivial discussion with the owner but, because it was a very impulsive visit we are both keeping our options open. He is though a very decent guy and I know we can somehow reach an agreement.'

She looked at him quizzically.

'You mean you just turned up on his doorstep?'

'Yes, if I had thought about it too much I would probably have chickened out.'

She leaned forward and took his hand; her face was alive with excitement,

'Tell me about it.'

He related the story of, how once again when in despair, he had returned to those great iron gates with the Rising Sun motif – realising once again how appropriate that emblem was to the family motto Ever to aspire to higher things. He remembered as if yesterday, how he had been drawn to this refuge as a fourteen year old boy who had just heard his mother pronounce his father's imminent death.

This time instead of looking through the gates at the great stone building that had belonged to his grandfather Sir Albert Staincliffe, he had found the courage to go through them and call, first of all at the lodge, where the former gamekeeper still lived. His wife Mrs Price had been so pleased to see him and had given him some background on Mr Gilbert, the present owner. Armed with this sketchy knowledge he had summoned up the courage to ring the doorbell.

She sensed his apprehension but did not interrupt as he described standing there not knowing what to expect.

He continued the story.

'After about a minute I heard the click of leather shoes on a tiled floor, a few seconds later the large oak door swung inwards and I was confronted by a grey haired man in his fifties. He gave me a knowing smile and greeted me quite unexpectedly as, 'J R Carrington Leicester and England number ten!'

He saw the mixture of astonishment and amusement on Sally's face.

'His son it turned out had also played rugby for the Leicester Tigers and he remembered my car registration, having seen it many times at the training ground.'

'The ice had been immediately broken and I was invited in for lunch, David Gilbert indicating that I should go through to the study. My heart was pounding as I opened the door that led into the short corridor at the end of which was the study door, its location firmly remembered from the many happy times spent in this room with my father.'

Sally listened attentively, thrilled to be party to such a moment, a privilege that she doubted had been afforded to Sally. In this she was right, his wife had steadfastly refused to even peek at the house from the end of the drive, as she feared this would encourage her husband's dream of living there.
 'Do go on, this is fascinating and so exciting.'
He described the study, which was exactly the same as when they left – even the whisky was Macallan and it was hidden in the same butler's pantry which was concealed in the bookcase.
 James hesitated and she sensed something emotional was coming. His lip trembled as he described the moment when he had opened a cream envelope addressed to David Gilbert; the handwriting which he had known instantly to be his father's.
He inhaled again before tremulously continuing.
 'Inside was a letter written in a firm sloping hand, it said,

Welcome to Milford Hall – look after it well
I have a feeling that my son might want it back one day!
Sincerely

Robert Carrington'

David Gilbert he explained, had been throughout, both understanding and encouraging as he rightly sensed the impact that the letter might have on his totally unexpected guest.
 The soup and sandwiches had, however, given them both the opportunity to acquaint themselves with each other's hopes and aspirations. The current owner it transpired, had played to a decent level of club rugby with Northampton so could understand just how good the Carrington and Lawson combination had been.

 'David had seemed very surprised that I had retired so young, as he put it.'
She looked at closely. 'And why did you?'
 'I was twenty seven, rugby had been very good to me but business was taking up most of my time and besides youngsters like his son Steve were snapping at my heels, so I got out before they flattened me!
She knew this was modesty. Her father had said when he first knew she was seeing James.
 'At the time he retired he and Edward Lawson would both have been selected in any journalist's Worldwide top rugby team.'

He appeared pensive. Rugby it is a team game, it taught me the importance of those around you and yet, I did not accord that belief to the best team mate anyone ever had and that will live with me for ever.'

He looked up into her blue eyes and saw a kind understanding face; it gave him the confidence to continue.
 'Forgive me; I have been rambling on a bit.'

Sally shook her head. 'Always remember that you did not cause Edwards death: Time is a great healer and it was that accident that denied you both the opportunity to have re-kindled your friendship.

'Your family background and your determination to restore your inheritance, I find it fascinating and want so much to be part of it. I think all of this history is something of which you should be rightly proud.'
She saw his spirits soar; He looked pleased as he challenged her.
'And what about your family history?'

'Gentleman Farmer is how someone once dubbed my father and I guess that is about right. He comes from generations of farmers who were constantly buying land and expanding. Apart from Manston Hall, which is in effect home farm, we have eighteen tenant farmers with a mix of arable and livestock. We all hunt and have ten or twelve horses around, so if Asprey is not up to hunting we have a big grey gelding that will suit you. My mother's family are all stockbrokers, as is my brother Guy who lives in Chalfont St Giles and works in the city, which is something I would hate. However, he seems to love the cut and thrust of London life; he is also very keen on sport, so was mightily impressed when Granny Parkinson told him who you were, well the England and Lion's part of it; he is not too keen about the Leicester connection.'
'Why, who does he play for?'
'Richmond, second fifteen I am afraid, although he occasionally gets called up for the firsts. He is also keen on squash and golf so you also have that in common and being my brother he is a really nice chap!'

'I look forward to meeting him and you, of course, will get to meet my sister, Louise, who is married to a barrister and they have two children and live in the Cotswolds. And then of course, there is my mother from whom I inherited my ambition; she will love you and before you worry about being regarded as the wicked witch, she knows all about my declining relationship with Kate and that you had nothing to do with it.'

He looked at his watch and suggested it was time to go, although he insisted it was only au revoir. The next time they visited the town it would be wearing its winter mantle of snow.
She clung to his arm, she had never been happier and she too was looking forward to being back in Rutland planning their future together and meeting his family.
They drove back to Appesbach, both with their own excited thoughts, both praying that somehow they could find a solution that would satisfy the dreams of four adults without demolishing the lives of two young boys, as yet unaware of the gathering storm; or maybe their intuitive young minds had sensed that all was not well, Sally hoped so.
The yellow walls of the Landhaus zu Appesbach was a welcome sight and although their wonderful holiday would be over tomorrow, they had had a fantastic time and the thought of going home and starting a new life together was even more exciting.
They skipped up the steps into the drawing room where Peter, the manager, was on hand to meet them.
'Mr Carrington you are leaving us tomorrow, may I offer you and your wife a glass of champagne on the terrace.'
They needed no further invitation and followed him to one of the tables shielded from the

sun by the yellow umbrellas. In silence they both gazed across the lake to the mountains on the other side.

James was the first to speak.

'What are you thinking?'

'Of just how much I want to be Mrs Carrington and how thrilled I was when Peter made that assumption.'

His hand reached across the table and stroked the third finger on her left hand.

'First I have to ask your father's permission; what if he declines my offer, weddings can after all be an expensive job?'

She tossed her head back and laughed.

'Mummy would kill him!'

As ever, laughter relieved the tension and they were soon planning the future, a new beginning that would offer four adults a new chance to rebuild their shattered lives, but one which might also crush the happiness of two young boys. Sally had been right, she and Johnnie Mortimer were fundamental to this and she prayed that Kate and James would accept and recognise that their future happiness would be best resolved with give and take. She and Johnnie were after all taking on a potentially new complication; she hoped not and secretly wondered if maybe she should meet Johnnie to explain her willingness for compromise and understanding.

'A penny for your thought, or should I say a pfennig.'

'James, if I keep drifting off on a cloud then that is because of what you have done to my life, there is so much I want to do with you and so many people I want you to meet and that I want to meet and at the top of that priority list is your two sons and your mother, I know she will give me the low down on 'Mr Wonderful'.'

He stood up and took her hand.

'You are coming with me and I will show you the low down, quite literally, on Mr Wonderful.'

'Oh you are awful, but I love you.'

He smirked at her.

'Thank you Dick Emery.'

They passed Peter on the stairs, once again his serious Austrian demeanour unable to really appreciate this handsome pair of Brits.

CHAPTER SIXTY

Kate and Johnnie arrived back in the UK and decided to spend a couple of days in Yorkshire to draw up a battle plan to integrate their three businesses into one.

Yorkshire and North Yorkshire in particular, is a closed shop to incomers; it takes twenty years to gain any credence and therefore the strongest part of their joint venture was the Mortimer name.

Kate took the initiative and suggested that as the Mortimer name carried more clout and also had a long commercial history they should call the reformed Estate Agency business Mortimer Associates.

Johnnie gave her what they call in Yorkshire, a canny look.

'I do believe we are on the same wavelength with that idea Kate, but only because it will include Mrs Mortimer - or have you forgotten the promise you made in Dublin; if you have, I have the telephone number of that Irish witness and her Dachshund!

The second part of the business did, of course, include her beloved Woolmington Manor and, as Johnnie had not as yet seen the building, she suggested that they should visit tomorrow so that he could consider the best way of integrating this into his existing 'health farm' business and also agree on the most suitable area for their accommodation

Having called Woolmington twice without getting a response she presumed that James and Sally - she somehow got her name out, must still be wherever their tryst had taken them.

His response was more than enthusiastic and became even more so as they swept down the drive that led them past the lake from which water filtered into the moat at the front of the house. She sensed his approval but not his response.

'Kate, I don't know how I can ask you to give up all of this, it is straight from a Hollywood movie, it is breath-taking.'

She put a finger on his lips and marched him into the house.

'If we can organise a wing of the house for our personal use, then in effect I will not be leaving and James Carrington will have to lump it.'

He still looked apprehensive.

'All this antique furniture; it is far too grand to allow to leave at the mercy of Joe Public.'

'Okay, but I can use it as a bargaining point with James, he is after all moving into a huge house which will surely need furniture to replace that which the present owner will remove, and in any case I intend to take the pick of it with me.'

The intensity of how she said it confirmed yet again to Johnnie just how committed she was to their future.

Johnnie had his thinking cap on and his lips were pursed as he blurted out,

'The stables and the horses what do you plan to do with them?'

'I have heard that James's new lady friend is very keen on hunting and so I imagine that he will take his mares and foals to Milford Hall.'

He looked at her quizzically 'His lady friend is called Sally Parkinson and until you can use her name instead of euphemisms you are not going to release James from your subconscious and you will not really be my Kate - my soon to be Mrs Mortimer.'

She pouted and flung her arms around him and they were thus embraced when James walked in with Sally Parkinson.

There was a long silence, finally broken by James.

'We had to meet sometime, so why not now? Please sit down everyone; let's do the civilised thing and have a drink. Kate, why don't you get the glasses and I will get the bubbly.'

They both disappeared in opposite directions leaving Johnnie and Sally to fidget around the embarrassment; she finally took the initiative and offered her hand to Johnnie.

'Neither of us deliberately caused the split which caused Kate and James to separate, so we have no reason not to be friends and I do genuinely hope that this is how it will work out for all four of us.'

He took her hand.

'I do so hope so because there are two young boys who are going to need a lot of love and attention.'

Sally interrupted him.

'Johnnie, you are so right and I promise you I will support you all the way on this.'

Their hands were still clasped when James and Kate appeared with the bubbly.

'So bonding proceeds, if you take my drift.'

The laughter came more easily as James poured the drinks and proposed the toast.

'Today's meeting was totally unexpected, but it seems that we are all prepared to adopt a very grown up attitude and I would like to propose a toast to us all and to the two young boys who will not understand what has happened.'

The response was muted but genuine and whilst the conversation gradually became less strained it had obvious limitations and, to break the ice further, Kate suggested that Sally might like to see the horses.

'Yes please and perhaps the groom might like to take me on a tour.' Realising as she said it that the expression had obvious overtones.

However, it did not elicit any comment and she followed James from the drawing room and into the hall and then through the kitchen and into the boot room where he collected a large circular key ring from which dangled a dozen or so keys.

Taking her hand, he kissed her gently and murmured, 'well done, in fact I think all four of us managed that quite well.'

She gave him a wry smile and effected to mop her brow.

'Hopefully that will be the ice breaker, now let's look at the real ladies in your life.'

He took her hand and led her into the stable yard where, with the exception of four boxes, all the bottom doors were closed. Peeping into one of the open doors, her closer inspection revealed that the straw beds were neatly banked against the walls and the hay nets stuffed with fresh clean smelling hay.

She sensed him watching her and turned to give him a thumbs up.

'Your stables lass is very neat and tidy and our visit was unscheduled; I like that.'

'Yes, I am hoping that you get on, as I would like Sue, that is her name, to maybe move with us to Milford Hall.'

He took her hand and guided her up the external stone steps that led to the office, the private sanctum where he kept all his racing journals, sales catalogues and endless other information on thoroughbred breeding.

Around the walls hung dozens of racing photographs including many famous stallions whose progeny had been instrumental in shaping the modern thoroughbred; descendants of which he had bred his own mares to.

On his desk she noticed a framed black and white photograph of two teenage rugby players; it bore the legend 'Carrington and Lawson, an unstoppable duo.'

She lifted the navy blue cap with its silk tassel which bore the logo. England v Wales 1948.

'Your first schoolboy international cap?'

He shook his head and his eyes were moist as he replied,

'No, that is Edward Lawson's second cap, my second cap sits on his desk or what used to be his desk,' he corrected himself. 'We exchanged them, it was a sort of schoolboy blood bond that could never be broken; which was how it would have remained, but for my stupidity.'

Sally realised that the magic of this day was in danger of drifting away and so, seizing his arm, she frog marched him down the stone stairs and back into the stable yard. Without pausing she led him through the archway that she rightly guessed led out to the paddocks.

Four mares with foals were in one of the larger paddocks and, the day being warm, were taking shade under the large chestnut trees. She stood enjoying the scene, particularly when every so often one of the youngsters would agitate the other foals and they would race away kicking their heels in the air. As a natural horsewoman, she was absorbed by their games, all of which helped build the muscle that would one day determine their ability to race.

They moved on to another ten acre paddock, which housed four yearlings standing in the shade of a group of oak trees. the horses heard the approach, causing the biggestof them to flick up his heels and race off to the bottom of the field; the others immediately springing in pursuit.

If you love horses as much as Sally and James, there is noting more exciting. He put his arm around her shoulder and without prompting, she whispered.

'The chestnut colt with the big black end is the looker but the bay filly she can outrun him every time.'

He nodded; Kate would never have spotted that.

They finally made their way back into the house and as the host, so to speak, James initiated the conversation they were all avoiding.

'We have now all met and it has all been very civilised, which is how I hope it will remain.

However, we have only crossed the stepping stones, several big bridges lie ahead.'

Johnnie held up his hand; James nodded.

'James if I might interrupt, we all know the big challenge will be to ask Charles and Edward to somehow be as remotely understanding as we are.'

He drew a deep breath, 'James and Sally, perhaps it will be helpful to let you know that I do have some understanding of what you are anticipating. A few years ago I lost my wife and two children in a car accident in the Alps. The thought that I would never ever see them again; it left me bereft and desolate of all hope, the future was for others not for me. You are lucky, you are going to see your children again and sooner than you think, the monsters that are Sally and me, will become slowly tolerable. Hopefully their friends and being away at boarding school should also help as they will have their pals and their routines to occupy them.'

The silence seemed endless as they each tussled with their own thoughts.

Finally, Kate looked across at Sally.

'Perhaps you are not such a bad old witch after all, but you are going to have your work cut out with this one!'

Despite protestation from James, Kate's aside further lightened the mood and the butt of her humour held up his hand in protest.

'As self- designated chairman of this meeting, I James Carrington, declare this meeting adjourned.'

Having said that, they all realised that two people were leaving and two should be staying, a problem resolved by Johnnie who offered to drop Sally off at Manston Hall.

'Only at the gate, as God knows what your parents might think!' he added.

CHAPTER SIXTY ONE

The house seemed suddenly very empty and neither James nor Kate knew how to begin the discussion that was both inevitable and essential. Instead they sat either side of the drawing room fireplace waiting for the other to begin.

He looked across at her, willing some words to come out. She looked up aware that he was watching.

'How did we get to this, we had everything?'

'And yet everything was not enough. You had to invent a problem and, despite all my pleadings to the opposite, you relentlessly insisted that I had been seeing Sally Parkinson, which I had not. However, it is now too late and maybe it was meant to be. In which case we are both fortunate to have met someone else and having met Johnnie Mortimer, I like him and you seem to have struck up quite a deep understanding. I hope very much that life will be to be kind to you and give you both the happiness that it seems was so ruthlessly snatched away from him. Have you been staying here or in Yorkshire?'

'James, you know very well where I have been staying.'

'I most certainly do not.'

She looked up.

'Your friend Andrew Travers, he will have kept you informed.'

'Kate, I have been to Germany and Austria with Sally, Andrew Travers had no knowledge of that and so why would you think that?'

She looked him squarely in the eye.

'How strange that he should be on the same aeroplane and staying at the same hotel.'

'Where have you been?'

'Dublin.'

'Okay, if I was going to Dublin, I would fly from East Midlands and the only hotel I know is the Shelbourne where we both stayed after the England game about ten years ago. Most of our friends would have taken that route; so is this where your paths crossed?'

She nodded uncomfortably.

'Kate, do yourself a big favour and stop being suspicious of everyone around you. You have met a nice man, in fact a very nice guy, give him and yourself a chance of happiness and stop believing that people want to hurt you. What is done is done and we must, for the sake of Charles and Edward and also Johnnie and Sally, remain good friends.

He held out his hands, her eyes were moist and so were his as she whispered.

'I want that.'

The situation was becoming emotionally dangerous, too many promises had been made and two other adults as well as two young boys stood to have their lives destroyed unless a realisation of where they had now moved to was accepted.

The new Kate, the only one that Johnnie had ever known, grasped the nettle.

'What about a cup of tea and you can tell me when you intend to move out; to Milford Hall, yes?'

This time he was on the back foot, surely Andrew Travers had not let this slip. He decided to do a little fishing of his own.

'Why should I be moving, surely it is you who are moving up to Yorkshire, to move in with Johnnie or at least that is what I had presumed from your comments when your parents last visited and you suggested moving the boys up north to Sedbergh.'

She set out for the kitchen, desperately needing time to think as what he suggested was the more practical option, but certainly not her preferred choice in view of the plans she had hatched with Mr M.

Her silence also had alarm bells ringing for him, as selling Woolmington Manor was essential for his purchase of Milford Hall.

Two wary people sat staring at the Aga, willing the kettle to boil, as the financial implications suddenly asserted a reality check. The kettle whistled and he leapt up to fill the teapot, which was part of a tea service given by Kate's parents. This in turn evoked the warm memories he had for Kate's father, Jeremy Palmer, it also reminded him of the tigress her mother had turned out to be, never more so than when he had defended himself by alluding to her unfaithful dalliance with her husband's friend from his student days at Oxford. His reverie was interrupted.

'James, since I have been running the estate agency business in Yorkshire I have adopted your attitude to Eating an Elephant. So why don't we sit down and compile a strategic way forward and reduce the problem into thin slices.'

He smiled as her poured the tea.

'I can hardly object to that, so let us be honest and make this a list of where we really want to be, which may include letting slip a few rather private thoughts.'

She nodded and he slipped into the study to collect pens and paper; they both scribbled away for twenty minutes or so.

Sally opened the proceeding and her first statement of intent really did shake him and lay down a high bench mark of integrity.

- 'Johnnie has asked me to marry him and I have said Yes - How about you?'
- I would like to marry Sally.'
- 'Have you asked her?' He looked up; she was staring at him, intently.
- 'Yes.'
- 'Do you intend to buy Milford Hall?'
- 'If I can finance it, but that would mean selling Woolmington.'
- 'Have you lined up a buyer?'
- 'No.' He looked at her, she knew he was telling the truth.
- 'What about the boys? I do know that it is important for their sakes that they stay at Uppingham, but can we afford it.'
- 'I believe so, but it will mean sacrifices.'

This time he asked the questions.

- 'Do you intend to live in Yorkshire?'
- 'Yes', she decided for the moment not to reveal Johnnie's offer to buy out James's share of Woolmington until she had discussed it in the reality of being back home.
- 'What about my investment in Braithwaite's?'
- 'I presumed you had accepted that it was my business.'
- 'As you accept that the property investments and my shares in Fordmill are solely mine.'
- 'I did not say that, but I will be reasonable!'
- 'Well I have to tell you that they are worth a great deal less since Edward's death.'

He attempted to scrutinise her mind; no doubt Johnnie would advise her, as would her father. However, the latter might well be the one to caution against unnecessary greed as he knew first-hand how lawyer's fees could eat into the assets being discussed. James mused the idea that he might speak with Jeremy Palmer or was that unwise, he was not sure.

He decided to continue firing the bullet point headlines.

- 'Kate, you also realise that this home we have put together has so many memories for both of us, when all this is settled and you look at a painting or piece of furniture, don't push away the fond memories, that way we can all be good friends.'
- 'Also I beg of you to remember that I did not precipitate these events. A combination of fate and chance combined to send you to Yorkshire for a break from the pressures here. You met JM and my best friend's untimely death threw Sally and me together.'
- He sensed that she was about to denounce him for falling out with Edward and he moved swiftly to nip this in the bud. 'I went to the scene of my friend's death because I was devastated and desolate. Serendipity, call it what you will, but that is how the fates construed to bring Sally and me together.'
- She interrupted him, 'Were you pleased to see her?'
- 'Yes, and when you met Johnnie at the health farm, were you pleased to see him?'
- 'I was flattered that someone should find me attractive.'
- 'But were you pleased to meet him?'
- 'Yes and I think that we have covered enough ground today.'
- 'I agree and I think we both know where our future lies, also that it is based on consideration and an understanding of each other's position and, most importantly, a mutual love and concern for Charles and Edward.'
- She stood up. 'Which bedroom would you like?'
- 'I'll have Tuscany.'
- 'And you have Wensleydale, that way no one has Our Room and you will feel almost at home,' he added mischievously.

She turned on her heels and was gone, so for the second time today he went out to see the horses, hoping this might free his mind of the emotions generated by the revelations made by both himself and Kate.

He trotted up the stone steps to his office, his heart as ever lightened by the prospect of positive thinking and planning. He pulled the latest edition of British & European Stallions from the library of breeding tomes and was soon lost in the myriad of observations and advice available as he flicked alphabetically through the coloured photographs. The variety in terms of looks and size could be confusing to the uninformed but he had by now, through observation and attentive listening to trainers and other breeders settled on a breeding pattern of mating his mares to stallions with known 'Nicks'.

The term 'Nick', refers to the results of analysed data which shows a pattern of success whereby certain stallions when bred to mares receptive to a particular pedigree, produce offspring designed to meet the mare owner's criteria. This of course depends on their preference for sprinters, middle distance horses or jumpers etc. Not only did it raise the chances of success as a racehorse, it also enhanced the sales potential when the offspring went through the sales ring. Buyers too are looking for these Nicks.

Perhaps the best way of understanding them is the explanation evinced by the great American stallion owner Bull Hancock –Best to drill where you have previously found oil!

Every so often of course a stallion arrives whose success on the racecourse or the success of his offspring is so appealing, that breeders forsake the traditional precepts and accede to the overwhelming desire to use this bloodline. In the USA and Canada, breeders are more likely to mate their mares to stallions with a proven track record, even if they are poorly bred. For instance, Northern Dancer was a small and immature two year old but he was very sound and very competitive and went on to win two thirds of the American Triple Crown as a three year old.

Many of his progeny did not look like him and it was one of these, named Nijinsky, a giant of a horse from his first crop, that would establish his fame. He was trained in Ireland by arguably the greatest trainer of them all Vincent O'Brien. So too was a horse that in size looked more like Northern Dancer, he was diminutive flashy chestnut also a Derby winner. They, like their sire, would breed a galaxy of stars that would dominate thoroughbred breeding throughout the world for the next thirty years.

However, if all breeders turn to this new phenomena, the stallion gene pool would soon become too small and to in-bred; outcrosses are essential, which is why 'Nicks ' are so important to the breeding industry.

James's head was immersed in this so did not at first hear Kate calling him from the stable yard below. He put his head around the door to be told that the boys were having an exeat from school and would be coming home after rugby on Saturday. His heart sank, it was a meeting he was dreading and he was also annoyed that she had arranged it without at least discussing it with him.

She was sitting in a determined mood at the kitchen table, two coffee cups and a percolator set out as if for a business meeting. He was agitated, but resolved to keep calm.

'Could you not have spoken to me before arranging this?'

'We have to face the facts and so do the boys, it might as well be sooner rather than later. How do you think we should present it to them?'

'As kindly as possible.'

'Obviously James, but when and where?'

'I have checked the calendar and Charles has a home match against Ampleforth and Edward is playing away against Oakham so there is very little in terms of distance. Why don't I go to Oakham?'

'So that you can bathe in the glory of your son's exploits on the rugby pitch.'

He fought hard to control his temper; the considerate truce they had agreed less than two hours ago was rapidly evaporating.

'Kate, I am just as happy - or sad, to collect Charles, so I will go to Uppingham but I beg you to remember what Johnnie Mortimer said, that unlike him, we do at least still have our children, although they will need a far more sympathetic approach than the aggression you are displaying right now.'

The mention of the latter struck a chord, her hand was trembling as she returned the coffee cup to its saucer and met his gaze, neither expression was any longer belligerent.

'You are right James, I will collect Charles and if you agree, I will make an appointment to see the Headmaster to make him aware that both boys will need some extra consideration to help them through this turmoil.'

'That is exactly what you should do and you are far more able to convey that need than I am.'

He stretched his hand across the table, she placed hers palm down in his and his eyes were drawn to her engagement ring, which was not the large single diamond he had presented to her on a '99' ice cream cone at Bucklers Hard all those years ago, but a large dark blue sapphire. She attempted to withdraw her hand and he gently let her go. Nothing was said, but everything had become even more crystal clear. He stood up.

'So that sorts out Saturday, meanwhile I am going back to the stable office.'

He was confused, the ring and its implications should have left him pleased and yet it had evoked a feeling of jealousy; still bewildered, he opened the small office fridge and poured himself a Macallan. Even this, his favourite tipple, took a few minutes to steady the ship and gave him a clearer insight into how Kate must have reacted to the rumours, albeit false, that she had experienced when so called friends had reported his attention to Sally Parkinson at the Architects and Builders Dinner. He continued to stare absentmindedly at the stallion book and finally the soporific effects of the Macallan gradually diluted his jealousy and instead he realised how intent Kate was towards Johnnie and, with spirits uplifted, he called Sally on her private line at Manston.

'Manston Estate Office, Sally Parkinson speaking.'

'Stevie here' - This was their private code - a reference to Stevie Wonder's I just called to say I loved you.

'This is a pleasant surprise; to what do I owe the honour?'

He related the events regarding the ring and its overt implications regarding Kate's obvious determination to spend the rest of her life with Johnnie. A very happy Miss Parkinson was anxious to see him and, bridges now burned, he suggested the White Horse at Empingham at around seven thirty this evening, a suggestion that was joyously accepted.

Rather than spoil the evening, he also related the plans for the weekend and she fully accepted that this would curtail any meetings they might have envisaged.

With so many imminent decisions he returned the Stallion Statistics to the bookcase, his star filly winner of the Musidora Stakes at York, was after all only a two year old and would hopefully race again next year, so breeding was not a pressing consideration.

He heard Sue calling the foals and decided to give her a hand getting them in. He grabbed a couple of the larger head collars and two of the foal collars from the tack room and followed her to the nearest paddock where all the mares and their offspring were waiting expectantly. They all knew where they were heading and that it meant supper time so it would have been easy to have opened the gate and let them make their own way home, but from day one they had been handled and this ingrained sense of discipline made the task of breaking them in so much easier.

The straw beds had been put down by Sue and less than half an hour later the residents were happily munching away and back in the tack room James passed on his visitor's compliment regarding the immaculate state of the yard and the neatly forked bedding.

The groom gave him a smile and a rather coy look.

'That would be Miss Parkinson then, in which case I will take it as a compliment.'
And with that she jumped on her bike and pedalled off down the lane to her cottage, leaving him with a wry expression on his face.

He returned to the house and joined Kate in the small sitting room where she was watching the six o'clock news. Neither had anything relevant to say and he watched the clock move slowly to six thirty, at which point he announced that as there was little point in maintaining this monastic silence, he was going out.

'No prizes for guessing where,' her curt response.
He gave her a sympathetic look and suggested that a couple of days in Yorkshire might be helpful but once again she went on the attack, his attempted consideration was swept aside.

'For whose benefit,' she snapped back.

'I was only...' He stopped himself, this was heading in the wrong direction and the longer it was protracted, the more she was going to spoil his evening and so he quietly closed the door and left.

With so much to discuss, the evening with Sally was nevertheless, relaxed and enjoyable and both agreed that the chance encounter with the other two had enabled all four of them to be above board with each other even though Sally was still very apprehensive that Kate might still refuse to give James his freedom. However, when he related the open conversation in which he and Kate had outlined their future she became more relaxed, even suggesting that she might help him choose her engagement ring.

'I am a man of impeccable taste, have no fear you will be proud to show it to your mother and granny, although first of all I have to seek your father's permission.'
She gave him a beguiling smile.

'Don't you worry, he has no chance against the three Parkinson women, in fact, you are invited for lunch a week on Sunday at twelve thirty sharp.'
Their conversation was interrupted by the landlord who invited them to proceed to the dining room as the food was ready. Over dinner, Sally gently probed for a timetable of events that would enable them to move in together. He shook his head and she saw the anguish in his eyes as he related his apprehension about meeting and explaining to the boys of the change in circumstances and the new people that would enter their lives.

She placed her hand on his, no words were necessary and in any case neither of them could think of anything remotely appropriate.

'Have you spoken with your mother, can she help?'

'Perhaps.'

'Why don't you go and see her tomorrow, she is after all fully aware of what is going on.'

He lifted his eyes and attempted a smile.

'I will go and see her tomorrow, I am sorry to have spoilt our evening but I guess we have to get used to sharing the lows as well as the highs.'

'Yes and don't you ever forget that.'

He settled the bill and they walked slowly back to the car park both silently praying that nothing would keep them apart.

'Let me know how you get on and when you do see your mother, please extend our lunch invitation to her, I am sure mother will be delighted to see her again - let's hope they can still recognise each other after all these years.'

'She will,' he promised, 'she has seen your photograph and immediately spotted the resemblance.'

Arriving home he found a note on the kitchen table. 'Took your advice and gone to Yorkshire for a few days to catch up with the paperwork - see you on Saturday evening.'

As promised, he called his mother next day from the office and went for supper with her that evening. It was a conversation that she knew had to happen and listened sympathetically, although she warned him that she would not take sides, 'Kate would always be welcome,' she declared.

CHAPTER SIXTY TWO

Finally it was Saturday and he set out for Oakham to collect Edward. As usual, despite a resolute display from the home side, Uppingham triumphed and his son displayed once again his relish for tackling and a lightening burst of acceleration as he glided past opponents.

The try he scored and converted evoked a comment from one of the other Uppingham parents standing alongside James,

'It looks like you could soon be only the second best Carrington to play for England.'

He nodded and laughed with the others. 'Let's hope you are right, Ian.'

The final whistle went and he joined the other parents for a cup of tea. He feigned an interest in their banter but his heart was pounding as he sought to imagine the right moment when he must deliver the shattering news to his son, his thoughts were interrupted by a familiar voice.

'Hi Dad, what did you think of the game?'

'You all played so well, particularly the forwards, they really stuck to their task, some of those Oakham lads were very big and well coached.'

'And you young man had another brilliant game.'

David Downes cutting in to confirm the observation his brother Ian had made earlier.

Finally with others they drifted back to the cars, some boys like Edward having an exeat, others climbed into the school mini-bus for the return trip to school.

Edward joined his father in the front of the car, his mood as effervescent as ever which heightened his father's apprehension and made the oncoming conversation even more daunting.

He started the engine and immediately his son switched the radio channel to Radio One and perversely the first song was the Rolling Stones version of It's all over now.

With a sigh he switched the engine off and sought his son's hand.

'Edward, you know how much mummy and I love you and Charles.'

The boys nodded his head, only slightly bemused by the question as this was an assurance they had received so many times.

His father drew a deep breath and heard himself saying,

'Mummy and me, we have been having a difficult time of late, we both love you and still like each other, but not enough to carry on living together.'

'Why not!'

The tearful accusation rang out; its words pierced his heart, which suddenly felt like a block of heavy stone in his chest.

'People fall out of love...'

'Does Charles know?'

'Mummy has collected him from school and she will have told him.'

'Please say you don't mean it Dad, please don't leave us.'

Even in the darkness of the car's interior he could see the small athletic figure of an hour ago was now suddenly a hunched up defenceless child; his child. Did he have the right to do this and how was Kate coping? What a nightmare and yet he clung to the hope that time and explanation this weekend might help them find a way out of the morass that he and his wife had created.

'Let's talk about it at home with Charles and your mother.'

'Yes, she won't let it happen.'

The small voice was stronger now; the defiance that had made his father successful was now exerting himself against that same figure.

He checked the impulse to say that it was Kate who had started this, he was too old to start hiding behind a woman's skirt and he also needed his wife to stand alongside and support what was happening.

James restarted the car and switched the radio back on. A small hand immediately switched it off, he did not intend to let his father hide behind this distraction, he would make him face the music of a more literal kind. He would gang up with his brother and mother to stop this happening.

The journey which normally took about forty minutes seemed to last forever, but finally they arrived and the drawing room lights confirmed that Kate had also returned. He opened the boot to off-load Edward's rugby kit but the small hand beat him to it and in a tremulous voice, Edward's pithy retort advised his father that he and Charles had to look after themselves in future. The father watched the boy disappear through the front door, the 'rock' in his chest growing heavier and heavier.

He hastened after Edward, anxious to make sure that Kate did not twist and weave the story in her favour, he was also anxious to see his eldest son whose thoughts would be deeper and more controlled than his brother, although the anguish would be just as raw.

He followed the voices to the kitchen where Kate stood clasping two sobbing boys. He joined them and they huddled together, tears streaming down all of their cheeks.

Finally Edward broke away from them and flopped on to the sofa and appealed to Kate.

'Don't let him do this mum.'

She joined him and to James's great relief declared that it was not just his father's fault.

'It is difficult for you to understand, but you must believe that we both love you and will always be here for you.'

Charles finally spoke.

'Is dad going to live with someone else?'

'Eventually.'

'So will we stay here with you?'

'Possibly, but whatever happens you will still see lots of him and we are still good friends even though we no longer love each other in the same way.'

She turned to James appealing for some help; he knelt on the floor with a hand on the knee each boy.

'When I was eighteen my father died and was taken away from me forever, but that is not going to happen to you, you will just see less of me but I will always be there to help and support you and, in any case, most of the time you will be at school with your friends, some of whom must also have parents who live apart.'

His eldest son looked him at him and his question was not anticipated by either parent.

'Are you going to live with Sally Parkinson?'

He saw his parent's bewilderment and knew he had hit the nail on the head.

Head in her hands and peering through her fingers his mother finally spoke.

'Whatever makes you say that?'

'I heard you and Granny Palmer arguing about her.'

'Did you tell Edward?'

Charles looked down, his voice much quieter as her replied, 'I hoped it wouldn't happen, so didn't want to worry him.'

James looked first at the boys and then towards his wife.

'We all need time to think and come to terms with everything. What your mother and I promise is that we will confide in you and promise that neither of us will suddenly go away and you two very special people need time to absorb what you have heard. We will do our utmost to prove to you that neither of us intend to disappear and will always let you know what is happening, and please be certain that we will always be there to help.'

Charles tapped Edward on the knee and they rose as one and made their way upstairs leaving two dejected parents to contemplate the bleakness they had created. Finally James spoke.

'We knew it was going to be difficult, have you still got the resolve to go through with it?'

Her reply was immediate.

'The lives of two other people are also on the line and in Johnnie's case I don't think he will get over it; more importantly, we are only putting off the next heartache and then we will be back in the same position, except that it will be worse, as the boys will think they can derail us again and they will start to see us in an even worse light. I really do think we have to be brave and see this through, that way we can remain as caring friends and I think that the boys will gradually see us in a different light, particularly when they have met Johnnie and Sally and I never thought I could contemplate that.'

'I agree, but God it is not going to be pleasant. I will get us a drink whilst you sort out supper.'

Meanwhile upstairs the atmosphere was still mutinous with Edward the main protagonist. His brother as usual, was contemplative and finally delivered his plan to his brother.

'We could go along with it just to keep the peace, but when Dad finally introduces us to this Sally Parkinson we can let her know quite clearly that Dad will have to choose between her and us and I think he will choose you and me.'

His brother gave him a cynical laugh and suggested this would be a good time to ask for the quad bike they had always wanted.

'Or two, what colour do you fancy Charlie?'

This bit of conniving lowered the atmosphere and both parents were more than surprised when they appeared in the kitchen in a more conciliatory mood, even more so when Edward's opening remark was so typical, 'what's for supper?'

'Beef Wellington'.

His brother's reaction a cynical. 'The fatted calf no less'.

James looked across at his wife and shook his head, but there was a small smile on his lips.

Dinner passed pleasantly enough, Kate reporting that the Headmaster had high hopes that, if Charles continued to produce the exam results achieved thus far, it should put him in with a good chance of being an Oxbridge candidate. To keep them both happy, James related the observation by Ian Downes that if Edward continued to play as he had this afternoon then his father would become only the second best Carrington to play for England. Charles's pleasure was a modest smile; his brother's was a cocky 'No Probs.'

After the meal they all went through into the drawing room and watched the Morecambe and Wise show, the non-stop humour helping to soften the mood and by bedtime a sort of normality prevailed.

It had been a difficult day for them all, but the boys definitely slept better than their parents whose dreams were tortured by the knowledge that whichever decision they made could cause grief to the other four lives concerned.

Sunday morning was awkward and, much as they wanted to talk about the future and give assurances, neither James nor Kate could find a way of broaching the subject. Also, neither of the boys was inclined to hold out an olive branch, quite the reverse, they were determined to make things as tricky as possible, even the sight of his mother standing ironing yesterday's rugby jerseys was subjected to Edward's far from innocent question on how they would manage when they went to stay with Dad and Sally Parkinson.

James looked up and was unable to keep the despair from his voice.

'Sally Parkinson is not a monster, please remember that and she will be only too pleased to wash and iron your kit.'

'Perhaps, but Mum is going to be lonely living in this house by herself so we are not just thinking about ourselves.' James looked at Kate hoping for some help which did eventually come.

'Edward, the truth is that I too have met someone else so you must not worry about me.'

His brother looked up astonished; this was clearly not what they were expecting to hear.

'When are we going to meet these people?'

'I think we should leave it for a couple of weeks so that you can come to terms with it.'

The tears welled in Edward's eyes.

'If we can ever come to terms with it!'

James looked his watch, it was eleven thirty.

'Why don't we have lunch at the Falcon on the way back to school, maybe a change of scene will help.'

The boys got up in unison, returning five minutes later with bags packed although they willingly opened them at the sight of a variety of chocolate bars on the kitchen table. James attempted to engage Charles re the Headmaster's conversation with his mother which prompted a few reluctant grunts, as did his praise for Edward's outstanding game at Oakham. He pulled the car to a halt outside the Inn and went to the bar hoping desperately that they would find other boys lunching with their parents who would form some distraction and, sure enough, they did spot other exeat returnees with whom they could share a coke.

'What are you having to eat?'

'Beef please.'

'And me too.'

They struggled through the main course and halfway through the dessert, the landlord's announcement for final orders afforded James the chance to glance at his watch and announce that exeat was over and it was time to report back to the boarding house.

They were met by a vigilant Housemaster, who greeted the boys with a warm welcome and for the parents a sympathetic and understanding smile. This was sadly not a new situation, several boys in his house had estranged parents and having their friends around them rather than bickering adults, often helped them cope better with the changing circumstances at home.

After the usual parental assurances he left them to say goodbye which was the most distressing moment of the whole weekend. Charles opened the door from the entrance porch to the hallway with a dignity beyond his years, advising his parents not worry as he would take care of his brother.

Kate and James bereft of speech could only nod as they watched the two boys, their boys, disappear into the sanctuary of the Brooklands boarding house.

The journey home was a desolate one, as was the rest of the evening. They did, however, both have their own thoughts which centred on how they could convey today's events to the new love in their lives.

CHAPTER SIXTY THREE

Minster UK was preparing to launch their new range of kitchen designs at the European Furniture Expo in Düsseldorf. This gave James the excuse to throw himself into work and spend as little time as possible at home, which also suited Kate. She had several pressing needs regarding her own business, one of these included converting Woolmington Manor into a health spa with a private wing for herself and Johnnie and of course the boys when they were at home during the holidays.

To assist her she had enlisted, at Johnnie's suggestion, an architect friend of his from Sheffield; hopefully this would be someone whom James would not know. This was confirmed when she answered the door bell and welcomed in Alex Brookes, a good looking tousled haired man in jeans and a Barbour jacket.

They went through into the kitchen and after coffee she took him on a tour of the house which seemed to make a very good impression although, like Johnnie, he was concerned that the furniture was rather too old and valuable to use in a public space.

Over more coffee he examined the plans of the Manor and suggested that the south wing with its fine view of Belvoir Castle would easily convert into a spacious apartment. He gave her a contemplative look.

'Rather than having to survey the property it would be much easier and less expensive if I could take these drawings away and copy them, is that possible?'

She thought for a moment.

It would be sod's law if James suddenly wanted them, but as both their names were on the title deeds she agreed. 'Why not.'

'I will post them back tomorrow, so look out for a long tubular package and in the meantime I will be on my way.'

Her heart was pounding as she watched his car snake its way down the lane and onto the road that led to the A1 and out of sight. Why should I worry about what James will think she argued with herself, he wouldn't flinch from what he was doing if he had decided to sell the house? Nevertheless her worst fears were founded when two days later James arrived home and left a brown cardboard tube addressed to herself on the kitchen table.

She tried to steady her nerves but the tremor in her voice gave her away.

'Where did you get that?'

'Sue stopped me in the lane, you were out and the postman left it with her.'

He looked at her enquiringly and saw the apprehension. His interest was immediately alerted.

'Aren't you going to open it, it is from Sheffield – and according to the label from Brookes, Challoner & Harvey. From recollection they are architects.'

His smugness emboldened her.

'Very well, you were going to know soon enough, it might as well be now.'

She removed the tape around the top rim and prised the lid off to reveal a set of plans stained by age and heard herself saying, 'I have been wondering how we can resolve this problem we have vis-a-vis Woolmington and Milford Hall.'

'Really?'

'Yes.' Her voice was steadier now.

'And what is this master plan you have hatched with your boyfriend; sorry, your fiancé?'

She outlined Johnnie's proposal to buy out James's share of the house, but omitted to mention the health spa idea.

He turned on his heel and was gone. She sat down, head in hands, not knowing whether to cry or call Johnnie for help and then she heard his footsteps in the hall and came back into the kitchen, his hands were behind his back and with a great flourish he produced a bottle of champagne and two flutes.

'I taught you too well. Congratulations, subject to the offer, I salute you both!'

He poured the fizz and offered her a glass and then more seriously,

'If we can be open and above board with each other we can remain as good friends. I personally liked Johnnie and hope that in time you will come to terms with Sally, because how the boys perceive our attitude to each other will also influence their happiness and in turn our own.'

Now it was her turn to muse about his plans and with a coy smile she probed for an answer.

'You have no doubt investigated the possibilities of buying Milford Hall, am I right?'

He nodded, unsure of how much to divulge.

Her expression was now anything but coy, it was challenging and she was clearly determined on knowing the truth. He sipped the champagne and returned her gaze.

'At the moment I have merely spoken to the owner and he has promised to seriously consider the proposal, but there is a lot to consider - the horses for instance.'

'Sod the horses!'

'So you have no objection to them staying here?'

'Not if Sue is still employed to look after them.'

He pondered his next move, trying to shift the emphasis back to her options.

'How will you live here and run the business in Yorkshire or is Johnnie prepared to move down here? If so, I find that very strange as everyone we have met in North Yorkshire consider it is God's own country and would not dream of living anywhere else, so I don't think you are exactly levelling with me?'

He had manoeuvred her into a corner, she had to regain control.

'What does the future Mrs C think of Milford Hall?'

'Truthfully, she has heard about it but has never even seen it, she is however happy to live there if I manage to buy it - which depends to some extent on what price Mr Mortimer has in mind which, him being an estate agent, as indeed are you, should not be difficult to work out. The sooner he makes me an offer, the sooner I can pursue my dreams of buying my inheritance. The ball is back in your court. I am going to Düsseldorf next week so why not invite him down for a few days and give me a ball park figure next weekend.'

'But the boys are home.'

'That will not preclude us from having some private time together, or will it?'

Her attitude became more resolute.

'Right let's get things moving, I feel like I am just wasting my life at the moment.'

'I know the feeling,' his curt response.

The following day he telephoned David Gilbert and asked if they could resume their discussions in earnest regarding Milford and was encouraged by his response. He also called his mother to remind her that they were lunching with the Parkinsons and that he would collect her on Sunday at eleven thirty. She admitted to being slightly nervous but was at the same time looking forward to meeting Sally's mother again after so many years.

Sunday finally arrived and at half past eleven he rang his mother's door- bell to find her, as anticipated, calm and elegant although she professed to being slightly nervous.

'Not as nervous as me,' he insisted, 'I have to meet my father-in-law to be.'

As they travelled from the outskirts of Nottinghamshire and into Rutland, he was very tempted to tell her about his dreams of Milford Hall but decided that he would not tempt fate and instead tried to prise some school day memories from his mother, particularly in respect of Sally's mother, previously Camilla Worthington.

'She was very pretty and easily the most intelligent girl in her year, so much so that her acceptance at Girton College, Cambridge, was regarded as a formality. So you will have to be on your toes with Sally, not that Kate is anything but highly intelligent.'

'All the women in my life are highly intelligent!' he assured her.

They were still laughing as they drove along the avenue of trees that guided them to the front door of Manston Hall. It seemed so long ago and yet he remembered so clearly how he had stood transfixed as he watched the hunt preparing to set off. How he had wished he could be part of it; he recollected too the jealous annoyance that he felt as Sally sipped a small stirrup cup accompanied by the irritating red haired Roddy Forsythe.

He cleared his head and parked the car. He opened the passenger door for his mother and before they could tug the doorbell it was opened by Sally. His mother's approving glance was followed by, 'I feel like I have stepped back in time, you are so pretty, a re-incarnation of Milly Worthington.'

They stepped inside to be welcomed by the aforementioned, whose beaming smile left no doubt the pleasure she felt at meeting her ex-schoolmate.

'Lizzie Staincliffe, this is so wonderful to see you again, please do come in, Robert is waiting for us in the drawing room. They followed their hostess along a wide hallway, its black and white tiled floor softened with Indian rugs, the walls hung with several gold framed portraits. About half way down, they turned right into the drawing room where the host was waiting, a bottle of champagne poised and ready for its cork to be withdrawn.

'Lizzie, how nice to meet you at last, I have heard quite a lot about you from Camilla but not quite as much as I have about Mr Wonderful.'

He gave James a knowing look and accepted his firm handshake.

'Of course in my day it was your father who was the talk of the county, no one has ever generated quite the same excitement and atmosphere as your father did on the day he scored four tries against the Ba-Ba's at Welford Road on Boxing Day - mind you, your own performances were not too bad!'

'Thank you Sir Robert.'

His host smiled as he handed him a glass of champagne.

'If you insist on calling me Sir Robert you will leave me with no alternative but to call you Mr Carrington and as I believe we are going to become family it would seem rather formal. Oh and by the way the answer to your as yet unasked question is YES.'

Sally clasped his arm. 'Mummy and I have ganged up on him as I told you we would.'

The drawing room door re-opened and an elegant old lady joined them and with a smile adding, 'and that includes Granny Parkinson.'

She took his hand; her expression was both warm and welcoming.

He returned her smile.

'I can see where the ladies in this family get their good looks from.'

She laughed. 'Camilla said you were a bit of a charmer.'

The banter remained light and pleasant and over a roast beef lunch the two mothers reminisced about their school days and James learned that his mother had been captain of lacrosse and tennis.

He looked genuinely surprised. 'You never told me that mother.'

Sally took his hand, 'Come on, I am going to take you to see the horses.'

As they walked towards the kitchen they heard the laughter but not the dry aside made by Sir Robert.

'Is that what they call it nowadays?'

He followed her into the boot room where she handed him a pair of wellies and a Barbour Jacket belonging to her brother Guy. Suitably suited and booted he followed her across the terrace at the back of the house in the direction of a series of paddocks separated by beech hedges. They arrived at a large American style barn which housed sixteen hardwood Lodden boxes, through the open doorways he could see the straw neatly banked up around the sides.

'I have to admit that much though I love my stable yard, the practicality of looking after the horses is so much easier in a building like this. In fact this will have to be top of our shopping list when we move into Milford Hall.'

He put his arm around her and lightly kissed the top of her head.

'Talking of shopping, I have been doing a little of my own, close your eyes and hold out you hand.'

Sally stood there, a mystified expression on her face, which grew ever more perplexed as she felt a small leather box being placed in her palm.

'You can open your eyes now.'

Nervously she slowly opened her eyes before letting out a great shriek as she focussed on the large single diamond that sparkled and danced as it caught the fluorescent light that shone down from the barn roof. There were tears in her eyes as she held him tight.

'James, I have never seen anything so beautiful as this; when did you get it?'

'I made a little detour to Asprey's in London on the way back from Dusseldorf.'

She grabbed his hand and marched him back to the house.

'I haven't seen the horses,' he protested and for the second time in two days a woman dismissed him with 'sod the horses.'

Back in the boot room, she grabbed his Barbour, threw it on to an armchair and hastened him minus shoes, back into the dining room. In an obvious state of ecstasy she waved her left hand at the ladies, all of whom immediately focussed on the large blue and white lights that dazzled even brighter as it picked up the reflections from the chandelier overhead.

Robert grasped James's hand and even his voice was slightly shaky as he saw his daughter's happiness. 'Well done my boy and welcome to our family.'

Whereupon he disappeared and left the ladies to continue the celebrations.

Five minutes later he was back with more champagne, this time Roederer Cristal 1949.

'This is the last of two cases with which we have, over several years, celebrated very special occasions in our family. I have been saving this survivor for a very long time, one day I knew it would be the right moment to open it and today is that day.'

He gently eased the cork out and finally with a small plop the cork was teased from the bottle and presented to his future son-in-law.

'The toast is to the future Mr and Mrs Carrington.'

Glasses were raised, the toast encored and reciprocal thanks were extended by the happy couple. Camilla left the room and returned and a few minutes later, putting her head around the door she signalled to Sally.

'It's your brother, he wants to congratulate you.' Sally needed no bidding and her mother returned to explain to Lizzie, as she continued to call her, that she just had to let her son know the exciting news.

As is the norm on occasions like this, they all remained seated around the dining room table with libations and anecdotes constantly flowing, so much so that as evening approached Robert suggested that it would be wiser for James not to drive home but rather accept a lift. He willingly agreed and Philip Tompkins, the farm manager, was prevailed upon to assist, with James also agreeing to spend the night at his mother's house, much to her delight.

CHAPTER SIXTY FOUR

The exhibition in Düsseldorf was opening on Tuesday and James was scheduled to fly from East Midlands at three thirty on Monday afternoon. He therefore had plenty of time to arrange a taxi to Woolmington where his suitcase was already packed and waiting, so with very little delay he travelled onwards to the airport.

Jack Priory and the sales team had gone over on Sunday to organise the display stands which had been assembled by the Minster joiners at the end of the previous week. The flight was uneventful and he proceeded from the airport to The Hilton Hotel where Jack was waiting in the bar.

He plied James with questions, confessing he would have loved to have been a fly on the wall at Manston and heard at first hand 'the moonshine that you came out with.'

As always happened when they were off duty the craic was good and was interspersed with business planning, both strategic and financial, which included the sale of Woolmington.

This was crucial to both of them, as a sizeable chunk of the money from that sale had been earmarked by James for investment in Minster Furniture, the success of which was rapidly outgrowing the existing factory workshops and offices.

Once again a business trip with no external interruptions provided the opportunity to use the time productively and by the time they finished their meal they had firmed up on several ideas. At nine thirty, Jack declared that business was over and suggested they strolled into town and grab a beer or two.

Düsseldorf is a university town and a centre for art and fashion and is famous for its congresses and trade fairs. It's most elegant shopping street and promenade is the Konigsallee, popularly known by the locals as 'Ko', at the north end of which is the famous Triton Fountain. Strolling along here on the banks of the Rhine, the visitor cannot but be impressed with streets that have none of the litter that infests so many towns in the UK. In the centre there are large glass cases displaying watches and other jewellery, none of them showing signs of damage or vandalism of any sort. Sadly not how it is in many parts of the Britain. It re-awaked the passion that James always felt when he was over here which was, hopefully, going to be more regularly now that ski trips with the Parkinsons was on the agenda.

It had been a calculated risk taking on the Germans on their own turf, particularly as they were acknowledged as the market leaders in kitchen furniture, particularly with regard to door fastenings and self-closing drawers. Both of which had been out-sourced over here and integrated in to the Minster range.

The Trade Show was a great success; in particular two new designs entitled Bavaria and Rhineland, perhaps not surprisingly, being the stars of the Minster collection.

The whole team had a celebratory dinner during the course of which a number of new ideas were initiated, several of them floated by a newcomer to the sales team whom James remembered from interviewing him.

He was a disenchanted architecture student named Mark Stonehouse; he was young, very presentable and, unlike the other members of the sales force, had come in from outside the furniture industry, bringing with him a different overview and an understanding of taste and design.

James intended to follow this young man's career with great interest.

They all travelled back together, the two directors foregoing their first class seats to continue the bonding and team ethic that had developed during the past week, the atmosphere on board the plane had a great buzz to it, and there was a tangible determination to ensure a kick start to the new sales campaign.

James arrived home to an empty house at six thirty, a note on the kitchen table advising that Kate would not be back until Monday evening.

This was a pleasant relief as he had anticipated a fractious weekend with his wife; instead he called the next Mrs Carrington and invited her to spend the next couple of nights at Woolmington, a suggestion that was jubilantly accepted, as was Sally's suggestion that she would cook supper for them.

In less than an hour she arrived with an overnight bag and a carrier containing the ingredients for spaghetti bolognaise, which she knew to be a favourite of his. Meanwhile he had lit the fire in the drawing room, decanted a bottle of Burgundy and was enjoying a Macallan when he heard the sound of a familiar engine.

'I thought I ought to return the Porsche, although I was tempted to hang on to it a little longer.'

'Very soon you will be able to use it every day; it will speed up the time it takes for you to travel to your office at Manston from Milford Hall.'

Her ecstatic face indicated that this was very much the future she was hoping for.

He poured her a G & T and she unwrapped the ingredients; minced beef - Manston bred of course, plus onions, streaky bacon, carrots, tomato puree, garlic and a packet of pasta.

'I imagine you will have some salt and pepper and a tablespoon of flour.'

'Coming straight up ma'am.'

He reached into the cupboard and produced the missing ingredients along with a red plastic apron with his initials emblazoned on the chest. She looked at it closely.

'I would venture that this has never been used.'

His raised eyebrows confirmed her deduction and he was ordered to sit down out of the way whilst she set about rustling up the food.

She was an assured cook who clearly enjoyed preparing a meal and like him she felt so happy that they had the evening together, although finding saucepans etc. in another woman's kitchen is not easy, so he was pressed back into service to find the various implements. The chef also ordered him to lay the table. Shortly after eight they had their first home cooked meal and then retired to the drawing room and the crackling log fire that danced in the elegant stone fireplace.

'Won't you miss living here?'

'No, because although Kate would never hear of it, I always had only one place that I wanted to live and, as things have worked out, you will be the first and only person I will share it with although...' He paused and gave her an anxious look.

'Would you be agreeable to mother having a wing of the house for herself - it would be self-contained? I haven't asked her, by the way, not until I knew how you felt about it.'
She sensed his concern and gave him a smile that convinced him of her sincerity.

'No, not in the slightest, I am delighted; I am used to having female company.'

'I do so want us to be together and I am going over to Milford again next week to try and agree a price that will be fair to both parties.'

'Don't you have to sell this house first and where will Sally and the boys live?'

'Fortunately, the sale of Fordmill Construction and the buyout of my shares means that I should be able to purchase Milford from the equity that it will produce and that is another meeting I have on Friday next week - the 13th - supposedly my lucky number.'

'So Kate will be staying here, that must be a relief?'
He gave her a wry look.

'Last week a cardboard tube, the sort used by architects to post plans etc. - was handed to me by Sue who, as you know, lives just down the lane. The postman asked her to take it as Kate was out. I spotted the label which indicated it was from an architect's practice in Sheffield and was addressed to Mrs Carrington. I asked her in all innocence what it contained and she opened it to reveal the original plans of this house and I could hardly believe it when she announced that Johnnie Mortimer was offering to buy me out so that she could stay here.'

'Wow!'

'Wow indeed, but it does not stack up because they both have businesses in Yorkshire, so why would they want to live down here?'
She gave him a perceptive look, trying to tease the answer from him but to no avail. She tried another tack

'They both have estate agency businesses, his company having several branches all in the Yorkshire area and what else does he do?'

'He has a health spa, it was where they met.'

'And!' She willed him to say it but, unusually, he could not see the obvious, finally she put him out of his misery.

'Don't you think this beautiful house would make a wonderful health spa?'
He shook his head in disbelief. 'Talk about the bleeding obvious.'

'So, how do you feel about that?'
There was a momentary silence as his brain sieved through the options and the downsides.

'I am all for it, my only concern is where we live and where the boys live and I am confident that whatever she does, it will not be detrimental to their welfare and having met Johnnie, I don't believe he would do other than look after them.'

'It looks like we could owe Kate a vote of thanks.'

'Assuming they come up with the right numbers, and I also expect to hear that next week.'
She snuggled up closer to him. 'It must be time for bed.'

'After what we have just unravelled I don't think I will be able to go to sleep.'

'That is just as well, as sleeping was the last thing on my mind.'
He drew the chain mesh fireguard across and took her by the hand and lifted her from the sofa.

'I will show you to your room.'

She followed him upstairs and across the landing into a corridor; he stopped when they reached the third door which, like the others, had a name engraved on a brass plate, this one said Tuscany.

She went in first.

'This room appears to be in use.'

'Oh dear, I seem to have brought you into my room.'

She turned and pouted.

'You are a naughty boy; but then I like naughty boys!'

He took her into his arms and peeled her shirt over her head before unclipping her bra to expose the generous breasts that jutted out. She nestled against him and gently pushed him down on to the bed and whispered.

'It is rather hot in here and these cord trousers must be most uncomfortable.'

'Not to mention your jeans.'

Neither of them needed any more encouragement and leaving the heap of clothes on the floor jumped between the sheets. The tentative first steps in lovemaking when in Germany were replaced by assured tantalising that went close but not quite to the limit, as he stroked and caressed her wonderful body and she in turn gently stroked those areas she knew would most excite him. Finally, however, she could no longer contain her emotions and as she began to shudder, he sought his own moment of ecstasy.

'I do so love you Sally Parkinson.'

'And I have waited all my life to meet you.'

They clung together, no words necessary as they luxuriated in the other's happiness, a joy she had never known. Her previous experience of sex had been lacklustre without the intensity of passion and excitement that she experienced when she was with James.

They were still lying there at daybreak as he tried to free his by now numb arm from under her shoulder. He finally extricated it, causing her to stir briefly before turning over and dropping off to sleep again..

Half an hour later she fluttered her eyes and gradually awoke from a deep and contented sleep, slowly she became conscious of his presence and the blue eyes intoxicated with affection that looked down at her. She held his gaze.

'Good morning Carrington, have you made the tea yet?'

'If you care to step on to the terrace mam, I think you will find everything to your satisfaction.'

He opened the French doors that led out onto a balcony and sat her down at a small table upon which he had prepared a pot of Earl Grey and croissants. Overhead the sun was already warm and she was captivated by the view, the backdrop of which was the stunning magnificence of Belvoir Castle. Between them horses grazed in the undulating paddocks, a scene that was so redolently English, so picture postcard perfect.

She was not surprised that Kate had refused to leave - an opinion she would wisely keep to herself! Instead she drew his attention to the yearlings she had seen on that fateful day that the two new couples had finally met. She pointed to the nearest paddock.

'The big bay colt is always agitating the others to run and, just as before, the chestnut filly speeds past him, you must keep her,' she pleaded.

'My strategy is to keep the fillies and sell the colts; firstly, they sell for more and secondly if the filly lives up to expectations, I will have another brood mare to breed me another colt that I can sell for profit. She stood up and embraced him. 'You are so romantic, just what every woman wants, not that anyone else is going to have you.'

'I will never ever look at another woman - well I might just look - but nothing else I do promise you. Now what are we going to do today.'

'Nothing, just potter around, check on the horses and pretend we are already married and go to one of the local pubs for supper.'

Which is how it turned out and the prospect of this togetherness made the future seem so wonderful that they managed to avoid worrying about the turmoil that might be vented upon them prior to living in Utopia.

The following morning he delivered her back to Manston before attending the monthly board meeting at Minster Furniture, after which he confirmed his Friday appointment with David Gilbert at Milford Hall.

Less than an hour later he received a call from Kate suggesting that she and Johnnie meet him at Woolmington at around six thirty to discuss the latter's offer to purchase his share of the house. This he readily agreed to, along with the suggestion that he stayed at his mother's house to save Johnnie the drive back to North Yorkshire. She was surprised at his consideration but more than happy to acquiesce.

The adrenalin was flowing and feeling on a roll he telephoned Anthony Jayes and arranged a meeting for four thirty.

He called his PA, Jane, handed over the correspondence he had signed and tasked her to blank out the afternoon as he had some private work to do.

He knew from Jack Priory's discussions that Fordmill Construction had been of interest to at least six parties, two of which were European companies that had a toe in the British market, the others were UK based. With so much at stake on both fronts he needed positive assurances before Friday's meeting with David Gilbert.

At four twenty he swept into the spacious Fordmill car park and, although his old parking space was free, he discreetly ignored it and parked amidst the staff cars. Glancing back the Porsche 911 did appear somewhat conspicuous sitting amongst the menagerie of variously aged Minis and other popular family cars.

Although no longer part of this company that had been his inspiration, he still felt a pride and allegiance towards it, almost everything was as he had left it, even most of the staff, every one of whom greeted him warmly, particularly Roger Blenkins, who had been his first operations manager.

'I am looking for a good deputy, if you are interested.'

'Best send me an application form, Roger; can I put you down for a reference?'

He declined the lift and strode upstairs to the top floor which housed the Directors' offices and the boardroom where Anthony Jayes awaited him.

The first thing he noticed was the new confidence and decisiveness that Jack Priory had seen growing month on month, why had he never spotted this, why had Anthony not pushed himself forward?

James answered his own question - probably because he personally had never truly learnt the art of delegation, of being less involved in day to day management, so that his employees would have had the confidence to express themselves, as Anthony was now doing.

'Earl Grey or Coffee?' Anthony brought his thoughts back into focus.

'Tea would be fine Anthony and I congratulate you, everything is spick and span, there is a good atmosphere and Roger even offered me a job!'

'I will second that James and in the meantime you will want to know how negotiations are going in respect of a sale. Well, as ever, your timing is impeccable. Last Friday we received an offer from Simmons International which you will know well, they have recently moved their HQ to Brussels and most of their key staff are moving to the new European base. Apart from acquiring a robust and dynamic company, Fordmill would become their new UK base. This was a strategy I suggested, as the cost indices in Nottingham are considerably lower than those they presently have in Kingston on Thames. If you also factor in the equity that will be generated from the sale of their premises, it goes a long way towards funding their new European head office.'

He looked up at James and was emboldened enough to add that Due Diligence would begin on Monday next and subject to this being successfully completed the sale would proceed.

'I don't think I will apply for the job Roger offered me; I think I might hold you back!'

Anthony accepted the compliment, but gave him a knowing look and an appreciative response.

'Every smart idea I have, emanates from the apprenticeship I served with you.'

James looked at the triumphant face across the table and remembered how he had been immediately impressed when he had first met the young lawyer who would not advise him of the misdemeanours of one of his clients; client confidentiality forbade that. He had, however, left the office to consult his senior partner, Jeremy Palmer. In his absence, the file which he had left open and the small window of opportunity it allowed, had enabled James to obtain the information he needed to turn the tables on the sole objector, who threatened to prevent the shopping precinct in Bournemouth becoming a reality.

It also reminded him of the man for whom he had the greatest of respect, Jeremy Palmer, his present father-in-law. He did still miss that kind and honourable man whose wisdom and advice he had so often sought; hopefully time would heal that wound.

He brought his thoughts back into focus.

'So do you have a probable timescale, as I need to commit a large slice of my buyout equity to purchase a house?'

'I can confidently guess that is your old family seat?'

'Yes, I am seeing David Gilbert, the current owner of Milford Hall, on Friday.'

Anthony sighed and pursed his lips.

'Entre nous, and I would rather that not even Jack Priory should know this, in the event of Simmons not going ahead, I am in talks with our bankers APP who have given me provisional backing for a management buyout, which includes funding your shareholding.'

It was now James's turn to sigh and shake his head in disbelief.

'I remember you telling me that accountancy had always been your calling, but the family legal background had ushered you into the law. Well don't regret it any longer because you are now accomplished in both professions and not just accomplished you have a Master's Degree in both. I genuinely wish you the greatest possible success.'

This time it was Anthony's opportunity to confer a compliment.

'James Carrington, sporting superstar and business genius, that vote of approval is the greatest compliment I could ever have possibly hoped for.'

'You are very kind and as you must have a mountain of paperwork in preparation for Monday's visit from the accounts people at Simmons, I will bid you farewell and wish you the very best of luck.'

He drove back to Woolmington, his mind trying to juggle the three pronged dilemma that was Milford Hall, Woolmington Manor and Fordmill Construction. The former was so dependent on the outcome of the two other parts, the first phase of which he hoped to conclude this evening. It was very nearly six o'clock when he arrived home, just enough time to pack an overnight bag before he heard a car draw up in front of the house. He felt strangely apprehensive, but reasoned that Kate and Johnnie would be equally anxious as their future also depended on getting the right result.

He deposited his bag in the hall and welcomed them at the front door.

'Shall we go through to the study? It seems the obvious venue for a business discussion.'

Kate appeared to be about to challenge this, but with too much to lose by spoiling the prevailing light mood, she acquiesced. He declined to sit at his desk and instead waved them to the sofa and planted himself in his favourite green leather armchair. They all looked at each other wondering who should begin; James finally assumed his role as host and took the initiative by suggesting a drink.

This was accepted and he dutifully handed round three Bombay gin and tonics which restored the harmony.

Johnnie kicked off the meeting by suggesting that both he and James write down their valuation of Woolmington Manor and from those baselines try to establish a deal that was fair to both parties.

James crossed to his desk and produced two notepads one of which he passed to Johnnie. He returned to his seat, his expression was serious but not hostile; it was a look that Kate recognised, except this time she was not on his team but on the other side of the negotiation.

'My estimation is based on two criteria. One is the value as a family home and the other is on the potential income stream that the investment could generate. In other words, as you both run your companies in Yorkshire and there is nowt better place to live, as so many of your Yorkshire folk tell me, why would you wish to buy this house?'

He gave them a moment to digest that he had rumbled their intent and that he was no longer valuing Woolmington as a domestic dwelling but as a commercial investment.

'I can only presume that you wish to develop this house as a business, presumably along the lines of your own family pile and have taken expert advice, which is why the plans of this property were delivered in a cardboard tube from an architect in Sheffield. To have persuaded Kate to give up her home is quite a feat Johnnie, I never could and I congratulate you, she must love you very much!'

'Yes I do.' Kate blurted out before adding; 'However, you should not be too cynical James, as we both realise the responsibility we have in ensuring that the boys still feel this is their home and that is why we intend to convert the wing looking towards Belvoir as a private family retreat.'

He gave her a kind and understanding glance.

'I think that is a really sympathetic solution to the problem and far from objecting to it, I applaud you most sincerely.'

They both turned towards Johnnie who seized the moment to suggest that they each wrote down their valuation of the property, which they did before exchanging the slips of paper.

Johnnie had written down £600k, James had pencilled in £700k which extracted a derisive snort from Kate.

He held up his hand. 'Let us take these valuations as only part of the solution, there are other pieces to this puzzle and I am quite happy to share my business finances, in confidence of course, with both of you.

- Apart from Woolmington I have 2 estate agencies on the South Coast and Kate, you have the York practice which I have already gifted you and which is worth circa £300k.

- The shares in Fordmill belong exclusively to me and their value, until sold, can only be estimated.
- In addition to my 50% ownership of Woolmington, I am prepared to offer you a share in the titles of both agencies in the south. I would like, if possible, that they should continue trading to protect the livelihood of the staff concerned.
- However, I am happy to be guided by your sentiments on this.
- The only caveat is that 50% of the Estate Agency earnings or their sales proceeds are put under the umbrella of an Investment Trust for Charles and Edward. This will pay their school fees and for any further education at university etc. Properly invested for the next ten to fifteen years, they will inherit a tidy sum at say age twenty eight, although this inheritance date is also open for debate.
- In appreciation of your concern for the boys, I will agree to your assessment of £600k for Woolmington.
- In return you will not suggest that the boys leave Uppingham and that we agree to have equal access to them.

She looked to Johnnie for guidance. He pursed his lips before attempting an answer.

'We do not know the value of the businesses in the south but presumably James you will have the balance sheets that will enable us to assess your offer?'

'Indeed I do and when you have examined them you will be able to fully appreciate that my proposal is more than generous as both pieces of the holding company are very profitable, due in no small part to the much higher property values on the south coast.

Kate was looking slightly on edge and sensing that he was running the show for his own benefit she challenged his division of their assets.

'It seems to me that this division of our joint assets is heavily weighted in your favour!'

'Okay, let's jot down a few numbers.

You have the York business value minimum	£300 k
50% payment for my stake in the house	£300 k
50% value in company in South min value	£500 k

Total value   £ 1,100,000

In addition, Kate you have a sizeable investment portfolio managed by Coutts Bank, the majority of which has been funded by me.

My assets are:-

The value of my shares in Fordmill - my most optimistic value is not in excess of the settlement figure I am proposing to you and may well be far less than that.
I too have investments with Coutts and APP Bank all of which have been funded by myself, with no input from Kate.

I also ask you to take into consideration that once you have bought my stake in this house, I do not even have a roof over my head which will, I hope, demonstrate why I want an early conclusion to our negotiations.

'I believe that this is a very generous offer; However, if you wish to challenge me in court, then I suggest Kate, that you discuss this proposal with your father, who has always counselled me that going to law has only one winner - the lawyers!'

He stole a glance at the sofa opposite, Johnnie was looking decidedly uncomfortable and no doubt fervently hoping that his advice would not be sought. However, James was determined to get this sorted, at least in principle today, so that he had a sound base from which to haggle a price for Milford Hall.

No response was forthcoming. He shook his head in exasperation, 'you both earn your living buying and selling properties, I have agreed to your offer on this house, what else can you want?'
Finally Kate spoke.
'What about the value of the horses, one of which, Wedding Belle was bought by me.'
He glared at her in disbelief.
'That was my wedding present; do you think I am going to ask you to give me the Morgan car back?
'What about the furniture?'
Johnnie patted her knee.
'Kate darling, I don't think that James is intending to be unreasonable about that and, as I commented when I first saw it, most of the pieces are too valuable and delicate to be left for the use of residents.'
James also sought to placate her.
'What Johnnie says is true and what I imagined was that any furniture or paintings etc. that had a personal affiliation to you would be yours, likewise items such as my grandfather's desk should automatically be mine. As to the remainder, I will give you first choice and then in turn we will choose pieces of approximately the same value - does this satisfy you?'
'That means that you still own the horses.'
'That is because I have spent my own money speculating on them, it is my pastime. However, as a last resort I will give you the pick of the yearlings that will be sold at the Tattersall's sale in October.'
'I will have the big bay colt.' Her immediate triumphal response.
'Then he is yours and will be catalogued as such. Do we now have a deal which is agreeable to both sides?'
'Subject to the balance sheets reflecting your valuation of the South Coast property companies.'
James held out his hand to Kate. 'I agree to that and will get a draft agreement drawn up whilst you and Johnnie seek your accountant's assessment of their worth.'
He took a key from his pocket and walked across to his desk from which he produced a large blue file which he handed to Kate.
'The properties were valued independently and the surveyor's report is enclosed, together with the balance sheets for the last five years, the last of which is dated only two months ago.'
He relocked the desk and, quietly satisfied with the outcome so far, he looked at Johnnie who returned his gaze with an expression that was positive but not yielding.
'James, I too want this matter sorted quickly, as does Kate. I will meet my accountant tomorrow and take his opinion on your offer, although of course the final decision has to be Kate's.'

'Then I shall bid you farewell and head off to steak and kidney pie at mothers. Bye the way Kate, she has no intention of taking sides and hopes very much that you will keep in touch.'

Whereupon he gathered his bag from the hall and set out for an evening with his mother, wondering as he drove how much of today's events he should reveal to her.

CHAPTER SIXTY FIVE

The negotiations appearing to be moving in the right direction, he arrived at his mother's apartment in good humour and looking forward to seeing her again.

He let himself in and followed his nose to the kitchen; where through the window in the oven door, he espied their supper.

'It smells marvellous mother, what lies under that crust?'

'All in good time, right now I need you to open the wine for me.'

'Batard-Montrachet; my word mother you really are spoiling me.'

'I don't get many opportunities to entertain these days so I decided to push the boat out, and there is also a bottle of red for you to open.'

She was interrupted by the door- bell.

'Will you get that dear, I can't imagine who it might be?'

'I will soon get rid of them,' he promised.

The pleasant evening suddenly became even more so as he opened the door to reveal two more guests, Camilla and Sally.

Hugging them both he called through to his mother. 'It's the Parkinson sisters.'

'Well fancy that.' His mother's droll reply as she took four champagne flutes from the drinks cupboard.

'Since you have the perfect name for a butler, James, perhaps you will do the honours and bring them through to the drawing room.'

She led them away, all smiling happily and pleased to see each other again, although Sally did break away to give the butler a hand.

'What a surprise, I had no idea. I was expecting a rustic supper in the kitchen, but was pleasantly surprised when the old bird had me open a bottle of Montrachet and a bottle of Chateau Neuf.'

She gave him a hug.

'I am so looking forward to being at Milford and having more rustic suppers together.'

'Me too, so let's go and help them drink this champagne.'

As Sally picked up the glasses he had a sudden thought.

'Whisper to your mother not to let on about Milford; I am not raising mother's hopes until the contracts have been signed.'

The evening went as pleasantly as it had at Manston and after a three course supper, of which the highlight was a Steak and Oyster Pie, the two mothers insisted on clearing away the dishes which gave James the opportunity to escort Sally into the drawing room and unveil the negotiations and proposals he had discussed earlier that day. She slid along the sofa and drew even closer to him.

'How difficult was it, how did they both take it?'

'Johnnie very wisely left any contentious issues to Kate but, to be fair, he did lend me support when she appeared to be getting too greedy. So the position is they have all the facts and the figures will stack up, so I am hopeful that this business can be settled amicably. Incidentally, your very astute observation re the health spa was bang on, although they do intend to keep one wing for themselves and the boys, which pleases me no end and I did give them full marks for this.

They rejoined the ladies who had effortlessly picked up the threads of their schooldays. The conversation flowed easily and they chatted with them until the clocked chimed ten at which point Camilla called a halt and, still talking twenty to the dozen, they took their leave.

He took his mother's hand and kissed her gently on the cheek.

'Thank you so much for a wonderful surprise and a marvellous meal.'

She radiated happiness and he was so happy for her, this was the mother he had known before his father's untimely death. That chance that had brought the two mothers together again after all these years was as unexpected as the twist of fate that contrived to him meeting Sally after Edward's fatal accident.

They enjoyed a final glass of wine together and although he was bursting to tell his mother about Milford Hall he resisted the temptation, he had a more dramatic plan up his sleeve.

CHAPTER SIXTY SIX

The rest of the week seemed to take forever but finally it was Friday and it was the 13th, which was his lucky number, or always had been!

First though he needed an answer from Kate; was she being deliberately perverse in not getting back to him? She knew very well know how desperate he was to get the Woolmington business sorted out. He decided therefore to take the bull by the horns and called her at Johnnie's house and it was he who answered the phone.

'James, you are wanting a decision I imagine.'

'Yes, I have been upfront with you in everything and would find it difficult to believe that you would think my offer was other than fair and generous.'

'Unfortunately James it is not my decision so I will pass you over to Kate.'

He heard them muttering in the background and finally she picked up the telephone.

'What is the rush James we haven't finished breakfast yet?'

'Kate, you promised me an answer by Friday and it is now Friday.'

'Well I have discussed things with our accountants and they feel that the least I should accept is one point two million pounds.'

He took a deep breath; he was not going to be played like some fish on a line.

'Kate, I have been scrupulously fair with you. I have offered you £1,100,000 plus the bank account I funded for you at Coutts and the pick of this year's foals which adds up to well over the one point one million I have offered.'

'Let me have a word with Johnnie.'

She put the phone down and he heard whispered voices in the background, finally Johnnie picked up the receiver and before he could say a word James took control.

'Johnnie, you appear to be a reasonable guy, so I think it is best that I tell you exactly how I feel. If Kate refuses the sum I put forward, this is what will happen. I will withdraw the terms I have proposed, including my acceptance of your offer for Woolmington. That property will be put up for sale and I will hold out for a bigger price than the ad hoc agreement we made. This will not inconvenience me, because I have already secured the funding to buy Milford Hall from my bankers. I will also be removing from Woolmington all of my personal pieces of furniture, and with regard to the estate agencies in the south a Trust Fund is being drawn up to hold them in the names of

Charles and Edward, that trust will be administered solely by me as they belong exclusively to me. As to my shareholding in Fordmill Construction, I will roll them over into the new company they are forming. I will give you thirty minutes to talk some sense into her and come back to me. Finally, I hope you will believe me when I say that my opinion of you is that you are a reasonable and fair man, whatever the outcome that will remain so.'

He put the phone down and looked at his watch, she had until ten fifteen to come to heel. Meanwhile, he felt the adrenalin rush through his veins, this was the James Carrington that had taken on the Martins Bank, had overcome seemingly impossible odds with APP Merchant Bank as well as the combined might of professionals assembled by Edward Lawson. If she wanted a fight he was up for it.

There was of course the one issue he did want to avoid, letting his sons see him at loggerheads with their mother. He was still pondering this when the call came through; it was Johnnie Mortimer.

'You have a deal James and for what it is worth, I have told Kate that it is a fair offer.'

'Thanks, I appreciate your co-operation and do sincerely hope it works out well for you both; will she speak to me?'

He heard them talking quietly, he was clearly advising her to clear the air and not sour the future. He sensed she had picked up the phone.

'Kate, please believe me, I do not want us to be at loggerheads and I want you to be happy and, as a little icing on the cake, I will pay for your colt to be prepared and entered for the sale and I hope he wins the Derby!'

'Okay James, for the sake of the kids I am going along with it but don't expect an invitation to the wedding.'

'Surely Johnnie needs a best man!!'

'Goodbye James.'

He leaned back in his chair, in less than two hours he prayed he would be in a position to return this chair and his desk to their rightful home at Milford.

He tried to visualise the scene, anticipated the dialogue, but only in broad strokes; from past experience he knew that if you tried to anticipate a two way conversation too closely you could get bogged down in the minutia and that hampers the ability to think laterally and spontaneously.

He tried to switch off by doing the Telegraph crossword but it was no use, today's meeting with David Gilbert had obsessed his thoughts and fuelled his dreams for thirty years. Finally it was midday and opening the sun roof, he fired up the 911 and set out to retrieve his legacy.

He cruised along the now familiar lanes until finally the great iron gates loomed in front of him. He kept his eyes firmly ahead, not wanting the door of the lodge to swing open and commit him to passing pleasantries with Mrs Price. Instead he concentrated on the sight of the great stone house reconstructed and enlarged by his ancestors, the house that he had called home until the age of fourteen. He drove to the front of the house and parked opposite the imposing stone tower which guarded the entrance. Above which a deep stone lintel bore the same family motto as the great wrought iron entrance gates, Semper Altiora Speramus - Ever to aspire to higher things, its pertinence had never seemed more appropriate.

The heavy oak door had been left ajar so, after pressing the large brass doorbell, he cautiously entered the hallway to be met by David Gilbert, his hand outstretched, the greeting undeniably welcoming.

It gave him courage, also the realisation that his host was probably as anxious as himself that this sale should go through; it also formulated the structure of their conversation as he now saw himself on the front foot.

'James how nice to see you again, shall we go into the drawing room?'
He gave James a warm smile.

'Why don't you lead the way and I will ask Mrs Jenkins to bring some coffee through.'
James instinctively turned left and headed for the pair of oak panelled doors that opened inwards to the vast drawing room that had hosted so many parties in its heyday and would host many more if today's visitor was given the chance.

James gazed around, the memories flooding back as he approached the huge windows which opened on to the terrace and beyond that a large manicured lawn in the centre of which stood a large oak tree, its sturdy waist surrounded by a circular bench. He remembered so clearly his mother and his sister Louise sitting there clapping as he caught the ruby ball kicked high into the sky by his father. That thought serving as a vivid reminder of why he was here today.

'Bringing back a few memories?'

'David, I didn't hear you come into the room, but yes, I was lost in pleasant memories.'

They both looked at each other, neither knowing quite how to start; finally David Gilbert broke the silence.

'I know that you want this house and at our first meeting I did originally indicate that I would contemplate selling as I wanted to be with my son, even though that would mean me upping sticks and emigrating to Australia.'

He saw the disappointment etched on his guest's face and sought to allay his fears, although the arrival of Mrs Jenkins with the pot of coffee unfortunately prolonged the agony. This was further compounded as she sought his preference of sandwich filling. David Gilbert held up his hand.

'I am sure that vegetable soup and a selection of sandwiches will be fine.'
He looked at James, who nodded, although his inclination was to decline and leave. Sensing this, David sought to bring the meeting back on track

'Now where were we? Oh yes, since then Steve has decided to return to the UK and, I hope you will be pleased to learn, has met a girl who lives in the Scottish borders. He is intent on buying a farm near to Hawick which is where her family hail from.'

'It is a great area David, in fact a real hotbed of rugby. Let's hope he has a son half as good as he was, although we may come to regret it if he decides to play for Scotland!'

'That would put me in a difficult position, particularly as I would have been living in the area for about twenty years!'

'So you are in fact going to emigrate after all!'

'Yes, and as I am financing his farm, I need to sell this place.'

'Your honesty does you great credit David, although I do have to admit that I thought that you had bad news for me when you started this conversation. So as one of us has to start this negotiation, what sort of figure do you have in mind?'
Whilst they momentarily considered this the soup and sandwiches arrived, although Mrs Jenkins was at a loss as to the humour her entrance invoked.

James waited until she had left and then handed David a small notebook.

'You may have heard on the grapevine that Kate and I are to be divorced.'

David Gilbert nodded.

'Yes it came as a surprise to everyone, but I am sure you both have good reasons; as I had when I split with Catherine and had to live in this great family house all on my own.'

He gave James a wry look and added. 'Maybe I will meet some lassie up in the Borders!'

'Let's hope so David. But to continue my tale of woe.

When I sold my share of Woolmington Manor to my wife's new husband-to-be, we found it easier to write down our expectations. Does that seem sensible to you? If so, after lunch I would like to have a look around and take a few instant pictures with my Polaroid camera to show my intended new wife and also my mother. You have been perfectly frank and honest with me and I do in turn promise complete clarity in my dealings with you.'

'Of course you must look around, at least you have the advantage of knowing where you are going.'

The conversation drifted to rugby and the latest England team and then out of the blue.

'Have you got a boy at Uppingham?'

'Yes, two in fact.'

'I guessed as much, a great pal of mine has his boys at Oakham and told me about this lightening quick lad called Carrington who single handed took their team apart!'

'That is a bit of an exaggeration as both teams were pretty evenly matched; Edward just seized the few chances that came along. He has of course the advantage of playing in the England squad so is getting the best of coaching.'

'You are as modest as ever Mr Carrington. Now, we appear to have finished lunch so why don't you give the house the once over.'

James needed no further bidding; he retraced his steps across the large black and white tiled floor that separated the drawing room from his next port of call, the oak panelled dining room. Once again his memory was not disappointed. To his left was a huge stone fireplace and in the centre of the room a long oak refectory table with a dozen elegant oak chairs along each side and at each end of the table a matching carver.

To each side of the fireplace was a long sideboard of the same period, all of which had been built by his forbear Sir Albert Staincliffe - The Furniture King - as he was known in the late nineteenth century.

These priceless family pieces would be included in the sale thanks to his parent's insistence that they be included in the purchase made by David Gilbert in 1948.

The windows to the front of the house replicated those in the drawing room and from here he could just glimpse the gatehouse at the end of the long drive.

From here he proceeded to the morning room which was adjacent to the kitchen, once again time had stood still, as it had in the kitchen. This however would be a temporary arrangement, as he could already visualise the Minster Kitchen fitters installing a new and contemporary look.

He bypassed the study and instead climbed the right hand side of the great oak staircase. Like the schoolboy of yesteryear he slid his hands along the classic handrail, barely able to resist sliding down to the great newel posts which supported balusters that echoed their design in miniature. He reached the landing and ignoring the temptation to explore his old room, he proceeded along the corridor to the east wing of the house which he fervently hoped his mother would occupy. It comprised seven rooms, all spacious and airy and he visualised immediately how they could be re-configured so that the largest would become a sitting room from where she would have access to a kitchen.

Two of the rooms would remain as bedrooms; the other two would conveniently convert to en-suite bathrooms. The views from them all overlooked open country and he could imagine his mother sitting in the window as the Belvoir Hunt swept by, in her mind she would see Robert Carrington fearlessly riding one of his grey hunters, as always just behind the Master.

He had to have this house and he had to have his mother here with him, it was after all her family home and he was so happy that Sally had responded so positively when it had had suggested... but then, she lived happily with her mother, as Camilla did with Robert Parkinson's mother, so she was already integrated into a communal family system.

He continued the tour, leaving until last the vast master suite that would be for him and Sally and then finally, he entered what had been his own bedroom. He sat on the bed his head between his hands as he remembered in total detail that fateful day when they had driven down the long drive to those great iron gates with the Rising Sun crest above the family motto.

He remembered too the youthful promise, that one day he would bring the Carrington's back to their inheritance.

He remained lost in his dreams until he heard a gentle tap on the bedroom door, it was David Gilbert.

'Can I come in? It must be about time for a snifter.'

'Good idea.' He opened his briefcase and produced a bottle of Macallan Malt Whisky.

'My shout I think.'

They returned down the other side of the staircase and made their way to the study where they sat in the burgundy leather chairs either side of the fireplace. David Gilbert produced two glasses from the butler's pantry and they drank each other's health, neither knowing quite how to start the negotiations.

The host seized the initiative by producing the notebook James had provided.

'I have written down what I feel is fair and this as promised, includes all the furniture and other pieces made for this house that your father assigned to me, together with the family portraits. He did after all point out that I was only the janitor, as one day you would be back to claim your birthright.'

His guest smiled and nodded before passing across his notebook.

'Sealed Bids, let's hope we can get somewhere in the middle.'

David Gilbert opened James's book, in it was written the three bold figures - 850.

James opened his book, there were no figures, it simply said As long as your offer is fair you have a deal.

He stood up and held out his hand which was firmly grasped by his guest; in unison they said 'Deal.'

'Now, good though the Macallan is, I think I have something even more appropriate.'

He walked across to the butler's pantry and returned with two champagne glasses and a bottle of Dom Perignon from which he gently eased the cork and promptly passed to his guest.

'Just to make sure you will remember today.'

'David I could never forget today, it is the 13th, which once again is my lucky number.'

They chatted on, two honest men with new aspirations whose short friendship would undoubtedly become a long one. Finally James called a halt, adding the proviso that David Gilbert must always regard Milford as his retreat whenever he visited the shires. This invitation was readily accepted and James with his precious Polaroid pictures set off to convey the good tidings to Miss Parkinson.

The original fortified building known as Milford Castle had been built by Sir William St Aubyn, a member of an ancient family whose ancestors came over from France with William the Conqueror. The building of the castle had commenced in 1655, at a time when Oliver Cromwell's Roundheads and often lawless mercenaries had constituted a potential threat to many of the population, particularly those with secret royalist sympathies.

It had been completed in 1661, just one year after the joyous return to the throne of Charles the Second. With the restoration of the monarchy the nation threw off the shackles of Puritanism; The returning monarch was at the forefront of this new age and one of the major beneficiaries was horse racing, particularly the Newmarket area, where he decamped with his court for months at a time.

When purchased by Sir Albert Staincliffe in 1891, the front elevation was essentially three sturdy towers linked by two great halls. Sir Albert, like so many other Victorian visionaries, espoused an admiration for the Neo Classical movement, A perception that was idealised by several notable designers such as John Ruskin and Augustus Pugin; the latter's visionary masterpiece St Pancras railway station, having been completed in 1868.

The Baronet's huge and rapidly expanding furniture empire had already adopted many of the ideals prescribed by the above luminaries. His furniture now incorporated the decorated tracery and other Neo Classical tenets and his immediate inclination was to incorporate these precepts into this rather tired old castle.

He had, therefore, surprised his architect and builder by instructing them to rip down the two end towers and replace them with two wings built in the Gothic manner.

In the ensuing design the roofs were steep, the chimneys were tall and decorative, and each wing he decreed would have a small turret with a pointed roof. It also had bathrooms with running water and most wondrously, to many at the end of the Victorian era, it was lit by electric lighting.

The central tower still rearing magnificently higher than the rest of the building, no longer looked forbidding; instead it exerted a commanding statement. 'This is an important family home'. With this emphasis in mind he confidently amended the title from Milford Castle to Milford Hall.

One day soon, James vowed to himself, he would stand on the rooftop and raise the family crest which would announce to his kinsmen and those who lived and farmed in the rolling acres of the Vale of Belvoir, that the Carrington's were back. Their legacy regained.

CHAPTER SIXTY SEVEN

James, always self-contained and jealous of his own privacy, considered the enormous feat he had engineered this afternoon and, as he drove back along the entrance drive at a steady pace, he was still unable to believe that the deal which had been his life's ambition had finally been put in place.

He was longing to tell his mother and to share the same tidings with Sally but, as ever, as had been the case with all his business deals and negotiations, James Carrington had to share his thoughts with himself. Whilst not entirely appropriate, he remembered the words of Martin Luther King addressing his supporters in Memphis in 1968: You can kill a dreamer but you can never kill a dream. His dream was now about to become a reality but sadly his father was not here to share it with him: Just as Dr King was not there to share his dream with the black people of America.

But, he was fortunate, his mother was here and so his dream would be shared. With that thought he switched back to the present and by the time he reached home he had formulated a plan. First he telephoned his mother to invite her out for Sunday lunch. To the question, 'was there a special reason', he had replied no, he was on his own, so he thought she might enjoy a treat. She readily accepted.

He then called Sally and confirmed that he would collect her at seven and that she would need an overnight bag, once again the offer was jubilantly accepted.

She was ready and waiting and after a Bombay and tonic they set out for...

'The George at Stamford?'

'Yes, miss smarty pants.'

She gave him an enquiring glance.

'Do you have something exciting to tell me?'

'Maybe.'

She snuggled up to him, her eyes sparkling with joy.

'Have we got a new home Mr Carrington?'

'Only if you like the look of it, Mrs Carrington.'

'When can I see it - have you told your mother?'

'I am taking her there on Sunday but she is unaware of that and I propose to ask David Gilbert if we can visit early next week; I can't tell you how happy I am.'

'You don't have to, it is written all over your face and I am going to buy us a bottle of the

George's finest bubbly to celebrate.'

They pulled into the car park at the rear of the hotel and made their way to the desk where the reception was as hospitable as ever. They divested themselves of the luggage and proceeded to the cocktail bar, whereupon Sally ordered the said champagne and excitedly sat down and plied him with questions.

He took an envelope from his jacket pocket and passed her the Polaroid pictures he had taken earlier that day. The expression on her face when she saw the front elevation was everything he could have hoped for.

'It's an ancestral home,' she stuttered.

He indulged her humour and passed her the photographs of the drawing room with its magnificent fireplace above which, was an enormous 'broken pediment' mantel mirror'.

The remainder of the wall was lined with leather bound books. The next picture was the great entrance hall with its impressive black and white marble floor and double staircase. It also housed a large inglenook fireplace occupied by the biggest firedogs she had ever seen.

The viewing was interrupted by the Maître d', who lead them to their favourite corner table.

She clung to his arm and whispered, 'I never expected anything so grand.'

'It is the seat of the Carrington's,' he jested.

They were both on cloud nine and between eating and poring over the photographs, drank a few too many cognacs so that his treat, as she described it, was put on hold overnight!

They woke to find the sun already high in the sky so breakfast was taken in the garden room, after which they set out for Manston. She implored him to stay for a coffee and show her mother the pictures of Milford Hall; it was impossible to deny her, particularly when Granny Parkinson joined them. They let him go only after promising that he would bring his mother back for Sunday lunch so that the whole family could celebrate together.

'Okay Granny, I surrender and I will leave you the photographs - no doubt you will have organised the décor by the time I return.'

With that and a cheery wave he sprinted towards the car and, in a cloud of dust, disappeared down the drive.

The following day his head still buzzing with excitement he set off to collect his mother from Watkin Hall, the stylish brick and stone Victorian house he had discovered a decade earlier.

He vividly remembered Mrs Watkin-Downes and her faithful companion Alice, and the expression of joy that lit their faces when he promised them that they would still live there even after he had converted the property into luxury apartments. Today, at least for the time being! - his mother had one of the ground floor conversions and it was her drawing room that now housed the magnificent large oil painting of the Quorn hunt gathered on the gravelled terrace at the front of Watkin Hall; Mrs Watkin-Downes had insisted that she should have it and that would be a memory he would see more of when it moved with them to Milford.

He finally reached the gravelled terrace and parked near to the front door that opened into the wonderful baroque hallway with its stunning staircase.

The door swung open and there she was, as fashionable and trim as ever.

'Come in dear.'

'No let's head for the hills and find a roadside café where we can get a cup of tea. It will be a new experience for you, mother.'

She chuckled. 'Okay, my treat.'

She slid into the front seat of the 911 observing, 'I don't think that Dr Porsche had people of my age in mind when he designed his motor cars.'

Suddenly however she became very quiet, a pensive expression clouding her face.

He waited, sensing something was concerning her.

Finally she spoke.

'James you are obviously planning to live with Sally and, as you have bought her that wonderful ring, you intend to be married.'

He nodded. 'Yes, things are developing but, as we are finding out the law moves very slowly. We have both taken legal advice, the upshot of which was that Kate or I had to petition the other. Although technically she struck up a relationship with Johnnie before I met Sally, I felt that for the boy's sake it would look better if I was the guilty party - i.e. your dad's been a naughty boy, preferable to your mother's been playing away.

His mother nodded sympathetically.

We were duly summoned to appear before a district judge who accepted our plea before instructing us to that we would be added to his list of those awaiting pronouncement of the Decree Nisi. This was issued four weeks ago, so in another two weeks the court will issue the Decree Absolute making us free to marry. I really should have kept you in the loop, but it is a tricky thing to discuss with one's mother, particularly as you have maintained a very fair and neutral stance. But I am glad you mentioned it, as I feel better having got it off my chest. Now we can enjoy the day, yes!'

'Yes we can I am looking forward to lunch, I presume this roadside cafe you have in mind has tables and chairs as I don't fancy balancing a cup of tea on my lap in the rather tight confines of this machine I am sitting in.'

'Hopefully mother we will find somewhere decent, although I can't vouch for the other diners.'

The good mood was immediately restored; likewise the weather was perfect as they set out in the direction of Grantham before diverting into the Vale of Belvoir. This elicited an astute observation from his passenger.

'We seem to be going a long way round.'

'I thought you would enjoy it, bring back a few good memories, in fact why don't we have a peep at that wonderful great stone house that used to be your home. You will have to remind me exactly where it is.'

'It has been a long time, James; I don't know how it will make me feel.'

His expression was understanding.

'Mother, it was thirty years ago and I have often thought about it, I would love to see it again.'

She gave him a whimsical glance.

'I remember a fourteen year old boy vowing to come back to Milford and reclaim his inheritance, so I suppose I cannot begrudge you at least seeing the place.'

'Because of Kate's feelings for Woolmington I have shut those thoughts to the very back of my mind.'

She squeezed his hand.

'Take the second left and after about two miles go right.'

He had never approached Milford from this direction so had no need to pretend not to know the way.

Finally the great iron gates came into view, he saw his mother glance at the lodge house.

'I still exchange Christmas cards with the Prices, I wonder how they are?'

'Shall we drive in; you can't see a lot from here?'

'In for a penny...,' she replied.

He swung in and tried to see the expression on his mother's face. She looked tense but expectant as he parked opposite the imposing entrance. Unexpectedly the door was locked.

'I suppose we could just walk around and have a look.'

They looked at each other, the atmosphere was electric. She dipped into her handbag and pressed a dark blue leather case into his hand.

He nervously opened it to reveal a large shiny brass key, above this on the underside of the lid, was a simple inscription in gold lettering, Charles St Aubin; Locksmith.

'You have brought us home James, as Robert and I always believed that you would. This was his idea, if only he could have been here to share this moment with us.'

He blinked away the tears and whispered. 'He is here, I can feel it.'

Elizabeth's eyes were also decidedly moist but she sought to keep the moment happy.'

'Why not try it in the lock she teased, you have only my word that it will fit.'

He did as he was bidden and the great oak door swung open to reveal David Gilbert in his morning suit holding a silver tray on which stood a bottle of champagne and three flutes.

The label on the bottle bore the legend Dom Perignon 1948. The year the Carrington's had moved out.

It was a marvellously expensive and poignant thought.

James was bereft of speech, but finally stuttered out the question on his mind.

'How did you know?'

'It is all my fault James; I was in Griffin and Spalding's department store in Nottingham looking at lampshades when your mother, whom I haven't seen in years, came in to the same department. I recognised her instantly and let slip that I was so looking forward to seeing her today. She was totally mystified but she put two and two together so I am afraid it is me who let the cat out of the bag.'

His mother interrupted.

'Having found out that today was The Day, I asked David to lock the door so that you could use the 'Brahma' key, which was presented to your great-grandfather by the maker Mr St Aubin, who I believe, was the greatest lock designer of his day and possibly ever.

He shook his head in disbelief but the bonhomie soon returned and he declared that it was not polite to keep a waiter standing around unemployed. They therefore followed David Gilbert into the drawing room where a selection of nibbles awaited them.

The atmosphere was totally convivial, Elizabeth and David Gilbert talking like old friends about the past and even about the future, as he explained why he was leaving and even produced the letter left by Robert Carrington which had forecast this day.

'Do you know Elizabeth, he even sent me a case of Macallan whisky and I have kept that last bottle for thirty years or so waiting for James to show up'.

He passed the cream envelope to James.

'And finally he did just that and claimed his legacy.'

His mother gave their host an understanding smile.

'Robert and I only met you two or three times David, but we were both struck by your integrity and appreciation of our finances at the time. This is why we decided to leave all the special pieces of furniture that were designed and made by my grandfather's furniture company which, at

the end of the nineteenth century, was the largest in Europe.'
He took her hand.

'And that is why Elizabeth, I have already promised to return them to James. They belong only in this house.'

'That is so kind and why don't you call me Lizzie, it is the start of a new life for me and it seems that all of my new friends have rechristened me anyway.'

'It suits you Lizzie. Now I must leave you to have a look round your new home.'
James took her hand.

'I wanted this as much for you as for myself. It is your family home even more than it is mine and you have suffered so much sorrow, widowed longer than you were married. You must always remember, as I do, the fortitude and determination to return us to our rightful home is because I carry your genes.'

'Maybe James, but the genes that made you famous, a national hero, the ability to play rugby for your country and the British Lions, you inherited those from your father and they have been passed on again, to my grandson son, Edward.'
He nodded, his expression was impassive, but she knew just how much warmth lay behind the mask.

'Okay, if I accept that then you must accept that my business acumen and the intelligence that Charles displays is definitely from the Staincliffe side of my family. Now let's start the tour, the hall you have seen albeit briefly but, as with elsewhere, things have not changed a great deal. Let's go and look at what I hope you will see as your wing of the house.'

She followed him up the great staircase and along a corridor to a very large bedroom which he suggested would make a splendid sitting room and then on to the proposed kitchen. She followed him into another generous room which, he suggested, would become an en-suite bedroom and adjacent a similar sized room that would become a guest suite.

'What do you think?'

'I am so excited, what does Sally think?'

'She insisted that you must come here first, but she is pretty excited by the photographs. However, you must ask her yourself as we have been invited to Manston for lunch. First though I must ask David when it will be convenient to bring Sally for a viewing.'

He left his mother still living yesterday's dreams and set off downstairs, trying the study first. It was an astute guess, he found his host watching the racing from Haydock Park and polishing off the nibbles.

'Sorry to interrupt David, I was wondering when it would be convenient to bring Sally, my fiancée, to have a look inside.'

The question evoked an amusing response.

'You have your own key, a rather special one at that; come whenever you feel like it. As for moving in permanently; I have signed all the documentation and I gather they are waiting for one last search to be returned. After that we can then start arranging with Pickford's to move me out and install you back where you belong.'

'Thanks David, I will let you know when we plan a visit as I would not dream of abusing your hospitality.'

He now had to find his mother and in a house as big as this it might have taken awhile but once again his instinct proved correct, she was in the kitchen.

'This,' he announced, 'will be the first room to get a makeover, I can't wait to get the designers over from Minster Kitchens and they will of course be working on your area too, which I think we should call the Staincliffe Wing, how does that sound?'

'A bit grander than it needs to be!'

'On that note then, let's head off to see the Parkinsons.'

They set out for Manston, his mother confiding on the way that much though she had and still did like Kate and her parents, Sally had through past connections, brought a new dimension into her life. The icing on the cake was Milford Hall which she realised would never have happened as long as he was married to Kate.

The reception at Manston was as cordial as ever but, unfortunately for James, Robert Parkinson was in London on NFU business so it was four against one.

Sally disappeared to collect the coffee and Millie directed Lizzie to the kitchen table on which the Polaroid photographs had been assembled. In no time the three older ladies were totally occupied, questions and suggestions flowing back and forth, every so often one of them evoking a source of great mirth as the reply was batted back at the others.

Sally took James by the hand and led him onto the terrace where a pot of coffee awaited.

'Would you care to pour Carrington?'

'Certainly mam.'

She patted the cushions of the swing seat and he joined her under the green and white striped awning; he felt so fulfilled and happy and there was no doubt that the euphoria was shared by his future bride. For a moment though she became suddenly serious.

'The boys seemed quite relaxed when we saw them last week, are they coming to terms with the prospect of new step-parents?'

'I believe they are and I have something to suggest which you may not be happy about. Kate called me yesterday and confided that she and Johnnie were considering a low key wedding as they felt the boys would handle this better than a big fancy bash. What do you think?'

'Actually James I have been thinking along the same lines but wasn't sure how to present it to you.'

He gazed into her blue eyes and saw nothing but understanding and compassion.

'Will your parents be happy to go along with this?'

'I will sound them out this evening; in the meantime can we now fix a day?'

He paused for a moment; she saw the cogs turning in his head, finally he spoke.

'I want us to move into our new home when we return from honeymoon, so let's allow say three months, by which time the major renovations will be complete. This means that you and I have to agree on the design for the kitchen, and mother has to okay the alterations to the Staincliffe Wing. He took out his pocket diary and flicked the pages to September.

'Unfortunately the thirteenth is not on a Friday, as it was when I agreed the purchase with David Gilbert but what about September the 12th and then when we wake up on our first day as man and wife it will be Saturday the 13th.

She stood and grabbed his hand.

'Come on let's go and tell the ladies.'

'What about your father?'

'As I have told you before he does what he is told - well inside the house at least.'

She propelled him into the kitchen and cupping her hand to her lips blew a fanfare before announcing that James Robert Staincliffe Carrington was to be wed to Sally Anne Louise Parkinson on Friday the 12th of September.

Needless to say this evoked yet more excitement which was in full flow when the father of the bride poked his head around the door. He shook his head but as affable as ever joined in the celebrations before disappearing and a couple of minutes later reappearing with a bottle of champagne and six glasses.

'As I believe I may have mentioned before, you are a very expensive chap to know Mr Carrington!'

After proposing the toast he signalled to James and they disappeared to the sanctuary that was his office, here James reiterated the suggestion of a small family celebration which, after brief consideration was approved. They agreed the date and the venue, Robert suggesting that the wedding breakfast be housed in a marquee on the lawn at the rear of the house; this had the advantage of several large trees where guests could wander out to sit and enjoy the fresh air, should the weather allow.

'You must help me choose the wines James, the rest if you agree, we will leave to the ladies?'

'With pleasure Robert.'

In the few weeks that the two had known each other, a very comfortable trust had been established and they chatted away, both very confident that the future boded well. The conversation had moved to Milford Hall when they were invaded by four slightly tipsy ladies who confessed to having raided the wine cellar and helped themselves to yet more of the sparkling wine of Rheims. They hauled Robert out of his chair and marched him off to see the photographs leaving the lovebirds to contemplate the future.

Normally the choice of church would have been Bottesford, but with the memory of Edward Lawson's funeral still very much in their thoughts, they decided to approach the vicar of St John's Church at Colston Bassett. This is a grade two listed building with a magnificent spire and is referred to locally as the Cathedral of the Vale.

As to the choice of guests, they decided that they must be essentially family with a few very close friends such as Jack Priory.

As to actual numbers, Sally recalled that at Granny Parkinson's eightieth birthday last year they had around fifty people comfortably seated in the marquee. So this was the round figure they would settle upon as it still had leeway for any last minute inclusions.

Another factor they had to contemplate was the date that Kate and Johnnie might choose as this may well mean James having to vacate Woolmington. After a brief thought he decided to pre-empt this by moving into Milford as soon as David Gilbert vacated the property. This would have the benefit of him overseeing the alterations without having to travel back and forth each evening. He lifted Sally to her feet.

'Come on let's join the revellers, we have achieved a lot and they might just have left us a drop of something alcoholic.'

On Wednesday evening he collected Kate from Manston and in a state of high excitement they set out for Milford, both of them just ever so slightly apprehensive over her reaction; so much depended on it - would all his dreams be dashed?

Finally she spotted the entrance and the attractive gatehouse that guarded it and as he swung onto the drive she spotted the impressive building with its great stone tower.

It had looked impressive on the photographs but she had not expected anything quite this imposing, He parked in the shade afforded by the tower; Sally had still not said a word.

'You don't like it?' His fearful reaction.

She turned to face him, tears running down her cheeks.

'It has taken my breath away, I can now properly understand what has driven you, what has so motivated you since you were fourteen years old, I cannot believe that Kate could have denied you this dream.'

'On one occasion she did actually back down, but it was in desperation, she soon resumed her spiteful rejection of this house; a property she had never even seen.'

She gave him an understanding look.

'As the Bard said, 'there is nothing sooner dry than a woman's tears.'

He took out his handkerchief and dabbed her cheeks.

'I know that yours are real tears and I can tell they are tears of joy.'

He slid out of the car and in a trice had opened her door and as she got out, not showing her knickers of course! He swooped down and picked her up.

'I am not sure if we have to be married to do this, but I am going to carry you over the threshold as this is our new home and always will be.

He nudged the door open with his shoulder and stepped through into the majestic hallway before gently lowering her on to the black and white marbled floor.

'David Gilbert is not here today so let's go explore and make plans.'

Still in a dream, her eyes slowly took in the great sweep of the staircase, the enormous fireplace and he basked in her excitement; likewise in the drawing room and the library and then the morning room. The study she suggested was his domain, so he would have a free hand in there but the kitchen and adjoining service areas she agreed did need serious refurbishment. They would of course utilise the expertise that was available from Minster Kitchens.

'How many bedrooms are there?'

'Excluding the wing which I hope will be occupied by Sue and Keith there are fourteen;

Although after the alterations, two of those will become mother's kitchen and sitting room and I think another should be converted into a den for the boys, and the one next to their bedrooms should become their bathroom.

So that reduces it to ten, but I really want your input so let's see what you think.'

He set off up the staircase expecting her to follow; instead she raced up the other side and waited on the gallery landing at the top. First he showed her the 'Staincliffe Wing' which she immediately recognised would become his mother's apartment and then on to ten more rooms from which the boys would select their domain, and finally he opened an oak door to reveal an enormous room with an impressively huge oak four poster bed.

It was not difficult to recognise that this was the master bedroom, attached to which was a large en-suite bathroom and a dressing room.

All the upstairs rooms were architecturally impressive but all were in need of a sympathetic overhaul. He turned towards her.

'Where do we start?'

'With those rooms upstairs that we are going to need immediately, the others we can do at a less frenzied pace. David Gilbert has kept on top of the decorating, although we may want to change a few colours schemes once we have properly settled in. Downstairs it is really only the kitchen areas that need immediate attention.'

She took his hand; her eyes expressed without words the depth of her feelings. 'I love you so much.'

He circled his arms around her and as she nestled against him he kissed the top of her head.

'And I love you so much, you have no idea how many times I had thought about you after that Architects dinner dance and I still find it difficult to believe that you are going to be my wife, I keep expecting to wake up from a wondrous dream.'

'Well when you do I will be in bed beside you.'

He looped his finger around hers and this time they came down the staircase together and agreed on how they would entertain Charles and Edward on Saturday.

CHAPTER SIXTY EIGHT

The following day he contacted Kate who was now, not unnaturally, spending most of her time in Yorkshire. He outlined the plans of yesterday and was slightly surprised that she had no objections and was prepared to work around September 12th.

With regard to letting the boys know, she also agreed but suggested that they each advise the boys of their separate plans rather than make it one big family affair. She was considering doing this in Yorkshire and tongue in cheek asked James if he would be confiding his news to them at his new address!

This had not occurred to him but, on reflection, he really quite liked the idea although he remained non-committal at this stage. He also resisted asking Kate if she was hoping to get an insight, albeit second hand, into the splendours of Milford Hall - the house that she had spurned.

He put the phone down, relieved that the truce between himself and Kate appeared to remain in place, hopeful that with the boys help they could all build on this.

It was a great relief, which brought added spice to the coming weekend when he and Sally were taking the boys to see Milford and hopefully, by getting their input into decorating their rooms would generate some enthusiasm for the move - he also had a surprise for them which he knew would prove to be a winner.

Accompanied by Sally, he collected them after cricket on Saturday afternoon and set out for home, a journey the boys knew only too well. It was no surprise then when an inquisitive voice from the rear seat enquired, 'Are we going to Sally's house?'

'Sort of,' he admitted.

Sally decided to help him out. 'We have to collect a parcel and it is for you two.'

As she had hoped, this generated quite a deal of excitement and much to the enjoyment of those in the front of the car, the guesses from the back seat all remained wide of the mark.

They were now quite close to Milford and to deflect their minds from the destination she appeared to look at the map and advised James to take the next left turn and look out for some large iron gates.

Edward saw them first and his excited voice rang out, 'there on the right.'

James swung in and the more considered tones of Charles posed the million dollar question.

'Wow, is this Milford Hall, is this the surprise?'

'Yes and no,' his father advised, as they drove past the front of the building to the stable block at the rear where Keith and Sue were waiting for them.

Edward spotted them, his voice tinged with disappointment as he added.

'We don't need a new pony.'

'Well at least have a look,' Sally implored him.

They reluctantly got out of the car and followed Keith through the archway and into the stable yard.

James and Sally hung back until they heard the squeals of pleasure as the boys stared, lost for words as they saw two quad bikes sporting the number plates 'EC 1' and 'CC 1'

They both raced back, red faces radiantly happy. In unison they cried out 'Thanks Dad.'

He gathered them into his arms. 'Actually it was Sally's idea.'

Whereupon, they ran across to her and hugged her tightly. 'Thank you Sally.'

When the excitement had died down, Sue produced two crash helmets and the protective vests they wore when riding the ponies. It took seconds to get them kitted out and once James had received their promises to always wear them, he handed them over to Keith and Sue for driving instructions.

They both stalled the Quads at the first attempt but they quickly got the knack and were soon riding confidently around the yard, at which point Keith led them out into the paddock nearest the house and they zoomed away.

James pulled the car through the open gate and into the field, followed by Keith and Sue. They unloaded the canvas chairs they had brought over from Woolmington and Sally, acting as hostess, collected and served the Pimms from the car boot. Her waitress duties over, she sat next to Sue and talked about - horses of course!

James meanwhile quizzed Keith about him and Sue relocating to Milford and taking charge of all the tasks they already did at Woolmington.

'I don't see any problems James, but the memsahib will have to be agreeable.'

'Absolutely,' James affirmed, adding that he was planning to enlarge his broodmare band, so another stable lass might have to be considered and that would fall within his and Sue's remit.

He was conscious that Sue's radar was picking up his conversation with Keith so he ran the idea past her, mentioning that the accommodation here would be larger, as they would see when they had a tour of the property.

Sally interrupted.

'There is just one slight problem, how do we communicate with the quad bikes?'

Keith jumped up. 'Sound the car horn James and I will wave to them.'

Amazingly it worked and two excited bikers roared towards them and collected a cool glass of Coke and a packet of crisps.

Meanwhile the adults gathered up the chairs and returned them to the back of Keith's Land Rover.

Edward identified the success of the quad bikes by anxiously asking if they would be coming again next week?

'There will be plenty more opportunities, meanwhile let's go and check out your bedrooms.'

They all trooped inside and whilst he took the boys on a tour of the house, Sally escorted Keith and Sue to the wing of the house opposite to the now so called 'Staincliffe Wing.'

Both the boys and Sue and Keith were more than delighted with what was on offer, even more so when the proposed improvements were outlined. After the tour, James led them over to the lawn that was dominated by the great oak tree with its circular bench, meanwhile Sally repaired to the kitchen where Mrs Jenkins had left a selection of sandwiches and cakes along with a note from David Gilbert which invited them to raid the fridge where a selection of drinks awaited.

The atmosphere was so convivial, everyone joining the merriment, James squeezed Sally's hand, everything was working out as they had hoped with no clouds on the horizon, and life was so full of expectation.

CHAPTER SIXTY NINE

Invigorated by the success of yesterday, James was at his desk at Minster Kitchens before seven. He ploughed through the mail, dictated several letters and telephone glued to his ear was not aware of Melanie, his PA, until she rustled a sheet of paper quite literally under his nose. This intrusion was so unusual and so not like her that he swiftly put his caller on hold.

Before he could say a word she placed the fax message in front of him - it was from Miles Stanhope Court, now senior partner at Abercrombie Pope & Plumber.

He quickly scanned the fax and wham - how quickly did yesterday's euphoria vanish, now it was the sword of Damocles that dominated the future - the sword that had in Greek legend been suspended from the ceiling by a single strand of hair. He now knew that precarious feeling.

The fax advised that Roger Blakeney, son-in-law of Herbert Simmons, the deceased founder of Simmons International, was seeking to organise an alternative option to the takeover of Fordmill Construction.

He apologised to the caller he had on hold and immediately called Miles and plied him with questions.

'What shareholding does he have - can he get enough support to form a majority?'

Miles, with the advantage of prior knowledge, suggested they meet somewhere halfway between London and Nottingham and The George Hotel at Stamford was quite naturally agreed upon.

James arrived at one thirty and was closely followed by Jack and Anthony. He was inwardly seething and they too were very agitated as they waited in the bar until Miles Stanhope Court and his assistant, Roger Gower, arrive just before two.

The pleasantries were very brief and no time was wasted before they repaired to a private meeting room. Miles kicked off the proceedings with a brief resume.

Herbert Simmons was an intensely private person who would never allow shares in his company to be traded: In his lifetime, the company was one hundred percent owned by himself. On his death the family retained eighty percent of the equity, the remaining twenty percent were left as gifts to long serving senior members of staff.

This is still the case although the pack has since been shuffled by the intervention of a stranger he had never met, and who he would never have countenanced as a suitable husband for his articulate and highly intelligent daughter. He nodded to Roger Gower who placed before each of them a summary of the current shareholders.

Arthur Simmons	son of founder and now CEO		30 %
Jane Blakeney	daughter of founder	30 %	
Mrs Simmons	wife of Herbert Simmons	20 %	
Roger Blakeney	husband of Jane Blakeney	12 %	
Four Small Shareholders	in total	8 %	

Miles pursed his lips and outlined some of alternative strategy options Fordmill might consider.

Private Equity Companies.
These have a culture of cost control; a liking for predictable markets; they are looking for Dynamic Management & Solid Historic Growth: both categories that fitted the Fordmill profile. However, he added, they are often short term investors who want a defined exit strategy.

Investment Banks
They too may not want permanent and long term commitment.
However, some are controlled by high net worth investors who will stay the course...

James held up his hand and cut him short.
'Gentlemen, we need to give this some very considered thought. When Edward Lawson and I founded Fordmill it was a business that had a driving force and a passion to succeed; now we are threatened by some jumped up bloody nobody. I thank Miles sincerely for dropping everything to come here this afternoon, but I suggest that we reconvene in two days and this time we will do him the courtesy of meeting at his office. Are you in agreement gentlemen?'
All the heads nodded, but optimism was not apparent.

They made their separate ways home, James deciding on a whim to go via Manston Hall where he might be able to gain some insight into background of the mystery objector, Roger Blakeney. Hopefully his conduit to this information would be Sir Robert Parkinson who regularly had business in the City.

The doorbell was answered by Camilla Parkinson who, seeing his demeanour, sensed that undue pleasantries were not appropriate.
'You know where his office is James, why don't you go through.'
He knocked on the door and shuffled his thoughts around in his head and decided to tell it as it was.
His host also realised that James was here on serious business so waved him into a chair.
'You have something of some import on your mind and you think I may be able to help.'
'I will cut to the chase Robert, you are aware of the basic tenets regarding the sale of Fordmill Construction. I am here because I know that you have extensive contacts within the City and I need to know the background to a character named Roger Blakeney and in particular his financial background.'

'I have heard the name but really little else. However, I know someone who should be able to help you and that is your brother-in-law to be. I will see if I can get hold of him.'

He picked up the phone and right on cue, Camilla arrived with a pot of Earl Grey. She looked up and they both nodded approvingly; she poured and left them to their thoughts although she did hear the start of her husband's conversation.

'Guy, hopefully I am not interrupting a meeting, but I have James with me and he needs some background on Roger Blakeney, yes the Labour MP.'
He picked up a pencil and started scribbling on a notepad, his only input was the occasional 'really' and 'cheeky beggar' and finally, 'thanks old boy, anything at all may be very helpful.'

He turned towards James.

'The CV as I know it so far is that Mr Blakeney was a hardly distinguished lecturer at a Midlands University where he taught politics. He is a socialist and a very active member of a local constituency party which led eventually, to him standing in that particular ward and being elected to Parliament. There are rumours that he has his nose in the trough, although he is not exclusive in that sense as this is a disease which is not unknown in all the parties. However, there was a rumour that he was a social climber who would willingly take cash for favours. He is very astute and every bill that he supported or opposed was usually a headliner. As a result he attended a good many City functions, particularly those relating to the law and finance; at one of these he sat next to Jane Simmons...'

'The daughter of Herbert Simmons and now Mrs Roger Blakeney?'

'Correct James and one last thing that Guy could recall at short notice, the same Roger Blakeney is a great friend of Paul Larkin and Ross Taggart, who were previously senior executives at...'

'Simmons International.'

'Right again James, but how did you know that?'

'I checked with Companies House for the names of the five people who had small shareholdings in Simmons and guess what, there were originally seven small investors, all of whom were Department Heads. The shareholdings were a reward for their loyalty when Herbert Simmons became a Public Limited Company. They did of course have every right to sell their shareholding but it was not in the spirit of the gift, as old man Simmons gave those rewards as a sort of private hedge fund for their retirement. And not content with that, the bugger screwed his way into the Simmons family by marrying Jane Simmons.'

They both leaned back in their chairs, neither said a word but they both knew that the other was trying to juggle the facts into a coherent strategy to bring down Roger Blakeney.

Finally Robert spoke. 'This will not be easy, James, he is artful and will have other low life in his team.'

'I am fighting for the company I founded and not just for myself, but for my family and the families of others such as Edward Lawson. I will not let this weasel bring us down.'

He stood up, his countenance that of a man going to war and with only one intention, do or die.

'Thank you Robert, you have given me a lot of ammunition, now I need a plan and one last favour. Dare I ask if Guy knows what Jane Blakeney does for a living?'

'Let's ask him.'

Whereupon he made the call and reported to James that she was a Financial Analyst for Gerlach's, a German Investment Bank whose British HQ was in the financial square mile, quite close in fact to the Bank of England. Finally, there is a well substantiated rumour that Blakeney is in a long term relationship with a woman who is the local party agent in Warwickshire. Apparently this began before he was elected to the House.

'Thank you once again Robert.'

And then he was gone; Robert Parkinson certain that if this man produced him a grandson, his farming empire would be in good hands.

James hastened back to Woolmington, the germ of an idea starting to grow in his head; this was a Staincliffe moment and he needed to be in his own study sitting at his ancestor's desk for what might well be the defining moment of his business career.

He checked the number with Directory Enquiries and plunged in at the deep end.
The reply to his call was prompt and business like. 'Gerlach's, how may I help?

'Jane Blakeney please.'
He spoke in a familiar way that often confused the receptionist and it worked.

'May I ask what about?'

'It is James Carrington, the call is personal.'

'A moment please.'
His heart was pounding, he had used this positive approach many times before, never had it been so significant.

'Is that Mr Carrington the ex- rugby player? How nice to hear from you.'

'Err, well yes it is.' She had caught him off guard.

'How may I help you?'

'Could we meet - tomorrow if possible - any time will be convenient.'

'Very well 5.30 am.' There was a pause and then she laughed, 'or perhaps 5.30 pm?'

'That is so kind, I really look forward to meeting with you. Shall we say the cocktail bar at Claridge's?'

'That would be perfect.'

'Auf Wiedersehen.'
He sensed the chuckle in her voice as she put the phone down and breathed a huge sigh of relief; he was still standing and still fighting.

CHAPTER SEVENTY

He did not sleep particularly well; his mind was in turmoil as it sifted through the various options. The first few seconds, they would be so crucial. Finally he fell asleep but at 6.16 the alarm went and he was immediately out of bed and into the shower. He was excited not daunted by the prospect of meeting Jane Blakeney.

He heard Sue arrive and went with her to check the horses but all she wanted to talk about was Milford Hall; let's hope I can make today's woman as excited as this one, he thought.

After a quick breakfast he packed his notes into a leather binder, gathered up his overnight bag and was away.

He was quickly on the A1 and although he was several hours away from meeting Mrs Blakeney he wanted to absorb the atmosphere and get a taste of London. He wound his way into the City and parked on the embankment, grabbed his notes and walked briskly towards St Paul's and Threadneedle Street from where he enjoyed a coffee on the pavement opposite Christopher Wren's great masterpiece.

Looking at this monumental achievement and considering the battles that the architect, who incidentally was a very accomplished engineer, had overcome to leave us this fantastic building put his own 'sortie' into perspective. Compared with Wren's undertaking, his task was akin to building a dog kennel, even though the dog owner would probably put up a fight!

Having broken down the problem into the proverbial way of eating an elephant - by cutting it into small slices, the problem was starting to recede and he walked back to the car with a spring in his step. He put the hood down and for good measure played a cassette of Edward Elgar's five Pomp and Circumstance marches which, even in the seemingly endless queue of traffic, raised his spirits so that when he finally reached Brook Street and his favourite hotel, Claridge's, he was in much better humour as he anticipated this evenings encounter.

By now he was a familiar figure to the man in the top hat who greeted him warmly.

'Good afternoon Mr Carrington, we are travelling light today.'

'Just overnight, William.'

He tossed the car keys over and they were relayed on to the parking attendant as he disappeared across the black and white tiled floor that led to reception. The magic of this totally British institution enveloped him with pride and the confidence to successfully accomplish today's mission.

Having arrived at base camp he re-examined his strategy in broad strokes, which included a few question marks where he expected any defensive statements.

He checked his watch it said five fifteen. It was time to go.

But she had stolen the high ground and although they had never met, he instinctively knew that the slim dark haired, long legged woman perched on a bar stool at the corner of this elegant art deco bar was his guest.

'Dr Blakeney I presume.'

He replicated probably the most famous introduction ever, although the setting was rather more luxurious than that famous meeting in Africa.

'And you must be Sir Henry Morton Stanley.'

'Indeed I am and I am hoping we can together negotiate our way out of this jungle.'

'I imagine you are here to discuss Simmons and Fordmill rather than Christianity.'

He looked slightly surprised.

'I am my father's daughter James, if I might be so familiar.'

'Only if you allow me to buy you a drink; champagne?'

She nodded and at his suggestion they moved to a corner table which afforded the privacy they needed.

The waiter poured them each a glass of Roederer Crystal and he sought to regain the high ground, but once again she beat him to it so he decided to let her initiate the negotiations as this way she may well reveal her hand.

'My father was born in Leicestershire and although the family moved to the home counties he remained a staunch supporter of Leicester Tigers, although the Carrington he so admired was of course your father. When you started to make the headlines he imagined with your looks and charisma that you had come via the Oxbridge route, but later discovered that you had as a very young man, founded the construction company that was so often mentioned in architectural and professional magazines.'

'That is very kind of you and you will not be surprised to hear that Simmons, Laings, and McAlpines were very much the template I attempted to model my own company on.'

'But then you deserted the construction industry to make kitchen and bathroom furniture?'

He paused, and looked at her intently; she returned his gaze, her eyes holding his. Fortunately, the waiter arrived to top up their glasses, so the impasse was removed.

'Jane, this is a topic that is never open for discussion but, as the stakes are so high, I will make you privy to details that I have never mentioned to anyone, other than family and very close friends. Edward Lawson was at school with me, we played rugby for Leicester and England and the British Lions, and we founded the business together. We were blood brothers if you like, until one day I made a great error of judgement and questioned his motives over a business deal that I believed he had made on his own behalf. Not until his untimely death did I come to realise that I had put two and two together and had come up with ten!

What he had done was entirely honourable, but I concluded that funds diverted to an outside contract was to finance a project for himself, when in fact it was to set up to fund a cancer charity for Elizabeth Lattimer - the wife of the bank manager who initially financed our business, and later introduced us to Abercrombie Pope & Plummer.

Unfortunately, for me the initials in the cash ledger were EL - sadly the same as his own. I only found this out when Edward's wife, Connie, told me at his funeral.'

She saw the effect this had on him and, negotiations forgotten for the moment, reached out and placed her hand on his.

'James, I so admire you for confiding in me; your secret will go no further. Now let us see what we can make of the conundrum we came here to sort out. Why should we acquire Fordmill Construction rather than other suitors who are keen to become part of Simmons?'

He passed her a sheet of paper which had his trade mark bullet point summaries, each identifying the advantages of the partnership.

Compelling reasons why Simmons International should integrate Fordmill Construction into their company:

- You need a company that is financially very sound with a proven track record of profitability over several years.
- Fordmill would ensure that your UK footprint would remain strong.
- You need strong and imaginative management - the present MD, Anthony Jayes is a qualified lawyer whose initial instinct was to study accountancy. Since joining Fordmill he has taken an external degree so that he now comes equipped with both qualifications. As such, you will acquire an extremely competent and loyal executive.
- We have won numerous awards for innovation and design.- Have the other people?
- Our developments, such as the Bournemouth project, were ground breaking and widely acclaimed by prestigious publications such as The Architects Journal.
- We also re-invented the wheel by buying and converting into living accommodation large run down country houses; riverside wharfs and industrial buildings such as cotton mills.
- Anthony Jayes' recommendations that you relocate your UK headquarters to the Fordmill HQ in Nottinghamshire will release considerable capital from the sale of your premises in Kingston on Thames.
- Furthermore the cost indices relating to salaries, business rates, etc. will be substantially less than London equivalents.
- Perhaps however, the most pertinent point is that your accountants and our bankers have already concluded that the synergy between our two companies is extremely conducive and you have already invested a great deal of money in reaching this decision.
- Why would you now wish to retract your intention??

She placed the sheet of paper on to the table. She turned towards him, her face was pensive, and for a few seconds she did not speak.

'Why do you think we are considering withdrawing?'
This time he considered his words very carefully, he was in deep water with no apparent signs of a lifeboat.

'During discussions with Anthony Jayes, your brother Arthur confided to Anthony that he was certain that they could work together, that they were both on the same wavelength. He also added that, and you have already disclosed this, your father had considered making an approach for

Fordmill as a means of establishing a foothold in the north. This made eminent sense as the cost of property and land is more attractive than in London and the Home Counties.

Our bankers advise me that you and your brother each own 30% of the shares in Simmons and you have also disclosed that you have a great respect for your father's business nous and intuition. So, as the two of you alone can trigger this acquisition, why do you hesitate?'

Once again her eyes challenged him, he knew he must tell her - but it was not easy.
'Jane, I know that your husband bought out two of the former directors to acquire a 10% holding. I know also that five other former department manager have a combine holding, also equivalent to 8%.

All seven of these former employees were given the shares by your father in recognition of many years of service in which they had helped him build up the Simmons Empire. I also understand that your mother holds 20% of the stock so as she will stay loyal to your brother you have in fact in a deadlock?'
She shook her head. ' My mother will vote with me to save my professional reputation.'

But he was not to be denied. ' I have recently become divorced so I understand very clearly the influence a spouse can bring to bear on matters financial - I have just finished fighting my own corner!

However, you are a Financial Analyst with a major German Bank; your husband with respect is a Member of Parliament whose background prior to this was lecturing in Politics. Surely a decision like this can only be made with industry knowledge, or has he a retainer from a rival competitor and do the five other former employees have a similar carrot? If so, of course, he will press their claims but you and your brother owe it to the present employee's and the memory of your father's reputation to vote with your head,'

He paused briefly. 'You also owe it to them to vote with your heart.'

Now it was her turn to hesitate and he waited anxiously for her reaction.

'James, you are very eloquent and have been very open and honest with me, particularly in regard to your trauma following Edward Lawson's untimely death. I will make you privy to my dilemma. My husband has borrowed a large sum of money to purchase his 12% stake in my family business and I believe that, without my agreement, he has used our London home, in which he has no equity, to guarantee that loan. If the alternative purchase of Fordmill does not go through, I do not have access to sufficient liquid funds to honour that debt. If that were to happen he would be vilified in the press and forced to resign his seat in Parliament, it would also ruin my financial standing professionally. Now do you see my problem?'
This time it was his turn to ruminate the extent of the enigma and after what seemed an age to Jane Simmons, his reply was short and cryptic.

'How much does he owe?'
Her reply was equally brief.

'£180k'
He held out his hand.

'You will tell him that you intend to vote with your brother and that to save his skin he will sell his shares to me. Failure to agree to this will bring into the public arena his large investment for personal gain which, to someone who has always lampooned those with wealth, will have ramifications that will almost certainly end his political career. Also his chances of going back into main stream education will be extremely tenuous, not to mention the much reduced income, even if he did find employment.'

She took his hand.

'Agreed James and thank you. How do you suggest we go forward?'

'What I would really like to do right now is give him a damn good hiding.'

'I would like that too, but the press would see it as British Lion eats Labour weasel and those who know nothing about rugby would see it as rich toff attacks college lecturer.'

Suddenly the professional demeanour cracked and he felt her tears on his face as she brushed his cheek and whispered in his ear, 'thank you James Carrington, thank you so much.'

He looked at his watch it was seven fifteen.

'Jane, the dining room will now be open, please say you will join me for supper.'

'I would love to.'

They made their way to the table he had already booked and his heart was light, he was back in the property business!

CHAPTER SEVENTY ONE

As usual he was up at 6.16 am and with the meeting at APP not scheduled until Ten O'clock he changed into a tracksuit top and running shorts. The doorman gave him a cheery greeting as he turned left and set off at a better than steady pace towards Hyde Park. A cursory glance at the Roosevelt Memorial in Grosvenor Square and he was into Upper Brook Street and finally Park Lane, his objective lay on the other side of this major thoroughfare and had he needed a breather, he would have had plenty of time. After what seemed an eternity the lights did finally change to red allowing the pedestrians to cross - if they were quick enough!

Once in the park, he chose to take the outer pedestrian path which took him towards Cumberland Gate and past Speakers' Corner. From here he followed the path around until he was running parallel with Bayswater Road, from the corner of his eye he saw the sign Stanhope Gate - could this possibly be associated with Miles Stanhope Court? He decided, humour once again near the surface; that in future he would certainly defer to him as Miles Stanhope Gate!

At the Serpentine he turned and headed back to Brook Gate and a few minutes later joined the ever thickening log jam on Park Lane. Not the most patient of men, this standstill would usually have provoked irritation but hey, he was in no hurry and he had joyful tidings to convey to two anxious business partners and Connie Lawson.

He was back at the hotel at just after seven o'clock and having showered, came down to breakfast feeling decidedly pleased that he had chosen to stretch his legs rather just his mind as had been the case yesterday.

At breakfast he opted for the continental option of cold meats and freshly squeezed orange followed by a black coffee. He spent half an hour or so completing 70% of the Telegraph crossword, despite his mind being elsewhere, and surprisingly, that was not in the APP boardroom. No, he had thought of the most wonderful way to celebrate Fordmill's victory yesterday and he made an appointment for 3 pm to facilitate that plan.

All packed, he asked for his overnight bag to be transferred to the Porsche and document case under his arm waited for William to signal him a cab. His first visit was at Trumper's. Set on the corner of Duke Street and Jermyn Street, it has been barber to the gentry since 1875 and his visits to the capital coincided with a haircut whenever possible. Suitably coiffured and with plenty of time in hand he continued his morning exercise by walking the short distance to the stylish Regency premises that housed Abercrombie Pope & Plumber. As he climbed the wide stone steps known colloquially in the banking community as the twelve apostles; he cast his mind back to that first visit when he fought for his company's existence under the scrutinising examination of that stiff backed ex-guards officer, Sir Julian Abercrombie and his fellow directors.

Now he was a regular visitor, instantly recognised by Peter the door man who greeted him with the news that Mr Priory and Mr Jayes had already arrived and were having the traditional morning glass of chocolate with Mr Stanhope Court. He walked purposefully to meet them in one of the smaller conference rooms and declining any refreshment he took his place at the conference table.

Clearly no one was in the mood for light-hearted banter and so, in an atmosphere which was very low key, almost funereal, James indicated that Miles should initiate the discussion, the outcome of which would have ramifications for all of them, none more so than Anthony Jayes who, unlike the others, may well not have a job if the Simmons takeover that he had orchestrated, was not concluded successfully.

Miles cleared his throat and glancing around the mahogany table summed up the state of play.

'Gentlemen we are fighting a rear-guard action, if it were war time we would hope that Sir Winston would summon our allies but, alas, there are no American or Commonwealth friends on the horizon – so, your suggestions please.'

He looked at Anthony who, like his next choice Jack, had nothing to contribute.

'There must be something that we have missed,' he urged them.

In desperation he turned to James who shrugged his shoulders; Miles stumbled on, uncertain for once to know how to proceed.

Eventually, James held up his hand.

'What do we know about the opposition? Think who they are, what do they have to gain, why did they not mount a more vigorous campaign at the outset; who has put the spoke in the wheel?'

Anthony finally found his voice, although he still appeared perplexed.

'It all seemed so clear cut, the son and daughter of Herbert Simmons both hold 30% of the shares and his widow has a 20% stake, so even if there was any opposition their 80% holding was enough to carry the day as the remaining group of small shareholders now have only 10% between them.'

James grimaced.

'Anthony you are in charge of Fordmill finances - does that add up to 100%?'

He received an embarrassed shake of the head.

'Mea Culpa I was just keeping you on your toes! - No it adds up to 90%.'

'But it still gives us a large measure of control.'

Miles chipped in. 'I have to agree with Anthony.'

James turned next to Jack Priory who was now stroking his lip with his index finger, a sure sign that he was seeing daylight.

'There is someone else, a Mr Ten Percent who is in someone's employ and has found a way to capture some of the other votes.'

'Correct Jack, but who is he?'

Miles leapt up. 'We have to get a name. I will send some coffee up and in the meantime I am off to our investment department to see what they can tell me.' With that he disappeared.

James looked at the others and wrote a name on a sheet of paper which he then placed face down in the centre of the table. The others looked at him, both craving an answer, which was not forthcoming, although the coffee did make an appearance.

Twenty minutes later an exultant Miles returned to the boardroom with the news that the unknown Mr Ten Percent was…

Jack leaned forward and turned James's piece of paper over.

'I suspect you are going to tell us that it is someone called Roger Blakeney?'

A crestfallen Miles nodded his head.

Anthony interrupted, 'So we have a name, but who is he?'

There followed a few minutes of conjecture, before James put them out of their misery.

'He is a Labour member of Parliament who was previously an undistinguished lecturer in Politics at a University in the Midlands.'

'Is he rich?'

'No, but he knows someone who is and what is more, she is the daughter of Herbert Simmons. As a result of his insider knowledge he was approached by the company now seeking to become part of Simmons and, seeing an opportunity to get on the gravy train, he sought out three of the original seven small shareholders and acquired a 12% stake, leaving the others with a joint 8% holding and also an assurance from these minority shareholders that they would vote with him in return for An Introduction Payment from the company aspiring to become part of Simmons International.

So to summarise;-

As a result of the financial black hole due her husband's deceit, not to mention the threat to Jane Simmons reputation, the opposition now have:-

Her voting rights	30%
Her Husband	12%
Her Mother	20%
Remaining Shareholders	8%
Total	**70%**

The M.D Arthur Simmons has made it known that he will not contemplate voting with them; in fact he will resign rather than renege on his handshake with Anthony Jayes.

Miles looked towards James; 'How did Blakeney fund the purchase of these shares?'

All eyes were on James.

'This is where it gets messy and this is highly confidential. In order to do this he borrowed a substantial sum, nominating his wife as the guarantor; a situation she was, until very recently, totally unaware of.'

Jack looked perplexed. 'But surely she signed the guarantee.'

'No, unbeknown to his wife, he kindly did that for her and she now finds herself in between the proverbial rock and a hard place as she either stands by him or votes against him, in which case he will go belly up and so will she as she does not have sufficient liquid collateral to cover his debts without selling their London home. It would appear that if the original sale does not go through, he has been promised a very good return on his investment and, according to his wife, so has she, as have the other minority investors.

The other dilemma; vote with her husband or risk financial ridicule, which as a Senior Financial Analyst at Gerlach's, the highly-esteemed German Investment Bank, would effectively end her career. And the plot thickens further, as about two weeks ago Mrs Blakeney discovered that he has been having a long term affair with one of his colleagues, his PPS, Helen Waterstone.'

Now they all started to chime in with ways of bringing him down. James held up his hand.

'Fear not, I have spoken with Jane Blakeney, in fact I dined with her last night and have offered to purchase her husband's shares, providing she votes her 30% to agree the Simmons take-over of Fordmill. She has more than willingly agreed to this suggestion and I am prepared to share my investment with anyone else in this room - don't all shout at once!'

Anthony Jayes a wide smile on his face indicated that he wished to speak.
'I believe my maths are correct this time. The vote would now appear to be :-

Arthur Simmonds	30%
Jane Blakeney	30%
James Carrington	12%
Total	**72%**

Their humour at the M.D's calculations was interrupted by Miles waving the 'phone at James. The words 'It is Jane Blakeney for you'. Interrupted the excitement; but not for long.

He replaced the receiver with a casual. 'Call that 92% - Ma Simmonds is coming on board.

The initial re-action was silence; once again he had worked a miracle, he dismissed their plaudits by suggesting that Miles Stanhope Gate take them to his club for lunch.

Miles picked up the phone and five minutes later the APP Rolls Royce appeared and they were swept in some style to White's Gentlemen's Club.

James had been here on a few previous occasions but still listened fascinated to the potted history with which Miles regaled his other guests.

'The club or at that time the coffee house, had been founded by an Italian immigrant named Francesco Bianco, whence it derived its name of White's and, as they stepped out of the car and cast their 'builders eye' over the classical façade, they could not but enjoy the symmetry of the building with its eight tall columns that, like so many of its neighbours, exuded an imposing statement of the wealth and tradition to be found in this great city that had once been the capital of the world.

By the early eighteenth century it had become a notorious gambling house, so much so that Jonathan Swift, he of Gulliver's Travels fame, described it as the base half of the English nobility. However its reputation did improve, so that by the turn of the 17th/18th century it became the unofficial headquarters of the Tory party and just down the street their opposition, The Whigs, had their praetorian.

They ascended the five stone steps guarded by two enormous black cast iron lanterns and as they reached the doorway Miles pointed out the large central bow window which, when they entered the building, they saw accommodated a large table, around which would gather the most influential members. These had included the regency dandy, Beau Brummel, who would sit in the window, preening himself to passers-by. He too was a prodigious gambler and a great friend of the Prince Regent until he defaulted on the large debts that incurred disfavour with his royal personage and he was forced to flee to France.

Others who held court from this 'seat of power' included Lord Alvanley whose legendary wager of £3,000 as to which of two raindrops would be the first to reach the bottom of the window pane, is still famously remembered.

Miles was a good raconteur and they were all in good humour as they followed him into the bar for a pre-prandial. As they sipped the drinks, Anthony still looking relieved, asked Miles whether he or James should contact Simmons.

James stepped in.

'I seem to recall Miles that you advised me that discussing business whilst at the club is definitely taboo?'

As usual the answer was understanding and designed to spare Anthony's blushes.

'My fault, I really should have told you - I only told James because he would have talked of nothing else! Now shall we go through to the Coffee Room?'

They dutifully followed him through into a spectacular room with an extraordinary vaulted barrel ceiling from which were suspended large glass chandeliers. The tables below were clad in crisp white linen and having sat down, Miles further entertained them by relating the very English nature of the food served here in the club's dining room.

Depending on the season, the club prided itself on only the very best of British gastronomic fare. French red-legged partridge for instance, would never be countenanced, only indigenous birds such as grey-legged partridge or grouse are on the menu. This extended even to eggs, where for five weeks gulls eggs are available from the coastline of the UK.

Today, Lincolnshire smoked trout was the speciality and they all opted for this, washed down by a full flavoured white Gewurztraminer. In the case of wine he admitted,

'This is where we break the English rule, as we will do with the Stilton cheese with which I recommend the Chateauneuf du Pape.'

James excused himself and repaired to the gentlemen's lavatory and, on his return, was greeted with the bonhomie they usually enjoyed over lunch. With James's assurances still in their ears they broke the club rules as Anthony agreed to take with Jack Priory a £50k stake each in James's commitment to Jane Blakeney.

On his way back to the table he saw them all huddled together.

'What cunning plan are you now devising?'

'We could not possible discuss it here in the club, particularly now that we are all going to apply for membership.'

'You could be in for a long wait, I applied three years ago and that means I still have to wait at least six years and getting enough people to support my application took ages, but you might just make it before you retire!'

After the most pleasant and relaxed lunch, James caused amusement by thanking Miles Stanhope Gate on behalf of Fordmill. Still smiling they shook hands and, as Anthony and Jack had travelled by train, they went their separate ways.

James chatted with Miles for five minutes or so and then signalled a cab, which delivered him to 167 New Bond Street and Messrs Asprey & Co; jewellers to the rich and discerning. His earlier conversation with the manager had outlined his requirements and, from their records and indeed his recent purchase of an engagement ring, had indicated to the manager the sort of price bracket that his client was prepared to pay. He therefore selected a tray of elegantly suitable rings for his client's consideration. They were all in white gold and within five minutes the choice had been made and as the engagement ring had been the correct size, the jeweller was able to advise the size required for the wedding ring.

'Do you wish to take it with you Mr Carrington?'

'No, but as this is for my wife, I would like our initials on the underside, separated by a heart.'

'But of course, and I can see yours from the name on the Coutts cheque; the lady's are?'

'S.A.L.C.'

'Thank you Mr Carrington, I will have it sent by carrier with the earrings to your address, which we have as Woolmington Manor.'

'Thank you Robert, by the way that is a splendid name.'

The Manager looked thoughtful for a moment and then understanding crossed his face.

'I imagine that the initial 'R' in your signature might also have that same illustrious connotation.'

'Indeed it does Robert; it was also my dear father's name.'

He bade them farewell with the warning that they should not rely on him requiring any further engagement or wedding rings.

'Perhaps one of our range of very exclusive eternity rings, Mr Carrington.'

'Maybe and au revoir Robert.'

By the time he had collected the Porsche he was wishing that he too had travelled by train, even more so by the time he got on to the A1. However, he had too many good memories of this trip and the prospect of supper with the Parkinson's and his beautiful fiancée kept his thoughts positive. Finally the traffic thinned out and his mind soared once again as he relished relating to her father - yet another Robert - how events had unfolded thanks in no small part to his family; in particular Guy Parkinson.

He arrived at Manton Hall where he was met by his host and a generous measure of a twenty year old Dalwhinnie Malt. The other guests were Sir Robert's accountant, George McIntosh, his wife Fiona and his solicitor, Gilbert Ruskin with his wife Pamela. With the Parkinson ladies, this made a convenient intimate gathering of nine making the table conversation personal and friendly.

Mrs Baxter, the housekeeper signalled to Camilla that they should go through and she seated them in the usual boy/girl arrangement which meant that James had Fiona McIntosh and Pamela Ruskin as his bookends. At the head of the table, Robert Parkinson observed his future son-in-law. He was effortlessly charming to the ladies but it was his shrewd interaction with the accountant and the lawyer that most intrigued him. He not only answered their questions, he questioned their reasoning and opinions and it was all done in a considered and measured style. But then Robert was not surprised, James's ancestor had been one of the richest men in England, he had been made a Baronet by Queen Victoria; had James been his son and not his great grandson then that vast furniture empire would surely still have been at the forefront of the FTSE 100 Share Index. But then he would probably not have been marrying his daughter and this pleasant little gathering would not have happened; he was very content with how things had worked out.

CHAPTER SEVENTY TWO

In the midst of all this manoeuvring in the hunting shires, Kate and Johnnie Mortimer were quietly making plans for their own wedding.

James's gifts of quad bikes had momentarily caused a small hiccup, which Johnnie had adroitly circumvented by praising their father's gifts and suggesting that the boys must have some fun options in Yorkshire.

The following weekend the boys were collected by Kate and travelled up North. They were slightly anxious although the times spent with Johnnie had always been pleasant.

They had supper at The Devonshire Arms and the following morning Johnnie hooked a trailer to the Land Rover and they set off for Skipton Cattle market, ostensibly to collect some hay. The boys spotted the sign for the auction mart, but Johnnie appeared not to have heard them as he continued past the entrance for another mile or so, finally turning into a car showroom and filling station.

He lifted the nozzle to top up the diesel and suggested that the boys had a look in the car showroom, in which they had already spotted some very sporty models. Like all boys they needed no further bidding from JM, as they now called him, and set off, as they thought, to sit in a few fancy cars.

The proprietor joined in the fun by asking if they would give him a hand to move a couple of bikes onto the forecourt. They followed him to the back of the showroom where from under a cream dustsheet two 50cc off-road bikes emerged.

One was red and the other was yellow; the boys stood there as stupefied as when they saw the quad bikes. Mr Farnell the manager looked at them, took a coin out of his pocket and flicked it into the air before catching it and pointing to Charles.

'Heads or tails?'

'Heads.'

'Correct, you have choice of colour.'

'Red,' the immediate answer.

Mr Farnell reached behind him and gave him the number plate 'Chas 1.'

Turning to Edward he handed him a plate numbered 'Ed 1.'

They were quivering with excitement as he took out a spanner and bolted the number plates into the pre-drilled holes. This done he looked at them both, his face was stern.

'Do not ever sit on a bike unless you are wearing a helmet and a back protector and remember, you are not licensed to go on public roads, besides which it is much more fun off-road.'

They jubilantly pushed the bikes to the Land Rover where a very happy Johnnie was waiting to help them load them on to the trailer.

'Thank you, JM,' they chorused in unison.

The bikes were secured and in a state of great excitement they set off for Nidderdale House. On the way, two happy teenagers were beginning to sense that their parents' divorce was not, after all, the end of the world.

They arrived in time for a late lunch which they scoffed at a rate of knots and unbelievingly declined a dessert, their one consideration was to be on those yellow and red machines.

Kate, like most mothers had, rather reluctantly, agreed to let them have the bikes but with the proviso that they wore helmets and back protectors she relented. Once again Johnnie was ahead of the game and he produced not only these safety garments but also leather gauntlets.

Feeling reasonably happy, Kate accompanied them into the parkland behind the house; those very same meadows where she had first cycled with JM, on her initial visit to the spa. Who could possibly have foreseen that this fateful meeting could have been the pre-curser to today's events?

As with the quad bikes, their natural athletic skills and balance enabled them to quickly acquire the basics to control these off-road machines. After twenty minutes or so they were left to enjoy themselves and as they disappeared across the field, their mother and Johnnie set off hand in hand towards the house - all four of them content and happy.

The following day the boys were up at the crack of dawn, anxious to spend as much time as possible on the bikes. However, as they entered the kitchen they were surprised to see their mother busily preparing sandwiches for them. She turned and smiled.

'JM suggested you might like to go for a little adventure around the farm, but please be back by one o'clock as we have to get you back to school by tea-time.'

They happily agreed and Kate equally pleased went back upstairs to Johnnie.

Bang on the dot she heard them ride into the stable yard and park the bikes in one of the empty boxes. Then followed the usual mayhem that was packing their bags and books and getting into school uniform, but finally they were ready to go.

Johnnie gave them a hug, at the same time slipping them a tenner each with the caution that it was not all to be spent on girls.

'Chance would be a fine thing,' Charles' cryptic response.

The following day Johnnie had meetings in York and Leeds so Kate, unbeknown to James, planned to stay the night at Woolmington, and so did he. He was therefore more than a little surprised when he returned home at 10.30 pm to see lights on both upstairs and down.

The thought that he was being burgled raised his hackles. He was six foot three tall and still very fit, so someone was going to regret this intrusion. He parked the car in the lane and, despite the pouring rain, walked slowly and quietly the couple of hundred yards toward the house, determined to defend his Castle.

He moved swiftly but quietly into the courtyard and spotted the burglar's getaway vehicle. It was Kate's Range Rover!

He tried the kitchen door, it was locked with key in the lock, so the by now bedraggled figure was obliged to ring the front door bell.

'Who are you?' Her voice was both nervous and angry.

'Kate, it is me.'

He heard the bolts being withdrawn.

'What are you doing here?' he demanded.

'I might well ask you the same question, as this is now technically MY house.'

'Okay, I apologise, but let me go and get changed before I die of pneumonia.'

He sidestepped her and raced upstairs to his bedroom where he dried his hair and changed into jeans and a tee shirt before returning to the kitchen where on the opposite side of the table sat a very serene looking Kate wearing a most seductive negligee.

She looked at him, her expression smouldering as she walked slowly to the fridge and started to mix a G & T. Through the silky transparency of the negligee the down-lighters of the kitchen units illuminated the outlines of the perfect body he knew so well and for the briefest moment his control faltered and she sensed the opportunity.

'It is not too late,' she began.

'Kate, if you are about to say what I hope you are not going to say, then please don't.'

She slowly and deliberately put her glass on the table and stepped out of her flimsy robe and attempted to embrace him.

He pushed her back into a chair, the expression spoilt bitch was on his lips, but instead he gave her a contemptuous look and sat down to face her.

'Sadly Kate, you really are your mother's daughter, which is what I always feared. I will forget what happened tonight, just as your father had to forget that his wife was seduced by his best friend from his time at Oxford and, in the process, mortified one of the finest men I have ever met. We are both lucky to have been given a second chance. You have met a really good man, someone who has already suffered the most appalling tragedy when he lost not only his wife but his two children. How can you contemplate wrecking his life again?'

She looked genuinely abashed and he continued, determined that this embarrassment would never recur.

'The boys have taken to him and I have met someone whom I love very much, she is also liked by the boys. Surely you must see that we need closure to our marriage or else the future will always be blighted...'

She held up her hand, her eyes roaming around the room as she sought to accept that he was right. Finally her gaze settled on him and this time her expression was sincere.

'James I am sorry, but as this is probably the last time we will sit here together in this room which holds so many memories, I want you to know that I now regret making those silly accusations about you and Sally, and I do realise that we are both very fortunate to be given a second chance of happiness. You are right to say that we have both met a special person, but please let us always be friends.'

He smiled and took her hand.

'Kate, I also hope, most sincerely, that we can remain as good friends - all four of us. But we can never be more than that - and why should we want any more?'

She looked at him, her expression was poignant.

'I know and I do accept that we are now on separate paths, but the boys will ensure that we stay in touch and you have been very kind whenever you speak of Johnnie and I want you to know that I do accept Sally, she is a beautiful woman...'

'And so are you - but then, I would never go for second best!'

She chuckled. 'I see she hasn't managed to make you any less conceited!'

He pushed his chair back and disappeared into the boot room, he returned flourishing a bottle of champagne and having extracted the cork, filled two glasses and inclined his towards her.'

'Here's to the past and to the future.'

She clinked his glass and repeated the toast, which was followed by trips down memory lane centred around their hopes for Charles and Edward.

As he poured a second glass she posed the question he was wondering how to ask.

'Re the wedding, have you thought of any dates?'

'Strangely I heard from my lawyers only yesterday, how about you?'

'Well I know we have less than two weeks to go and then, as they say, I will see you in court. We should get the Decree Absolute, that is assuming that there are no outstanding financial arrangements.'

He nodded. 'We are both anxious to get this matter sorted, I have signed the necessary documentation so I don't see any reason for any delay. I do though think it a good idea if we agree on dates for the wedding as we don't want them to clash. Have you decided yet?'

'JM thinks the beginning of September - just before the boys go back to school.'

'That sounds fine, let's have a look at the calendar.'

Sally thinks a Friday as any people who have a distance to travel can stay over for the weekend - I will go for the second Friday...'

'Which is,' she interrupted. 'The 26th, yes?'

'Correct, so will the previous week do for you?'

'I guess so, but will confirm it tomorrow after I have spoken with Johnnie.'

Finally the bottle was empty and as she put the glasses in the dishwasher, he gave her a thoughtful look.

'Please remember me to your father, I do miss him.'

'He misses you James, you are the son he never had, why don't you invite him to join you the next time you go to Twickenham and then stay over at his club? That way you don't have to meet mother!'

Now it was his turn to offer a wry smile.

'How strange Kate, I quite often have lunch at Whites, in fact I am on the waiting list, so what a great idea. Please tell him to expect a call.'

The following morning he came down to find a note on the kitchen table confirming last night's resolutions and he set off for the office hardly daring to believe that the emotional downside of the last few months was at an end. He reversed his new Aston Martin into his reserved parking space almost in unison with the arrival of Jack Priory, who greeted him with one eye raised.

'You are looking pretty chipper this morning; shall I get Samantha to send up some coffee so that you can tell me the gory details?'

James nodded and as they strode through reception the coffee was requested. The interrogation continued as they made their way upstairs to Jack's spacious office.

They parked themselves at the far end of the superb burr oak conference table.

Jack looked at him quizzically 'Well?'

James related the gist of events over supper at Manton Hall and then hammed up the seduction scene at Woolmington.

Jack's expression remained cool but this was not at all what he was expecting.

James continued and regaled him with the transparency of Kate's negligee and her attempt to embrace him.

'You didn't?'

'No, although I admit that just for a fleeting second I did waver and then I regained my senses and spelt it out to her, after which she apologised and we made amends over a bottle of Bollinger and we have even decided on provisional wedding dates.'

Jack shook his head. 'You are unbelievable but then, after your performance at Claridge's and APP, why am I surprised? Your whole bally life is a series of impossible circumstances and stubborn refusal to lose.'

He gave his old friend an admiring look.

'That is why I wanted you to join my company and I was right, your flair when added to our solid reputation for excellence is proving to be a great success, particularly our fitted kitchens and bathrooms.'

They were interrupted by a tap on the door followed by Samantha and a jug of coffee, which brought them back to talking business and the forthcoming Furniture Expo fair in Milan.

James had been involved in the decision making but, in view of the mass of other projects on his desk, was hoping he would not have to attend.

Jack Priory, sensing his colleague's reluctance, offered a possible solution.

'That young guy, the one who switched from architecture, I have spent quite a bit of time with him recently and I think we should give him the chance to prove himself.'

'How old is he?'

'Twenty six.'

'Plenty old enough, I was running my own business when I was nineteen and the only person I could refer to was Edward Lawson and he was two months younger than me. Mark Stonehouse strikes me as having great potential and I sense he will have the nous to ask Trevor and the other members of the fitting team if he is unsure about any protocols and, of course, you will be around to educate him in the black arts of entertaining and customer bonding - you know dining establishments that always have a plethora of nubile young guests, or is it just chance that you always happen upon them.'

'Kismet, old boy.'

'More like slipping the hotel porters a quid or two. At which point, I have a site meeting with Fordmill at noon so mustn't be late, you never know what these builders get up to!'

And he was off, loping down the stairs and across the car park as if his life depended upon it. Jack observing him from the window reflected on the difference having him on board had made to Minster Kitchens. The family owned company under his stewardship had grown and with it had become extremely sound financially, so that when James had come up with his ideas for diversifying into kitchens and then bathrooms, followed by conservatories, the finances were readily available. James's concept of Mr and Mrs Average having dreams of the stylish living previously only seen in expensive magazines was spot on and ahead of its time. Minster was now the acknowledged leader and the army of joiners and plumbers 'franchised to them' by referring new clients, excluded the necessity to market the product through retail outlets and incur the discounts that they paid the department stores to sell their traditional furniture.

The building site that James was heading to was out of town in a business park that Simmons International was building on the outskirts of Nottingham. Minster was the first client to sign up for this project giving them the advantage of selecting its location, which was facing the city ring road. This announced their presence not only to Nottingham but also to passing motorists and, as they were the showcase for the entire business park, the road surface and lawns that would surround them would be immaculate.

James would relocate his office to this site which inevitably made his juices flow, he liked being in charge but he was heedful of the promise he had made to Jack after the meeting with the joiners at Trent Bridge Cricket Ground. 'That he would always be upfront with Jack.' He was now part of a team; He liked it that way, the split with Edward Lawson and its consequences were etched on his brain for ever.

He arrived ten minutes early but Anthony Jayes, ex-lawyer now CEO of the Fordmill division of Simmons International, was already on site, sitting behind the wheel of a black Porsche 928 busily speaking into the handset of a Dictaphone.

The dust caused by the arrival of his former boss, now very close friend, alerted Anthony who quickly deposited the handset on the passenger front seat and grabbed his leather bound jotter, rammed his red hard hat on and set off in pursuit. Thirty seconds later he was in the cabin where he found James already bent over the drawings with Tim Cooper.

They acknowledged each other in the casual off hand way born out of longstanding respect. This took seconds; Anthony meanwhile braced himself for the usual barrage of questions from The Client.

Unusually there were very few, instead he was congratulated on the progress being made and was able to report that they were two weeks ahead of schedule: Second fixings were almost complete and the painters would be moving in next week.

James handed Anthony a schedule of the various colour schemes, smiled wryly at the other two and paid them the ultimate compliment.

'I don't know why I bothered coming over, everything is so under control.'

Evoking a shocked response from Tim, 'Bloody Hell are you feeling unwell!'

An affable smile and he was gone, the departure confirmed by a similar cloud of dust to that which had marked his arrival.

Six weeks later the engineers had installed the machinery and the Lord Mayor had pushed the switch that brought their aspirations to life. The offices and particularly the workshops were to a standard that even Sir Albert Staincliffe would have applauded...

The launch of the new Minster HQ and the publicity that ensued produced a volume of business well beyond that which James and Jack Priory had envisaged.

More fitters were recruited and with a view to the future also twelve apprenticeships were awarded. The trainees' first month was spent in the workshop learning how to assemble the flat packs of furniture after which they were sent out to work on site with those joiners that James most trusted to train them in the Minster Way. Which was 'That everything is in the detail', the mantra that had been the philosophy of the Bauhaus School of Architecture in the 1930s, before the Nazis came to power in Germany and destroyed such expectations.

In this frenzied atmosphere, time seemed to hurtle by and it was suddenly the end of August and the realisation that in two weeks he would be married. Fortunately all the arrangements, apart from organising the honeymoon, had been deputed to Sally, assisted by Camilla and his mother.

CHAPTER SEVENTY THREE

Friday September 26th

Once again the sun shone on his wedding day and with his best man - Jack of course, he set out with the boys, both looking very proud wearing their morning suits.

'Much better than our school uniform,' observed Edward, admiring himself in the mirror.

'You should pack him off to Eton father, then he could wear one every day!' His brother's smiling riposte.

The friendly banter continued and they were all in good humour as the car delivered them to the church of St John at Colston Bassett. With half an hour or to spare, they sought out his mother and sister's family with whom they chatted, before mingling for the next twenty minutes with the large gathering outside this beautiful church, known affectionately by the locals as the Cathedral of the Vale.

Leaving the boys with his mother and his sister Louise, he and Jack moved into the church and made their way to the front pew, nodding and smiling along the way to those already seated. He knelt, with Jack at his side, and silently asked that this marriage would bring happiness to Sally and himself and that the same good fortune be granted to Kate and Johnnie. As he sat down the clock struck eleven and two minutes later the organist announced the arrival of the bride prompting an aside from Jack that it was, 'nearly time to put your head on the block.'

The usual low bubble of expectant conversation went up a few decibels as the ladies, many of them standing on tiptoe, strained to catch a glimpse of the bride and her two bridesmaids. At the head of the procession came the choir and, as they moved to their allotted places in the choir stalls, James and his best man followed the vicar to the steps leading to the altar. A few seconds later she stood at his side.

He turned towards her and through her veil saw the breath-taking woman who was to become his wife. He felt the emotion well up in his throat but managed to whisper, 'You are so beautiful.' The delight in her eyes radiated her happiness as she muttered, 'I love you.' He was brought out of his daze as the assembly of friends and family were welcomed by the Reverend Dalton and invited to express their pleasure with an upbeat rendition of the first hymn.

Guide me, O though great redeemer, Pilgrim through this barren land...

As the last notes faded away, the sunlight came streaming through the stained glass windows to bathe the happy couple in a warm spectrum of colour as they stood facing each other to make their pledges. The ring was produced by the best man and a slightly tremulous James slipped the white gold wedding ring on to his wife's elegant finger.

The vicar gave them a warm smile and invited Sally's brother Guy Parkinson, to deliver the first reading.

At the conclusion of which, he challenged the congregation to once again out-sing the choir, this time the choice was Dear Lord and Father of mankind...

As the last notes drifted away and much to everyone's amusement he declared that, despite the large number of strapping rugby players on James's side of the church, the farming community on Kate's side now had a slight lead in the volume competition.

In this atmosphere of goodwill and happiness he led Kate and James to the altar where their marriage received his blessing followed by prayers and the final hymn.

Now thank we all our God with hearts and hand and voices...

At the conclusion of this and a further blessing, they made their way with the Reverend Dalton to sign the register as Mr and Mrs Carrington.

Whilst this ceremony was being enacted the organist entertained the gathering with the Beatles song All you need is love, love, love...

It was the couple's adopted favourite piece of music and the one they had first danced to at the Architects and Builders dinner dance those few years ago.

Eventually all the formalities were complete, except for the photographs which, though the captured memories would prove so precious in the future, the demands of the photographer as usual seemed endless. Finally they escaped his clutches and joined the well-wishers gathered in the grounds of the church before the selected elite friends repaired to Manston Hall.

The original suggested guest list of fifty had swelled to ninety eight but they still fitted comfortably into the marquee, the sides of which had been drawn back to allow in a welcome cool breeze.

The atmosphere amongst their relatives and friends was warm and convivial and glancing across the room, the two most important guests, Charles and Edward, were obviously enjoying themselves judging by the laughter that was generated by them and their new cousins, Pippa and Olivia Parkinson.

He gently squeezed his wife's hand as the toastmaster invited the Reverend Dalton to bless the happy couple and propose a toast to their happiness.

After which the first course was served.

In tribute to the Vale of Belvoir, its signature starter dish Cream of Stilton Soup with croutons or for those not partial to cheese the alternative was Prawn Newburg on a bread bake sprinkled with paprika and watercress; the wine Sancerre, dry and very refreshing.

The main course not surprisingly was home grown, Fillet de Boeuf grille béarnaise, courtesy of the Parkinson's herd of Aberdeen Angus. This was served with vegetables, also home produced; accompanied by a full bodied Chateau Neuf du Pappe.

Next the dessert, Meringue Basket with summer fruits served with a choice of dessert wines. This was very much the ladies' favourite, although it was noted that quite a few gentlemen also requested a second helping.

Finally the ceremonial cutting of the cake, this was greeted with the usual badinage about saving the top layer for the christening. Job done, the cake was wheeled away to be cut into plate sized slices.

Once again the toastmaster orchestrated the proceedings by banging his gavel and calling upon the father of the bride to say a few words.

Sir Robert Parkinson rose to his feet and in his eloquent tones welcomed all those gathered to bask in the happiness that this day had brought to his family.

'This is the third time I have made a wedding speech. On the first occasion the bridegroom was one of the most handsome men you could wish to meet. His bride must surely have be the envy of all those ladies present. Over the years that young man has lost none of his charm. But that is enough about me!

He paused, until the good humoured amusement subsided.

'My second speech was at my son's wedding and as today, Camilla and I could not be happier at our children's choice of partner.

It is an honour for me to stand here today and, as the father of the bride I have the dubious honour of making this first speech. I am of course the warm up man for the Groom and the Best Man - they top the billing and I get to pay for this privilege!

Distinguished guests, those of dubious distinction and also those of no distinction whatever.'

This was interrupted by hoots of laughter and cries of scandalous - and 'we will sue' from the younger contingent.

'You are all good friends of James and Sally and as such they had great difficulty with the seating plan, so I offered to step in and sort things out. What we finally agreed on was to seat you according to the size of the wedding gift. So if you can hear me at the back there Arthur and Celia, yes the ones seated behind the eighteen electric toasters, thanks for the oven glove - could you send a right handed one for their anniversary as James will by then doing all the cooking.'

He turned to face his new son-in-law.

'Having run your own business since the age of nineteen you are used to giving orders; the best advice I can give you is - from today on get used to obeying orders!

Finally I ask you all to join in the toast to the James and Sally.'

He sat down to warm and generous applause. The master of ceremonies then invited the Groom to take the floor. As he did so James glanced at his two sons; Charles gave him a thumbs up which, simple gesture that it was, it allayed any slight apprehension he had about making this speech with them present.

'Ladies and Gentlemen; I first met Sally at a dinner dance in Nottingham and although we spoke only a few words, I did manufacture an excuse to dance with her and she was often in my thoughts.'

His voice faltered as he strove to continue, leaving no one in any doubt that this was both a joyful and difficult day for him.

'That we did meet again was the last gift that my best friend gave me. Edward Lawson's tragic death was the reason that took me to Stamford where, quite by chance, serendipity perhaps, I met Sally at the George Inn and from the depths of my despair she gave me hope and I know

Edward is up there giving us his blessing.'

The room was still, everyone sharing his grief but then, as when under the cosh playing rugby, he found the resolve to carry on.

'Having met Sally again, my life took surprising new directions, she has not only introduced me to hunting, I have also acquired a new family who have made my mother, to whom I owe so much and myself, extremely welcome, Quite amazingly it turned out that Mother was at school with Camilla and I know how much they are enjoying this re-launching this old friendship.

Naturally meeting someone new can bring surprises; On my first visit, Robert led me to the drawing room where I found my darling Sally reading a book which she swiftly hid under a cushion. I was of course intrigued to know what sort of salacious literature she was reading. My chance came when she was called to the kitchen by her mother. I swiftly took this opportunity to glance at the hidden Mills & Boone. It was entitled How to boil an egg.- Can you imagine how I felt? However, all the other books in her library, How to slice a cucumber etc. have been most assiduously learned and she is now, since meeting me, a very accomplished hostess.

I have known my new father-in law for only a comparatively short time but he is the font of all knowledge so I have woven my speech around the principles he advised.

My speech today is like a mini skirt - Long enough to cover the essentials and hopefully short enough to hold your attention.

Part of my duties is to thank the best man who has so expertly carried out his duties. Without his help I would probably have slipped the ring onto the wrong finger and ended up marrying the vicar, - who by the way, is already married, so I would have started married life at the centre of a bigamy trial!

Finally I come to my main task which is to thank our beautiful bridesmaids, Pippa and Olivia. These two stunning young ladies have attracted many admiring glances, not least from Charles and Edward. - I see now why they gave me the thumbs up sign. They are not actually related so watch this space in about ten years' time!

Ladies and Gentlemen please join me in a toast to two wonderful bridesmaids who have been such a help to Sally today.'

Glasses were raised and two blushing young ladies accepted a silver photograph frame for which James promised he would send photographs of their big day.

The Maître d' then called upon the Best Man, Mr Jack Priory, to say a few words which, after a lot of feigned coughing and spluttering, he began the traditional assault on the Bridegroom's character.

He surveyed the room, raised an eyebrow and before speaking took James' hand and placed it on Sally's. Then surveying the room, he turned again to the happy couple.

'Firstly James I congratulate you on making the most of your sixty minute speech - well it seemed like an hour to most of us. This is however the last time you will enjoy the luxury of rattling on, as speaking for one minute uninterrupted will now become an achievement.

My duties as Best Man are to prepare you for the new rules of Mrs Carrington but first I would like to remind her that not many people can boast that their best mate is Kind; Honourable; Ambitious; Charismatic; Reliable and incredibly Handsome... but James can!'

He held up his hands to halt the howls of derision and laughter before continuing.

'The origin of the word 'Wedding' is derived from the Olde English meaning to unite and the word 'Ding' which is the sound of a frying pan as it hits you on the head.

Married life James, can be compared with your illustrious career on the rugby field - Each day train hard and make sure you score every weekend. However, Sally assures me that playing away from home will result in serious groin injuries and will certainly end up with you being put on the transfer list.

You may also be wondering why I am wearing this Davy Crocket hat. Well I bumped into Prince Charles the other day and he had mentioned to the Queen Mother that I was attending your wedding in Colston Bassett. To which she replied 'Wear the Fox Hat!'

This went over the heads of several of the older ladies but brought howls of laughter from the majority of guests.

He continued in similar vein but decided that the many tales accredited to James on his many rugby tours, which had been mentioned at his previous wedding should not, with his two young sons being present, be mentioned today. Instead, he shared with them the embarrassing experience he had experienced earlier today.

'Can you imagine what it is like having to struggle with a grown man who is almost paralytic and you have to get him into the church… you really would think a vicar would know better!'

By now the audience were in really good humour and eagerly awaited his next assault.

'First however the toast. As I speak on behalf of your beautiful barmaids; I am so sorry, I do of course mean bridesmaids. Will you all raise your glasses to The Bridesmaids?'

Before they could sit down he raised his glass.

'Also to the most important people here today, the Bar Staff.'

He waited until they were seated.

'Finally Ladies and Gentlemen, the reason I asked James to put his hand on to Sally's, was so that he could experience, ,for the very last time, the feeling of having the upper hand.'

He sat down, his droll wit had been enjoyed by all and it occasioned a round of genuine applause.

At Five O'clock James and Sally retired to divest themselves of their finery and to change into their 'Going away outfits.' Needless to say their departure was assailed by a barrage of banter suggesting the guests knew what they might get up to. Wearing broad smiles they cheerily accepted the advice and retreated into the house and thirty minutes later returned to a round of applause.

The amusement was however drowned by the heavy rhythmic sound of helicopter blades as a dark blue machine landed in the paddock adjoining the marquee.

Clinging to her husband's arm, a bewildered Sally was clearly as surprised as everyone else.

'James Carrington, what have you done now?'

He held her tight, his blue eyes twinkling with delight.

'The Friday traffic on the A1 can be so heavy, particularly as you approach the turn off for the airport. So now you know why Ralph Burton, my old Tigers team mate was not at the wedding; instead he will be flying us down to Sussex.'

She shook her head. 'Am I allowed to know where we are going?'

'Certainly not, although when we check in you will probably guess.'

She pretended to pout, but it was momentary, instead she clung to his arm as they made their way through cheering friends and across the paddock to a smiling Ralph Burton.

'Welcome aboard Mr and Mrs Carrington, we are ready for take-off as soon as you are.'

Sally looked more than slightly alarmed as she blurted out, 'What about the luggage?'

The pilot indicated she should turn around, whereupon she saw her brother Guy in a Land Rover, in the back of which were two large suitcases and two pieces of hand luggage.

Guy waved aside James attempt to assist with the loading.

'As you can see Mr Carrington, I am dressed in my flunkey's tailed suit and apart from a generous tip, I must decline your involvement.'

The newlyweds climbed aboard, pausing briefly to slip the flunkey a fiver and give a royal wave to the onlookers before donning their ear defenders and strapping themselves in ready for take-off.

They heard the whirring blades above them and then with a small lurch forward they began a sweep around Manston Hall before setting off for a small private airstrip ten miles from Gatwick, where a private taxi was scheduled to take them to Gravetye Manor in West Sussex.

The flight, which was a new experience for them both, conveyed them effortlessly south on the first leg of their exciting honeymoon. What made the journey even more satisfying was the predicted sight of the slow moving traffic below them on the motorway.

Their reverie was interrupted by the pilot who invited them to open the cool-box located behind his seat. To their delight it revealed a bottle of champagne and two glasses.

James popped the cork and glasses filled he proposed a toast.

'Cheers Ralph, here's to you and your enterprise - a very considerate thought - not exactly what you would expect from a front row forward.'

'Well I know it's the sort of drink you girls who play in the backs would prefer!'

The rugby banter flowed back and forth until Ralph pointed out the English Channel a few miles ahead and at two o'clock the bustle of Gatwick Airport and just beyond it, he promised them, was their immediate destination.

Five minutes later they swooped on to the airstrip and came to a halt. As the blades slowed down a dark blue BMW approached to convey them to tonight's lodgings.

Their seamless journey lasted for a further twenty five minutes before they were decanted outside a charming ivy clad house that seemed to grow organically from the exciting garden that surrounded it.

The building itself, a rambling Elizabethan manor house with splendid panelled rooms and large open fireplaces exuded warmth and welcoming to its guests. Scarcely had the driver switched off the engine before the front door opened and a porter emerged to gather the luggage and direct them to reception.

They checked in and followed their luggage to a large, airy bedroom with a huge four poster bed and the most marvellous views of the garden. This landscape had been envisaged and planted by William Robinson, a celebrated gardener and botanist who bought the manor in 1884.

Not surprisingly in this romantic idyll as they feasted their eyes upon each other and the bottle of Dom Perignon resting in an ice bucket bearing its name, amorous feelings were evoked which, after the first sip led them to make love for the first and second time as man and wife.

'Mr Carrington,' she murmured, 'I do hope this is how you intend to carry on!'

He ran his fingers down her spine. 'You may rely upon it.'

Coyly she assured him, 'I will hold you to that.'

'Well that is a very good starting point.'

And then once again her impersonation of the comedian Dick Emery; which he had so enjoyed in Bavaria.

'You are a very naughty boy - but I like you.'

The following morning they were awake at seven thirty and after a continental breakfast their second cup of coffee was interrupted by Simone from Reception with news that their car had arrived and, sure enough, a silver Mercedes with chauffeur in full uniform awaited them.

Forty minutes later they were in the airport and with queues already long and busy, the additional costs of flying first class once again seemed so worthwhile as they were fast tracked through to the executive lounge.

'I know where we are going.' She whispered in his ear.

'And where might that be?'

'Frankfurt,' she whispered triumphantly.

'You are partially right, but that is only a short stopover, because we have another stopover in Dubai and then, I might as well tell you, we go on to Singapore where we are staying at Raffles Hotel. And then, I have been dreading telling you this, because things are so hectic at the office, we come home. I do hope you understand - can you forgive me?'

She looked at him, smiled sweetly and nodded. 'Of course, darling.'

They both burst out laughing but she refrained from further questions, she knew how he loved surprises; she had after all been more than pleased with the honeymoon so far. He would have an ace up his sleeve of that she had no doubt.

CHAPTER SEVENTY FOUR

The journey to Singapore was uneventful and having cleared customs, they picked up an airport taxi which carried them through the bustling streets to the centre of the colony, before coming to a halt in front of the large colonial hotel that is Raffles.

In front of the great white portico is a covered veranda and from this shaded area emerged a tall dignified Indian impeccably dressed in a white uniform surmounted by a red turban. The effect is stylish and dramatic; it is the cocktail before the main course, as they would find out when they sampled the hotel's exotic delights. Like so many before them, they would come to appreciate why this iconic building is one of the great hotels of the world.

It is named after Sir Stamford Raffles, former Governor General of the British East India Company; universally acknowledged as the man who established the colony from which the modern Singapore has emerged.

When the hotel was first established by two Armenian brothers in 1887 it stood on the waterfront but, due to continual reclamation of the harbour, it now stands more than a quarter of a mile inland; only it's address Beach Road, offers a clue to its former location.

A bellboy relieved them of their luggage and after registering they were directed through the great hall with its galleried landings to their suite which, thanks to the large overhead fan, they found to be deliciously cool.

Feeling decidedly excited they quickly unpacked and set out to explore this fascinating piece of colonial history. The dining options catered for all culinary requirements but the taste they were looking for was the legendary Singapore Sling which for complete authenticity, has to be drunk in the famous Long Bar.

James was not a cocktail man, beer or Macallan was his usual poison, but today at least he would succumb to this iconic drink invented by the head barman in 1910.

They chose to sit on bar stools to see at first hand this famous elixir being prepared and they were not disappointed. With a great flourish the barman, having shovelled a copious quantity of ice into the shaker, added Gin followed by Cherry Brandy; a good slug of Pineapple Juice, Orange Liqueur, Grenadine and finally a dash of Bitters, all of which received an acrobatic final shake before being poured into tall glances and garnished with cherry and pineapple.

'I can't see me doing this at home,' he admitted to the barman.

'This may help you sir.' He handed James a list of ingredients which fortunately identified the volumes of each constituent.

Anxious to see as much of the city as two nights would allow, they finished the cocktails and made their way out of the hotel grounds to walk the few hundred yards to the Harbour. Here boats of all shapes and sizes, including the native Junks, were actively plying their trade to a cacophony of hooters and ships' whistles. Beyond the harbour, a continuous stream of tankers and cargo ships awaited their turn to unload or take on board cargos destined for ports spread across the world.

At the end of the waterfront, thanks to similarly inclined holidaymakers, they posed for photographs in front of the great statue of a lion, the symbol of this city.

Leaving the harbour they wandered through the maze of sightseers until they came upon the Old Parliament House, a grandiose Victorian Villa built in 1827 as a home for the Scottish merchant, John Maxwell. To underline its importance, a majestic bronze elephant presented by the King of Thailand, stands proudly in front of the building.

That evening two people very much in love dined at a Chinese restaurant on the quayside, soaking up the atmosphere of this city which never sleeps. It had been a memorable if somewhat hectic day but the jet lag was starting to kick in as they retired to Raffles for a quick nightcap.

The following morning, anxious to see as much of the city as possible, they set out to explore the frenzied hive of activity in the central area of the city. A passing Trike; a three wheeled bike with a seat for two behind the driver - the modern version of the original Rickshaw, was flagged down and to their great delight the young rider, no doubt to impress his passengers, seemed anxious to overtake any other such vehicle or indeed any car that he could squeeze past on the inside. He was also keen to impress with his local knowledge as he reeled off the names of bars, casinos and restaurants his passengers must visit. After an exhilarating hour of savouring the sights and sounds they instructed him to head for Beach Road.

'So you stay at Raffles, bloody good hotel,' he assured them with all the panache of one who was a regular visitor, which they thought- not!

But he had been good company and James added a handsome tip, in return he received a business card with instructions to call him at any time, he would come straight away he assured them.

After two long flights and a further day of frenzied sightseeing they once again felt in need of a nap; the suggestion of which was viewed suspiciously by Mrs Carrington.

'I am not as gullible as you might think Mr Carrington, I suspect you have ulterior motives, or at least I hope you have!'

'Maybe we should have a shower first, just to cool us down. Let me help you Mrs Carrington.'

She slipped out of the light cotton dress, unclipped her bra and hung it around his neck.

'I need to work up a good appetite so don't forget to bring plenty of shower gel as I need to protect the white bits.'

Seconds later he joined her under the two large shower heads and obeying her instruction he gently applied the lotion to her voluptuous white bits. They luxuriated in each other's embrace and as he put it, made love under water.

They finally emerged from the shower satiated and fulfilled and snuggled together they drifted off into a light sleep. When they awoke it was dark and, imagining it must be the middle of the night, both were relieved to find it was a little after seven o'clock; they had of course forgotten they were more or less right on the equator. Slipping on his white bathrobe, James poured two flutes of champagne and leaving Sally to pamper herself he stepped out on to the gallery outside their room and looked down into the Courtyard Restaurant below. It is a wonderfully timeless alfresco setting of tropical plants complete with a piano player who evokes memories of a different era with his repertoire of music from yesteryear. To his right was the colonial cocktail bar and closer to the music, table three, this evening it was reserved for the Carrington's. Lost in his thoughts he became slowly conscious of a fragrance he knew well, Must de Cartier, it announced the presence of his wife.

She snuggled into his arms, still unable to comprehend how magical her life had become since they had met under those sad circumstances in Stamford. But she pushed this thought from her mind, Edward Lawson she felt sure, would not begrudge his friend his new found happiness; how bizarre though that they should be staying at the 'Stamford' Raffles hotel.

He gently stroked her neck. 'A penny for them, what is going on in that brain of yours?'

'I was thinking that although ties are not de rigeur, your bathrobe is somewhat long to pass off as a jacket!'

'Give me five minutes and I will spruce myself up - you never know you might even fancy me.'

In just over the allotted time he returned in a pale blue shirt and white linen jacket set off, as always, by an appropriately coloured pocket handkerchief. He took her hand and they strolled casually to the cocktail bar to sample once again, the signature house drink.

They tilted their glasses in salutation and three sips later, as if my magic, the head waiter appeared with menus which he opened with a great flourish, his slight Italian accent confirmed by his name badge which announced him as Luigi.

'Shall I give you and your wife a few minutes to consider?'

They readily acquiesced to his suggestion and after three or four minutes of consideration, they both decided on the same light starter; Red and Yellow Peppers with Scallops.

After more consideration they finally opted to continue the fish theme with Langoustine Thermidor with Rice Pilaf.

Luigi returned, his nodding head seemingly approving their selections.

'And to accompany your meal?' He raised his eyebrows quizzically.

'What do think to a Chassagne Montrachet, maybe a seventy six?'

'A perfect choice Mr Carrington, that is one of the great years, it compares favourably with the vintage of sixty nine.'

With a click of his fingers he was gone and a most attractive waitress appeared to divest them of the unnecessary cutlery and glassware. From her accent they deduced that she was Australian and she likewise assumed that Sally was English.

To the question, 'Have either of you ever been to Oz?'

Sally had to confirm that no she had not, but would very much like to.

'You are more than halfway there.' Was her parting shot, at which point James quietly steered the conversation in a different direction by suggesting that as their flight home tomorrow was not until seven thirty in the evening, they should take a day trip into Malaysia, an option to which Sally enthusiastically agreed.

At this point Luigi delivered the cool bottle of Montrachet and proceeded to perform an extravagant opening ceremony, at the end of which, having sniffed and considered the cork, he presented a fine example of what is generally regarded as the greatest of all the white Burgundy's. The flavour was strong and intense, dry yet luscious. It complemented both courses to perfection and as they sipped the wine in this romantic location it was not difficult to forget the outside world, although his thoughts did briefly travel across the globe to North Yorkshire. He fervently hoped that Charles and Edward would continue to understand and accept that the future would bring happiness.

Sally reached across the table with an expression of understanding.

'I know what you must be thinking; everything will work out for the best.'

He gave her a wistful smile and then to lighten the mood again.

'So you are on for this trip into Malaya?'

'You bet, after all we go home tomorrow.'

He tried to appear nonchalant but a smirk lingered on his lips.

'What say we order the coffee and have a nice large brandy to round off a wonderful day?'

She nodded, her expression leaving him in no doubt that the evening had been as magical as any honeymooners could wish for and they retired to bed eager for tomorrow and the next port of call.

Morning arrived and after a light breakfast they opted for a guided coach tour rather than taking a car, reasoning that the extra height would enable better views. It was a good choice and as the guide unfolded the history of Malaysia, they discovered that it was formed in August 1963 when Malaya, Singapore, Saba and Sarawak jointly declared independence from Britain.

The Republic is, as they were to discover on today's guided tour, a fascinating and wondrous mixture of ancient rainforests and towering mountains; the scenery was breath-taking. They visited a rubber plantation and a lakeside village in which all the houses stood on stilts, they also briefly visited a Hindu Temple. The entire experience was magical and so different from the frenetic hive of commerce that is Singapore.

They were also to sense the tension that exists between Malaya and the smallest of the original quartet, which is Singapore. The Singaporeans had originally believed that Britain would not consider them viable as a nation due to scarcity of water and other resources. A further vital consideration in joining this uneasy alliance with its three neighbours was the extra military muscle they needed to flush out the communists from their midst.

However, after two years of internal strife and bickering, Singapore was ousted by the other members of the Malaysian Government and became an independent republic within the British Commonwealth. A decision welcomed by the British as Singapore with its naval base, the largest in East Asia, had a huge strategic value and was often described in the press as the Gibraltar of the East.

They returned from the tour in high spirits; today had been informative, it had provided the opportunity to see beneath the surface of these differing cultures.

They arrived back at Raffles at five, collected the suitcases and thirty minutes later were en- route to the airport where they were due to board at seven thirty, which gave them time to relax and take some refreshment in the first class lounge.

As they waited to board the flight, Sally was in a state of high excitement as she tried to spot which gate number he was keeping an eye on. Conveniently for him the Air France flight to Nice was just above the Cathay Pacific flight to Sydney. She could wait no more.

'Do at least tell me what time we fly, pretty please.' She implored.

'From memory I think it is seven twenty five-ish.'

She scanned the departure times before turning triumphantly and blurting out'

'We are going to Nice, oh that is so romantic.'

He looked surprised. 'Really, - in that case our flight must be the seven thirty.'

She spun round to view the overhead board and her jubilation when she turned was ecstatic as she clung to him.

'You monkey, you wonderful, wonderful, horrible monkey!'

He hugged her; all the planning and scheming had been so worthwhile to see the happiness that enveloped her.

'Now I see why you were so keen last night to avoid conversation with that pretty Australian waitress.' She shook her head, 'I am so happy.'

Finally the flight was called and they made their way to gate twenty six and were finally walking down the gangway to the aircraft. She snuggled his arm and confided,

'As soon as Granny saw you she said you were 'A turn left chap'!'

He looked slightly bemused and then chuckled as she advised him.

'Turn left chaps; always turn left when they go aboard an aeroplane, because that is where you will find the first class seats!'

'Not just first class but right at the front where you get the extra leg room,' he added.

They settled into their seats and very soon the champagne arrived, the cabin doors were locked and the pilot proceeded to the slot on the tarmac ready for take-off. Sally was by now on a frenzied quest for information.

'How far is it to Sydney... how long will it take... where are we staying?'

'Near enough four thousand miles and about nine hours depending on the wind speed and we are staying at the recently refurbished Park Hyatt Hotel which I am told is the place to go, overlooking as it does, the Harbour and Opera House. But as we arrive in the middle of the night I guess we will have to wait until morning to check that out.'

His interrogation was interrupted by the arrival of the menus and more champagne. The airline, Cathay Pacific, had established a big reputation for comfort and style, never more appreciated than on long flights during the hours of darkness. So much so that after a couple of hours even Sally's enthusiasm wilted and they hunkered down into their blankets and pillows.

The cabin lights were dimmed and they both slept well until the lights came back on and the bustle of cabin staff preparing a light breakfast awoke them.

His rejuvenated wife could scarcely contain herself, although being at the very front of the plane meant they were almost the last of first class to walk down the tunnel and into Sydney airport. The great advantage of arriving very early in the day was that their flight was the only one checking through customs. Forty minutes later they were in a taxi and heading towards the Park Hyatt Hotel. They were soon checked in and excitedly headed for the top floor and a first floodlit view of the harbour and it's iconic Opera House; it was just as they had been told: It was Fantastic.

CHAPTER SEVENTY FIVE

As expected they awoke to a blue sky and tingling with expectation had breakfast before setting out to walk the short distance to the harbour. Here not only the most distinctive musical arena in the world awaited them, but also the equally famous Sydney Harbour Bridge.

Nicknamed The Coathanger, because of its arched shape, the bridge was built by the British company Dorman Long Ltd of Middlesbrough in the North East of England. Taking nearly nine years to build it was, when opened in March 1932, the widest long span bridge in the world; it was also the tallest.

As they gazed in awe and not a little British pride, they saw a continuous stream of cyclists, trains, motor vehicles and pedestrians heading to and fro from the North Shore to the central business centre of Sydney and then, just to complete a full house of transport, a large ocean liner hooted her presence as she made her way under the bridge and outwards to the Tasman Sea and onwards to the Pacific Ocean.

Turning their backs for the moment on the bridge they walked around the harbour to the Opera House. This, one of the most distinctive buildings in the world, was designed by the Danish architect Jorn Utzon who had won the competition with an Expressionist Design in 1957. Contrary to its name, it is a venue for multiple music and artistic performances and is constructed from a series of large precast concrete shells supported by concrete ribs; these in turn are covered by more than one million Swedish made tiles. Its dramatic exterior is further enhanced by its setting in the Royal Botanical Gardens where, walking amidst its exotic flora, one can still appreciate the exciting impact these plants must have made on the botanist Joseph Banks when Captain Cooke landed in Botany Bay.

Sally and James were both enchanted and impressed by this wonderful city, it was so easy to understand how anyone having tasted its many delights, might want to emigrate and bring up their children in such a setting. However, having only recently restored Milford Hall to his family's ownership, this idea was clearly not on their agenda.

Hand in hand, still clearly infatuated by each other, they drifted into an Italian style bistro overlooking the harbour. Sally ordered a starter size portion of cannelloni, whilst James opted for a lasagne and a small carafe of Aussie style Chianti.

As he was pouring the wine Sally became aware of being watched, lifting her head she saw a tall fit man of about James's age thoughtfully smiling at her. She whispered her thoughts to James who looked across at the other table before blurting out.

'Bloody Hell, is that you Bruce.'

The smiling face opposite came across and grasped James with both hands.

'How are y'mate?'

He followed this with an admiring look at Sally and wink at James.

'Still know how to pick 'em. I see.'

And then to a still mystified Sally he explained.

'I did a history degree here in Sydney and not ready to settle down and also being keen on sport, I applied to and was accepted by Loughborough PE College in the UK. I got into the first fifteen and Roger Gillow, the guy in charge of rugby sent me for a trial with Leicester Tigers - I taught this guy just about everything he knows about rugby - or maybe it was the other way round!'

Sally gave him a wistful smile. 'I am sure you taught him everything, so at least we owe you is a drink. Why don't you join us?'

He took no persuading, so whilst waiting for the waiter, Sally plied him for information about his native city.

'Bruce, as you have a degree in history, you are just the person to tell me why Captain Cook named this place Sydney.'

'Well, contrary to popular myth he did not, in fact he never even saw this harbour. Having charted both the North and South Islands of New Zealand, the Endeavour sailed into the Tasman Sea and found what they were looking for, the legendary southern continent.

He landed at Botany Bay, collected a large selection of unknown plants and set off on what was to be a perilous journey home with the joyful news that the British Empire had suddenly become very much larger with the discovery of Terra Australis.

Subsequently the British, seeking somewhere isolated to set up a convict colony, chose Cook's remote discovery, the outpost at Botany Bay and dispatched a fleet of eleven ships under the command of Captain Arthur Philips to implement this decision. However, on arrival he found it unsuitable for habitation as the soil was poor and the water supply unreliable. He therefore sailed north to the next inlet, now called Port Jackson, where an appropriate site was found and two weeks later on February 7th 1788, he discovered this place and contradicted orders to call the colony Albion; instead naming it Sydney after the British Home Secretary Lord Sydney, who had issued the charter authorising him to establish the colony.'

The one drink turned into several, Fosters of course, and they arranged to have dinner with Bruce and his wife in two days' time at the Park Hyatt Hotel.

Their newfound guest stood up and kissed Sally briefly on both cheeks, adding,

'By the way my name is Mark - it was the hooligans at Leicester Tigers who re-named me Bruce, it being the perceived name of every Aussie bloke: My wife, however, really is called Sheila!'

Seeing him stride away along the quay activated their own impulses to continue exploring this fascinating city. Having paid the tab they walked steadily around the circular quayside to the ferry terminal and on impulse, bought tickets for a cruise that would take them to Botany Bay, the landfall site that had changed the map of the world.

Thirty minutes later the boat cast off and as they lazed on deck seeing the bridge slowly recede, they sailed past beaches alive with surfers and sun worshippers and on to areas where millionaire homes abounded in glitterati areas reminiscent of Hollywood.

As the current increased and the waves began slapping against the boat they saw the headland eight miles from Sydney harbour that Captain Cook had seen from the Tasman Sea and where he had anchored at what is now the township of Kurnell. Originally, the ferry guide explained, he had in fact designated the area as Stingrays Harbour on account of the vast quantities of those fish to be found in this place. However the great quantity of plants collected by the botanists Mr Banks and Dr Solander prompted him, when later writing his log, to rename the area Botany Bay. And, they were advised, the first European to set foot on this vast continent was Isaac Smith, whom Captain Cook ordered to jump out as the ship's boat beached itself on the shore.

The skipper brought the ferry to a halt enabling everyone on board to point their cameras and take photographs of this historic location that could so easily have been a Dutch colony had the explorer Abel Tasman, who in 1642 was the first European to land on the southern continent, sailed on a little further to the land mass of Australia.

His historic landfall was on the island now called Tasmania, which had originally been designated by him as Van Diemen's Land in honour of Anthony Van Diemen, the Governor General of the Dutch East Indies Company. Strangely he sailed on unaware of the giant landmass of Australia which remained merely a rumour until Captain Cook arrived more than a century later in 1770.

The clicking of camera shutters was suddenly eclipsed by the loud blasts from a ship's foghorn alerting them and any other vessels in the area to make way. Five minutes later the mouth of Botany Bay was obliterated by a large passenger liner heading for Sydney Harbour. As she sailed proudly past they saw on her prow that she was the SS Canberra.

This superb vessel, commissioned by the P&O Shipping line, was built by Harland and Wolff's shipyard in Belfast to operate between the UK and Australia: Her name appropriately taking the name of the capital city of the southern continent. Amongst her many public rooms the appropriately named Cricketers' Tavern, houses a collection of bats and ties and other cricketing ephemera from all over the world; not surprisingly it rapidly became a popular venue for the many passengers addicted to that sport.

The decks were lined with excited holidaymakers, many of whom waved cheerfully to the passengers on the ferry, most of whom, even James Carrington, much to Sally's delight, happily reciprocated this greeting.

After a few minutes pitching around in her wake, the skipper judged it safe to make their way back to port and as they entered the harbour; the final icing on the cake was the sight of a large three masted wooden vessel with sails billowing and a piratical crew dressed in Captain Cook style outfits belligerently shouting and waving their cutlasses, inevitably this triggered another bout of camera activity.

The ferry docked and after slipping the guide a few dollars they stepped ashore; it had been a thoroughly exciting and interesting day.

As they made tracks for the comforts of the hotel she became aware of the intensity in his eyes.

'A penny for your thoughts.'

'I am descended from centuries of farming stock, country people who recognise the vagaries of the elements and the seasons and how we have so little control over them.

It makes me very conscious of the bravery and resolve of men like James Cook who would, for King and country, leave his wife and family, often for periods of up to three years. In that time he would suffer not only the vicissitudes of the sea, but also temperatures and weather that ranged from howling icy storms of the most southern seas to the unbearable heat as they neared the equator. Here they would sail through that area known to mariners as the Doldrums, where the Trade Winds would produce a baffling and unpredictable mixture of light winds, storms and calms.'

She grasped his hand.

'Come on Captain Cook, after that long sea trip you need to enjoy a few home comforts.'

He seized her hand and immediately increased his pace, causing a few raised eyebrows as they dodged in and out of the other pedestrians.

They trotted up the hotel steps collected the room key and Kate silently closed the door behind them. She unbuttoned her dress and stepping out of it she discarded her bra and cupping her breasts and looking at his trousers she whispered,

'From where I am standing you seem to have a problem fitting into your shorts.'

She dropped her hands and drew him by his belt to the bed; he offered no resistance as she pushed him on to his back and felt her smooth silky hands untying the cord on his shorts.

'My word skipper, you appear very pleased to see me; just feel how my heart is pounding.'

He needed no further bidding and for the next half an hour they toyed with each other, both revelling in the other's lithe body as they squirmed enticingly together. They both wanted the ultimate satisfaction but wanted also to delay that ecstatic moment for as long as possible.

Finally he could bear it no longer and slid effortlessly into the centre of his desires; by now they were both too excited to delay the moment any longer and almost simultaneously felt the waves of ecstasy engulf them.

They slowly recovered from their exertions and lay, two prone figures with perspiration pumping out of every cell; exhausted but deliriously happy.

They finally mustered enough energy to take a shower and dress for an evening reconnaissance of Sydney which found them sauntering and stopping at one of the many open air bars for a G&T, before progressing further into the city where they found a most attractive pavement restaurant.

The following day after a Full Aussie Breakfast they set out to explore the central business district which led them into George Street where they stumbled upon the Queen Victoria Building, proudly referred to by the locals as the QVB.

Designed in the late nineteenth century by George McRae in a Romanesque style, it was, when opened in 1898, the Harrods of the Southern Hemisphere.

This formerly most imposing structure, which occupies a complete city block, is over 200 metres long and 30 meters wide. Sadly it was now threatened with demolition although the city authorities had stalled this petition in the fervent hope that some brave entrepreneur would save this iconic landmark.

Sally's initial retail enthusiasm when she saw the magnificent 'cart wheel' entrance was quickly dashed as they moved closer and observed at first hand the faded glory of this masterpiece.

They continued into town, their disappointment assuaged by a bottle of 'Aussie Champagne' and a light lunch of lobster and crab salad. Afterwards they wandered through the harbour side walkways of the botanic gardens before inevitably drifting back towards the Circular Quay and the majestic vessel that dominated the harbour.

They wandered alongside, gazing in awe at the beautiful lines of the vessel, so much so that Sally was prompted to suggest that one day they should consider a cruise.

James meanwhile pondering the secret that was in his head was very nearly caught off balance but recovered in time to agree with her.

That evening Mark aka Bruce and his wife Sheila joined them, as arranged, in the hotel cocktail bar. Both girls hit it off immediately, leaving the men to discuss, inevitably, rugby and golf until Sheila interrupted.

'Sally tells me you breed racehorses, which has prompted a good idea. What say you to us all having a day out tomorrow at...?'

'Randwick Park racetrack,' interrupted James.

'Go to the top of the class Mr Carrington.'

Inevitably with Sally's love of horses, the conversation at the dinner table revolved around all things equine. The meal was excellent, both the food and the Australian wines chosen by Mark. The quality of the latter was a revelation to James who, like so many Europeans had all too easily, pompously dismissed the products from this distant part of the globe.

The following morning, determined to see as much of the area as possible, they took the ferry from Circular Key for the half hour trip to Manly Bay. This service opened in 1855 was, prior to the bridge, the only way to directly access Sydney itself. They arrived to find the harbour a hive of activity as ferries, yachts and kayaks vied for the rights of passage and the beach even at ten in the morning, was heavily populated with sun worshipers and surfers.

This seaside suburb is a laidback escape from city life, which advertises itself as 'Seven miles from Sydney, a thousand miles from care.' On one side you have a mile of sandy beach with a back drop of Norfolk Island pines; on the other side one mile of multicultural al fresco restaurants.

'Typical of the Aussie's to name a place Manly.'

James smiled. 'Au contraire ma chérie, it was in fact named by Captain Philips, he who became the first governor general of NSW. He was apparently so impressed with the manly confidence and behaviour of the native Aboriginal population that he chose that name to honour them. Although he may have regarded them as a little too manly when at a presentation ceremony he was speared through the shoulder by an Aborigine who misinterpreted his raised hand in greeting as an indication that he was about to attack him.'

Sally gave him a whimsical smile.

'Where do you get all this information from?

And what is even more pertinent Mr Carrington, is that we have not yet had even so much as a dip in the ocean, it is not like you not to want to show off your physique; It must be the competition from these life guards.'

'True, true, but I promise in the next few days we will get a tan to take home.'

At eleven they took the short return trip and by twelve thirty were seated in the cocktail bar booted and suited waiting for the taxi. It was on time and as it wound its way through the three miles of traffic to the Eastern suburbs they were eagerly anticipating the afternoon's racing.

Randwick Park is the premier racecourse in the Sidney metropolitan area; it is also home to the Australian Turf club, which annually stages the AJC Australian Derby here in April which is, of course, autumn in this part of the world.

By sheer chance the feature race was The Epsom Handicap and there outside the members' entrance, their hosts were waving Owners & Trainers badges that Mark had persuaded Richard Thompson, a friend and steward of the course, should be made available to his friend and wife who were, he had assured him, well known racehorse owners in the UK.

He led them into the corporate area of the grandstand from where they had an excellent view of the course and the many facilities it provided.

In a similar fashion to American courses, there are not only race tracks, they also have training facilities, both grass and all-weather, which accommodate more than twenty trainers and in excess of six hundred horses.

'Wowee.' Sally summed it up in one word.

James just shook his head in astonishment, it was not what he expected, but then Epsom Downs, unquestionably the most famous flat racing course in the world, is equally surprising to anyone making their first visit. The Americans for instance, were so impressed by the bowler hatted spectators that they adopted them back home and dubbed them 'Durbies.'

Socially the afternoon proved to be a great success, thanks in no small way to Richard Thompson who introduced them to not only Bart Cummings and Colin Hayes, two trainers both very much at the top of their game, but other members of the great and the good of racing down under. From a fiscal point of view it was not so successful although Sally, thanks to Bart, did land the winner of the feature race, the Epsom Handicap.

After racing they dined in town with Mark and Sheila and were introduced to a friend of Marks, Murray Ryan; who turned out to be an interior designer. From across the table, Sally saw James's brain click into business mode and when he learned that Murray regularly flew to Germany to purchase designer items of modern furniture, it was not long before an invitation was proffered and accepted to visit the UK.

'Bring your wife and we will take you racing at Ascot or Newmarket or York, there are so many racecourses within easy reach of Milford Hall.'

As she said it, her heart leapt, it was the first time she had felt so proudly possessive of their wonderful home. James noticed it and he too felt a similar warm glow, he didn't want the honeymoon to end but they had so much to look forward to on their return home, both business and pleasure.

They moved on from the restaurant to the Sydney Yacht Club, where once again they were made to feel most welcome and understood very clearly why so many visitors end up emigrating to this fantastic corner of the world. Finally they retreated to the hotel and bed. Both with their dreams, in James's case he was so excited about tomorrow that he spent an hour or so mulling over how to present his latest surprise.

He was awake at just after seven and made rather more noise than necessary in the shower, which had more than the desired effect as he was soon joined under the cascade of hot water by a now wide awake wife. An event that delayed his intended surprise!

Feeling refreshed they both donned bathrobes and as she made coffee he flung open the curtains to reveal a marvellously blue sky and there anchored beside the Harbour

Bridge was the sight he had been dreaming of ever since they had reached Sidney. He attempted surprise, although he had to turn his face away as he called her.

'Sally, just take a look at this.'

She joined him, her reaction was perfect.

'Wow, I thought the ship the other day was special but this is even more so, we must go and have a look after breakfast.'

At that point she returned to the bathroom, her mind whirling with ideas on how to persuade him to consider a cruise for their next holiday. He had his own thoughts on that matter.

Breakfast over, they once again retraced their steps towards the harbour and finally stood gazing in awe at the majestic lines of the QE2. She was built by the famous John Brown Shipyard in Clydebank, Scotland, on the same plot as her famous forebears from the Lusitania to her immediate predecessor the Queen Elizabeth.

She was launched and named in September 1967 by the Queen who was using the same gold scissors that her mother and grandmother had used to launch her two immediate predecessors.

They were unaware of the historical details, in fact, all Sally wanted to know was would it be possible to go on board. He declared himself unsure but, at her insistence, he climbed the gangway to find out.

She saw him having an animated conversation with one of the white clad officers and returned with the news that they could go aboard but not until four thirty. A smile played on his lips; prompting her to ask, 'What is so amusing?'

'It only gives you five hours to repack the suitcases before we have complimentary drinks on board and then at eight, sail for Cairns and the Great Barrier Reef and then onto Darwin: After which we stop off in Bali, before finally docking at Singapore prior to our flight back to the UK.'

Her mouth fell open; she could not believe that even James could have planned such a surprise without giving some hint of what he was up to.

She hugged him before planting a kiss on his cheek and still trembling with excitement set off at high speed for the hotel. They skipped up the steps to the entrance foyer and this time she took command.

'Off you go to the bar; it is now my time to be in charge. Knowing you as I now do, you will inevitably find someone to discuss horse racing or rugby with and I will join you in one hour after which we will wander into Sydney and find a nice pavement restaurant where I can buy you lunch.' And with that she was gone.

The afternoon was spent discussing the further exciting options that Australia had in store for them and then finally after endless looks at her watch, a nearby church clock proclaimed that four o'clock was finally upon them.

Adrenalin surging through her limbs, she jumped up, hauled him to his feet and marched him in quick time to retrieve their luggage; the hall porter hailed a cab and five minutes later they joined other expectant passengers at the cruise terminal, all waiting to go through customs and up that magic staircase that would take them on deck.

Suitcases identified by cabin numbers, were deposited with the crew and then finally they climbed the stairway to heaven, as she now identified it. Here they were welcomed aboard by a posse of Cunard officers in their best 'whites', and directed to the Midships Lobby on Two Deck, a circular room with a sunken green leather seating area where they joined other incoming passengers for champagne cocktails. They chatted easily with those around them, many were cruise veterans who congratulated them on choosing Cunard - 'The very best', they were assured. After half an hour of pleasantries, Sally, anxious to check out their cabin, led him in search of a steward who directed them to Signal Deck. Knowing him as she now did, it was no surprise to find that they had a penthouse suite with its own private terrace.

This extra luxury had been added behind the ship's bridge in 1972, making the QE2 one of the first ships to restore this privacy, which was so reminiscent of the great days of cruising in ships such as the Normandie in the 1930s.

A tap on the door announced the arrival of the suitcases accompanied by a butler ready to unpack them. Sally declined this invitation and instead ordered James onto the balcony to enjoy the now familiar view of the Opera House and botanical gardens.

Within half an hour she had unpacked and was champing at the bit to explore the ship. The first impression was one of surprise at the advanced interior styling; the first class lounge, the Queen's Room, was decorated in white and tan, with a recessed ceiling lit by indirect lighting. The supporting columns were flared with more indirect lighting, which reflected the shape of the table bases and the leather shell chairs. Even more avant-garde was the Theatre Bar on Upper Deck in which the chairs were red, as were the drapes and indeed so was the baby grand piano which evoked another Wow from Sally.

Still buzzing with excitement they returned to their penthouse and prepared for dinner. As this was the first night on board, the dress code was less formal. Sally opted for a sleeveless pink dress which showed off her newly acquired suntan, James choosing to wear a cream linen jacket.

They headed for the cocktail bar, observing on the way the numerous photographs and paintings of the royal family. These, like the silver plaques, are traditionally commissioned by Cunard to mark such occasions. Everything had an aura of majesty and Sally was completely fascinated by it all.

At eight o'clock, the Captain's voice came over the loudspeakers to advise that they were about to cast off. This prompted an exodus to the deck by many of the passengers including the Carrington's, who wanted to say a fond Gud Day Mate to this dynamic city.

Looking over the side they saw a hive of activity as the enormous ropes that restrained the QE2 were released. On the quayside dozens of onlookers waved farewell, their gesture replicated by most of the passengers. Once again the atmosphere was charged with anticipation and excitement. - One passenger in particular who was still pinching herself; She had been expecting to fly home tomorrow!

The QE2 slipped her moorings and leaving the Harbour Bridge in her wake she glided past the Rocks and the Opera House on her starboard side. Meanwhile on the port bow the lights of the many restaurants and bars in Port Jackson and Manly twinkled as they prepared to feed the hungry sunbathers and welcome home the throng of bustling young executives who had the great good fortune to live in this exciting resort.

As they approached the open sea the QE2's fog horn announced her presence to other shipping before she nosed elegantly towards the harbour entrance where, as on their ferry trip, they saw once again the spot which Captain Philips had chosen as the site for the penal colony. On the starboard bow they said farewell to Watson's Bay and directly opposite, jutting out from Manly Cove, the Sydney Harbour National Park and then quite suddenly as the sun started to go down, they emerged into the Tasman Sea and the adventure had really begun.

The excitement was palpable as those on deck made their way below to the various dining rooms; Sally and James, with two full days and 1,500 miles at sea ahead of them were in no particular hurry, so repaired to the Cocktail Bar to discuss again the anticipation of yet more wonderful experiences. After dinner they retreated to the seclusion of their private terrace where a full moon bathed the ship in a romantic glow and an excited Sally pointed to the sky insisting that the bright constellation of stars was in fact The Southern Cross.

Now courtesy of an information leaflet in their cabin it was her turn to educate him. The indigenous people of Australia she advised, believed that the arrangement of the stars represented a Stingray (the cross) being pursued by a shark (the pointers). As Captain Cook had discovered, the stingray was indeed a very populous occupant of these seas, making it a very appropriate design with which to embellish the Australian flag.

The night was warm, the only sound they heard was the romantic lapping of the ocean against the hull as the QE2 sliced her way through the Tasman Sea, towards her next port of call which was to be Cairns.

With that excitement still way over the horizon they turned in for the night in a bed that they had already found to be comfortable!

The following day was spent acquiring more of the suntan Sally was intent upon, the highlight was the cocktail party as they crossed the Tropic of Capricorn, approximately half way to Cairns. Later needing a break from the fierce sun, they spent further time exploring the ship and it's many treasures. In the Midships Lobby they found a solid silver model of the QE2 made by Asprey of Bond Street, the very same jewellers from whom James had purchased Sally's wedding and engagement rings.

Passing the Yacht Club whose entrance was guarded by a bronze bust of Sir Samuel Cunard, they decided on an impromptu libation, two Singapore Slings, to remind them of the past and the near future.

The following day promised yet more sunshine and enjoyment, highlighted when they returned to their suite as there, perched on the desk, was an invitation to attend the captain's reception.

At seven thirty prompt, this time dressed for the occasion, she in a stunning designer blue dress, he in a white tuxedo with a blue bow tie to compliment his wife's outfit.

In the captain's suite they mingled with a couple of dozen selected guests as the captain nodding and smiling circled the room, finally he reached them.

'Mr and Mrs Carrington, or may I call you James?'

And before James could reply, the captain continued,

'My ship was docked in Durban when the British Lions played South Africa and like every Brit. there, I was on my feet and cheering you on as you took on three South African backs before kicking that enormous drop goal from inside your own half of the field. It won the match for the British and Irish Lions, it was the most outrageous piece of genius any of us had ever seen. You were the hero of the hour and when I saw you come on board in Sydney, I asked the purser to check if it was you, and now here you are with this beautiful lady who, I presume, must be Mrs Carrington.' He paused before adding.

'It would seem that your skill at choosing ladies is as good as your skills were on the rugby field.'

Sally's blushes at this compliment were heightened by those joyous words, Mrs Carrington.

As the reception drew to a close and the passengers took their leave, the first officer handed James an envelope in which, he confided, was an invitation to join Captain Trenchard's table for dinner on Saturday evening.

'It will be an honour and a delight,' James assured him.

After a further day at sea sailing along the Great Barrier Reef and within sight of shore he woke on Friday morning, slowly becoming conscious that the ship was motionless. He slipped out of bed and the view from the terrace confirmed that the ship was indeed tied up in Cairns. The gang planks were down and the crew were erecting the awnings ready for the anticipated exodus of passengers heading out on their chosen day tour.

The Carrington's were in a majority who had opted for a visit to the Great Barrier Reef, some to explore it from the confines of a submersible boat, those of a more energetic nature opting to go snorkelling. The air was full of excitement, particularly amongst the would-be divers as at ten thirty, they boarded the air-conditioned bus which was to deliver them to the dock. Here a ferry awaited to transfer them to the floating pontoons which housed the offshore HQ of the diving operation. After a brief introductory talk they were issued with wet suits and snorkelling equipment.

Encumbered by the flippers and dressed in black wetsuits they resembled a colony of penguins as they stumbled through the door to the outside deck. They listened to a few final instructions and then hand in hand James and Sally jumped into the ocean.

Below the surface the experience was incredible, instead of miles of endless blue sea they were met by a staggering galaxy of colour, as fish of every conceivable hue and shape swam in great shoals all around them. No wonder this phantasmagorical environment is rated as one of the Seven Wonders of the World.

The coral reef supports marine life of all colours and there nestling in the soft fleshy tentacles of the sea anemones was many people's favourite, the Clown Fish, which, according to the Dive Master, was the most photographed fish in the world.

In the next hour they saw dozens of the Reef's fifteen hundred species plus Turtles and other marine life. As they returned yet again to the surface, James tapped Sally on the shoulder and pointed to his watch; it was only five minutes from midday when they had been assured they would experience the most exciting experience of them all, the Goliath Grouper Fish.

Often nicknamed Wally, they can grow up to eight feet long and have the most enormous elephantine head. Despite this fearsome appearance they mean no harm to the strange creatures in rubber suits and are quite happy to be stroked; an indulgence they allow because they have learned that the pontoon is a great source of food as twice a day the staff tip bins full of food scraps overboard.

Despite promises from the dive team that these leviathans would not harm them, Sally along with several others, could not help squealing as one of these monsters brushed against her legs. James meanwhile had re-adjusted his goggles and slipped back below the surface where he saw close-up this unbelievable creature, something out of a Walt Disney film, the head from some angles was almost grotesquely human. He shot back to the surface and persuaded a reluctant Sally to take a peek. He flapped his arms like a chicken. 'You will regret it if you don't.'

Momentarily she paused, but then she too disappeared beneath the surface and joined her husband, pausing briefly to give him a thumbs-up before to his total amazement she swam alongside this monster fish and stroked its head. The mask covered her mouth but he sensed the twinkle in her eyes. They spent a further thirty minutes or so in this wonderland before changing for lunch.

Appetite sated they bought tickets for the glass bottomed boat for the alternative experience. The submersible's floodlights brought everything, fish, corral, turtles etc. into sharp focus, it was not as exciting as the diving but it enabled them to take photographs that would remind them of this truly magical experience on grey days in the UK.

On the bus returning to the ship, the atmosphere was very upbeat and full of good humour with everyone anxious to share their experiences and personal highlights of what had been a spectacular day.

Back on board after their exertions, James recommended they had a little snooze to recharge the batteries. She flashed him a knowing smile but did not demur, although as she snuggled down with him she guessed that sleep was not on the agenda. But hey, she thought, he hasn't mentioned work since we came on board and she knew how to keep his mind off that!

They made love tenderly, each wanting satisfaction for the other, and when that moment arrived they clung together before drifting into a light slumber.

Despite being on the fastest cruise vessel in the world - max 39 miles per hour, most of the next two days were at sea so the suntan craved by Sally was now well advanced and at Saturday night's dinner was shown off to great effect as she sat next to Captain Trenchard who was dressed in his white Cunard dress uniform. The round table made for easy conversation and the selected guests had, as you would expect from a company with Cunard's long experience, been chosen with several overlapping interests and occupations. James found himself seated next to a merchant banker's wife whose husband it would transpire, had similar interests to himself. To his right an elegant blonde in her thirties whose husband, he discovered was a property developer.

Introductions were made, the captain proving to be an accomplished host who's PA had armed him with thumbnail sketches of his guests enabling him to cleverly initiate conversations between James and the banker, whose interests included rugby; likewise, Susie the blonde lady, a keen horse woman whom James introduced to Sally. At the end of the evening, cocktail dates on board were arranged for following day.

After which Mr and Mrs Carrington strolled hand in hand back to their suite and anticipated over a brandy, tomorrow's arrival in Darwin, the capital city of the Northern Territory.
James of course, with his craving for facts, was able to advise his wife that in 1839 it was originally named Port Darwin by the captain of The Beagle, this in honour of Charles Darwin who had sailed with Captain Wickham on his previous visit of exploration in 1836. The name was shortened to Darwin in 1911.

As with their arrival in Cairns, they awoke to find the QE2 moored and with preparations well advanced to transfer the passengers ashore. As usual they were both impatient to explore their new environment.
'Before it gets too hot, let's take a turn around the deck and get our bearings.'
Sally nodded; it was no use protesting, although she did demand time to brush her hair.

They headed for the stern of the ship and gazed out over the Timor Sea, the surface of which today was as still as a millpond; quite unlike the picture painted by Captain Trenchard as he described the devastation wrought by Cyclone Tracy back in 1974 when dozens of people and 70% on the buildings were destroyed. As a result, 30,000 people out of a population of 43,000 were evacuated in what is still Australia's biggest airlift.

From the stern they could see a long jetty reaching out into the sea; During the Second World War this had housed the anti-aircraft guns used to defend Australia's northern coastline against the Japanese. In February 1942, two waves of some two hundred aircraft attacked Darwin; many of these kamikaze pilots had been involved in the attack on Pearl Harbour; the number of bombs dropped here was far more than the assault on the American fleet. Australia responded by deploying in excess of 10,000 troops to defend the northern coastline. As with cyclone Tracy the damage to the city was immense.

Sally squeezed his hand.

'I have to admit that life with you is one great learning curve, you really should have gone up to Cambridge and read history. However, on second thoughts, I am not sure my brain would be able to handle it!'

He gave her bottom a smack.

'Any more comments like that and I shall send you back to your cabin.'

'Yes please professor!'

By the time the history lesson was complete they had circled the deck and had worked up an appetite for breakfast - a *Full Aussie* of course.

Today they planned to visit the capital of the Top End as Darwin is known, most of which is built on a low bluff overlooking the harbour.

Near the dock gates Sally noticed a bus stop and suggested they would gain a more authentic experience of Darwin if they hopped on a bus. He readily agreed and having checked with the security guard at the harbour gate, they jumped on to the next bus heading for city centre. The passengers were a mix of white Australians and the native Aboriginal people who speak a version of that tongue known as Larrakia.

As advised by the guard, they stayed on the bus until they reached the largest shopping precinct which is in Casuarina Square; Their first purchase was prompted by the morning temperature which had risen from 82°f to 93°f. Sally's female antennae spotted a department store, so the first shopping visit was to buy a panama hat for James and a yellow baseball cap emblazoned with the city emblem for Sally.

Inside the shopping malls it was deliciously cool so for once he indulged her female obsession to look at just about everything, well nearly everything; he blocked her attempt to look at microwaves, insisting instead on lunch.

The day spent with different cultures and a different language - Australian! - was good fun although retracing their steps to the bus terminus was not quite so straight forward, but eventually they were back at the dock gates where under the lea of the harbour wall the guard, just for one moment, caught them on the hop when he announced that due to the unexpected arrival of two more cruise ships the QE2 was now moored off-shore.

James slipped him twenty dollars and asked him to call Captain Trenchard with a request to come about as his mate James Carrington was stranded. The guard clearly enjoyed this droll repartee and they returned to the ship already anticipating their next point of call which would be Bali.

CHAPTER SEVENTY SIX

First though they had arranged to meet with Clive Somerville the banker and his wife Emily, and Rupert Erskine the property developer and his wife Susie, with whom Sally had got on so well at the captain's dinner table.

At five minutes to the hour they were seated at the bar and just about to order when they recognised Susie Erskine's infectious laugh, a moment later and they were joined at the bar by their fellow guests.

Every so often, by chance, people meet as strangers and immediately bond as friends; tonight's gathering did just that. Clive Somerville it transpired had represented Oxford at rugby on several occasions but not, sadly, in the match against Cambridge at Twickenham.

Unfortunately he missed out on getting what all sportsmen dream of at our two senior universities; that much sought after accolade, the right to call oneself A Blue.

James gave him a wry look. 'What year did you go up?'

'Coronation year, 1953.'

'I too had high hopes in 1953; sadly, my father's death meant I could not take up my offer at the Other Place, St John's College; otherwise we may well have met on the rugby field.'

'That is very kind of you James, but I don't think for a moment that you would have not been selected for the match at Twickenham, albeit for the other lot.'

Sally cut in, 'enough of rugby, Susie and I want to talk about horses.'

Now it was Rupert's turn to steer the conversation.

'And so do I, as long as they are racehorses.'

'Me too,' piped in Emily.

And so as the cocktails slipped down, Rupert Erskine introduced the idea of a racing partnership. This quickly elicited several suggestions for the syndicate name - Darwinian; Captain Cook; Endeavour; Southern Cross...

The atmosphere was light, conversation came readily, all six of them had an easy sense of communication and enjoyment and it soon became evident that horse racing was a common denominator and, because of his experience and involvement, the others naturally turned to James to guide them along this exciting path.

'Okay, but first of all you must recognise that this is not an investment in gilt edged stock, it is as haphazard as the roulette wheel. There is an oft quoted axiom, breed the best to the best and hope for the best - but, when you do get it right it is one hell of a great feeling.

The first consideration is how much would you wish to invest?'
Rupert Erskine, his brow slightly furrowed, was the first to respond.

'To get something half decent, how much will we be spending?'

'A ball park figure based on last year's prices would be £50k for something well- bred and around half that for an athletic type without quite so much pedigree. If we go to the sales, you will see plenty of good types for less than £10k. However, if they are not out of a mare with Black Type, i.e. one that has been placed in a listed race, then the re-sale value or the valuation of its offspring would almost certainly be much reduced.'

He pursed his lips. 'In Europe and in particular in the UK and Ireland, such animals no matter how well they perform, will always be regarded as Chance Bred. Whereas in the USA owners and trainers are more concerned with racing ability.'

Sally tugged his sleeve and whispered in his ear, which elicited a wry smile as he continued,

'Most trainers are looking for precocious types, usually colts, who will be ready to race as soon as possible after the flat racing season opens at the end of March. I feel rather awkward mentioning this, but we do have an entry in the Tattersall's sale at Newmarket in October.

This I should advise you, is the principal sale for yearlings and he is a well bred colt by Habitat whose progeny are always in demand. He is very forward in his development, which is typical of his sire, and is a hell of a looker. I am confident that he will go for around the £50k - £60k mark. We also have a filly, equally well- bred who is not entered in the sales as she is one I plan to keep and race, after which she will join my broodmare band. I do not want to part with her but would be prepared to join you in a three way syndicate based on leasing the filly for two years.'
Once again Rupert Erskine initiated the conversation.

'That sounds interesting, what does everyone think?'
Clive Somerville with his banker's head on pursed his lips and declared,

'If this is the option that James has chosen, then it will also be my preference.'
Rupert nodded before turning to James. 'And the maths for this one are?'

Sally glanced across at her husband; his head was in business mode as he declared, 'Her breeding is impeccable, but as the colts generally sell for more than the fillies and as I will also retain ownership after she retires I think that £30k split three ways is a fair price. On top of which will be the training and entry fees of around £20k per year split three ways which will hopefully be offset by the prize money!'

Now it was Susie Erskine who joined in. 'When do we get to see this Cunard Lady?'
Sally answered for him.

'Next weekend will be rather hectic, but the following week you must all come to stay and we will visit the Sales at Newmarket.' She turned to her husband.

'And now James will treat us to a celebration glass of bubbly, won't you darling?'
He raised his hand to attract a waiter. 'I am already doing it.'
That set the tone for a very convivial evening; the main concern for the men was a name for the filly and for the ladies the colours of the silks she would carry.

The following day racing receded into the background when the purser delivered an unexpected telegram from James's bankers, Abercrombie Pope & Plummer; it intriguingly read:

John St A Shorthouse

James,

> *Trust all going well and that you are not yet countenancing divorce!*
> *Not sure when you get back but would appreciate seeing you ASAP on your return.*

Regards,
Miles

He passed the telegram to Sally who was also perplexed but confident that Miles would not have interrupted their honeymoon with bad news.

'It will be a formality, some document or other you need to sign, probably relating to tax.'

He was not so confident, but did agree that Miles was not the sort of chap who panicked.

'What time is it now in the UK?'

Sally checked her watch; 'About 10 pm.'

'In that case I will call him this evening.' It must be important he mused.

The day at sea passed slowly and to wile away the time he spent a couple of hours reading the financial reports in the various newspapers available on board, none of which reported or predicted financial turmoil and, having had time to reflect, he decided to park the problem and send Miles a cable rather than telephoning him.

'Intrigued by your message but assume no great threat to my financial future!
Will see you on Monday next at 10 am and then if I am still solvent, maybe lunch at White's?'

Yours,
James

CHAPTER SEVENTY SEVEN

After another long haul of nearly 3,000 miles, they reached the romantic idyll that is Bali and dropped anchor 800 metres or so from the quayside. With typical Cunard attention to detail, the QE2 operations director had despatched a reception crew at dawn; their mission to set up a temporary terminal to receive those passengers wishing to visit this honeymoon paradise.

The first boat of visiting passengers, which included the Carrington's, departed the ship at 8.30 am and as they approached the landing jetty they became increasingly aware of the hiatus of sound created by a myriad of cab drivers and vendors of every possible type of souvenir, all pleading for attention. James, on the advice of the purser, had pre-booked a car. Surveying the horde of drivers all of whom appeared to be waving a sign, he finally spotted one sign embellished with the name Carrington.

Fortunately the local police were on hand to control the locals, so he was able to enlist their assistance to clear a passage which enabled them to gain access to a fairly ancient white Mercedes. To their great relief the air-con was working and the interior was mercifully cool.

'The Bali Hyatt Hotel and don't spare the horses.' A quip from Sally that required an explanation, although judging by the cabbie's amusement, it seemed that it would soon become local parlance.

This destination had been recommended by the Erskine's, whose son had spent his honeymoon here a few months previously.

They were not to be disappointed, although the journey itself was not for the faint hearted; indeed it made the Hanger Lane gyratory system seem positively pedestrian. However, after an hour's journey, along a route besieged by giant potholes, they were introduced to the other side of this rural paradise. From the cool interior of the car they saw picture postcard scenes of paddy fields ploughed by bullocks and wooden ploughs; ornate Buddhist Temples; market stalls which lined the routes to each village or town; beautiful stepped hill sides, but most of all the wonderful smiling dignity of people who had so little in comparison to the western world.

Finally, they reached the gated entrance to their destination where they were immediately absorbed into the friendly ambience that pervades in this magical country; even the guards who manned the barrier were innately welcoming and polite.

Once through the gates, they walked hand in hand along the pathway that followed the perimeter of the nine hole golf course.

'Don't even think about it buster, golf is not on today's menu and this is not the clubhouse, this is the great meeting hall where I shall sit whilst you announce us to the manager and find out where the swimming pool is located.'

She watched him stroll towards the desk and wait until the manager arrived and greeted him with hands clutched together as if in prayer, after which they shook hands and the manager handed him a key. He returned to collect her with the news that they had a day room in the picturesquely named Bougainvillea wing of the hotel. It was surrounded by these beautiful flowering plants and turned out to be as enchanting as its name. They swiftly changed into swimwear and headed for the pool area where, having bagged a couple of beds in the shade, they quickly deposited their towels before slipping into the pool and swimming the few strokes to the thatched roof bar that dispensed drinks and snacks. They spoke very little as they sipped the cool orange juice, content to listen instead to the ocean crashing on to the hotel's adjacent private beach; both cocooned in their own bubble of happiness.

Sally placed her glass on the bar and snuggled against his tanned body.
'Less than a year ago you were but a memory of someone with whom I had danced at an architects' ball in Nottingham. Little did we know the awful circumstances that would bring us together, but out of that tragedy has come great happiness, with yet more to come.'

She took his hand and placed it on her stomach.

'Say hello to George.'

His reverie was broken. 'You mean! – He searched for the words. 'We are going to have a baby - are you sure?'

When you were in the bar in Sydney and I was packing, I suddenly realised that my monthly visitor had not arrived and if you remember, when we were queuing to go aboard ship I said I needed to visit the ladies room, well I was telling porkies, I actually nipped into the chemists alongside the ferry terminal and bought a pregnancy test kit.

She saw the handsome face looking down at her, she felt him willing her to say yes we are having a baby.

'This morning before we docked I used it and have been trying to find the right moment to tell you.'

He shook his head but she saw the happiness there. 'Well I suppose this is an appropriate time although I guess this might be a bit big for a birthing pool!'

'James that fateful day when we met again at the George Hotel in Stamford was when I dared to dream of this moment, but never expected it to happen and now that we have spent part of this fantastic honeymoon at the hotel named after Stamford Raffles, I think that there can be no other name for this baby, it must be George - or Georgina!'

Finally, conscious that their fellow pool residents must be confused at this unusual display of British emotion, they recovered their composure by inviting their pool mates to a celebration glass of champagne.

After which to his suggestion, 'You should go and lie down.'

She raised an eyebrow. 'Don't you think you have done enough damage!'

They spent the rest of a wonderful afternoon swimming in the warm but thunderous ocean before returning to their room in Bougainvillea to shower and change in preparation for the switchback ride back to the ship. With so much to think about, the journey passed largely unnoticed until they reached the quay side, where the tumult from the street sellers brought them back to earth.

Back on board they retreated to their balcony both suffused in happiness and longing to share the news with those back home, meanwhile they would be unable not to confide the news to their syndicate friends.

After a further day at sea they made their penultimate visit, to the cosmopolitan city of Semarang, the capital of Central Java. Here they took a trip in a Becak or tri-shaw, first to the main shopping district known as Jalan Permuda, a wide tree lined boulevard with a myriad of local traditional delicacies, cookies, ice cream and numerous local breads all made on the premises. Then having given their driver a break, they pushed on to the Kota Lama or, as it is popularly known, Little Netherlands, whose charming collection of Dutch styled houses were once the residences and offices of the Dutch East India Company.

It was a fascinating day made all the better by their mode of transport which allowed them to feel the cool sea breezes which made the ninety six degrees Fahrenheit tolerable. The real highlight of the ride however was sneaking up behind the Erskine's and then, with the advantage of a flying start, leaving them in their wake much to the chagrin of Rupert who responded with cries of 'Foul play, we will lodge an objection with the stewards!'

He duly reported the incident to his 'Fellow committee man' Somerville; the result of this breach of gentlemanly conduct resulting in a fine of one bottle of Champagne, vintage of course.

As expected the evening was enjoyable with the ladies talking about babies and the men concentrating on horse racing and the planned visit to the Newmarket yearling sales.

CHAPTER SEVENTY EIGHT

They docked in Singapore on Friday morning and enjoyed a farewell breakfast on board with their new racing partners, both of whom who were due to fly to Heathrow via Frankfurt that evening.

Sally and James had instead, opted for an overnight stay at Raffles. Their invitation to spend the day with them for some R& R at such an imposing venue was enthusiastically welcomed by the others.

The men shared a cab and the ladies likewise and once again they were welcomed by the tall Indian in his white suit and red turban. As before, an imperceptible click of his fingers and the luggage disappeared from the taxi's to a vault beneath this iconic building.

The ambience of history and the charisma of its many famous residents meant they inevitably drifted in the footsteps of Hemingway and Somerset Maugham until they found themselves once again in the Long Bar. With the exception of Sally, now conscious of her responsibility to George, they downed a couple of Singapore Slings. This elixir prompting Susie Erskine to suggest they called the filly Miss Raffles which was applauded until Sally stole the show with her observation that, as they had not yet seen the filly, perhaps Pre-Rafflelite might be more appropriate, a clever pun that was not only approved but was celebrated with a third Sling to christen the baby as it were.

After which they drifted out into Orchard Road and followed James to The Istana, a Palladian mansion set in one hundred and six acres which offers views of the sea and the endless stream of tankers and container ships heading or returning from the South China Sea. This magnificent building, built between 1867 and 1869 was formerly the residence of the British Governor. It continued as such until a century later when in 1969 Singapore was granted independence and it was renamed The Istana, the Malay name for a palace.

Turning their backs on the maritime activity, a variety of pastoral delights awaited them in the park that surrounds the palace. This spacious green space provides the lungs to an area otherwise totally urbanised and was for Emily, a keen gardener, her moment in paradise, as it offered several idyllic botanical sights such as the marsh wetland with swans swimming on the small river that runs alongside, or the Lily Pond, where fabulously coloured blooms, some of them nearly two metres high, were quite breath-taking.

For the gentlemen, unbelievably, there was a nine hole golf course – 'Not today chaps!'

Susie emphatically closed that option.

Finally, out of respect for the sacrifice of those who had given their lives in the Second World War, they followed the directions to the compound where they viewed the Japanese field gun presented to Lord Mountbatten after the Japanese surrender in 1945.

After an uplifting experience in which they had felt enormously proud to be British they retraced their steps to Raffles and marvelled at man's ingenuity and stubbornness – James recounting how, when he and Sally had taken the coach trip into Malaysia, his suggestion to the Malay driver that, rather than continually filling in the shrinking harbour – Raffles Hotel for instance had once stood on the quayside – why not purchase land from Malaya and move the Singapore border a mile or two into that comparatively vast country, it was after all, only jungle. This suggestion he recounted, had produced a string of expletives, which you did not have to be Malay to understand!

They wandered back to Beach Road and as they approached Raffles, a nearby clock striking five galvanised the men folk to accelerate towards the lobby where the tall statuesque figure in the red turban once again clicked his fingers to send his minions scurrying into the luggage room, whence they soon re-appeared with two sets of luggage. These were swiftly deposited in the two taxis that had been lurking out of sight awaiting a coded message.

Goodbyes were exchanged and confirmation and assurances given that they would all re-group at Milford Hall on the Wednesday prior to attending the Newmarket October Race Meeting and the Yearling Sales which were held each day before and after racing.

Sally and James watched them disappear from sight before returning to their suite to change into swimwear before heading for the roof terrace and the welcome cool water. Here they contemplated the pleasure of going home and imparting the exciting news to the family.

The following day, unlike the usual last few hours of a holiday did not flash by, in fact it seemed to pass quite slowly, but finally they headed for the airport, climbed the boarding steps, took a left turn and settled into their seats in the front row of first class. With twenty hours of flying and stopover time ahead of them, this is the moment when most passengers promise themselves that they will have short haul holidays in future. In this instance, the holiday had been so memorable and the tidings they were taking home would generate so much joy and excitement that they were both unfazed. There was of course that intriguing summons from APP Merchant Bank that had to be resolved before they arrived home with the news of George Carrington Esq.- But could life possibly get any better?

The first stop-over was Dubai where Sally excused herself, for a make-up call he wrongly presumed. She returned thirty minutes later with a small beautifully wrapped box which, when opened contained, much to his astonishment, a yellow and white gold Rolex Oyster watch. Attached to which was a message in childlike script.

To my darling Daddy with love from George xxx.

He shook his head, his eyes distinctly moist. 'I have to say the boy has excellent taste!' She smiled, 'Rather like his father.'

An hour later their flight was called and the final leg of this momentous honeymoon was about to get underway. James instinctively looked to his wrist with a view to advancing his watch to UK time; what he saw of course was the embryonic gift from George or would it be Georgina? – Either way as long as the child was born strong and healthy, he would be happy.

He leaned back in his seat; life was so good and now with a new baby on the way he had even more to anticipate. He was looking forward to telling the boys; He could imagine Edward in particular, itching to get his new brother into rugby boots; Charles on the other hand would probably be more the responsible older brother.

In this contented frame of mind he drifted off into a deep sleep; a slumber unbroken until daylight when morning was announced as usual by the sound of hostesses preparing to serve breakfast.

He slowly opened his eyes and removed the blanket to find Sally very wide awake and in the latter stages of applying her cosmetics. She flashed him a smile and anticipated his first question; 'We land at Heathrow at eight thirty so you have two hours to have breakfast before we set off to your, and now my favourite hotel, although Raffles runs it close.

The thought of London immediately triggered thoughts of Miles Stanhope Court and the mysterious cable he had received from the bank earlier in the week. But that was for the morrow; today he intended to devote to his wonderful wife.

Finally they saw the channel below them and then the hive of activity that was Heathrow, the busiest international airport in the world.

The sun was shining and as it was Sunday the traffic was comparatively light, allowing them to be in Brook Street at ten thirty. William the head Doorman, resplendent as always in his tailed coat and top hat recognised James immediately and a tiny flick of his fingers summoned one of his staff to receive the luggage.

'I imagine by your tan and amount of luggage that you and the lady must have been on holiday Mr Carrington.'

'Quite right William and this lady I am proud to say, is my wife.'

'I am very pleased to meet you Mrs Carrington; will you require all the luggage taking to your suite?'

'No thank you William, just the two smaller cases.'

Once again as if by magic the two larger suitcases were immediately transferred to a trolley and disappeared into the bowels of Claridge's myriad of store rooms. James and Sally checked in and rather than climb the large gracious staircase, she led him to the lift simply to enjoy the wonderful rocking horse, except that, in order to conform with the stylish black and white tiled floor, this rocker was a zebra and it was perfect in every respect, even to the mane where the black and white stripes exactly matched those on its body.

As it was Sunday, instead of the usual business clientele huddled in intensive commercial propositions, the atmosphere was altogether more relaxed and family orientated; the perfect environment to clear his mind ahead of tomorrow's meeting with APP.

Hand in hand, they meandered out into the stylish streets of Mayfair and headed for Hyde Park where, along with so many other visitors and locals they enjoyed the sunshine. They strolled with no planned destination, simply luxuriating in the pleasure of being man and wife, albeit that the third member of the family was never far from their thoughts.

Tomorrow's business at the bank was not for discussion; their only conversation revolved around the exciting pleasure that their news would bring to the as yet unknowing grandparents.

They skipped lunch, settling instead for an ice-cream eaten on the hoof as they strolled along the Bayswater Road before turning back into the park. Here in a leafy glade they came across the bronze statue of Peter Pan. There he stood on the stump of a tree blithely blowing his pipe and as James gazed at him, Sally burst into laughter.

'You are thinking he looks like you!'

'Well, rather like young George, he arrived in the middle of the night and is supposed to stand on the spot where he landed after flying out of the window in Kensington.'

He gave her a cheeky smile.

'However, it is true that I have been accused, a few times maybe, of putting on my little boy's face when I am pleading my cause and like his creator James Barrie, I like surprises. Did you for instance, know that the author arranged for the statue to be installed in the dead of night in keeping with the storyline?'

She snuggled against his arm. 'Don't ever stop being that little boy. It melts my heart!'

They returned to the hotel - from one magic location to another.

CHAPTER SEVENTY NINE

The following morning he ordered breakfast for Sally to be taken to the room at nine thirty whilst he went down alone at seven thirty, to try and formulate in his head the reason the bank had requested today's meeting. Try as he might he could not visualise why or what might be the urgency; one thing was for sure, the little boy look would cut no ice with the directors of APP.

At nine fifteen he set off for a leisurely stroll along Brook Street, skirting Hanover Square until he reached Regent Street and the impressive Regency façade that was APP Merchant Bank. He climbed the now familiar twelve steps to be greeted by Kenneth in his navy blue and gold livery. 'Good morning Mr Carrington, Mr Stanhope Court asked me to take you straight up to his room.'

As he followed his escort along the now very familiar route, his mind went back to that very first visit and the meeting with Sir Julian Abercrombie when, against all odds he had, thanks to his grandfather's legacy of APP shares, been invited to bank with this prestigious city icon.

His reception from Miles was extremely cordial, although he declared himself unable to explain the purpose of today's meeting, his body language did however help to mollify James's slight apprehension.

The announcement that the meeting was to be held in the executive boardroom did somewhat surprise him, jilting the relaxed mode in which he had arrived. His business acumen had now switched to red alert; the casual dismissal of any real importance regarding today's meeting, instantly evaporated.

The Executive Boardroom, it sounded ominous, his agile mind was whirring as he mentally reviewed his business record with the bank. This had over several years been propitious for both parties. He had prospered and so had APP: In every single year his companies had all made considerable profits.

He studied Miles's expression; it remained non-committal but his eyes displayed a   mischievous twinkle.

He attempted to draw a stronger reaction. 'Is this how they get rid of a chap?'

'Well yes it is, but the Board would have to be seriously concerned about an individual and I don't believe they see you in that category.'

With that he stood up and led his visitor up the great staircase with its 'Floreat Cacahuaquchtl' carpet, the translation of which, James recalled, bore testimony to the elixir of the South American

Gods - drinking chocolate.

He remembered the trepidation he had originally felt, particularly when first being presented to the main board of APP. The then formidable chairman, Sir Julian Abercrombie, had since retired from active involvement in the company; his son Marcus now steered the ship. So it was with some surprise that Miles's tap on the door was answered by the patrician tones of the former chairman, whose response, 'Come', left no excuse but to do so.

'My dear James; the original formal greeting of Carrington had long since been dropped.

'Julian, I understood that Marcus was now running the show?'

'Indeed I am James, but father insisted on crashing this particular party.'

Thus the tone was set as an equally warm welcome was extended by two of the original five main board directors; Sir Marcus Partington and Jonathan Fox King who were joined at the table by the newer appointees, Rufus Mainwaring and Miles Stanhope Court.

Sir Julian indicated that James should join them at the oval Hepplewhite table he remembered so well.

Marcus Abercrombie shook hands with James and immediately ceded authority to his father who continued in those clipped tones which still resonated with evidence of his military background.

'Gentlemen we are here today to mark a strategic and modernising step forward for APP.' His eyes swept the conference table; held their gaze and without further ado he continued.

'I believe that for APP to go forward in the spirit of those Tea Clipper days of two centuries ago, we need, and I emphasis this, we need a man at the helm who will once again fill our sails with the leadership and authority that exemplified our forebears; We do have such a man sitting at this table.'

He once again scanned the boardroom.

'I ask you, as directors of this bank, to invite Mr James Robert Staincliffe Carrington to accept the role of Managing Director of Abercrombie Corporate Developments, which I am sure will, in the near future be simply referred to as ACD.'

Sir Julian resumed his seat, allowing the mantle to pass to his son who immediately seconded the proposal and asked for a show of hands. Four of the five directors immediately pledged their allegiance; the uncertain abstainer was Rufus Mainwaring who sat with pursed lips, apparently in a dilemma.

The others turned to James, who was by now in full financial mode and he did not disappoint them. The challenge immediately excited him, what had he to lose, to recruit him was in the interests of APP; he did not need the income they would be offering, equally he would not sidestep the challenge - Sir Julian knew that, indeed his proposal depended on it.

The abstainer leaned back, his position suddenly very vulnerable as he realised he was facing an exceptionally astute operator, as Sir Julian himself had found out when he first locked horns with the then young Mr Carrington some twenty or so years ago.

James however did not go for the jugular, unanimity was essential.

'Gentlemen, this is a most unexpected proposition; I have had dealings with most of you for several years. Mr Mainwaring of course only joined the board a little over a year ago, so we have had no opportunities to get to know each other. I am confident, however, that he must be very astute and highly regarded by the other members around this table or he would not be sitting here.'

He turned to Mainwaring, the fish was on the hook, and it was time to reel him in.

'In business there always has to be another point of view; When necessary, both parties must accept an alternative opinion, as I had to when I first set out in business. My first partner was, as is common knowledge, Edward Lawson. He was the strongest big man I have ever met and that includes those gigantic Springbok forwards that faced the British Lions in South Africa. He would never take a backwards step and that inspired every member of that side to be equally resolute but, in business he was always prepared to negotiate and this sense of fairness generated far more respect than his physical presence. This is why Fordmill Construction has consistently set new standards and innovations in the construction industry; many of those concepts are of course relevant to other commercial scenarios and I will not hesitate to share my experience with suitable potential clients. Ironically of course, I have through my family connections dating back to my great grandfather Sir Albert Staincliffe, been associated with this merchant bank and all its ambitions since 1890, though little did I ever expect to be so honoured as to sit amongst you. True my own close involvement has been for twenty years or so, but having experienced at first hand, the APP ethos of constructive and informed banking, I am acutely aware that only well informed arguments will be acceptable. Needless to say those propositions have to be undeniably legitimate.'

Sir Julian, not for the first, appreciated his protégée's subtle ability to take control: When they first met, James was extremely well prepared, his proposals were augmented by architectural drawings and skilful watercolours with which to seduce not only the bankers but also would be clients.

This time however the earnest face opposite did not have the advantage of preparing his address, he was thinking on his feet, not in an over-bearing way but in an empathetic style that diffused resentment. He observed closely how Rufus Mainwaring had absorbed James's words and how his expression had softened. His posture was no longer belligerent; the other directors could sense his awakening desire to be part of this 20th century renaissance of APP's glorious past.

Rufus Mainwaring had listened carefully to Mr. Carrington's pitch. He had to admit that for someone with no prior knowledge of today's proposition he had quickly grasped the nettle. If the other main board members had confidence in him, particularly Sir Julian, he would go with the majority vote. Should they be wrong, he would remind them of his earlier apprehension.

Like the other main board members he would have an important part to play, James Carrington would need their help, he might spot the winners but the other members would initially have to discover suitable candidates and ultimately place the bets and gambles, and long shots would not be considered. Mentally he allowed himself a smile; Mr Carrington was going to have to be very good at his job or... but if he was, they would all be acclaimed. He had nothing to lose by giving him the nod. James continued with his own potted history.

'Because of the demise of Sir Albert's company, I had to create my own empire, which was constantly predicted by the financial press to be acquired by our larger competitors. That did not happen on my watch, but the management structure I left in place has acquiesced to a takeover and entre nous I was asked to help broker that deal which has given me a further insight into the art of negotiation. In essence gentlemen, I am truly excited that I should even be considered to be asked to be MD of ACD and very much hope that Rufus, if I may be so presumptuous, will welcome an alternative view and agree to differ when necessary, as will I, because this will be pivotal to our success. In essence, if we all play to our strong points – your knowledge of banking and my ability to assess the probability of a company's likelihood to succeed, then we will prosper.'

There was plenty for the board to consider but James's address to Rufus Mainwaring, very much on a one to one basis, albeit disguised as an affable conversation, had certainly convinced the other directors that they had made the right decision, this was not an uninformed choice, they had chosen well.

There was a silence, maybe half a minute, before the Doubting Thomas in their midst stood up and offered his hand across the table.

'I am now totally convinced. What you don't know about banking we will teach you, on condition that you educate us in spotting winners, companies like yours who have the potential to become blue chip.'

As he had done at that memorable meeting when James had first been accepted as a member of APP's clientele, Sir Julian rose from the table and instead of pouring glasses of dry sherry he opened instead a small refrigerator cleverly disguised as a chest of drawers, Hepplewhite, of course.

He expertly removed the cork prompting James to observe,

'When I saw the clear glass bottle I knew you were being exceptionally generous, but surely you did not anticipate a bomb scare, particularly as Marcus is still in the room. I also imagined that cavalry officers always opened the bottle with their sabre.'

'As ever James you are well informed and yes, for those who don't know; Tsar Alexander the second feared, in the unstable days of 1876, an assassination attempt at his Three Emperors' Dinner. He therefore ordered Louis Roederer to supply the champagne in clear glass bottles, whence it became known as Cristal; a vintage not commercially available until the end of the Second World War. Marcus joined his father in passing around this most exquisite wine from Rheims, not in the increasingly popular tulip glasses, but in the traditional glasses which, Miles could not resist advising them, were replicas of Marie Antoinette's bust. This elicited a rather dry riposte from Sir Julian: 'Thank you Stanhope Court.'

A toast to the new director was drunk and a contract was brought in by Marcus' PA for James's consideration. He scanned the remit, studied the proposed salary and performance benefits, before willingly agreeing a date with Marcus Abercrombie to develop the strategy in more detail.

Handshakes all round and the meeting was closed.

Whilst the others returned to their desks, Sir Julian accompanied James and Miles to White's for a celebratory lunch. As of course they were not by tradition allowed to discuss business at the dining table, Sir Julian took the opportunity during their brief car ride to pass James a key ring. The keys he explained were to two adjoining fully serviced apartments in a mansion block overlooking Hyde Park; owned by the bank, so one is usually available.

'Give Annabel a couple of days' notice to make sure one of them is free and make sure you use the correct key - I don't want you bursting in on me!'

The conclusion of lunch at one thirty prompted a final round of handshakes before James in a state of great excitement retraced his steps to Claridge's and Mrs Carrington who would be anxiously awaiting his news.

His pace quickened as he approached Brook Street and there she was, anxiously sipping coffee at a table adjacent to the piano which gave her a full view of the hotel entrance. Two seconds later she was hurtling across the black and white tiles and into his arms.

'Tell me, tell me everything, I have been thinking of nothing else since breakfast.'

He attempted to keep a straight face; 'Well the good news is that we are not bankrupt, in fact I have an opportunity to earn quite a bit of extra income, if you agree of course!'

He gave her a quick overview which, knowing his need for new challenges she found exciting for him and to his observation, 'why did they choose me?' Her reply was instant and pertinent.

'Your great hero is Captain Scott; my personal champion is the founder of the suffragette movement Emily Pankhurst; the dictum she preached most in her campaign was, 'We need deeds not words' and that is how the bank see you, a man of action who makes things happen. They also know you have never failed at anything, so this will be another notch on your office chair!'

Secretly she had been hoping, particularly with a baby on the way, that they might spend more time together, but she did her best to conceal her disappointment. It would be selfish and unfair to spoil the accolade that such a highly esteemed city blue chip had bestowed upon him.

He sensed that as a new mother she would need support, particularly in such a large house; she would of course have his mother for company, plus June and Keith who were living in the old coach house organising the horses and farm. No doubt too, her mother and grandmother would be regular visitors plus Mrs Thompson the daily help. Plus most of all she was a tough cookie who had always coped.

He took her hand and stroked her engagement ring.

'I will only be in town occasionally, most of the time I will be visiting would-be clients at their premises so that I can absorb at first hand the ethos and the management style of the company. And, as you have a great eye for detail and assessing people - there will be occasions when I will ask you to accompany me to meetings.'

The tension was immediately gone, it was time to be off to the station, they had a train to catch and exciting news to convey. Nothing was going to spoil their homecoming.

'I have already arranged with William for the luggage to be made ready the moment you arrived and there it is and yes this is the best hotel in the world!'

They arrived at Kings Cross with time to spare and were soon ensconced in first class and eager to be at Grantham where Camilla would collect them unaware of the joyous tidings they would announce. Ninety minutes later they saw the Range Rover, but it was the farm manager who had been despatched to collect them so the suspense was heightened for a further twenty minutes.

At last they were on the private road that led to Manston and there parked at the front of the house was his mother's BMW, which solved the problem of who to tell first; They did not have long to wait as one side of the large oak door opened to reveal an excited Granny Parkinson.

He took Sally's hand, muttering as he did so; 'Try not to spill the beans until we are all together and take that grin off your face.'

After an enthusiastic hug they followed Granny into the kitchen where the other ladies awaited, a minute later Robert Parkinson joined them.

'Sorry I could only send the Range Rover, I have been unable to trace your pal with the helicopter! So how are you both, you do look extremely well.' His daughter kissed him on the cheek before blurting out.

'We are all very well.'

It took a few seconds to sink in but finally, after what seemed an age, Elizabeth Carrington posed the question.

'You mean?'

'Yes.' No clarification was required, but did elicit a deep sigh from the Grandfather.

'Mr Carrington as I have mentioned several times. You do seem intent on emptying my wine cellar of Champagne!'

'Not quite Robert, courtesy of Duty Free I bring replenishments.'

Whereupon he produced from his hand luggage, two bottles of Dom Perignon.

'It really should be Roederer Cristal but I am afraid that not even the Heathrow store stocks that.'

The ladies meanwhile were engrossed in matters far more important.

'Do you want a boy or a girl - what names have you chosen - when are you due...?

Robert signalled his son-in-law to follow him and en route to the cellar he turned before taking James by the hand.

'You have made my daughter so happy, she is such a beautiful girl but after that dreadful disappointment with that Cavalry officer, we never thought she would ever trust a man again. I cannot tell you how happy you have made this family.'

James looked the older man in the eye before declaring, 'You have been so welcoming, not only to me, but to my mother and in all my adult life I have never seen her so energised and carefree. She has thanks to Camilla, even started to play golf again. Having her living at Milford Hall again is just the cherry on the cake because I owe her so much.'

He followed Robert to the wine cellar and had his first glimpse of Manston's hidden treasure trove. His host pointed to the first rack and identified these as Bollinger Grande Année, a label James had only rarely tasted.

'The very best from this vineyard - only produced when the company believe they have an exceptional harvest.'

He smiled at James. 'For family consumption only! Likewise, your Dom Perignon will also be saved for a very special day, my Grandson's christening!'

James would have loved to have spent more time exploring this vintner's paradise but the ladies would be getting impatient so, carrying their cargo carefully, they returned above ground where six crystal flute glasses, one of them containing orange juice awaited them.

Toasts and more toasts were drunk as the afternoon continued in high spirits. The suggested baby's name George was appreciated and approved; in a lower key so was Lawson and in a much more euphoric tone so was the third name of Robert, although that too had intensely emotional overtones for Elizabeth.

Finely however, knowing the others had to drive home, Robert sent for his farm manager and the evening was declared closed.

Apart from the hand luggage the other cases were left in the Range Rover for Camilla to deliver tomorrow.

The three guests with Sally at the wheel of Elizabeth's BMW were despatched to Milford Hall. It had been a long day, but a momentous one.

On the way home, Sally looking in the rear view mirror saw Elizabeth snuggle up to her son. Please God let my relationship with my baby be as loving and caring as this.

CHAPTER EIGHTY

Two days later the holiday gear had been washed and ironed and stowed away ready to receive their guests and co-owners of Pre-Rafflelite. The Erskine's arrived late morning the Somerville's minutes later.

After an approving tour of the house, Sally took them to meet the filly who would carry their colours; she was led out by June and even to the uninformed she looked magnificent: Susie Erskine the one horse person amongst the guests was particularly impressed.

'She has a magnificent back end and a wonderful shoulder, she could be a colt at first glance, but those long ears and kind expression are very compelling. I think we are lucky to be part of James's syndicate as this filly would surely be well beyond our budget.

June took the lead rein off and clapped her hands.

The bay filly flicked her heels before setting off at high speed across the paddock in the direction of four foals in the adjoining field, this in turn got them excited and provided a thrilling spectacle for the visitors as they all thundered into the distance and then back towards them. June, eyes sparkling with pride, confided.

'This young lady is going to the top; you rarely see such power and balance, I am so thrilled to be associated with her.

Rupert Erskine wanted to know more.

'Which is the best of the four youngsters?'

Quick as a flash his wife took up the challenge.

'When we come back this time next year I think that the big dark bay will be the one, he was first out of the blocks and the others were never going to catch him - judging by his physique I presume he will probably be a sprinter.'

James who had crept up on them confirmed that was indeed their expectation but, as a colt he would be sold.

'That is great news James because by then we will have won so much money we will be able to buy him and let you join our syndicate!'

The joyful expectations were interrupted by the housekeeper who advised that lunch was served; they dutifully followed her to the breakfast room where lobster soup followed by salad and a selection of cold meats awaited them, this was washed down with one of the great wines of France,

Montrachet.

In between bites the conversation turned once again to the filly. James was able to confirm that he had spoken with Weatherbys, the custodians of all matters relating to horse racing in the UK and confirmed that she was now named Pre-Rafflelite. However, the application for the owners to be known as the Cunard Syndicate was rejected. The registrations department feeling it unlikely that the shipping line would be agreeable to what they might feel to be an invasion of their company profile.

Instead he had reserved the name Serendipity Syndicate which, subject to their approval, would be accepted. In view of the propitious circumstances that brought them together, the others approved his choice.

Lunch over, the ladies moved upstairs to have coffee with James' mother. The men meanwhile, both of who had clinical and enquiring minds, continued to grill James on the importance of pedigrees; a subject on which he was only too happy to indulge them. He stood up.

'Let's go where we can find a few answers'.

They dutifully followed him across the yard and up the stone steps to his private domain; the office where the walls were smothered with paintings and photographs of famous horses. He pointed to a photograph that hung directly in front of his desk.

That gentlemen is Habitat, sire of Pre-Rafflelite. On the track he was the champion miler either side of the Channel, a horse that has consistently produced fast stock. He was owned by the man who also owned Nijinsky, in whose shadow he dwelt, like every other horse in the world.

Only multi-millionaires can afford to send a mare to the all-conquering Nijinsky and that mare will herself will be worth a fortune. Whereas Habitat, who was a late developer, did not really announce himself until half way through his three year old career. After two attempts over ten furlongs, where he finished second on both occasions, his very experienced trainer Fulke Johnson Houghton dropped him back to a mile. This was a distance over which he would never be beaten, as he went on to win the Lockinge Stakes ; Prix Quincy ; Goodwood Mile and the Prix du Moulin de Longchamp. In the Moulin he comprehensively beat the seasons Two Thousand Guinean's winner Right Tack. This earned him the crown of European Champion Miler.

He was an instance success at stud; his first crop made him leading first season sire and also leading sire of two year olds. His popularity with mare owners is the speed and precocious talents he transmits to his offspring.

He is more affordable than Nijinsky, but because of the demand for him, only quality mares can visit him. His only negative is that, like most horses that are so speedy, a mile is the maximum distance for his progeny. If you want to win the Derby go elsewhere; ironically if your horse did win that race he would, in most instances not be a popular choice as a stallion, because these days speed is king...'
Rupert Erskine's furrowed brow summarised his perplexity. He waved his hands at the serried rows of pictures.

'How does one get to understand the complexity of all this.'
James gave him an understanding smile.

'Go to Allen's bookshop in London and buy a few books and bury your head in pedigrees. Once you get hooked you will find it fascinating. Also listen to people like Henry White, who will train our filly, but don't believe all the people who will offer advice, many of them have their own agenda. But you are a successful business man, you will soon sort out the wheat from the chaff.'

After which James looked at his watch and suggested that they might like to take the dogs and help June do evening stables. This was immediately approved and they retreated through the boot room to collect the dogs. Sally, with similar thoughts was pulling on her Barbour wellies and sensing Susie's desire to help and guessing she was the same size kitted her out with another pair.

When they all arrived at the stables the star of the show, Pre-Rafflelite was already in her box with her head buried in the manger as she busily munched her evening meal.

June meanwhile had already set out to collect two of the foals; Sally handed a head collar to Susie before setting out in pursuit, the expression of confident ecstasy on her helpers face convincing her that her new friend was a proper horse lover. Hearing Sally's call June walked back to join them, closely followed by four inquisitive youngsters.

'Susie, you might as well take the bay as you are planning to buy him next year! His pet name is Monty.'

'Yes boss.' Susie rubbed the small white star on the colt's head and fondled his ears before expertly slipping the head collar on. Sally was similarly ready to go and so was June who was leading the other two.

Their ecstatic helper smiled, 'They are so well mannered.'

'That is because from the very start we handle them and bring them in every evening to feed. From spring until autumn we put them back out to harden them off and even in the winter the top door of the box stays open. So many people unnecessarily pamper horses. They do not feel the cold like us and even when they are out with a field shelter to hide in, they will very often choose to stand outside in the snow.

Susie nodded; 'I appreciate what you are saying, National Hunt horses in particular, have to run in the cold and rain so, apart from when they are parading under a sheet they have to put up with it.' This appreciation confirming once again Sally's liking of her new friends understanding of horses, it boded well for the future.

The evening, after a splendid meal, was spent anticipating tomorrow's trip to day three of the Newmarket Sales which would take place before and after racing. The colt that James was selling was in the evening session with all the most fancied lots.

They awoke to a slightly overcast day but a few taps on the barometer encouraged James to forecast a dry day ahead, 'well in Leicestershire!' he added.

As there were six of them, they decided that Sally would take the girls and Rupert would drive the boys. They would meet up at the Owners and Trainers Bar where Henry White had arranged for a quick lunch before racing began.

Newmarket has a rich history and just as Queen Anne was responsible for the development of Ascot, it was the Stuart reign that launched Newmarket from an insignificant small market town to become the centre of world racing.

James 1st built the first grandstand on Newmarket Heath; and his son Charles 1st was in residence here when the Civil War broke out. Perversely his protagonist Oliver Cromwell was born only a short distance away in Huntingdon and completed his education at relatively nearby Sidney Sussex College, Cambridge.

After the reformation the newly crowned King Charles 2nd was so obsessed by racing that twice a year he would move his entire court to his Palace here.

Newmarket racecourse is unique; for a start it has two courses, The Rowley Mile Course, very much the choice of the connoisseurs, which stages the first two classic races of the English racing calendar - the 1,000 and 2,000 guineas in early May.

It also has the July Course which is much more of a fashion statement, sometimes advertised as 'Where fashion meets passion.' A claim much disputed by Royal Ascot which is undoubtedly the most chic event of the racing calendar.

These facts outlined by James, further heightened the appetites of his travelling companions and with no traffic delays they arrived on time and in good spirits. The Badges provided by Henry White enabled them to park with access to the Premier Enclosure where, as anticipated, the girls excluding Sally, were already seated with G & T's to hand. Opting for the same, they then set about finding a winner. Clive Somerville, perhaps not surprisingly given his banker's background closed his race-card, announcing that he intended to follow the Long Fellow.

An amused Sally, knowing who he was referring to, declared that she was impressed with his knowledge but she would be relying on Smokin' Joe.

At which point Emily Somerville threw her hands in the air. 'Will someone de-code this gobbledygook?'

The ball was back in her court, so Sally quickly explained that the Long Fellow was racing's nickname for the housewive's favourite, Lester Piggott who was tall for a jockey and Smokin' Joe was how that supreme stylist Joe Mercer was known.

Finally their selections were made and the ladies went to war with the Tote, the men taking on the serried rows of rail bookmakers.

As it turned out the bookies won and the ladies almost broke even but this afternoon was merely a precursor to their mission at the Tattersalls' Houghton Sale.

Tattersalls, auctioneers of thoroughbred horses, was founded in 1745 by Richard Tattersall who left Yorkshire to purchase an interest in a repository in London. He later became racing manager to the Duke of Kingston before leasing land and premises at Hyde Park Corner, where he staged twice weekly sales of horses and even packs of hounds.

Today's venue was at the Park Paddocks, a stylish and spacious facility opened in 1965. The seating arranged in tiers around the circumference of the ring is lit overhead by a large lantern roof. Despite being circular, buyers not wishing to show their hand somehow contrive to keep out of sight of those bidding against them. The task of the younger members of the sales team - referred to as Spotters - is to catch sight of the almost imperceptible nods and slight wave of the sales catalogue and point this out to the man on the rostrum.

This building, the final block in Kenneth Watts' great development scheme, was designed by Sir Robert Richardson, President of the Royal Academy who had also in 1934, designed the Jockey Club Headquarters in Newmarket High Street.

He was also responsible for erecting the famous Fox statue, which had sat at Tattersalls' London HQ for two centuries; it now sits on a column under the iconic cupola, the top of which is capped by a bust of George 1V.

Bloodstock sales are exciting events which evoke great pleasure and great disappointment in equal parts to vendors and buyers alike, as the Somerville's and Erskine's would find out.

On a night such as this, the yearlings parading in front of the packed audience had probably never travelled until they were sent to a handler to be prepared for today's sale. The preparation and exercise they receive is designed to build up muscles and posture to prepare them to be fit enough to do themselves credit when they are hopefully pulled out several times to be viewed by prospective buyers.

Each time they are paraded the new viewer will expect them to walk with purpose so as to show off their athleticism. Many breeders with small studs, such as James, will have walked them back and forth to the paddocks etc. but just as people are taught to dance, so they are taught to prance.

The evening of day three is when the big hitters gather to battle for the cream of the yearlings on offer. That James, representing his ex-wife, had an entry so late in the sale was a testimony to how well his breeding strategy was evolving.

As the big strapping bay colt, nicknamed Rebel, strutted around the ring his heart was pounding. The initial bid of 20,000 guineas was quickly eclipsed as Kenneth Watt, sometimes leaning forward on his rostrum, sometimes standing upright to view his arena, continued to encourage a buyer with his trademark pleas, 'One more sir.' Then having extricated a further bid, his spotters will have drawn his attention to another bidder whom he rounds on with 'Don't lose him for a thousand.'

If after a further sortie this does not elicit another bid he will sympathise with 'No, thank you for your help sir.'

Finally, he could extract no further bids for Rebel so his hammer came down and at sixty two thousand guineas, with the unbelievable revelation, 'Sold to Captain White.'

James sank into his seat, what a fantastic price, Kate should be more than happy! But he was also delighted for himself as the policy originally hatched to sell the rather boisterous colts and keep the fillies was working. If the foal the mare was currently carrying looked as good as this one, then another good payday was possible next year.

The surprises though had not yet finished as, over dinner at the Trattoria Ristorante, where the conversation had been animated and excited, Rupert Erskine summoned a waiter and asked for two bottles of champagne.

'Your very best, it is to celebrate something very special.'

'Surely Susie is not having a baby?'

'Not exactly,' came the reply, 'but sort of, I will leave it to Captain White to explain.'
Henry waited for the glasses to be charged before he broke the news.

'Rupert and I have bought the horse and we are looking for one more partner, have we any takers?'

The table went quiet, but only briefly.
Sally glanced at James and raised her hand.

'How about letting me join you, sort of keep Rebel in the family.'
James left his seat at the other end of the table and hugged her.

Rupert proposed a toast to the new syndicate and also challenged them to come up with a racing name for the colt.

Susie suggested they keep the link to Australia as it was that voyage that had brought them together, 'How about 'Botany Bay?'

'Nice one Susie - he is after all a Bay!'
Emily came up with 'Darwin.'

Clive opted for 'Manly' after the town across the harbour from where they met, it would certainly suit the big strapping colt he reasoned.

Sally suggested, 'maybe we should call him 'Sir Philip Sydney', it is the sort of classy name that mare owners will like.'

James for once was struggling. He was too astounded at the turn of events.

Thus ended a truly momentous day,

They returned in two taxis to Belvoir Lodge Stables where, at Henry's kind invitation, they were all spending the night. - As owners they might well expect more invites in the future particularly now that they would have two runners boarded here.

As in every aspect of his life, James Carrington had arrived. However, travelling not arriving was his mantra. But today, not far from his beloved Cambridge, he would afford himself the luxury of a dream.

He contemplated his past, an unusual consideration for a man whose mind was always focussed on the future:

- Age 14 evicted from his family home
- International sportsman
- Successful entrepreneur - Founder of 3 highly successful businesses
- Director of a leading Merchant Bank
- Successful Racehorse Owner and Breeder
- But, there was one last goal that his family must achieve and it was in this same county...

EPILOGUE
CAMBRIDGE OCTOBER 1980

The tapping grew louder and a befuddled James Carrington slowly became conscious of where he was and what the noise was all about.

The lady traffic warden saw him regain consciousness and waited until the window finally slid down.

She wore a slightly bemused expression as she greeted the good looking but somewhat tousled head which appeared in the now open window of the Aston Martin.

'I am sorry to wake you sir but this is a non- sleeping zone.'

He smiled one of his small boy expressions.

'I wasn't planning an overnight; in fact, sleeping in the day is something that always seems to elude me whenever I need a kip. I have just dropped my eldest son off at St John's College and it brought back some rather poignant recollections from the past; my father's death you see, prevented me taking my place here.'

He had obviously touched a nerve and this time it was she who had the uncomfortable expression.

'Sadly I never really saw my father, he cleared off when I was two. Family is important, well it is if it is loving and caring; sadly my second father so to speak, did not have a lot of time for my sister and me, he just wanted to be out with my mother; which is why I have tried hard to stay close to my kids, not too close of course. I have always encouraged them to try hard at school and make something of themselves: Like you, my eldest has just gone off to college, to Hull in fact, to train as a teacher and whilst it may not be Cambridge, it is a big step up for my family.

This time it was his turn to nod his understanding.

'I think all parents share our dreams and don't you disparage Hull, you just be proud of your son.'

He saw her demeanour soften; despite the fancy car they had become kindred spirits.

He returned her smile and to lighten the mood took up the conversation.

'This conversation means I have gone another ten minutes over my time - I see through your cunning ploy to extract even more money from me.'

She laughed and then assumed a more stern expression.

'I have decided sir, that as you were on official university business at St John's College, I have inadvertently issued you with a parking fine.' She winked. 'For that I apologise and if you will return

the incorrect ticket, I will of course cancel it, and I do hope that this has not spoilt your day.'
He reached into the glove pocket and handed her the parking ticket.
With a smile she turned on her heel and walked a couple of yards before turning round.

'Mind you, in future, just remember that I have your number!'
With that she stepped into the centre of the road and halted the traffic and signalled him to pull out.
He mouthed 'thank you' and headed for the A1 North sign.
This had been the most wonderful ending to an emotional day -'Lucky Jim' his father used to say
when, even as a child, he would somehow have these fortunate coincidences.

In an even better frame of mind if that was possible, he negotiated his way through the city centre
until he saw the sign for the A45 and St Neots and, as the traffic gradually became less, he was able to
let his beloved Aston Martin show her paces. He joined the A1 North and settled down to consider
the sequence to this memorable day; a laying to rest of the demons that had driven him since he was
fourteen years of age and in particular, the final commitment to the bond and affection between
himself and his father.

He was quickly upon the sign for the A47 and turning left followed the well-known signs;
for Uppingham, originally the alma mater to the male members of his father's family briefly indeed
his own school, until the collapse of the family fortunes. That link he had restored for his own sons
and today's visit to Cambridge, despite the memories of his own misfortune, had finally closed the
circle; well almost.

He drove slowly through the town, a place that had become so familiar since Charles and
Edward's schooling; past the Falcon Inn, another place with warm memories although they were
tinged with the sadness of Edward Lawson's death.

And yet, but for that tragedy, a meeting with Sally Parkinson may never had taken place.

He made a conscious effort to rekindle the mood of Cambridge and leaving the town he headed
towards home. First though he had one final act of reconciliation and it lay behind the heavy iron
gates that guarded the entrance to the churchyard where he was now parked.

From the passenger foot well he gathered a Martins Bank money bag and briefly checked the
contents before getting out of the car and walking to the plot where lay his father's remains.

The grave was sited next to a large yew tree which afforded both shade and shelter and
as always it was immaculate, with fresh flowers in the stone vase as he knew there would be. Every
week, whatever the weather, his mother arrived with seasonal flowers and an ancient trowel which
she used to tease out any weed that had dared to show its head in the gravel that covered the grave.
The headstone was simple, it read:
Robert Carrington 1903 – 1952 and below the name *Much Loved and Much Admired.*

He opened the blue money bag and this time it was he who took out a trowel which he used to
scrape out a hole at the foot of the grave. About ten inches down he found the small heavy steel
chest that only he knew about. He removed the polythene bag that protected it and with a slightly
reluctant creak the lid with its tarnished brass bands opened to reveal the contents.

There were three photographs, one showed Robert Carrington in his prime playing for
the Leicester Tigers, an athletic horizontal figure diving over the try line for the last of his record

breaking four tries in the annual Boxing Day match against a world class Barbarians Rugby team; a side that included players from six nations. The second photograph was of the England team when James had won his first cap at senior level, and the third was his mother with 'Their' two children James and his sister Louise.

All three pictures rested in a dark blue England cap that bore the legend England v Scotland 1954; it was James's first full cap and it had lain with the photographs, undisturbed in the chest for a quarter of a century.

From his bag he now he retrieved a dark blue leather case about eight inches long and three inches wide. He opened the lid to reveal a large brass key, the handle of which was embellished with the rising sun motif of Milford Hall.

The blue silk lining on the underside of the lid bore the name Charles Aubin: Locksmith. and on the line below By appointment to her Majesty Queen Victoria.

Aubin's most famous work, the Aubin Lock Trophy was made for the great exhibition held at the Crystal Palace in 1851. This amazing piece of work comprised a series of forty-four different movements in the shape of a five tiered wedding cake, some three feet tall. In her private journal the Queen wrote that Mr Aubin had demonstrated that whilst each lock had its own key, all but the bottom tier could all be closed simultaneously by turning the large Bramah key situated at the top of the wedding cake. Those locks on the bottom tier had their own challenging problems, number forty-two for instance was designed to cause injury to anyone making an unlawful attempt to open it - the deterrent, her Majesty's journal confides, is a harpoon like steel barb!

James placed the box in into the steel chest and from his inside jacket pocket took the letter from St John's College which explained the reason for today's visit to Cambridge; the confirmation of his son's place to read for a PPE degree. The choice to read for this degree, which was an appreciation of Politics, Philosophy and Economics would prepare Charles for opportunities across a broad spectrum of career options.

He placed the letter with the other items and returned the chest to its hiding place and carefully replaced the soil and gravel. For a few moments he stood contemplating his father's headstone and with tears streaming down his cheeks as he spoke quietly to his father.

'It has taken me thirty two years to make good my promise, but Milford Hall is once again the family home of the Carrington's and that includes your darling Elizabeth, which I know was your greatest concern.'

He gathered his thoughts and regained the sense of fulfilment that he had experienced when standing with Charles in the first court of St John's College. The great monkey that had sat on his shoulder since he was fourteen years old was finally removed, he had fulfilled his youthful promise, Milford Hall was restored to the Carrington's.

He headed for the gates of the cemetery, deviating only to drop the blue bag and trowel into the litter bin, he had no further need to disturb his father.

James Carrington for all his outward confidence, was a very private man and, as with his business triumphs, he needed to be alone to soak in the pleasure of the moment; only then could he share it with others. Today was no different and driving home on this very special day of atonement was something he had dreamed of for many years and there were two very special people with whom he needed to confide, his beloved wife and the woman to whom he owed all his business acumen, his mother Elizabeth Carrington.

Opening the sun-roof to make the most of this fine autumn day he imagined them excitedly anticipating his return, longing to hear about today and to share with him the bottle of Roederer Crystal 1962, a vintage born in the same year as the new undergraduate, Charles Robert Staincliffe Carrington.

This day, like the champagne, was indeed, very special.